GOD BLESS THE DEAD

by Evan Geller

Published by Evan Geller

ISBN: 147829969X
ISBN-13: 9781478299691

Dedication

To strong women
because life is hard

to my wife Sheri
one strong woman

and to my three children
Kaitlin, Sarah, and Ethan
in whose hearts I see
their mother's strength,
quiet courage,
subtle grace

TABLE OF CONTENTS

Prologue

Like most great discoveries, it owed more to circumstance than scientific method. As years passed, he learned to omit the more personal, embarrassing details, allowing the episode to become iconic, until now it was both as famous and fictive as Newton's apple incident. Gabriel held his wife's hand. He tried to remember the true moment, his epiphany, without the layers of embellishment added over almost thirty years, trying to make some sense of how events had come to this point. He couldn't; his head swam. Gabriel glimpsed the small piece of paper clutched in his wife's lifeless hand, a token that gave testament to this impossible, inexorable, chain of events. He remembered clearly the evening he had given her that note, on their wedding night. In this moment of complete loss, he agonized over how their lives, so long shared, had somehow come to this. He was alone now; alone with his thoughts. Utterly alone, and without any answers. He wept.

CHAPTER 1

Gabriel awoke, having no idea where he was or what he was doing there. His head hurt. As he opened his eyes, he could not make any sense of what he saw. Slowly, elements of memory trickled back to his consciousness. He remembered the girl, of course: Helena. He remembered her from that ridiculous class he had TA'd last year. Any course entitled "Exobiology" was obviously destined to be an embarrassment. Though not intended to be, it became one of those almost science courses that liberal arts majors used to fulfill their science requirement. He was sure that of the hundreds of students he had taught since starting grad school, she was the only one whose name he could recall for longer than twenty minutes after the course. As a doctoral candidate in bioengineering, Gabriel had been roped into teaching the class run by an adjunct visiting pseudo professor. Helena, he clearly recalled, was the one intelligent, serious student in the whole course. He had realized this fact early on; actually during the professor's opening lecture, when Helena had raised her hand and interrupted the lecture to ask, in a matter-of-fact manner, whether the entire course was going to be devoted to batshit crazy malarkey or just the introductory lecture. For reasons unfathomable, she had not dropped the course, turning up in Gabriel's study section. She was undeniably brilliant, and had blown away the course by, to his astonishment, devoting exceptional effort to a subject that clearly merited none. It was an embarrassment to give her the A on her final paper, it was that good. It had almost a hundred citations; unbelieving, he had checked over twenty. Not only was every reference he checked real, each actually said what she claimed. He probably still had it on his laptop.

He recalled why he remembered her name so clearly. Gabriel usually was awful with names. Gabe uniformly addressed his students as "Yes, you" while pointing at them for clarity. Helena, though, made an immediate impression. Her appearance was striking. She looked alien, immediately distinct from her Midwestern classmates. Intensely green eyes set off by absurdly pale skin; a complexion that must be what they mean by alabaster. Once, early in the semester, she had stood before him to ask a question after class: Gabriel thought he could watch blood coursing beneath her surface. Her most striking feature, though, even from a distance, was her hair; a cartoonish explosion of red curls. She looked like no one Gabriel had ever met before in his twenty-nine years, every one of which had been spent in Ann Arbor. Since he had never met anyone from Montana, he immediately christened her to be Helena, from Montana. Actually, he didn't have a clue where she was from.

That's why Gabriel had recognized her the night before. It was Friday night, and he felt particularly compelled to go through the motions of being social. He had joined a couple of his fellow grad students from the engineering department in an uninspired bar cruise. They all three knew, in their hearts, that they were far too unappealing to have much luck in the Ann Arbor bar scene. This was their home, however, and they felt compelled to rail against their monastic fate, despite the obvious futility. Gabe had been lecturing his colleagues on just how futile their prospects were when he spotted her at the bar. Helena couldn't be missed. Her appearance was well suited to standing out in a crowd, for though of diminutive stature, her huge crown of curly red hair gave the impression from a distance that her head was exploding, or on fire. He watched her for a few minutes, ignoring the beer-addled conversation of his friends. She was with a physically imposing guy, obviously a football player. He seemed pretty drunk and, as Gabe watched, the tight end put his hand on Helena's butt in a very familiar fashion. Oh well, Gabe thought, as he turned to scan the bar, disappointed and embarrassed. He swiveled back as he heard a loud crash, and saw that the football player's stool had flipped backwards, landing him on his back. Reflexively, Gabe hustled over to find Helena standing over him with her stiletto heel on the man's neck. She wasn't saying anything. The guy's face looked like he was in fear for his life. As Gabe came up to them and caught sight of the expression on Helena's face, he could see why.

"Hey," Gabe called to her as he stepped up to the bar. Helena turned slightly to look at him. She smiled in recognition.

"Hey yourself, Professor." He remembered then that she had always called him that. He always assumed it was to piss him off, but Gabriel smiled in return. She still had her heel on the guy's neck.

"Friend of yours?" Gabe asked, nodding slightly to the floor.

"Not yet. We were just getting acquainted."

"My opinion, not really your type."

"You think?" She pressed down slightly harder and the guy actually yelped. It was a sound usually heard from a Yorkshire terrier. Gabe thought the guy might be turning a little blue.

"Gonna kill him?" Gabriel asked, smiling. She took uncomfortably long, considering.

"Thinking about it." Gabe looked at her face, and detected a troubling lack of humor. "What do you think?" she asked, giving him a considering look.

"Not worth ruining the rest of the night for, I think."

"Got a better idea, Professor?" She arched an eyebrow.

"Let's find a better bar."

"Take me away," she said, smiling and spreading her arms wide, beer in hand. Before he did, she took a moment to empty her glass onto the gentleman beneath her heel. Helena set her glass back down on the bar and took Gabriel's arm. They left.

Gabriel remembered a series of increasingly decrepit drinking spots, the last two unclassifiable as bars. Somehow little redheaded Helena knew a lot about where bikers drank in neighboring Ypsilanti. He remembered an impressive array of tattoos, but not much else. He did recall a remarkable variety and volume of alcohol. Some of it came out of a still-like contraption in a garage they visited towards the end of the evening and, he believed, was just that, plain alcohol.

He tried again to make sense of what he was looking at, and again failed. He closed his eyes again and concentrated. He tried other senses. Distant music, filtered through cinderblock—he remembered now. He was in her dorm room. And he now was aware that he wasn't wearing any clothes. He was definitely making progress. More events from last evening came to mind. Gabriel remembered being impressed that Helena did not shave her legs, but not in a positive sense.

Was she still here? He didn't think so. He began to turn his head to check and was immediately struck by the impression that this was not a good idea. An immense wave of nausea washed over him. Gabriel closed his eyes again, breathing deeply. He was somehow quite sure that he was alone. He kept his eyes closed and considered the possibility of a roommate walking in unannounced. From the little he had learned about Helena overnight, he thought a roommate unlikely. The poor girl would probably have run screaming back to some small hometown in the Upper Peninsula, now intent on applying to convents. He breathed easier. It was Saturday. He was alone. He was at peace with his thoughts. He certainly wasn't going to try to move his head again anytime soon.

She had left him, asleep. There were implications to this fact, implications too subtle and convoluted to fully understand in his current state. She might have left him a note. He suddenly wished for a note, could see it in his mind's eye. "Gabe," it said in a loopy feminine script, "I'm sorry but I had to go. I'm hoping you're still here when I get back." He smiled. But thinking more, he wasn't sure if she even knew his name. Hadn't she called him "Professor" all night? She never even asked him his real name. Hell, even the bikers had been calling him "The Professor" by the end of the night. His smile vanished as he envisioned another note, this one scrawled in angry block letters on the back of a scrap of paper: "Prof—BIG mistake! Hope you're not the stalker type. Lock the door on your way out."

He sighed. Once again, he chanced opening his eyes. He stared as things started to come into better focus. He realized now what he was seeing. Gabriel was staring at the screen of her laptop. It couldn't be more than two inches from his face. And it was upside down. Why was it upside down? He thought some more, analyzing his position. He was lying, naked of course, on her bed. He now recalled the bed to be a basic mattress on floor situation. His head, he now deduced, was hanging off the edge of the mattress. This was all making so much more sense. Now he even knew why his head hurt so much. He stared deeply, unmoving, at the upside down screen. He brought to bear his considerable graduate student intellect in analyzing the screen. He had seen this before. It was her screensaver. Of course; she had told him at some point that she was an astronomy major, or in the astronomy department, or something like that. He had been amazed, expressed genuine drunken disbelief for an inappropriately long time. "She was to be an astronomer!" he enthused, though she had just shrugged. Gabriel now realized that he was looking at her *de rigueur* SETI screensaver. It was at that moment, that exact moment, when Gabriel Sheehan experienced his epiphany.

An epiphany does not occur in a vacuum. It is a bolt of lightning only for denizens of the Old Testament. A moment of epiphany can occur only as the result of a delicate and intricate latticework of prior events, couched in a precariously perched nest of emotions, and emerging, trembling, as the newly hatched fledgling of a pure idea. Alternatively, metabolic breakdown products of toxic quantities of alcohol will suffice. In the epiphany of Gabriel Sheehan, all of these elements combined to initiate an extraordinary chain of events.

Gabriel Sheehan was in the third year of his doctoral program in bioengineering. He was smart, having earned both his bachelor's and master's degrees in engineering with honors from the University of Michigan. His parents, both on faculty at U of M, had hoped their only son would choose to become a real doctor, a physician. Gabriel disabused them of this dream during his freshman year, when he quickly realized that over half of his fellow freshmen were premed and every one of them a calculating, self-absorbed asshole. He enjoyed math more than biology anyway, and was a hard worker. He made the difficult jump to engineering—no easy feat, as U of M's engineering school was regarded as one of the best in the country, particularly by the folks at U of M. In a nod to his parents, whom he loved deeply, he chose to dedicate his considerable skills to the strikingly-similar-to-being-a-doctor field of bioengineering.

In some ways, he was brilliant. He was insightful and creative, unusual traits for an engineer. He asked good, elegantly simple questions; the kind of questions that an engineer, with hard work, could answer. Gabe was a very hard worker. He had come to decide on a topic for his post-graduate studies early on. He was lucky in that he knew exactly where his interest lay. Gabriel wished to devote his life to understanding the bioelectrical basis for human thought. It was his type of question. It was big and important. And, he naively believed at the time, it was elegantly simple. The basic electrical properties of the mind were well known. His particular proclivity lay in bioelectrical engineering, particularly in the study of microcurrents, an interest born of a summer during under-grad working in a research lab. Later, Gabriel had successfully defended his master's thesis on a new method of controlling artificial limbs by incorporating both movement and sensation in the two-way detection of microelectrical signals to the brain. The technique had been hailed as brilliant beyond his years, and rapidly brought to market to the benefit of the large number of limbless veterans recently returned from the wars. As a young recipient of a master's degree, he was honored and acclaimed, and when he decided to pursue his doctorate, his mentors at Michigan wouldn't let their rising star even consider another program. He had spent, as a consequence, his entire adult life in Ann Arbor.

He didn't mind. He was comfortable here. His parents were here. It was easy to focus on his work. He quickly wrote and defended his pro-posal. He would improve the already burgeoning field of microelectronic signal detection to identify and define individual, single thoughts. Once he had perfected the technique, he could dedicate his life to defining the entire encyclopedia of human consciousness. It was simple. It was bril-liant. It was important. He would be the greatest bioengineer in his-tory. It would be even more important than being a doctor. Way more important.

It started well. He was enthusiastic and confident, as recent discov-eries on the physiology of the brain proliferated in almost every aspect of biology. New techniques of identifying the actions of single living neurons had been developed and were being successfully applied to the human brain. Gabe was the one to study the field from the electrical side, surely to summate with his biochemical colleagues in an eventual, and ultimate, synergy culminating in the true understanding of the human mind. When he dreamt of his future, his parents were proud.

It was early in the second year when his troubles began. Cruelly, the problems were in the very aspect of the field that he felt most confident, the detection of microcurrents in the brain. It was proving difficult to refine his measurements to the necessary levels of specificity and detection. He was coming up against unanticipated practical problems. Initially, he was sure it was just a question of better technique, better equipment. It wasn't. He spent long hours brainstorming with researchers studying mentation from the biochemical approach, trying to leverage their new single cell dye technique with his own microelectrical studies. The biochemists, though, were having a similar problem—single neuron activity couldn't be equated to any meaningful definition of thought. They could figure out the neurons required for movement, sure—but not thought. No one was too impressed by discovering which signal translated into a twitch of the finger. The biochemists were just as frustrated as he, and their enthusiasm waning. The international meetings, the symposia and colloquia, the journals and reviews, all reflected a tide rapidly ebbing from Gabriel's shore.

Gabe was not to be deterred. He returned more forcefully to his engineering talent, redoubling his efforts for more precise measurements. He got funding to travel to Germany, and spent two weeks in the lab of a brilliant physicist who had discovered an indirect method of measuring microcurrents utilizing nanotechnology. He spent the next four sleepless months adapting the technique to his brain studies, generating a huge volume of data that he only recently had begun to analyze. His initial analysis was a body blow: The data were garbage. All noise, no signal. No meaningful anything, not a shred of a result to even pretend was pointing to a way forward. Six weeks ago, Gabriel had presented his initial findings to his advisor, then to the committee. There was stunned silence, then sympathetic murmurs. The golden boy had gone bust, big time. This wasn't supposed to happen. Hell, this never happened. The reason why your proposal had to jump so many hurdles was precisely to prevent this exact scenario. Gabriel had literally wasted over two years of his young adult professional life. He had expended over forty thousand dollars, granted with the confidence born of his young reputation, to generate a mountain of completely meaningless trash.

The committee had endorsed his embarrassed advisor's recommendation that Gabe submit his raw data to a colleague in the mathematics department, in the hope that, through some arcane sophistry, meaning could be found. It was the last hope of a fool's notion, he knew. Yesterday, Gabriel had gotten the formal report from the math wizards. In a brutally brief summary, it was concluded that "all applicable approaches and analyses failed to yield a significant result". Gabriel had tossed the entire hundred-page report out his office window. He decided that evening that going to the bar was his only option. His life had failed to yield a significant result.

Against this tragic veil, subsumed by chemical and emotional melancholia, Gabriel experienced his epiphany. At that exact same moment, in mid-epiphany, Helena returned. She stopped in the doorway; staring down at his naked, prostrate form. She was unaware of Gabe's epiphany.

"You're still here."

Gabriel looked up at her by looking down over the laptop screen. He was disoriented, but amazed. Not just amazed by his recent epiphany, though that would amaze him very soon. At this moment, Helena amazed him. She stood there, inverted and more beautiful than he remembered. Her statement hung in the air, amazing him. It was the simplest of statements, uttered with a perfection of intonation that gave no hint of meaning or judgment. It held no inflection of the interrogative; "You're still here?" Such a question, at that moment, where he lay naked and exposed by an epiphany, would have pierced him to his heart. It was, rather, a plain but elegant statement of his very condition: "You're still here." He swelled with joy.

"Damn right I am!" He felt deliriously happy.

She averted her eyes from his nude form as she closed the door behind her. "Why?" Definitely a question this time.

He was undeterred, unfazed in his utter giddiness. "Helena! I have had an epiphany!" He knew it to be true.

"Yeah, I think you had about three epiphanies last night. I'm gonna have to wash those sheets today." She sat down in the chair at the desk, facing the wall. "How about you get some clothes on, sport. Nothing personal, but I have a problem seeing you this way, in the light of day."

He tried to understand this statement, but was still quite muddled by the epiphany. His wrackful hangover didn't help either. He misfired, audibly. "Are you gay?" he asked, twisting to see her at the desk. She didn't turn. He immediately feared he had misspoken.

"Excuse me?" she asked of the wall.

"I mean, what you said. And your legs, and all." He felt himself sinking quickly.

"My legs? What about my legs?" She turned to glare at him with this. He remembered her expression back in the bar, dangerously similar. "Are you a fucking moron?" she asked. She stared more, finally shaking her head in seeming disbelief. "Please," she continued, "Get dressed. I'm going for some food. Be dressed when I get back. Please." She left, not quite not slamming the door behind her. Bright white light exploded in his head.

She returned with two scrambled egg bagels with cheese, orange juice, and huge buckets of black coffee. Gabriel was dressed, busily typing at a frenetic pace on her laptop at the desk. Helena sat down cross-legged on the mattress. She handed him his food and drink. Gabe paused to thank her, then returned to typing at a comically rapid rate. "Listen, sport..." she began softly.

Gabe stopped typing and turned to look down at her. "Do you know my name?" he asked. This gave her pause.

"Is that important?"

He tried to look wounded. Actually, it was his most convincing expression. "I think it is." He continued to look hurt.

Helena rolled her eyes, took a bite encompassing half the sandwich. "Ok, sport, I'll bite. What's your name, Professor?"

"I'm not a professor, you know." He decided to be truculent.

"Geez, still a postdoc after two years?"

"Huh?" He was getting confused. He realized he really was not at his best at the moment. "I'm not a postdoc."

Helena feigned incredulity. "You are not trying to tell me I've been impregnated by a fucking candidate! Please tell me you're defending next week. Leave me a shred of self respect, I beg you."

Gabriel had only heard the word 'impregnate'. He went white with panic. "You're pregnant?" he gasped.

Helena stood up and poked a finger hard into his forehead. "You," she gave him another, harder poke, "are a fucking moron."

CHAPTER 2

Gabriel returned to working at her desk. Helena spent the first hour cleaning up, doing the sheets. She repeatedly glanced at Gabe, typing feverishly on her computer. He was in a kind of trance, completely focused on whatever he was doing. He was, to her eyes, a man possessed. She could stand it no more.

"That's my laptop, you know." Gabe paused, looked at her with a bovine stare.

"Sorry?"

"Your magnum opus. It's on my computer." He blinked. "You," she said, speaking slowly and pointing to him, "are using my computer." Here she gestured to the machine before him. "You could've asked, Professor."

"It's Gabe, actually."

"It's 'jake'. Actually, the phrase is, 'It's jake.' "

"No, it's not Jake. It's Gabe."

"No, it's not Gabe. And it's not jake, either. You should've asked." For the umpteenth time since meeting her last night, Gabriel was completely at sea. He returned to typing. He belched. That did it. Helena leaned over and gently closed the cover on the laptop. He looked at her.

"I'm sorry," she continued softly. "Last night, I didn't have you pegged as an idiot savant. Or brain damaged, or whatever's screwed you up, mentally speaking. Thanks for an okay night, Professor. But this is the part where I give you the peck on the cheek and you never call me again, okay? I'm sorry, I don't do pity very well. Just not me."

"It's Gabe."

She rolled her eyes, put her hand on his wrist. "Perseveration. I'm thinking a car accident, brain injury, huh? Time to go, Professor." Helena began to lever him up off the chair with an Aikido technique that usually didn't cause fractures if she was careful. She had him halfway to the door.

"My name is Gabe, Helena. I think you should stop calling me that."

She had him at the door. "That's just jake, Gabe. Time to go, Professor. And my name isn't Helena."

He twisted his head to look at her quizzically. "Of course it is. I've been calling you Helena all night." He tried to slow his exit and felt a stab of pain shoot up his forearm. His arm went numb. "Ow, careful."

"Doesn't make it Gabe, Jake. And I am being careful. You really don't want to stick around for the 'not being careful' part. Time to go." She opened the door with her free hand and spun him to face her, quickly kissed him on the cheek, and sent him backward out the door by striking him sharply in the midchest with the heel of her palm. She slammed and bolted the door as she heard the breath knocked from him and then the smack of his head against the far wall. She went back to straightening up her place.

Eventually, she opened the laptop and began to read. She whistled softly, rereading what Gabe had written. She rose and opened the door. Gabriel was still sitting on the floor in the hallway, alternately rubbing the rising bump on the back of his head and trying to get the feeling back in his arm. He looked up at her, grinning sheepishly. "Hey, Helena."

She stared down at him hard, thinking. "What the fuck is that?"

"I had an epiphany."

She stood over him, deciding. "Listen very carefully, Gabe. If you ever say that word to me again, for any reason, I swear on the grave of my sainted sister that I will kill you as you sleep. Do you understand me,

Gabe?" He nodded solemnly, but couldn't help smiling. "My name's not Helena." She let him back in her room.

They talked for hours, the room eventually getting twilight. Actually, Gabriel talked, nonstop. Helena listened, not interrupting, not a question. She was a very good listener, encouraging him with appropriately timed nods and eye contact.

"Almost three years, Helena!" he continued. "Three years of trying harder and harder to measure smaller and smaller currents. It couldn't be done. It was impossible. I was coming up against principles of nature, you know? But I kept trying to get more precise, more focused.

"I was going the wrong way completely! I see that now, because of you, of your laptop. Your screensaver, the SETI thing program. It uses distributed computing, thousands of computers linked together, each running a small program that network together to crunch some gigantic problem. I don't even know what problem SETI is crunching. I just know the distributed computing thing." She knew what it was crunching. Helena had rewritten the code for the front end as a project for one of her astronomy seminars. Before that, it hadn't been upgraded in over ten years. Running for almost thirty years, the *Search for Extra Terrestrial Intelligence* still hadn't found a damn thing.

"That's the answer, you see?" Gabriel continued without pause. "Not improved equipment, not trying to filter out all the noise so the signal of a single firing neuron can be detected. That's fucking impossible! I spent three years proving it. No! Go the other way, upscale the signal. A thousand subjects wearing electrodes, you know? You could almost use a hospital EEG, but I can do better than that. But you really don't have to, see? Just up the numbers. More subjects, more signal! I think the S/N ratio would be exponential, you know? Sorry, signal-to-noise ratio."

"I know what S/N ratios are." It was the first thing she had said in almost an hour. He caught his breath. He was actually winded, he had been talking so fast. Or maybe that was left over from the shot she'd given him to the sternum earlier, she thought.

"You do?" He suddenly seemed to realize he hadn't been talking to himself. "Why do you keep saying your name's not Helena? I remembered from when you were in my class." He was proud of that.

"Yeah, I remember. 'Helena from Montana.' Witty, that. You used it about a hundred times. Never got old, that one. Except it's not HELL-in-a. It's Hel-AIN-a. I corrected you the first forty-two times, then gave up. It just ruined your little joke, I guess." She smiled at him.

Gabe was crestfallen. He'd been mispronouncing her name all this time, just for his little play on words, all semester long? He looked at her, smiling at him. She had a beautiful smile, he thought. Then another thought came to him, and he knew it immediately to be true. Smiling back at her, he knew. If, all this time, he had been calling her 'Hel-AIN-a', he'd still be wrong. He could see it, in her eyes, above the smile: "No, you silly fucking moron! It's 'HELL-in-a'. You know, like the capitol of Montana." God, I love this girl, he thought.

They worked from her room for three days straight. Empty pizza boxes piled up in the corner. Gabe continued to monopolize her laptop, completely rewriting his thesis proposal. There were huge gaps to be filled in, but he knew now the direction he had to go. He knew this was right. This was the exact polar opposite of his previous work. Where before he felt he was slogging through academic quicksand, struggling against the forces of nature, now he was on the Titanic, arms spread wide as he stood on the bowsprit, feeling the wind and the spray on his face. He was having a hard time typing as fast as the ideas were coming. Every once in a while, he'd be brought up short. A large portion of the technical aspects, the stuff where Gabriel usually was most at home, was completely foreign to him. The nature and design of the distributed computer network, for one thing. Gabe looked up from the laptop, suddenly lost. He looked over at Helena, sitting on the mattress with her back against the wall. She was filling yellow legal pads with what looked to him like the blackboard scrawls from a bad fifties science fiction movie. Occasionally, she'd tear off the sheet she had been working on, ball it up, and send it arcing across the room towards the overflowing wastebasket. Every time, the wadded paper struck the piled waste and bounced off onto the floor.

"Why do you bother?" he asked, gesturing to the mountain of paper covering the floor in the opposite corner. She looked up at him.

"Do I criticize your Quasimodo working style?"

"Who was Quasimodo? Was he brilliant?"

She looked sincerely troubled. "How hard did your head hit that wall, anyway?"

"Not that hard." He couldn't help smiling at her like an idiot.

"Then you're a moron."

"Is that better than a fucking moron?" he asked brightly.

"No, it's not. I was trying to be kind. I see that was a mistake. Now shut the fuck up, I'm trying to work."

"I've got a problem."

Helena sighed expansively and tossed her pad to the foot of the bed. "What?"

"I'm not sure about the architecture of the distribution network. It's not really my thing. And until I design the network, I can't come up with the number of nodes I'll need. I'm not even sure how the statistical modeling is gonna work. And without all that, I can't even begin to work on a budget." He looked troubled.

"Don't worry about that."

"Don't worry about what?"

"What, what? What you just said."

"Which part?"

"All of it."

"What do you mean?"

Helena jumped to her feet, visibly making an effort to control herself and coming up a bit short. "Jesus, Mary, and Joseph! You are killing me here!" She paused, taking a deep breath. "Do us a favor and say the word, Gabe." She was wringing her hands fiercely, staring at him.

"What word, honey?" he grinned.

"Just say the fucking word so I can kill you now."

"Epiphany?"

She lunged for his throat. They took a break.

They worked for three more days in her dorm. Gabriel showered late at night in the communal bathroom. People probably noticed, but no one seemed to mind. He sat at Helena's desk in his underwear, tapping incessantly on her laptop. He thought that when they woke up on Monday morning, she'd start getting ready to head to class. Once dressed, though, she resumed her posture, cross-legged in the corner of the mattress, picking up pen and pad. He glanced over from the desk.

"What?" she demanded. He just shrugged, gave her a wan smile and resumed his typing.

It was as if they were fated to work together on this particular project. Gabriel knew everything he needed to work up the detection side of the experiment. He had spent years working on how to detect, analyze, and process electrical signals from the brain. The techniques required from this new approach were child's play for him, compared with the techniques he had developed during his futile three years prior. He wrote lengthy protocols right from his head. With time and effort, he was sure he could improve on existing methods, but for now he was well within his comfort zone.

The rest of the project, however, was a whole different matter. Gabriel was completely unfamiliar with the practice of distributed networked computing, except as a concept and a tool for what he needed to do. Perhaps most fatal to his plan was his suspicion that he lacked the knowledge of the mathematics that would be required. He thought he knew a lot of math, and was fluent with the statistical methods he employed in the course of his previous studies. He feared, however, that he didn't have the knowledge of the right math for this project. While you could always hire a mathematician to collaborate on the work, the truth of the matter was that, if you didn't understand the math, you really weren't competent to design the experiment. His élan, so powerful for the last two days, was at low ebb. He had hit the proverbial wall.

"I'm toast," he declared, snapping the computer shut. He looked over at Helena, still scribbling on her yellow pad. He realized with a start that she had filled a stack of legal pads half a foot tall next to her on the bed. Of course, he could hardly not notice the mountain of crumpled yellow sheets in the opposite corner, now threatening to pour over the windowsill. He realized he could no longer see the minifrig for the mess. "Leena." He had started calling her that and she hadn't stopped him yet. "We need to talk."

She didn't look up from what she was writing, but furrowed her brow in concentration and answered. "I'm sorry, Gabriel. I'm just not ready to start going steady yet."

"What are you talking about?"

"What are you talking about, angel?" It was unnerving to hear her talk like that. He still wasn't sure if he was being played. Actually, he was pretty sure he was being played.

"I've got to quit for a while. I'm spent. I'm going to go home and get changed. Maybe shave," he added, rubbing the stubble on his chin.

She brightened, looking up at him and smiling. "Great. Dress up nice and pick me up at six. You can take me someplace expensive to celebrate. Someplace with champagne."

"Celebrate what, Leena?"

"Gabby, sweetheart," she stood to give him a childlike kiss on the forehead as he bent to put on his shoes, "You're going to change the world."

He had to smile at her. "You really think so?"

She nodded and pushed him gently toward the door. "And Gabe..."

"Yes, Leena?"

"Don't shave."

CHAPTER 3

He hadn't shaved, but now sported a tweed jacket and tie. Helena sat across the table from him, her red hair piled high on her head and wearing a black dress that would've gotten her an audience with the queen. She toasted him with her flute of champagne, her third since they sat down.

She gave him a wink. "You clean up nice, sport."

"You too," he replied with approval. Her face grew stormy.

"A woman shouldn't have to fish for a compliment, Gabriel."

"Of course, Helena. You are very beautiful tonight."

"Thank you, Gabriel. But, to be honest, I had set my sights on 'ravishing'. I'm sorry to have fallen short."

"You are certainly ravishing, Leena. Very ravishing."

"Thank you, Gabe. I believe 'very ravishing' may be a personal best. You've made me happy."

Gabriel blushed. He was certain that this was the happiest he had ever been. He knocked over his water glass.

By the time the entre arrived, they had stopped mooning at each other and were earnestly discussing the project. This time, she was the one talking animatedly and brooking no interruption, though Gabriel kept trying.

He was taken aback, and not just by the pen and ink diagram she sketched on the heavy linen napkin, cursing the fact that she hadn't brought a pad of paper along. What had she been thinking, she asked, that they were just going to stare at one another all evening? No, he was quite literally astonished, for as she talked on and on, Gabriel began to understand that this girl was something of a genius. What other explanation could there be, he wondered, as he realized that his Helena had been filling those yellow legal pads with all the knowledge and insight that he did not possess. The whole of his ignorance, his weakness, was the subject of the seminar this young woman was presenting over broiled lobster tails. Here was a schematic of how the computers would be networked, the nodes connected to internodes—he had never heard of internodes, had no idea what they were. He tried to interrupt her for an explanation, but failed as she sailed further on into the tricky aspects of packet sequencing, problems to be expected with hardware clock synchronicity that would require at least three months of damn hard work to finally get right. But he would get it right, Helena assured him, he wasn't reinventing the wheel here, it had all been done a hundred times before. When she finally lost steam while summarizing the generally accepted statistical model useful for first pass analysis of the signal variation inherent in any network geographically larger than the fourth order harmonic, he raised his hand to interrupt.

"What? You interrupted me. That was rude."

"But only to point out that you've hardly touched your lobster."

She looked down at her plate. "Oh, well I don't really like lobster, Gabriel. It's just a huge underwater spider, you know."

"But you ordered it!" he spluttered.

"Only to see the look on your face. You do know what 'market price' means on a menu, don't you, Gabe?"

"Yeah, but I wasn't going to bring it up. You really don't like lobster? Why don't you order something else?"

"No, I'm fine. I'll just have a little bite of your dessert, if you don't mind."

"Why did you order lobster if you don't like it?"

She looked at him through narrowed eyes. "I cannot tolerate misers, Gabriel. We cannot be together if we have conflicting views on money. It's the most common cause of disharmony between lovers, you know."

"My money, you mean. Conflicting views on my money."

She stiffened and suddenly seemed to be looking down on him, despite her being a full head shorter than he. "Do not be crass, Gabriel. It doesn't suit you."

A brief, uncomfortable silence ensued. He chanced a thin smile. "So is that what we are then? Lovers?"

She smiled back and reached across the table to put her hand on his. "Ask me again after dessert."

He helped her move into his place the next day. He owned a two-bedroom condo off State Street. His parents had given him the down payment as a graduation gift from undergrad, when it became apparent he wasn't leaving town for graduate school. No sense paying rent for the next six or seven years, they explained. It was a great investment, they added. He suspected it was a way to be sure their only child stayed close to home, but he was grateful nonetheless.

Gabriel nearly died moving Helena in. She offered to provide a couple of strong, young men to help with the move; something about owing her big-time for when she kept them from getting kicked off the football team by intensely tutoring them in math for the week before finals. She seemed to know a lot of football players. She admitted that football was a passion of hers.

Gabriel was still puzzling over that statement, and seriously regretting his refusal of steroid-strengthened assistants, as he dragged the sixth box of textbooks up the stairs to his second floor unit. He could not believe how much stuff Helena had squirreled away in her tiny dorm room, like some trick Escher painting. The books were the killer, the boxes packed full and weighing over a hundred pounds each, he was certain. He vowed to never let a woman pack things for him to carry again. He would never again refuse help, either. Manual labor was not his strong suit.

He fell, drenched in sweat, into the living room, heavily depositing the box on the floor. Gabriel lay supine on the carpet, limbs spread-eagle. "That's it," he gasped dramatically, trying to spit up some blood for sympathy. "Last box." He looked up to see Helena on a step stool, putting books neatly on shelves. "Lotta books," he gasped, not entirely acting.

"So I'm guessing you want me to carry that box the last three feet, so I can put them away. Is that what I'm guessing, tough guy?"

Gabriel dragged himself up onto his hands and knees and, crawling, pushed the box over to where she was working. He rolled back onto the floor and watched her as she continued shelving.

"Lotta books," he repeated. He wasn't sure she had taken his point. There were a damn lot of books. He had carried a lot of very heavy books up the stairs for her.

"'Bout half."

He blinked. "Come again?"

"This is about half my books."

He sat up, cradling his knees—which hurt quite a bit, by the way—and laughed. "You are cruelly funny, girl. I emptied your place. Bare walls, kiddo."

"Storage unit."

"Storage unit? Where?"

"Ypsi"

"No way. What's in it?"

"Books, mostly."

The rest of her books arrived late the next morning, delivered by two of the biggest guys Gabriel had ever seen—defensive linemen. They hauled twelve more boxes into the living room while laughing and joking with Helena, not breaking a sweat as far as Gabe could tell. Yeah, well—where were these dudes yesterday, when the real work had to be done? Gabe mused. Probably at the spa.

Finished, the guys were joshing and catching up on old times with Helena. Finally, each gave her a bear hug, lifting her two feet off the floor in turn.

"Thanks, guys," Helena said, her feet touching down after a hug that Gabe had started to feel was lasting a bit overlong. "Thanks for taking the time. I know you're busy."

"Hey, Helen, anytime, you know that," the bigger of the two replied in a deep, molasses drawl. "You saved our lives, girlfriend."

Gabe walked up to join them and Helena introduced him to the two, James Earle and Barry. James Earle was the bigger and had to be well over 300 pounds, Gabe figured. Both of them towered over him, though Gabe himself was almost six foot.

"Wow, that's great," Gabe chimed in. "I've tutored a lot of students, but I don't think any ever called me a lifesaver." He shook their huge hands and grinned at them. Each of them smiled back, looking confused.

"Come again? Tutored?" Barry replied.

"Yeah, Helena told me how she met you guys. Glad it worked out for you." Gabe noticed Helena doing a little jig next to him and saw that she was blushing. He had never seen her blush before. Her entire body, usually the shade of bones bleached for years in the desert, had gone crimson, matching her hair. She looked like a dancing fireplug.

James Earle and Barry were grinning like circus clowns. "Oh yeah, yeah," Barry picked up, just a beat late on the uptake. "Helen's a great teacher, got us through the rough parts, no problem."

James Earle nodded assent, both still unable to stop smiling.

"Math can be a bitch," Gabe added. James Earle's smile drooped.

"You told him you tutored us in math? I majored in math, woman!" James Earle said in his syrup drawl, facing her. Helena kicked him hard in the shin. "Ow! Damn, girl, that hurt." Helena said nothing, hands on hips and still the color of a stop sign.

"You do know I saw that, right?" Gabe asked, hoping he wouldn't have to get between these two. He didn't like the visual he was getting as he played that out in his mind. "Alright then," Gabriel said, addressing the two guys now and reaching into his pocket for the fifty bucks he was planning to give each of them to get them on their way. Not that he wasn't really enjoying their first time having friends over as a couple. Gabriel realized they hadn't even offered these guys a drink.

Barry noticed the money in Gabe's hand and was waving him off, taking a slight step back. "Thanks, Gabriel, not necessary, man. Happy to help out, Helen. Anytime, Helen."

"Come on, guys. It's just a token," Gabriel said, trying to give them the bills. "That was a lot of work, going to Ypsilanti and all. Helena and I wouldn't feel right."

Helena glared at him. "Bull shit, Gabe. I feel fine about it. It's you waving money at my friends that's pissing me off." She looked like she was about to kick him in the shin next. At least her color had drained back to normal.

James Earle put his giant hand gently on Gabe's shoulder, defusing the situation. "No, no, guys. It's not like that at all. We appreciate the gesture, but like Barry said, happy to have gotten to see you guys. Really. Anyway, man, we're on the football team, you know?"

"Really, James Earle?" Gabriel asked. "Play much? Math major not taking up all of your time?" Gabriel was ticked off. He had just been trying to do the right thing, and Helena had embarrassed him. She had moved in less than 24 hours ago, and they were already having their first fight. He had thought that wouldn't happen for at least another four or five days. Maybe this wasn't such a great idea after all. After dessert two nights ago, it had sounded like a great suggestion. Hell, Helena still hadn't even offered these guys a drink of water.

James Earle interrupted his reverie, ignoring Gabe's sarcasm. "Naw, man. I graduated cum laude last spring," he said, beaming. "I still got a year of eligibility left though, tore up my knee junior year." James Earle pointed out the nine-inch scar running down the side of his knee. "But this is my year, man. Starting NT by opening game. Count on it." He gave a little dance step that Gabe would've bet twenty bucks a guy this size couldn't do on the moon.

Barry was shaking his head in an apologetic fashion. "Yeah, Gabe. No offense, man, but the NCAA kinda frowns on the whole 'taking cash while on scholarship' thing. They're pretty stressed around here about that stuff."

Gabe thought he saw Barry actually shoot a glance around the room, furtively checking for hidden cameras or assistant coaches. Gabe hadn't even thought of that. "Sorry, guys. I wasn't thinking. You're right. But we really appreciate your help. I could hardly drag my ass out of bed this morning."

Barry and James Earle were both grinning at Helena again. "I believe that, my brother," Barry replied. He gave Helena a burlesque wink and danced back, allowing Helena's kick to miss his shin this time. She was the color of a fireplug again. "Shit, Helen, don't you know I am a collegiate athlete? Back off, girl." He held his hands out defensively. "Listen, though. We brought all the books, I think, but there's still a lot of shit in there, and your bike. You want James Earle and I to make another run while we got the truck? We got time, wouldn't be a problem."

Gabriel thought having a lot more of Helena's shit delivered was a bad idea, but would like her to have her bike. Gabriel owned a Pinnarello road-racing bicycle that was his special toy. Thoughts of Helena asking to ride it suddenly made him swallow hard. She was way too small to fit, for one thing. And you had to wear the special shoes with cleats. His shoes were way too big for her tiny feet; he thought she had like size four feet. "Hey, babe," he said, turning to her. "Maybe the bike's a good idea. We could keep it in the front closet and you could use it, to get around a little when I had the car."

She stared at him icily. She was white again. "Hey, babe," she replied with a dangerously frigid tone and the slightest emphasis on the 'babe' part. "It's not that kind of bike, babe."

"It's a sweet machine," James Earle interjected, suddenly worried about the tone the conversation was assuming. "Hey, Helen, you remember that time you tried to teach me how to ride it?" James Earle was working hard to get them back to a happy place.

Helena laughed. "You learned, James Earle. You were a good rider. The Ducati's just really not your ride, I told you."

"Girl, I put that machine clean through the back wall of your garage! I almost killed myself." The big man turned to Gabriel. "I'd never take that thing out on the road, man. It's wicked powerful," he added, for Gabe's benefit. Gabe was enraptured though, listening to Helena's laugh. He had never heard her laugh before. She's got a great laugh, he thought to himself. He collected himself, returning to earth and the conversation.

"Wait, you had a garage?" Gabriel asked.

"Not after James Earle was done, I didn't." She was wiping away tears from laughing so hard.

"And a Ducati?" Gabriel asked, incredulous.

"Still got the Ducati. Fork's a little bent, though." She gave James Earle a playful scowl.

"Where'd you get a Ducati?"

"It was a gift. Kind of."

"What kind?" he asked, not really buying this.

"1199 Pinagale"

"No friggin' way you ride a Pinagale. That bike must weigh like 300 pounds!"

James Earle's eyes were getting wide with panic. "Don't go there, man," he stage whispered to Gabe.

"It weighs 361 pounds, with an empty tank," she answered in a dangerous *sotto voce*, hands now on hips again. Gabe was thinking how beautiful her laugh had been, just a couple of seconds ago. "Why would there be no fucking way I'd ride a Ducati 1199? You one of those cretins that think anybody who rides anything other than a Harley with tassels is a pussy? Is that what you're saying, motherfucker?"

"You're kidding, right?" Gabe soothed, raising his hands apologetically.

James Earle leaned in to Gabe again, trying to play peacemaker. "She's not kidding. Word of advice." He put a protective arm around Gabriel.

Helena took a step closer, still staring up at him wickedly. "Still listening, Gabby. Maybe you've got some gang tats I just hadn't noticed while we were rolling around the last few nights? Maybe I missed your badassness, Gabby Hayes motherfucker?"

"Okay, then," Barry interjected, physically placing his not insignificant self between Helena and Gabriel. "You all are starting to lose me with the sophisticated conversational references and all. I'm thinking we leave the bike for another day. James Earle, we should be going."

James Earle had gone very pale for a person of African-American descent. His eyes were still wide with concern. "Yeah, Barry's right. We should be getting to the weight room."

They said their goodbyes at that point. Each lifted Helena up in turn again so she could give them a kiss on the cheek. As he heard the door click shut behind them, Barry turned to his friend. "I give it two weeks, tops, before the bitch pops a cap in his sorry ass. Serious." James Earle nodded in agreement.

"Poor dude hasn't a clue. He's got a wicked-ass tiger by the tail. Think we should tell him?"

"Nobody warned us, worked out okay."

"Yeah, worked out great. Cost me a year rehabbing." James Earle rubbed his knee as they descended the steps to the truck.

Chapter 4

Gabriel started opening the new boxes sitting on the floor. He stole frequent glances at Helena, trying to gauge which way this seesaw was riding now that James Earle and Barry had left. She was back on her step stool, putting up more books from yesterday's boxes. Her body English told him nothing. He didn't know her well enough for that yet. He could tell she wasn't whistling, though. And this silence was really dragging on. He took a shot.

"James Earle and Barry seem like great guys." Lame, he thought. Oh, well.

"You have no idea."

Okay, he thought. She sounds happy enough. He waited for her to continue. She didn't. He waited, couldn't wait any longer. "You said I had no idea." Too perky, he thought. I sound like a freaking Jack Russell here.

"You don't, Gabe. Have no idea, trust me."

He laughed, waited for her to elaborate. She didn't, just kept filing away books. "Love to hear a story or two." Sitting up begging here, pant, pant. Toss me a bone, a ball, anything.

"It was before we met."

"Well, yeah; I figured that. We met less than a week ago."

She sighed and sat down heavily onto the step stool, leaning elbows on knees. "What is it, Gabriel? You starting to panic here? Just starting to figure out that you let this girl move in that you don't know shit about? Thinking, hell, sure, she's a great lay and all, but what if she's a psychopath, or a serial killer, or something? What will Mom and Dad say if they drop by with cookies this weekend and you don't answer the door, so they go away thinking that's pretty odd, our Gabe usually gives us a call if he goes out of town for the weekend, and you're sitting here in the living room, gagged and bound with duct tape to your Ikea dining chair and trying to make enough noise so they'll come rescue you with the spare key they made you give them, even though you didn't want to, but it is, in some ways, their place too, since they helped you buy it, so you gave them the key, but shit, what if they walked in when you had a girl straddling you naked and making so much noise they stop dead in their tracks right here in the living room and let themselves out quietly without you even knowing they were here? Is that what we're talking about, Gabby?" She stared at him.

He stared back, jaw slack. All he could think of was how pretty she was, with a curl of red hair stuck down in the middle of her forehead. "How'd you know my parents helped me get this place?" he asked.

"You don't have to be freakin' Columbo to figure out you can't buy a condo on State Street on a grad student's salary."

He couldn't stop staring at her, didn't try. "Who's Columbo?"

"Does it matter who freaking Columbo is, Gabe? Is that what we're talking about here? Focus, partner, focus! Because I don't want to have this conversation every time your suburban guilt-fueled insecurities well up when I introduce you to two of my African-American former lovers."

"You SLEPT with those guys?"

"No, I didn't sleep with those guys, but shit, Gabe, you really don't look like you're paying attention here, and I was just seeing if you were listening. That's quite an image when you think about it, though. I mean, wow." She smiled wistfully.

"I didn't really think you had slept with them."

"Why, because they're black? Little white girl like me shouldn't lie with Mandingo? You a racist, Gabriel?"

"Not a racist, Leena. Just not your type."

She smiled at him. "Oh, the whole football player at the bar thing, right? You are smooth, Sheehan." She came over and sat on his lap, putting her arms around his neck. He bent to give her a kiss, just as he realized he wasn't really sure he knew Helena's last name. That was crazy, he thought. He would ask her right after this. And didn't those guys keep calling her Helen?

"How'd you know my parents have a key?"

Chapter 5

After lunch, they went back to putting away her books. He was helping, as it was apparent she wasn't using any particular filing system and there were a lot of books, more than were going to fit on his shelves. He was starting to pay attention to the books themselves as well, rifling through them casually. He had already noted four different names written on the inside covers, none of them with the first name of Helena. Almost every book was filled with notes written in the margins in her script, however. Over and over, he ran into whole paragraphs that had been circled or crossed out. Tattered notes, always on yellow legal stationary, were to be found in every one. He picked up another book from the box, this one in Cyrillic and smelling of mildew. Pages were stiff and many stuck together, but here were the same notes in the margins.

"I'm thinking, Leena, that since we're not going to have room for all of them, maybe we should leave the rotting Russian math books in the box."

She turned to look. "Let me see." She bent down to take it from him and put it on the shelf. "We're going to need that one, I think."

"You can read Russian?"

"That's not Russian, silly!"

"Oh." He picked up a book he recognized. It was a text from a graduate math seminar he had almost taken last year. The course was a concentrated study of an advanced statistics method that he thought might help him massage his data. He had realized after twenty minutes that he lacked about three prerequisites that were needed for him to even have a shot at passing the course, and dropped it the next day. "Hey, I know this book."

"Yeah, right. What did you do, read it during the twenty minutes you were actually in the class? No, wait—I remember now; you spent that twenty minutes asking the professor to review all the shit you should've known before signing up for the freaking class." She smiled.

"You were there? Why? I don't remember seeing you."

"Yeah, I was there, moron. You were like the running gag of the whole semester. Even that prof—Professor Jackshit—he'd say right up till the last week of class, like whenever one of us would completely screw up a problem, Jackshit would say, really serious like, 'Don't Sheehan on me, mister.' We all cracked up every time. Great class."

"Jacoby. His name is Jacoby."

"Yeah, I know. But he can't teach worth jack shit, so that's what I called him. He loved me, gave me an A."

"You're teasing me again, aren't you?"

She looked shocked, hurt. "I don't tease you, Gabe."

"That really happened?" She nodded solemnly. "But Jacoby's one of my advisors. He's on my committee."

"Then dear, I'd say you're pretty much fucked." She smiled at him.

Over the next three weeks they settled into a routine. They were both early risers. She'd go for a run in the morning, while he took the Pinarello for an hour past North Campus. When they got back, they'd shower and eat. Then he'd get to work at the desk in the spare bedroom he had set up as his office. Once, he asked her if she was going to ever go to her classes. "Dropped 'em," was all she said as she flipped through some five-pound math textbook in her lap. She worked sitting cross-legged on the bed, propped by pillows against the wall. He shrugged and went back to his desk.

Most days, they'd work all day in their separate rooms, hardly speaking, unless they passed on the way to the bathroom or the kitchen. Other days, Gabe would hear the door close and go check to find Helena had left without a word. Often, he'd notice she'd taken his car keys from the kitchen counter. She never said where she had gone and he never asked. Once, she came back and asked him to help her bring in the bags of groceries she'd bought.

Once, she was gone for three days. He was thinking about calling her cellphone, and then realized he didn't know her phone number. He finally heard her come home at two in the morning. Gabriel was still awake, working but not really waiting up. He walked around the condo looking for her, found her dumping clothes out of a duffel bag into the washer. He came up behind her and gave her a hug.

"Hey, Gabe. Working late? How's it going?" She added soap and closed the lid, turned and jumped to sit on the machine.

He leaned into her, smelling her breath. No alcohol, no smoke, no weed. Not that he was checking. He laughed, a little at himself. "It's going great. I think I'll have the proposal done in another day or two."

"Wow, that's great."

"Yeah, wow is right. My last proposal took almost a year."

"You didn't have me."

"No, that's right. I didn't have you." He leaned in again and gave her a kiss this time. "Listen, Leena. We need to talk."

"Shit, Gabe. Sounds ominous. Maybe we should screw first?" She rubbed her nose against his. "You know, lighten the mood? Maybe even skip the whole talking part until morning? Whaddya say, sport?"

Seemed reasonable.

The next day, she ran, he rode, they showered and sat down to breakfast together. Through a mouthful of Fruitloops, she asked, "Whaddya wanna talk about?"

He laid down his spoon carefully alongside his bowel of Grapenuts and looked at her. "I don't have your cell number."

"Don't have one." He looked down at his bowel of cereal. "Geez, Gabe. That was a short conversation." She shoveled up another soupspoon full of Fruitloops. "God, I love this stuff. Never even tasted it until I moved into the dorm. It's like little molded rings of pure sugar infused with artificial dyes and shit. It's amazing they can serve this stuff to kids, but get caught toking one little joint in sixth grade and—you okay, there, Gabby? You're not eating your ground up human remains there with your usual zeal, partner."

Gabe looked up at her and watched a small rivulet of purple tinged milk drip down her chin. Who could not love this girl? he thought. "I'm not really sure what your last name is," he said slowly.

She spluttered, spraying him with Fruitloops and pastel milk spittle. "Sorry Gabe, honey. That was rude." She leaned over to dab at his face with her napkin. "You have got to be shitting me!" He shook his head like a Bassett hound. "Hell, Gabriel! Why didn't you just go through my wallet while I slept, like any other freaking paranoid?" She leaned back in her chair to grab her wallet, fumbled with it for a moment and tossed him her driver's license. He scanned it carefully. It was an Alabama license, with the name Helena Fianna. He handed it back to her. "Happy now, Gabe? Honey?" She raised the bowl to her lips to drink the rainbow colored milk. "Best part," he heard through the fake china.

"It's fake," he said matter-of-factly. Helena froze momentarily, lowered the bowl to the table.

She stared at him levelly. "No shit? Why do you say that?"

He looked at her curiously. "That says you were born over thirty years ago. And Alabama? Come on, Leena! Helena Fianna from Alabama? Sounds like a bad limerick."

She laughed with him. "Busted! That's my drinking license. Dude who forged it for me was a real comedian. Said that Alabama still didn't use the crazy holograms, that he couldn't do the hologram thing. I almost killed him when I saw that date of birth, the bastard. Worst part?" Gabe shook his head, waited. "Crazy moron cut up my real license for the picture."

Another week and Helena announced that if she didn't get a desk to work at, her back would be so fucked she was going to start sleeping on the floor, and that meant that nothing else but her back was going to be fucked for the indefinite future. Gabriel enthusiastically offered his study, but she pointed out that his middle-aged spine probably wouldn't hold up to switching places. A new desk was needed, a workspace to call her own.

"Let's get in the car, I'll take you to Ikea."

"Oh, catch me," she feigned a swoon. "The man has proposed to take me to Ikea. What the hell is it with you guys and Ikea? Does every guy still have to stare at that poster of Bridget Bardot while he's jacking off as a teenager? Do you have like lingonberry wet dreams? Really, what is it?"

"Who's Bridget Bardot?" He followed her to the car and, starting the aging Subaru, turned to her in the passenger seat. "What's wrong with Ikea?"

"Drive, Gabriel."

"All my furniture in the place is Ikea."

"Noticed that."

"You never complained."

"Not my place. Drive. South."

"Where're we going?"

"Ypsi"

"I think there's an Ikea in Ypsi."

"Yeah. We're not going there."

"Where in Ypsi, then?"

"Not the Ikea, Gabe. Get over it."

"If it's about paying for a desk, I don't mind. Really, it's not a problem."

Helena looked at him in profile, driving. Profile wasn't his best angle, she decided. The nose was a problem in profile. From straight on, you didn't notice the nose so much. The beard was filling in nicely, though. There was hope. She sighed deeply. "Really, Gabe? Not a problem?" He turned to look at her, wondering yet again what he had said wrong. Face on now. Definitely better. "Before I moved here, I could eat for a year on what you'd pay for the cheapest desk they sell in that place."

Gabriel sensed an opening. "Really? Where was that, Leena?"

"Not here, Gabe. Way not here." She laid her head back and closed her eyes, giving him directions to her storage unit.

Gabriel pulled the Subaru over some train tracks and up to a low sheet metal building covered with graffiti and gang tags. This was easily the worst neighborhood he'd ever seen at less than sixty miles per hour. "Nice neighborhood," he said, reluctantly turning off the engine.

"Don't worry, cupcake," she said, climbing out of the car, "you'll protect me."

"I'm not worried. You don't have to be faster than the bear, you know." He gave her a wink.

"I've seen you run. If that's your plan, you should worry."

"Plan B, then. Offer them the girl, they always want the girl."

"Not in this neighborhood, they don't." She pulled up the big roller door with a squeal.

"No lock?"

"Why bother? Wouldn't last two minutes. No lock, most of the derelicts assume there's nothing but shit inside." She pulled on a string dangling in front of his face and a florescent light sputtered to life.

"What about the rest?"

"The rest know who owns it." She began heading towards the back of the unit, stepping between chest high piles of who-knows-what covered with tarps and moldy blankets. Gabriel poked around, mostly lifting tarps with the toe of his shoe. He found the Ducati and whistled softly. Unlike everything else he saw in here, it looked cherry. He pulled the tarp off and ogled. It was red.

"You ride, Gabe?" Helena had come up quietly behind him, putting her arms around him.

"What do you mean, do I ride? You've seen me on the Pinarello. I am an awesome rider!" He turned in her arms to look at her. "Bike's pretty much the same, right?"

She smiled at that. "Yeah, Gabe, pretty much. Just picture yourself on your bike, going the wildass fastest you've ever ridden, down the biggest, steepest monster hill you've ever seen, and the road is wet." He was smiling, nodding, as she continued. "And you're coming up to a sharp left with loose sand and gravel, and there's like a fifty foot cliff if you miss the turn, with no guardrail. And a dumbass truck taking up both lanes."

He was still smiling, nodding enthusiastically, "Yeah, yeah! I've done that, exactly! Stupid-ass truck! That's the Ducati all the time, huh? Wow."

"No, Gabriel. That's first gear." His smile drooped.

"Oh."

"Sweet though, huh?" she asked. He nodded appreciatively. "Sorry I can't let you take it for a ride."

He used the hurt face. "What, you don't trust me? You let James Earle ride it and you never even slept with him."

She shook her head, smiling at her pouting friend. "Not real gas in her. I've got her juiced for storage, long-term. Sorry, she's a rip. You'd like her. But she's no Pinarello." She smiled at him knowingly.

"What? I'd let you ride my bike!"

"No, you wouldn't. Your heart skips a beat if I get too close to it with a can of coke in my hand."

"Coke could hurt the finish. Listen, why don't we trailer the Ducati to my place? You could fix it up and we could race."

She shook her head as she replaced the tarp carefully. "Not a good idea."

"Chicken!"

Helena laughed. "Can't park it at your place, sorry Lance."

"Lots of bikes parked in front of our place."

"Not hot ones."

"What, your bike is too cool to hang with the Vespas? Some of those bikes are pretty hot."

"Not like mine. Mine's stolen. Come on, help me drag out my desk."

It took them the rest of the day to get the desk trailered back to the condo and manhandled up the steps into their bedroom. It was a compact rolltop, beautifully handcrafted in oak with brass fittings. Gabriel made appreciative noises as he helped Helena wipe it down with oil and lubricate the slides with surgical wax. Finished, they fell onto the bed and lay on their stomachs, chins in hand, admiring the oaken glow in the fading twilight. "It's pretty," Gabe offered.

Helena nodded. "It feels good to have it here. It was a sin to have it in that shitpile."

"Is it stolen, too?"

She shook her head. "Don't think so. It was my Da's. He always claimed he brought it with him from Ireland, but I never really believed him."

Gabe perked up, listening. She had never said a word about her family before. "Why didn't you?"

"Because he was Irish, for one."

Gabe didn't understand the comment, but wanted to keep her talking. "And for another?"

"For another, any Irishman rich enough to bring his desk to America would've left his family with something more than empty whiskey bottles. We're all misers, you know."

"Yeah, I've heard. Misers and drinkers and storytellers. And good music. I like your music."

"Do you now?" she asked in a thick brogue. She laid her head on her hands, smiling at him.

"So your folks are dead, then?"

Her smile evaporated. "They are to me." He was about to ask her what that meant, exactly, but she had rolled away from him and went to sleep.

CHAPTER 6

Two days later, Gabriel finished his part of the proposal. Helena was still working, spending several hours a day at the astronomy building. Two more weeks passed, Gabe doing minor rewrites until he realized he had started changing some bits back to the same way they had been in the first draft. Finally, Helena returned at four in the morning and startled him from a sound sleep, slamming the door shut and screaming in her loudest Irish pub brogue, "Break out the booze, Gabriel! It is finished!" the last in a loud, quavering falsetto.

They toasted the seven-inch thick pile of single-spaced pages, an opus of intense brilliance (her phrase) that she had deposited ceremoniously in the center of the kitchen table. Halfway through the second bottle of champagne, Gabriel went and got his equally thick and just as brilliant proposal (his phrase), setting it next to hers. They finished the champagne and started on a bottle of single malt whiskey that he didn't even know he had in his liquor cabinet. Actually, he drunkenly explained to Helena—he was drinking on an empty stomach and had never started drinking at four in the morning before—he didn't even remember he had a liquor cabinet. She reminded him that he had been saving the $200 bottle for just this occasion. They composed more eloquent toasts to the proposal, toasted his parents, toasted that rat bastard, Jacoby Jackshit. Helena tried to teach him a few Irish drinking songs, but Gabe could never be drunk enough to sing anything with lyrics that embarrassingly offensive. By ten in the morning, both of them sat passed out at the kitchen table, surrounded by the empty bottles and their magnum opus at its place of honor in the center of the table. They never heard his parents let themselves in or, having determined that their son and some pretty redhead were unarousable but breathing, let themselves back out.

Gabriel thought the next step was to get to work combining the products of their hard work, resulting in the complete, final proposal. Helena convinced him that, as great as that sounded, it wasn't that easy. She proposed that they take a week taking up each other's report for a thorough, critical reading and review. He realized immediately she was right. He also immediately agreed that they were both too fried from the work of the last three months to dive right back into it.

"We should go on vacation!" he exclaimed. "Together!"

"Couldn't agree more."

"A week lying on the beach! You got a passport?"

"Several."

Gabriel let this pass, too enthused with the image of Helena lying next to him on a white sand beach. "That's it then—I know a great place. Fantastic condo right on the beach, Turks and Caicos. Sunny and mid-eighties every day, really great. You'll love it, I—what?"

He had finally slowed down enough to notice her heavily sighing as she shook her head lugubriously. "Not gonna happen, partner."

"What, you said!" He heard himself sounding like a truculent nine year old, but couldn't help it. He was still holding on to his bikini-clad vision.

"Sorry we can't relive your Bar mitzvah trip with mom and pop in the islands. Not this time around, Gabe. Sorry." She sounded deeply sorry, for some reason he wasn't seeing.

"We don't have to bring my parents, if you really don't want to." He smiled at her, concerned that she suddenly looked so sad. "What else, Leena?"

"So much, Gabriel. We're wrong on so many levels here."

"Tell me."

"Honestly, I don't know where to start."

"What's the worst?"

"Depends."

"On what?"

"Well, on whether your parents gave you a Netjets card for your birthday, for one."

Gabriel shook his head. "They wanted to. I insisted on the yacht, instead."

She brightened. "You've got a boat?"

"No, Leena. I do not have a boat. I don't have access to a private jet. I didn't have you pegged for this high maintenance. Work with me, will you? It's just a week's vacation. Hell, we can drive up to Sleeping Bear dunes and camp on the beach, that'd be great with me."

She jumped to her feet. "What is it with you with the beaches and the dunes? Shit, Gabby, are you a moron or what?"

"What? What's wrong with the beach?"

"Look at what we're working with here, moron! Why don't we just lay out our blanket on the patio? You can pour kerosene on me and just fucking light me on fire, save travel expenses. I'm Irish, Gabriel—did you run into many bonnie lasses last time down in the islands, mon? No? You may have missed them. If we stand still we look like a flaming Tiki torch, moron." She sat back down and blew her hair up off her forehead.

"Oh. Not the beach, then. Somewhere else."

"Yeah, somewhere else. And no flying."

Gabriel sat down in front of her. "I'm just taking a wild guess here, but I'm betting taking the train for a screaming good time in Toronto is out, too."

"Tempting, but not gonna happen."

"No borders, then. No airports. Probably not up for a DC getaway, take a tour of the freaking FBI Headquarters."

Helena flopped back on the couch, covering her head with her arms. "Don't fuck with me, Gabe. I'm too tired."

He said softly, "You're not the one being fucked with here, Helena."

"I can't do this now, Gabe," she said from the shelter of her encircling arms. "I'm too tired, or too hung over, or too old, but I can't do this now. I just want to get away for a while. With you would be great. If not, then..."

"With me, Leena. Definitely with me, but—"

She propped herself up on her elbows and looked at him, interrupting. "Let's just work on the how and where right now, Gabe. Please? We'll do the why later, okay? On vacation?"

"Promise?" She nodded and made a cross my heart gesture. "Should I bring extra money for bail?"

She gave him a weak smile. "Won't be necessary."

"Where are we going?"

"My pick?" He nodded. She flopped back and considered, staring at the ceiling. "You seem in pretty good shape."

"Better than you!"

She snorted derisively. "We'll see, Gabe. You're not afraid of heights are you?"

"No, I don't think so. Why, where are we going?"

She sat up and gave him a wicked smile. "The Gunks!"

"Really? The Gunks? Is that like a grunge Six Flags? I love those old wooden roller coasters."

As soon as Helena decided on their destination, she returned to her usual frenetic self. Helena directed Gabriel on what to load into the Subaru. They stopped at her storage unit. Helena loaded in two backpacks and several large ditty bags of camping supplies. He waited in the car, listening to her noisily rummaging around the storage unit, cursing like a sailor. Finally, he heard her whoop in triumph, "Found it!" Gabriel didn't start worrying until she emerged wearing two bandoliers of climbing equipment and carrying six huge coils of multicolored rope. She tossed it all in the back of the car and climbed into the passenger seat. "Onward!" she cried, smacking the dashboard with a loud crack. He didn't start the car.

"That's a lot of rope."

"You have got to be shitting me!" Gabriel squealed as he peered over the granite cliff. "No fucking way, Leena!" He refused to approach the last four feet to where Helena was working with their packs.

"Chickenshit! I thought my Gabby wasn't afraid of heights."

"Yeah, I thought you meant like those really high Ferris wheels, no problem. This is like five seconds of me screaming and splat!"

She tossed a dramatic look over her shoulder "Closer to thirty or forty I'd say. But you're right about one thing—you're awake and screaming the whole way."

"You are so fucking with me!"

"No, really. It's true. I've done it."

"WHAT? You told me in the car you knew how to do this shit! What happened to 'Don't worry, Gabe, it'll be fun'? I'm starting to think we have different ideas of fun, crazy fucking girlfriend..." He trailed off as he crawled on his belly the last few feet towards her and peered over the edge. He screamed again and rolled onto his back, looking skyward. "Why not parachuting, instead?"

"No way. That shit's really dangerous. Never get drunk enough to do that again."

He watched her rechecking the ropes, inch by inch. He had seen her check every inch of every rope three times in the car ride here and twice more since they pitched camp this morning. She had rejected two coils, cutting them into smaller hafts to use the good parts for harnessing. She double bagged the bad parts and threw them in a dumpster, after drawing a picture of a skull and crossbones on a piece of paper and enclosing it with the rope, murmuring that if they didn't get the point they deserved to die.

"Deep, cleansing breaths there, cowboy. Everybody's scared at this point. At least, the ones who survive are. I'd be worried if you weren't scared. Though you could take it down a notch, wouldn't bother me." She smiled at him as he kept looking at the clouds, hyperventilating. "Do you remember what we went over this morning?" She had spent an hour explaining the rig to him and going over knots and basic climbing technique.

"Not a fucking thing."

She laughed. "You're my favorite kind of pupil, Gabriel."

"Yeah, what kind don't you like? The ones who puke on your shoes at this point? I hope not."

"No, the ones who so want to please you they pretend they got it all and nod a lot. They usually don't say much, but they'll step right off, still nodding like an idiot."

"Yeah, then what?"

"Then they're in it up to their ass and they realize they don't have a clue what to do next. And Gabe, honey, I'm not saying this to scare you. I know you're going to be just fine. I won't let you fall, but I can't do the climbing for you. Once you're on the face, I can't get you off. Look at me, hon—" she waited till he met her eyes. "Climbing is not a team sport. It's just you and the rock, baby."

"And gravity." He smiled weakly.

"No, not gravity, not for you. I'm in charge of gravity. Your job is just to move: up, down, sideways; you are in charge of moving. No matter what you do or don't do, I will not let you fall, understand? Say it, Gabe."

"You will not let me fall." She nodded and gave him an encouraging smile.

He sat up, took a shuddering breath, and smiled back. "You're not going to let me fall, are you?"

"Nope. You're going to be great. Now come over here so we can check your harness again." Gabriel started to scoot towards her. "Oh, for the love of Pete, Gabe, stand up and walk. I'm not gonna sneeze and knock you over the edge. Be a mensch!" He stood warily and walked over to where she sat on her haunches in front of him. She made him trace the knot at his waist with her twice. Then she made him do it himself again. "Happy with it?"

"Ecstatic."

"Check it again."

"I was kidding, Leena."

"There's no kidding at the top, Gabriel. You kid at the bottom. Too much kidding, you're kidding at the top and the bottom at the same time." He checked it again and declared himself ready to climb. "Good. Follow me." She picked up the coil of rope she'd just checked and walked away from the cliff to a big oak tree set thirty feet back in a clearing. He followed. "Look at this tree, Gabriel. See how big and strong this tree is, Gabe?" He nodded. "How old do you think this tree is, Gabe?" Gabriel shrugged. "This tree is over a hundred years old, Gabe. Nothing has budged this tree in a hundred years."

"Got it. Tree big. Tree old. Tree strong."

She squinted at him with green steely eyes. "See the rope marks around her, here?" He nodded. "This tree has held thousands and thousands of climbers. You and I are going to be tied off to this tree, got it? This tree won't let you fall. This tree won't let you pull me off, no matter what happens. And no matter what you do, I will not let you fall. Now watch as I tie us off." He watched her encircle the tree over and again, then made him check over everything again after she clipped herself in with her harness. Then she made him show her how to move his rope through the metal belay plate to control his descent, which she had taught him that morning.

"Ready, sport?" He nodded, not willing at that moment to trust his voice. "Then over you go." He shuffled backwards toward the precipice, stood with his heels a safe distance from the edge. She made him show her his hand position and demonstrate again that he knew how to move his ropes. "Climber ready?"

"Ready to climb," he said with a squeak, reciting the ritual she had taught him that morning. "On belay?"

"Belay on. I've got you, Gabe. Have fun."

He nodded, gave her a smile. He didn't move.

"It's all good, Gabe-baby. Look at me, hon. Cliff's that way." She pointed behind him. Not smiling now, Gabriel took a step back with his right foot, found empty air, and disappeared below the edge of the cliff.

CHAPTER 7

They were home ten days later, having decided to splurge on two nights of high rent resort living on Lake Placid to 'clean up and scrape the mud off' before making the drive back to Ann Arbor. Gabriel was addicted, having quickly proven himself an agile, yet thoughtful, rock climber. He wasn't going to win any speed climbing championships, Helena's specialty, but he spent surprisingly little time dangling in midair from Helena's belaying rope for a novice. He had the balance expected of an avid bicyclist. Helena was surprised, however, that he had better upper body strength than she had anticipated, and the endurance bought from daily riding made up for his semi-flailing climbing style. She was generous and sincere in her appraisal of his first expedition. He felt it was the best vacation, ever.

They tossed their duffels of dirty clothes in the laundry room and plopped onto the couch. They both tried not to see the twin piles of neatly stacked paper still waiting on the kitchen table.

"So now," she said with evil relish, "I get to ride the Pinarello, right?"

Gabriel blanched slightly but managed a jaunty, "Only fair."

Helena guffawed. "Yeah, Gabe. As if you could let me touch that bike without getting angina."

"I'm not really like that."

"You're kidding right? Gabe, you fondle that thing like it's your second dick. You start panting when you wax it, which is every night. If I were the jealous type—"

"Got it, made your point. We could get you your own bike, I know a guy—"

"No way."

"Oh, yeah, that's sweet. Toss your buddy Gabe off a cliff, but too weak to ride with him, huh? Yeah, I can understand, what with your endurance problem and—"

"Endurance problem? Last time I say something nice about your body, lardass! I can probably run farther than you can ride that thing. Besides..."

"What? Besides what, my melanin-challenged mate? What other lame excuse? Too sunny, honey? Bunny?"

She rolled her eyes. "I'm not riding around Ann Arbor with you dressed like that. You're going to want to get a latte at Cappy's, and there's no way I'm being seen with you like that."

"Like what?"

"The shorts, Gabe. The freaking Spandex shorts!"

"What's wrong with the shorts? I look good in the shorts."

"No, Gabe, you don't. Nothing personal, dear. Nobody looks good in the shorts, Gabe. Nobody wants to have to see that stuff. Guys don't like to see other guy's stuff. Girls don't want to see guy's stuff. And I sure don't want to have to see your stuff all hanging out and—"

"We take a shower together almost every morning."

"No choice. There's not enough hot water in this shit hole. And I never look down. Remember that time I dropped the soap and—"

"You made me get out and get a new bar. You said it was more sanitary."

"Yeah, well, I lied. Jeez, Gabe, it's soap. Think about it."

"Forget it, then. You're not getting a bike, ok?"

"Fine. Get me a puppy or something."

"That would be cruel."

Finally, they could procrastinate no longer. After breakfast the next day, each reached across the table and picked up the other's report, then retired with coffee mug in hand to their respective desks. Ten minutes later Helena barged into his room and waved a page in his face. "What is this shit?" she demanded.

"You're kidding, right? You've looked at my stuff for what, ten minutes?"

"It took me all of two minutes to figure out you're a fucking moron! I waited the extra eight to spare your feelings. Dickhead!"

"You're really mixing your metaphors here, Leena."

"I mean this dickhead, Dickhead. Is this a joke page? In your doctoral proposal world, you guys throw in a Farside every few pages, lighten the mood?" She put the page down in front of him on the desk. It was an illustration of the putative test subject, wearing Gabriel's design for an electrode array skullcap.

"What?"

Helena collapsed onto the loveseat next to the desk. "Oh, fuck me sideways, Gabe. He's bald!"

"Well, yeah, babe, the electrodes gotta—"

"Oh by the blessed Virgin, Gabriel! No wonder they're throwing you out on your ass! Let's think about this. The SETI model, remember? Tens of thousands of people, sitting down at their computers, you said, each having their brainwaves recorded while viewing some picture on the screen." He nodded. "Non synchronous but massively, multiply redundant, same stimulus repeated over thousands and thousands of subjects, allowing the electrical fingerprint of a single, pure thought to be recorded from every volunteer's home computer, networked together and filtered until it's like a perfect little gem. And we repeat with another picture, and another, and we record, and we accumulate, and we analyze over and over with every college student and computer geek and who knows who else we can get to—"

"Yeah, Helena, I got that. It's my idea! What's your point?"

She stabbed a finger down on the illustration, voice rising. "You never mentioned that we're only going to figure out how to read the mind of a fucking skinhead, Dickhead! Oh, hold it! I'm sorry—was I too hasty, and didn't get to the part where you explain that every volunteer gets a free Gillette and a can of fucking Barbasol? All ten or twenty thousand freaking volunteers? Hey, it could be like a fashion statement: See my shiny head? I stayed home last night and dedicated myself to the study of Gabriel Fucking Sheehan's neuroscience project, give me a hug!" She collapsed back on the couch. Softly, she added, "Please tell me you're just fucking with me and I picked up the fake proposal. Please, Gabe."

He shook his head. "The electrodes need to—"

He stopped as Helena slid to the floor, wailing. She curled up on the floor hugging herself, rocking back and forth. "No, no, no, no, no, no!" she moaned, eyes squeezed shut as she rocked on the floor. She was crying, he saw.

He knelt to hold her, but she kept rocking and crying, rocking and crying. "Helena, please," he whispered in her ear, "Please, stop. I'll fix it."

She slowly stopped rocking and looked at him, eyes over brimming with tears. He wiped tears from her cheeks as he held her face close to his.

"You promise?" she asked, looking at him and stifling a sob.

He had made her cry. Helena never cried. He nodded.

"I promise."

CHAPTER 8

They went to bed early that evening, barely speaking. The next morning he awoke to an empty house. She had left his proposal on her desk, untouched. He showered, dressed, and went to the kitchen table. He looked for a note that he knew wouldn't be there. Helena didn't do notes, except for the skull and crossbones variety. He sat down at his desk and put his face in his hands. His picture of the Dickhead was still sitting there, accusingly. He crumpled it up and flung it aside. He put his head in his hands, and sat.

For the next three days, he sat at his desk. Ate, showered, and returned to his desk to bury his face there in his hands. He knew he should drag himself to the lab, start the experiments he'd need to design a new sensor. He couldn't force himself out of the chair. He kept imagining Helena's face as he held her, could see her eyes filled with tears. He had known great success before; god knew he had experienced professional failure before. But Gabriel had never known the pain of so cruelly and profoundly disappointing someone, someone he deeply cared about and wanted to please more than himself. He sat, capable only of seeing her face, feeling her head in his hands as she wept. And in that vision, he saw his answer. He raised his head, put his hands before him as he had when he had held her, and he saw it—the thing he had promised her, was right there. Almost a vision but not really, just so right it was tangible. He stood shakily and giggled. He ran to the kitchen and had his cellphone in his hand before he stopped, feeling stupid and impotent. He couldn't call her, couldn't tell her 'I did it, come home'. He so much wanted to replace that image that had haunted him these past three days with the face of his Leena smiling, laughing.

"Jesus Fucking Christ," he yelled to the empty room, "who the FUCK doesn't own a cellphone?" He raised his arm to throw the worthless thing against the wall, but knew he wasn't going to do it even before he began the gesture. He just looked at it there in his hand. Who doesn't own a cellphone? Every single person in North America, from the poorest ditch digger in El Paso to the prime minister of Canada, carried one of these around. Who didn't own a cellphone? Nobody. Except for his Leena, that's who. He looked at his phone and dropped heavily into a kitchen chair. He had another idea. It was done now, he was certain. This was going to work. He had to find Helena.

He started backing the car out the driveway, not knowing where he was going, only knowing he had to find her. He didn't know if she had any friends, didn't think she had any family. Shit, he suddenly realized, they never had the conversation. She had promised. She had promised she would tell him the 'why' when they were on vacation, but she never had. Well, he had made her a promise and kept it. He'd make her keep hers.

Gabriel started driving to the dorm, her old dorm where they had spent their first days together. He had cleared out her stuff but given her back the key, he was certain. Had Helena returned it? No, that wasn't the Helena he knew. He tried to envision his Helena curled up on the mattress on the floor, to make the vision real, but as he approached the dorm, he shook his head and kept driving, finally turning south.

Gabriel pulled up the rusting garage door to the storage unit and peered in.

"Helena?" He could see shafts of sunlight cutting through the motes of swirling dust and in the corner, Helena. She lay curled up like a child on the concrete floor near the motorcycle, it's tarp half pulled down and covering her like a blanket. He knelt by her and gently touched her cheek. "Hey, baby. You asleep?"

Her eyes fluttered open. "Hey, Gabe." She seemed to take a minute to focus on him. "Did you fix it for me?"

"I did, Leena. I fixed it for you. It's time to come home."

She stretched her arms up to him dreamily. "Take me away."

CHAPTER 9

Again, they were sitting at the kitchen table together. Gabriel felt deliriously, dangerously happy. It was like he had a huge diamond or something even better, because he thought this girl probably didn't give a flying fuck about diamonds, hidden in his hand, and his Helena, smiling again because she believed beyond a shadow of a doubt in him, in his having fixed it just as he had promised, was sitting here with him, and now waiting for that moment when he flipped open the little box and he could watch her eyes go wide as saucers. She had slept in the car on the way home, snoring like a truck driver. When he got her home, she stripped off her clothes as she walked back to the bathroom and took a shower, blissfully alone, for thirty minutes. She stepped from the steam filled bathroom and fell into bed, where she had slept like the dead for almost twenty-four hours.

Gabriel spent the time filling in details, but he knew, just as he had known yesterday, that his solution to the sensory electrode problem was so simple and elegant that it couldn't not work. And his added idea, that additional insight, was just the crazy, perfect hot fudge sauce on top. He was at his desk when he thought he heard her stirring in the bedroom. He was convinced that his friend was indeed awake by the drill sergeant scream of "WAFFLES! Stacks of waffles, with EGGS. Lots of eggs! Bacon! No, not bacon, SAUSAGE! No, no—bacon AND sausage! And orange juice, fresh squeezed, not that frozen shit! COFFEE! Black as tar and hot enough to kill, in that mug I like." By the end of her rant she had emerged dressed in his oversized robe and joined him in the kitchen, plopping down in a chair and leaning her elbows on the table, chin in hand. She looked about ten years old, swimming in that robe.

Gabriel brought her over a bowl of Fruitloops and put it down in front of her. "Hungry, huh?" She nodded, attacking the cereal before her.

"COFFEE!"

Gabriel set down a chipped mug of black coffee before her and sat in the chair opposite. He couldn't help smiling as he watched her eat. A distant memory of a childhood visit to the Detroit zoo came and passed.

"WRONG MUG!"

"Yeah, well, sorry, your highness. Your mug's dirty. I'll fire the maid. She's been missing for a few days." She gave him a rueful smile. It was hard, but Gabriel waited until she finished her meal and her second cup of coffee. Helena leaned back in her chair, smiling at him. "Ready?" he asked. She nodded imperceptibly. Gabriel placed a picture on the table, smoothed the wrinkles from the page and dramatically slid it before her. He waited, watching her face. She looked down at it, a scowl briefly crossing her face before being replaced by a comically huge grin that, more slowly, elicited the same response in Gabriel.

"Gabriel Sheehan," she whispered, still smiling down at the picture, "you are a genius." She looked up and met his gaze. "Genius."

"It is. I know." He couldn't say any more for a bit. It was the illustration of Dickhead, now sporting a huge head of curly hair that Gabriel had drawn in with a red Sharpie, obscuring the electrode-bearing skullcap. In its stead, Dickhead now sported a pair of ear buds with cord trailing down his chest to a rectangle labeled "Dickhead's cellphone".

He beamed at her. "It was amazing, Leena. Not the way it should've happened at all. I kept thinking that I would have to beg to be let back in the lab, to at least get started on a new electrode design. I couldn't get myself to do it. Hell, I don't know if those guys would even talk to me at this point. I kept thinking how stupid it was to think anyone would actually sit down in front of a computer and pull a skullcap on, even if I could figure out how to get the electrodes to sense through hair. Which I'm not sure I could do, not reproducibly, at least. The resistance would be an unmeasured variable, you know?" She nodded, enraptured. "And then, it was the strangest thing, like the opposite of deductive reasoning—"

"That would be inductive."

"What?" he faltered.

"That would be called inductive reasoning, the opposite of deductive."

"Yeah, right, whatever," he waved a hand dismissively, "I could never keep that shit straight. It might've been the opposite of inductive—"

"That would be deductive."

Gabriel's head thunked face down onto the table. He continued with his face pressed into the tabletop. "Did I say how much I missed you?"

"No, Gabe dear, I don't think so."

"Missed you," muffled by the tabletop.

"Missed you too, Gabe."

"Want to hear about this idea I had while you were gone?"

"Sure, Gabe, I'd love to. Was this something you deduced in my absence?"

"I'm not sure, I may have induced it."

"Why don't you tell me about it?"

He raised his head, a red mark on his forehead. "I was thinking I needed a window to the brain, you know, not trying to listen through the scalp, that was just too hard. I kept thinking that the eyes, man, the eyes are the window to the mind. But I was having a hard time with it because, for one thing, we're going to have to pay a pretty heavy incentive to get the volunteers to shove needles in their eyeballs. So, I thought about some sort of contact lens electrode, which was stupid, even I couldn't put in the stupid things. I tried contacts when I was fifteen, couldn't do it, and besides, how are they going to see the stimulus if they got electrodes in their eyes? And then—"

"Then you thought, 'In through the eyes, out through the ears'!"

Gabe looked at her, nonplussed. "No, I didn't think of that. But that's good, I like that! But I guess it was kind've like that, because I thought the eyes won't work and then, bam! Right out of the blue. The earphones were just there. And as I thought more about it, it just made more and more sense. Bam—no hair at the ears, no variable resistance. Bam—everyone wears these things while at the computer, all the time. Bam—no need for conductive gel or anything, it's like a window straight to the brain. It just all fell into place, like seeing dominoes falling—and it just kept getting better and better. Not like the usual thing, where you think you have a great idea, but the more you think about it, the more ways you see it's not going to work. With this, it was the gift that just kept giving. I thought, what the hell, they could be real, working earphones. I mean they could play music and everything, because I don't think that'd interfere at all. How cool would that be?"

"Pretty cool, Gabe, pretty damn cool."

"But listen to this, this is the best part!"

"But wait! There's more!" Helena intoned, as a TV barker.

"No, really, this is almost as good. I was going to call you—"

"But Helena doesn't have a phone."

"Exactly! I thought, who doesn't own a phone?"

"Nobody!"

"Exactly! And then I realized how last century the whole SETI thing is—no offense, I know you worked on it, Leena—but people don't sit at a desk using a computer very much any more. They walk around doing most of their shit on a smartphone. And then I thought—"

"Please, don't say it, Gabe."

"There's an app for that!"

They spent the next two weeks combining their reports and producing the final, glorious masterwork that Helena christened Gabe's Fantastic Mindreading Machine. It came off the tongue more easily than Gabriel's official title: A Proposal for the Development of a Transaural Electroencephalographic Pattern Study Employing Metachronous Massively Multifocal Distributed Networking with the Goal of Establishing an Encyclopedic Dictionary of Human Thought. Gabriel returned from the printers with a box big enough to hold a fair sized St. Bernard. He grabbed out one of the six-inch thick, bound manuscripts and let it fall on the kitchen table with a ceremonious thud. Helena joined him in staring reverently at the boldly printed cover.

"I still say your title sucks."

Gabriel sighed, reverie over. "I like it."

"I think electroencephalographic is the wrong word. I don't think that's what you mean. How many did you print, in case you have to fix it?"

"Fifty."

"Fifty? Wow. I thought you'd get, maybe, six. You know, so we could give a couple to your Mom or something."

"Dropped off three copies on the way home."

"Really? Three, Gabe? How is Mom?"

"Mom's great. She's great when she thinks I'm great. She always thinks I'm great."

"That's Mom, Gabriel the great, even when he's been shitcanned by the Harvard of the Midwest."

"That was last year's motto—now she calls Harvard the 'University of Michigan of the East'. And I don't think she knows exactly how extraordinarily well my doctorate is progressing; we haven't been talking much."

"She mad about that?"

"No. I thought she would be. We used to talk a couple of times a week, so I thought I'd catch hell when I walked in."

"Probably doesn't love you anymore. Or she's distracted by your new little brother arriving soon from Thailand. Or—"

"Couldn't figure why I was getting off the hook so easy until I was on my out the door."

"She's not really your Mom, is she? I'm so sorry, Gabriel..."

"Get this. As I'm almost to the car, she says to call her 'if that cute little redhead ever gives me a chance'. And then, 'love ya, Gabe' and closes the door on me."

"Fuck me."

"Yeah, I think that's pretty much what she meant. Mom can be pretty subtle, teaching philosophy and all."

Helena was blushing, but Gabriel couldn't tell if she was embarrassed or angry. He was betting on angry, as he watched her percolate.

"They have a key?" she asked, coldly.

"Well, yeah, you knew that."

"I was ranting. It was a stab—I thought I was employing hyperbole in my description of what a total jackass, shit-for-brains, cracker, suburban momma's boy you are. I guess I was wrong."

"No, you were right, babe. They really do have a key. They must've somehow—"

"You've got to get it back." She looked like a lit stick of dynamite, fixing his gaze with an icy stare.

"Sure, babe. That was my thought, too. When I see them next—"

"Now."

"What do you mean, babe?"

"Once more with the 'babe-shit', Babe-Gabe, and I'm getting the duct tape. Not kidding."

"I only say it when I think you're angry, you know. Babe."

"Call your Mom."

"What, to tell her the ransom or her little Gabe's ear will be in the mail?"

"Tell her you're bringing over dinner for her and Dad."

"What? When?"

"And you're bringing the cute little redhead. Tonight. Six."

"No way. They're liberals, they're like completely unarmed. At least give them a couple of days to get a gun or a Taser or something."

"Call her. Now."

"Okay, sounds nice. What can we bring for dinner? Hey, maybe we can pick up some hemlock at the farmers market on the way, make a nice salad. Or that free range chicken with the strychnine sauce. This is going to be great."

"Gabe—"

"Yeah, babe?" He gulped.

"You get the key back. Or I come home without you."

Gabriel pondered that last statement for the entire drive over, wondering if Helena meant she'd be going home alone because he'd be lying dead beside the blood spattered bodies of his parents. Within ten minutes of arriving at his parent's house with the bag full of delicatessen takeout and two six packs of beer (Gabriel had told Helena that his parents wouldn't even finish a bottle between them, but she had insisted), he had stopped worrying. An hour later, he doubted if his parents would've noticed if he had left through the back door, they were so taken with 'his Helena'. He must have had to come up with six different answers through the evening to his parents' question of why he'd been keeping his charming little Helena a secret for so many months. As tempted as he was, he never veered close to the truth. He had been wrong, anyway. Gabe was sent for more beer by ten and no, he couldn't take 'our Leena' with him. It was after 2 am by the time Gabriel had managed to convince his parents that he and Leena had to get going, as they had a lot of work in the morning. His dad had tried insisting that they remain for at least one more round of drinks and a couple more of those great songs Helena had taught them. Before tonight, Gabriel thought, the piano in the living room probably hadn't been touched since he quit taking lessons at age ten. And he couldn't remember ever seeing his folks actually drunk before. It was disturbing to hear his parents sing lyrics laced with slang references to genitalia. Thankfully, Helena's melodic alto pretty much drowned out the tone-deaf Sheehan clan, one and all.

During the car ride home, Gabriel tried not to sound too relieved. His mother had actually insisted that he take the extra key without his even asking, telling the story of how embarrassed they had been to walk in on them 'sleeping so soundly'.

"Geez, Gabe. Your parents can't sing worth shit."

"Tell me about it. Not the Sheehan strong suit, that's for sure. We're great Scrabble players, though. Kick butt Scrabble players." He turned onto the main road. "You can sing. You sing like an angel, Helena."

"Aye, fucking Angel of Death."

"No, really. Between the piano and your voice, you're better than most guys working the bars in this town."

"Did that some, when I couldn't find honest work."

He let the silence linger, wondering if all the beer might make her a little more historically inclined than usual. She wasn't; not without prompting, at least.

"Where'd you learn?"

"Wasn't taught. Where I'm from, the ones who can't sing are put out on the curb for the gypsies to take."

"Sounds rough."

"Not so rough. During the famine, they ate 'em."

"Cannibalism?"

"Not cannibalism, Gabriel. My people believe that if a thing can't sing, it ain't human."

"I'd be—"

"Stew meat."

They drove on in silence for a while.

"My Mom really liked you, Leena."

"All the moms like me, Gabe. I'm likable." He looked over at her with raised eyebrows. "Your parents are just relieved because they thought you were gay." He ignored this.

"I mean she really liked you. Mom pulled me aside just before we left. She asked me if you're the one. Can you believe it?"

"Your Mom was shitfaced, Gabriel."

"True." He looked at her. She still had her eyes closed, head back against the seat. "I told her I thought so."

Helena didn't open her eyes. "You shouldn't be driving. You're going to get us killed."

CHAPTER 10

Gabriel told his parents of their engagement at Sunday brunch three weeks later. He and Helena had brought over bagels, lox, and cream cheese. They were retired to the couch, drinking their coffee, when Gabriel made the announcement as casually as he possibly could. In spite of his delivery, his mother let out a whoop that scared the dog, jumping up and down on the couch and gathering Helena in a suffocating hug. Gabriel caught Helena's wink, noticing that she was genuinely returning his mother's embrace. Gabriel's mother suddenly broke away and held Helena at arms length, snatching up her left hand for inspection.

"Where's the ring?" she demanded. Gabe cringed.

"No ring," Helena replied.

His mother rounded on him. "You cheap cad! Is this the way you were raised?" She turned to her husband. "Daniel, this is your fault. How could you let this happen?" Both Gabriel and his father began to stammer in defense, ineffectually.

"No, it's not like that at all, Mrs. Sheehan," Helena said. Gabriel held his breath in fear.

He knew exactly how it had been. Gabriel had not waited two days after that first dinner with his parents before, taking a large portion of the royalties he had received from the licensing of his prosthetic limb interface, purchasing a diamond engagement ring of sufficient size and quality so as to not embarrass his future wife for the rest of their lives together, or so the jeweler downtown had assured him. Two weeks later, he formally professed his love to her and proposed marriage, on bended knee and with ring in hand, at their condo after he had conjured a suitably romantic meal accompanied by two bottles of wine. He knew his Helena well enough by now, and didn't dare try this in public. As with most things with Helena, he didn't have any idea of her response; just in case, he had been certain to remove the steak knives from the room while cleaning up for dessert. Gabe had been astonished and relieved when she had taken his hands in hers, kissed him tenderly, and given her assent. She had then instructed him to return the ring. No, it hadn't been the wrong ring, she explained. She wouldn't be wearing any ring. Perhaps, she had offered instead, they should publicly profess their undying commitment with matching spiked leather dog collars. Alternatively, she had offered to take him to a tattoo parlor she knew in Ypsilanti, in which they could obtain matching tattoos. She had recommended a bodily location for his tattoo that would, he had to agree, be especially appropriate for the occasion. He didn't think a tattoo could actually be applied there, however. She had assured him it could, taking great care to explain the exact method of application. Gabriel was desperately hoping that most of this wouldn't be revisited now with his parents.

Helena was speaking again. "Gabe presented me with a beautiful ring, but I made him return it. I'm sure it was way too expensive, being over two carats and all. I think it a sin to spend so much money at this stage of our lives together." His mother was obviously impressed, though the truth had been well under a carat. "I made your son promise, Mrs. Sheehan, that he would give me one even prettier on our tenth anniversary." Gabriel's mother burst into tears, giving Helena another passionate hug and insisting to be called mom from now on. Gabe let out an audible sigh.

To Gabriel's surprise, the next several weeks saw his mother frequently dropping over the condo to engage his fiancé in close discussion regarding the impending wedding. He was genuinely astonished that

Helena appeared to enjoy his mother's visits, enthusiastically discussing all things nuptial. Gabriel would happily attend these sessions, if only to listen to that tinkling laugh that he had heard so seldom before, to stare smiling at this previously unknown side of his fiancé. It was made increasingly clear to him, however, that his presence wasn't really required, or even desirable. It was suggested that Gabe might better spend his time doing constructive man-things, such as yard work or car repair, or something else that required him to be outdoors.

As it happened, Gabriel was awaiting an appointment with his dean, so far without success. While the secretary had been perfectly happy to give him the appointment, on two occasions, as the day approached, he received an apologetic notice that something had come up which required the dean to reschedule. He was growing increasingly frustrated, now that the proposal was complete and he was eager to make a presentation. Not welcome at his own home, he sought refuge most evenings at his parent's house, sharing a beer and the occasional cigar with his father. Up to this point, he had always had a close relationship with his father, but had not spent a great deal of time alone with him. His father was a quiet, equanimous man. When all three members of the family were together, as they almost always were, it was his mother who dominated verbally and emotionally. Gabriel found these sessions sitting with his dad new and enjoyable, as did his father.

They sat side by side this evening, feet up on the small patio's railing, enjoying the settling twilight. His father broke the comfortable silence, offering his son another beer. Gabriel declined. "Watching your weight or feeling guilty about never bringing any over for your old man?"

"Ouch! Fine, I'll bring tomorrow night. Getting a little tired of this watered down piss you buy anyway. And I see you're not really worried too much, speaking of weight."

"Screw you, son. I'm old, I'm supposed to be fat. It's a sign of wisdom, like Buddha."

"Then you're getting wiser by the day, Dad. We should go to the gym or something."

"One of us works for a living. Speaking of doing nothing constructive with your life, what's going on with your project, by the way? Going to be married soon, might want to have a job or something."

Gabriel explained the situation of trying to get an audience with the dean. His father, a physician and department chairman in the medical school, understood immediately.

"He's hoping you'll give up or die, either one. What's your standing with the department?"

"I haven't formally given up my position, if that's what you mean. I didn't sign anything, just haven't been around for most of the year."

"No registered letters telling you to clean out your office?" Gabriel shook his head. "Good, then he can't throw you out on your ass. Do you have an appointment?"

"Yeah, next Monday. Which means I can expect the call to cancel or reschedule any minute now."

"Just don't answer it. No matter how many times the secretary calls or leaves messages that the dean can't see you, just waltz into his office on Monday like you were expected. Once you're standing there, he'll see you."

"Really, you think? Why won't he just tell her to send me packing?"

"He won't, not if he's actually in his office. All deans are pricks—not the way they work. Once you're there, he'll want to just get it over with."

"Worth a shot. Thanks, Dad."

"No problem. I'm afraid that getting in is going to be the easy part, though."

"Gotta start somewhere. I think staying in the department is my best shot." His father nodded. They drained their beers, flung the bottles toward the recycling bin and both missed.

Each muttered, almost in unison, "You suck." They laughed.

"Your mom has really taken to Helena. The daughter we never had, I guess."

Gabriel nodded. "How 'bout you, Dad? You haven't said much." The ensuing pause concerned Gabe. "What?"

Daniel Sheehan looked at his son. "Your mother said something funny last night. She loves Leena, don't get me wrong."

Gabriel had a feeling what was coming. "Okay."

"Mom said that she's had a great time getting to know Helena, that she's really excited to have her as a daughter, and all..."

"But."

"No 'but', Gabe. We're really happy for you. But Mom said that after all this time, she realized she really hasn't gotten to know her at all. Every conversation is about us, or you. Mom says she's very good at steering a conversation, you know, deflecting questions." Daniel looked at his son with concern. Gabriel stared out across the small, trim lawn of the backyard. "Is there a problem, there? Gabe?"

Gabe shook his head slightly. "I don't think she's a serial killer, if that's what you mean."

"So like, you asked her?" His dad forced a smile. "And she said she wasn't?"

"Not in so many words."

"How many words is, 'No, I'm not a serial killer', about five?"

"She's not very open about personal stuff, is all."

His dad paused, considering, before deciding to take it up again. "Have you met her folks?"

"Don't think they're alive."

"You don't think? That seems like something that would be pretty clear cut, you know, alive or dead."

"She's pretty protective about her past and stuff."

Both stared out at the yard, the colors changing as the late summer afternoon faded. "You mind if I do some checking? I don't want to insult you or anything, but—"

"I'm not insulted, Dad. But don't bother. I've Googled her up, down, and sideways. I've seen more hits on 'Ann Arbor celebrities'. There's nothing there."

"Well, how about the Myface? Or the Spacebook your mom's always on?" Gabe smiled, shook his head. His dad was thoughtful. "I have some better resources, in the department. Medical stuff that's not available to you. If you want—I don't want to pry."

Gabriel looked at his dad. "Give it a shot, Dad. If you want." He shrugged his shoulders. "Tell you the truth, I stopped trying a long time ago. Doesn't even bother me anymore. I love her."

The elder Sheehan nodded sagely. "She's a good girl. I think you'll do fine." He paused, and added more softly, "Wouldn't hurt to check a little, though."

"Be my guest, Dad. I'm gonna get going. Hopefully, they'll let me back in my place by now."

Monday came, and Gabriel Sheehan, MS was dressed in his best (only) suit, about to leave for his meeting with the dean. There were four voicemails on his cellphone from the secretary. He had two copies of his proposal in his messenger bag.

"Wish me luck, Leena."

Helena came out of the bathroom, toweling off her hair. "Why? It won't help."

He kept smiling at her. "Thanks, I was afraid I was getting overconfident. That's okay, I don't need it. I'm going to be brilliant."

"You will be brilliant. He's going to throw you out on your ass, Gabe."

"He can't. This is going to change the world. It's too perfect to stop. He'll be blown away."

Helena gave him a sad smile. "Gabe, love? Promise me something?"

"Anything."

"Promise me you won't get mad or start yelling at him. Or try to pummel him to death with the proposal."

Gabriel smiled at her. "Won't be necessary. I'll be brilliant. See you later, Leena." With that, he gave her a kiss on the cheek and closed the door behind him. Helena stared at the door.

"Hope you don't kill the little prick. I would."

Gabriel was back less than an hour later. He was deflated and angry. He had managed to leave one copy of the proposal with the dean. The dean said there was no reason to leave two.

"Hey, Gabe." She was already hurting for him before he came home. Gabriel sagged back against the door, allowed himself to slide down onto the floor, where he sat staring up at her. "You didn't get mad, did you?" she asked.

He shook his head. He looked like a Basset hound who had just peed the floor and knew he'd screwed up, waiting for his owners to start cursing. "No, Helena, I didn't get mad." He sat. "A little, I may have screamed a little, just towards the end. Just before he asked me to leave."

Helena tried not to cry for him, he looked so pathetic. She knew that wouldn't help at all. He looked up, met her gaze. "He asked me to clean out my office. Didn't want to hear much about the proposal." She nodded, arms crossed. He gave her a weak smile. "Time for plan B."

"Which is what, exactly?"

"Working on it."

Helena handed him a shot glass of whiskey. "Here, this is for you." He drained it in a gulp. Standing, he leaned against the door. "I suggest throwing that as hard as you can. At the wall, not the window." He looked at her. She nodded. Gabriel flung the glass at the far wall with a suitably shouted epithet. The glass made a highly satisfying hole in the plaster. He had just missed their only framed picture.

"Better."

"Come sit at the table, Gabe. Time for plan B, hon."

They sat, quietly for a time. He broke the silence. "Plan B then," he said. She nodded. "Haven't a fucking clue, Leena."

"I have a suggestion."

"Shoot."

She brightened. "There's no way they're going for the whole proposal, Gabe. Your budget's over forty thousand—"

"That's what this shit costs, Leena! I spent more than that on my last—"

"Yeah, and pissed the whole thing away without any results, remember? That's part of why they shitcanned you, Gabe. That, and not showing up for most of the past year, of course."

"Yeah, I guess I kinda burned that bridge. Time to start looking at other schools, I guess."

"Not going to happen, Gabriel. I don't think your letters of reference are going to be all that glowing, you know?"

He looked even sadder. "So much for plan B. Time to apply at the burger establishments, huh?"

She shook her head. "You can get them to go for this, Gabe. But not the whole proposal. A pilot project, something cheap, that won't require the whole funding application thing. Something that can be paid out of the department." He brightened a little, listening to her. "I'm listening."

"Maybe a couple of hundred subjects, maybe just using a computer for now. Save the mobile app for later."

"A couple of hundred? I don't think it'll work. Not enough discrimination."

"I think it will, Gabriel. Not for the whole thing, no, but a focused study. Just three or four ideograms, something really simple. Shapes or colors or something. Just to show efficacy, you know?"

"Shit, yeah! If we did it in lab conditions, paid volunteers to wear the dickhead cap, it would be easy. I think. I'd have to work this out." He thought for a while, then appeared saddened again. "Tell you the truth, though, Helena..." He looked very sad, almost defeated. "...Dean was pretty negative. Like wouldn't bother him if the door hit me in the ass on the way out, negative. I'm not sure he'll even see me again."

"Not the dean. Dean's are pricks, that's why they're deans. Go back to your Chair, try to get your committee to listen to you. They probably have to give you some sort of exit interview, just to formally get you out the door anyway." She took his hand across the table. "Here's the important part. You'll make them see how brilliant you are, how awesomely brilliant the whole idea is, I'm sure of it. You are fucking brilliant, after all." She smiled at him. He nodded. Less the Basset Hound, more the Golden Retriever. "They'll see how freaking brilliant the whole thing is. You paint them the 'we can change the world' thing. First step on the road to a bright new tomorrow! And then you tell them the price."

"And that's when they ask for my keys back."

"Yeah, exactly. They're not going to want to give you a dime, Gabe."

"Great plan, Leena. You want fries with that?"

"So you tell them how dedicated you are to your department, how you appreciate everything the department of bioengineering has done for you, stuck by you despite your missteps, you know, that kind of—"

"Bullshit."

"—bullshit. Yeah, exactly. And then you tell them how bad you'd feel if you had to take this to another department." She paused, smiling.

"What department? I don't have any standing outside of bioengineering, Leena. Nobody'll even—"

"Astronomy, Gabriel. Half of your proposal is stolen from the astronomy literature, half the technique. More than half."

"That's crazy, Leena. No offense, I appreciate what you're trying to do. But this stuff is bioengineering, there's no way the department of astronomy will—"

"Not the point, Gabe! You know how these things work. Or maybe you don't. I can tell you, though, department chairmen hate to get shat on by other chairmen. Makes them feel small, you know."

"But it's an empty threat, Helena. One phone call to the astronomy Chair and I'm toast. Bluff called, thanks for playing."

"No, Gabriel. It's not a bluff. You probably think that all I've been doing these past two weeks is talking about sex and wedding dresses with your Mom."

"Yeah, pretty much. Wait—you talk to my mother about sex, about us? Oh, god."

"Oh, we found the perfect dress, by the way. Really, really expensive."

"Great! You were saying…"

"Oh, yeah. Not a bluff. Or only partly a bluff. My Chairman read your proposal and, of course, thinks it's brilliant."

"You presented my proposal to your Chair?"

"Yes, Gabriel, I did. I hope you don't mind. There did seem to be about forty-two extra copies in the box, just sitting there."

"No, I don't mind. It's just that, you know, if you had asked, I would have been happy to make a presentation to your Chairman. We could've both—"

"Oh, Gabe. I know it's your proposal, your project. But, hey, we're a team, you know. Besides, this really wasn't a formal presentation or anything. I know the Chairman, Dr. Lipscomb, pretty well. I took his seminar last year and he really enjoyed having me and my cleavage in his class. Really enjoyed it, like constantly. So I made an appointment and wore that low cut slinky thing, you know, the grey, clingy one that you said shows my nipples—"

"You wore the streetwalker outfit?"

"Yeah, that one. He thinks you're brilliant, by the way."

"You're shameless, you know."

"We knew that."

CHAPTER 11

Six weeks later, Gabriel had approval and funding for a pilot project involving two hundred fifty volunteers. Helena received an email from the astronomy Chairman relating in great detail how he had sat down over lunch with the Chairman of bioengineering, how he had spent over thirty minutes extolling what a genius he considered Mr. Sheehan to be, and yes, Mr. Sheehan could certainly count on him for support if the opportunity were to arise. The email was far too lengthy and familiar in tone for Gabe's liking. He hoped Helena wasn't expected to make a return visit in appreciation.

Gabriel had projected the pilot study to require six months and twenty-eight thousand dollars. It required half as much money but twice as long as expected. In order to save money and startup time, they employed the skullcap electrode array Gabriel had developed as part of his previous, failed experiments. This required them to solicit volunteers willing to shave their heads. As he was paying fifty dollars for ten eight minute sessions that required no more effort than to stare at a computer screen, he had no trouble attracting volunteers. The entire ROTC signed up en mass, followed by almost every male athlete on campus and several of the female athletes. Twenty-two faculty members with male pattern baldness enrolled, in the interest of research, of course. None of them declined the check, however.

The real challenge lay in the experimental design. Mistakenly, Gabe had believed the selection of simple ideograms would be straightforward. It was Helena who convinced him that he should undertake a cheap and quick pretest, a focus group exercise to confirm the suitability of Gabe's "simple pictures, like in those kindergarten IQ tests". He was shocked when he brought in five groups of twenty subjects at twenty-five bucks each (an expenditure he considered at the time to be a gross waste of his tight budgetary resources). Each subject was given a set of flashcards with a picture and asked to write down the very first thought that came to mind. To his amazement, many of the simplest ideograms generated a range of responses. A large black circle was a circle to only eighty-five percent of respondents, the rest responding with "dot". Even worse, the same respondent, upon seeing the ideogram a second or third time, might see a circle or a dot, seemingly at random. A large black "X" was interpreted as "cross" amongst twenty percent of volunteers of European descent, though this interpretation was never given by US native-born citizens. It went on and on. Even an amorphous smear of green gave them fits for two weeks, with five percent of respondents responding "blue". They finally figured out that these were the patients suffering blue-green color blindness. They switched to red with better result. Brown was a disaster.

Gabriel was humbled by the realization that, if he had gone ahead with the study using the simple ideograms as he had initially conceived, he would have succeeded only in generating a colossal mass of useless data. He had done that before and didn't think his career would ever recover from a second such debacle. He declared Helena to be his muse and his guardian angel, vowing to never disagree with her again. A package was delivered to his lab ten days later. In it, Gabriel found a Lucite paperweight inscribed with the words: "Helena is my muse and guardian angel. I will never disagree with her." She also left one on his desk at the condo. Also, one on the kitchen windowsill where he could see it while he did the dishes. She also dropped one off to his parents. Gabriel would find additional copies randomly over the next two years; his sock drawer, under the bathroom sink behind the spare toilet paper, glued to the dashboard of the aging Subaru. He prayed she wouldn't drop one in his coffin, the woman was killing him.

Finally, he arrived at a set of six ideograms with a uniformity of thought response over 95 percent. His pilot set consisted of a triangle, the number 3 (not zero, that's for sure), a smear of bright red, a picture of a shoe (not a sandal, not a tennis shoe, not a loafer), a car (not a VW beetle, not a convertible, not a sports car), and a baseball (not a beach ball, not a soccer ball). Gabriel added in ten others of fractionally lesser stability, as he felt he needed to generate greater variety and randomness for the test subjects.

Gabriel returned home to his waiting fiancé. He was a happy man today.

"Got it!" He held his copy of the signed research contract aloft in triumph.

Helena gave him a hug. She popped the cork off the champagne she had chilling in the refrigerator, filled two glasses. They toasted and sat together on the couch. She took the contract from him, and began to flip through the eight pages of densely packed print. "They went for it?"

Gabriel was still beaming. "Yeah, it was really straightforward. I was surprised, they had it ready and waiting."

"You went through it? No surprises?"

"Yeah, I went through it with them line by line. Gave me the entire budget, to the penny. I was shocked."

Helena whistled, still reading. She had no experience with this and was having trouble finding what she was really interested in. "What about ownership? Does it say anywhere in here about intellectual property rights, all to the university, that sort of thing?"

Gabriel gave his friend a sly smile. "That's the really great thing. I was worried about that, too. It took me almost two years to get my royalties out of these bastards with my master's work, you know." She nodded, still trying to listen and read the arcane document at the same time. "You can quit flipping pages, Leena. It's not in there. This isn't that kind of contract at all. I knew right away when they handed it to me, actually. When you're spending big money, the kind that requires granting agencies, the contract is like a hundred pages. I wasn't going to sign that without letting a lawyer look it over this time. But they handed me this. This is nothing, it's a departmental contract. All the funding is in-house, so I think they just boilerplated it. There's not a word in there about ownership rights, resulting patents, anything." He smiled again, as did Helena.

"Probably because they expect you to fuck the whole thing up again, honey."

"Yeah, I set them up real good. My strategy all along, you know."

They toasted again. "To fucking the whole thing up."

Gabriel wasted no time in initiating the study. He had already obtained his approvals, as he couldn't obtain the funding without all the regulatory paperwork in place. He reopened his old lab, and was able to set up the entire human testing station with equipment he already had in house. His setup basically consisted of a subject testing booth (a study carrel Gabriel borrowed from the departmental library in the middle of the night), with a chair, a monitor, and his skullcap electrodes. This was connected to an amp and a laptop for examiner monitoring and data recording. Initial expenses for capital equipment had been budgeted for eleven thousand dollars. Gabriel spent nothing. He planned on twenty-five sessions of ten subjects each, each subject to be tested ten times at sessions assigned randomly. Testing was to be done on Mondays and Thursdays, with the rest of the week devoted to data analysis and killing the inevitable bugs that would crop up with each session. He was afraid that Tuesday sessions would lead to three-day weekends. Too tempting. He realized that he had been doing this grad student thing way too long.

Gabriel was loath to interrupt his work for the wedding. Whenever he complained about taking time away from the lab, for his tux fitting, or arranging for the liquor, or the few other assignments he was entrusted with, Helena relished pointing out that he was the sucker who had come up with this idea. He had no reply to that.

"What about rings?" he asked. "Is that on my list of to-do's, too? Because I'm going to have to find a different jeweler, you know. Last one was pretty pissed off when I walked back in to return—"

"What is it with you and rings? No rings. No dog collars, no tattoos, no fucking rings. Get it?"

"But it's tradition. You know, with this ring, I thee wed..."

Helena rolled her eyes at him. "Yeah, we're not saying that either, so don't worry about the rings. No rings."

He looked disappointed. "We're really getting married, though, right? Not one of those things where we just cut open our palms and mix our blood or anything, I hope, because I'm a little squeamish about—"

"No, Gabriel. You won't have to hurt yourself. That's my job. Actually, it's going to be a pretty standard Jewish ceremony."

"You're kidding."

"No, I'm not. Your mother was very gracious and never actually asked, but you're her only child and I could tell it was important to her. With all the disappointment you've caused her over the years, I thought she deserved a wedding that the whole bridge club could enjoy."

"Yeah, right. What's the angle?"

"It happens to also be the shortest wedding ceremony of any of the world's major religions, if you must know." She smiled. "And I like the stomping on the glass part. It's like foreshadowing, you know."

"I don't think that's what it means. What's this going to cost me?"

"What do you mean, Gabe?"

"Emotionally, in servitude, whatever. You know, the *quid pro quo*. You're doing this just to make my mom happy, huh?"

"Well, there is—"

"Knew it!" he fist pumped.

She gave him a scowl. "Shut up, asshole. The least you can do is honor my traditions, since I'm sucking up big time to yours."

He sighed and sat. "Let's hear it. This is going to cost me, big."

Helena sat with him on the couch and took his hand, "There is one thing."

"Here we go. It is blood, isn't it? I knew it, I knew there'd be blood."

"No, not blood, not money. Just the opposite, love. My people have a tradition—"

"That would be the Druids, right?"

"Shut up, we're being serious now, Gabriel. I'm not joking. My people have a very long tradition, that on the night of our wedding, we will exchange a gift."

Gabe looked relieved. "That's it, a gift? No blood?"

Helena sighed in exasperation. "Don't belittle this, Gabriel. This is very important to me. Which means that it's very, very important to you. A real gift, a meaningful gift. A gift that each of us will treasure for our entire lives together, Gabriel." She gave him a hard look. "Not a fucking ring."

"That's it? A gift on our wedding night? But not a ring."

She nodded. "Don't disappoint me, Gabriel. A girl doesn't like to be disappointed on her wedding night."

"I've heard that. That's it, huh?"

"Well..."

"I knew it! Too easy! Tell me the other Irish wedding night tradition I'm about to experience, please."

"Well, there is the three months of complete abstinence."

"Alcohol?" he asked hopefully.

The wedding was small and satisfying for all concerned. The same could not be said of the honeymoon. Gabriel's parents had arranged for them to spend a week in the honeymoon suite of the Grand Hotel on Mackinac Island as their wedding gift. As they drove the Subaru north from their reception, Gabe explained that it probably would have been cheaper for his parents to just sign off on the mortgage to the condo. As he also explained, however, they were in no position to complain about such a magnanimous gesture.

After five hours of driving, Helena felt she was in a perfect position to complain.

"What is this shit, no cars?"

Gabriel sighed, leaning over the rail of the ferry taking them to the island. "That's right, no cars. Just horses, buggies, that sort of thing. You're going to love it, you'll see." He knew better.

"Just horses? What is there to do? And don't tell me it's our honeymoon, wiseass."

"I haven't been here since I was ten. I remember a fort, though."

"Great."

"And fudge. I remember fudge." Helena stared out over Lake Michigan, hoping the boat would start sinking. Nothing fatal, just enough to make them turn around. "It's not as if my folks had an easy time figuring this out, you know. They wanted to send us to somewhere in the Caribbean."

'Yeah, well, I'm sure this will be just like Turks and Caicos. Just without the white sand beaches, the warm cerulean surf, the nightlife, stuff like that. At least we'll have fudge." They stared out over the water for the rest of trip.

They disembarked with their bags and stood, each staring down the dirt road towards the white-pillared hotel on a grassy hill in the distance. A horse drawn buggy pulled up for them.

"Are you the newlyweds for the Grand Hotel?" asked the driver of the buggy. He was dressed in a bright red formal coat with white gloves and top hat. He smiled. The horse defecated.

Gabriel nodded. Helena just stared. "We're in fucking Oz."

They were eventually shown to their ornate, period style suite. Helena sat on the bed. "We're in Hell," she said. Gabriel chose not to reply. He began to unlatch the suitcase. "Don't unpack." Gabe stopped, looked at her with raised eyebrows. "We can't stay. We'll have to go in the morning."

"A week, babe. They booked us a week."

"Your parents hate us."

"My parents love you, Leena. You know that."

"You're right. Your parents hate you." Gabriel sat on the bed, put his arm around his new bride. Helena shook her head slowly. "We can't stay here, Gabe. Seriously. Did you see 'The Shining'? Forty-eight hours in this place, I'm going for that axe I saw in the hallway. Seriously."

Gabriel flopped back on the bed. Helena did the same. They looked at the ceiling. It was ornate. "Where do you want to go?"

"Home," she said. He sighed. She turned to look at him. "Did you get me a gift?" He turned, smiled at her, and nodded. "That's great, Gabe. I'm sorry. I probably shouldn't have married you."

"I love you, too, Leena." He stared at her. He smiled. "Is this when we exchange gifts?"

"What do you mean? Was I supposed to get you something, too?" She smiled back and, laughing, jumped up to get a small box from her backpack. Helena knelt, smiling, in front of him and handed him a small, plain box. "For my husband," she said, handing it to him. She rested her elbows on his knees, chin in hand, watching him as he opened it. From it, he removed a heavy gold ring. It was a Claddagh, the two encircling hands embracing a crowned heart.

"It's beautiful," he said. "Thank you." He leaned forward and kissed her. He stared at it, feeling its extraordinary weight in his hand. "It's a ring, you know."

She returned to sit next to him on the bed. "No, Gabriel, it isn't." She took it from him, took his left hand in hers, and placed the ring on his finger. It fit. She smiled, satisfied. "It's an heirloom. My Da wore it every day. He said it had been worn in my family since forever. He said," she said seriously, "that it had been given to us by the Uncrowned King of Ireland, for our service and our loyalty."

Gabriel looked at it, there on his finger. It was amazingly heavy. "Thank you," he said, kissing his wife again. She looked at him, waiting, smiling like a child in anticipation. Gabriel took a small box from the pocket of his coat hanging on the chair. He handed it to her. "For my wife," he said. She looked at him dangerously. "It's not a ring," he reassured her. Smile returning, she unwrapped the beribboned gift box and withdrew a small piece of parchment paper. She stared at it, read to herself the short poem he had written. Lips slightly moving and eyes tearing, she read it again and again to herself.

"It's perfect." She held the paper against her chest, giving him a kiss.

"Thank you." She looked down at it again, reading the poem aloud in a soft whisper to herself:

Like reflections
deep within a mirror,
I am
only when you are.
—your loving Husband,
Gabe

"It's a haiku," she said finally. "Did you write it, for me?" He nodded.

"What's a haiku?"

The next morning they bought two pounds of fudge and left the island. They decided to skip the fort. They took a lot of pictures on their way out of town. Their plan was to lay low, keeping to the condo and the lab as much as possible. They would periodically post the honeymoon pictures over the next five days; laced with the occasional 'having a great time' email to Gabriel's parents, they'd spare their feelings. Of course, Helena ran into Gabe's dad at the grocery store on their second day back. When Helena saw him at the end of the deli counter, she made no effort to hide.

"Hey, Pops!" she called to him. Daniel Sheehan turned and saw his daughter-in-law. He hurried down the aisle to her, smiling. She kissed him on the cheek.

"I told Cheryl you'd hate that old place! Told her honeymoon or no, you guys wouldn't last a night there." He laughed.

"We made it one night. We had to get out though, Gabe was starting to go all Jack Nicholson on me." Daniel laughed, appreciating the reference. He loved every Kubrick movie ever made. They finished their shopping together and walked out in the rain to the parking lot.

"Can I give you a ride home?" he asked her.

"I've got the car, Dad. I dropped Gabe at the lab. I'm picking him up later for dinner. Thanks, though."

Daniel grasped her elbow gently, bending closer to her. "Listen, Leena. Do you have a couple of minutes?"

Helena heard the catch in her father-in-law's voice as he asked the question. She looked in his eyes. She wanted to drop her groceries and run, but knew she couldn't. "Sure, Pops. Let me just put my bags in the Subaru. I'll be with you in a minute." Helena put her bags in the back of the station wagon and reluctantly joined Daniel in the car. Her wet hair was plastered to her forehead. He looked at her, shook his head a little.

"I can see why my son fell in love with you, Leena."

"Yeah, well. It's not as if I gave him any choice. What are we doing, Pops?"

"Do you mind if we go for a drive? Just for a bit?"

"The kind of drive where we have a heartfelt father-daughter chat, or the kind where I end up gagged and bound in the trunk?"

Daniel couldn't help but laugh. "I promise you won't end up in the trunk. But after you hear what I have to say, you may try to stuff me back there, Helena." He started the car and backed out of the parking space.

"If this is about your son being a lousy lay, please don't blame yourself, Dr. Sheehan. I had pretty low expectations going into this thing, you know."

Daniel tried to smile but was now caught up in what he had to tell his daughter-in-law. "Leena, you know Cheryl and I love you." He looked at her in the passenger seat, gazing at him intently. She wasn't smiling now. He couldn't read her expression. She nodded at him. "Cheryl and I love you and couldn't be happier to have you as our own. I hope you feel the same about us." He paused, but she said nothing. "I made a mistake, Leena. Like most, I thought I was doing the right thing at the time. Looking back, though, I did a stupid, stupid thing. And I want to apologize up front, before anything else." He turned toward the arboretum, the windshield wipers slapping and squeaking. He gave her another sidelong glance. She was still looking at him intently, giving away nothing. He knew she wasn't going to make this easy for him. But then, he didn't think he really deserved easy. "The worst mistakes I make are when I think I'm doing the right thing, but I'm so stupid that I can't even see how wrong I'm being. This was one of those, a big one." He paused, took a deep breath. "We know you're a very private person, Leena. That's putting it mildly. Actually, my son doesn't really know much about you."

"And you, Dad? Do you know much about me?"

"I'm sorry, Leena. Cheryl and I, we're Gabe's parents. He's our only child, and we felt we had a duty, in a way. No, that's not fair. Cheryl had nothing to do with this. And the parent thing, that's just an excuse, I know." He stopped the car in the parking lot of the arboretum. In the rain, it was empty. He turned to look at her, but she was now staring ahead at the rain running in streams down the windshield. "I did some checking. I'm a doctor; I have a friend in the medical society in London. I found out things. I'm sorry, Leena. I had no right."

"What things?"

"Your medical history, mostly. Your childhood. I know you were abandoned at six. I know you were raised in the Irish Catholic orphanage system, the Sisters of Mercy." He looked at her; so hard, unmoving.

"What else?"

"I didn't try to find any legal records, any criminal records or anything. Just medical history, but I shouldn't have—"

"What else, Daniel?" She looked at him now, fixing him with that icy green-eyed stare that was so unnerving.

"I know you were hospitalized as a teenager, the diagnoses you were given. The treatments." His voice was pained, almost breaking. "I'm sorry, Leena. I had no right." It was all he could do to keep his emotions in check. He thought about trying to take her hand, but she was too remote. "I'm sorry, Helena. I'm a physician—I, more than anyone, I should have known that I had no right. But you have to know, I love you as my daughter, Leena. I didn't mean to hurt you." He paused. "I haven't told anything to Cheryl or Gabe. I won't say anything to them."

They sat in silence.

Helena spoke softly. "If Gabe asks, Daniel, you tell him what you know. Don't lie for me, Daniel." She looked at him again.

Daniel nodded. "I won't lie, Leena. But I'm hoping this will stay between us. I'm hoping you can forgive me, Leena."

Helena laid her head back against the seat. "Take me to the car, Daniel. The food will spoil."

Chapter 12

Gabriel began testing two weeks later. Helena served as his research assistant. She managed the volunteers from solicitation, through scheduling, and finally to payment. Gabe was, therefore, free to concentrate upon the technical aspects of the testing. In the evenings, they had dinner together and went over the raw data they had generated earlier that day. They soon fell into a productive routine.

The proposal was for twenty-five testing sessions of ten subjects each. After only five sessions, however, Gabriel started to recognize patterns in the data. By five more sessions, he could hardly contain himself. He was almost giddy as he and Helena ate pizza in the lab, sitting at the console in front of the big computer monitor.

"Look at this, Leena." He pointed at the tracing on the screen, smearing it with pizza sauce. "Do you see?"

"Yeah, I see the same crazy lines you showed me last night."

"No, here. Look!" He traced a line again with his finger, looking at her hopefully. She shook her head, blew her hair up off her forehead.

"Shitstorm in the Sahara, Gabriel."

"No, hon, it's there. I've been seeing it the last three sessions. Here, look at this." Gabriel used a stylus on the tablet next to his keyboard, highlighting a particular tracing in red. "Here's today's subject looking at the triangle. And here's from last week, same ideogram, different subject." He made this tracing green. He dragged the two tracings to the second monitor, made them overlap. "You see?"

"Christmas shitstorm." She shook her head.

"Right here!" He pointed at the initial peaks and valleys in the complex tracings. "Just the first twenty-two milliseconds. Ignore the rest. Here." He enlarged the scale, highlighted the first part of the tracing.

"Holy shit," she said. Gabe smiled.

"You see, right?" She nodded. "Now, watch this. All subjects to date, just the triangle. He selected more tracings, overlapping the various colors. The tracings superimposed over the first milliseconds of recording, then diverged in a colorful tangle.

"Jesus, Mary, and Joseph," Helena whispered under her breath.

"I started focusing on just that initial response. I had to change the way we tested, though. In the first two groups, the transition between the ideograms wasn't crisp, the responses weren't distinct. Kind of echoing or something, like blurring. So I changed it. Now there's fifteen seconds of black screen, then the ideogram snaps on. It's that first snap, that's where the money is. See?" She nodded. He talked faster, more excited. "The rest of this is crap, secondary thought patterns or something. Forget that. Just the first snap, the blink. I call it the blink." He looked at her, smiling like an idiot.

Helena looked at the screen. "It really works."

"Shit yeah, it works."

Helena sat, staring. "Maybe it is a blink, though. Maybe it's not—"

He shook his head violently, stabbing at the keyboard. "No, no, I thought of that. Look, look—shit, I screwed it up. No, here, look—" He stacked more tracings beneath the first, brought up more and more in superimposition. "Here's the tracings for the baseball, see? Just look at the first part, here. They overlap with each other, but not with these, see? Distinct, right? But these are consistent, you see what I'm saying?" He looked at her, pleadingly. "Tell me I'm not crazy, Leena."

She stared. "Show me the rest. Can you do the rest, overlapped like that?" He nodded, punched keys, cursed, punched more keys.

"It's early, I know," he said, "too early. But it's there, I can see it already and we haven't gone halfway into it yet." Gabriel leaned back in the chair as Helena studied the screen, densely covered with the tangled multicolored tracings. "It's the opposite of what happened last time. Last time, Leena, every time I looked at my results, they just got more and more squirrely. Not this—," he stabbed his finger into the monitor, rocking it. "Not this. This is getting tighter and tighter. I'm telling you, I can tell you what picture the subject is looking at, just watching the tracing as it comes up."

"No fucking way."

He smiled and nodded. "It's like I can read their minds, Leena."

The study moved faster and faster. Now with a fixed routine, they moved the volunteers through like an assembly line. Gabriel's analysis crystallized as each subject tracing added to the previous data. With the increased amount of data and Gabe's insight into where to focus, they were able to apply some crude filtering algorithms, cutting away the tangle that tried to hide the fingerprint of the pure thought. Gabriel and Helena took turns watching the monitor during testing, seeing if they could name the ideogram being viewed by the subject as he blinked. Well before the last set of volunteers were paid and sent home, both Gabriel and Helena had achieved near flawless accuracy with their limited picture set.

Gabriel spent three months writing his dissertation. Despite months of haranguing, Helena was unable to get him to change the title. It didn't help that she kept suggesting "I Can Read Your Motherfucking Mind" by Gabriel Sheehan. After a successful defense and a total of almost eleven years at the University of Michigan, Gabriel Sheehan received a doctorate of science in bioengineering. He was now officially unemployed.

Gabriel's parents and Helena toasted him with Mimosas at Sunday brunch. To all present, it seemed a bit of an anticlimax. They sat on the porch, enjoying the sunshine as they ate.

"So when's commencement?" asked his father.

"Don't know, don't care, Dad."

"What? You're not going to commencement?" his mother asked.

"No, I'm not going. I didn't go when I got my master's, remember?"

"Yeah, and your mother and I were very disappointed, you know."

"Yeah, well, get used to disappointment."

"I'm sure they have, Gabe," Helena interjected.

"Seriously, why not? You earned it. You should go. We should go."

"Not going, Dad. Besides, we're not even going to be in town. Helena and I are going out of town, to San Francisco."

"Really, Gabe? That's great. Celebrating?"

"Not so much. My paper has been accepted for presentation at the national bioengineering conference."

"That's great, hon," his mother said. "You guys flying?"

Gabe shook his head, smiling at Helena as she finished her bagel. "Helena and I thought we'd take the train. Make a vacation out of it."

Gabriel stood at the podium, in front of the plenary session of the conference of the International Society of Bioengineering and Biomechanical Professionals. Over eight hundred attendees sat before him in the audience. Gabriel was wearing a splendid new suit, which he had purchased for the occasion. He squinted out over the crowd before him, trying to see Helena, who he knew to be seated in the back of the great hall. He couldn't see much beyond the first few rows, however, due to the strength of the stage lighting. He relaxed, knowing she was there. He was thankful that he had never shared that most common of all phobias, the fear of public speaking. Actually, he always enjoyed presenting, though he had to admit that this was a much bigger deal than he had ever experienced before.

Gabriel heard his name spoken in introduction and gave the audience his practiced stage smile. The light on his podium lit green. He touched the button to initiate the PowerPoint presentation.

"Good morning, ladies and gentleman," he began in a strong, public speaking tone. "I thank the society for the honor of allowing me to present my research to you today." His title slide appeared on the huge screen behind him. "Before I begin the substance of my presentation, I would like to take a moment to acknowledge the expert assistance of Ms. Helena Fianna," he thumbed the control and the image changed to a discrete picture of Helena, "without whom this work would not have been possible."

He touched the control again, advancing the slide. Gabriel was remotely aware of a mild commotion towards the back of the hall, but could still see nothing as he smoothly transitioned into his presentation. "As you are undoubtedly aware, despite vigorous efforts to elucidate the discrete electrical signals and patterns associated with cognition..."

Gabriel concluded his presentation before the light on his podium turned red. His conclusion was greeted by far more enthusiastic applause than he had anticipated. He smiled in appreciation, then spent the required fifteen-minute period answering questions from audience members who lined up at the standing microphones in the aisles. He was surprised at the number of questioners and their effusive praise preceding each question. Seven or eight questioners remained when the moderator had to end the session due to time. They converged on Gabriel as he descended the steps from the stage. He took up a position at the side of the hall, patiently answering the questioners and thanking the well-wishers. Gabriel kept looking over their heads for Helena, but didn't see her yet. One last questioner remained and stepped up to greet Gabriel.

"Dr. Sheehan, my name is Arthur Schlessel," he said as he shook Gabriel's hand. "Great talk, really impressive work."

"Thank you. Are you in the field?"

"Only in a manner of speaking. I'm not a scientist, if that's what you mean. I'm a businessman, Dr. Sheehan, and a big fan of your work. I bought your patents three years ago or so, relating to—"

Schlessel was cut off as he was roughly shoved aside by Helena.

"Hey, Leena—"

Helena grabbed Gabriel's lapels in her fists and jerked him down hard so her nose was a fraction of an inch from his. She met his astonished gaze and, in a menacing hiss, said, "If you ever, ever pull that shit again, I swear I will take a fucking butcher knife and stab you through your fucking heart as you sleep. As you sleep! Do you hear me?" Gabriel nodded, ashen. She released her grip on him, spun on her heel, and strode away, out of the auditorium.

Schlessel was agape, said "Holy shit, what was that?" Gabriel was straightening his lapels as best he could. "Who was that, a stalker? Someone you knocked up in high school? Shit!"

"Actually," Gabe tried to say nonchalantly, failed. "That was my wife."

"Really?" Schlessel asked. Gabe nodded, color starting to return to his face. Schlessel tried to give him a weak smile. "Oh, well. It's okay, then, I guess. I mean my wife says stuff like that to me all the time..."

"Really?" Gabe was relieved.

"No, no fucking way. Are you crazy? She said she was going to kill you. Listen, we need to talk, but I'm starting to think this might not be a good time, you know? Here's my card," he said, handing it to Gabriel. "Call me in the morning, okay? We can get together in my office tomorrow."

Gabriel looked at the card. "I'll have to bring my wife along."

Schlessel turned to go, said as he left, "I'll notify security."

Gabriel and Helena waited for their appointment in the art deco styled anteroom of Schlessel's office on the fortieth floor of the Transamerica building. They looked out of the large windows at the San Francisco Bay, the bridge nearly hidden in fog. Gabriel was in his suit, Helena in a dress for the second time since they were married.

"Mr. Schlessel will see you now." The receptionist held open the door, waving them in. Arthur Schlessel stood, came around his desk to shake their hands. Gabriel was surprised; the man hadn't looked so young to him yesterday. Of course, he had been distracted at the time.

"Gabriel, Helena. A pleasure. Please, sit. Coffee, water?" Schlessel motioned them to chairs around a low coffee table. Gabe and Helena both declined. "Thank you for coming. Enjoying San Francisco?" They both nodded. "First time, then? I'm sure you'll like it. It's the Ann Arbor of the west, you know." He winked at Gabe. "How in hell have you been able to stay at that place all this time, Gabriel?"

"Family, mostly. But I think Helena and I are glad to get away, at least for a bit." Helena nodded. They waited for Schlessel to begin.

"Again, thanks for coming all the way out here. If you had asked, I would have come to you, you know. Least I could do, Gabe. You've made me a shitload of money, you know."

"Actually, I don't know. How did I do that, exactly?"

"I bought your patent three years ago, the prosthetic limb interface."

"You're the one signing my royalty checks? I didn't recognize—"

"No, no way. I sold it a year later to that company, Prime Interface something, something. I forget. They've done well with it, though. They went public last spring. I probably should've asked for something on the back end, but what the hell, if I were that smart, I'd be retired by now like everybody else, right?' Helena and Gabriel just looked at him. "Anyways, when your new patent apps, what are there, like six of them? When the patents crossed my screen and I saw your name again, I was intrigued. So I got your dissertation—I hope you don't mind, I know it's premature, not accepted yet, not peer reviewed." He looked at Gabriel, who was alternating nods with the occasional shake of his head. "Anyway, read it and bingo, man. Effing brilliant. Seriously, fucking brilliant." He waited for a response, got none. "Really."

Helena leaned in. "I'm sorry, Mr. Schlessel—"

"Arthur, please."

"Arthur, then. I'm wondering why Gabriel and I are sitting here."

"Of course, Helena. I'm sorry, I haven't really been clear. I was getting there, though. Normally, I'd just offer to buy the patents, like the last one—"

"Only, they're not for sale." Helena gave Schlessel a smile. He smiled back at her, looked back at Gabriel.

"Yeah, Helena, no surprise. Let's not do the 'good cop, bad cop' thing, okay? I've seen you in action and, no offense, but I seriously do not want to piss you off. We're all on the same team here, you know."

"What team, would that be, Arthur? Exactly?"

"The team that changes the fucking world, Helena. That's what you two want, right? You two change the world, and I make more money than god."

"Sounds like a plan," Gabe agreed.

They met that evening for dinner at Schlessel's house in Half Moon Bay, overlooking the Pacific. Dinner conversation centered mostly on the relative differences between Detroit and San Francisco, as Arthur's wife, Samantha, had been raised in the suburbs of Detroit before moving to California and meeting her husband. Helena stayed behind with her as Gabriel and Arthur moved to the deck. The two men settled into chairs with the remains of the wine from dinner.

"Thank you for dinner, Arthur. You have a great house."

"Pleasure, Gabe. Thanks. Yeah, it doesn't suck, does it?" He took a sip, set down his wine glass. "She's tough, your wife."

"I'll assume you mean that as a compliment, since I'm your guest."

"Oh, I most certainly do. Very impressive, your Helena. Intimidating, too. She could help us a great deal, Gabe."

"That's not why she's here, Arthur."

"I know. I'm just saying, though. Here's how I see this going. You've got proof of concept. I don't think we're going to have any problems with the patents, though the U of M bastards will try—"

"They won't." Arthur looked at him, eyebrows raised. "They think it's a crock of shit, to tell you the truth. Didn't even offer me a postdoc to continue the work. Thought it'd probably be unfundable."

"That's fantastic, Gabriel. Never underestimate the stupidity of the academic. You know what Churchill said?" Gabe shook his head. "Churchill said, 'Man will occasionally stumble over the truth, but most of the time he will pick himself up and continue on.' I depend on that in my business. Anyway, if they try, and believe me, Gabe, they'll eventually come back and try, that's what the IP lawyers in Chicago are for. By the time they come back around, we'll have the patents nailed, I'm sure." He took another drink. "I assume you have a proposal, a plan to scale this up?"

Gabriel nodded. "Twenty five thousand subjects."

"Are you shitting me? Can't be done, no way."

"It can be done." Gabriel explained the SETI distributed computing concept, the plan for networking smartphones with his ear bud electrode.

"Does that really work? Have you tried it?"

Gabriel nodded. "Almost. It'll work." They sat together in silence, watching the colors change on the surf.

Arthur stirred from his reverie. "I can do this, Gabriel. We can do this. This is going to be big, a lot bigger than I thought. And a shit-load way more expensive. I've got to make some calls, get some people together. You and Helena will stay with us tonight, okay? We've got a lot to talk about, no sense spending half the time running back and forth to the city."

Helena and Gabriel spent three days with the Schlessels. In addition to working on the proposal for Gabe's Mind Reading Machine study, the four toured the area and walked the beach. In the end, they had a fully fleshed out proposal for Arthur to sell to his cadre of venture capitalists. As Arthur kept telling them, this was going to be big, and it was going to be expensive. They would change the world. They would make more money than god. Gabe and Helena returned to Michigan to await Schlessel's call.

Gabriel started working on the new ear bud electrode as soon as they got back to Ann Arbor. His department hadn't kicked him out of his lab yet, and he was intent on utilizing their resources for as long as they let him. Two weeks later, Gabe and Helena sat side by side on the couch in their condo, staring at the laptop open on the coffee table. Arthur Schlessel's face swam onto the screen.

"Hey, guys. Good to see you."

"You too, Arthur."

"Sorry this took so long. Nothing should take two weeks to put together, I know. But, Gabe, I had some people go over the project we put together, with your proposal and the budget, and no surprise, the budget was fucked. Badly."

"What, eight hundred fifty thousand too high, Arthur?" Gabe asked. "I told you, we could stage it—"

Arthur shook his head on screen, broke into distorted pixilation, regrouped. "No, not too high, Gabe. Too low; like really, really too low. Like order of magnitude too low, guys."

This took a minute to register. Helena recovered first. "You mean, eight and a half million?" Arthur nodded.

"That's a lot, isn't it?" Gabriel had found his voice.

"I won't kid you, guys. That's starting to get up there."

"Can you do this, Arthur?"

"Gabe, I'm going to pretend you didn't mean to hurt my feelings. Of course I can do it. This is my job, guys. It took a while, though, to put together the right group."

"But you got a group to back you?"

Arthur shook his head on screen, refocused. "I got a group to consider backing us, Helena. We—meaning you two—are going to have to sell it. I'm setting the date for the pitch meeting for next week, if you think you can be ready by then."

"What kind of pitch, Arthur?"

"This is what I'm thinking, Gabe. It's going to have to be a mind reading show, of course. But we're going to have to be careful, keep away from the circus fortune teller vibe, you know?" Gabriel nodded at the screen. "We have to sell the science, you know? The cold, objectiveness of the thing. Make them understand that at the end of the day, ordinary scientists like you can read the thoughts of anybody willing to sit still for a scan.

"Do the PowerPoint, you know, the academic professor shtick. You've done it before, I remember when you did the amputation thing, you did really well. Same thing; no limbless veterans, though, so it's going to lose some punch, can't be helped. Questions, answers, change the world, yada yada. Cue music.

"And then, we give them the dog and pony show. We do a nice, objective demonstration of how you can interpret Helena's brainwaves real-time—"

"No." Helena became rigid next to Gabriel.

"Did Helena say something, Gabe?"

Gabriel looked at Helena beside him. He realized that there was no way Helena was shaving her head, but maybe: "Hey, Leena. I think I can rig the electrodes so that you won't have to—"

"No."

She looked him full in the face. Gabriel saw something in her expression; he had seen this sudden fierceness, the look of taut, restrained anger, many times. This Helena, though, showed all that and something else; a deep fear, a hurt that he could see in her eyes. He remembered the one time he had seen his wife look this way before. "No," she repeated to him.

Gabriel turned back to the screen, taking his wife's hand in his. "No, Arthur, I think—"

"Gabe, Leena, listen. I've been doing this my whole life, you know. I really, really think it sells best with Helena wearing the—" Helena snapped down the screen of the laptop computer. She kept her hand on the lid, seeming to hold Schlessel trapped in the device. Helena took a deep, shuddering breath. She sat rigid as Gabriel held her hand.

'Listen, Leena. You don't have to," he said softly, still holding her hand. The phone began to ring. Gabriel picked it up, looked at the caller ID. "It's Arthur." He didn't dare answer it, not yet. It continued to ring incessantly. "We'll do it another way, Leena." Gabriel's cell phone began to vibrate on the coffee table next to the laptop, then began to both ring and vibrate, adding to the cacophony of the wall phone. "Shit, he's persistent." Gabe said. Helena stood and, walking to the door, left.

Gabriel answered the phone.

"What the fuck, Gabe? What was that?"

Gabe waited, took a deep breath. "Arthur, that's not the way we're going to do it."

"I'm telling you, Gabe, we got one shot at this thing and I think—"

"Shut up, Arthur. This is my show, so shut up. Set it up for two weeks from now. I'll send you the outline for the presentation and I'll get you a copy of the PowerPoint. Bye." Gabriel went to find his wife.

Helena agreed to accompany Gabriel for the presentation, on her terms. Arthur had reluctantly agreed to Gabe's plan, realizing that to choose otherwise would cause him to lose any shot at this. They met the group of eight venture capitalists in Arthur's office conference room. Dr. Gabriel Sheehan, PhD., gave his twenty minute presentation accompanied by visuals polished by Arthur's media consultants. Gabe answered their questions politely as Helena and Arthur looked on from the back of the room. Then they all moved to the next room where the demonstration was to be held. Four chairs were arrayed on one side of the rectangular conference table. On the table, a simplified version of Gabriel's electrode headset rested before each seat. Each was wired to the amplifier and laptop computer that faced the other side of the table.

"Gentlemen," Arthur began, ushering them into the room. All eight were men, apparently ranging in age from forty to the early seventies. The older wore suits, the younger three in all black, tight slacks and shirtsleeves. One wore shorts. Thankfully, Gabe thought, they were all either bald or had their hair trimmed close. Or maybe Arthur had bought them all haircuts before they arrived, Gabe didn't know.

Arthur continued to herd his flock of angels. "Four of you may sit, it doesn't matter which. You'll see, you'll all have a chance. Obviously, this is the demonstration portion of the presentation. I suggest the rest of you stand for now behind the chairs, thank you." They positioned themselves as suggested. Gabriel took a seat near the wall, watching. Helena stood across the table from them, dressed in a designer dress that had cost the project over eight thousand dollars the week prior. "I'd like to introduce Ms. Fianna." Arthur gestured and Helena gave her audience a slight bow, smiling at them. "Ms. Fianna is Dr. Sheehan's wife and research assistant. She assures me that she possesses no extraordinary psychic powers. She will lead our demonstration. Helena?"

"Thank you, Arthur. Gentlemen, what you see in front of you is obviously not the electrode sensing device that Dr. Sheehan described in the presentation. Rather, this skullcap device is purely for this demonstration, being the prototype that Dr. Sheehan utilized in his pilot study. Though inconvenient, it will serve our purposes for today. Those of you who are sitting may go ahead and put the device on. Thank you. You see on the laptop in front of me," and here she spun the computer around on the conference table to let them all see the screen, "are your brain wave tracings being amplified and displayed in real time." She let them watch the multicolored waveforms dance across the quartered screen, each reflecting the thought patterns of an individual. "In an effort to convince you gentlemen that I am capable of reading your minds, we will have a brief demonstration of the device. As you are aware, our current mastery of brain wave interpretation is limited to a vocabulary of six thoughts. Each of these thoughts is represented by a picture, what we call an ideogram. In front of each of you is an envelope containing flashcards. Please open the envelopes. Thank you. I encourage you to shuffle these cards, exchange them between yourselves, do whatever is necessary to convince yourselves that I could not have memorized the order in which you will be studying the cards in the coming minutes. We will go around the table. Each of you will, in turn, close your eyes briefly. I'll ask you to open your eyes and look at the card. I will watch the monitor before me and hope to impress you with my accuracy in reading from your brainwaves which ideogram you are looking at. Those of you who are standing, I encourage you to view the process by walking around the table, watching my monitor, looking from my vantage point to confirm that there are no mirrors or window reflections giving me an advantage.

At whatever moment you choose, any individual standing should tap one of the seated and take his place. Have I been clear?" They all nodded. "Are there any questions or concerns before we start?"

"I have one thought," Arthur said. "Just to make this more entertaining. Here's five thousand," he dropped crisp bills in the center of the table, "to go to the first person Ms. Fianna gets wrong." Helena looked at him, forcing a smile, despite her thought that Arthur was being an idiot. She reconsidered, however, when she saw the smiles and laughter of those across from her. These guys liked a show, after all.

"I've got ten," a participant in too-tight black pants said, leaning up from his chair to dump a wad of crumpled bills in the middle of the table, "for our pretty redheaded wizard, if she gets us all right." This guy, Helena thought as she smiled at him and gave him an acknowledging nod, is an ass.

Helena continued. "Thank you both. I appreciate your enthusiasm, if that's what it is. If we can get started, please shuffle and arrange your cards as you see fit. Ready?" They nodded. "Let us begin then."

Helena pointed to the man seated to her far left. "Mr. Hangstrom, if you would close your eyes, please. Thank you and now open—triangle. Mr. Fishberger, thank you, the number three." She moved smoothly, at a theatric pace, working her audience as a carnival barker might work a crowd. The others circulated around the room, often looking over her shoulder but moving on with a shake of the head, as they could make nothing of the complex display on her computer. As subjects were replaced with new participants, she passed over those arranging their headgear, continuing to read the thoughts of those around him until he was ready to participate. It wasn't long until she had read the thoughts of all participating over thirty times each and the money still remained on the table. She couldn't help noticing that Mr. Tight Pants had spent a large portion of the demonstration looking over her shoulder from an uncomfortably close position. He was still there when Helena decided the demonstration was complete.

"Gentlemen," she said with finality. "I don't wish to make this tedious. If you are satisfied, I suggest we end here." With that, she leaned over the table and began to gather up the fifteen thousand dollars. "I believe this belongs to me, if I understood the wager correctly."

"Half a second, dear." Mr. Tightpants leaned past her to put his hand on hers.

Helena straightened, withdrawing her hand. "Yes, Mr. Chen? Is there a concern?"

"Concern? No. Very impressive. Ms. Fianna, was it?" She nodded. "I was just hoping to be even more impressed, is all."

"How so?" Helena asked as Chen sat down across from her, redonning one of the electrode caps.

He pulled out a deck of cards. "How about you tell me what card I'm looking at?"

"That would be great, Kwon," Arthur interjected, stepping forward. "But you know, right now we're limited to the pictures. Ms. Fianna certainly can't—"

Helena leaned over the table to Chen, palms flat on the table. She gave him a wicked smile. "Double or nothing, Mr. Chen?"

Chen returned her smile, leaning back in his leather chair. "You'll have to trust me for it, I'm afraid. If you win, that is."

Helena straightened, took her position behind the laptop. "Close your eyes, Mr. Chen." She stared intently at the display. "Do you have your card ready?" Chen nodded, eyes closed and holding the card before him. Helena waited, letting the suspense build dramatically. "Open your eyes!"

Helena gave her husband a smile. He gave her a wink from across the room. Helena took especially long to ponder the tracings on her screen, then leaned over the table toward Chen, drawing out the moment. "Six of diamonds, Mr. Chen."

Chen smiled, turned the card around to show the group that the card was indeed as called. "Now, Arthur, I am impressed." The small group applauded appreciatively, laughing.

Helena swept the money up. "I'll have to trust you for the rest, Mr. Chen," she said, smiling at him. She looked at her monitor again, snapping the lid down. Helena leaned over, even closer to the man. "Oh, and Mr. Chen," they smiled at each other, "you're right. I am kind of a bitch." She reached over and removed the electrodes from the man's head as he reddened.

Arthur wanted to treat Helena and Gabriel to dinner to celebrate. He was ebullient. They declined, preferring a quiet meal in their room at the hotel. Arthur had been effusive in assuring them that after that show, investors would be lining up to pour money into their project. The budget should be even higher, he thought. He just hoped those bastards at Google didn't get wind of this, he added.

Gabriel and Helena lay next to each other in bed, staring out the wall sized window at the glittering nighttime skyline of San Francisco. They each sipped at the leftover wine from their room service dinner.

Gabriel gave his wife an appreciative look. "So how did you know, Helena? How'd you know Chen would do that?"

She shook her head. "Didn't, Gabriel."

"Bullshit. You told me to be ready with my phone. You knew. How?"

Helena shrugged. "There's always an asshole, Gabe." She looked at her husband. He obviously wasn't buying it. "Fine! Take away my mystery! I saw the pack of cards in his pants before your presentation. Girls notice these things, you know. Shit, in those pants I could tell he was circumcised." She put her head on Gabe's chest. "You were pretty quick on the draw there, partner. Picture came up on the screen in about eighty milliseconds. Did I look good?"

"Beautiful, Leena. You were beautiful." He kissed the top of her head. "You are beautiful."

They had almost dozed off. Gabe opened his eyes at Helena's voice, soft against his chest.

"You know, hon; I think I could've done it."

"Done what?"

"Before the picture came up on the screen, I think I saw it. In the tracings. I was thinking I saw red, and triangle. I was thinking it was a diamond before your picture popped over."

"Seriously? You could get two thoughts, like that?' She nodded. "Still would've been screwed with the six part, though." They were quiet, thinking. "And the part about 'kind of a bitch?'"

"Didn't need the machine for that."

Gabriel and Helena sat at the conference table in Arthur's office. Contracts had been signed, corporations and limited partnerships formed, office space rented. The new offices of "Thought Technologies, LLC" were not yet ready for occupancy, however. Torrents of money were being expended under the direction of their managing partner, Arthur. He assured them that once his designers were through, they would be very pleased with their headquarters in a converted warehouse off the Embarcadero.

As for now, they sat with Arthur and his latest team. It seemed to Gabriel that Arthur had many teams, and that these teams never included the same players on any two consecutive meetings. When Gabe pointed this out to Arthur, Arthur explained that only the successful were allowed a second visit. Gabriel was frequently confused, not only by the members of the team, but also by their purpose and intent. Such was the fact today.

Gabriel looked about the table at the fourteen individuals gathered. Helena and Arthur were the only faces he recognized. As he was sitting at the head of the table, and all seemed to be looking at him, he felt obliged to lead off.

"Tell me again what we're meeting about?"

Helena rolled her eyes. Arthur was more helpful.

"This is a meeting of our product development team, Gabe."

"Correct me if I'm wrong here, Arthur, but I thought we met with product development last week. For like three or four hours. And I don't remember seeing any of these people there." Gabriel gave a smile to all around the table.

"Yes—no, you're right, Gabriel. They're gone."

"Gone?"

"Gone, Gabriel. Wrong approach, poor timeline, lack of vision, under resourced. They weren't going to cut it. They're gone. New team." Arthur gestured grandly around the table, smiling.

"Did we pay them? The old team, I mean?"

"Yes, Gabe. You always have to pay them to make them go away. But they're gone now and it's time to move on. I'd like to introduce Caitlin Mallory, she's founder and CEO of Mallory Marketing, here in San Francisco. This is her team. Caitlin has a presentation for us."

An athletic appearing woman with short hair and angular features stood from her chair. Gabe didn't think she could be over thirty years old.

"Thank you, Mr. Schlessel," she said, standing. She smiled at Gabe, then Helena. "Dr. Sheehan, Ms. Fianna."

"Did we pay them a lot, Arthur? Because I don't think they did—"

"Gabe? Really, you care?" Helena interjected. Gabriel shrugged.

Mallory continued with an indulgent smile. "I know you all have reviewed Mallory Marketing's proposal, so I don't intend to bore you with all the details."

"Actually, I haven't. There's a proposal? Because I haven't seen it."

"Gabriel," Helena answered. "we went over it together, yesterday."

"Oh, that. I thought that was the old product development team's proposal. No?" Helena and Arthur shook their heads. "Oh, then great. That was a great proposal."

"Should I continue? Thank you." Mallory started to slowly circle the table, making eye contact with the three principals, ignoring the others. "I trust everyone shares Dr. Sheehan's opinion that ours is a great proposal. With your approval and incorporating any modifications which you see fit, Mallory would like to go active as of next week. I can assure you that we are very enthusiastic about this opportunity. We have the experience and resources necessary to bring this endeavor to successful fruition. Our plan—"

"I'm sorry, Ms. Mallory," Gabe interrupted. "It's just that I've heard so much of this crap lately. I mean, how can you say you have all this experience; you're like, what, twenty-nine? Thirty?"

Mallory stopped circling, eyed Gabriel and smiled. "I assure you, Dr. Sheehan, that Mallory Marketing brings to the table over twenty five years of experience in—"

"Yeah, sure," Gabe said, gesturing around the table. "There's like twelve of you. That's what, two years each?" Helena watched the exchange, absently spinning a pen around her fingers.

"Dr. Sheehan, I certainly don't wish to take up your valuable time reviewing my personal credentials and that of my company. I trust that the materials we provided in submitting our proposal were sufficiently impressive to cause you to invite us here today."

"Actually, I had no idea you were coming."

"I propose, therefore, that we provide a brief presentation of our initial efforts on behalf of Thought Technologies." Mallory touched a button on a remote she produced from her pocket. The lights dimmed as blinds whirred down over the windows. The projector came on, displayed a video accompanied by a stridently inspirational soundtrack. The eight-minute movie concluded with the Mallory Marketing logo, an animated silhouette of a pole-vaulter clearing the bar. The room brightened as the blinds retracted.

"Loved the logo," Helena commented. "Rest of it was crap, though."

Gabriel blinked. "Hold it. Really? You're selling my process, already? We don't have a process." He turned to Helena, then Arthur. "Oh, I know we're pretty damn good at six words, but really? I thought we were doing the project to create the product. Then we'll have something to sell."

Arthur leaned in. "Gabe, this is how we're going to develop the project. We have to sell it, Gabe."

Gabriel looked confused. "I am genuinely confused, guys. I thought we'd use the ear bud electrodes, you know, the cellphone app, to gather the data. Remember, twenty-five thousand subjects looking at ideograms on their cellphones?"

"Yeah, Gabe," Helena answered. "And how are we going to get those twenty-five thousand subjects to do that?"

"What do you mean? Why wouldn't they?"

"Why would they, Dr. Sheehan?" Mallory asked, returning to her seat.

"Because it's easy. It's a good thing to do. They can help in a great cause. You know, like the SETI thing." Everyone around the table except Helena was obviously lost at the reference. "You know, the computer thing that searches for extraterrestrial intelligence."

"Yeah, Gabe, we know," Helena said. "How's that SETI thing working out, by the way? Been running for, like, over twenty years, at least. Unless I missed that issue of Time magazine, no real breakthroughs on the intelligent alien front."

Arthur said, "Gabriel, we don't have time to wait for twenty-five thousand altruistic computer geeks to do this for us. This is business, we've got a timeline. Our funding horizon is eighteen months, give or take. And by that I mean, at the end of eighteen months, either we give my backers a product or they take this all away."

"So we're going to pay people to use our app?" Gabe looked pleadingly at Arthur.

"No. We thought about it, but it doesn't work. We focus tested paying people just to use the device for a couple of minutes. Anything less than twenty bucks a pop, they told us to get lost."

"Twenty bucks?"

"Yeah, wasn't going to happen. But what they do want, well—Caitlin, sorry. I'm stepping all over you here."

"No problem, Mr. Schlessel. Dr. Sheehan, Ms. Fianna; people respond to money, but only in quantities that aren't practical for our project. So we had to find other motivations. What do people want?"

"You mean, besides money? Sex."

Helena gave her husband a look. "Give it a rest for a while, Gabe."

"We thought of that, too, Dr. Sheehan. Also not practical. So we look for lesser motivations, but motivations that still lead to the behavior we desire. We want tens of thousands of people to wear our ear buds and use our cellphone application. We have to make the app do something that they want, or makes their lives better.

"What people want—besides money and sex, of course—is convenience, entertainment, nutrition, refreshment. And, if they can get it, some form of cachet at the same time. Some element of prestige or superiority. We can give them all those things.

"When we focus tested a group of undergraduate students at Berkley, only nine percent said they'd be interested in using our app because it's important and will make the world a better place."

"Young people are ungrateful bastards." Gabe shook his head.

"And that nine percent said they'd do it once. And then they'd delete the app. What they told us they want, Dr. Sheehan, is convenience, a better use of their valuable time, and the cachet of a new way to interact with their environment."

"No clue what you're talking about."

"They want this." Mallory slid her cellphone down the table at them. "They want that device to read their thoughts. They loved that idea.

One hundred percent penetration, five plus enthusiasm, right off the charts. Your nineteen-year-old undergraduate female nonalcohol ingesting, nonsmoking Caucasian wants to be able to look at her iPhone and think, 'I feel like a Coke'. And then, poof, she's got a coke in her hand. She thought that was pretty damn cool. She'd do that all day. You know who else thought that was cool? Every single demographic we tested. Every single subject, in every age group, loved it. Kids loved it. Seventy-year-old grandmas, who didn't know how to use the phone their children had gotten them, loved it. Hipsters, college professors, day laborers, lawyers? All loved it. Most wouldn't leave the room until we told them how to get the app, were willing to pay for an app like that."

Helena was smiling with excitement. "We can do that," she said.

"No we can't," Gabriel responded in exasperation. "What are we, fucking magicians? We can't make a coke appear or anything else."

One of the young men who had been sitting in silence until now interjected. "Actually, Dr. Sheehan, we've developed an app—"

"Who are you?"

"Sorry, Dr. Sheehan. My name is Jay Tedesco, I'm the app developer."

"The app developer? And you're going to tell me we have an app that does that?"

"Well, yes, Dr. Sheehan. In a fashion. If the subject is wearing your ear bud electrode device and activates my app, she can initiate a purchase of coke just by thinking about it."

"Initiate a purchase? Not materialize in her hand?" Everyone around the table nodded at that. "And that's good enough, you think? Walk into a Seven Eleven thinking, 'Gee, I feel like a coke, and Mohammed behind the counter..." Gabe saw Helena wince, glance at the young gentleman of obvious Indian descent sitting next to Gabriel. "Sorry, whoever you are. This was like, fantastic, that instead of pulling out a couple of bucks from your pocket—"

"That's right, Dr. Sheehan. The person walks in, thinks 'I'd like a Coke', and holds her phone in front of the register. The app displays a barcode for payment and the transaction is complete."

"You do realize that the subject still has to walk to the cooler and grab the stupid can of coke herself, right?" Jay nodded. "And they were good with that?"

"They went crazy for it, Dr. Sheehan. Wanted to keep the demo device, wouldn't give it back."

There was silence for several minutes while Gabriel digested this. "I see two problems. I hate to piss all over this, guys. You all seem so nice and enthusiastic and all. But I see a couple of problems."

"Please, Dr. Sheehan," Mallory encouraged. "We'd like to hear your concerns."

"Oh, good. Because here are a couple of my concerns. Concern number one: We don't know the freaking mind pattern for 'I'd love a freaking coke right now'. You know why we don't know the freaking mind pattern for that? Because we can interpret exactly six friggin' thoughts, that's why. As a matter of fact, that's the whole reason we need to do the project, kids. Because we can't read minds yet! Ironic, isn't it?"

"That's not a problem, Dr. Sheehan." Gabriel rounded on Jay, who had spoken.

"Not a problem, Jay? Your app reads minds?"

"No sir, not really. But it looks like it does. It just uses your electrode as a trigger. I figured if someone starts an app titled 'I feel like a Coke', we can just use the blink spike to trigger the barcode."

Helena leaned onto the table. "We can do a little better than that, even. We can detect the thought for the color red, use that to refine the trigger."

Gabriel was still not impressed. "Okay, I get it. Better not market this to the Mountain Dew folks, though. Simple enough, smoke and mirrors. We're good at that. But there's still problem number two. My company isn't about streamlining the convenience store purchase experience. How the hell does this do anything for my project?"

They all looked at Jay. "Well, sir, that's the point, isn't it? The app really isn't about buying a coke. That's just the Trojan."

"You're losing me with the prophylactic metaphor, son."

"No, Dr. Sheehan, I meant Trojan horse. It's just a ruse to get the subject to put on the electrode device and perform a behavior. In this case, to look at their phone and activate my app. The real purpose of the app runs every time the behavior is performed."

Gabriel smiled at him. "So every time they buy a coke, your app runs through ideograms, and they're wearing the buds. And the app stores the data?"

Jay smiled back. "Exactly correct, Dr. Sheehan. Focus testing shows that people will stare at three images for two seconds each, no problem, while they're waiting for the app to complete the purchase cycle."

Gabe asked, "What's the name of your app?"

Jay looked embarrassed. "I Think I'd Like to Change the World. It plays that Coke song from the eighties."

"I hate that song," Arthur said. Arthur turned to Mallory seated next to him. "So how much do we pay to get Coke to play along?"

Mallory shook her head. "We took a different approach, Mr. Schlessel. It looked more attractive to their marketing department when we showed them the app and told them it would cost them twenty-five thousand up front and fifty cents per download. That will allow us to distribute the app for free and still cover overhead. Also, they agreed on a two-tenths of a cent royalty payment per purchase for utilizing our innovative purchasing modality." She smiled.

"Yeah?" Arthur smiled back. "Who gets the royalty? You or me?"

"Well, Mr. Schlessel, that depends on how we write the contract, doesn't it? I'm just having a great time with their national marketing director. I've got her by the balls, she wants an exclusive on this so badly. Yesterday, she tried to give me ten grand under the table if I'd cancel my meeting tomorrow with Pepsi."

Helena frowned. "I'm having a problem with the whole gender confused bribery corruption thing. Just tell us one thing, Ms. Mallory. Is this going to work?"

"I think it will, Ms. Fianna."

It worked better than they had hoped. While the initial apps were fairly crude affairs, they benefitted from their innovativeness and exclusivity. It was the "next great thing," making several magazine covers. Nobody had anything to compete with the concept. By the time the novelty of manipulating single purpose apps with thought had begun to grow thin, Thought Technology had accrued enough data to make the technique much more sophisticated. The effect was synergistic, its growth exponential. More and more people wanted to use thought input technology to interact with their smartphones in more and more ways. People became annoyed if they actually had to touch the things; they'd rather just think about what they wanted it to do. And every time they did something, anything, it generated more data for Thought Technology to refine and expand their burgeoning encyclopedia of thought patterns.

Thought Technology, LLC rapidly expanded its offices to take over a block of warehouse buildings on the Embarcadero. Despite aggressively outsourcing, subcontracting, and outright selling as many aspects of the exploding technology as possible, Arthur was overwhelmed. Caitlin Mallory rode a wave of "New Thought Marketing" expertly, buying out two other marketing firms in San Francisco, with additional subcontractual agreements to multiple firms in New York and DC.

Helena and Gabriel had long ago moved into a cottage they bought on the ocean in Half Moon Bay, less than a mile from Arthur's home. They usually commuted with Arthur, and the three often dined late with Arthur's family at his home. On this evening, they sat on the beach in chairs pulled around a low fire in a sand pit. The sun had set brilliantly, and now they watched as the sky darkened through shades of blue to purple, bright points of light starting to appear in the sky above.

"I'm sorry, guys," Arthur said. "I don't think I can go in tomorrow. I'm spent."

"Come on, Arthur," replied Gabriel. He and Helena shared a chaise. "We need you. You're the driver."

"Take the keys, Helena can drive."

"No way, I'd rather take the bus. Have you seen Helena drive?" She gave him an elbow to the ribs. "Hey, ouch. It's true and you know it; you drive like Steve McQueen."

"Yeah, that's the point; we're in San Francisco."

"He's dead, you know."

"Not from driving. Come on Arthur, you've said this before. Yesterday, actually."

"Mean it this time, Helena. It's time to bail. We did what we set out to do and a shitload more. I've already made more money than god five times over with this thing, and so have you guys. I'm old now, time to retire and kick back."

"What are you talking about, Arthur? You're what, thirty-eight?"

"Exactly. I'm the only guy I know over thirty-five that's still working. And working my ass off, I might add."

"But we haven't changed the world yet, Arthur. That was part of the deal."

"Changed it enough. Sell it off, guys. All of it. Google's been trying for it since we started. Give it to them."

"Not all of it," Helena said soberly. The other two looked at her. "I think Arthur's right, Gabe. The project's done and we got what we were after. We sell everything except the salmon."

Arthur asked, "I'm sorry, what? The salmon?"

"Yeah, Arthur. We sell the technology, the hardware, the marketing rights, everything. Everything except the salmon of knowledge, the encyclopedia we've built. We never sell that."

Gabriel was nodding. "It's all I wanted out of this, anyway. Never even conceived of everything else that spun off. Fine, if you want. Go ahead, Arthur, get rid of everything. But Helena and I keep ownership of the master cylinder or whatever, the..."

"Salmon. We let people use the salmon, we license its use in various products and whatever people want to use it for. But we maintain control of the salmon. Nobody ever touches the salmon, except us."

They smiled at her. Arthur poked at the fire, sending up a shower of sparks. "Your analogy sucks, by the way. I prefer the crystal of knowledge, like in that Henson movie. Did you ever see that one? The one with the talking vultures? I love that movie. My kids hated it. Too cerebral for them."

"It's not an analogy, Arthur. It's history," Helena replied. "And your kids probably hated it because the actors were all fuckin' puppets, Arthur. Really ugly vulture puppets."

Gabriel had heard too many discussions between these two regarding the merits of obscure cult films to allow this to continue. He deeply feared they would start quoting dialogue from "The Princess Bride" again. He pre-empted Arthur's retort. "Since we're talking about work, there's one thing I've been thinking about. Something besides quitting and writing a blog about how great Jim Henson was—"

"He was a genius."

"Yes, Arthur. Taken from us too soon, I agree. None of us will be the people we could have been, if only he had the time to complete that Muppet version of 'Gone with the Wind'."

"Henson was working on that? Really?"

"No, Arthur. I think I made that up. Listen, we're talking transition here. I think we're hitting a wall with our current research technique."

"Why, Gabe?" Helena asked. "The database, the encyclopedia is growing deeper and deeper. We're getting better at reading—"

"Better at reading ideograms, Helena. We have a giant database of single blink responses to a lot of pictures, a lot of words. We keep calling it an encyclopedia, but—"

"It's a salmon."

"It's a crystal."

"No," Gabe continued. "It's just a dictionary. Thoughts defined by individual words. That's not an encyclopedia. We guess at meaning, we assume meaning from context, from single thought pictures. But we don't really have any idea of the grammar, the full sentences. We don't really read what they're thinking."

They thought about this for a while.

Arthur stirred. "You're right, Gabe. It's not the crystal."

"It is the salmon, though," Helena said.

"I think I speak for Arthur, Leena, when I say that we'd like you to stop with the stupid fish analogy."

Helena pouted. "It's not an analogy. Bloody Americans, you have no culture, no history. Fucking Philippines."

"Philistines."

"Exactly."

"What is it you want to do, Gabe?" Arthur interrupted.

"I think we need to go back to the lab. We know what to look for now. I want to go back to volunteers wearing full electrodes, better recording. We know how to filter now, we have better analytics. I think we do a large scale study in a more controlled setting, in a lab setting."

"Back to skullcaps?" Helena asked.

"Yeah," Gabe answered. "We can afford to pay a lot of volunteers to shave their heads now. We can do it right."

"You're not talking about going back to Ann Arbor, are you?" Arthur asked.

"Well, yeah, but not just Ann Arbor. We do have to get back at some point, don't we, Leena?" Helena just looked out at the ocean. "Well, I think we build the main lab here. We can use most of the space we already have, at Embarcadero. We'd just need one or two testing rooms. But I think we should have satellite labs in six or seven sites, you know. Around the country, a couple overseas."

Helena sat up and moved to the foot of the chaise. "Yeah, who's going to run those labs, Gabe?" she asked, tossing a twig into the dying fire.

Gabriel was silent. Arthur eventually filled the silence, saying, "If you set them up, Gabe, I'm certain we can get some PhD types to run the actual testing, if that's what you want." More silence. Arthur prodded at the fire, trying to revive it.

"What do you think, Leena?" Gabe asked.

Silence, save for a couple of crackles from the reinvigorated fire.

Arthur was studying Helena's face. "Hold it," Arthur said. "How long have you guys been married, two years?"

"Three," Gabriel replied.

"And in three years, how many nights have you slept apart?" Silence. "Oh, that's sick, I gotta tell you."

"Fuck you, Arthur," Helena said.

"Well, that's not going to happen, is it? Not unless we convince Gabe here to leave town for a few days."

Helena turned to smile at Arthur. "No, it's not going to happen because you're too fucking old."

Gabriel winced. "Ouch."

"I can't believe my geek friend Gabe is that great you wouldn't want to try, Leena."

"He fucks like a mink, Arthur."

"Okay," Gabriel interjected, glad it was now dark. "I'm feeling uncomfortable."

Arthur wasn't. "Gee, I hope my wife says that about me."

"Arthur," Helena said, "she doesn't."

Mercifully, the fire had now completely died. Arthur failed in his attempts at resuscitation.

Helena spoke from her seat on the foot of the chaise, watching phosphorescent waves break in the darkness. "Why the hell would you want to set up labs around the world? That's just stupid, Gabe."

"I don't think it's stupid, babe. I think we need to—"

"No, it's fucking moronic, Gabe-babe. Fuckin' waste of time and money."

"We need to study thought patterns outside—"

"Outside what? Outside humanity? People think alike, Gabe. You want to start testing aliens, call my old department. Oh, here's an idea. We can branch out to pets. You know, what is your dog really thinking?"

"Hey, that's not bad, Leena," Arthur interjected.

They both looked at him, shook their heads.

Gabriel looked back at his wife. "How do you know? How do you know that people all think alike?"

"Because I'm not a fucking moron, that's how."

"You guys sleep together every night, really?"

"Shut up, Arthur. Prove it, Leena."

"Give me three months and five hundred thousand, I'll prove it."

"Arthur," Gabe said. "You heard the lady."

Arthur converted nearly the entire complex at the Embarcadero to research facilities, fitting out five separate laboratories with everything Gabriel and Helena needed and about twenty times more. For reasons unfathomable to Gabriel, Arthur felt it necessary to include huge flat panel display screens on almost every surface. In addition, Arthur installed state of the art, high-end sound systems in every lab, despite the fact Gabriel said it was completely useless. As Arthur realized that his two friends would be pursuing independent research projects in the same building, he felt that anything he could do to prevent competition for facilities might prevent bloodshed. Also, he felt the sound system might come in handy to drown out the yelling.

Helena and Gabriel hired a cadre of postdoctoral fellows and technicians as research assistants. Gabriel claimed that Helena's hiring criteria was "male, under thirty, former Abercrombie catalog model". Helena replied that she was going to show that Gabriel was "so fucking wrong that the dumbest studs on earth could prove it". At least, that's what she claimed was her rationale.

They pursued parallel research projects, hardly encountering one another in the huge facility until they met to ride home with Arthur at the end of each day. Gabriel had developed an advanced electrode array that provided improved sensitivity in thought recording. It did, however, require the subject to completely shave their head. At an incentive of two hundred dollars for thirty minutes in a testing booth, Gabriel didn't have much trouble recruiting from the two dozen colleges and universities in the greater San Francisco area.

Helena took a different tack in the recruiting of test subjects. She desired non-English speaking Hispanics and Asian nationals. Once word got out that her brightly colored vans (driven by damn good looking guys) were recruiting volunteers at fifty bucks a head to spend thirty minutes doing the easiest work an undocumented alien had ever seen—and really weren't just dropping everyone at the INS detention facility—there were crowds lining up on street corners, flagging them down. She used the ear bud electrode system so as not to trouble her subjects with the stress of cutting their hair. The sensitivity of their standard system was entirely sufficient for the purpose of her study. In just over two months and at forty percent of budget, she crossed the hallway to her husband's office.

Gabriel was seated at his desk, staring at an array of ridiculously huge flatscreen monitors in the semidarkness. Helena kicked open his door, causing it to crash against the wall. Gabriel shot of his chair, knocking it over.

"Holy shit! What was that?"

"You dear," Helena said, striding into his office and throwing an inch thick report on his desk, "are officially proven to be a fucking moron." She smiled at him, arms crossed.

Gabriel's heart was still racing as he picked up his chair. "Like I've never heard that before."

"Yes, but now it's official." They sat and stared together for a while at the colored tracings on the monitors. "What is this shit?"

"Oh, you're asking the moron to interpret thought waves for you?"

"This is what you've been staring at for the last two months? What is it?"

"That," Gabe said, gesturing at the screen, "is my test subject telling the interviewer about his mother."

"Wow. Looks like he has a very confused idea of his mother."

"Don't we all." They stared some more.

"No, seriously. What is this, Gabe?"

"Ah, you're intrigued. Watch this, grasshopper." Gabriel keyed the input tablet on his desk. Spikes in the tracing became bright red. "Here are thought patterns that correspond to our dictionary definition of 'mother'."

"Wow, how cool. Of course, we could probably just listen to the audio and pick out every time he says 'mother'."

"No, that isn't the same. Watch, grasshopper." Gabriel manipulated the tracings with the keyboard again, now displaying three layers of multicolored tracings, each occasionally showing the red spike pattern. "The top tracing reflects the subjects thought pattern relating to his speech. If you listen to audio at the same time, there's direct correlation between the spoken word for 'mother' and the thought wave pattern 'mother'. The second and third tracings, however, reflect simultaneous, but distinct, thought layers. They also involve the concept 'mother', but they in no way correlate with the subject's speech."

"So what do they mean?"

"I call them 'the subconscious'."

"In other words, you don't have a fucking clue."

"Exactly. So," Gabe picked up Helena's report, "what wise and wonderful things have you discovered, grasshopper?"

"I'm discovering that I'm sick of you calling me 'grasshopper', for one. And like I said, Gabe, you're wrong."

"Yes, I know. Tell the moron what he's wrong about today."

"People think alike. It was very straightforward to prove it. Native foreign language speakers, despite utilizing different words for just about everything, display identical thought patterns in response to all ideograms tested. The language may be different, but the thought dictionary is universal. I should have put money on it."

"I thought we put about half a million on it."

"Came in at under two hundred thousand, with tips and bar tab for the guys."

"She's smart and cheap."

"And beautiful."

"And cheap." He thumbed through the report. "Nice. What are you going to do with it?"

"I figured I'd just use it to humiliate you at random moments for the rest of our lives."

"A noble goal, I admit. But I have a thought. Can I steal this?" Helena shrugged.

"Might as well. That shit," she gestured at the monitors, "isn't getting you anywhere."

Helena promptly declared herself on vacation, spending almost every day jogging at the beach or solo rock climbing up and down the coast. Gabriel continued to spend weekdays at the lab, riding in with Arthur, who was happily accomplishing almost nothing in his own offices downtown. After two weeks, Gabriel had completed his little side project. He announced this to Arthur on the car ride home to Half Moon Bay.

"Really?" asked Arthur. "And what project was that?"

"Just a little thing that grew out of Helena's study."

"The one that proved you're a moron?"

"Yes, that one."

"I'm intrigued."

"You should be. I think it'll turn into something you're going to make a lot of money off of."

"Okay, now you really have my attention. Tell me."

"I don't think so, not yet. It kinda works in the lab, but I really haven't had a chance to trial it in the real world."

"So why the hell did you even bring it up? I could be listening to NPR right now, you know."

"You were telling me about that new restaurant last week, right? That was you?"

"Yeah, it was me. What, are you trying to pretend you have another friend in the world?"

"No. You said it was French, right?"

"Yeah, it's supposed to be great. The chef is from Lyon. Expensive, must be great, right?"

"French wait staff?"

"Yeah, the whole nine yards. Takes about three months to get a reservation."

"Let's go Saturday night. The four of us."

"What? Why? There's no way we get a reservation for this weekend."

"Come on, Arthur. Send over one of your minions to rain down some cash and get us a reservation. What good is it to have more money than god if you don't use it to get us into a decent restaurant? That's what the ancient Greek gods did with all their money, you know."

"Didn't know that. I'll see what my minion can do."

The two couples were shown to their table by a suitably effete maître de. Eventually, menus and drinks arrived. Gabriel turned to Arthur's wife, asking, "Sam, you speak French, right?"

"I speak French," Helena said.

"Yeah, with an Irish accent. I'm not trying to get us kicked out before the entre arrives. Sam, you lived in France, right?"

Samantha nodded. "Four years at the Sorbonne. Oui." She smiled. "I can handle these guys, don't worry, Gabe."

"We'll see, Sam." Gabriel pulled a device from his pocket. They all stared at the thing. It appeared to be a large smartphone with Thought Technology mind reading ear buds. "I want you to get the waiter to wear this whenever he's at our table."

"How is she supposed to do that, Gabe?" Arthur asked. "This guy's nametag says 'Surly'."

"I don't know. Tell him I'm hard of hearing so he has to wear the device."

Helena slapped her forehead. "That makes absolutely no sense. Then you should wear the stupid thing."

"He's a waiter," Arthur said. "Perhaps he wants a tip."

"I'll try," Samantha said. Twenty minutes later, their waiter returned. "Pardon me," Samantha said to him in Parisian-accented French, "But it will be necessary, please, for you to wear this device. Our companion is deaf." She smiled at the waiter, who did not smile back. The waiter surveyed his four charges, expertly palming and summing the five twenty dollar bills Arthur passed him beside the table.

"Certainly, madam," the waiter replied in French. He was shown how to don the ear buds as Gabriel kept the device in front of him. "Would you like to hear of our specials this evening?"

"Oui," replied Gabriel, reading the English translation of the waiter's question on the device he held. As the waiter described the evening's specials in thickly accented French, Gabriel read the translation from the screen before him aloud to the group. "Steamed mussels in white wine sauce with tarragon, rack of lamb with chestnuts and potatoes, sea bass with turnips. How did I do, Sam?"

"Perfect, I think," Samantha replied. "His accent is quite unusual, I think."

"I think he's just being a dick," Helena added.

They each ordered in turn, with Samantha translating their selections into French. The waiter removed the ear buds and left with a "Merci" that even the non-French speaking amongst them found impressively insincere.

"Well," Arthur said, "we won't see him for at least half an hour."

Gabriel was fiddling with the device he had brought. He smiled and chuckled to himself.

"I'm impressed, Gabriel. Did that thing translate from the French?" Arthur asked.

Gabriel was grinning like a kid. "Yeah, I think it did a pretty good job, too." He showed the device around the table where the previous conversation was displayed. "This is based on the work Leena just finished in the lab."

"Really, Gabe?" Helena asked, obviously pleased. "That data was good for something else besides gloating?"

Arthur took the device, reading off the display. "Gabriel, this is fantastic. Is this what you were talking about in the car a couple of days ago?" Gabriel nodded. "It's a translator. This is great."

Gabriel was nodding. "Yeah, Leena proved that our dictionary was accurate across languages and cultures. So it was easy enough to use the database—"

"The salmon," Helena interjected.

Both Gabriel and Arthur rolled their eyes. Gabriel continued, "—use the database as a universal translator. Language, accent, lisp—doesn't matter. This sees the thought behind the spoken word."

Arthur wouldn't let the device go. "This is going to be a goldmine."

It was Helena's turn to roll her eyes. "No it won't. Geez, Arthur, sometimes I think you're as big a moron as my husband."

"Oh, he is," Samantha said.

"Thought so, Sam. Sorry," Helena said. "Like the perfect universal translator requires the speaker to wear ear buds all the time. Good luck with that, Arthur. Maybe if you include a hundred bucks for incentive with each device, you know, to give to the speaker so he'll wear the stupid thing..."

"So what's this, Gabe?" Arthur had hit a button on the side of the device, and the screen had changed to display a long string of italicized script. He began reading aloud, "If the ugly little fucker wants to give me a hundred bucks, I'll wear his underwear on my head."

"That," said Gabriel, "is my part of the project. I call it 'Level Two'."

"What is level two?" Samantha asked.

"You're kidding, Gabe. That shit you were showing me on the screen?" Helena asked. Gabriel nodded. "You found a way to filter down in real time? And interpret?"

Gabriel nodded again, enthusiastically. "It's just filtering, knowing how and where to look. The interpretation is pretty lame, still."

"Kind of screws up the whole universal translator thing, doesn't it?" Arthur asked.

"I don't think that was going to work, honey," Samantha said, patting her husband's arm.

"No, not that," Helena said in a reverential tone. She looked at her husband, amazed. "You invented a lie detector, Gabriel." He was grinning at her like an idiot. Helena took his hand, saying, "I think you finally did it, Gabe. I think you just changed the world."

Their food arrived, cold.

Gabriel was more enthusiastic about his research now than he had ever been since graduate school. After many years, he had reached the point where he could see his invention affecting the fabric of society. His enthusiasm was infectious, and while Helena continued her extended vacation, Arthur was caught up. He met with Gabriel several times a day to discuss the way forward.

"If you think this is ready, Gabe," Arthur began, "then we should talk about patents before we go much farther." They were sitting in Arthur's office, drinking coffee as they stared out over the bay.

"It's ready. You need to call the lawyers, I think. And I need a cadre of new volunteers to test, people who can lie and deceive."

"Lawyers and liars? Sounds like one phone call to me."

Gabriel utilized the full resources of the lab to research the complexities of multilayer analysis of mentation. While the business of continually expanding and refining the dictionary of thought patterns went on automatically in the back labs supervised by employed researchers, Gabriel directly supervised this new area of investigation. Utilizing improving analytic resources and techniques, he endeavored to sort through the multiple layers of thought patterns he had discovered to exist in every subject. His problem, he quickly realized, lay in the overwhelming complexity of the patterns and data he was gathering. Despite several weeks employing various techniques of displaying and filtering the patterns, Gabriel was often lost due to his inability to maintain visualization of the layer of thought he wished to analyze.

Gabriel was becoming frustrated with the problem. He returned home to meet Helena for dinner every evening, but lately had become an unentertaining dinner companion.

"So, how was your day?" Gabriel asked his wife.

"Definitely better than yours."

"What? Why do you say that?"

"Because I've had better dinner conversation in prison, Gabe."

"Really?" She nodded. "I told you what's going on in the lab, right?"

"Every night for the last week, yeah."

Gabriel sighed, put down his fork. "I hit a wall, I think. It's too much, too complicated. If I filter all the levels enough to make sense of what's what, I lose all the definition."

"The shitstorm problem again, sounds like." He nodded. "Use what we used last time. Brute force: Networked analysis of large data sets, like we did the first time, Gabe."

Gabriel shook his head. "Been trying that, but this is different. Way too complex. I'm looking at longitudinal patterns, really complex thoughts with grammar and syntax, not just snapshots. It works on a single level, but gets overwhelming when I try on multiple levels. More subjects in the pool just goes to garbage in a couple of seconds." He pushed his food around on the plate.

"You know, I don't think I've seen you ride for a couple of months now."

He looked up. "What, the bike you mean? Yeah, it's probably been a couple of months. Too windy now."

"Never used to bother you. You're getting old, Gabe."

"Is that it? I don't think it's old age. Just work."

"Fine, quit for a while. Been working for me, I can tell you."

"Yeah, well. We can't both be on indefinite vacation, you know."

"Yeah? Why not?"

Gabriel shook his head. "You'd kill me, for one thing."

Helena chuckled, a sound that always made Gabriel think of wind chimes. "You're right. But come out with me tomorrow, we'll have fun. Maybe it'll help you see things better."

"What do you have planned?"

"Bouldering with a couple of the guys. From the lab. But if you're coming, I've got a better place. We could go up to Arcata, great bouldering right on the beach. Best in the state, I hear."

"How far?"

"Take five or six hours to drive there. We could borrow one of Arthur's cars. He can't drive them all every day. We can stay a couple of days, it'd be fun."

"Bouldering, huh? Is that like the Gunks thing?"

Helena shook her head. "No, this is different. No ropes or anything, Gabe. You're only a couple feet off the ground. No sweat, you'd like it."

"You think?" She nodded, seeing he was warming to the idea. "Okay, what the hell. I'll call Arthur and get us a ride. You pack."

"I always pack. Borrow the Porsche, the convertible one."

"I'm driving, Leena."

"We'll see. Maybe we could bring the guys along."

"The Abercrombie PhD's? Forget it. You can drive."

She smiled at her husband.

They left before sunrise the next day with Arthur's black 911 Cabriolet Turbo packed full, which basically meant one duffle of climbing stuff and one duffle for clothes and toiletries. Helena had to leave the crash pad behind, there was no room.

"No problem, Gabe. We can rent one once we're there. Probably should've borrowed a bigger car, but that wouldn't be fun. Could've fit the guys in, though."

"Enough with the guys, wiseass. You just wanted to drive." She smiled wickedly. "I thought you said this was going to be fun. Somehow 'crash pad' doesn't imply fun to me."

"Crashing's the fun part. You are going to have a great time."

It was cold, but Helena insisted on having the top down as they crossed over the Golden Gate Bridge, the sun just rising. She immediately decided against the more direct route, cutting west to catch Shoreline Highway. It was early, with almost no traffic. Helena's hair was a curly red cloud trailing behind her as she took the swooping cliff-side curves, never dropping below ninety miles per hour. Gabriel was just thankful that they were on the inside lane, going North.

"I am definitely driving home," he yelled over the wind noise. "Holy shit, Helena—," he screamed in cracking falsetto as they rounded a curve and suddenly closed on a slow moving stake truck on the two lane highway.

"You are such an old woman," she said, turning to look momentarily at his horrified expression just before double clutching, dropping into third gear and snapping into the left lane. Gabriel's pathetic scream was drowned out by the sound of the engine redlining. Helena whooped, pleasantly surprised to find no oncoming traffic in her new lane. She was by the truck and swerved back to the right in a split second, upshifting again smoothly. "You better not throw up in Arthur's car, Gabe."

Gabriel stopped clutching the dash in front of him, leaning back. "Yeah, like they'll ever notice vomit in the middle of all the gore and broken bones when we're at the bottom of this cliff. I am so driving home, Helena."

"We'll see. Did I tell you we might be meeting some of the guys in Arcata?" She gave him a sideways smile, hair streaming across her face. "Uh, oh. Can't see!"

Their scenic route should have taken over seven hours. Somehow, they arrived at the bed and breakfast in under six. They found an outdoor sports shop and rented their crash pad. Helena joshed with the storeowner for a bit, got directions to the boulders. They grabbed burgers in town and settled back in their room at the B and B.

The next morning, Helena and Gabriel grabbed an early breakfast in the dining room and headed out with their crash pad stuffed behind the seats. It was a short drive to Moonstone Beach, where they parked and carried the pad over to a series of boulders.

"This doesn't look so tough," Gabriel said, as Helena threw the pad onto the sand beneath the rock face.

"It isn't," she said. "Thought I'd let you get the hang of it first."

"Any pointers for the beginner?"

"Yeah, land on the pad."

"That should be the easiest part." Gabriel chalked his fingers from the bag on his belt, stood looking up at the rock face of a twenty-foot boulder. Seizing a handhold, he began to climb. Hand, hand, foot, foot, up, repeat. He occasionally paused to find the best route, then climbed again. In fifteen minutes, he was sitting on top of the boulder, winded.

"Very nice, Gabe. Was that fun?"

"Yeah," he said between pants. "Great. How do I get down?"

"Any way you can."

Gabriel walked around the top of the boulder until he saw a point he could half crawl, half climb down until he could safely drop to the sand.

"So that's bouldering, huh?"

"Pretty much, yeah." They sat together on the empty beach. "Ready for something a little more challenging?"

"Sure."

They walked down the beach to another, larger boulder. This one had a face jutting outwards about two thirds of the way to the top. Helena plopped the pad down beneath it.

Gabriel shook his head. "Your turn, beautiful. Show me how it's done."

Helena rubbed chalk over her hands, studying the rock. "You got a second hand on that watch?"

"I'm an engineer, what do you think? It's a friggin' chronograph. Why?"

"Twenty bucks says I'm standing on top in under three minutes."

Gabriel looked up at the boulder, shaking his head. "No way, Leena."

"Forty bucks."

"You're on."

"Start when I touch the rock. Ready?" He nodded, watch in hand. Helena stood for another minute, studying the rock. She took a half step back, then sprung onto the boulder, catching a double handhold almost ten feet off the ground. She scrambled up the sheer face like a crazed spider, in constant motion until she reached the outcropping. Here she paused momentarily, then reached far out on the overhang. Helena let free with all but one hand, swinging out over Gabriel.

He jumped back, certain she was about to fall on him. "Holy shit, Lena!" But before he had finished his sentence she had completed her pendulum swing to a small ledge on the other side of the outcropping. She grabbed with her free hand and heaved up over the ledge, flopping onto her back at the top and screaming "Time!". Gabriel looked at his watch again. Two minutes, two seconds.

"Aw, sorry, hon. Forgot to hit the little button thing."

"Bullshit! You owe me forty bucks!"

"I think it was, like three and a half minutes, Leena."

"Bullshit. Pull the pad out a ways from the rock, Gabe. There, good." Helena climbed out onto the outcropping, hanging from straight arms. She swung front, back, front, back, and then, with a yell, fell with a lazy backflip, landing with a huge whump onto her back in the center of the pad.

"Didn't quite stick the landing, huh?" Gabe commented, helping her up.

"Always land on the pad. That's the secret. Your turn, Gabe." She pushed the pad back to the rock and sat in the sand a ways back.

"Here, time me. Double or nothing."

"Take your time, Gabe. Figure out how you're going to get over that outcropping before you leave the ground."

"I was just going to do what you did."

"I don't suggest it, but go for it, big guy. That's what health insurance is for."

Gabriel stood for a few seconds, then started to climb, deliberately. He got to the outcropping and paused, considering. As he reached out for his handhold, his cellphone in the pocket of his cargo shorts started to ring.

"You brought your phone?" Helena asked in disbelief. Gabriel was in no position to answer at this point, hanging from both hands spread too wide for comfort and reaching with his left foot for a toehold. "Who brings their phone climbing?" She began throwing pebbles at him. "Who the hell brings a phone climbing? Aren't you going to answer that, hon?" She threw another stone, catching Gabriel between the shoulder blades.

"Hey!" he just got out as his left hand slid from its handhold. He managed a short scream as he fell almost twenty feet, landing with a thud onto the pad. It knocked the wind from him. As he lay on his back, the phone kept ringing. Helena walked over and stood over him.

"You gonna answer that, Gabe?"

Gabriel struggled to get his wind back, couldn't. Finally, he managed a deep, rattling breath. "You," he gasped, "threw a rock at me!"

"Expecting an important call?"

Gabriel looked at his phone, which at this point had become silent. "It was Arthur." He sat up on the pad with a wince. Helena sat in the sand beside him, cross-legged. She threw pebbles at him.

"Did you tell him we were going away?" she asked.

"Yeah. It might be important. I'm going to call him back. Later. Like when I stop peeing blood."

"You don't want to try again?"

He looked at her. She threw another pebble at him. It bounced off his forehead. "No."

"Loser."

They drove back to the inn and showered. Gabriel was already bruised along his entire left flank. Dressed again, they headed back to town.

"Let's find someplace where my dinner will be at least forty bucks."

They ended up at a restaurant with a French sounding name, specializing in local produce. Helena easily exceeded her goal before dessert.

"Call Arthur," she said between mouthfuls of white chocolate crème Brule.

Gabriel dialed. "Hey. You called." Pause. "Yeah, I was busy. Fracturing my kidney, that's what. What's up?" He listened for a couple of minutes. "Okay, I'll tell her. I don't know. I'll let you know. Bye." He replaced the phone in his pocket and took up his fork.

"So what was so important that he had to knock you off the rock."

"You knocked me off the rock."

"Yeah, right. But it was his fault, for calling. What did he say?"

"He said he was by the lab today. He talked to Faith."

"Receptionist Faith or Faith the tech?"

"He didn't say. We have a tech named Faith?"

"It's California, Gabe. What did Faith say?"

"Must've been receptionist Faith, because she said a guy stopped by the lab earlier today and she thought it was funny."

"He was dressed as a clown, funny?"

"No, she thought it was funny because he asked for you, not me."

It was Helena's turn to put down her spoon. "Who was it?"

"She didn't know. He didn't leave a card. Said he'd check back."

"Give me your phone, ok?"

"Why?"

"Because I want to talk to Arthur."

"Why? Who was it, Leena?"

"I don't know, Gabe."

"You're lying."

"I'm not lying."

"Yeah, you're not lying because you're not saying anything. But you're thinking something that you're not saying and that's kinda like lying."

"No, I don't think that's like lying at all. Could I borrow your phone, Gabe?" He handed her the phone, watching her. Her body English had completely changed, her jaw clenched. "Arthur? Leena. What else did Faith tell you? Just one guy? Suit or jeans? Ponytail, really? Just the one time? Okay, listen. How much do you like the

Porsche? That much, huh? No, forget it then. Plan B. You still have the Netjets account? Good. There's a little business airport here in Arcata. Book a flight. For the morning, as early as you can, okay? Tell them you're picking up Gabe to fly him home. No, just Gabe for now. Okay, Arthur? Thanks a lot, love. Bye." She handed the phone back to Gabriel. He took it, waited.

"Waiting," he said.

Helena returned to her dessert. "Shouldn't have brought the phone, Gabe."

"I could go toss it in the ocean, if you think that's important."

Helena considered, finishing her dessert. She pushed the plate away. "No, I think it's a little late for that."

"Actually, I was just kidding."

"Just as well, then."

"You going to tell me what's going on?"

"I told you, I don't know. Probably nothing."

"Just because you're paranoid, doesn't mean—"

"Don't call me that, Gabriel."

He sighed. "So if I'm flying back, where are you off to?"

"Actually, you're driving back in the Porsche. I'm taking the plane."

"Why? Why don't we just drive back?"

"I'm not going back right now. And Arthur won't let me take his precious Porsche. You get to drive after all, hon."

"Where are you going?"

"I think I'll visit your folks for a while, Gabe. We haven't seen them for a while."

Gabriel considered this. "Not since they visited last year. They'd like that, I'm sure. You don't think I should go along?"

Helena shook her head. "No, Gabe. I wish you could. I'll miss you terribly, you know."

"How long?"

"Just until you figure out who the guy with the ponytail is. And Gabe, hon? Don't tell your folks I'm coming. Let it be a surprise, okay?"

"But they could pick you up at the airport."

"Don't tell them. Please."

"You're not really going to see them, are you, Leena?"

"Yes, Gabe, yes I am. I'd never lie to you, Gabe. Okay, we both know I lie a little, sometimes. But this isn't, I'm going to see your folks. Just, please, don't tell anyone where I'm going. Not on the phone, at least."

"I can tell Arthur, when I see him?"

"Sure. Just tell him when you see him, not on the phone, okay?" Gabriel nodded.

"I don't like us being apart, Leena."

"No, Gabe, either do I. I'm not sure if I'm even any good at it. Believe me, if there was any choice..." She shook her head. "It'll be good to see your folks again."

Gabriel and Helena waited the next morning on the tarmac of the little airport as the Gulfstream business jet taxied over to where they stood. The engines spooled down with a whining decrescendo, the door opened. Arthur waved as he descended the air stair.

"Hey, guys," he said. He gave Helena a kiss on the cheek, Gabriel a brief hug. "Nice day for flying."

"Didn't know you were coming up, Arthur," Gabriel said.

"Seemed a waste, flying an empty plane to get you. Didn't seem right."

Helena was smiling at him. "I like your thinking, Arthur. Have you eaten?" Arthur shook his head. "We should get you something to eat. Before we go, do me a favor? Tell your pilot there's a change in plans. We'll be leaving in two hours for Ann Arbor airport. Make sure he knows it's the little business airport in Ann Arbor, not Metro, okay?"

Arthur shrugged. "Sure, Leena. Why are we going to Michigan?"

"Not you, Arthur. Just me. You and Gabe get to drive home in your car."

"Sounds fun. I'm driving, Gabe."

"Why don't I ever get to drive?"

"Because you drive like an old woman," both Helena and Arthur said, almost in unison.

"Listen, Arthur," Helena continued. "Don't change the passenger manifest, though. Let the pilot file the new flight plan with Gabe still listed as the passenger. And ask him to file just before wheels up, okay?"

"Is that how I should say it, 'wheels up'? Like real pilot talk? Sure, Leena. For you. Though it sounds like it might've been a better idea to just let you steal my Porsche."

"You could've gotten a new one with the insurance, too."

"Now you tell me. Older one's best, though."

Helena smiled at Arthur and said, "Isn't that the truth?"

The three of them had lunch at the small diner in the airport. While Arthur paid the bill, Helena stopped at the sundries shop and came back wearing a hooded sweatshirt.

"You cold?" Gabriel asked.

Helena just smiled at him. "Listen, Arthur, how much cash do you have on you?"

"What?" Gabriel asked. "We have money. We don't need—"

"Quiet, Gabe," Helena said, and gave him another smile.

"It's not a problem, Gabe," Arthur said. "I've got about two, three hundred. Why, you need some, Leena?"

She nodded. "Where did you get it?"

"I didn't steal it, if that's what you mean."

"No, I mean, did you get it from an ATM or the bank's teller? Did you cash a check for it?"

"No, I got some of it from the ATM at the airport. Most of it, I don't really know—bank, probably, but I don't think I've cashed a check in the past decade."

"Can I see it?" she asked.

Arthur produced his clip of money, handing it over to Helena. Helena went through the pile, separating out the twenties. She counted what remained. "Gabe," she said, "we owe Arthur two hundred thirty-seven bucks. Thanks, Arthur."

Gabriel looked mildly hurt. "I could've given you some money, you know. I've got like twelve bucks."

"I know, dear," she said, giving him a kiss. "Listen, guys. I'm going to go soon. Gabriel, in a few minutes I want you to go to the plane and tell them you're ready to go. Tell them you want to sleep the whole flight, don't want to be disturbed. Then come out and walk straight to the car, ok?" Gabriel nodded, starting to feel a little sick. He felt like he was losing his wife. "Arthur, thanks for coming. You wait in the car. Put the top up, ok?" Arthur nodded.

"Just till we get on the highway, right? Gotta have the top down the rest of the way, Leena."

"That's fine, Arthur. Only do me another favor, and put it back up before you hit the bridge, okay?" Arthur nodded, now also somber. Helena turned to her husband. "I know, Gabe. It looks weird. Geez, you look like a Basset hound." She gave him a vicious hug. "I love you. It's probably nothing, but let's not take chances, okay?" She looked up into his eyes. Gabriel thought she might be a little teary eyed, then thought it was probably just him projecting. "I'm going to see your folks, really. I'll call you every day."

"Promise?" Gabriel asked. Helena nodded. "How long will you be gone?"

"Not long, I don't think. Just until you find out what's going on."

"What if I can't? What if this guy doesn't show up again?"

"I'm not that lucky, Gabe. You'll figure it out, I know you." She kissed him and hugged him again, this time more emphatically. "Here, put this on, okay?" She gave him another hooded sweatshirt, the same color she was wearing.

"Cute, matching sweatshirts. Do I have to put the hood up?"

"Your call, hon. I love you. I'll miss you. Now, go."

Gabriel put on the sweatshirt, left the hood down. He walked out to the tarmac and disappeared into the plane's cabin. Helena turned to Arthur. "Take care of my husband, Arthur." Arthur nodded. "Thanks for your help. You're a good friend, Arthur." Arthur shrugged, gave Helena a kiss on the cheek and hugged her.

"I'll see you, Leena." He left to start the car. Helena waited until she saw the pilot disappear into the cabin. Once Gabriel stepped off the plane, she pulled up her hood. She waited another couple of minutes, then walked to the back of the small jet and curled up in a backward facing seat. She went to sleep.

Gabriel and Arthur watched from the car as the small jet took off. Arthur put the car in gear and headed for the highway. They were silent for a while, each with their thoughts.

"You have a nice vacation, Gabe?"

"While it lasted."

"You have any idea what's going on?"

"Not a fucking clue, Arthur." They were silent again.

Arthur looked over at Gabriel, who had the expression of one who had been recently kicked in the stomach.

"You know I love your wife, Gabe—"

"But you think she's fucking crazy. Yeah, I know, Arthur. Sometimes, I think the same thing."

"Is she?"

"To be honest, Arthur? I'm not always sure."

"You've been with her every day for over three years and you're not sure?"

"Yeah. Crazy, huh?"

They got in late. Gabriel dropped off Arthur at his house, asking if he could borrow the car for a few days.

"We're not riding in together in the morning, Gabe?"

Gabriel shook his head. "No, Arthur. I'm going to get in early. I need to check some things. I'll call you tomorrow, though."

"Night, Gabe."

CHAPTER 13

Gabriel drove in to work early, arriving at the lab just after seven. He was thinking he'd go through the receptionist's records before she came in, try to get a lead on Mr. Ponytail. He stood at the door with his key in his hand. All the lights were already on. He pushed on the door. It was unlocked, and he walked in.

"Hello?" he called. No answer, but Gabriel could hear music. Loud music, coming from down the hall from where the labs and his office were. All the lights in the place were on. He walked down the hall, towards his office and the source of the sound. Opera, Gabriel thought. Sounded German.

The door to his office was open, the light on. The music was very, very loud. He stepped into his office to find a young man seated in his chair, sandaled feet on his desk. The man looked up at Gabriel and smiled. His dark hair was pulled back in a ponytail. The man reached back to the stereo system Gabriel had never touched and the music stopped, leaving an echoing silence.

"Wagner," the man said. "You have got a fantastic sound system, Dr. Sheehan."

"Yeah, and I love the smell of napalm in the morning. Who the hell are you?"

The man, dressed in tee shirt and board shorts, rose from the chair. Gabriel read the shirt: World Inferno Friendship Society. It had a picture of a burning police car. "Sorry, I hope you don't mind me sitting at your desk." He offered his hand to shake. "Chuck Parnell, Dr. Sheehan." Gabriel didn't shake his hand, but tossed his messenger bag onto the desk. Gabriel came around the desk and sat down. Parnell sat in one of the chairs in front of the desk. They looked at each other.

"What do you want with me and my wife, Mr. Parnell?"

"Please, call me Chuck." He smiled, a grin of orthodontic perfection. "I'm from the government and I'm here to help."

Gabriel snorted. "How'd you get in here?"

"Same way you did."

"It was locked up."

"I used a key."

"The alarm?"

"I turned it off."

"What are you, some kind of CIA spook?"

"No, I said I used a key. If I was CIA, I would've broken a window, set off the alarms, then realized I was in the wrong building." He smiled again.

"You're really with the government?" Parnell nodded. "Which one?"

"Ours."

"Huh. You talk like my wife. Which is your government?"

"Funny thing to say, that. The US government, Gabriel. May I call you Gabriel?"

Gabriel shrugged. "You don't much look like a civil servant."

"No, I don't. I must admit, I kind of cultivate the antiestablishment thing. If I were wearing a dark suit and sunglasses, you probably would've hit me over the head with your bag and thrown me out already. I'm disarming you with my charm, aren't I?"

"The pony tail?"

"You're embarrassing me. But since it was rude of me to show up like this, well, whatever. An affectation, I admit. I keep imagining this scene in the Oval Office where there's been a crisis, an attack or something, and the President turns to the Security Director and says, 'Dammit, man, this is a crisis—get me that guy with the ponytail to save our ass!'" He smiled again. "Just my little trademark."

"Could've worn a bowtie. Less time in the morning, same effect."

"Don't get me started on bowties, Gabriel."

Gabriel stared at the man. "Why did you come here asking about my wife?"

"Pleasantries over, then? I had to get you apart, Gabriel. You guys are like, inseparable."

"Why?"

"I don't know. Personally, I think it's creepy. But that's just me."

"Why did you want to get us apart?"

"Oh. So we could have this little talk."

"Could've made an appointment with my secretary." Parnell shook his head. "How did you know where we were?"

"I didn't. That's the problem. Your wife," he said, wagging a forefinger at Gabriel, "is very good, very consistently good. You have no idea how hard it is to be that good. I couldn't do it, I tell you."

"Good at what?"

"Oh, you know. Staying off the grid, off the radar. Low profile. No profile, really. That's why I had to do it this way. Her one weakness, I think, her one predictability. Predictabilities are weaknesses, you know. She knows that."

"You're losing me, Chuck."

"Am I? I doubt it."

"So you didn't know where we were, but you knew if you came here asking for her, she'd run?" Parnell nodded.

"Exactly. It was my only play. I'm sorry."

"You don't actually seem very sorry."

"I thought it was important that we talk. Matter of life or death, Gabriel."

"Without my wife around." Parnell nodded again. "What is it you want to talk about?"

"Your work, Gabriel."

"We could talk about my work anytime, with or without my wife."

Parnell shook his head. "I think you'll see why I did it this way."

Gabriel sighed, put his feet up on the desk. "Talk."
"Can we have coffee? Breakfast? A doughnut?"
"Maybe later. If I haven't thrown you out on your ass."
"Oh, you won't want to do that, Gabriel."

Helena stayed in her seat until the pilot opened the door and dropped the stair. Then she walked, hooded and hunched over, brushing past the smiling pilot and went straight out the door, not pausing. She heard the pilot mutter something about 'rich assholes' as she descended the stair. Helena grabbed a taxi at the front of the small airport and had it drop her on a corner of Washtenaw Avenue in Ypsilanti. She hitchhiked most of the way to her storage unit, walked the rest.

Helena stood behind a tree overlooking the storage unit, watching for five minutes. Seeing nobody, she circled the building, finally arriving at the entrance. She checked that the scratch on the jamb exactly lined up with the one on the door, meaning the door was as she had left it over a year ago, half an inch up from full down. She opened it with its usual squeal and stepped inside.

She looked around, satisfied that all was undisturbed. She walked over to the motorcycle, pulling off its covering tarp. Helena reached up under the rear fender and pulled off the package she had taped there. She tore off its waterproof wrapping, counted the neat stacks of cash. She pocketed the passport and driver's license, checking first that both hadn't yet expired. Getting close, though. She unwrapped the oilcloth from the small pistol, a Beretta. She tore it down quickly and checked for rust. Oiled and reassembled, she worked the action. It felt smooth to her. Satisfied, she reset the safety and loaded it with the ammo from the package. She carefully wiped the gun down and, using a roll of duct tape from the storage unit, taped the gun to the inside of the entry door. Then she returned to the motorcycle. She sat down, cross-legged, beside the machine and began the task of draining the storage fluids and making it rideable.

"It was really luck that I came across your work at all," Parnell said. "All those different companies, the marketing crap. Never really crossed my radar, not my interest."

"What is your interest, Chuck?" Gabriel asked the man.

"Signals. I do signals intelligence. For the National Security Agency."

"Oh, here we go."

"What? It's a job. Please don't tell me you're thinking black helicopters and shit. Because that's bullshit, you know." Gabriel just raised his eyebrows. "Oh, give me a break, Gabriel. Check our website. 'The NSA/CSS mission is to protect national security systems and to produce foreign signals intelligence information'. We don't have a budget to get me a decent laptop, let alone buy a helicopter. No helicopters, no black Suburbans. Just little old me and a bunch of other geeks scanning a lot of electronic chatter."

"So, what's this about, then? Helena and I aren't a threat to national security and we haven't produced any foreign signals, either. Why are you fucking with us?"

"You are so defensive, just because I'm from NSA."

"And you broke into my office."

"I did not break in."

"You stole a key."

"I did not steal a key." Gabriel stared. "I had one made. At the hardware store. It's legal, you know."

"You must have stolen a key to make a copy, Chuck."

"We're really getting bogged down in details, here, Gabriel. But if you have to know, I didn't steal a key. I just looked up the lock codes from the office construction detail sheet. It's in the public domain. Kind of. If you know where to look."

"And the alarm code? I set that code myself. Public domain?"

Parnell shrugged. "I like to think that if it's on the web, well, that's my personal definition of public." He held up his hands. "I admit, it's a stretch."

"My alarm shutoff code, which I personally set, is on the web?"

"Of course it is, Gabriel. What, you think people write this stuff down nowadays? Nothing gets written down. Everything on the computer, you know."

"And you can access my alarm company's secure files?"

"Secure files? What, are you joking? I mean, yeah, that is my job, to access files and shit, but this stuff we're talking about? There's nothing secure about it. Every police precinct and fire department in this county has access to your personal alarm code. How do you think they get in? Not to mention the maintenance service, now there's a high security outfit—every one of their employees is probably an illegal. Hell, the company's probably got two or three ex-cons on work parole programs. The alarm company's own maintenance contractor, their software service vendor—am I boring you, yet? Probably two hundred people can walk in here and turn off your alarm. Not counting the smart people like me. That's a huge number. But none of them give a shit about your alarm code."

Gabriel thought about this, thought about the information they had worked so hard to produce. He thought about how Helena had made such a point about how they had to maintain control. He scowled at his visitor.

"Hey, don't look at me like that. It's just the world we live in, brother."

"Okay, so why bother? Why come pay me a visit?"

"Well, like I was saying before the tangent we took, eventually I came to understand what Thought Technologies, LLC was really about. All that smartphone crap, that marketing stuff, was a front, a means to an end. Don't shake your head, Gabriel, I'm up to speed now. I've done my homework. I even watched a recording of that entire tedious speech you gave at the Moscone Center."

Gabriel flushed, remembering the day he had met Arthur Schlessel.

"So why should my work interest the government?"

"I'm not sure it does. Not yet. It interests me, though. And if you're going where I think you're going with this shit, yeah, the government is going to be interested. Count on it."

"So you're not here as a representative of the government?"

"No, I don't think so. I mean, that's not even my job. I'm just interested, that's all. For now."

"What does that mean, 'for now'?"

"Well, we were kicking that around the office last week."

"At the NSA? In Washington?"

"Well, yeah, Gabriel. That is where I work."

"What, exactly, were you kicking around?"

"We were discussing whether what you're doing, or trying to do, comes under our mandate."

"How so?"

"Well, NSA exists because of Executive Order 12333, from 1981. We looked it up. Amazing, we had to look up why we go to work every day, huh? Anyway, we're charged to 'collect (including through clandestine means), process, analyze, produce, and disseminate signals intelligence information and data'. It's on our website." Gabriel looked unmoved. "So I was arguing that what you're doing, the mind reading stuff, is a type of signals intelligence, you know?" Parnell smiled at him.

"You're shitting me."

"No, I think it might be. I gotta admit, the other guys thought I was nuts."

"Good."

"They're idiots. They think you're nuts, too. They don't think you can really do it. But I do. I think you can, Gabriel."

"Can what, Chuck?"

"Read minds."

"Not quite yet, Chuck. Not quite yet."

Helena finished prepping the Ducati in a little over two hours. It was starting to get dark. Any longer and she'd have a hard time bumming a ride into Ann Arbor. She made it back to their old condo just after dark. Despite living full time in San Francisco, they still hadn't gotten around to trying to sell the place. Gabriel felt that they could use it to visit his parents, but with Helena's aversion to public air travel, his parents had made all the visits. Unfortunately, circumstances had prevented her from bringing a key to the place; that was back in their home in Half Moon Bay. And they had never given Gabe's parents their key back.

Helena walked around to the back of the condo, now dark. She had brought a screwdriver with her from the storage unit. She used this to jimmy the aluminum window frame and popped the lock, sliding the window open enough to crawl through. Helena closed the window behind her, waiting for her eyes to acclimate to the deeper darkness. She went to the kitchen, found the flashlight they kept in the drawer. Helena systematically went from room to room, pleased to note it was just as they had left it.

Helena went into Gabriel's study and examined his desktop computer. It seemed undisturbed. She sat on the floor next to the big computer and unscrewed the case. She removed the hard drive and carefully reclosed the case. She repeated this process with her computer in the bedroom. Helena then sat down at her beloved roll top desk. Holding the small flashlight in her teeth, she reached into the back of the second cubbyhole from the left and found the tiny, elegantly crafted switch. With a faint click, the hidden shelf softly dropped onto her lap. She removed the gun, this one already loaded. She checked it, then took out more neatly wrapped packets of money, two more passports, one expired. Helena put everything, including the hard drives, in a canvas tote she found in the kitchen.

She was tired. She was also dirty, greasy, and sweaty from her activities since landing. Shower first, then sleep, she decided. Though it disturbed her greatly, she showered in the dark, afraid that any light might be noticed by a neighbor. She slept alone in their old bed. It still smelled like her Gabe.

"You still haven't explained why you're screwing with my family. We could've had this conversation with my wife. Why did you have to scare her off?" Gabriel was losing patience with his intruder.

"You're kidding, right?" Gabriel just stared at him. "If you had walked in here with your wife, I'd probably be a corpse wrapped up in the area rug by now."

"Give me a break, Chuck. No offense, but let's not be melodramatic here."

"Hey, maybe I'm wrong. She's your wife. I've never met the gal."

"Yeah, so I'll ask you again, nicely. Why did you scare off Helena?"

Parnell shrugged. "Listen, Gabriel, I'm sorry to screw with you. But really, knowing what we do about your wife—"

"Knowing what, Parnell? I'm getting a little pissed off at all the innuendo shit you're spewing."

"You know what I'm talking about, Gabriel. I just know the file. You know from your Dad, from living with the chick—"

Gabriel pulled his feet off the desk and leaned forward. "What the fuck are you talking about? What file? What about my Dad?"

"Gabriel, I know what your Dad told you about your wife. I know he accessed her medical records, after you guys married, I think. He must have told you." Gabriel sat back. He remembered his father saying once he was going to talk to a friend of his, but he hadn't heard anything of it. Parnell was watching him closely. "Shit, Gabriel. I'm sorry. I just assumed your Dad told you what he found out, that's all."

"What did he find out, Chuck?"

Parnell looked nervous. He realized he had made a mistake with this approach. "Maybe you should talk to your Dad. I could come back."

"What does my Dad know about Helena, Chuck?"

Parnell swallowed hard, hunching in his chair. "Well, her name's not Helena, you know. For one thing. You know that much, right?" Gabriel just stared at the man. "Shit, Gabriel. He just got some of your wife's medical history, I think. I don't think he could've accessed the rest—or didn't even want to."

"Tell me."

"I don't know what to tell. I don't know how much to—"

"You came here, Parnell. I didn't invite you here. Tell me."

"Your Dad knows your wife's medical history. That she was raised an orphan in the Irish state system, with all that implies, if you know what I mean." He watched Gabriel's face. "You don't know what that means, do you?" Gabriel shook his head. "Well, I'll let you look it up, watch the documentaries if you want. It's not a popcorn on the couch with the missus thing, though." He swallowed hard, again. "We really need coffee, don't you think?"

"Later."

"Your wife was hospitalized during her teens, for treatment."

"Treatment for what?"

"She's a paranoid schizophrenic, Gabriel."

Daniel Sheehan heard the knocking on his front door. He pulled it open to see his daughter-in-law, as beautiful and radiant as the day she married his son, standing with her tote bag, smiling.

"Hey, Dad!" She dropped the tote, threw her arms around her father-in-law in embrace. Daniel hugged back in surprise and stepped back, smiling.

"Wow, surprise! Hey yourself, Leena. You look great. Come in, come on in." Helena picked up her tote bag from the porch and followed him into the house. "Mom's in the back, pulling weeds. You're lucky I heard you knock." He led her to the patio door. Helena left her bag in the kitchen. "Cheryl, look who's here, babe!"

Cheryl Sheehan looked up from her hands and knees in the garden and squealed. She came running to Helena, kissing her on the cheek. "I can't hug you, I'm covered in dirt. You look great. What a surprise!"

They sat outside around the patio table. Daniel was sent inside for lemonade. "You should've called, we could have picked you up from the airport," he said, returning with the pitcher and glasses of ice.

Helena poured for everyone. "It was kind of spur of the moment. Gabriel wanted to come too, sends his regrets. He's in the middle of something in the lab that's not going well, I think. He's been pretty grumpy about it."

"So what brings you? We have to go out for dinner," Cheryl said.

"I fly out tonight, but I can probably do an early dinner. We needed some stuff out of the condo, so I just dropped in to pick it up. It's not like I have a lot on my plate right now, you know."

"That's crazy, Helena," Daniel said, then blushed slightly. "We could've gone over and gotten the stuff for you, mailed it out to California."

"Gabriel was going to call you to ask you to do that, Dad. Then we realized that we never even left you guys a key to the place. Anyway, he needed the hard drive from his old computer," she gestured to the tote bag she had left in the kitchen. "He didn't want to ask you to tear down the computer to get at it, and it would've been a waste of money to mail out the whole machine. So I volunteered to get it. It was a good excuse." She polished off her glass of lemonade and poured herself another. "So what's up with you guys? You two look great."

They exchanged pleasantries, talked about how the summer was going. The phone rang. Daniel went inside to get it. "Hey guys," he called through the patio door, "It's Gabe."

"Don't use her name," Parnell stage whispered. "Say wife or spouse or something. The filters won't pick that up."

"Hey, Dad," Gabriel said into the phone.

"You will not believe who just walked in, Gabe!" his dad replied.

"I know, Dad. I know my wife is there, right?"

"Yeah, just now—"

"Listen, Dad. Listen for a second, okay?"

"Sure, Gabe," Daniel said, hearing the strain in his son's voice. "What's wrong?"

"Listen, Dad. Please don't say my wife's name on the phone, okay? Say wife or whatever, not her name."

"Okay, Gabe. What's going on?"

"It's okay, Dad. Probably nothing. Is my wife with you now, in the room I mean?"

"She's outside with your mom, why?"

"Is she okay?

"Yeah, Gabe. She looks great. What the hell is going on, son?"

"Dad, I found out this morning, just now. About my wife." There was silence on the phone. "You know what I'm talking about, right? You knew for a long time, right?"

Daniel walked deeper into the kitchen, stood by the tote bag. "This isn't the time to have this discussion, Gabe." Daniel pushed absently at the bag with his toe.

"Why didn't you say something?"

"This isn't the time, Gabe. I'll just say this for now—people have problems, doctors put a label on them. It's not always right. My friend in London said the records were very sketchy. And I made a promise to Hel—to your wife. That's all I'm going to say on the phone." He raised his voice, "Here, let me put her on the phone." He covered the mouthpiece. "Hey, Leena, it's Gabe. You want to talk to him?"

Helena called from the patio. "I just got off the phone with him this morning, Dad. Tell him I'll call him after we have dinner. I need to tell him when to pick me up from the airport."

"Did you hear that? Here, I'll let you talk to your mother." Daniel carried the phone out to the patio, let his wife talk for a minute.

"I gotta go, Gabe. I want to talk to Leena some more. Call me later, darling. Bye."

Gabriel hung up the phone, looked across his desk at Parnell. "She's there now."

"Yeah, I got that part. Is everything okay?"

Gabriel shrugged. "Seemed to be. He said he promised Helena something."

"That can't be good."

"You said there was a file."

Parnell pulled a tattered manila file from his backpack on the floor. He handed it over to Gabriel. It was stamped "Top Secret, burn date." Nothing was written in the blank. There was no name, just a long number along the filing window. Gabriel started to go through the pages carefully.

"Top Secret, huh? Pretty lame, Chuck."

"What do you mean? Everything is top secret, Gabriel. That's the lowest classification we have. Everything else goes out on the web or gets burned." He watched Gabriel leafing through the record. "I'm sorry I can't leave that with you, it's signed out in my name. It wasn't supposed to leave the building. You can make a copy if you want." Gabriel looked over the top of the file at Parnell, eyebrows questioning. "I mean it is against the law and all, but I don't give a shit."

"What am I looking at, Chuck?"

"Not much, like I said. Almost nothing from the last four or five years. Your wife has kept a very low profile, particularly the last five years."

"Tell me about before, then."

"It's thin, the whole thing is weird. Very nebulous, very few confirmed events. A lot of maybe's, speculative shit. I'm not even sure how old your wife is. She's either twenty-two or thirty-eight or something in between. And you can choose from about six or seven names. None of them Helena, by the way."

"You're kidding me. What about a birth certificate?"

"There isn't one. She was abandoned. Parent's names were unconfirmed, there's a couple of Irish names in there, but who knows. No known living relatives. Lot of orphanage bureaucratic bullshit, some of the hospital records we talked about, then—"

"What the hell is this?" Gabe asked, holding up a color photograph of a leather clad motorcyclist racing through a crowded turn, leaning to the point where the rider's knee was touching the track, sparks flying.

"Look at the hair."

"No shit, really?" Gabriel saw the curly red hair escaping from the back of the racing helmet.

"She raced MotoGP for Ducati, two years. European circuit."

"Was she any good?"

"Well, we know she wasn't killed, so I guess she was okay. I don't know anything about racing motorcycles, the things scare the crap out of me. There's another picture in there, though." Gabriel found it. It was a very young looking Helena, dressed in black racing leathers and getting sprayed with champagne. She looked like she was about sixteen, though she must have been older, Gabriel thought. Parnell said, "I think they only do that if you win or you're on fire."

"So the whole 'paranoid schizophrenic' thing is a load of crap," Gabriel said. Parnell shrugged. "You don't do all this if you're mentally ill, Chuck."

"I don't know, Gabriel. I won't pretend to know. I've gotta say, though, I don't think they treat a girl over forty times with electroshock just because she's refusing to change for gym class, you know?"

Cheryl convinced Helena to join her in driving to the nursery to pick up plants for the garden. Daniel declined to join them, saying he'd rather cut the lawn before it got too hot. Once the girls had left, Daniel called his son back.

"Gabe, it's Dad. What the hell is going on?"

"I don't know, Dad."

"How did you find out?"

"I'm sitting across from someone who knows things, knows that you found out things."

"Who the hell is he?" Daniel demanded.

Gabriel looked across the desk at Parnell. "My dad wants to know who the hell you are." Parnell shrugged again. "I haven't completely figured that out yet, Dad. Is my wife okay?"

Daniel sighed. "I guess that depends on what you mean by okay, son."

"Why, what's going on? You said you didn't believe that stuff about her."

"I didn't say that, son. That's why I don't want to get into this on the phone. I said my source felt there was room for doubt. I never pursued it. I didn't think it was my place."

"Could've told me, Dad."

Daniel sighed. "Not now, Gabe."

"So is she acting okay, or what?"

"She seems great."

"But?"

"But I'm looking in her tote bag, here. And I'm looking at a couple of hard drives, about fifty thousand dollars, and a loaded gun."

"Holy shit."

"Yeah, son. Holy shit."

"Put it back, Dad."

"Did that already, Gabe. Listen, I've got to cut the lawn now. I'll call you later, after dinner. We're taking your wife to dinner, you know. Hopefully, we won't fight over the check. Love you, bye."

Gabriel heaved another sigh, felt like he was sighing a lot this morning. They heard the staff coming into work. Gabriel's secretary poked her head in the door.

"Morning, boss."

"Morning, Faith."

"Can I get you two some coffee?"

"That'd be great—," Parnell began.

"No, thanks, Faith. Chuck here has to run and I have a lab full of subjects in a little while."

"I can't run with a cup of coffee in my hand?"

"How long are you in town?" Gabriel asked. Parnell shrugged. He did that a lot, Gabriel thought. "Come back here at five. We'll get dinner with my partner." Gabriel put the file in his desk drawer and locked it. "See you later, Chuck."

Helena spent a pleasant afternoon with her in-laws gardening and working outside. They all cleaned up and had an early dinner at an outdoor cafe on Catherine Street. Helena insisted on picking up the bill and was surprised that her father-in-law hardly protested at all. He did, however, insist upon dropping Helena at Metro airport for her flight home.

"No luggage, Leena?" Daniel asked as she prepared to walk into the terminal.

"Just this," Helena said, indicating the tote bag she carried. "Like I said, spur of the moment."

They gave hugs and kisses, waving as Helena went into the terminal. Daniel sat with his wife in the car.

"I think she's gone now, hon. We can go," Cheryl said to her husband.

"Huh? Yeah, just waiting."

"For what, Dan?"

For shouts and gunfire, Daniel thought to himself. "Nothing. Let's go home." He pulled away from the curb and headed back to Ann Arbor.

Helena watched them finally pull away, wondering at the delay. Then she hailed a cab and rode back to Ypsilanti. She had the cabbie wait while she ran into a downtown electronics store. She paid cash for ten prepaid cellphones, extra batteries, electrical tape. She gave the cabbie fifty dollars for waiting and had him drop her a mile away from her storage unit. This time she watched the door of the unit from a different vantage point than before, finally approaching with her bag of supplies from a different path. She quickly checked the tell, went in and closed the door.

Helena sat cross-legged on the floor as she worked on the phones. She found her soldering iron in the cluttered workbench and used it to rig extra batteries to four of the phones. She shorted the call answer buttons on each of them. She wrote all the phone numbers down on a small sheet of paper, which she folded and set aside. Helena then taped each of two pair of the extra-batteried phones face to face with black electrical tape. She wrapped each in the dirty rags from the Ducati and loaded up the bike with the phones and the contents of her tote bag.

She pawed through boxes in the storage unit until she found her old racing leathers. Shit, she thought, as she wriggled and struggled to squeeze into the skintight suit, this could be a problem. Must've shrunk. Five minutes of cursing like a longshoreman and she finally managed to get it zipped. She could barely get the little piece of paper into a pocket of the suit.

Helena rolled the bike out of the unit, closing it behind her. She stood for a bit, balancing the motorbike, considering what to do with the storage unit. There certainly were enough flammable materials inside to either burn it down or rig a trip to blow it if anyone were to try to get inside. After a bit, she couldn't think of anything inside that was worth the attention that would attract. She thought about taking the Beretta from the door. She already had a gun, she thought. One gun is self-defense, two is a crazy person. She decided to leave it where it was. She closed up the storage unit and rolled the heavy motorcycle to the street.

Helena mounted the bike and scraped spider webs from inside her old helmet. It smelled musty as she buckled it on. At least her head wasn't any bigger, she thought. Crunch time. This bike hadn't been started in years. Let's see how good a bike mechanic you still are, she thought, punching the starter. The engine spit, coughed, and roared with the deep-throated sound that always made her smile a little. She tore off down the street. It felt great to be riding again.

Helena had a couple of errands she needed to accomplish before hitting the road in earnest. For starters, she was riding a stolen motorcycle with expired plates. That was not a recipe for staying inconspicuous. She had a number of options, each with its own risk of complications. She needed someplace with parked motorcycles, preferably dark, definitely unattended. She figured it was about one in the morning by now. Helena sorted her options, turned towards St. Joseph hospital. The day had been nice and warm; she felt the odds were worth a shot. Once at the hospital, she cruised around until she found the doctor's parking lot. There were several motorcycles parked all over the hospital lots. This lot was the best, though, if one of the surgeons or anesthesiologists were on call, preferably two or more. She found the doctor's lot, not difficult what with the sign, the gate she had to skirt, and the number of overpriced sports cars. Lucky me, she thought. Tucked in the corner slot was a brand new looking Harley. Doctors are the best, she mused. They rode about twice a year, so their wives wouldn't scream about what a middle age crisis waste of money the thing had been. And when they did ride, they rode so slowly there was no chance that they'd be pulled over. Unlike about every other bike parked at this hospital, most of which were owned by twenty year old orderlies popping wheelies down Washtenaw on Saturday nights.

Helena killed her lights and parked beside the Harley. Two bikes for a double switch would have been best, but her luck wasn't that perfect. One would have to do, she thought. She fished a driver out of her bike and switched plates in less than two minutes. She was gone in three.

Helena pulled in at a truck stop on I-94 to fill up the tank. She spent some time chatting up the long haul truckers, not difficult when a gal is wearing a skintight leather racing suit. Eventually, she settled on two rigs headed in opposite directions, taping a phone pairing to the undercarriage of each. She bought a map, a small flashlight, and all the beef jerky she thought she could carry on the bike. After studying the map for a bit, she took off, heading off the expressway for Ellsworth Road, taking the backroads west past Jackson.

Gabriel sat with Arthur and Chuck Parnell, eating sushi at a restaurant in Pacifica. Parnell was describing every sushi restaurant he had ever eaten at in DC, a surprising number but unsurprisingly tedious. Arthur finally steered the conversation back to the pertinent. Gabriel had returned the file to Parnell earlier in the evening, having made two copies. Arthur was looking through his copy as they ate.

"Most of this stuff seems like speculation," Arthur said, wiping a drip of soy sauce from the page with his little finger. "And the rest I think they just made up."

Parnell agreed. "I told Gabriel this morning, there's not a lot you can be sure of."

"Like none of it," Gabriel said. The more times he went through the file, the angrier he had become. About the only parts he believed fully were the medical files, and those only convinced him that his wife had been the victim of many, many years of institutional abuse. He suspected that the reality was probably much worse than what was reflected in these sterile records.

"You can be sure of a few things, Gabriel. Your ring, for one thing," he said, gesturing to Gabriel's hand. "Can't help but notice. Gift from your wife?" Gabriel nodded, took a drink of his beer. "Nice. Just so you know, friend, be careful where you're seen wearing it."

Arthur looked up from the file. "Why? It's just a ring, I've seen dozens like it."

"You have, have you? Don't think so. Or, maybe like it, but like a zirc is to the Hope diamond, you know? Shit, the thing's as big as the Hope. I spotted that from across the room this morning, and I'm not even native Irish. You get off a plane in Dublin or Galway wearing that monstrosity, you'll make a lot of friends very quickly. Probably same thing would happen if you walked into one of a dozen bars in Boston, too. Might find your bloody carcass in the alley. Or get a lot of free beers, depending on the bar and the crowd that night."

"Why, what of it?" Gabriel said, fingering the heavy thing.

"Like I said, I'm no expert, Gabriel. Where did she say she got it?" Parnell asked.

Gabriel thought back, trying to remember their wedding night. "I didn't really catch it exactly. Said it had been in the family forever."

"Well, that's a lie, I'll tell you. Not unless—"

"No, I remember now. She said it was a gift from her dad."

"Your wife didn't have a dad, Gabriel. She was lying. I'll bet fifty bucks it's stolen." Parnell took a pull from his beer.

" 'From my Da', she said, 'a gift from the uncrowned king of Ire—'"

Parnell choked and spewed beer from both nostrils. He was beet red, coughing and laughing uncontrollably.

"Judas Priest, Chuck," said Arthur. "What the hell was that?" He and Gabriel were wiping spewed beer from their faces.

"Holy shit, Gabriel," Parnell finally said, gathering himself. "Your wife said that?" Gabriel nodded, looking at the man, then the ring. "Of course she did. You couldn't have made that shit up!"

"What do you mean?" Asked Arthur.

"Gawd, I love your wife, Gabriel. I have got to meet this woman! She's just as full of shit as I am."

"What do you mean, full of shit?"

Just then, Gabriel's cellphone rang. He pulled it from his pocket, looked at the screen. "Shit, it's her." Parnell pulled out his own cellphone, sent a text as Gabriel answered. "Hey, hon. Speak of the devil."

"Hey, love. Good to hear your voice. Miss you."

"Miss you, too. We were just talking about you."

"Really? Who's we, hon?"

"Well, I'm having dinner with Arthur and a guest." Gabriel and Arthur were watching Parnell texting like a madman, making no effort to conceal his activity.

"Is that right?" Helena said on the phone. "Give Arthur my love."

"She sends her love, Arthur."

"Hi, there, Leena. Shit, sorry, Gabe. Can I say that?" Arthur blushed.

"Arthur says hello back, hon. How are you?"

"I'm great. I had a nice visit with your parents, we gardened all day and had dinner just before I had to go."

"Sounds nice, hon. Are you coming home? I miss you."

"Miss you too, hon. Depends, though. Does your guest there have a ponytail?"

"Yes, he does. A very striking hairstyle." Parnell looked up from his phone, gave Gabriel a smile.

"Who is he, Gabriel?"

Gabriel looked at Parnell, who was chuckling as he continued to exchange text messages with someone. "She wants to know who you are."

"Tell her I'm a new friend, Gabriel."

Helena snorted softly. "I heard. Ask him his name. I want the name of our new friend, Gabe."

Gabriel looked again at Parnell, who shrugged. "He said his name is Chuck Parnell, hon."

There was silence for a moment, and then Helena asked lightheartedly, "Ask him if he's expecting Winston Churchill to join you guys later for cigars and brandy."

Parnell was still smiling, shaking his head slightly. "Tell your wife," Parnell said loudly enough for Helena to hear, "that I was just admiring your wedding ring, but I don't remember giving it to her dad."

"Did you—"

"I heard, hon. Listen, I gotta go, but I'll call you again tomorrow. Enjoy the rest of your dinner, boys. Love you, Gabe. Miss you."

"Love you, too, hon. Talk to you tomorrow. Bye." He looked up from the phone, watched Parnell chuckle at his text message again. They both put away their phones and took a drink.

"Well, like I was saying," Parnell said, "I am so looking forward to meeting your wife, Gabriel."

Arthur looked angry, staring at the man. "Doesn't sound like Leena is going to want to meet you, Chuck."

Parnell looked offended. "Why do you say that, Arthur? She didn't say that, did she, Gabriel?"

"Not in so many words," Arthur continued, "but I'm not stupid."

"No, you're not stupid, Arthur," Parnell said to him. "Just uneducated. And in way over your head."

"What the hell are you talking about, Parnell?" Arthur said, turning even redder.

Gabriel laid a hand on Arthur's arm. "I didn't get much of that, but I got enough to know your name's probably not Parnell." Chuck smiled at them, nodded.

"I was about to address that concern when your wife called."

"Maybe. I assume your furious texting there was an effort to trace my wife's call?"

Chuck nodded again. "Yeah, I texted the shift chief back at NSA." He chuckled again, drinking.

"Did you find her?" Gabriel asked. Parnell shook his head as he set down his glass. "What, she wasn't on long enough to trace? Good for her." He took a deep gulp of his beer, finishing it.

"No, that's a crock," Parnell replied. "That, 'oh, keep 'em on the phone for ninety seconds so we can make a trace'. Yeah, back in 1972, maybe. Now, we can trace instantaneously." He snapped his fingers. "Actually, you don't even have to be on your phone, once we know which phone you're carrying."

"Yeah, okay then, sport," Arthur said. "Where is she?"

"My chief says your wife is heading south out of Toledo at sixty miles an hour." He finished off his beer and smacked the glass onto the table. "And, simultaneously mind you, she's heading west from Chicago at almost seventy. I said it this morning, Gabriel, and I'll say it again—your wife? She is very, very good."

Helena tore the SIM card out of the phone. She wiped down the cell-phone and tossed it into the dumpster. The card she crushed with her boot. She had stopped at a convenience store in Jackson. Helena blended well with those loitering in the parking lot here. She declined the friendly offers to ride with a gang of bikers heading to Chicago. They were obviously disappointed. She started her bike and headed back the way she had come, now heading east. Her original plan, a nice cross country back roads run back to San Francisco, looked less appealing after her conversation with Gabriel. Now, going to ground and reestablishing contacts in Boston looked like a safer path. She thought she could make Pennsylvania before stopping for the night. "Chuck Parnell, my royal ass," she said aloud. She hadn't any idea of this man's angle and that disturbed her. Until she figured it out, though, she had no intention of sticking her head up anywhere it could be seen.

Arthur and Gabriel suggested Parnell grab a cab back to his hotel, or wherever he was staying. Before dinner, Gabriel had half suggested the man could stay at his place. He thought better of that idea now. Gabriel followed Arthur back to his house. They sat on the deck and reviewed the events of the day.

"What now, Gabe?" Arthur asked.

"Back to work, Arthur. I can't figure out this whole business with Parnell or whoever he is. I can't talk to Helena; I have no idea where she is. So, I might as well do what I can, back at the lab."

"Do you think he's a threat to Helena in any way? I can't figure him, and I make my living figuring people out."

"I don't think he can hurt Leena, or us. I don't think he wants to. What bothers me, is that I don't know what he wants."

"He went to a lot of trouble to pull our strings. He has to want something, Gabe."

"I'm sure he'll tell us eventually, Arthur."

The next day, Gabriel again arrived early at the lab. Once again, all the lights were on, music blaring. Verdi, this morning. He walked back to his office to find Parnell at his desk, again. This time, though, he was using Gabriel's computer.

"What is this, 'Groundhog Day'?" Gabriel shouted to him over the music.

Parnell turned off the music. "Different aria. Verdi."

"Heard of him. Listen, do I have to change the locks, or what?"

"What good would that do?"

Gabriel threw his messenger bag on the desk. "You mind? Can we pretend it's my office?"

"Sorry, sure. I'll get out of your way. Listen, do you have maid service back there or should I pretend to straighten up?" He gestured to the small apartment Gabriel kept behind his office. Gabriel had never used it.

"You slept here last night?"

"You said I could. Last night, before dinner," Parnell said. Gabriel dropped into his chair, rolling his eyes. "You said."

"What are you, seven? Listen, Chuck. I don't think we ended on very good terms last evening. Arthur and I were hoping that maybe you headed back home. Which would've been fine, if I'm not being clear."

"We still need to talk, Gabriel."

"I don't think so, Chuck. About halfway through dinner, I lost interest in any more conversations. See you. And why are you on my computer, anyway?"

"Just work stuff, don't worry. I didn't screw up anything or look at any porn sites or anything."

"I should hope not. Bye, Chuck. Don't let the door, etcetera, etcetera," Gabriel waved at him as he reset his computer, just in case.

"We could have Faith bring breakfast. That'd be nice."

"No, it wouldn't, Chuck. And that's not her job. She doesn't do breakfast."

"Really, she didn't mind, Gabriel. She bought for the whole lab."

"Hey, guys," Faith called as she came in. "Breakfast is up."

Gabriel dropped his head on the desk. "Let me guess—my credit card, right?"

"Hey," Parnell answered, "I'm just a civil servant, you know."

They ate breakfast with Faith and the techs in the lab. Somehow, everyone thought that this was going to be a standing practice from now on. They all thanked their boss profusely.

Gabriel again found Parnell seated across his desk.

"I didn't lie to you yesterday, Gabriel. It was all true."

"Except for your name, you mean."

"Well, yeah. That's complicated. Everything else, though."

"So why not tell me your real name, Chuck? Or whatever?"

"Is it important, really?"

"I think it's more of a trust thing, Chuck."

"I could tell you another name."

"Would it be your real name?" Chuck shook his head sheepishly. "Don't really see the point, then."

"I don't think it's a good idea to tell you my real name. Not right now, at least." He brightened. "Maybe in the future, though."

Gabriel was not heartened. "Why not, Chuck? Most of the people I know use their real names. All of them, I think."

"You'd be surprised, Gabriel. Listen, Gabe. To be honest, it's your wife. I wouldn't mind you knowing, or even Arthur knowing, my real name—but your wife, well, I have reservations. I'm probably being silly, I know."

"Maybe not. Maybe she'll kick your sorry ass, I don't know. I can tell you this though, Chuck. It won't matter what she's calling you when she does it."

Parnell appeared to be considering this. "Could you just keep calling me Chuck? You know, pretend?"

Gabriel put his face in his hands. "Sure, Chuck. Whatever."

Parnell smiled, seemed pleased to get past that. "Did you go over the file any more, last night?" Gabriel nodded, head still in hands. "So, what do you think?"

"Same as last night. Crock of shit. That's not my wife."

"Some of it is, though, Gabriel. Parts of it. The important part. The really, really scary part."

Gabriel looked up again, already weary of this conversation. "Which is what part, exactly? The entire thing is scraps of speculative bullshit and innuendo. Most of it is nuts, half of it I can't make heads or tails out of."

"I admit, it's pretty sketchy. I don't look at enough of this stuff to know how to evaluate it. But when you see reports from Interpol and MI-5, FBI; shit like that doesn't accumulate for no reason."

"Maybe it does. From what I read, it makes no sense. One report on Irish Nationalists has one line mentioning a person who may or may not now be my wife. Something called SOCA—"

"Serious Organized Crime Agency, they're British."

"—has a whole report on gambling involving motorcycle racing, speculating about a certain team with a certain redheaded driver and another driver who was seriously injured—"

"He died—the guy lost his brakes at 150 miles per hour, Gabe."

"Like racing motorcycles isn't dangerous, Chuck? What does that have to do with my wife? Crock of shit. A nearly dead guy in Boston that somebody in an FBI file says was at a bar with a redhead the night before he's in some kind of car accident. Hard to believe my wife is the only redhead in Boston—shit, I don't even know if Helena's ever been in Boston."

"She lived there for three years, Gabe. But like I said yesterday, her name wasn't Helena."

"It's ridiculous. The government can have a file like that on me, or anyone."

"Yeah, but they don't. They do have a pretty thick file about your wife, though. Because, big picture, a lot of very scary shit happens around her."

"So you say. But I've known her for a long time now, spent every waking moment with her for over three years without any scary shit. Well, actually a lot of scary shit, but no one's ever died because of it. I'm pretty sure. Anyway, I shredded the whole thing, last night. My wife doesn't need to see that shit."

"You may be right, Gabriel. But that's not what has me scared."

"Please, Chuck. Tell me. Tell me and then leave. Tell me and leave so I can have my wife back."

"Well, that's it, isn't it, Gabriel? That's the thing."

"What's the thing?"

"Why did she leave?"

"You scared her, that's why."

"All I did was show up and say hi, Gabriel. What is she so scared of?"

"What are you scared of, asshole? You said you were scared of her. Kind of a double standard, don't you think?"

Parnell shook his head. "All that other stuff, Gabriel? Fine, throw it all out. Like I said, not my field. I have no way of evaluating its credibility, any of it. Forget everything in that file. But I'll tell you what is my field. SigInt. Signals intelligence. And not to toot my own horn here, Gabriel, I'm pretty good at it. I've been doing this a while and I do it well. And I'm telling you, your wife scares me shitless."

"Why, Chuck? What has she done? I've never seen her do anything remotely scary."

"Now who's kidding whom, Gabriel? I know you must have seen it, you've lived it. Shit, man. When was the last time you took a vacation out of the country? Or even took a commercial airline trip? Who doesn't get on a plane? Who do you know doesn't carry a cellphone? Don't tell me that's normal. I've never met your wife, but I know how she must live. She is fucking off the grid, brother."

"So? What's wrong with that, who does that hurt?"

"I don't know, Gabriel. I don't know. But it is very scary to a professional like me. Look, you need some perspective on this. Pick up a phone book, if there still were any phone books. If you picked up a phone book listing every person, from any random city in this country, ok? With me? Pick any name, any city, circle the name and give it to me. Give me about three minutes, max, and I am not kidding, I'll give you his location to within ten feet. And that's without pulling any extra req's or satellite time or asking some submarine skipper to pop an antenna up someplace or shit like that."

Parnell waited for a response.

"You do shit like that?"

"Every day. That's our job, at the good old NSA."

"Why?"

"Lots of reasons, but that's not the point. You don't care about what I do. What the hell do you care if your government can find out where you're sitting? You don't. You sure wouldn't go to any trouble to keep me from being able to do my job, would you? You never knew me, and now that you do, you still don't care."

"Your point, then?"

"My point is, there are about six people in this country who can consistently do what your wife does, long term. One of them is the President of the United States."

"And the other five?"
"Really, really bad people."

Helena woke up in a motel in Erie, Pennsylvania. She had gotten in late and slept in. She did not like sleeping without her husband. Gabriel always kept the bad dreams away. She was not good at being away from him, at being on her own. She used to be, she reminded herself. Maybe should could be again, for a while at least. She hoped so.

She needed breakfast and she needed some real clothes; she couldn't walk around in leathers all the time. And she wasn't having beef jerky for breakfast, either.

Helena showered, squeezed back into her riding suit. Breakfast at the local diner, where her appearance didn't elicit a second glance. Then to Walmart for clothes and toiletries, today's paper, a backpack, running shoes; again, just the occasional leer. Back to the motel to change clothes, go for a run. She was planning to cover a lot more distance on the bike tonight; she'd need some exercise. Then, a nap.

When she awoke, it was dark outside. She showered again, then squeezed back into the riding suit. She packed her purchases in the backpack. She checked the room. She hadn't done much, never touched the television remote or telephone. The maid would wipe down the bathroom; she'd have to with the mess Helena had left in there. Satisfied, she wiped the doorknob on the way out.

She checked out at the desk. Using cash for motels had become a problem. The managers didn't like not having a credit card on file, particularly from a biker arriving late at night. She had been forced to leave a two hundred dollar deposit at the desk to get the room. In a pinch, she could leave without it, but that would be noticed. She squared with the same night manager she had met the night before, gave him a nice smile and an extra fifty bucks before she left, implying to the man that she'd prefer not to be remembered; abusive boyfriend problem, eyelashes batting, slightly moist eyes. That was the tough part, to leave enough of a tip to encourage the individual to answer any subsequent questions in a friendly, dismissive manner, but not so much that the tip itself raised suspicion of trying to cover up something really bad. It was a constant calculation. It helped that almost everybody disliked the kind of people who might show up to ask questions, government employed or otherwise. They never left a tip.

Helena decided to take I-90 eastward. She preferred traveling by back roads, particularly in Pennsylvania on a bike. That would have been a treat. Unfortunately, that also would require that she travel during the day, not trusting herself to navigate rural roads all night in the dark without repeatedly getting sidetracked or lost. She thought it best to travel at night, even if it meant using the expressway. As long as she didn't blow the doors off a state trooper, a single biker riding in the dark should be pretty inconspicuous.

It was a perfect, cool night for riding. The road was dry and smooth and there was just a light wind. Even expressway cruising was beautiful in upstate Pennsylvania. I-90 was pretty sparsely traveled, winding through hills and valleys in broad swoops that made riding the Ducati an unadulterated pleasure. In her current situation, she wouldn't risk going more than five miles per hour over the speed limit, since in her experience there were as many speed traps in this state as there were hills to hide them. And there were a lot of hills. She got lucky, though, when she was overtaken by an eighteen wheeler. He must have been really, really behind schedule, as he blew by Helena at over ninety-five. Helena, switched off her lamps, dropped her gear and shot up behind him, closing to his right rear corner within five feet of the bumper. This way, she wouldn't be limited to fifty-five all night. This way, she could do ninety plus and remain completely invisible to both the rig's driver and any radar guns pointed her way. And five feet off the bumper at ninety-five with no view of the road ahead, she certainly didn't have to worry about being bored to death. Maybe smashed to death, but not bored. A good-sized pothole or any road debris would probably kill her before she could react. If she stayed just in line with the rig's tires, however, the chances of that happening were minimized. Just like the old days, she thought, it's all statistics.

Gabriel thought about what Parnell just said. He still wasn't impressed. He knew his wife, this joker didn't, he thought. "I don't get it, Chuck. If Helena is so dangerously, antisocially, invisible, how did you find her?

"I didn't find her, I stumbled over her. I told you yesterday, I actually was coming out to see you. It's you and your work that interests me. Still interests me a lot, you know."

"Great. Big fan, I understand. Flattered, genuinely."

"We do the same stuff, you know. Signals intelligence. I do it from, you know, the thirty thousand foot level. You do it at sea level, in the face. Same stuff. I'm sure we can help each other, work together."

"Fat chance, Chuck."

"Don't say that, Gabriel. Really, this is going to be great, it's why I'm here. And believe me, you'd be better off with me than those other yahoos that will kick in that door and flashbang you in the face, if we don't work together."

"Are you threatening me, Chuck? Is this the badass NSA threat you told me yesterday was a figment of the Hollywood imagination?"

"No, I'm not threatening anything, Gabe. What I said yesterday was true. We don't do anything except stare at screens or electrical engineering shit. You know, find the little signal, clean up the little signal, record the signal, jam the signal. I told you. But if you keep going down this road, other people are going to notice. Those people are the people who tell the people with the black body armor which doors to knock down. Not that I'm saying they're bad people, they're not. Some of my best friends. It's just that, if you're successful, I don't see any way they let you keep this. It's too important for the government not to have it. And they really don't like to share."

"It's my salmon, Chuck. I'm not letting the government touch my salmon."

"What's the salmon?"

"It's an analogy, Chuck." Parnell shook his head, looking confused.

"I can help you, Gabriel. I've read your papers, reviewed your talk like seven times. I'm sure I don't know the half of it, that you're much better by now. But this is the same exact stuff I do. I find it very exciting."

It was Gabriel's turn to shake his head. "I'm still not buying this, Chuck. I have to admit, we'd be better friends if you hadn't done the fake name, screw with my wife bullshit."

"We're not past that? I thought we got past that." Gabriel shook his head again. "I told you, I didn't think it was safe to meet you with her around, that's all."

"You can't say, 'that's all'. That's the whole problem. It doesn't hold water, because I know my wife. She's not dangerous, or a sociopath, or some kind of superspy or professional killer. So I can't trust someone who thinks she is. Period."

"Maybe I overreacted."

"You think?"

"Not really, no. Truth is, she's a problem."

"That problem is my wife."

"I wouldn't even know about her except for you. Maybe it's your fault. Except for you, I just would have walked in the front door with an appointment, you know."

"You're blaming me? You're an asshole, Chuck."

"I'm not, quit calling me that. We're going to work together."

"Not seeing that right now, Chuck. Why is this my fault? I can't believe I care, but after three years of marriage, somehow that's the first thing that rings true, you know?"

"I was doing research on you and watched the video of your Moscone talk. Great talk, convinced me I had to come out here. Just to be thorough, you know, they teach us to be thorough, to run down everything, I followed up on your research assistant. At least, I thought she was your assistant, that's what you said she was in the talk. I just figured I'd see what her research was, see what angles she was working on, that kind of thing. 'Helena Fianna', you said her name was. Well, no joy with that on first pass. That was a huge red flag, right there. I've got resources, you know. Real, big time resources for this sort of thing. My problem should have been, whoa, too much information, you know? All the government stuff, medical hits, insurance claims, naked web postings, high school suspensions for grass, I mean that's the kind of stuff that pours out. If you're a normal human being, that is."

"Really, Chuck? No naked pictures of my wife? That disappointed you?"

"You're twisting this on purpose, Gabe." Parnell paused, thought it best to go on. "So I pull in the backroom guys, say here's an interesting person. They love interesting people, you know, that's their job. And like I said, there aren't very many really interesting people, not interesting in the way they'd be interested, you know? But they loved your wife, Gabriel. They were very excited about your wife."

"Please don't tell me they were passing around naked pictures of my wife in the backroom, because that will really piss me off, Chuck."

"No, not excited that way, Gabe. Though, there is a strange picture of her in a bikini. Did you know your wife has a tattoo?"

Gabriel flushed, angry. "She's my wife, asshole, of course I know she has a tattoo. It's in a place where you shouldn't know she has a tattoo."

"Don't be silly, Gabriel. Can I ask a question, though?" Gabriel just glared at the man. "Why does she have the number 42 tattooed there? On her upper thigh, like that?

"It's the answer."

"What?"

"That's what she said, 'It's the answer'".

"What's the question?"

"Exactly."

"What?"

"That's what my wife said, when I asked her."

"And you don't think she's a serial killer, Gabriel? Maybe, that's like, the number of dead bodies she's left in her wake or something."

"You're not winning me over here, Chuck."

"Just let me finish, Gabe. So the boys—"

"—in the backroom?"

"Yeah, them. They did a facial recognition scan on that nice photo you showed. They usually have to work on some blurry satellite thing of a guy half-hidden behind a window shade, so they loved the picture of your wife. It was easy to get a really high probability match, you know. And bang, sirens go off and the supervisor says she's got Langley on the phone, and what the hell am I trying to do, get her fired? You have no idea how much trouble you caused, you almost got me fired, Gabriel. I'm the one who should be pissed off here, if you really think about it."

"Really, Chuck? Almost fired? I'm so sorry."

CHAPTER 14

Helena felt like she was eighteen again, racing the circuit back in Europe. It wasn't nearly the same, of course, but she hadn't been able to do much of any riding for years. What she was really enjoying, she realized, was the mile after mile of intense concentration. Just like racing, she had to maintain that razor focus every second or something really bad would happen. Probably happen so fast that she'd be dead before she even noticed a problem. That was the challenge in racing motorcycles at speed, the same as racing cars. The challenge wasn't the technical aspects of driving, or the strategy, or the line you raced. Thousands of drivers, motorcycle and car, could turn in a really fast lap, maybe even a few in a row. The great drivers, though, the ones who stood on the top step, could maintain intensity of concentration hour after hour without a split second lapse. Helena could do that, usually. She was doing that now, three feet off the tail of a semi doing almost a hundred in the dark, mile after mile.

It was too good to last all night, she knew. After two hours and over 160 miles, Helena was almost blinded by the truck's right hand turn signal lighting up like a blinking sunburst in her face. She downshifted in a fraction of a second, shedding speed without daring to touch the brakes. Even a little wheel lock up here would put her under the rig, probably headless. She clicked her lights back on as the truck drifted into the right lane, slowing. She saw the rest stop up ahead that the guy was probably aiming for. She was coming alongside the cab, thinking of maybe pulling off herself to call Gabe. She was too low on her bike to see the driver of the truck, but as she started to pull ahead, the driver gave her a heart stopping blast on the air horn and flashed his headlights at her. She was so startled she almost dumped the bike right in front of his rig. He must have known I was drafting him the whole time, she thought. She couldn't tell if he was signaling camaraderie or if he was pissed off, as she'd seen both reactions from long haul truckers in the past. She decided not to find out. She flashed her lights back at him and left him in her rear view.

Helena settled down into a cruise. After an hour, she realized this was going to be a problem. Sixty miles per hour on a well-maintained highway in the dark, the drone of a perfectly balanced machine; this was not good for the mind. Not Helena's mind, anyway. Monotony was dangerous for her, she knew. She sang at the top of her lungs for a while, spent a few miles slaloming between every fifth white lane reflector, then every third. She started alternating slaloms of every fifth and third, tried a few miles of slaloming between every prime numbered reflector. At the fifty ninth marker she looked at her speedometer to see she was doing over one-twenty. She dropped her speed back to sixty, started slaloming to a Fibonacci sequence, forward to 144, then backwards. Despite these efforts, however, she started to feel the tickle, the faint tickle in the very back of her brain. It started so faintly, was so subtle, she didn't recognize it at first. On some level, she was probably blocking it out, intentionally ignoring it. It grew, however, grew to the point where she couldn't pretend any longer. When she became conscious of it, she was swept with a wave of nausea. She let the bike slow. She tried to focus, tried to will the sensation away, but it would not leave. She needed Gabriel, she thought. She let the bike roll to a crunching stop on the shoulder of the road. She pulled off her gloves, her helmet. She concentrated on putting her gloves in her helmet, watched as her hands set her helmet on the ground. She sat down on the gravel shoulder and tried to will the buzzing to go away.

She needed Gabriel, she kept thinking. What was she doing, why was she out here, alone and without him? She pawed through her backpack, found a new cellphone. She used the light of the phone to read the numbers from her cheat sheet. Her hands were shaking so hard that she had trouble reading the numbers, punching the little buttons, screwed up, started again. Finally, she heard the series of rings that meant the call was going through her mash-up. She desperately hoped that Gabriel would answer.

"So that's how you found Helena and got her file. I get that, Chuck. Great story." Parnell nodded. "There's still nothing there that scares me. Or should scare you, really."

"It's not the stuff in the file that got me scared, Gabriel. Once we had her framed up, we started pulling records, doing the surveillance thing. The thing we do, you know, to find a person and trace back where they've been, who've they've been in contact with. We build a contact map, like a spider web. Only in your wife's case, it's like a web with no spider. That's when I realized what she is. She is nowhere in there. It's like that file. It's about her, but she's nowhere in there. We got a touch of her in some classes in Princeton, maybe her as an undergraduate student at U Penn. A lot of probably her for a month or two at various universities. No passport hits, no TSA screenings."

"You can see who goes through TSA, every day? Everyone?"

Parnell blushed. "Don't spread that around, okay? You're not really supposed to know that."

"But you have her registered as an undergrad at UM and those other schools."

"No, Gabe. She's there and she's not. Sometimes she's living on campus, but names and socials, birthdates, phone numbers, are meaningless with your wife. She shifts all the time."

"So how do you even know this stuff?"

"Like I say, random acts. We get a hit, we start checking. Pulling up surveillance camera archives, running facial recognition sweeps. We got a ding here and there, luck mostly. Usually, we have a lot of luck with voiceprint, cross check a lot of archived phone chatter, lecture hall recordings, anything where people are talking near a recorded mike, posting to the web, you know? Nothing. Not a thing, Gabriel. Nobody can even put a voice to your wife, can you believe that?"

Gabriel shook his head. "It sounds like you spent a lot of time and effort dogging my wife, Chuck."

"She was kind of a project, I admit."

"None of this means shit. None of this means anything, Chuck."

"It means a lot to me, Gabriel. It's what your wife is: a wraith, a will-o-the-wisp."

"A will-o-wisp? What are you, Dickens now? You don't know my wife, and you don't know what my wife is."

"I know how she lives. I don't know why."

"Fine, let it go then."

"I can't, Gabriel. Because it makes no sense. Why would a person who spends her whole life living like that—"

"Paranoid, you mean."

"Let's just say, 'intensely private', okay? Why would she help you do what you're doing? It doesn't make any sense."

"You mean, because what I do is a kind of an invasion of privacy. Is that what you're driving at here?"

Parnell nodded. "It's like the ultimate invasion of privacy, Gabe. What we do at NSA is nothing compared to you; we just locate people or listen in on their conversations. You're trying to listen to their thoughts. You can see, Gabriel, that this has got to be your wife's worst nightmare, what you're trying to do. It doesn't make any sense, unless—"

"Unless what, Chuck?"

"Unless it's a trap, Gabriel. Unless she's setting you up, you know."

"Like to make me disappear or something?" Parnell nodded, wringing his hands. "You think Helena lived with me for five months, married me, and suffered through over three years of marriage so that..."

Parnell was nodding with increasing vigor. "Yes, Gabriel, I'm afraid so. Your wife is going to kill you. Maybe me, too."

"Chuck, to quote Dickens, you are a fucking moron."

"I should've realized that you wouldn't believe me, since she's your wife and all."

"No," Gabriel said, "You should've realized that you're an idiot, Chuck. I'm done with this. When Helena calls back, I'm going to tell her that."

"Tell her what, Gabriel?"

"I'm going to tell her that you're a moron and not worth running from. I'm going to tell her to come home."

"Oh."

"So maybe you should leave."

"I don't have to leave right away, do I?"

"I think that would be best, don't you? Really, Chuck?"

"But I came all this way, set this all up to work with you. How about just the rest of the day? You could show me the lab, the research you're doing now. I'm sure I can be of help."

"But you've done so much already, Chuck."

Parnell just sat, hopeful. Faith came in, knocking.

"Guinea pigs in their cages, boss. Showtime." Parnell looked like a Jack Russell, Gabriel thought. He remembered feeling like that, once.

"Fine, Chuck. Come on; let's go to the lab. I'll show you what we're up to here." Gabriel was relieved when the man didn't jump up to lick his hand.

Gabriel spent the day with the second group of subjects, continuing to work on the multilayer problem, which continued to be a problem. He had one of the research fellows give Parnell a tour of the facilities, implied that the fellow should show him at great length how the other researchers were broadening the recognition dictionary with a steady stream of subjects on the other side of the building.

Unfortunately, Parnell reappeared in Gabriel's office while he was eating lunch.

"Eating in, Gabriel?" Parnell asked, plopping down in a chair. "I'd thought maybe we'd grab something together, maybe a sandwich."

"Thought wrong, Chuck. Working here. Hope you enjoyed your tour." He stood, brushing crumbs from his shirt. He offered the man his hand to shake. Parnell just remained seated.

"I can grab something later, no problem. Show me what you're working on. Everything I saw this morning is pretty much more of the same. Not what I came here for."

Gabriel sighed, sat back down. "Fine, Chuck. Pull your chair around here, let me show you this." Parnell smiled, pulling a chair next to Gabriel's.

"You gonna eat the other half of that?" Parnell said, pointing at the half of a sandwich on the desk.

"Help yourself, Chuck."

Gabriel presented Parnell with a thorough explanation of his current research project. Once finished with their lunch, he brought him into the lab and let him spend the afternoon watching Gabriel work with the deep subject testing. Parnell sat next to Gabriel, frequently asking questions that exhibited an understanding and insight that surprised Gabriel. Evidently, this guy really did do this sort of analysis for a living. And he was right, he seemed good at it.

By six that evening, the subjects were gone and the other employees had left for the day. Arthur dropped in to see if Gabriel wanted to talk about the Parnell situation.

"Surprised to see you still here, Parnell," Arthur said, walking into Gabriel's office and interrupting a vigorous technical discussion that made no sense to Arthur.

Parnell looked at him, interrupted in mid sentence. "Really? Why?"

"Thought that would be obvious, Chuck. Heard from Helena yet today, Gabe?" Gabriel shook his head.

"No, but I was telling Chuck here, earlier," Gabriel said, "that when she does call, I'm going to tell her to come home."

Arthur nodded. "Problem solved, then."

"What problem, guys?" Parnell asked.

"You," Arthur said, standing. "How about dinner?"

"Sure, great," Parnell replied. The other two just looked at him.

Helena was afraid. Old sensations, sensations that had been at bay for many years, were steadily creeping over her. She felt cold and shivered slightly as she held the phone, ringing, to her ear.

The ringing stopped, hissing silence, then her husband's voice.

"Hey, Leena," he said over the slurred connection.

"Gabriel," was all she could manage in reply. She was breathing steadily, deeply, trying to hold back the buzzing sensation swelling slowly in the back of her head. Her fingers were numb.

Gabriel could sense immediately in the one word that something was very wrong with his wife. "Helena, what is it? Are you okay?"

"No, Gabe. I'm bad." She had to stop talking for a moment, breathe. Pinpoints of light had appeared, distantly. The smell of burnt toast. She knew it was inevitable now. She could feel the seizure approaching.

"What is it, hon? What can I do?"

"I need you, Gabe." Helena had struggled to her feet, stood at the side of the road unsteadily. The white lights were growing brighter. She thought she could hear a roaring starting to build in her ears, still faint yet.

"Tell me, hon. Tell me what to do."

"Come get me, Gabe. Like before."

"Where, Leena? Where are you?"

"Side of the road. Come get me. Please."

She dropped the phone. The white light was blinding now, she could see nothing else. There was a huge roaring, a building wind. She flung her backpack at the light as hard as she could, dropped to her knees, buffeted by the violent rushing. With numb, shaking hands, she stuffed a riding glove in her mouth, lay down, and waited for the seizure to take her.

The trucker was way behind and moving fast. He wished he hadn't stopped at the rest area, but he wasn't a young man anymore, had needed coffee and a bathroom. He was rolling again now, almost back up to speed. He wondered if he'd catch up his pesky mosquito again, that drafting biker who had ridden his ass for the better part of two hours. The trucker's name was Randall Mosgrave, three days out of Little Rock and way behind. He didn't like being drafted by the biker; not that he cared about anyone saving gas or avoiding a speeding ticket at his expense. He just didn't like the idea of killing anyone. He'd feel bad about that, though he thought he might not even notice if it happened. Probably be a lot of delay and paperwork involved, too. He was already so far behind, if he didn't make up at least six hours, he'd be making this run for free.

For a split second, Mosgrave thought he saw someone standing on the side of the road, a motorcycle, and then something exploded into his windshield, like a bomb going off without warning inches from his face. He cursed loudly, but had the presence of mind to fight the reflex to throw up his hands in protection, a move that probably would have jackknifed his rig. He laid on his airbrakes, the emergency Jake system cutting in. The huge heavy rig stuttered and hammered slowly to a stop as Mosgrave pulled it off the highway. He cursed, looking at the broken windshield in front of him. He'd been hit by geese and other large birds before, scared the shit out of him every time. But geese didn't fly into your windshield at 3 am. He waited until his heart stopped racing, then hit the emergency flashers and dropped out of the cab, leaving the big engine turning. He started walking back to see what had hit him. He still had a fleeting image in his mind of a motorcycle and someone standing at the side of the road, barely glimpsed in the glare of his headlights, an instant before the bang. The thought occurred to him that the asshole might have thrown a rock at his rig. He had to see. That asshole could have killed him.

It had taken him almost half a mile to stop the rig. He trudged back, starting to think that the image may have been an illusion of some type, maybe a deer or something. He was thinking of turning back, thinking of how much time and precious diesel it was going to cost him to get back up to speed, when he saw the motorcycle parked in front of him. He couldn't see any rider, though; probably taking a piss in the woods, he thought. He hoped the dude wasn't taking a dump, because he didn't have the time to wait and besides, he wanted to beat the shit out of the guy. Mosgrave kept walking, and then saw movement on the ground by the bike. Not natural movement, though; a twitching that he immediately recognized.

"Hey, there," he called, trying to get his massive frame into a run. He managed a faster shuffle, looked down on the slight, leather-clad figure, lying curled up on her side. He could see in the dark that she was a young, redheaded woman, and that she was in serious trouble. He knelt down with a grunt, trying to cradle the girl's head as she convulsed. Her eyes were open and she made guttural, grunting sounds, spittle coming from her mouth around teeth clenched on a leather riding glove. Her arms and legs beat rhythmically against the gravel.

Mosgrave had seen a seizure before, knew that he just had to protect the head until it ended. His little brother had suffered a brain injury serving in Iraq, and Mosgrave had seen him seize several times when he went off his meds. Randall made little calming sounds, cradling the girl, though he knew she couldn't hear him. After a few more minutes, the jerking diminished, then stopped altogether. Helena took a deep, reflexive breath. Randall held her, knew that despite her open eyes that she wouldn't be really conscious for a while. 'Post-ictal,' the doctors called it. He rocked the little girl in his lap as he pulled his cellphone from his pants pocket and dialed 911.

Helena awoke in the emergency room, lying on a stretcher and dressed in a hospital gown. An intravenous flowed into her right arm. She hurt all over. No buzzing, though. That was good.

She was staring at her riding suit, neatly folded at the foot of the bed. Those are my feet, down there, she thought. She wiggled her toes experimentally. They seemed to work fine.

"Hey, darlin'."

Helena was startled by the deep mahogany voice, turned to see a huge bear of a man, overflowing a too small chair beside the gurney. He was round faced and bald, looking at her with concern.

"You're awake, huh?"

"Seems so," she answered. "Who might you be?"

Mosgrave leaned over her, blocking out the light and offering his hand. "My name's Randall. I picked you up off the side of the road."

Helena shook his hand. It was the size of her head, she thought.

"Well, thank you for that, Randall. That was kind of you." Her head hurt, always did after a seizure. "Where are we, Randall?"

"Hospital. Amsterdam, New York. Just outside of Schenectady."

Helena nodded, taking this in. Events of the evening were coming back to her. They sat quietly for a while.

"Didn't get your name, honey," Mosgrave said after a bit.

Helena looked at the hospital bracelet on her arm, saw 'Jane Doe 1' typed on it.

"How'd we get here, Randall?" She tried a smile, was halfway there when it changed into a wince. She must have split her lip, she thought.

"I called an ambulance. You were having a seizure."

"Then I thank you again, for saving my life."

"I didn't save your life, girl. You weren't dying, just seizing. You ever seize before?" Helena nodded, which hurt her head. "You shouldn't be riding if you're prone to seizing, you know." He gave her a studied look. "You sure as hell shouldn't be drafting my rig at a hundred miles an hour, that's for sure."

Helena smiled at him, winced again. She touched her lip and her fingers came away bloody. "I don't suppose there are any doctors or nurses in this hospital, are there?"

"Nice young doctor was in examining you before you woke up. Looks about sixteen."

"Great. Because I could use some drugs right about now."

"I'm sure he'll be back, good looking patient like you. He probably sees old geezers all night."

"That'll be fun. Long as he has drugs."

Randall was still staring at her. "You threw something at my rig, didn't you?"

Helena blushed, nodded. "Yeah, Randall. Sorry. I was just trying to flag you down."

"No, girl. 'Flaggin' down' is waving your arms around, like this." He waved his arms in her face. "You nearly killed me, that's what you did. Broke my windshield, too. What did you throw at me?"

"Backpack. Sorry, Randall. I meant no harm, really."

"Backpack full of rocks, must be."

'No, actually, backpack full of gun, money, and fake ID', Helena thought to herself, 'Must have been the gun struck the windshield.' Helena sincerely hoped that the backpack had been launched into the woods in the collision. "No rocks, Randall." She looked around the room. "I don't suppose they found it, did they?" She thought they hadn't yet, since she wasn't handcuffed to the stretcher.

"Nooo, not exactly," Randall answered. He was watching her again, closely.

"What does that mean, Randall? Not exactly?"

"Well, the sheriff was kind enough to drive me back to my rig a while ago. Sun's come up, clear sky morning. But, girl, it looked like it had been raining money all over the interstate."

"You don't say, Randall."

"I do say, girl."

"Well, I hope you got a couple of pocketfuls for your kindness, Randall," she said, managing a sly smile.

"Managed a little, before the Sheriff noticed and started collecting the rest. I think he's going to pocket most of it, that was my impression."

"Sheriff didn't call anyone, then? Didn't say anything about evidence of a crime or anything?" Helena met the man's eyes, studying him.

"No, girl, didn't say anything about any crime. Though I think you committed a crime." He waited, Helena waited longer. "Throwing that bag at me, I think you could have killed me."

Helena smiled, less painful now. "Well, I'm very glad I didn't kill you, Randall. I'm lucky I encountered such a good and decent man, not the kind who'd like to press charges against a girl. And I'm glad you were able to secure some compensation for all the trouble I've caused you."

"You made your point, missy. Don't have to hit me on the head again, you know."

The white-coated doctor appeared around the corner of the curtain, carrying a clipboard.

"You're awake."

"You must be the doctor," Helena replied.

"I am," he answered, missing the tint of sarcasm in Helena's Irish lilt. "How are you feeling?"

"Awful, thanks for asking. I hurt all over, but mostly my head."

"Well, you had a seizure. Lucky thing Randall stopped to help, otherwise you'd still be on the side of the road."

"So I hear. I am very grateful to both of you. I hope you're not one of those doctors who allow their patients to suffer needlessly, Doctor."

"Not usually. We'll get you something for the pain in a second, it's already ordered. I just need to examine you first."

"Randall tells me you already did that, while I was unconscious."

The young man blushed. "Not completely. I need to do a neurologic." He proceeded to examine her, starting with shining his penlight at her eyes. "What is your name, ma'am?"

"You didn't recover my effects, then? My ID and all?"

The doctor paused, straightened. "No, I don't think they found anything. They have you as Jane Doe. You do remember your name, right?"

"Of course, doctor. Not much else though, I'm afraid."

"That's pretty common after a seizure, amnesia around the event. It'll all come back, though." He smiled at her. "Your CAT scan looks okay, and your labs are fine. Let me check on the pain medicine and I'll be back, okay?"

"Thanks, doctor. That'd be great."

Mosgrave waited until the doctor had left, then gave a low whistle.

"Damn, girl, you are good." He was smiling broadly at her, shaking his head.

"I'm sure I don't understand, Randall."

"Bullsheet, sugar, I'm sure you do. Maybe that doctor can't see past it, but I'm not so young and foolish, sister. All of a sudden with the Irish accent for the white country boy? Wasn't going to do anything for me, huh? And I've heard you asked twice point blank for your name and both times you slipped that hook and took the minnow with you, without so much as a tug on the line. Damn."

"I appreciate a man who can elegantly employ a fishing analogy, Randall." She smiled at him.

"Shit, girl, don't bother batting those green eyes at me. I'm just having fun watching you work."

"It seems to me, brother Randall, that you have done more than can be reasonably expected from even the kindest stranger. I hate to think I'm making you even later for your delivery."

"Oh, so now you're giving me the boot. No way, girl, I'm sticking around for act two. I want see how you play this out. Haven't quite figured your angle yet, but I'm listening."

Helena dropped the smile and stared at the man. In a quieter voice and less agreeably toned, she said, "Well, Randall, I'll tell you how this is going to play out. Two choices, your call, and believe me when I say, I certainly don't wish to presume or impose any more than I have."

"I'm listening, sugar." He was still smiling, enjoying this. The chair creaked as he leaned back, hands clasped behind his head.

"Play number one," Helena said, " I get admitted to hospital and we say our goodbyes. And I will be ever thankful." Randall nodded. "Play number two, you walk me out of here and take me back to my bike."

"And then that's it, we go our separate ways? Your money's gone, all your stuff. Don't even know where they took your bike, no keys. Sounds like a risky play for a young girl."

"Your call, Randall."

"It seems to me, though, that plan number two allows you to avoid a lot of potentially embarrassing questions."

"It does have its advantages. But please don't feel like you need to put yourself out any more than you have. Plan two has its own potential pitfalls."

"Girl, you are wiser than your years."

"Actually, Randall, I'm just older than I look." He looked at her, appraisingly. "And Randall?"

"Yeah, sugar?"

"You've got about fifteen seconds to make up your mind."

"I don't need no fifteen seconds, sugar." Mosgrave stood up, gave Helena a paternal kiss on the top of her head. The doctor walked in with the syringe. Mosgrave bent to whisper in her ear. "Old Randall's going with plan number C. Good luck to you, sugar." And then he left.

The doctor paused, surprised. "He's leaving?"

"I believe so, yes. Is that for me, doctor?"

"Oh, yeah. This'll help." He attached the syringe to a port on the IV and slowly infused the clear liquid. "Ketorolac, non-narcotic. Works great." Even as he spoke, Helena could feel the pain evaporate like smoke, her head clearing. "See, told you."

"Thank you, Doctor. You're very kind."

"Listen, if he's not coming back, then we've got a problem. I can't release you after a seizure unless there's someone who can watch you for at least twenty-four hours. Do you have any family in the area?" Helena shook her head. "Then we've got to admit you, at least for a day or two."

"Doctor," she asked, "is there an inpatient psychiatric unit in this hospital?"

The doctor looked surprised. "Yes. Yes, there is a small unit. Why?"

"Doctor, I'm afraid that I may be a danger to myself. Riding a motorcycle in the dark, so fast and all, knowing about the risk of a seizure; I think I was hoping this would happen. Only worse, you know?"

A sudden look of concern and confusion appeared on the face of the doctor. "Are you saying that you're suicidal? That you've had thoughts of killing yourself?" Helena nodded. "But just a little while ago, you seemed okay. I don't think it'll be necessary to—"

"I'm sorry, doctor. I didn't realize that psychiatry was your specialty."

"Well, no. It isn't. I'm emergency medicine, but my training includes—"

"I just think that it may be dangerous to discharge me without a psychiatric evaluation, given my behavior and severe depression."

"You're depressed?" Helena nodded. "It's," he looked at his watch, "six on Saturday morning. There's no way I have a psychiatrist in to see you until Monday, at the soonest. You don't want to—"

"I don't think either one of us would feel comfortable any other way, Doctor. I'd like to voluntarily commit myself for psychiatric evaluation. Formally." She looked the young man in the eye.

The doctor stared back at her, puzzled. He knew he was being played here, couldn't figure out just how. This girl was depressed like he was George Clooney. "Fine, I can't argue with that." He grabbed up the clipboard and took out his pen, writing. "I'll need your name, for the admission."

"Actually, doctor, I don't think you will. Not for a psychiatric admission. Let's just go with Jane Doe, for now. I don't want my family finding out. And Doctor—," he looked up from the clipboard, "I hope you'll stop by, see how I'm doing." Helena smiled at him.

"Yeah, we'll see. I'm going to go get this started. Jane Doe."

CHAPTER 15

Gabriel was sitting bolt upright in his bed, in the dark. His wife had just hung up on him. He had seen her in bad shape, once, completely devastated. This sounded worse. She had never asked him to rescue her. It was so far out of character that he was deeply shaken. He would help her, but he had no idea how he was going to do it. He looked at the clock; saw that it was after one in the morning. He called Arthur.

Arthur was still awake and answered on the first ring. Gabriel explained the short conversation with Helena to Arthur.

"Shit, Gabe. What do you think is going on?" he asked.

"I don't know, Arthur. The connection was awful, like yesterday, but she sounded like she was in deep shit."

They were both silent for a while, thinking. It was Arthur who thought of it first.

"Where's Parnell? Where did he go?"

"Back to DC, I guess. I don't think he left a card, if that's what you mean."

"Fifty bucks says we don't need a card, Gabe. I'm picking you up in fifteen minutes. Are you dressed?"

"Not yet, Arthur. Where are we going?"

"Get dressed. I'll be right over. I just have to tell Sam I'm going."

Ten minutes later, Gabriel was sitting on his front porch in the dark. Arthur pulled up, Samantha in the passenger seat. Gabriel got in and Arthur drove north to San Francisco.

They pulled up and parked in front of the Embarcadero lab. It was dark, the door locked. Gabriel let them in, turning on lights as he led them back towards his office. No music. He unlocked his office, clicked on the light. No Parnell.

"Shit," Arthur cursed, "I would've bet the little fucker would still be here."

Gabriel sat down at his desk. "Well, Arthur, we did pretty much ride him out on a rail, you know."

Arthur and Samantha sat down in the other chairs.

Parnell appeared in the doorway to the back bedroom, rubbing his eyes. He was dressed in Gabriel's pajama bottoms.

"Hey, guys. What's up?" They looked up at him. Arthur smiled.

"It's my job, man. Knowing people. That's my job," Arthur said.

"Sit down, Chuck," Gabriel said. "We need to talk."

Faith appeared behind Parnell, pulling on a shoe. She squeezed past Parnell and hurried out the door with a backwards wave. The three of them watched her go, and then looked at Parnell.

"What?" Parnell asked.

"In my bed?" Gabriel asked.

"You said you never sleep here."

"Never going to now, that's for sure."

"Surprised the hell out of me," Arthur said. "That's a bet I would've lost."

"Yeah, knowing people, that's your job. Don't be a hater, Arthur," Parnell said. "What's going on, guys?"

"Helena's in trouble," Gabriel said.

"She killed somebody, didn't she?" Parnell asked.

Gabriel shook his head. "I need to find her, Chuck."

"Just wait, Gabriel. She's probably coming for you next."

They all sat around mugs of coffee. Parnell was not optimistic.

"Look, Gabriel; two possibilities. If your wife does not want to be found, we're not going to find her, period. She would have to make a significant mistake, probably a series of mistakes. I don't think she makes mistakes like that."

"And the other possibility, Chuck?" Gabriel asked.

"That she might want to be found. Then it'll hinge on how she wants to be found and by whom."

Arthur said, "Well, of course she wants to be found. She said so when she called Gabe."

Parnell scratched his head. "Tell me again, what she said. Exactly."

Gabriel thought, and then said, "I'm bad. I need you. Come get me." He thought some more. "Something else, though. She said, 'Come get me, like before'."

Parnell looked up, asking, "Like when before? What was she talking about?"

"She must be talking about the time before we married, when I came and found her sleeping in her storage unit, I think." They all looked at Gabriel. "Long story."

"Do you think she could be hiding there, again? Is that what she means?" Arthur asked.

Gabriel brightened. "Maybe. I could ask my parents to check."

"But that's not what she said, Gabriel," Parnell said. "Before, you told us that when you asked your wife where she was, she said 'on the side of the road'. Isn't that what you said?"

Gabriel deflated again. "Yeah, that was the last thing she said, before she hung up."

"How did the call end, Gabriel?" Parnell asked. "Did you hear her hang up, disconnect? Was there any sound after she stopped talking?"

Gabriel thought again. He had been waiting up when Helena had called, wondering why she hadn't called earlier. He ran through the whole thing in his mind again, remembering. "No, I don't think she hung up. There was a noise—I think she dropped the phone. It sounded like she dropped it onto something hard."

"Like the side of a road, maybe," said Parnell. They all looked at him. "What? This is what I've been talking about, Gabriel. This is so your wife. It's all clues and subterfuge."

"What do you mean?" Sam asked. "What subterfuge?"

"If I asked you, 'where are you?'" Parnell said, "What would you say? You'd say, 'in San Francisco', or 'on Embarcadero', or 'sitting in Gabriel's office'. You wouldn't say, 'sitting in a chair', would you? Of course not, that's not helpful, it's stupid."

"You're saying Helena doesn't want to be found, then? Then why did she call?" Arthur asked.

"I think she does want to be found," Parnell slowly replied, "but she's afraid of who might find her. She didn't want to say straight out her location, somebody might be listening."

"But you said nobody could be listening. You tried to trace her yourself and couldn't."

"That's not the same thing. She used some kind of trick to prevent a trace, but anyone could still listen in. That call is open air, probably recorded in half a dozen different databases. So she gave you clues, something you could figure out but nobody else would."

"But I can't figure it out," Gabe said, exasperated. "I don't know what she's trying to tell me."

"Something about the storage unit, I think," Parnell said. "And about being on the side of a road." He shook his head. "It's not much, Gabriel."

Parnell again broke the ensuing silence.

"She said 'I feel bad'?" Parnell asked, "When you asked her what was wrong?"

Gabriel thought some more, shook his head. "No, not 'I feel bad'. She said 'I'm bad'. Just like that, 'I'm bad'."

Samantha said, "That's weird. That doesn't sound like something Leena would say."

"That 's not something anybody would say, not normally, in response to Gabe's question," Parnell said.

"So why say it?" Gabe asked.

Parnell looked brighter. "Again, I think she's trying to imply something. She's thinking fast, she's on the side of a road, she's in trouble. 'I'm bad.' That could me she's feeling bad, she's sick—but that's not how you'd usually say that. She could mean she's a bad person, which makes no sense—"

"Unless," Arthur interjected, "she meant she was about to get arrested."

"I think you're right, Arthur," Parnell said, nodding.

Samantha was shaking her head, confused. "Why would Leena get arrested?"

"I think I know," Gabriel said.

They all looked at him, waiting. "My dad called during Helena's visit. He said she was carrying a loaded gun and a lot of money in a bag with her."

They were stunned for a minute.

"Have you talked to your dad since then. Is he still alive?" Parnell asked.

"Yes, he's still alive," Gabriel answered, exasperated. "He said he and mom dropped Helena at Metro airport for her trip back."

"Well, that can't be true, Gabe," Sam said. "No way Leena got on a plane carrying a gun."

"She may have dumped it, before she got to screening," Arthur said.

"Then why carry it at all? That doesn't make sense," Parnell said.

"And Leena doesn't do planes, not commercial at any rate," Gabriel said.

"So why go to the airport?" Samantha asked.

"To ditch my folks, that's why," Gabriel said. "And I think I know what her message means, now. I think."

"Really? Because I'm lost," Arthur said.

Gabriel stood, paced as he talked. "Helena kept a motorcycle in her storage unit. A stolen motorcycle."

"Let me guess," Parnell said. "A Ducati racing bike."

Gabriel nodded. "She wouldn't let me ride it, said it was too hot."

"Okay, I got it. She took off from Ann Arbor on a stolen bike, she's getting pulled over, she's carrying a loaded gun—," Parnell said.

"Shit, Gabe, she's in jail!" Samantha exclaimed.

"This isn't a jail!" Helena said, louder than she meant to. The other patients turned to look at the new girl, arguing with the supervisor at the nursing station. Helena had spent a quiet night in her room on the psychiatric ward, washed up and had breakfast. Now she was trying to reason with the charge nurse, attempting to look both sane and imposing while holding closed the back of the hospital gown she was wearing.

"I signed myself in voluntarily yesterday," she continued, trying to sound more pleasant. "And now I'd like to sign myself out, please." She smiled.

The charge nurse, a severe woman in her late fifties, was having none of it. "I understand what you're saying, young lady, whatever your real name is. But I can't let you sign out. You'll have to talk to the doctor."

Helena blew a red curl off her forehead in exasperation. "When do we expect him, then?"

"We expect her," the nurse replied, writing on a chart at the same time, "When she comes in to make her rounds."

"And when would that be?" The nurse shrugged, turned her back on Helena and headed to the med room, leaving Helena fuming at the desk.

A too thin, blond woman that Helena judged to be in her late teens or early twenties, approached. "Won't be too, long, Ma'am," she said to Helena. "Dr. Hussein usually is in by nine or ten, especially on weekends. She likes to round early and get out, before all the relatives show up, you know, asking why we're not all better and ready to go home."

"Oh," Helena said. "Thanks." She gave the girl an appreciative nod and headed back to her room to wait.

The doctor arrived an hour later. She appeared in Helena's room and introduced herself. After sitting down on the chair across from Helena, she explained that she was just covering for the staff psychiatrist for the weekend, and that no, unfortunately, she would not be able to allow Helena to sign herself out. The doctor explained that Helena would have to wait until Monday when the psychiatrist in charge of the unit could formally evaluate her and make a determination. Yes, the doctor explained, she understood that Helena had signed herself in voluntarily, and yes, under ordinary circumstances she should be happy to allow her to sign herself out, but in view of the fact that the patient had suffered a seizure, and additionally, had expressed suicidal ideation, that to release her without the signature of a responsible adult was not possible. Particularly problematic, the doctor pointedly added, was the patient's reluctance to provide them with her actual name. Helena was considering this when she heard the familiar, booming voice of her friend Randall from the nursing station.

"Darlin', I understand that visiting hours don't start for another two hours, but I don't have another two hours to kill, you understand? I'm here to speak with my little Irish friend, Jane Doe. Won't take but a minute, I promise. Nice lady down in the ER told me she was here now."

Helena swept past the doctor and out to the nursing station, holding her gown closed behind her. Randall gave her a smile as she appeared.

"Hey there, Irish. Good morning," Randall said, smiling.

"Good to see you, Randall," she smiled back. She noticed the grocery bag he was carrying. "You brought me a gift?"

He nodded. "Thought you might need some clothes and things, since your backpack never turned up". He gave her a wink. "I hope I guessed your size right, sugar."

The doctor had trailed Helena out to the nursing station and introduced herself to Mosgrave.

"Are you a friend or relative of this patient, sir?" the doctor asked.

"Just a friend, doctor. No relation".

"Would you be willing to accept responsibility for the patient?" the doctor continued, studying him.

"Well, I'm not sure that—"

"Of course you would, Randall," Helena said brightly, as she took the bag from him. "I'll just go and change while you and the doctor take care of the paperwork." With that, she disappeared into her room while the doctor allowed Randall to sign the forms necessary to release Jane Doe to the custody and responsibility of Mr. Mosgrave.

Twenty minutes later, Helena sat in the passenger seat next to Randall as he pulled his rig back onto I-90 eastbound. Helena was dressed in the Yankees tee shirt and overlarge gray sweatpants Randall had acquired from the Salvation Army store, along with a pair of orange tennis shoes. He had also picked up various toiletries and makeup supplies that he thought she might require.

Helena finished brushing her hair and surveyed the makeup items in the bag critically.

"I trust, Randall, that you didn't actually kill the prostitute that you acquired these items from," Helena said.

Randall gave her a sideways look before continuing to accelerate and rechecking his mirrors. "If by that, Irish, you mean thank you, then you're welcome."

"That's exactly what I mean, Randall. So this is plan number C, is it?" Mosgrave nodded, shifting gears. "You are too kind, Mr. Mosgrave. It will get you in trouble someday, I fear."

"I think it has already, Irish. I just signed my name about sixteen times on a bunch of papers that probably will get me sent up if you go and do something stupid."

Helena smiled at him, shook her head. "You don't have to worry about that, Randall. And thank you for signing me out, you didn't have to do that."

"I didn't? I guess I missed that part back there, the part where Randall had a choice."

Helena just smiled again. "If you'd like, you can drop me anywhere and I'll head back for my bike."

Randall fished her keys out of his pocket, tossed them to her. "Bike's in the back. No need to go back and talk to those folks again. Wouldn't suggest it, either."

"A girl could fall in love; big, kind, resourceful man like you."

"Now, Irish, why'd you have to say 'big'? I was starting to like you."

Mosgrave settled his truck into the flow of traffic, relaxed. They sat quietly for a while, watching the traffic and the road.

"How far behind are you, because of me?" Helena finally asked.

"Too far to matter, Irish."

"I'm truly sorry for being so much trouble for you, Randall."

"My choice, my problem, Irish. Besides, I probably got more of your money in my pocket than I was likely to clear from this run, anyways." He smiled at her.

"Keep it, then. Least I can do."

"No argument there, Irish. Where were you heading, before?"

"Boston." Helena checked the big side view mirror.

"You got people in Boston?"

"I'm Irish, like you keep saying. Half the town is my people, Randall. Where are you headed?"

"Boston, same as you, it seems."

"Quite a coincidence. Lucky for me."

"Luck of the Irish."

Helena shook her head, put her feet on the dash. "Never really applied to me, Randall."

Gabriel, Arthur, and Samantha all looked again to Parnell. They had gone out for breakfast and now sat once again in Gabriel's office.

"Like I said before," Parnell repeated, "If she doesn't want to be found, she isn't going to be. Period."

"She wants me to find her, I'm sure. Just not anyone else. What if she's been arrested; can you find her then?" Gabriel asked.

"She won't be using her real name, if that's what you mean. Shit, Gabriel, she doesn't even have a real name, you know."

"What, then?" Sam asked. "What can we use?"

"You really want to find her?" Parnell asked. They all nodded. "One play has the best chance of finding her. You call the San Francisco office of the FBI; tell the duty officer that you have reason to believe that your wife is considering an act of public terrorism. That'll get their attention. Usually, they'd let something like that spike and fade in twenty-four hours, without a credible threat. But your wife, Gabriel—one look at her file and they will go ape shit ballistic, guaranteed."

"You have her file, remember?" Arthur said. "They'll see you took it, wonder what's going on."

Parnell shook his head. "No, no one will even look for the real file. It's scanned into a dozen different databases, I assure you."

"But you said before that they'd probably burn her file when nothing turned up about Helena in a few years," Gabriel said.

"They will," Parnell answered. "It's the law, part of the 'open government' movement, you know. They burn a ton of stuff; it's all in the computers, anyway, nobody cares about the file."

"So they'll find her then? If Gabriel calls the FBI?" Samantha asked.

Parnell nodded. "They'll find her, eventually, even if she's gone to ground. She might be able to keep under the radar for a week or two, but if Gabriel really lights the fuse, they'll use a lot of resources on her. Two weeks, tops."

"Then what?" Gabriel asked.

Parnell shrugged. "That, Gabriel, depends on why your wife is really running. Like I said yesterday, she's got something she's hiding. Once the FBI has her, they'll find out everything. They won't stop until they've filled in all the blanks. That's what they do."

"So what?" Sam said. "Leena hasn't done anything wrong."

"Yes, she has," Parnell said. "Probably killed a few people, you ask me."

"Shut up, Chuck," Gabriel said.

"Then call them, Gabriel," Parnell said. "Go ahead and pull the trigger. Only, I'm telling you, I bet you don't ever see your wife again. Except maybe, through a thick glass window, on visiting day."

Gabriel and Arthur were both shaking their heads.

"Yeah, see? My feelings exactly," Parnell continued. "Plan B, then. Let me do some low-key stuff; ask my office to look for any arrests of red-headed women with a stolen motorcycle, that sort of thing. Guys in my office, they already have a warm feeling about your wife, you know. They won't mind running with this, as long as we don't ask for something that'll show up in an expense report."

"You think it'll work?" Arthur asked.

"Might," Parnell said. "Worth a try. Won't set off any alarms."

"You gotta find her, Gabriel," Samantha said. "You can't let her sit in some jail."

"Yeah," Parnell said. "Not fair to the other inmates, they don't know what they're dealing with."

"Enough of that shit, Chuck. Just talk to your friends; keep it quiet, though. No alarms, okay?"

"Sure thing, Gabriel, I'll make a call right now." He smiled, adding, "Guess I'll be staying a while. You wouldn't mind if I stayed here, in your office bedroom, would you?"

"Now you ask?" Gabriel said. "And stay away from my secretary, at least during the day. We still have work to do here."

"Yeah, about that..." Parnell said.

"Oh, here we go," Arthur said, standing to leave.

"No, really, guys. I've got some ideas about your problem here, been working on it most of the night."

"That's not what it looks like you've been working on, from what I can tell," Arthur said.

Parnell rolled his eyes. "Still can't get past the 'I know people' thing, huh, Arthur? Time to move on, partner."

Arthur turned to Gabriel. "Now he thinks he's a partner."

Helena had her head back, eyes closed. Randall gave her a glance every few minutes, sighed and shook his head.

"What?" she finally asked, not opening her eyes.

"Just wondering, is all. Is it an abusive husband or did you kill somebody?"

"Seems to me, Randall," Helena said, opening her eyes and looking at Mosgrave, "that you have a fairly ungenerous view of me, if those are the only two choices."

Mosgrave met her glance, smiled. "Irish, I love the way you talk. Still haven't answered my question, though."

"For your information, Mr. Mosgrave, I am happily married to the greatest man on earth. In fact, three days ago was the first time I left his side since the day I met him, four years ago."

Randall checked his mirrors, looked at her again, this time without the smile. "Killed somebody, then."

"Randall," Helena said, "I'm afraid you have a rather unperceptive attitude on the subject of women."

"Oh, I'm plenty perceptive, Irish," Randall replied. "You don't get married six times without gaining some perception on the subject."

"Six times? You're not wearing a ring," Helena asked.

Randall shook his head. "Neither are you, sugar. Kind of between marriages, right now, you could say."

Helena laughed. "Not a man who is easily dissuaded, are you Randall?"

Mosgrave shook his head again. "No, Irish, not at all. Loved all my wives, in their time. I pray to God every day to send me another."

Helena was less sanguine. "I knew a priest," she said soberly, "that claimed that more tears were shed for prayers answered than those that were never fulfilled."

Randall nodded, thoughtfully. "He sounds like a wise man, your priest."

"He was the man I killed."

CHAPTER 16

Arthur and Sam left for home. Parnell made his phone call and now sat with Gabriel in the lab. There were no subjects today, just the two of them in the control room. Parnell had already set up a recording from a recent examination, having been experimenting the night before with an idea he had.

Parnell sat at the console, demonstrating. "Here's one of your recent subjects. You labeled this 'Dissembling on the Reasons He Left His Wife'. I don't know where you get this stuff, Gabriel."

"His idea. I asked him to speak on a topic with which he could comfortably lie. Pleasant enough guy; not very monogamous, though. You want a different recording, this thing is a mess. I remember him."

"You're not kidding, it's a mess. Here." Parnell started the playback. Multicolored tracings began to crisscross the monitors as the subject's narration filled the small control room. "Right here, not even thirty seconds in—" He pointed to the screen.

"Yes, Chuck, I know. It's the same problem I showed you yesterday. Anybody of any intelligence who's not concentrating on exactly what they're saying, the waveforms become impossible to follow. Can't analyze a thing starting right there."

"Right," Parnell agreed. "But look. Here's the tracing of him speaking, the top layer, the thinking behind the verbalization."

"Yeah," Gabriel agreed. "That's the easy one, like I said. We can use that for universal translation, that's about it. It's the more fundamental—"

"Yeah, just watch for a second, Gabriel." Parnell clicked the controller and the subject's narration cut off, along with the top yellow waveform. "There, I just cut out that channel, okay?" He looked at Gabriel, who nodded in the sudden silence. Parnell spun in the chair and switched on the stereo system that Arthur, unbidden, had put in almost every room of the building. Gabriel had never even turned the thing on.

"Please, spare me any more Wagner, Chuck. Not in the mood."

"Quiet, philistine. Listen. This took most of the night."

"Not the entire night." Gabriel smiled at him.

"Let it go, Gabriel. Most of the night. I had to find some patch cables," here he indicated some wires strung around the consoles that Gabriel hadn't previously noticed, "that I took from another lab. I probably screwed up somebody's experiment but good."

"Great," Gabriel replied. "I'm surprised I haven't heard about that already."

Parnell swung back to the main console and began activating several controllers. One of tracings on the monitor became brighter as the sound of a violin began to swell.

"That," said Parnell, pointing at the brightened tracing, "is a second level waveform, something to do with his thought process, maybe the lying part."

"Maybe not," Gabriel retorted. "Maybe that's the one where he's thinking about scratching his balls."

"Could be, could be. Doesn't matter."

"Yes, it matters. That's the point, Chuck. Since I don't know which waveform represents which thought process, I can't keep them straight. Even when you eliminate the top layer, the rest begin to merge and cross to the point they can't possibly be kept separate long enough to analyze." Gabriel started to rise from his chair.

"No, sit down, Gabriel. You're not listening." Parnell paused. He said nothing.

"Fine," Gabriel answered after a moment. "I'm listening. You're not talking."

"Not to me, Gabriel. Listen to the violin." Gabriel listened, heard the sound of the violin rise and fall in pitch. It was atonal, not a melody.

"Got it. I see what you're doing. The violin pitch follows the amplitude of the second level tracing. I can't dance to it." Gabriel shook his head.

"No, but you can follow it. Now listen." Parnell quickly snapped and slid controllers across the console. With each of his actions, another instrument was added and another of the waveforms brightened. "You see? Each waveform has its own unique voice. Just like the top level, but instead of words, I give each level an instrumental voice. You can follow the pitch of the instrument to follow the waveform. It's a freaking symphony, Gabriel! I can follow the entire thing, down to eight or nine levels." He smiled at Gabriel as the sounds of more and more instruments filled the little space.

"Symphony? More 'The Clash' than 'LA Phil', don't you think?"

The two men sat in the control room, listening to the strange atonal music of the inveterate philanderer's mind. As they listened, a widening grin overtook each of them.

Helena let her last statement sink in for a few minutes. "How about you let me drive, Randall?"

Mosgrave gave a start, then forced a laugh, shaking his head. "Are you crazy, girl? You can't drive this rig."

"Why not? I'm a great driver. I used to race, you know."

"Not eighteen wheelers, you didn't. This isn't a motorcycle, sugar."

"Doesn't seem too hard. You could teach me."

"Now why would I want to do that, Irish?"

"Might be fun."

"Watching us go into the ditch while you had another seizure? That doesn't sound like much fun to me." Randall thought that settled it, shook his head slowly. "Obviously, Irish, you are not a god fearing person."

"I'm not going to have any more seizures, if that's what you're worrying about," Helena said.

"Oh, yeah? How do you know that?"

"I can tell. I made a mistake last night, that's why it happened. I hadn't had one for over ten years."

"Yeah, well, letting you drive this rig would be another mistake, let me tell you."

They pulled into a rest stop for lunch an hour later. As they pulled out into traffic, Helena was driving.

"Where'd you learn to double clutch like that, girl?" Randall asked from the passenger seat.

"Been driving too fast my whole life, Randall," she smiled back, not taking her eyes from the road. Her brow was furrowed in concentration as she worked steadily through the gears and checked the big mirrors, working on bringing the rig up to speed as she merged with the highway traffic. At Helena's insistence, Mosgrave had spent the entire rest stop explaining how to drive the truck over lunch. Helena hadn't let the conversation drift anywhere else.

Randall kept checking his mirror as well. "Well, this run's cost old Randall enough already, Irish. Keep it at fifty-five or I'll have to demonstrate the secret emergency ejection seat thing."

Helena nodded, still concentrating but now unable to stop smiling, settling into the rhythm of the powerful machine. She relaxed a little as she got the knack of alternating power with the changes in the terrain.

"That a girl, Irish," Randall said, approvingly. "It's all about maintaining momentum, keeping it rolling. Keep your distance. Don't touch those brakes, girl. Every time you touch those brakes, you're costing me money." Helena swore as a Corvette cut close in front of her, requiring her to back off the throttle and lose speed on a gentle uphill grade.

"Where's the fuckin' air horn, Randall? I wanta blast this asshole."

Mosgrave just laughed. "It don't help, sugar. He'll still be an asshole. It's the assholes that make the driving interesting, that's all. Try not to kill anyone."

An awkward silence ensued. Finally, Randall said softly, "Sorry, Irish. Didn't mean it that way." But the awkward silence returned.

Helena settled into her driving. Almost an hour passed without a word between them. Randall pretended to sleep but kept checking the outside mirror through half-closed eyes.

"My sister and I never knew our parents, Randall, neither one of them," Helena said softly, still looking straight ahead at the traffic. The sun was starting to set behind them. Randall opened his eyes, watching her. "I have no memory of them. We were raised in orphanages, one orphanage after another. They'd move us every two or three years, never told us why. They always kept us together, though.

"When I was twelve, me and my baby sister, we were moved to an orphanage run by the Sisters of Mercy, in Dublin. Ever hear of 'em?" Randall was watching her closely, just shook his head silently. "Just as well. Some of the sisters were nice. Most weren't. The sisters weren't the real problem, though.

"Every Thursday evening, the priest of the diocese that ran the orphanage would come to say mass for us. There was a chapel in the convent, same building as the orphanage. All the children, there were over fifty of us, had to attend. I was one of the oldest there. That's probably why he picked me, I guess. My luck, I probably had the only straight priest in Dublin.

"I don't think three weeks passed before that priest decided I needed special, private sessions. Every week, every Thursday, he'd say mass and then have the sisters collect me for my special sessions with that fat, drunken bastard. He was an evil creature, Randall."

Helena was silent for a few minutes, watching the traffic. Randall checked the mirrors with her, turned back to watch her again. She seemed calm to him, serene. Her voice was soft. The twilight was deepening behind them.

"After three months of being raped nearly every week, I'd had about enough of that shit. So the next time he had me alone, I told him we were done. Told him if he touched me again I was going to tell the sisters. I told him I didn't care what he did to me. He didn't really care about the sisters, but he didn't like being threatened, I'll tell you."

"Did you tell them?" Randall asked, softly.

Helena shook her head, still staring straight ahead, concentrating. "Never really had the chance. Don't think it would've made a difference, anyway. Can't believe they thought for a second anything else was going on in there.

"He knocked me around some, more than usual. Threatened me. He was a big man. So I bit him. I bit off his finger. Index finger of his right hand, bit it clean off. Screamed like a motherfucker, I'll tell you."

"You didn't!" Randall exclaimed softly. "Good for you, Irish."

"No, Randall. It wasn't good for me. I thought it was. Rat bastard didn't show up for almost two months. Never heard anything, was feeling pretty proud of myself. Stupid twelve year old girl, thought I bested the bastard."

Helena was quiet for a bit. It was growing dark in the truck. Randall could see her expression intermittently, from headlights streaming through the broken windshield. "What happened, Irish? What did they do to you?"

"To me? Nothing. One Thursday, though, the old bastard finally shows up again, missing a finger; says his mass. Never even looks at me. After mass, he walks right by me and takes my sister by the hand, walks her right past me to his study."

"That bastard."

"That's right, Randall. She was my baby sister." Helena paused. "When she came back up to the dorm that night, I promised her that I would never let that happen again. I promised to hide her. So we prayed hard, Randall. We'd put our heads together and pray, prayed so hard that an angel would come down and carry us away, fly us away from that place. Every night we prayed for that.

"But Thursday came again and there wasn't any angel, Randall. Just that fucking molesting bastard of a priest. Well, before we had to go down to mass, I hid my baby sister. Like I promised. You know where I hid her? I hid her on the ledge outside the window of the dormitory, just until we all had to go down to mass. I left the window open a little so she could get back in, while we were in mass. It was winter, it was pretty cold. I didn't want my baby sister to catch cold. I just wanted to hide her. So we told Sister that she was sick and wasn't coming to mass. But the bastard, he was looking especially for her. And when he didn't see her, when Sister told him she was sick in the dormitory, he and Sister went upstairs looking for her. He was a determined old bastard, Randall.

"I don't know if one of the other kids ratted her out. Every kid knew where I had put her. Kids will do that, too. They're as nasty and evil as any adult, I'll tell you. I don't know how he knew. Maybe he just noticed the window was unlocked. So he locked it. He locked my baby sister out on that ledge, where I had put her. In the middle of winter.

"The priest said an extra long mass that evening. I still remember his drunken sermon, rambling on and on, about sin this and sin that, and the sin of pride and the sin of not obeying. We all heard the pounding. After a bit it was so loud, the pounding on the window from upstairs, that even the sisters couldn't pretend not to hear. But he wouldn't let them go. He kept them all there, all of us listening to the pounding. I thought I could hear her, hear my sister's voice calling my name, crying out in Irish for me to come and unlock the window so she could come back in. It was really cold, that night. I probably was imagining that, her voice. But we all heard the scream. We all heard her scream, and then the sound of her hitting the stones, right outside the chapel. Right outside where I knelt, praying the whole time for an angel to come carry her, carry her off that ledge.

"He couldn't keep them in then, of course. They all ran out to see, to see my baby sister. I couldn't move. I just stayed there, kneeling. I kept praying that maybe, at that last second, that angel had taken her."

It was dark now, but Randall could see from the light of reflected headlights that Helena's cheeks were wet with tears. He didn't have any words for this, just shook his head.

"And do you know what Father Donovan did then, Randall? The good Father, he came down from the altar, he comes down to where I'm kneeling there, the only one left in the pews. Father Donovan bends down to me, puts his hand so gently on my shoulder, puts his mouth close to my ear. I can still smell his stinking drunken breath, feel it on my neck.

"And Father Donovan whispers real softly to me, 'On your hands, child, on your hands'. That's what he said to me, before going out to my baby sister, to give her last rites."

Gabriel returned to his office the next day to find Parnell sitting at his desk, working on his computer. They greeted each other, Gabriel handing the other a hot cup of coffee.

"Anything?" Gabriel asked, gesturing to the computer screen.

"A lot of nothing. And I mean a lot. I sorted through several hundred partial hits, all zip. First pass, a bust," Parnell said, leaning back in the chair.

"So what now? What do you think?"

"Not good, Gabriel. Not excited by the odds, to tell you the truth. If your wife was saying what we thought she was saying, all the pieces should have been in place by now, it should've popped. You might want to think about the other approach."

"What, call the FBI?" Parnell nodded. Gabriel shook his head. "No, I'm not going to put my wife in that situation. Too risky."

"You sound like her. You don't even know what the risk is."

They were both quiet, looking at something meaningless on the computer.

Gabriel said, finally, "You're right. I don't. But I'm still not going to do it. I'm going to wait another couple of days. You'll keep trying, right?"

Parnell shrugged, nodded. "Sure, no sweat. But I'm not holding my breath."

"Come on, Chuck," Gabriel said, heading back to the lab. "I want to try something. Something I was thinking about after I left last night."

They sat down at the console. The recording from the night before was still set up. Gabriel started the recording from the beginning, set all the instrument voices to play at once, though he kept the speech track muted. He turned up the volume and the strange, atonal music filled the lab. They both sat and listened. It was, for the most part, dissimilar to anything either had ever heard before. The great majority of the recording sounded discordant, but for periods of time, some brief but others lasting for a minute or two, there was a vague musicality to the strange sound. After ten minutes, Gabriel stopped the recording and began it again from the beginning. He repeated this process two more times, each time the two men listening in silence as they watched the multicolored waveforms dance over the multiple monitors in the darkened laboratory.

Gabriel stopped the playback and looked at Parnell. "There's something there, I can feel it. But I'm not musical enough, I guess. I can't put my finger on it."

"I can," Parnell said. "I'm sure I'm hearing patterns, several themes recurring. Do you play an instrument?"

Gabriel shook his head. "Never learned. Not in the genes, I'm afraid. We need Helena here, she's fairly musical."

Parnell was mildly offended. "Well, I'm more than fairly musical, Gabriel. And I'm telling you that there are definite motifs and themes that recur in that recording. I don't know how to describe them to you, but I can point them out." Parnell restarted the recording, decreased the volume so he could be heard. "Here," he said, stopping and restarting the recording several times to replay a passage that lasted about ten seconds. "Hear that?" Gabriel nodded. "Now listen for that as I play the rest of the recording."

Parnell let the recording run, turned the volume back up. Each time the passage recurred, Parnell said 'here', and 'here'. Gabriel nodded, hearing the pattern clearly now and pointing at the monitor each time it recurred. He nodded, smiled.

"Now all we have to do," Gabriel said, "is figure out what that pattern represents."

"Shouldn't be too hard, now that we know what to look for. We'll listen to dialogue simultaneously and, if that isn't enough, we can have the subject sit in and tell us what was going through their head at that moment. Kind of."

Gabriel said, shaking his head, "I don't think that'll work, though we can try it. Most people don't know what they're thinking, especially after the fact. It's like a Heisenberg Uncertainty Principle of the Mind: if you think about what you're thinking, you don't know what you're thinking about, you know? But that's another problem, for down the road. First, I want to know if that passage exists only for this individual recording or is it more general? Does it recur if we reexamine this individual, thinking about a totally different subject, or the same subject on a different day, or in a different mood? Is it generalizable between people? Do all people think like this or does everyone have their own crazy mental music?" He shook his head again.

"Sounds like a project. It's doable. We just need the data," Parnell said, muting the sound but watching the screens.

Gabriel said, "We have the data. I have hundreds of recordings like this. We need a better system, though. We can't sit through thousands of hours of recordings and try to listen for patterns. Even if you are musical."

Parnell thought silently for a few minutes. "We can do this. I think there's some signals processing algorithms that NSA has, used to analyze voice print data. It identifies patterns, something like this. Let me work on this a bit."

"Go to it, Sherlock." Gabriel left for his office, leaving Parnell bent over the console.

Randall turned to stare ahead, out the broken windshield. It was getting late, and they were approaching the outskirts of Boston.

"There's a nice place to stop in a couple of miles, good place for dinner," Randall said, softly. "Not too hard for you to get in. We'll take a break, next exit after this one. Okay, sugar?" Helena just nodded, kept her eyes on the road. "Do you still think about her, your sister?" Randall asked.

Helena nodded. "All the time. She doesn't talk to me anymore, though."

"You mean she used to, after she died?"

"Every day. All the time, for a while. After I left the orphanage. When they sent me to hospital."

"You were in the hospital? Is that when she talked to you, sugar?"

Helena nodded again, smiled at him.

"I miss talking to her."

"They thought you were crazy, huh? Talking to your dead sister?"

"Didn't help, that's for sure. Doctors were all over the 'hearing voices' thing. I told them I only heard one voice, my sister's. They thought that was enough. I think they put me in there before any of that, though. To tell you the truth, I don't remember most of it."

"So when did you stop hearing her voice?"

"Long time ago, years ago. The treatments stopped it. That's what they were for, I guess. Cured, and out on the street."

"And your seizures? Did they cure those, too?"

"I think they caused them. I never had a seizure before they started the treatments. But, yeah, they stopped, too. With her voice."

"Until a couple of nights ago." He looked at Helena inquiringly.

"I'm not hearing her, if that's what you're asking."

Randall smiled, relaxing in the seat. "Just checking, sugar. You are driving my truck, you know."

Helena and her new friend sat quietly across from each other, tentatively eating huge plates of pasta. They each had a beer in front of them, untouched.

Randall put his fork down, looking at Helena with new eyes. Now, he saw, she wasn't just a runaway, not some con or sharpie. Sharp enough, certainly, and with a certain mastery, a certain set of skills, no doubt. But now he could see the hurt and brokenness that sat at the other side of the table. She looked up from her plate, forcing a smile.

"I'm not buying, if that's what you're thinking," she said.

"No. I'm wondering how you killed him."

She looked at him quizzically. "Why?"

"Don't see a little twelve year old girl killing a man, I guess."

Helena sighed, putting down her fork. She took a sip of her beer and looked at Randall.

"He presided at my sister's funeral. Stared at me the whole time, spoke like I was the only one in the place, the whole time. 'Pride leads to the fall,' you know? He was real big on that one. The next week, he came back that Thursday like nothing had happened."

"No way. He must have known how much you hated him, must've known what you'd try to do," Randall said, unbelieving.

Helena nodded. "He knew. I made quite a sight, I'm sure. Everyone knew. That was the problem for him, I think. He couldn't stay away, because of me. He had to make me submit, get everyone to see me accept his authority. Big time priest needed that. Instead, everyone could see I hated him worse than ever; I think he had to finish it. That's what I think, anyway."

She took another drink, looked back into Randall's eyes. "That night, he beat me up double, just to prove the point. Before starting in on the usual, that is. I just took it. Waiting. Because I knew, eventually, he would be ready. And when he was, when he was on top of me and good and distracted, I shoved a sharpened length of coat hanger up under his breastbone. Shoved it in that far, at least," she said, holding her hands almost a foot apart.

Randall watched her. She was unemotional now, telling a story that might have happened to someone else. Just a story.

"He just stopped what he was doing. His eyes got big and he looked me in the eye, surprised. 'Child,' he said, all bug eyed, 'you have killed me'. The only thing that bastard ever said that gave me any satisfaction." She picked up her fork again.

"But what happened, then? They must've all known what you'd done, sugar."

Helena started back on her pasta, shaking her head. "I don't know what they thought. It was a scene, I'll tell you. I was screaming at the top of my lungs for the longest time, no one would come in. I just lay there naked under him, screaming. I shoved the wire into the mattress, all the way in so it'd disappear. Sisters wouldn't come in. They had heard girls screaming from the priest's study before I suppose, but I wouldn't stop, so they had to come, eventually."

"They must have known, Irish. The priest dead, the blood and all."

Helena shook her head. "I don't really know, Randall. There was blood all right, but not as much as you would think. And it was mostly on me. They might've thought it was mine. The sisters were kind of distracted, you know, seeing the Father with his pants around his ankles, lying on top of a screaming, bloody, naked girl, you know? It was upsetting for them."

Randall pushed his plate away. He waited for Helena to finish.

"The next day," Helena continued, "they came for me. Just me and the clothes on my back. No more orphanages, no more Sisters of Mercy."

"They just threw you out?"

"Not out. Threw me away, though, for four years. Four years institutionalized at the Central Mental Hospital."

Randall shook his head. He pulled out a twenty and laid it on the table, over the check. "Time to roll, Irish." Helena nodded, stood. "What's the plan, sugar?" Randall asked.

"Me? You can drop me anywhere, Randall."

"Yeah, I know I can drop you anywhere, Irish. I wouldn't feel right about dropping you just anywhere, though. I'm heading over to Cambridge, but I can drop you wherever you like."

Helena shook her head. "Randall, you've been a good friend. And a good listener. Thank you." She stretched on tiptoe and gave him a kiss on the cheek.

"Right here, then, sugar? This is it?" Randall asked. She nodded. "Okay, then, that's what you want. I'll help you get your bike down. And you better take some of your money back, just so you don't have to roll anyone before morning."

"Thanks, Randall. I'll take your help with the bike, but keep your money. I have enough stashed on the bike, unless they stole it at impound. I need one more favor from you, though."

"Anything, Irish. As long as you'll do something for me."

"Who first, then?" Randall gave her a nod. "Fine. Call this number for me, tomorrow, okay?" Helena scribbled a telephone number on a corner of the check, tore it off and gave it to him. "Not from your cell, though. You'll want to use a pay phone, if you can find one. Try to put all this behind you, that way." He nodded. "Ask for Arthur. The secretary won't put you through, she never does. Just tell her you'd like to leave a message for Arthur."

"What's the message, Irish?"

"You just wanted to let him know that you had breakfast with a mutual friend, in that Irish bar in Boston. Okay, Randall? You do that for your friend?" She held his hands, looking up at him like a child.

Randall nodded. "No problem, sugar. Seems kind of vague, though. Won't use the cellphone, like you said."

"Now, what can I do for my friend, Randall?"

"Just want to know your name, that's all, sugar."

"You're going to make me cry, Randall." She gave him another kiss on the cheek. "Thank you, Randall. You are a good, good man."

"Good luck to you, Irish."

"My name is Fiona."

"Good luck to you then, Fiona. Godspeed."

"*Slán agus beannacht leat.*"
"What's that you said?"
"It's Irish, Randall. 'Good bye and blessings with you.'"
"You too, child. You too."

CHAPTER 17

Randall helped Helena get her motorcycle off the big truck. He waited as she went back inside and changed into her riding leathers. She threw out all the clothes and supplies Randall had gotten her, not out of meanness, but simply because she had nowhere to stash them. He pretended not to notice as she came out, looking like her usual cocky self again. She checked that her emergency stash was still taped to the underside of the bike's seat. Randall insisted she take the scrap of paper on which he had scribbled his cell phone number, made sure she tucked it into the pocket of her suit. Helena gave her friend a fierce hug and climbed on her bike, donning her helmet. She gave a wave without looking back. Randall waved back and watched as she tore off, too fast, towards Boston in the dark. Shaking his head, he climbed back into his cab and slowly followed in her wake. He didn't expect to ever see his new friend again.

Helena decided to stay off the expressway this time, afraid of possibly inducing another seizure. She didn't think she was in any danger if she stuck to regular roads. She was close enough to the city that she could make her way by dead reckoning, and she'd make her destination in plenty of time either way. The night was warm and dry and, though she missed the company of her new friend, she enjoyed the ride.

In just over two hours, Helena could see the lights of downtown Boston. She easily picked out the Prudential Tower from the skyline ahead and pointed her motorcycle in that direction. It had been over ten years since she last was in this town, but she expected to be welcome. Hopefully, she thought as she drove through the dark suburbs towards the city center, her friends hadn't sold the bar on Boylston.

Helena parked her bike in the alley behind the bar, pulled off her helmet and stashed it behind the seat. The back door was unlocked and she walked up the narrow back hallway of the bar, listening to the familiar noises of the kitchen as she made her way to the front.

Helena emerged into the busy, noisy bar. A fair crowd for a Thursday night, she thought as she surveyed the room. She was looking for familiar faces, but saw none.

Helena climbed up on one of the less occupied tables, ignoring the protests of the young couple grabbing for their drinks. "If this is a fucking Irish bar," she yelled as loud as she could over the din, hands on hips, "where are all the fucking Irishmen?"

Silence rolled like a wave around the bar as the other patrons turned to look at her. A couple of the more obviously drunken souls started to redden and looked like they were thinking of something witty in response, albeit slowly. Helena was beginning to think that her introduction might be ill suited if her friends no longer owned this establishment. With relief, she caught sight of the bartender at the other end of the room, looking at her with a grin.

"Holy mother of god, look who walked into my bar!" exclaimed the bartender, putting down the mug he was dry washing and coming around the bar to stand below her. "Thought you was dead!" He beamed up at her as the crowd watched.

"Not yet, Billy." With that she jumped off the table and let him catch her.

Helena gave him a kiss and stood back to look at him. "There was a time, Mr. McDougall," she said to him with a lilting brogue, "that you would've jumped over that bar to catch me." Billy McDougall, thirty years old and wearing a bartender's apron, shook his head.

"Too old now, Fiona. You're lucky I didn't drop you, just now." He smiled broadly. "Thought you was dead, really. Good to see you, girl."

"Good to be seen, Billy. How's Ma and Da, and your handsomer brother?"

Billy jabbed a thumb towards the kitchen. "You must've walked right past them. Same as ever, just older. Sean's as fat and stupid as ever."

"Yeah, you were always the skinny one, Billy. Go back to tending your bar and I'll see you later. I'll go say hello to the family. Is Kate still around?"

"She better be," Billy answered, "I married her two years ago." He gave Helena a wink.

"She married you, Billy? Well, congratulations on marrying so far above yourself, then. Good for you. Of course, if it's lasted two years already, she must have someone on the side, let's her put up with you." Billy feigned to hit her; Helena hit him for real in the shoulder. He went back to his bar, shaking his head and rubbing his shoulder. Helena went back to the kitchen, to be greeted with hugs and kisses from all those she hadn't seen in so long.

Hours later, Helena was helping clean up after closing. She put the mop back in the closet as she'd done years ago, sat down at a table to a waiting beer with the barkeep and the McDougall family.

Billy kept shaking his head. "Thought you was dead, Fiona," he said again.

"That's why he married me," Kate said, sitting back with an arm around her husband.

Helena smiled at them. "Why do you keep saying that, Billy?" she asked.

That was met with general incredulity from the extended family. "Cause you disappeared without a word, girl, for one thing," the elder McDougall said, draining half his pint. "And for another," he continued, "cause there were about half a dozen guys wanted you dead by the time you left. That's why."

Helena smiled as she shook her head at him. "Can't love 'em all, you know, Da. Certainly not when your handsome son here was around."

"It's not the boyfriends I'm talking about, Fiona, and you know it. It's been quite a while, I know, but there's some around that will be just as surprised as Billy here to see you, and just as surprised that you're not dead. Less happy about it, too." He spun the glass, looked at her red-faced. The others nodded, looking into their glasses.

"I don't know what kind of stories you guys have been dreaming up since I left. Trying to scare me into the bosom of another bar, that's what I think." Helena finished her beer and thwacked it onto the table. "I don't plan on being in town long enough to see all my old friends, anyway."

"Oh, the really important ones will know you're back by morning. Count on it, girl," McDougall said. "But if you're planning on lying low, you're welcome to stay upstairs, if you want."

She nodded, eyes twinkling. "I was hoping to stay with Billy, but I'll settle for my old place, Da. With pleasure." She gave Billy a wink, causing him to blush monstrously. Kate gave him a look that portended explanations later.

"I'm telling you," Parnell was insisting to Gabriel, back in the lab again, "you can listen in if you want, but it's not necessary. The whole process can be automated, I'm sure of it. I'll have a test program ready in a day."

Gabriel watched the monitors as Parnell's voice recognition software ran through a subject recording. Small samples of the colored tracings were highlighted, several every minute. He turned up the sound and listened to the instrumental nonmusic rise and fall in concert with the waveforms on the screen.

"I agree this will help," Gabriel responded, still watching and listening to the analysis. "But I can't believe this is going to go the whole mile, you know. It'll show us the patterns to look for, but I don't think it will take us to meanings, not to that level."

Parnell turned the volume back down. "It will, because you can integrate your dictionary into the algorithm. It may not be a final product, I'm sure there'll be a lot of nuance that we'll miss initially. But with repeated passes, this will keep getting more and more refined. It's just a matter of brute force and time. I bet we have full interpretative capability in a couple of months, if you put the resources into it."

Gabriel turned the volume back up and listened for a few more minutes. "Resources won't be the limiting factor. I'm pretty convinced we're seeing a generalizable, reproducible language. It stands up between sessions and between individuals. That doesn't mean, though, that it isn't much more subtle than we realize. It could go much deeper than we've been able to study."

Parnell snapped a switch, turning off the sound entirely. "When did you get to be so pessimistic, Gabriel? This is exactly what you've been working towards. Now that you have the tools to deliver it, you're getting cold feet? Why?"

Gabriel opened his mouth to answer when the door opened and Arthur stood, silhouetted in the bright light behind.

"Helena—" Arthur began.

"Still no word," Gabriel said, squinting in the glare. "Chuck just checked his office." Parnell nodded.

"Well, I think I found her."

"What? How?" Gabriel asked, rising from his chair. The three moved into his office.

"I just got off the phone with a trucker in Boston, guy by the name of Randall Mosgrave. He called the office twenty minutes ago, wouldn't let my secretary blow him off, insisted on being put through to me. He says he gave a ride to a good friend of mine, redheaded Irish girl named Fiona. He was told to tell me that he had breakfast with her in an Irish bar in Boston. He says, though, that they actually parted ways just outside of Boston." Arthur dropped into a chair.

Gabriel remained standing. "Yeah, and what else? What did he say about Helena?"

Arthur shrugged. "That's it, the whole thing. Never said anything about Helena, called her Fiona."

"Not surprised," Parnell said. "Who the hell knows what her name is."

"He must've said something else, Arthur. What else did he say?" Gabriel implored.

"Just that I should come and get here quick as I can. That she's a very troubled young lady, and needs to be home."

"What did he mean?" Gabriel asked.

"I don't know, Gabe," Arthur answered. "But I think we need to go to Boston and find her."

They were in Boston, the three of them, less than twelve hours later. That was the easy part. They sat in their hotel room, wondering how they were going to find Helena.

"How many Irish bars serve breakfast?" Gabriel asked the other two.

"Depends on what you mean by breakfast," Parnell answered.

"Food."

Parnell shrugged. "Not that many, I imagine. If we split up, we can probably do a pretty good job covering the downtown pubs in the morning. Let's get a list together and divvy it up."

The next morning, they each headed to a separate neighborhood downtown to canvass the breakfast serving Irish bars. Parnell walked into his second bar, a wood lined taproom with booths and a pool table in the back, past the large, ornate bar. He immediately saw the unmistakable back of Helena's head seated in a booth at the back of the restaurant. She was seated across from two men in black leather jackets. Parnell stopped and watched from the door. Neither man looked particularly friendly or pleased, one obviously speaking in a very animated fashion, though Parnell couldn't hear what was being said from his vantage point.

A large man in a bartender's apron came around the end of the bar to greet Parnell.

"Morning. Just the one of you, then?" the man inquired.

Parnell stood quietly for a moment. He gestured toward the back of the bar. "I'm a friend of the lady, there."

The bartender didn't turn around at the gesture, just eyed Parnell suspiciously. "If you know Fiona, then you wouldn't call her that. And if you're a friend of hers, I'd turn and leave before those two blokes she's with see you. Just a suggestion."

Parnell nodded, pulling out his cellphone from his pocket and speed dialing Gabriel. "Found her. 'Killian's', on Boylston. You might want to get Arthur and get here pretty quick. And bring a baseball bat." He hung up and turned back to the heavyset bartender who had been patiently listening.

The bartender looked Parnell up and down. "Don't think the bat's gonna help, lad. Best to come back a little later. Most likely, Fiona'll still be alive. Not for certain, though."

"You really think they'll hurt her?"

The bartender nodded. "Oh, yeah. If they don't kill her first. But probably not for a while yet. There's a lot of talking to do first."

"What do they want?" Parnell kept watching, could almost make out what the one guy was yelling.

"What does everyone want? Money. A whole lot of money, from what I gather."

"Why? What does Hel— Fiona have? Who are they?"

The other man just shook his head and started back to his bar. "If you don't know, then you're probably no friend of Fiona's. Best to come back later."

Parnell put his hand on the man's broad shoulder. "Do me a favor. When my friends come in, stop them at the door. They're going to want to join us, but that doesn't look like a good idea. Keep them here at the bar, okay?" The bartender just shrugged and moved off behind his counter.

Parnell took a deep breath and slowly walked to the back of the bar. He slid into the booth next to Helena. The two men across the table, faces reddened from yelling, looked at him sharply.

"Who the fuck are you?" the older man asked.

Parnell slid his business card across the table to the man who had spoken, ignoring the other man. He placed his palms flat on the table.

"Gentlemen," Parnell said amiably. He smiled. "Good morning to you both. My name is Parnell and I'm from the government. The National Security Agency." Helena and the other two were watching him intently, waiting for him to go on. "Fiona, here," he continued, nodding to Helena next to him, "is the subject of an active federal investigation." He waited for this to sink in. The others said nothing. "As the subject of a federal investigation, we have been closely monitoring her activities. And from what I've been listening to from the van outside, I'd advise you to end this conversation. Now."

The two men didn't move, but the older man looked at the card on the table. He leaned over to Helena. "You know where to find me, love.

Don't make me wait too long." He stared at Parnell for a minute. "You don't look like you're with the feds."

"Oh, I am. And so are the guys outside. Just a word of advice, gentlemen: I'd keep my face down as you leave the building. Makes it harder for the photographer in the truck." He smiled at them. They slid out of the booth and left the bar, almost running into Gabriel and Arthur on their way out.

Helena turned to Parnell. "You must be Chuck. Nice to meet you." She shook his hand, picked his card up off the table and looked it over. Gabriel came over and pulled Parnell bodily out of the booth by his shirt. He gave his wife a kiss and a hug.

"Missed you," he said, smiling at her. She smiled back at him. Arthur and Parnell slid into the booth across from them.

"Who the hell were those guys?" Arthur asked.

"Them? Just some old business partners."

"Well, that's a relief," Gabriel said. "I was afraid they were more of your old boyfriends."

The bartender came up, wiping his hands on a small towel at his waist. Helena brightened further, introducing them.

"Hey, Da! Meet my husband, Gabriel. Gabriel, this is my Da." Gabriel shook the large man's hand, though the bartender was obviously shocked.

He recovered himself and asked Helena, "You're married?" Helena nodded, smiling like a little kid. The older man looked at Gabriel, unbelieving. "You married her?" Gabriel nodded, also smiling. "You're an idiot," the man said, turning and walking back to the bar, shaking his head and muttering something unintelligible.

They all looked at Helena questioningly. "He's just surprised," she told them, looking about sheepishly.

"'Surprised' doesn't sound like it quite catches it," Parnell said.

"How about some breakfast?" Helena said. She left for the kitchen. In her absence, Parnell described his impression of Helena's business associates. Unfortunately, he hadn't dared take their picture with his phone before approaching them and didn't have enough information to start any type of inquiry. He did manage to convey his apprehension regarding the possibility of violent death in the immediate future. By this time,

Helena returned wearing an apron and expertly balancing a large tray of food. She served up four breakfasts and mugs of coffee, and then slid back into the booth next to Gabriel.

Arthur stared at the plate in front of him. "Okay, I'll ask. What is it?"

"Breakfast, Arthur," Helena replied, starting in on corned beef hash, sausages, and scrambled eggs.

"Doesn't look kosher," he responded, dubiously.

"I'm pretty sure blood sausage is kosher," Helena replied.

"That's just a name, right? Not a literal description?" Arthur asked, stabbing at the sausage.

"Right," Helena said between mouthfuls, "kind of a metaphor. It won't kill you, Arthur. Don't insult me." They all ate.

"Speaking of killing people," Parnell said as he ate, "how long till your business associates return, you think?"

Helena shrugged, took a sip of coffee. "Couple of hours, I guess. As soon as they figure out you're not really NSA—"

"I really am NSA." Parnell looked hurt, as usual.

"Seriously? With the pony tail and all?" He nodded. "Well, as soon as they figure out you were bullshitting about me being the subject of a federal investigation, then—"

"You are the subject of a federal investigation."

Helena put down her fork and stared at the three of them. She began to flush with anger.

Parnell almost cowered. "But not a full fledged investigation or anything. I kept a lid on it. Ask Gabriel. Tell her Gabriel." Parnell looked about to bolt from the restaurant.

Gabriel nodded, putting his hand on his wife's arm. "Chuck's a friend, Helena. There's no investigation. He's just screwing with you. It's his own megalomaniacal delusion. We go along, so he doesn't get too sad." He finished his coffee. "Where do I get more?" Helena gestured to the kitchen and Gabriel left to get the pot.

Parnell smiled nervously at Helena, who was staring at him in a fashion he found very disturbing. She said nothing. Gabriel returned and filled everyone's mug.

"That was great," Arthur said, finishing the last bit of food from his plate and leaning back. "What was in that, really?"

"Blood," Helena said, still staring at Parnell.

Helena took Arthur and Parnell into the kitchen to clean up and help get ready for the lunch crowd. Gabriel helped at the bar.

"What should I call you?" Gabriel asked the older man, helping to stack glasses and mugs from the night before.

"Might as well call me 'Dad' like everyone else. You've got better reason than most, I guess."

"You're like Helena's foster dad, then?"

The older man shook his head, looked at Gabriel. "We know her as Fiona, you know. And no, I'm not her foster anything."

"You took care of her though? She obviously cares for you."

"More like she took care of us, at least for a bit. Before she disappeared. Fiona's family, that's all." He gave Gabriel a serious stare. "She's a good'un, Gabriel. Can't believe she got you to marry her. You need to get out of that, good and quick."

Gabriel laughed, grabbing for another mug to stack. "You're kidding, right, Dad?"

"No, I'm not. Lose her or die trying, I'd say." The big man took Gabriel's hand, looked at his ring. "She give you that?" Gabriel nodded. "You're gonna want to put that in your pocket for a while. People will get the wrong idea."

"It was yours, right?" Dad just looked at him, seeming at a loss. "What kind of idea, then?"

"People'll think you're something you're not, that's all. They'll already be thinking that, they hear you married Fiona."

"Think I'm what, then?"

"Crazy, for one thing. Fucking crazy."

Helena came out of the kitchen trailing Chuck and Arthur in aprons. "My boys," she said, giving Gabe and McDougall each a kiss on the cheek. The older man returned to the business of wiping and stacking mugs.

"So, Helena here has been telling us about the good old times in Boston, gave me a couple of names to run," Parnell said amiably to Gabriel. Helena nodded. "And I'm thinking, Gabriel, that we really should leave. Now. Not kidding."

"So he's the smart one in the group," McDougall said.

Parnell smiled at him. He offered the older man his hand. "You're right about that, sir. Nice to meet you. Chuck Parnell."

McDougall shook his hand, laughing. "Seriously? Chuck?" Parnell's smile wilted as he nodded. "The king's right, boys and girls. You should go. Been a pleasure." He gave Helena an emphatic hug. "Good to see you, girl. Stay well, okay?" Helena nodded.

"You too, Da. I'll be back. Love you lots."

"Just write or something."

The four of them went back to the hotel, Parnell checking frequently over his shoulder as they walked. As they walked, they talked about how to get back to San Francisco. Helena wanted to take the train, eliciting strenuous objections from Arthur, who pointed out that this would probably take a week. Helena again vetoed any commercial airline travel as usual, and Parnell, who thought that any flight out of Logan airport, commercial or private, might be a bad idea, supported her. None of them liked the idea of renting a car for an extended road trip. As they packed up in the hotel room and Helena relaxed on the bed, they agreed to a hybrid approach. Taxi to the Back Bay station, and then they would pick up the high-speed train to Washington. During the train ride, Arthur would arrange for a jet to pick them up at Dulles for the flight home. Parnell would take advantage of their time in DC to check in at his office.

Much to Parnell's obvious relief, the group was finally seated together across a table in first class on the high-speed train to Washington. Helena sat next to Gabriel, apparently asleep with her head on his shoulder. Arthur sat down next to Parnell, distributing bags of pretzels and cans of soda from his foray to the lounge car behind.

"How long until DC?" Chuck asked Arthur as he sat down.

"Couple of days, if we're lucky," Arthur said, shaking his head.

"No, really. This is the high-speed train, how long can it take? You can drive Boston to DC in like, what, seven or eight hours?" Parnell asked.

"Yeah, something like that. Which means we'll be lucky to be there in two or three days."

"What's the problem, Arthur? Don't like trains?" Gabriel asked.

"What's to like? They're slow. They're obsolete. We oughtta be listening to eight tracks and sipping sasparilla. We should be flying home. This sucks."

Parnell shook his head. "I don't think we would've made it out of Logan, not after what Mrs. Sheehan told us."

Arthur made a scoffing sound and settled back in his seat, closing his eyes.

"Why, Chuck?" Gabriel asked. "What did Helena tell you two, in the kitchen?"

"For one thing, the names of those jackals who were talking to her in the bar. If I had known who they are, I sure wouldn't have jumped in front of them like I did."

"Who were they?"

"Rory and Ryan Lonegan. Two brothers who run half the rackets on Boston's south side. And they were none too happy with your wife."

"What do you mean? What do they have to do with Helena?"

"Well, your wife was a little vague in her explanations. But from what I can gather, the man Helena calls her dad was in hock up to his eyeballs to those two. On top of the protection racket, liquor distribution, trash kickbacks, all the usual stuff of doing business in that neighborhood, you know? Helena shows up a few years back and proceeds to play one brother against the other somehow."

"My Helena? Mixed up with those thugs?"

Parnell nodded. "I didn't have time to get details, but the bottom line seems to be that Helena, aka Fiona, splits the brothers, gets them somehow fighting an all out turf war over the South side, with both ending up in jail doing ten to twenty. They come out missing about half a million dollars and thinking Fiona's dead. Oh, and somehow Killian's bar pays off its mortgage that year." Parnell glanced down at Helena and saw her smiling as she napped on Gabriel's shoulder. "Seems like a stupid place to visit, you ask me," he added in Helena's direction.

Helena snuggled closer to Gabriel's chest and said sleepily, with eyes still closed, "Didn't know they'd get out on good behavior. Didn't really call ahead."

Gabriel looked down at his wife and shook his head silently. "You think they were coming after us?" Gabriel asked Parnell.

Parnell shrugged. "Ask your wife. They sure didn't seem too friendly when I met them. But I doubt they'd venture outside of Boston. At least, I hope not."

Gabriel stared at the top of Helena's head, asking finally, "Well?"

She shook her head against his chest. "I don't think those two even know there is anything outside of Boston. Now let me sleep."

They took rooms in a hotel in downtown DC several blocks from the Capitol building. Parnell immediately left to check in at his office in the NSA. Helena and Gabriel walked hand in hand down the mall towards the reflecting pool, enjoying the warmth of the spring afternoon. The cherry blossoms had already peaked, but many still clung to the trees on either side of the sparse grass. They talked of Gabriel's work since Helena had left. Gabriel tried to ask about her activities in turn, but was rebuffed with an inconsequential shrug. They sat in sunshine on the steps of the Lincoln Memorial and watched the tourists milling on the mall stretching away beneath them.

Helena laid her head on his shoulder, holding his hand in her lap.

"I don't think we should take separate vacations anymore," she said.

He smiled. "You left, not me." He gave her shoulders a hug, growing more serious. "You were right, though. I'm sorry. He wouldn't have found you except for my presentation. We're lucky it was Chuck, though."

"Are we?" she asked, looking at him.

"Yeah, I think so. He's not a bad guy. And he knows his stuff, that's for sure. I'll show you when we get back to the lab."

"He works for the fucking NSA, Gabriel."

"Yeah, that bothered me for a while, too. But I think he's okay. Are you worried?"

"Too late to worry."

"Sorry."

"You meant well. You're forgiven."

"Several ironic quotations come to mind. You're back on the radar though, Leena." She nodded, looking pained. "Is this a problem? You're not going to disappear again, are you?"

She looked at him and smiled sadly. "No," she said, "I'm not running anywhere, Gabe. You'll just have to protect me, that's all. Let's head back and see if the others want to get some dinner. I've been eating Irish food for the last two days."

Parnell had returned and was waiting with Arthur at the bar when they got back. He waved them over.

"Thought you two would be hiding under the bed, not strolling around DC," he said as they approached.

"Do I need to?" Helena asked, sitting down at their table with Gabriel.

Parnell shook his head and took a sip from his martini. "Not yet. I'll let you know when there's trouble."

"Even if the trouble is you, Chuck?" Helena asked, looking at him levelly.

"You won't have any trouble from me, Helena. The rest of the world, though, that's your problem."

"Thanks for the warning, Chuck."

"No problem." He gave her a wink. Gabriel ordered a round of beers.

"Small problem on this end, though," Arthur added. "No plane for a couple of days." They all looked at him incredulously. "What? Since when am I the logistics guy? Two days is the best I can do, Dulles to San Francisco."

"You're not getting frugal on us, are you, Arthur?" Gabriel asked.

"No, I'm not, Gabe. It's going to cost a fortune as it is. But two days is the best I can do without going commercial."

"Well, let's go to the Holocaust museum tomorrow, Gabe," Helena said.

Gabriel looked surprised. "Are you kidding? Really? Why?"

"Just want to see it. Never had the chance before."

"You still don't. You can't get tickets," Arthur said.

"Sure we can," Parnell said. "I can get you guys in tomorrow. You ever been, Gabriel?" Gabriel shook his head. "Then you have to go. It's amazing. Should be required of every citizen, my opinion."

Gabriel and Helena arrived at the museum the next day to find two VIP tickets waiting at the will call window. Helena declined the offer of a privately guided tour that Chuck had arranged with the tickets.

At first, Gabriel wasn't sure why they were there, standing in the austere lobby with its imposing gray fortress walls. Within fifteen minutes of entering the exhibit hall, holding his wife's hand, he knew. He was swept up in the terrible power of the place, almost from the instant they entered. There was little here, he thought going in, that he didn't already know. He realized as he walked the museum, however, that he knew the history, but not the story. He didn't know what it meant, didn't feel the heavy weight of its terrible importance, until he was within the museum's dark hallways. Knowing as much as he did about his wife, and just as little about her past, he was worried for her. But he immediately understood why she wanted to be here.

They walked hand in hand from room to room, moving slowly. They read everything, they stared at the exhibits. She gripped his hand tightly as they listened to the terrifying sounds of Kristallnacht, the Night of Broken Glass, all the more terrible for their veracity. As hours went by—Gabriel would not have guessed the museum to be so large, so exceptional—the imposing weight of the subject lessened. They moved more lightly, sometimes one moving ahead and the other catching up at the next exhibit. They pointed out a particularly interesting or surprising item to one another, always speaking in a hushed tone, as did everyone in the place.

They came together in the room with the shoes. Helena stood at the back of the room, staring, as Gabriel moved forward to read the plaque. Having read it, he stood and stared at the display; a mountain of shoes of all sizes, many those of children, representing a small fraction of the inventory of shoes the victims were ordered to remove just before going to their death in the murderous chambers. Gabriel felt his heart heave as he stared at this testament. Deeply moved, he finally walked on with the surging crowd, all sensing the close relief of the exit. He walked about the final room, the large, high ceilinged room of contemplation, and finally sat down to await Helena.

Helena didn't appear. He waited, looked at his watch, continued to wait. He didn't want to disturb her, knowing they would never return to this place. He was appreciative for having done it, would not have missed it; would not do this again. He looked at his watch again. This was too long, he thought, concerned now. He moved back into the hall from which he had come, excusing himself against the tide of patrons surging against him.

Gabriel came into the room with the shoes again; he saw his wife still standing immobile against the back wall. He approached her, sensing something amiss. She stood stock still, staring.

"Helena, dear," he said, gently touching her hand at her side, "we should go." She gave no response. "Helena," he repeated, but now saw that something was certainly wrong. She didn't turn to look at him, didn't acknowledge him at all. Her breathing was wrong, a staccato of inhalation, long sighing expiration, repeated. Gabriel felt panic rising in him. He shook her arm, calling her name more loudly but without response.

Others in the room had begun to notice and, when he called out in a quavering voice filled with panic, "We need some help here!" the guard and several patrons were already approaching his side. They gently lowered Helena, unresisting but unresponsive, to lie on the floor by the wall. The guard spoke into his walkie-talkie as a young woman knelt by their side.

"I'm a physician," she said brusquely, beginning to gently examine Helena. She felt her pulse, put her ear to Helena's chest and listened for a minute. "What is her name?"

"Helena. Helena Fianna. Is she okay, doctor?" Gabriel asked, feeling nauseous with fear.

"I think she'll be fine. Are you her husband?" Gabriel nodded. The doctor spoke softly into Helena's ear. "Helena, dear. It's okay, just relax and breathe deeply for me, nice and slowly." The doctor turned again to Gabriel. "Does she have a psychiatric history? Depression? Is she on medication?" Gabriel shook his head, and then remembered what Parnell had told him. Actually, he thought, she might have such a history. But no, not like this. Certainly not depressed. "No, doctor, no medication or anything. She was fine when we came in." They both turned to look at Helena as she took a deep, sighing breath.

The EMT's arrived and placed Helena on a stretcher. They placed an oxygen mask on her face and attached electrocardiographic leads. The physician stared briefly at the monitor, as a technician pronounced her blood pressure to be one twenty-six over eighty-four. The doctor nodded. "She's going to be okay, Mr. Fianna"

Gabriel started to speak, but noticed his wife's eyelids fluttering strangely as she lay on the stretcher. She appeared to be mouthing something. Gabriel put his ear close to her mouth, listening.

"Tá mé go dona, deirfiúr"

He could hear the words she was repeating softly, but could make no sense of them. She continued to repeat the same unintelligible phrase over and over. Not entirely knowing why, Gabriel took out his phone and placed it close to his wife, recording the phrase she kept muttering. After a few minutes, she became silent and her eyes fluttered open. Suddenly, Helena sat up on her elbows and looked around blankly.

"What?" Helena asked as they all stared at her. "Did I pass out or something? Did I have a seizure?"

The young physician looked closely into Helena's eyes. "You've had seizures in the past?" she asked Helena.

Helena was rapidly recovering herself. She removed the oxygen mask and started to swing her legs over the side of the stretcher in an effort to sit up. The EMT gently restrained her, pushing her shoulders back down.

"Listen, Mac," Helena said, fixing him with a glare. "I know you're trying to help. But if you touch me again, I'll put you on your ass. You hear me?"

The EMT looked at the doctor, who nodded. Helena sat up and swung her legs over the side of the stretcher. She began to remove the EKG leads.

"Have you had seizures in the past, Mrs. Fianna?" the doctor asked again.

Helena looked at her suspiciously. "Who are you?" Helena asked her.

"I'm a doctor. Your husband called for help."

"Why?" Helena asked, turning to Gabriel with an accusatory glare. Gabriel opened his mouth to answer but the physician interjected.

"Because you were completely unresponsive for several minutes. He was very concerned. We all were concerned."

"Well, thanks for your concern, all of you. Sorry to have caused any trouble. But you can see, I'm fine now." She stood, swayed unsteadily for a moment and Gabriel caught her arm. Helena gave him a weak smile.

"You really should be evaluated in the hospital, Mrs. Fianna," the physician said, as much to Gabriel as to Helena. Gabriel nodded.

"Thanks for your opinion, doctor. I'll be fine." She made to move off, but the physician and Gabriel remained unmoving in front of her.

"You didn't have a seizure, if that's what you're thinking," the physician added. "If you have had seizures before, that's not what just happened to you. I'm concerned that you may have had a mild stroke, something we call a TIA. And there are other possibilities, as well."

Gabriel had been feeling relieved at his wife's sudden recovery, but now was overwhelmed with concern again as he heard this. "Really?" he asked the doctor, "a stroke? But she's so young."

"It happens," the doctor replied.

"It didn't," Helena said, taking Gabriel's arm in hers with a purposeful step forward. "Again, doctor, my husband and I thank you for your concern. Good bye."

"At least take my card," the physician said as Helena started off, pulling Gabriel along with authority. The doctor fished a business card out of her pocket and offered it to Helena. Helena strode past her outstretched hand, but Gabriel held back long enough to thank her and take her card, which he pocketed.

Half a dozen steps down the hall, Helena muttered to Gabriel, "Fine, save the lady's card. It'll make it easier in case we have to have Parnell make her disappear."

"What's wrong with you, Leena? She stopped to help you."

"What's wrong with me? What's with you that you have to keep telling my name to every stranger you run into?" Helena snapped, still setting a fast pace towards the museum exit.

"I was scared shitless, that's what was with me. I thought you were dead."

"Yeah, well, you were a bit mistaken, weren't you?"

"I'm not a doctor."

"Sure was lucky there was one just standing around then, huh?"

He had no answer for that. He just shook his head and they headed back to the hotel.

Back in their room, Helena had planned to take an afternoon nap; "in order to get a head start on the month of nightmares that museum's going to give me". Gabriel noticed the light on the phone flashing, and found a message from Parnell, saying he had made reservations for all of them for dinner at the best new French restaurant in town. Helena heard the end of the message as she came out of the bathroom, realized that she had taken almost no clothing with her in their escape from Boston.

"Change of plans, partner," she announced, tossing Gabriel his shoes from the end of the bed. "Shopping!"

Gabriel spent the next two hours carrying a rapidly enlarging cluster of bags from a dozen high-end shops as they cruised up one side of M Street in Georgetown and back down the other side. Displaying yet another side of her personality heretofore unknown to Gabriel, Helena purchased a wardrobe suitable for one leaving to become ambassador to France, with accessories and matching shoes. Hot, tired, and overburdened, Gabriel finally dropped into a chair at a street side table at the Ben and Jerry's, unceremoniously dumping their parcels on the ground next to him.

Helena was halfway down the block before she noticed he was gone. She turned and saw him sitting at the little table. She waved. He waved back. After a moment, she walked back to him.

"We're not done yet," she admonished, standing over him with hands on hips.

"Double scoop hot fudge sundae with Cherry Garcia and Chunky Monkey," he answered, squinting up at her in the afternoon sunshine. She sighed, blew her hair off her forehead and stalked into the ice cream shop. She emerged a few minutes later with two single scoop cones, one Cherry Garcia and one Chunky Monkey.

"Your pick," she said, holding them out for his evaluation.

"That's not what I ordered."

"And I suck as a waitress," she said, handing him the Cherry Garcia. "This is all we have time for. We have to hit Moda Nova and a couple of others before we go back." She sat at the little table across from him. He sighed and started on his ice cream, staring at her as she ate hers.

"What?" she asked after a bit, meeting his gaze.

"Are we going to talk about it? Or is this something else that I'm just supposed to ignore?" Gabriel asked.

"What? What's bugging you?"

"Don't play, Leena. What happened this morning, in the museum?"

She shrugged her shoulders and continued eating her ice cream.

"Have you had something like that before? A seizure you said?" he asked, finishing his cone and looking at her seriously.

"You have some on your nose, Gabe," she said, wiping her ice cream against his nose. She smiled at him.

He wiped his nose, leaned over and put his hand on hers. "You're not going to tell me? One more thing on the list of 'don't go theres'?"

She tossed the rest of her cone in the wastebasket and met his gaze. "I don't want to talk about it. We're having fun."

"You scared the shit out of me, Leena."

"I know. I'm sorry Gabe. It wasn't on purpose, believe me."

"You owe me something, some kind of explanation. I can't just wait for it to happen again."

"I don't know what happened, Gabe. I don't have an explanation, even if I owe you one. I don't know, but it's over and I'm fine. Let it go." She gave his hand a squeeze.

"You were saying something, before you came to. Something I couldn't understand."

She looked at him curiously. "What was I saying? Why couldn't you understand it?"

He shook his head. "Didn't make any sense. You kept saying the same thing over and over, but it was like gibberish."

"I'm sorry, Gabe. I really don't remember."

Gabriel pulled his phone from his pocket. "I recorded it," he said, laying the phone on the table between them. He played the recording, listening to his wife again muttering that same unintelligible phrase repeatedly. He looked up from the phone to see his wife had gone pale, obviously distressed.

"What?" he asked, concerned. "What is it?"

"That doesn't sound like me," she said weakly, looking stricken.

"It is you. It's you just before you came to and opened your eyes. What is it you're saying?"

Helena shook her head forcefully, standing up and gathering the bags. "We need to go," she said. She started back up the sidewalk. Gabriel gathered up the rest of the bags and trailed after her.

"Hey," he said, trying to catch her up, but she had already turned into another boutique. He sighed, and took up his position outside to wait. Helena sat down in a dressing room. She closed the curtain and soundlessly began to cry.

Dinner was at eight. Helena and Gabriel arrived to find Arthur and Parnell already seated at the table. The two men stood as Helena approached.

"You look ravishing, Leena," Arthur said, giving her a kiss on the cheek.

"Thank you, Arthur." She turned to her husband. "Arthur thinks I look ravishing, Gabriel."

"Arthur's right," Gabriel replied, holding out her chair for her and then seating himself.

Helena smiled at Parnell. For some reason, Parnell had seen fit to wear a tuxedo with full regalia, including a very distinguished gold lapel medallion that, on closer inspection, proved to be his high school National Honor Society badge. "You're looking very regal yourself there, Mr. Parnell."

Parnell nodded as formally as he could, given the incongruity of his plaited ponytail. "How was the museum?" he asked.

"Moving," Helena answered. The sommelier approached and opened a bottle of red wine, allowing Parnell to pass judgment before pouring for all.

"I took the liberty of ordering the first bottle," Parnell explained. He raised his glass. "Never again," he toasted.

"I'll drink to that," Arthur said, clinking his glass against Parnell's and taking a drink. The others did the same.

"I think I'll have nightmares for a month," Helena said, setting down her glass.

"I almost couldn't move in that room with the shoes, I was in tears," Parnell said.

"Helena had the same problem," Gabriel said, taking the menu being offered by the waiter. Helena flushed and looked steadfastly at her menu as the waiter recited the specials for the evening.

They spent the first course discussing Arthur's arrangements for the next day's flight back to San Francisco. Helena finished her first glass of wine as the soup arrived.

"So, Mr. Parnell," Helena said lightly.

"Call me Chuck, please," Parnell said, finishing his second glass.

"Only if that's your real name, Chuck." Helena accepted a refill from the sommelier.

"It's what they call me," Parnell replied.

"Then I sure would like to meet your Dad," Helena said, smiling.

"Me, too," Parnell said.

"I'm sorry, Chuck. Did you lose him as a child?" Helena asked.

"Lost him before I was born, I guess. Just another Irish bastard, Helena."

"You or him?" she asked, motioning for the sommelier.

"Both, I suppose," Parnell replied. Helena asked the sommelier for something suitable, white, and not French this time. He nodded and retreated from the table. "You?" Parnell asked of Helena as the other two listened and ate.

"Orphaned."

"Here or there?"

"There. And here, too."

"Then I'm sorry," Parnell said, shaking his head before starting his soup. "Rather be an American bastard than an Irish orphan, any day."

"If there was a choice involved, I must've missed it."

An awkward silence ensued as they ate their soup, the others not able to find a suitable subject to broach. Eventually, Parnell felt the need to continue the conversation. He put down his spoon.

"So, Helena?" he asked. Helena nodded, looking at him. "So, Helena, who did you kill in Ireland?"

Helena stared at the man, as did Gabriel and Arthur. Gabriel reddened with anger, opening his mouth to speak. Helena stopped him, laying a hand gently on his arm.

"My husband tells me you're a friend, Chuck. I believe my husband to be a good judge of character."

"He married you," Parnell said, smiling at her. Gabriel opened his mouth again but Helena tightened her grip on his forearm. She smiled back.

"Until you give me a reason to think otherwise, Chuck, I'll trust my husband on this."

"That's not a denial, Helena," Parnell said.

"And that's not how friends talk over dinner, Chuck. If you'd had a father, you'd know that." The sommelier returned with the second bottle of wine.

"And if you weren't raised in a effing gulag, you probably wouldn't have spent your whole life hiding," Parnell retorted, raising his voice.

"Enough!" Gabriel snapped, knocking the elbow of the sommelier that was trying to listen and pour at the same time. The man doused the table with wine.

"Pardon, monsieur," the sommelier said, beginning to mop at the wine.

"Give me a break," Gabriel answered in irritation, "you're about as French as I am."

The man flushed and excused himself to bring another bottle of wine. Helena and Parnell glared at one another. Finally, Helena returned to eating. She said softly, looking at her plate, "You don't know me as well as you think, Chuck. You presume too much."

Parnell also lowered his tone. "I'm sorry, Helena. You're right. It's part of the job."

They ate on in silence for a bit. Finally, Arthur adopted a lighter tone, saying, "Yeah, Chuck, about that job. How's that going by the way?"

Parnell looked at him, asking between forkfuls, "What do you mean, Arthur?"

"Well, you had a chance to check in at the office. What's going on? Pertinent to us, I mean."

"Oh, not much. I took Helena off the watch list, not that it mattered. They had nothing," Parnell answered, dabbing at his face with his napkin. Helena looked up, eyebrows raised at him. "Yeah, your cover's intact, at least as far as the government is concerned. Can't say the same about the Lonegan brothers, but I don't think they got your real name, or your current name, or whatever. They know you're alive now, but I doubt they have the resources to follow up the few traces we left behind."

"They obviously know about your dad, though. They may try to get to you through him," Gabriel said.

Helena shook her head, leaning back in her chair. "Dad and his boys can take care of themselves. It's just business. I wouldn't worry about them." She looked back at Parnell, leaning forward again. "You're sure about my being clear?"

Parnell nodded. "Yeah, we kept it in house, just signals. Gabriel wouldn't let me pull the trigger on a full-fledged notice."

Helena leaned over and kissed her husband on the cheek. "Good for you, Gabe."

"I came close, though," Gabriel said. "If we hadn't heard from your friend, I wasn't going to wait much longer."

Helena nodded and the sommelier returned to restart the second bottle of wine. He appeared disappointed that civility had returned to the table, lingering as he waited for Helena to approve her tasting. She nodded and he circled the table, pouring.

"So, Chuck," Helena continued, "will you be staying here, then?"

"Oh, no," he said, trying the white wine. "Oh, that's great. Nice choice, Helena."

"I'm glad you like it. But how can you leave with us? Don't you have a real job, here? At NSA?"

"Yeah, but it's not a problem. I'm assigned to you guys indefinitely. Section 93 action, extended off-site activity, assigned." He smiled. The entrees arrived.

"I don't understand," Helena said. "Why are you assigned to us? I thought you said I was free and clear."

"Oh, you are. This has nothing to do with you. It's about Gabe," he said, gesturing at Gabriel with a forkful of lobster before drenching it in drawn butter.

Helena frowned and started her fish. "What is the NSA's interest in Gabriel?"

"To be honest, it's really more my own interest than an official NSA project, like I told Gabriel."

"Really, more of your own interest?"

"Yeah. I was telling Gabriel while you were gone, I think the work has great potential, from the point of view of my specialty."

"Which is, exactly?"

"Signals intelligence. Finding needles in the global electronic haystack."

"I'm not following. How does our work fit in with electronic surveillance?"

Parnell shrugged, washed down his food with more wine. "I don't know either, not yet. It's interesting though."

"I'm sorry to hear that," Helena said, turning to Gabriel. "How do we get rid of him, Gabe?"

"I'm sitting right here. I heard that, Helena," Parnell said. Helena ignored him.

"What?" Gabriel said, looking at her. "Chuck's been helping out. Like I was telling you, he helped me make a major breakthrough while you were gone."

"Yeah," Parnell said, nodding like a clown, "I've been helping a lot. You'll see when we get home."

"You are home, Chuck. We're the ones going home," she said. Parnell looked hurt.

"What are you worried about, Helena? Chuck's okay," Arthur said.

"Oh, Chuck's great," Helena said, smiling at him. Parnell brightened. "It's just that he works for the fucking NSA, that's the problem. That's a great big problem."

Parnell's face fell again. "That's not a problem. Not yet."

"Not yet?" Gabriel asked.

"Yeah, I told you, Gabe," Parnell answered, "When I first arrived. You're under the radar so far. But at some point, the government's going to be involved. Gotta be."

"No, notta gotta be, Chuck," Helena said. "Not going to happen." She looked from her husband to Arthur, back to her husband. "Right? Not going to happen? The government doesn't get to touch the salmon."

"How was the salmon?" Parnell asked her.

"It was great, Chuck. Drink some more wine. Gabe?"

"No, you're right, Helena. Same as before, nobody touches the salmon but us."

Parnell took another gulp of wine. "Really, guys, the lobster was enough. It was great. I don't need your salmon. Dessert would be great, though."

"She means," Arthur interjected, "that you and the government don't get possession of our technology."

"She said salmon," Parnell said.

"It's a metaphor," Gabriel said.

"Oh," Parnell said, and after a pause, "I don't get it. But like I said, it's not going to be up to you. It's not going to be up to me, either. It's just inevitable, fish metaphor notwithstanding."

"Can't happen, guys," Helena said.

Parnell shrugged. "Gonna happen, guys." Parnell signaled for the waiter. "Coffee and dessert?" They each stared at him. "What? You can't all be on diets."

"Maybe we can ditch him during dessert, leave him with the bill, Arthur," Helena said.

"Not a chance," Arthur said, taking the dessert menu being offered by the waiter. "Chuck never pays, not in his nature."

"I make like one one-thousandth what you guys make," Parnell protested.

"You sure don't order like it," Arthur replied.

"So why don't you quit that government job, Chuck?" Helena asked, declining the dessert menu. "Just coffee, please. Why don't you come work for Arthur and Gabriel, full time?"

"You'd do that? Really?" Parnell asked, smiling like a kid.

Gabriel looked at Helena questioningly.

"If we can't get rid of him, Gabe, why not? You said he was smart."

"You said I was smart? Really?" Gabriel rolled his eyes. "Do you guys get benefits? I've got great benefits. I'd hate to give those up."

Now it was Arthur shaking his head, saying, "I don't think we can afford to buy this guy off. He'll be bumming meals off us for the next twenty years."

"I don't see what all you guys are worried about, anyway," Parnell said. "We're the good guys. What's wrong with the NSA using your technology? We're all on the same team, you know." Helena snorted derisively, shaking her head. "What? You don't think you're on the same team as the government?"

"No, Chuck, I don't. The government doesn't believe in teams. It doesn't even play the same fucking game."

"Well, you're a product of your unfortunate upbringing, that's all. I've worked for the government my entire professional life—"

"Yeah, that's about what, six or seven years?" Helena scoffed.

"—and I don't think there's anything evil about the government or the NSA."

Helena was still shaking her head as the coffee arrived. "When was the last time you visited the Holocaust museum, Chuck?"

"A couple of years ago, why?"

"You probably don't remember, then. You know what I'm talking about, though, don't you, Gabe?"

"Honestly, Leena? No. Not the shoes?" Gabriel asked.

"No, not the damn shoes again. No," she said, turning back to Parnell. "I'm talking about the room with the Hollerith machine. Right in the beginning."

"The what?" Arthur asked. "I've never been, so enlighten me, Helena." The others looked equally confused.

"The Hollerith machine," Helena repeated. "Don't you guys learn about this stuff in Jewish school or anything?"

"Hebrew school," Gabriel said, shaking his head. "And no, we don't really go on field trips or anything."

"The Hollerith machine," Helena continued, "was invented by IBM, before the war."

"The American IBM? They existed before World War Two?" Arthur asked.

Helena nodded. "The same one. They're over a hundred years old, actually. They invented the first computational machines. Their machines were used in almost every factory and manufacturing facility in the nineteen twenties and thirties. They sold a lot of them to Germany."

"Before the war, you mean? So that's not evil, Helena. They weren't specifically helping Hitler, not like Ford and the others," Parnell said.

"That's the point I'm making, Chuck. They sold all those state of the art computing machines to Germany. The German government then used those new machines to catalog, find, and systematically round up all the Jews for extermination." She let this sink in for a moment. "That's what the government does with technology."

"I don't know, Helena," Parnell said, eagerly watching his Bananas Foster en flambé. "We don't live in Nazi Germany. People may be evil, but technology isn't."

"It's all the same, Chuck. No government can be trusted with what we're developing."

"Is that your goal, then?" Parnell asked.

"What do you mean, Chuck?" Helena asked.

"Gabriel knows what I mean, don't you, Gabriel?"

Gabriel looked at his wife. "Chuck doesn't understand why you married me. He doesn't think you support the research. Doesn't fit with your personality, he claims."

Parnell nodded. "So what's your angle, Helena? Sabotage?"

Arthur smacked his forehead with his palm. "Gad, Parnell," Arthur said, "You are such a moron."

"If I'm such a moron, let's hear what Helena has to say. How about it, Helena? What makes you want to help develop a technology that allows Big Brother to listen in on our thoughts?"

Helena put down her cup of coffee and looked at Parnell coolly. "You're doing it again, Chuck. Don't presume to know somebody because you've read their file or some intercept transcript. You don't know who I am. Gabriel knows me, you don't."

"Then why? Why the deep interest in this research? Love?" Parnell scoffed.

"Someday, Chuck," Helena said to him, "you might find out. If I don't kill you first."

Parnell turned sharply to Gabriel. "What did I tell you?" Parnell snapped.

They flew home the next day. Settled back in Half Moon Bay, Helena was anxious to see what had been accomplished in her absence. Gabriel promised to give her a demonstration later in the week. First, he said, he had to work some things out with Parnell. The following morning, Gabriel met Parnell in the lab, where the younger man had again taken up residence.

Gabriel walked in to the sound of Ligiti playing at ear splitting volume. Parnell was sitting in his underwear in the semidarkness, staring at the monitors and oblivious to Gabriel's approach until Gabe gave the other man's ponytail a yank. Parnell screamed and nearly fell over backward, kicking the console and knocking over his mug of coffee. He screamed again as the hot coffee streamed onto his lap.

"Holy shit, Sheehan," Parnell exclaimed, jumping to his feet and trying to wipe the steaming coffee from his crotch. "I got second degree burns here. Don't you knock?"

"It's my office, remember?" Gabriel turned down the music and dropped into a chair. "What are you doing?"

"Here, look," Parnell said, sitting back down. He mopped up the rest of the spilled coffee with a dirty shirt he had left on the floor. "It's pretty much all done."

"What's all done?"

"That program I told you about before we left for Boston. I had it running while we were gone. It's all done."

"Done with what, Chuck? I'm not following."

"Done analyzing the database you gave me. I was just starting to look at the results when you nearly neutered me, but I think it worked. Let me show you."

"In a minute, Chuck. I want to talk to you first." Gabriel flipped off the monitors and the music.

"Oh, oh."

"It's not like that."

"When they say 'It's not like that', it's always worse than like that. Helena told you to have me whacked, didn't she?"

"What are you, some mobster wannabe? No, Chuck. She was the one who suggested we hire you, remember? At dinner?" Parnell nodded. "Have you given that any thought?"

"Yeah, a lot, actually. About a lot of things Helena said that night. Your wife is right about a few things, Gabriel."

"Actually, everything."

"Wouldn't go that far. I'm afraid, though, she might be right about the government. I don't know."

"But you think you might want to leave the NSA and join us?"

Parnell shook his head. "No, I think I need to stay on. If Helena's right, the best thing is for me to be the one on the inside, the contact with NSA."

Gabriel thought about this for a while.

"And I've got great benefits, Gabriel," Parnell added.

"Fine," Gabriel said. "That's fine. Let me know if you change your mind."

"I will. Thanks for the offer, anyway."

"Yeah, no problem. There's something else; about Helena."

"I'm a dead man."

"Why do you think she killed someone, in Ireland? Really?"

Parnell leaned back, putting his feet on the console. "She's obviously running from something, like I said before. She's not the kind to hide from a jealous wife or an abusive lover. She's too confrontational. But she's right, I'm making a lot of judgment calls here."

"What about the stuff she was mixed up with in Boston?"

"No," Parnell said, "that's all after the fact. I'd have found traces of anything like that if it happened stateside. No, it was something in Europe, and probably something as a juvenile, so the records, if there were any, were expunged. It just makes sense. And now that I'm sure she was an orphan, raised in the state Catholic system, it all fits. They specialize in making things disappear, you know what I mean?" Gabriel didn't, but he nodded anyway. "No offense, Gabriel, but now that I met your wife, I haven't changed my mind a bit. Just the opposite. Short fuse, and I don't want to be around when she goes off. No offense."

Gabriel sat, considering. Parnell misinterpreted the silence, as usual.

"Really, I meant no offense, Gabriel. She's great, really."

Gabriel leaned forward, pulling out his cellphone from his pocket. "Forget it, Chuck. We both know you just fear strong women. Most women, actually. Here, I want you to listen to something." He put the phone on the console and played the recording he had made of Helena at the museum.

"Play it again," Parnell said. Gabriel replayed the recording and sat back.

"Well?"

"That's Helena."

"Yeah, I know that. I made the recording. What is she saying? Is it nonsense or what?"

"Nonsense? No, I don't think so. Play it again." They listened through the recording two more times. "I'm almost certain, but I'd have to check—"

"Almost certain of what?"

"I'm pretty sure she's talking in Irish. I can't make out the words, wouldn't understand it if I could, anyway. Been too long since my grandmother passed."

"Irish? That's a language?"

"What's wrong with you? Of course it's a language. It's the language spoken in Ireland. Mail me the recording. I'll forward it to the office and have it translated."

"Hey, boys," Helena said, appearing through the doorway.

Parnell flushed, recoiled, and nearly fell out of his chair.

"Hey, Leena. Didn't expect to see you down here today," Gabriel said. "We were just talking about you."

"Yeah, I know. Stop it." She gave Parnell a look that made him cringe. "So, show me your big discovery. I'm all excited." She smiled at Gabriel.

"I thought we'd put together a demonstration for later in the week," Gabriel said, blushing. He looked at Parnell, who gave a considered nod.

"A demonstration? We're not pitching a grant here, Gabe. Show me what you got, darlin'."

"Okay, then," Gabriel said and turned back to Parnell. "Actually, Chuck was just getting ready to show me what we've got. Go ahead, partner, show us what you got."

Parnell gathered himself and hunched over the console. He spoke with his back to Helena, but grew more effusive as monitors sprang back to life. "I was just starting to tell Gabriel," he said, "that I had a linguistic analyzer I pirated from the office running while we were in Boston."

"Cool. Running on what?" Helena asked.

"I set it up with the library of subject recordings from Gabriel's prevarication study and, actually, just about all the full-lead monitored sessions he had recorded here in the lab. A ton of stuff." The monitors filled with the multicolored tracings once more. "So here's the multichannel recording from a subject, don't know which one. Doesn't matter." Parnell spun in his chair to turn on the audio feed. The lab filled with the dissonant tones from the subject recording.

"What the hell is that?" Helena asked over the cacophony. Gabriel reached past his wife to turn down the volume.

"That's one of the things we came up with while you were on vacation," Gabriel said, smiling. Helena scowled at him. "I was having no luck trying to sort out the multiple channels for analysis, remember? Too complex, too much overlap."

"I remember."

"Well, Chuck had the idea to assign instrumental voices to each of the channels. That way we can more easily follow each track, like an orchestra, you know?" He looked at his wife. Parnell also looked at her, waiting for approval with an expectant expression.

"An orchestra? More like the elementary school band from Hell. Can I hear just one channel at a time?" Helena asked.

"Sure," Parnell said, making adjustments on the console. "First, here's the oral—," he cut off all the sound except for the voice of the test subject. He let this drone on for a few more seconds, and then reduced it to a murmur. "Here's channel one," and the sound of a violin rising and falling in pitch filled the room. They all listened to the strange melody for a few minutes. "Do you want me to add the other channels?" Parnell asked Helena.

"Just one at a time, equal volume but slowly." Parnell gradually added each voice to the room. Helena listened intently. She nodded finally, smiling at them. "That's brilliant," she said to them over the sound. They both beamed at her.

Parnell turned down the volume again. "But that's not the real breakthrough," he said. He stopped the playback, fiddled with the keyboard. After several minutes, a new subject recording appeared on the monitors, the soundtrack playing softly beneath the subject's voice. "And now, voila!" he said, flipping a switch on the console. Subtitles appeared along the lower edge of the monitor. They all stared.

"Subtitles?" Gabriel asked? "Of what?"

"His thoughts! That's the translation of his waveforms, using your dictionary, the salmon," he smiled, "run through the NSA processor. Great, huh?" He looked back and forth between them, waiting.

The other two watched the subtitles crawl along the screen, reading. "Turn the sound up on the vocal track," Gabriel said. They listened and read. There was a correlation but it was certainly not identical. The two streams approached and diverged, approached again and separated.

"Interesting," Helena said.

Parnell's face fell. "Interesting? That's it? That's the best we can do?"

Helena shrugged. "It's great, Chuck. Really great. Great work, kid."

Parnell turned to Gabriel, waiting. Gabriel slapped him on the shoulder. "Brilliant! This is fantastic!" Parnell smiled, nodding. "It's just that—"

Parnell rounded on him. "What? It's just that what? It's brilliant, you said. Can we leave it at that?"

Gabriel looked at the monitors, intentionally avoiding Parnell's gaze. "It's just that I'm not sure what the interpretation is based upon, you know? We've been here before, a couple of times actually."

Helena was nodding but said nothing. Parnell looked like he was in pain. He said plaintively, "What do you mean? I told you: it's based upon the dictionary, your work. It's interpreting the waveforms by applying your dictionary to the recorded thought patterns and—"

"Yeah, Chuck. That's the brilliant part. I agree. But we did something similar before, though not nearly as well, I'll grant you. But I'm just not sure it's that simple, that's all," Gabriel said.

Helena was nodding again, said, "Exactly. Not every French waiter is an asshole."

Parnell grabbed at his hair, almost pulling it out of its plait. "Exactly? Really? What's with you two? Why does it have to be even more complicated? It's pretty fucking complicated already. I analyzed a crazy complex signal using a crazy sophisticated algorithm and it generated this. Look at this! It's not gibberish. This is real! It makes sense. This is what the dude is thinking."

Helena shrugged. Gabriel was shaking his head. "That's the thing, though, Chuck. What is the dude thinking? What does that mean?"

"What are you talking about, Gabriel?" Parnell asked, slumping back again.

"Well, when you say, 'This is what the dude is thinking' there are so many levels. There is the level of what we say when we speak—"

"It's not that," Parnell interrupted with irritation. "You can see it's not that." He gestured at the monitor.

"Yeah, yeah. I know. But beneath what we say, there's what we're thinking."

"Exactly," Parnell said this time.

"Not exactly. What we say, what we think, what we believe, what we remember, what we feel—where is all that? What level are we reading here?" Gabriel asked.

"Lost me," Parnell said.

"I agree," Helena said.

"So he lost you, too?" Parnell asked.

"No," Helena said. "I agree with him."

"Really? You're agreeing with him? You think we need to see into this man's soul," he gestured again at the monitor, "before we can use this?"

Helena shook her head. "I'm not sure, that's all. You may be right, Chuck. It is a brilliant start. But we don't know what we're reading. Just because it's not gibberish doesn't make it right. The product could be the result of the process you used. It's a basic question. It's too soon."

"I don't think so," Parnell said.

"Then you're not a scientist," Helena said.

"I'm more of a government surveillance engineer," Parnell said.

"There you go," Helena said, smiling at him.

"I think we have a working mind reading program," Parnell said stubbornly.

"That's what we're going to find out," Gabriel said.

"Another study?"

"That's science, Chuck," Gabriel said.

"Hey, Gabe," Helena interrupted, "does my lab have a sound system like this?"

"Arthur put one in every lab," Gabriel answered. "Don't ask me why."

"Great. Chuck, could you set me up with this satanic synthesized symphony you guys ginned up? In my lab?"

"Sure, Helena," Parnell said, "I can do it right now."

"Hold on a second, Kimosabee. We've got to talk."

"Is this something that can wait until later, maybe let me get some clothes on, something really unimportant and unthreatening?" Parnell asked, blanching.

"Actually, no. I think it's important to talk about this now. You said you used our dictionary for this program, our salmon?" Parnell swallowed hard and nodded. "How did you do that?"

"Gabriel gave it to me," he said, his voice cracking. "Tell her, Gabriel."

"I let him use it for the analysis, Leena," Gabriel said. "Is that a problem?"

"I don't know," Helena said, looking back at Parnell. "Is that a problem, Chuck?"

"I don't know what you mean, Helena," Parnell said.

"When you said you used the dictionary with the NSA program, did you mean you sent our dictionary to NSA? Has it left this building?"

"Oh, I see what you mean. No, absolutely not, Helena. I imported the program from NSA to our lab. Nothing went out, promise."

Helena nodded. "Good. Here's the thing, Gabriel. I was thinking this morning during my run, thinking about the whole government thing we were talking about in DC. We haven't been careful enough with the salmon."

"We talked about this before you left, Leena," Gabriel said. "We maintain control. It's not leaving."

"We have to make sure, Gabe. I think Chief What-the-Chuck here is our man to make sure we are secure. What do you think, Chuck?"

Parnell looked between them, confused. "What are we talking about here?"

Helena leaned forward. "Well, Chuck, being an engineer and from the NSA, you should have some insight into how the salmon could be stolen from us. We want you to help prevent that, don't we, Gabriel?"

"Sure. Chuck could help with that. But he's not working for us, he's working for the NSA."

"Really, Chuck?" Helena asked. "You decided to turn down our offer?"

Parnell nodded. "Just for now, Helena," he said. "I'm really flattered, though. I've got—"

"Great benefits, yeah, I know," Helena said. She leaned forward and put a hand on his boney knee. Parnell leaned away. "Chuck, you strike me as a man who's easily intimidated," she continued. Parnell nodded. "Great. Listen. We're putting you in charge of security concerning our salmon. Talk to Arthur, hire whoever you want. But Gabe and I are holding you personally responsible for preventing our intellectual property from ever leaving our complete and total control."

Parnell was relieved. "I can do that, Helena. We can set up a system, no problem. What do you mean by 'personally responsible', exactly?"

"Just so we understand each other, Chuck," Helena said. "I'm glad you're willing to take this on. But if we ever find that the salmon has even been touched without our authorization, if it ever gets pirated by the government or any other organization, if a copy ever leaves our control—" Parnell was leaning so far back now he was against the console. "—then Gabriel and I will know exactly who to blame. You." She stabbed a finger into Parnell's chest, smiling. Parnell flinched, cowering back. "Okay, then?"

Parnell nodded, and then shook his head. "But what does it mean, 'who to blame,' exactly?"

"It means, Chuck, that I hunt you down like a dog and squeeze the life out of you with my bare hands. Okay?"

Parnell nodded.

"Then boys, let's get to work."

Over the next several weeks they set up in their separate labs. Gabriel solicited a new cohort of volunteers for a prospective study of the new program. Two hundred volunteers with orders to say anything they wanted for ten minutes; truth, lies, stories, or any combination. Gabriel and Parnell watched each subject from the control room in real time, Parnell using his program to parse the subject's "thoughts", while Gabriel studied the tracings on the monitors and listened to his musical synthesis through headphones. Gabriel marked up each recording as it was made, electronically noting phrases and tracings, highlighting particular sections and passages. After each session they sat with the subject and compared notes and impressions, challenging the subject on which sections were true, which falsifications. Gabriel pursued his questioning of the subjects on a different plane, questioning why they had said one story or another, what was true and to what extent, what was based on memory or provoked some strong sentiment in the subject.

Several times a day, Gabriel walked down the hall to look in on Helena in her lab. Every time, she'd be sitting in the semidarkness, staring at the tracings on the monitor or the recording of the subject's face as he spoke, listening to the musical interpretation of the mental recordings. She appeared enraptured and he hardly ever interrupted her. They usually met for lunch, often with Parnell. This routine stretched beyond the next several months.

Gabriel walked down the hall to see if Helena wanted to grab lunch. He walked into the lab to see her again sitting behind the console, electric bright tracings reflecting on her alabaster complexion in the semidarkness.

"Hey, Leena—" he began. He stopped, looking at her. Helena's eyes were open, staring at nothing. He felt his throat tighten as he recognized the expression, her posture, from that day in the museum. He stood watching her as she sat immobile, oblivious to his entrance. As he approached, he saw her lips moving in speech, though the words were lost in the sound of the recording. He sat in the chair beside her and gently touched her knee.

"Leena," he called to her softly. He could hear her speaking softly now, but could understand none of it. He couldn't tell if it was the same thing she had recited before. She remained unconscious of his presence, unresponsive to his touch. Gabriel turned to the console and switched off the recording. The screens went black; the strange warbling song abruptly went silent. As he turned back to his wife, Helena took a great shuddering breath. He saw her eyelids do that same brisk flutter he had seen the one time before.

"Leena," he said again, leaning in front of her. Helena's eyes focused on his own, and she smiled at him.

"Gabriel," she said. "I didn't hear you come in."

He smiled back at her in relief. "Are you okay, Leena?"

"Yeah, fine. Want to grab lunch?"

"Sure, Leena. How about just you and me today?"

"Don't be silly, Gabe. Chuck would be sad. You'd spend the rest of the day trying to console him and get nothing done. Let's see if Arthur wants to join us."

They met Arthur for lunch at a restaurant by his office downtown.

"So, gentlemen," Arthur said, looking at Gabriel and Parnell across the table from him and Helena. "Do we have a product?"

"Yes," said Parnell, simultaneous with Gabriel's, "No".

Helena laughed as Arthur just shook his head. "So which is it, yes or no?"

Gabriel opened his mouth to answer but the words came out from Parnell. "Gabriel has us scheduled to listen to two hundred lying homeless derelicts. We're singlehandedly propping up the under-five-dollar-a-bottle wine industry in this city. It'll be two years before he's satisfied. But I can tell you, the program works. We've sat through over sixty so far and it's spot on."

Gabriel was shaking his head angrily. He opened his mouth to speak but Parnell again preempted him. "Gabriel's still worried that I'm not reading what the subject is thinking, that the program may be mixing up deeper issues."

"What issues, Gabriel?" Arthur asked.

"Gabriel thinks I might be seeing what the subject is remembering, or what he thinks he thinks, not really what he thinks. Isn't that right, Gabriel?" Parnell looked at his boss.

Gabriel started to flush, explaining, "We don't know if—"

"What did I tell you?" Parnell interrupted. "We don't know if maybe the subject is projecting a childhood fantasy, or is emotionally involved in his response, or some other nonsense. Who cares? We can see what he's thinking, when he's thinking it. I say, who cares why he's thinking what he's thinking. Am I right, Arthur? Helena?"

"Gee, Chuck, I don't know," Arthur placated. "Gabe?"

"What, you're taking his side on this?" Parnell asked.

"I'm not taking anybody's side. I just want to know if we have a product, that's all."

"Well, we do," Parnell said. "We have a program that reliably translates brain wave patterns for interpretation. We can read minds, period."

Gabriel had twisted his napkin into shreds by this point. "Can I talk now?" he asked Parnell. Parnell shrugged. "Chuck is mostly right. The program needs more work, but it's getting very accurate at putting words and structure to the brainwave recordings."

"Getting? It's already really accurate. Almost perfect," Parnell interjected.

"It's doing well on that level, I admit. Much better than the French restaurant gambit, for sure. But there still is the problem of meaning. We know what we see, but we don't know what it means."

"Same shit, different day," Parnell muttered under his breath. Gabriel picked up his butter knife, then gently put it back on the table.

"Chuck thinks we're done, obviously."

"Not done. Just really close."

"It's not that black and white. We need more time, Arthur."

"That's fine, Gabriel. I just don't quite grasp the problem."

"Thank you, Jesus!" Parnell exclaimed.

"Shut up, Chuck," Helena said. "Give us an example, Gabe."

Gabriel gave a weak smile. "Thank you, I will. Say we market this product like Chuck wants to do, sell it to the justice community—"

"Or security," Parnell said.

"Or for security, fine. We hook up the suspect, or the job applicant, whoever, to the machine and start asking him questions. As he's answering, we can see what he's really thinking—"

"Exactly," Parnell said. "We can see if he's being truthful." He nodded for emphasis.

Gabriel spread his palms on the tablecloth and sighed. "Say I ask him, 'when did you stop beating your wife?' He says, 'I never beat my wife'. But on the mind read, we can see something different."

"Then he's lying."

Gabriel picked up the butter knife again, toying with it. "Maybe he's lying. Maybe we triggered a memory of an incident when he was six, when he saw his parents fighting. Maybe he's thinking of the time he saw a movie with his high school girlfriend and there was a scene in the movie where a guy beat his wife."

"Why would someone think about that during a job interview? Huh? Why?" Parnell asked, looking plaintively from Arthur to Helena.

"We can't tell why someone is thinking what they're thinking. There's no discrimination yet. It's not ready."

Helena and Arthur were both nodding appreciatively. "I can understand that," Arthur said. "So when do you think?"

"So then, never," Parnell said. "Ask him. Not gonna happen. Not in our lifetime."

Gabriel was spinning the knife on his fingertips. "I'm working on it. I'm just saying, it's not that simple. It's not black and white, like Chuck wants it to be."

"Then we wait," Arthur said.

"Till Hell freezes over," Parnell added.

When they made it back to the lab, Gabriel pulled Parnell aside. "Give me a minute," Gabriel said.

"You're pissed off about what I said at lunch, aren't you? I knew it."

"No, screw that. You know you're wrong."

"I'm not wrong. You're just stubborn."

"Whatever, Chuck. Shut up a second. Remember that recording I played for you a couple of weeks ago?"

"Helena's? Yeah. You never sent it to me."

"I know. I'm sending it to you now, though."

"Why?

"Can you check it out, yes or no?"

"Sure, Gabriel. Send it to me, I'll get right on it."

Parnell walked into the lab an hour later to find Gabriel reviewing a study at the console. Gabriel hit pause as Parnell sat down.

"I was right," Parnell said. "So were you. She's saying the same phrase, over and over, the whole recording. And she is speaking Irish."

"Could you tell what she was saying?"

Parnell nodded. “She keeps saying, ‘I’m so sorry, sister’.”

“That’s it?”

“Yup. ‘I’m so sorry, sister.’ That’s it, about forty times.”

“Then she came out of it?”

“I guess. You were there, not me. Why did we do this today? What’s up?”

“It happened again, this morning.”

“Shit.”

“Yeah, shit is right.”

“I guess that means it wasn’t a stroke, huh?”

“I guess it wasn’t.”

“What are you going to do?”

“Not sure yet.”

Two days later, Arthur showed up at the lab. He walked into the office to find Gabriel and Parnell arguing. Helena, he noticed, was lying on the couch in the corner with a wet washcloth covering her eyes.

“Headache?” Arthur asked her, sitting down on the couch at her feet.

“Assholes,” she replied without opening her eyes, jerking a thumb toward the other two in the room. Gabriel and Parnell stopped arguing and looked over.

“Arthur,” Gabriel said, “didn’t see you come in. Didn’t think you remembered where we lived.”

“Just followed the sound of the yelling. What’s going on?”

Parnell dropped into Gabriel’s desk chair, saying “Same old shit, Arthur. Freud, here, wants to psychoanalyze our subjects. Ask them how they feel about their mothers—”

“Not psychoanalyze, exactly,” Gabriel said defensively, sitting down in the only remaining chair. “What’s up, Arthur? Do I have to sign some more forms for the pension account?”

“You guys get a pension?” Parnell asked.

Arthur ignored him, turning to Gabriel. “I think it may be time to give your program a try, Gabriel.”

“Great,” Parnell said, leaning into the conversation.

“Not time yet, Arthur,” Gabriel said, shaking his head. “Why, what’s up?”

"I got a call this morning from a friend of mine, guy I play bridge with sometimes. He's the director of the FBI field office here in San Francisco."

"And you figure you two can tighten up your bidding if you can read his mind while you're playing? Smart thinking, Arthur," Helena said from her end of the couch.

"Go back to sleep, Helena," Arthur said, smacking her feet. "Ed's working a case that he needs our help with."

"Great! Fire up the Batplane, Arthur. We're there," Parnell said, starting to rise from his chair.

"Sit down, Chuck. What are you talking about, Arthur? How does the FBI even know about our work?" Gabriel asked.

"Yeah, Arthur," Helena said, rising up on one elbow and pulling off the washcloth to give him an evil stare. "How in Hell does the FBI know about our work?"

"It's bridge," Arthur answered sheepishly. "We talk. Listen, this is potentially life and death."

"Yeah, because Gabe and I are going to kill you," Helena said. "Bridge, my ass. You're such an *alter kocker*, Arthur."

"What's an *alter kocker*?" Parnell asked.

"Shut up, Chuck," Gabriel and Arthur said simultaneously.

Arthur continued, "There's a nine year old girl missing in Sausalito. Ed thinks the stepfather is involved; they have him in custody. A really disturbed individual, like Steven King novel disturbed. Keeps saying that the girl's alive but won't tell them where she is."

"Where's her mom?" Helena asked, interested in spite of herself.

"Also missing," Arthur replied. "It can't be anything official. Ed thinks he can get you into an interview room, try to pull it off as some sort of lie detector test."

"He'll refuse," Arthur said.

"No, he won't, he can't," Parnell said. "I can do this. We can do this." Parnell sketched out his plan enthusiastically for the three of them. Gabriel was shaking his head throughout.

"It's not ready," Gabriel repeated.

Helena put her hand on her husband's arm. "Maybe not, hon," she said, "but we have to give it a try. A little girl's life may be in danger."

"It's not going to work, Leena," Gabriel said to her.

"I'm almost more afraid of what'll happen if it does work," Helena replied.

"I'll call Ed and set it up for tomorrow," Arthur said.

"Shit, Arthur," the FBI agent said, staring at the machinery in front of him. "You didn't say he'd have to wear electrodes on his head. This guy will go ape shit. The guy's a whack job. No way he's gonna sit for this."

"No, no, officer," Parnell stammered, stepping in front of Arthur. "We know. That's the decoy. All we have to do is get him to put in these earplugs."

"I'm not a traffic cop. Quit calling me officer, asshole," the agent replied.

"Okay, officer asshole," Helena intoned. "We're here to try to help you out. Listen to the guy."

"Fine," the agent said. "Tell me how this is going to work, because his attorney is going to want to be in the room the whole time, guaranteed."

"That'll work," Parnell said. "Just tell them I'm the technician and Gabriel is in charge of the examination. You tell the lawyer that his client can refuse to answer any and all questions. Ask whatever you want. Doesn't matter."

"Doesn't matter?"

Parnell nodded. "Not gonna matter. Just get him in the room. Oh, and we need a picture of the missing girl."

Gabriel was holding his head in his hands. The FBI agent left the room. Gabriel looked up at Parnell. "It's not going to work, Chuck. You're screwing with people's lives here."

Parnell looked at him, smiling. "Hey, Gabriel, I'm with the government. That's what I do."

Parnell walked into the conference room to find the subject sitting next to his lawyer. The subject was a huge guy, with a matted head of hair and a beard straggling over his belly. His handcuffed wrists were in front of him on the table as he rocked slowly back and forth. Parnell tossed his ponytail about him as he dropped down handfuls of electrical equipment onto the table before them.

"You'd think that someone of my pay grade wouldn't have to carry all this shit around, wouldn't you?" Parnell said to the two of them, smiling. The guy just kept looking at his hands, rocking. His attorney, sitting next to him, shook his head slightly. Parnell got the feeling he was trying to warn him off.

"Maybe not, then," Parnell continued, beginning to untangle cords and plug in his recorders. "Which one of you handsome gentlemen is my client?" The older, gray haired man in the expensive suit just rolled his eyes. The other man, taciturn with a bland face and uncommitted expression, just kept looking at his hands on the table. "Okey, dokey, then. Time to dress for the ball, Prince Charming."

The man quit rocking and stared at Parnell as Chuck applied a blood pressure cuff and clipped an oxygen sensor to the man's index finger. Parnell met his eyes and was immediately seized with a strong desire to leave the room. The subject had a deeply disturbing gaze, a dead stare that caused Parnell to look away as he wrapped an elastic band around the subject's chest. Parnell sat down in front of the recorder, watching the readout. "What kind of music do you like, sugar?" Parnell asked the man. The other man looked at him, appearing confused.

"Why do you want to know?" the lawyer answered for him.

Parnell pulled an iPod from his pocket and began fiddling with it. "Because we need to get a baseline, need him relaxed. It's my own little trick, you see. You sit and listen to music while I calibrate the machine." He smiled at them.

The attorney shrugged. "Suit yourself. He's not answering any questions anyway." Parnell looked expectantly at the subject, waiting.

"Country, I guess. Whatever," the man finally said softly, staring down Parnell again with his dead eyes.

"Your lucky day, that's my favorite, too! Here we go, got my own mix tape all ready to soothe." Parnell adjusted the settings on the iPod and slid it across the table to the other man. "Just go ahead and listen to that and close your eyes and relax. This'll be done in a jiffy."

The man did as Parnell asked, putting the ear buds in with difficulty due to the handcuffs. He finally got them in place and began rocking slowly again as he closed his eyes and listened to the music. Parnell took a pen and stack of papers from a briefcase he had brought in with him, placing them on the table in front of him. On top of the pile was the picture of the missing girl provided by the FBI. Parnell pretended to watch the tracings for a few minutes, adjusting dials as he hummed tunelessly to himself.

The attorney began to fidget, obviously getting annoyed. He pulled out his Blackberry and began to check his messages.

"I'm sorry, Perry Mason," Parnell said, looking up. "You'll have to turn that off. Screws with the recording." He smiled. The attorney scowled at him and put it back in his pocket.

"Are we almost done with this?" the attorney asked.

Parnell nodded. "Looking really good." Parnell held up the picture of the abducted girl in front of him, facing the subject. He kept looking down at the pile of papers, pretending to rifle through them.

"What the hell?" the attorney began. Parnell looked up at him and smiled. Suddenly, Parnell smacked his palm down hard on the tabletop in front of the subject. The man's eyes snapped open as he jerked forward, looking at Parnell but seeing the picture right in front of him. He suddenly reddened with anger.

"What the hell is this?" the attorney repeated. "Where did you get that? You can't do that!"

"Sorry," Parnell replied, smiling as he made a mark with a grease pencil on the tracings and pretended to note the time on his watch. "Startle response. Part of the calibration."

"Not that," the attorney continued, agitated. "That picture, get rid of that picture. My client is not going to be subjected to—"

"Oh, this?" Parnell said, turning the picture over to look at it and replacing it on the pile of pictures. "This stuff belongs to the interrogator, I think. I'm just the technician." He smiled again.

"That's it, we're outta here. My client is not agreeing to be subject to any prejudicial materials. That wasn't part of the deal. We're leaving." The attorney stood, began packing his briefcase. The other man looked at him, obviously angry and bewildered, still wearing the ear buds and not hearing a thing. Gabriel and the FBI agent came into the room, having seen the activity through the window and wondering if Parnell was about to be pummeled.

"What's going on?" The agent asked.

"We're leaving, that's what's going on," the attorney said. "I said my client wouldn't answer any questions during this session, it was to be just a formality."

"Fine, then have a seat. We're all set."

"Not a chance, agent." The attorney pointed to the stack of papers on the desk with the picture on top. "That's not part of the deal. We're walking." He grabbed his client's shoulder, pulling off the blood pressure cuff. "Take that stupid thing off, will you?"

The other man pulled off the ear buds, still looking confused. "What's going on?"

"We're leaving," the attorney replied. "Get up." The other man gave Parnell a sheepish grin and slid his iPod back across the table. "Thanks, man. Great mix."

"Glad you liked it," Parnell said, retrieving the iPod and replacing it in his pocket. They all watched as the subject and his attorney stalked out of the room, letting the door slam behind them. An officer escorted the two out. The others dropped into the chairs beside Parnell.

"Shit," the agent sighed. "I thought they'd at least give us a shot."

"Just as well," Gabriel said, shaking his head.

"Give me ten minutes," Parnell said. He reached back into the briefcase beside him and pulled out his laptop. He pushed all the wires and the recorder away, clearing a spot on the table before him. He connected the iPod to the computer and began tapping furiously, his nose inches from the screen.

"What gives? You never had him hooked up," the agent said.

"Oh, shit. You got it, didn't you, Chuck?" Gabriel asked.

"Just shut up and give me a minute, okay?" Parnell snapped. The other two watched him as he continued to work. Gabriel came around the table to stare over his shoulder at the screen. He gave a soft whistle under his breath.

"That is one fucked up tracing, Chuck."

Parnell was shaking his head and swearing softly and continuously. "What the hell is all this?" Parnell said. "What's with this guy? This isn't right..."

"Maybe because he's batshit crazy, did you think about that?" the agent said.

Gabriel hunched closer. "No, it's there, see?" he said to Parnell, pointing at the screen. "Not that one, this one here." Parnell stopped tapping keys for a moment, staring with his nose almost touching the screen.

"You're sure? How do you know?" Parnell said, shaking his head.

"I've looked at a lot more of these than you have, Chuck. Focus on this. Process this track," Gabriel responded.

"What's going on?" The agent asked. "I thought he walked out before—"

"Shut up," Gabriel and Parnell said in unison. The agent sat and fumed as the other two continued to work. Parnell stopped his repeated swearing, and then began to smile as the text started to scroll across the screen.

"That's what I'm talking about!" Parnell exclaimed, pumping his fist. He offered his palm up for a high five from Gabriel. Gabriel ignored him. After a minute, Parnell dropped his hand. Gabriel was reading the text, shaking his head again.

"We can't be sure, Chuck," Gabriel said.

"Bullshit!" Parnell replied.

"It has no context. He's obviously very disturbed. We don't know what we're reading here." Gabriel sat down as the agent got out of his seat to come around and look at the screen.

"What? What is it? You have something?" the agent asked.

"Yeah, we fucking have the whole thing, Mr. Agent, man. Officer agent, whatever. Don't know about the mother, but the girl is in a hotel room, somewhere. I think. There's a name."

"You can't be sure, Chuck," Gabriel said. "You're making a lot of assumptions."

The agent was leaning over Parnell now, reading the screen. "Holy shit. This is him?" Parnell nodded. "When?"

"Near the end, when I flashed him the picture. Startle response. No doubt about it," Parnell said. Gabriel groaned.

"Print this out for me," the agent commanded. Parnell started to tap again.

"No way," Gabriel said, closing the laptop onto Parnell's hands. "We're not printing anything, we're not putting this on a thumbdrive, burning a disk, anything. You want to read over our shoulder, that's your call, Agent. I will not take responsibility for any of this. Read it over, do what you want with it. But do it quick because when we leave this room, it's gone and this never happened."

It was Parnell's turn to shake his head. The agent looked between the two, questioning. "Whatever," Parnell said. "He's the boss. Be my guest, officer." He pushed his chair away from the table. The agent pulled his chair over and sat down in front of the computer, reading the text through several times. He picked up the phone on the desk.

"Get the others in here, now. I think we have something."

Less than an hour later, the FBI found the little girl, scared but alive and well, in a motel room three miles from their location. The girl's stepfather confessed to abducting her, but continued to insist he had no clue what had become of the girl's mother.

During the week after arresting the stepfather, Ed the FBI agent had called the Embarcadero lab six times, asking for Gabriel to set up another session. Gabriel had stopped taking his calls.

"You can't just ignore this guy, Gabe," Arthur said, sprawled on the couch in Gabriel's office.

"Watch me," Gabriel said, seated at his desk and trying to catch up on his emails.

"He's the FBI, Gabe. You gave them the location for the girl, they're just looking to give you a little credit."

"Bullshit, Arthur. This isn't about pinning a medal on me for community service and you know it. He wants more. He wants more and he's not going to get it. You can tell your bridge buddy that. No trump, or whatever."

Arthur sat up on the couch to stare at his friend. "Say what you want, Gabriel, but you may have saved that little girl's life."

"Swell. He can still go to hell, Arthur. I shouldn't have let you guys talk me into it."

"Ed's in a bind, Gabriel. He's got to explain to a lot of people how the FBI managed to storm the right hotel room. He's trying to figure out what to tell his superiors about where he got his information. Not to mention that asshole of an attorney. And the press, the press is all over this, you know." He watched his friend shaking his head as he typed his emails.

"Maybe he should've thought of that before he let us experiment on his person of interest. Probably broke a few regulations, you think? Maybe blew his whole case against this whack job. Anyway, not my problem, Arthur."

"You saved that girl, Gabe."

"Like I said, Arthur, that's just swell."

"It's out now, Gabriel. Face it. You can't put it back in the box."

Gabriel sighed and pushed back from his desk, turning to face his friend.

"Yeah, Arthur. I know. Helena was right."

"About what, this time?"

"Before we left for the FBI. She said, 'the real trouble is if this works'. And now we're in it, deep."

They stared at each other for a minute, silent. Parnell sauntered in, drying his waist length hair with a towel as he dropped into the chair across from Gabriel's desk. A puddle began to form at his feet. "Who died?" he asked.

"Our research," Gabriel answered.

"This goes one of two ways, Gabe," Arthur said slowly. "We either get out in front of this, make a public announcement about our new technology with the FBI standing behind us—"

"Yeah, yeah," Parnell said. "That'd be great, have the girl there with her parents and all."

"Yeah, you think?" Gabriel said. "Her mom's missing and the lunatic stepdad probably did her. Great publicity. No thanks, Arthur."

"Okay, maybe not with the parents. But the girl would be a nice touch, I think," Parnell said brightly.

"What's the other way, Arthur? Let me guess—"

"The other way?" Arthur interrupted. "The other way, this comes out like a Molotov cocktail, probably from the FBI itself."

"And blows up in our face," Gabriel said. Arthur nodded. "Thanks a lot, Arthur."

"Let's go with the first choice, then," Parnell said.

"I'll get public relations cranking on it," Arthur said, standing.

They tried all the usual tricks to deflate the announcement as much as possible; Sunday morning press conference, pitched only to the local crime media, Gabriel doing his best absent-minded professor shtick. He tried to baffle them with arcane terminology, unimpress them with smokescreens of marginal utility and conditional veracity, disabuse them of any thought of scientific or social import. He failed spectacularly. Despite their efforts, every national news report on Monday led with the story of 'New Mind Reading Technology Saves Kidnapped Girl'; the picture of the smiling, now rescued, child hovering angelically behind the shoulder of every major television anchor.

"We are so fucked," Gabriel said, burying his face in his hands. They had gathered at Arthur's home and were arrayed in front of his giant flatscreen, seated behind beers and guacamole.

"Fucking famous," Parnell yodeled in two-tone falsetto from his spot on the couch, pumping both arms, palms up. He leaned over to give Gabriel a high five, who ignored him. Parnell dropped his hand, took a scoop of guacamole on a chip, adding, "Shame your press conference didn't make the national feed, Gabriel."

"Yeah, those twenty minutes of mumbling into your shoes would've made great television," Helena said, draining her beer.

Gabriel looked up at his friend. "We gotta lay low awhile, Arthur. Let this blow over."

Arthur snorted derisively. "Yeah right, Gabe. Blow over? Have you checked your email today, buddy?" Gabriel shook his head. "Yeah, well, keep living your fantasy, then. The phones at the office have been ringing nonstop all day. Tomorrow will be worse."

"I'll hide in the lab," Gabriel said, laying his head on Helena's lap and covering his face with a pillow.

"Bullshit, you'll hide in the lab," Arthur said. "You think I'm going to be the face of this thing?"

"I'll do it," Parnell said through a mouthful of chips, raising his hand.

Arthur shook his head. He leaned over and pulled the pillow off of Gabriel's face and chucked it at Parnell's head. Parnell ducked in time to avoid the pillow but face planted in the bowl of guacamole.

Arthur just shook his head again and continued in Gabriel's direction, "I'm setting you up with half a dozen interviews by the end of the week, buddy boy. National press, too, not those Sausalito crime beat stooges. Science types, NPR, New York Times, the Post. Hell, you'll probably be on 'Meet The Press' next weekend. Start whitening your teeth, Mr. All-Knowing Swami. You are the man of the minute." Gabriel groaned and buried his face in Helena's lap.

"Why can't I do some interviews? I actually saved that girl, you know," Parnell said, wiping his face with the pillow and looking from Arthur to Helena.

"Because," Arthur said, "you're a moron, Chuck. And you got guacamole all over your eyebrows. Mostly, because you're a moron. Really, Chuck? My pillow?"

"Arthur's right, Gabe," Helena said, tickling her husband until he sat up on the couch. "You have to go full tilt on this."

"Why? I hate this shit."

"I know," Helena continued, "and god knows you're not any good at it. But it's your invention and you've got to get in front of this, before it spins out of control."

"It's already spun."

"No, not yet, not if you set it up right. Define the reality of it. If you don't, this is going to get ugly, fast. By next week, there'll be ads on Home Shopping Network for do-it-yourself mind reading devices. Every wife in the country will be buying some rejiggered first generation iPod that's labeled as "FBI approved" and using it to try to find out where her husband really went last night. Or worse."

Arthur was nodding. Gabriel looked morose.

Helena gave her husband a supportive smile. "Cheer up, darling. It's what you always dreamed of."

"Yeah? Which dream was that?"

"Changing the world."

"I never said that."

Helena just rolled her eyes and turned to Parnell. "Chuck, where do we stand with security?"

"What do you mean?" Parnell asked.

Arthur saved him from Helena's nearly thrown empty bottle of beer, grabbing her arm as he interjected, "Chuck and I have a meeting with the consultants next week, at the lab."

Helena set down the bottle, turning to Arthur. "That's not good enough, guys. And we put Chuck in charge of this, not you, Arthur. This is Parnell's responsibility." She picked the bottle back up and leaning over, tapped it against Parnell's forehead. He flinched away.

"Arthur's helping, that's all," Parnell said. "What's wrong with next week?"

"Because this is out now, today. We're exposed," Helena said, exasperated. "I want you to go straight to the lab, Chuck. Disconnect the lab from the internet, completely. Until we have a real security system, that'll have to do." She glared at Parnell.

"What? Now?" he asked, incredulous. She nodded. "But how will we work without the internet? That's ridiculous." Helena just stared at him. "Fine," he said, "I'm going. But we're getting a real security setup before next week, then. We can't not have internet. Geez." Parnell stood and, grabbing a last fistful of chips, stood to leave. "Enjoy dinner without me, guys. See you, Sam, thanks for nothing," he called towards the kitchen as he walked out.

They watched him go. "Okay, Helena," Arthur said after the door closed. "What was that about?"

"Security, Arthur."

"You don't trust Chuck? Come on."

"You know where this is going, Arthur. It's inevitable. The government has gotten wind of this. And Chuck works for the government."

"You're crazy, Helena. Chuck is a friend."

"What's on your mind, Leena?" Gabriel asked from his place on the couch.

"Chuck knows he's on notice, that if anything happens, it's on his head. But that'll only work for a while. When the shit really starts to hit the fan, and it will, I don't think intimidation is going to do it."

"What do you propose?" Arthur asked.

"Let Chuck set up his system, I'm sure it'll be great. But we keep a single copy of the salmon on a removable hard drive that goes home with us every night. It never leaves our hands."

"Yeah, like that'll work, Helena," Arthur said. "This is going to take off, there'll be a huge demand for access to this technology. That's the whole point."

"I've been thinking about this," Helena said. "We have the program, the salmon, on a single server, in the middle of the lab. Like it's on an island. The only access to that server is from direct hard wired lines to the individual consoles, in the labs."

"Like bridges across a moat."

"Whatever," Helena said. "But that network, the network that accesses the central server, has no connection to the Internet or the outside world. No way for anyone or the government to hack into the system because there's connection to the outside world."

Gabriel was nodding. "That could work," he said. "We could have a separate computer network at the lab, one for administrative use and all, that accessed the internet."

"Yeah, but it would have no physical connection with the internal network, the one that accessed the salmon. And we physically protect the salmon from the outside world, so no one can touch it," Helena said, nodding also.

Arthur wasn't nodding. "You guys are nuts," he said. "Paranoid wackos, both of you."

"No, Arthur," Gabriel said. "It's not paranoia. Well, maybe a little paranoid," he said, gesturing at his wife. "We can't let this get out. I agree with Helena."

"But it's going to get out, Gabriel," Arthur said. "That's what we're talking about here. We're going to have to license this or something, so that it can be used. The public is going to demand it. Every court in the country, every investigative agency, every police force, they're all going to want one of our devices. To pursue truth and justice, you know? It's going to be everywhere."

"No," Helena said emphatically.

"You won't be able to stop it, Helena. Like you said yourself, if we don't get out there with this, the conjurers will take over." Arthur looked at them defiantly.

"No, Arthur," Gabriel said. "Helena's right. Not just because it's ours. This technology is too dangerous."

"Well, let's not get all melodramatic about it, Gabriel," Arthur said; now smiling at him. "I agree we have to maintain some sort of royalty system, establish some sort of payment scheme so this doesn't just get everywhere, but—"

"No, Arthur, I'm not kidding. And I'm not talking about the money, either. This is genuinely dangerous, like Manhattan Project dangerous," Gabriel said.

"I'm not following you," Arthur said. "The technology works, it reads minds pretty well, Gabriel. I saw that. The world saw that."

"We got lucky, Arthur. That's the whole problem, the Parnell problem. He thinks because we can read a guy's thoughts that we're seeing the truth, with a capital 'T'. It's two different things."

"It worked, Gabriel. You can't argue with his methods. It saved that girl's life."

"Aargh. Stop saying that, Arthur. We got lucky, that's all. All we needed was a location, a single thought, and that's really all we got. Hell, I don't think Chuck could've even picked it out if I wasn't there to make sense of the tracings. This isn't something we can load up in a box and sell to every law enforcement agency in the country. We'll fill up the jails with everyone who ever had a passing thought of knocking over a convenience store."

"We'll just have to train them to use it right, that's all," Arthur said.

"No, it's not like that. That's what Chuck believes, that it can be distilled and simplified, if we get good enough at it. It's not like that, that's why it's so dangerous. The more I work on this, the more complicated it's getting. Look, we could attach electrodes to my head, right now. There are multiple layers of thought going on in my head, dozens. Every improvement shows more layers. I'm having a conversation with you, but at some deeper level a tracing may show some transient emotion, some sexual desire or—"

"What?" Helena said. Arthur sat up straighter.

"—anything, you know? That doesn't make me gay or anything, just because a tracing at some level shows a passing thought," Gabriel finished.

Arthur was just staring at him.

"Yeah, Gabe," Helena said. "I think that makes you gay."

"No, it doesn't," Gabriel insisted. "That's the point I'm trying to make here."

"Really gay, Gabriel," Arthur said.

"This explains so much," Helena said. "I should've seen this day coming. Your mom was right. I'll just let you two have some alone time, to work out your feelings."

"Don't leave me with him, Helena. I'm happily married," Arthur said.

"That's not what Sam tells me," Helena said.

"That's because she's a little gay," Arthur said.

"That explains the haircut," Helena said, smiling.

"I'm going to tell her you said that," Arthur said. At this point, Samantha walked in, carrying a platter of barbecued chicken. She set it down on the dining table.

"Tell me what?" Sam asked.

"Gabriel's gay," Arthur said.

"Not surprised, he's so neat and all," Samantha said. "Dinner's ready. Where's Chuck?"

"Will you guys knock it off?" Gabriel said. "I'm serious about this."

"You sound so gay now, Gabe," Helena said. She turned to Arthur. "How could I not have seen this?"

"Love blinds us all," Arthur said, heading into the kitchen to help his wife with the rest of the food.

Gabriel and Helena just looked at each other, looking thoughtful.

"I think I have the answer," Helena said after a bit.

"To what?" Gabriel asked.

"Both problems, silly gay boy," Helena said. They all sat down to dinner.

"Food's great, Sam," Gabriel said. "And I love the new haircut, by the way."

Samantha smiled. "Thanks, Gabriel. Arthur hates it, says it makes me look butch."

"That's because Arthur is threatened by independent minded women, aren't you, Arthur?" Gabriel said. "And he's homophobic."

Arthur wiped his hands. "If you mean, I'm not having homoerotic fantasies about my coworkers all day, yeah, I guess you're right."

"Where is Chuck, anyway?" Samantha asked.

"Actually, hon, I was referring to Gabriel," Arthur said.

"Oh," Samantha said, giving Gabriel a weak smile.

"Chuck's going to be a problem," Helena said.

"No way," Arthur said.

"Wait, Arthur. You'll see," Helena said. She gestured to the empty place at the table. "Judas Iscariot. Nice guy, gonna stab us in the back."

"I don't think so, Leena," Gabriel said. "He's on our side."

"Can't see past your man crush, Gabe," Helena said.

"Okay, we all love a running gag. Time to move on. So what's your big idea, hon?"

Helena put down her fork and brightened. "This may be brilliant, just warning you." She paused for effect as they waited. "We have two problems, not counting Chuck. First problem—security. Keeping control of our technology, though we all realize that it's out of the bag. We need to develop it commercially, whether we want to or not."

"That's right," Arthur agreed. "It's going to be distributed, no doubt about that."

"Maybe not, Arthur. Give me a chance here. That's problem number one. But Gabriel has another concern. He's worried that if we license the technology, just put it out there, it'll be all screwed up. Inappropriate use, misinterpretations, oversimplifications. Am I getting this right, Gabe?"

Gabriel nodded half-heartedly. "In an inarticulate manner that doesn't nearly do justice to the subtlety of my argument, yeah, hon. Perfect."

"Fuck you too, dear. I hope your gay lovers are more sensitive to the subtlety of your arguments. Let's move on."

"Well," Arthur interrupted. "Maybe we don't sell the technology. Maybe we license its use, make sure we train the operators so it gets used appropriately."

"You're halfway there, Arthur. I've got something better, though. We license the technology to make the recordings, train and control the operators. But the interpretation stays in house. The recordings get sent to us, we keep the salmon in house and do all the analysis. Gabriel maintains control, we maintain security. The salmon stays on the island. We send them back our analysis." She stopped, smiling around the table.

"That's brilliant, Helena," Samantha said.

"Thank you, Sam. I think so, too."

"That's perfect," Gabriel said. "I can keep Chuck from screwing it up."

"And we can charge for every step," Arthur said. "Split up the process. Charge for the data collection, charge for the interpretation. Hell, charge for every certified copy of the interpretation that's distributed. Brilliant."

"Always seeing the profit angle, aren't you, Arthur?" Helena said.

"Hey, it's what you pay me for," Arthur said as he stood to gather up plates. Gabriel stood to help, leaned over to kiss the top of his wife's head.

"You're just lucky I'm not intimidated by strong, brilliant women," Gabriel said.

"You should be," Samantha said. "Like my husband. You should try cutting your hair short, Helena."

"What, me? Never!"

"But who will love us now that our husbands have switched teams?" Samantha pouted.

"Younger, stronger men," Helena said, smiling.

"We can hear you, you know," Arthur called from the kitchen. He returned with cheesecake. Gabriel followed with the coffee urn, and poured around the table.

Arthur was ebullient as he sliced and distributed dessert. "We could dress them up, you know? The recording technicians. Create a sort of cult of mystery, a brand, you know?"

"Now you're getting weird, Arthur," Samantha said.

"No, it'd be more formal like that. Add an air of drama to the recording session, make it more important. More intimidating."

"Like a deposition, or a lie detector session," Gabriel said, sitting down.

"More intimidating than a lie detector session," Arthur said. "That's our competition. We're better than that, more special. We actually read minds."

"What did you have in mind, Arthur? Tuxedos and top hats?" Helena asked, laughing.

"No, better. Heavy brown robes, with deep hooded cowls. Like Capuchin monks, you know?"

"What? We're using formally dressed primates?" Helena asked. "I don't think we need to go cross species with this, do you, Arthur?"

"What?" Arthur asked, confused.

"Capuchins are monkeys, Arthur," Samantha said, embarrassed. "You mean Friars, or Jesuits. He's Jewish," Samantha added to the others, apologetically.

"No, they're monks, too. Capuchin Friars, I'm pretty sure," Arthur said, defensively. "This is what I get for marrying out of the faith, constant anti-Semitism."

"Your mother warned you about me," Samantha said.

"Mom told me you were a metrosexual. Until the haircut, I didn't know what she meant."

"Always listen to your mother, Arthur," Gabriel said. "I did. Look where it got me."

The security consultants arrived at the lab the following week. The consultants listened to Arthur and Chuck as the two of them explained Helena's ideas. The consultants nodded, took notes, and poked around the lab for three days. Then they produced a plan that cost eighty eight thousand dollars (without hardware) and was a strict retelling of everything that Helena had said, though in completely altered jargon. Instead of Helena's 'island with a moat' concept, it became 'room within a room'. Not as poetic but far more costly. It took another six weeks to install.

The consultants were appalled at the concept of physical removal for protection of the central server hard drive. Not the way to go, they insisted. Just the opposite, they insisted, multiple copies of offsite backup were absolutely required. Helena stood toe to toe with the lot of them, hands on hips as she insisted that she would flail each of them if she discovered any type of backup system anywhere on the premises. Custom built hardware with no port or electronic interface of any kind, she insisted. Permanently sealed chassis, no physical access possible, ever. If it breaks, we'll replace it. Further, she would hunt down and dismember every last one of them and their closest relatives if she found any hint of an offsite backup system or any connection between the island, or 'inner sanctum' as they insisted on calling it, and the outside world. They were appalled, they shook their heads in disbelief, they referred to Helena as "Keyser Söze" behind her back. The consultants tried to go around her to Arthur, who obviously would be more sensible. He laughed at them. They finally gave in, built the system Helena had laid out at the outset, took their ridiculous sums of money and left.

Arthur and Parnell sat down with Helena, concerned. You do realize, they explained, that we do have to back up everything, don't you? This is a business; there will be reports, invoices, everything involved in everyday operations that could go 'poof'. Earthquakes, fires, floods, sabotage, power failures, spilled coffee; we'd be wiped out. Not to mention a lifetime's work. Copies must be made, multiple backups in multiple locations, all over the globe.

Of course, she told them. A second security firm was brought in from Israel. Helena found them; a firm of two brothers that had set up a small in-house network for the Mossad, when they updated their system two years ago. She sat down with them and explained what she wanted: a multiply fragmented backup system that would break up the information generated every day into randomly sized and ordered pieces, each fragment then being backed up to multiple randomly selected locations; some domestic, most not. The randomization keys for each day until the year 2050 listed only on the single hard drive kept on the central server and physically in Helena's possession. One list of key codes, encrypted with a unique key number known only to the three principals of the company. A random twelve-digit key, memorized, not written down anywhere. The only physical encrypted list of keycodes for the fragmented backup system mailed in a nondescript manila envelope serially between every UPS office in the world, the next address being randomly chosen from their branch offices list, the tracking number being mailed each day and piling up in a decrepit storage unit in Ypsilanti. To Helena's face, the Israelis smiled and marveled at her deep appreciation for their field. Once out of the room, they called her a fucking paranoid mushigannah, and worse. They were paid more than the last group, and once the system was in place, left wondering what in the world this crazy woman did in this lab, and if she had a sister. Their kind of gal. Never got her name, they realized.

Arthur went back to doing what Arthur did best. He built a new industry from scratch. He met with investors, set up another complex network of companies, hired contractors who hired, in turn, more contractors and subcontractors. Marketing, patents, office space, training, staffing. Legal teams, teams of programmers, launch dates, beta testing of software, pricing, contracts, insurance. The list never grew shorter.

Gabriel visited Arthur at his downtown office almost daily. Chuck was left to run the lab and ready themselves for the coming influx of mental tracings to be interpreted. Parnell headed a small team of programmers charged with the task of automating the interpretations based upon accessing the salmon of knowledge. Parnell and Gabriel would do quality assurance, reviewing every interpretation before releasing back a report. Gabriel was not looking forward to that part, but could see no way out of it. He certainly wasn't going to let Chuck review the interpretations alone, based on his own software. He already anticipated the looming battles.

"Working way too hard here, Gabriel," Arthur said, pushing back from his desk.

Gabriel dropped into a chair, gesturing at the immaculate glass desk. "You don't have a single piece of paper in front of you, Arthur. How hard can you be working?"

"Paper? Who uses paper for anything? I'm working my tail off here," Arthur replied indignantly.

"So? When do we start seeing some output?"

"Six weeks, big rollout. You'll get the invitation. Clear your schedule."

"For how long, you think?"

"Probably the next decade. This is going to be big, Gabriel. Too big, maybe."

"Never heard you say that before, Arthur."

"Well, you heard it now, my friend. Couple of months from now, you'll be quoting me. We're going to be ass deep in this."

"Investors should be happy."

"They're going to make a fucking fortune, no doubt."

"So what's the problem, Arthur? Just working too hard? You love this shit, the startup is your favorite part."

Arthur stood up, walked to the windows and looked out. "You're right, Gabriel. This is the fun part. That's not what's got me worried."

"So what's the problem?"

Arthur turned to face his friend. "No exit strategy this time."

Gabriel nodded. "I see your point."

"We're not going to be able to just pull the plug on this. This is going to change the way the world works. Once it starts, it's not going away. Ever."

"We'll just have to figure out a way to hand it off, like everything else we've done. Worked before, Arthur."

Arthur returned to looking out his window at the city. "I don't see how, Gabriel. Not this time. Between you insisting on being the last word on every report, and your wife's paranoia about the technology getting stolen, I don't see the door on this."

"Helena does feel pretty strongly, I agree."

"You're both fucking crazy. No offense, Gabe."

"What do you want to do then? Call it off?"

"Can't."

"Then what? Give me some options here, Arthur."

Arthur shrugged at the city below. "Just going to have ride this tiger for a while, Gabriel. Don't see any choice at this point."

"What happens when we get tired of riding?"

"Usually, you get eaten. Isn't that what the analogy is all about?" Arthur turned to smile at his friend.

"Is it an analogy or a metaphor?"

"Might be a simile. What's Helena up to?"

"You mean since she locked down the lab tighter than the Fortress of Solitude? She's back in her lab, listening to tracings like before."

"I'm worried about that girl, Gabriel. So is Sam."

"Not half as much as I am, Arthur."

After hours of focus testing, they decided against the hooded monk robes. They were deeply intimidating, but conjured up a combination of grim reaper and coffee flavored liquor that proved counterproductive. Ultimately, the technicians were chosen to be youthful, serious, and professional in demeanor. They were dressed in identical pinstriped dark gray suits with a solid black vest, white button down collared shirt, thin solid charcoal gray necktie tied in the single Windsor fashion. They wore identical name badges, always naming them as Mr. or Ms. Smythe. It was pronounced 'smith'. They were to speak as little as possible, using short, clipped sentences. And they all maintained a smoothly shaved head—both men and women. They were awesome. Parnell wanted dark glasses, but he was outvoted. Too much "Men in Black", Arthur said.

The service launched in eight major metropolitan markets across the United States. The startup was called "Insight Services". They marketed to all comers, made no restrictions or claims. Gabriel, always trying to limit expectations and exposure, came up with the idea that the Insight technicians would only function to record the subject's thoughts. This further distanced them from the concept of lie detection, as they were not the ones responsible for asking the questions. That task was left to the discretion of whoever signed up for the service. Subjects signed a release stating that they were submitting to the examination voluntarily. They were required to don a lightweight electrode cap, though no shaving of the scalp was required. It was Gabriel's latest invention.

Sessions were billed by the minute of questioning with an initial basic fee covering the setup period. A quiet room was required, to be furnished by the contractee. The session could be videotaped if the contractee desired and the subject signed the necessary release. The videorecorder was built into the laptop, which each technician carried in his or her standard issue black attaché case.

Arthur and Gabriel were surprised by the reality of the business once it started. Arthur had been concerned prior to the launch about Gabriel's insistence that he review every recording, believing that such a policy would inevitably lead to delays and a backlog of reports. He had tried to talk Gabriel into some sort of sampling protocol to maintain workflow, but it proved unnecessary. Insight sessions proved to be astonishingly brief and to the point. As the questioners were usually the paying clients, they didn't spend much time before getting to the gist of what they wanted to know. Questions were direct and almost always factual in nature. Often, clients hired lawyers to act as questioners, mimicking some form of deposition. The lawyers were quickly reigned in when they became verbose, however, as the client was painfully aware that they were paying the lawyer by the hour and the technicians by the minute.

Gabriel's concerns about the interpretations being complicated by emotional overlays or misremembrances proved equally unfounded. Chuck had been closer to the reality of the thing. A typical question was, 'Did you sleep with my sister, girlfriend, husband?' An emphatic 'no' was either true or false and easily interpreted by the most cursory review of the recording. They never asked, 'Do you find my sister attractive?' or 'Have you been thinking of sleeping with her?' That sort of questioning would have required application of Gabriel's interpretive skills, but it never came up. Nobody asked why or how, it was always 'did you?' or 'didn't you?' Factual questions with a straightforward answer, easily identified as truth or fiction. Gabriel was almost bored with the simplicity of it all. Parnell was insufferable.

To simplify things even further, subjects almost never lied. Gabriel realized that they should've anticipated this, though they hadn't at all. They also didn't anticipate how emotionally wrenching the sessions were for some of the subjects. Many walked into the sessions worried that their every thought was to be laid bare, not just the veracity of their answers. In many ways, this fear was appropriate, though technicians reassured the subjects that the recording was limited to those thoughts 'pertinent to the question'; whatever that meant, which was nothing, really. The subjects felt naked and exposed in a manner more penetrating than anything society had experienced before. Some subjects winced with each question, staring at the technicians for some hint of feedback. Those who did try to lie frequently became distraught, breaking down and reversing their statements before the end of a session. More than once a subject simply couldn't or wouldn't proceed, removing the electrode cap and bolting from the room.

It became necessary to formalize the sessions, create a kind of Kabuki dance to emotionally support the subject. It was explicitly stated by the technicians at the outset that the subject was there voluntarily and was welcome to end the session at any time. The clients, the questioners, often bristled at this, but were allowed no argument. Technicians were trained to be empathetic and supportive to the subjects at all times, even if this meant offending the client who was paying the bill.

The teams realized early on that it was important to end the sessions in a formal and dramatic fashion, to emphasize to the respondent that he was no longer subject to having his thoughts monitored. Therefore, at the conclusion of the session, the technician formally thanked the subject and made a show of removing the electrode cap. A little Japanese style bow on the part of the technicians was required. The recording was transmitted in an encrypted fashion immediately to the lab in San Francisco. A printed proof of transmission was given to the contractee and the subject. All recorded data was then deleted from the laptop with a dramatic flourish. This helped prevent the technicians from being assaulted or threatened on the way out the door. Early on, it was decided that all technicians were to work in teams of two for added security. The results of the examination were mailed back to the contractee in five working days as a printed transcript, certified. A copy could be mailed to the subject separately if the contractee desired. Rush service was available for an extra expense.

Gabriel had hoped they would start under the radar and build slowly. Arthur's marketing firm had a different vision. They made the evening news and front page in every significant media market in the country, some using footage from the kidnapped girl incident. Insight Services took off like a rocket. Within a week, they were booking in most markets over three months in advance. Arthur was forced to scramble to get more technicians in the training pipeline. Recruiting was not difficult. The job of Insight technician held a great deal of cache for reasons that baffled everyone but Parnell. Out of work actors throughout the country stopped waiting tables to apply; no scientific background was required, but an air of authority and competence was necessary. Stage presence helped a great deal. It paid well, lots of travel was involved, and so far no technician had been assaulted. Just in case, though, the standard attaché case carried by each technician included a can of pepper spray.

At first, clients were private citizens with a burning need to know something; something so important that they needed to know the truth. Everyone had something they wanted to ask, if they could be sure of the veracity of the answer. In fact, many newspapers began to run a daily feature where questions were proposed by readers to famous subjects. The Wall Street Journal ran two such features daily, one on the business side and one on the cultural. It didn't seem to matter that the questions were never answered. The public was caught up in the idea of knowing the truth. That had never been possible before.

Before long, there came a wave of requests from business and financial firms, subjecting possible candidates to Insight screening as a precondition for employment. This was extremely popular at the middle management level, though rarely employed at the most senior levels. After a while, customers included security firms of course, but also hospitals and nursing facilities, universities, and professional societies with a particular care to prevent fraudulent employees or faculty. All of these examinations proved mundane for the interpretative processes put in place by Parnell and Gabriel. The system whirred along without a hitch. Volume steadily grew, as did acceptance. Controversy was conscientiously avoided. Though Insight Technologies refused to become involved, inevitably a spate of reality television shows appeared, always utilizing feigned bald headed technicians. Arthur's legal team was kept busy pursuing a steady stream of injunctions. The concept of mind reading slowly and pervasively seeped into the public consciousness.

The judicial system did its best to pretend the technology simply didn't exist. It didn't help that the FBI had been embroiled in a public lawsuit resulting from that first use of Insight technology in a criminal investigation. Police forces of every size and type were loath to consider any new technology that didn't involve shooting or being shot at. Insight technology remained a creature exclusive to the private sector. This was fine with the principals of the company, though they knew it couldn't last.

Helena walked unsteadily into Gabriel's office. Gabriel looked up from his computer where he had been reviewing the last case of the day. Helena gave him a weak smile, leaning on the doorway.

"Hey, good-looking," she said. "Want to take a girl to dinner?"

Gabe looked at her with concern. She looked like someone who had just awakened from a prolonged coma. He smiled back. "Sure, beautiful," he said. "You miss lunch?" He watched her closely, seeing the cloud pass over her face as she considered his question. "You don't remember, do you? You don't remember if you had lunch?"

She straightened, becoming defensive. "Of course I do. I just grabbed a yogurt from the frig. I was busy, working."

He knew she was lying. They knew each other too well. She knew it too. "How's the work going?" he asked.

"I'll tell you over dinner," she replied. "Finished?"

"Finished. Let's go someplace nice."

"Let's go to a bar."

They ended up facing each other over burgers and beer in a noisy bar a few blocks from the lab. They had talked little over the first two beers.

"So," Helena began between mouthfuls. "How go's the business?"

"Not bad. Pretty dull, actually. I haven't had to swear at Chuck all week," he smiled.

"Still looking over his shoulder?"

He nodded. "Every time, yeah. But I'm pretty much just going through the motions now. Not much controversy, now that the software's up to speed." She nodded back. "How about you, hon? What's going on back there?" He inclined his head back toward the lab as he ate his burger.

"Just listening."

"Still? You've been listening for over four months, darling," he said.

Her expression hardened for a moment. "You think I'm wasting my time back there, Gabriel? Need help with the profit side of the business?"

He shook his head, polished the last of his beer and gestured to the waiter for two more. "You know that's not what I meant. Finish your beer, there's another on the way." He looked at her soberly. "What are you listening to now?"

She finished her own beer and looked at him with a wicked smile. "Well, since you ask. I've been listening to the kidnapper."

"What? The FBI thing? Why? That recording is trash." He stared at her, concerned.

"It's not trash, Gabe. It's different, that's all. Weird, actually."

"Why are you studying him, Leena? He's a sick guy. He never went to trial, ended up being declared criminally insane."

"The medical term is schizophrenic, Gabe. 'Criminally insane' is just what the lawyers call it when the FBI fucks up so badly they can't file charges."

"I'm not arguing with that, Leena. I just thought you were listening to the recordings from the normal cohort, and the prevaricators."

"I did. I finished them."

"There were over two hundred recordings, hon."

"Finished 'em."

Gabriel leaned back as the waiter delivered their beers. "No way."

She nodded. "Way."

"So what'd you learn? That's a lot of listening to noise."

She shrugged, leaned back in her own chair and blew a red ringlet from her forehead. "Not noise, exactly. Definitely not noise, Gabe. I learned a lot about how normal thinking sounds, what it looks like. Now it's time to look at the other side, I think."

"Mental illness, you mean? Schizophrenia?"

"Yeah, and other illnesses. Depression, bipolar disorder. Of course, so far I only have one subject recording to go over."

Gabriel was quiet for a moment, thinking. "So what do you think about the one subject?"

"Very different in some ways, same as all the others in a lot of ways. It's weird. But I've only listened to him a few dozen times so far."

Gabriel was shaking his head, questioning. "But you're just listening, right? That's not science, Leena. How are you going to quantitate anything, generate any data?"

"Yeah, that's a problem. I've been thinking about that a lot. I've listened to so many recordings, I can tell a lot about what the subject is thinking at multiple levels, you know, all at the same time, just by listening to the waves. I can tell abnormal, or lying, or fantasizing, or whatever, just listening to the music of the thing. But I couldn't describe to you how I do it or document it in any way. It's a problem."

"Sure as hell is," Gabriel agreed. "We need coffee and dessert."

"You do."

Gabe ordered cheesecake. "Does San Francisco have a music school? A conservatory or something?" Helena asked, between huge forkfuls of cake.

"Did you want your own, because you said you 'just wanted a bite' of mine, remember?" She smiled at him wickedly. "Yeah, San Francisco Conservatory of Music. Why, thinking of changing majors again?"

"Thinking of getting some help with this listening thing. Trying to figure some way to document what I'm hearing."

"What, like a music theory major or something?"

"I don't know. Maybe a composer, one of those new music or electronic guys, you know? Maybe they could help."

"Interesting thought. Worth a shot, I guess." Gabriel made a stab for the last piece of cheesecake, a fraction of a second too late.

Deacon Zacharias sat next to Helena in the semidarkness of her lab, his face reflecting the multicolored hues of the monitors around them. He was young, certainly much less than thirty by Helena's estimate, and a doctoral student in composition and music theory. He had been recommended to Helena when she called the chairman of the department at the San Francisco Conservatory. He was shaking his head.

"Sorry, Ma'am. Can't help you," he said.

"Call me Helena, Mr. Zacharias," Helena replied. "Why do you think you can't help me?"

"You can call me Zeke," he said.

"Zeke?"

"It's what they call me, Ma'am."

"You need to stop calling me that or I'll take back my five hundred dollars, Zeke."

The young man shrugged as he swiveled his chair to face her. "Gonna have to give it back anyway. Can't help you."

"Why do you feel that you can't help me, Zeke?" she asked again.

"Cause it's not music."

"Zeke, I've listened to some of your work. No offense, but I think this sounds a lot more musical than some of your stuff."

He shrugged again. "None taken, Ma'am. Helena." He smiled sheepishly. "It's still not music, though."

"But you can hear rhythms here, phrases that repeat, a lot of harmonies in there, right?"

He nodded, looking back at the screens. "Still not music, though."

Helena did her best to hide her frustration with the young man. "Can you explain to me why it's still not music, Zeke?"

He pointed to the monitor above them. "For the same reason that EKG tracing there ain't art. That's why."

"I'm not following you, Zeke."

He swung back to face her, leaned closer to her. "Look, Helena. You may not appreciate my music, but it's music nonetheless. I created it the way I did for a reason. Sometimes, the music lacks what you would appreciate as tonality, or rhythm, or some other elements of what you expect in music. But I wrote it that way for a reason, I created it that way. This," he said, gesturing over his shoulder at the screens, "ain't the same thing at all."

He leaned back in his chair. Helena digested this statement for a few minutes, studying him. She wasn't in the mood for a philosophical discussion, but didn't like having her idea blown up in her face. And she knew she had been working alone too long. She needed a collaborator.

"Go on."

Zeke looked at her with curiosity. He thought she'd want her money back by now.

"Okay. That EKG tracing, it's just a line of light tracing an electrical signal from your patient, or whatever. You can make it yellow or pink, doesn't matter. It's just a pattern of a guy's voltage. Now, I've got a friend who could print out about a thousand copies of that tracing and cut and paste 'em into something so pretty and abstract that you'd buy it for a couple grand and hang it in your living room. It would manifest our inevitable mortality, or some such shit. That's art. That," he said, jerking a thumb back toward the screen again, "ain't."

"Same with the sounds we're listening to. You just assigned a voice to some electrical signal and let it rip through these speakers. There maybe thought behind it, as you say, but there isn't any thought in it, you understand? It's just a signal. Now I could sample some of this, loop it, maybe manipulate it in some ways, and use it to create a piece of music. You understand me?"

She nodded, disappointed. She liked this young man. She was beginning to believe, however, that she was pursuing the wrong approach.

"I understand what you're saying, Zeke. But I don't want you to change it. I want you to help me describe it, to catalogue it in some way. Even if it isn't music."

"Wasting your time, I think. Look what you're doing, Helena. You're taking a signal, converting it to sound, and then you're going to try to describe the sound you made. That's nuts. Just go back to the original signal. Hire yourself an engineer or physicist to describe it at the source. Save yourself a lot of trouble."

Helena shook her head. "Doesn't work, Zeke. We tried that, a lot. It's too complex, too many layers. It didn't make any sense at all until we started listening to it. I've been listening to it for over four months now and I can understand it this way. The sounds create a gestalt, a pattern that can be appreciated in a way that the tracings or a formula doesn't capture."

"If you say so. Still don't think I can help you, though." He reached into his jean's pocket to give her back her money.

"No, keep the money. But I'm not done with you yet. Here, listen to this for a bit." Helena cued up a new recording. Zeke leaned back and put his sandaled feet up on the console. He closed his eyes to listen. The room filled with a staccato phrase that rose and fell eerily, repeating, pausing, and repeating again. Zeke's eyebrows raised over his closed eyes.

"Cool," he said softly. The phrase broke off and was replaced by a sonorous bass sound that filled the room for a few seconds, and then was joined by the repeating phrase again. Zeke's eyes opened. "Cool," he said again.

Helena stopped the playback. "Humor me. Pretend it's music. Tell me what you heard."

Zeke sat up again. "You could call that an ostinato, no problem. You could describe it musically. Is there more like that?"

Helena smiled at him. "A lot more. Like that and not at all like that. A whole lot more."

"You know what you need, Helena?" She shook her head. "You need an ethnomusicologist."

"A what?" Helena asked.

"Holy shit," Zeke said. He looked shocked.

"What? What's the problem?"

"I don't think that's ever been said before. Never in the history of civilization. 'You need an ethnomusicologist.' Wow." He shook his head in amazement.

"What the hell is an ethnomusicologist?" Helena asked.

"Kind of a musical sociologist. Or anthropologist. I'm not really certain which you'd call it."

"I don't think that's what I need."

"I think you do. They're really smart, some of them. Well, one of them I know, at least. They know a lot of music theory. Well, some music theory. Some of them. They might be better at this cataloguing part, too."

"You're trying to blow me off, aren't you Zeke?"

Zeke smiled at her. "Just trying to help, ma'am."

"Fine. You got any ethnomusicologists at your school?"

"No, not at the conservatory. But I know a couple in the area. There's a department at Berkley, and another at Davis."

"Fine. Come back tomorrow. And bring me an ethnomusicologist. Bring the smart one."

The ethnomusicologist proved to be very smart. She was Zeke's older sister, an assistant professor with a PhD, teaching 'Ethno' at Berkley. While her area of expertise was in the interpretation of hip-hop lyrics as social criticism, she was immediately enthralled with the concept of musical interpretation of thought waves. "Kind of like cutting out the middleman," she claimed. Helena had no idea what she meant. Helena did appreciate the enthusiasm she brought to the project, however. Particularly since Zeke was making every effort to excuse himself and return to his own work, working on his doctoral project. His sister Hannah, however, wouldn't let him off the hook. She insisted that Zeke could do both. It's a doctorate, she said; what's another year? He stayed on, though it was obvious he was just trying to be agreeable to the two of them. At least, at first.

The three of them spent three days a week together in Helena's lab. Helena spent every other day sifting through the recordings to prepare the material for the other two for their interpretation. From the start, it became obvious to Helena that her associates were coming at this project from a perspective completely different from her own. While Hannah was a soft scientist, Zeke was an artist. Hannah was the bridge between Helena's hard science and Zeke. It worked.

At first, Zeke treated the project like that of an orchestrator. It wasn't his music, he figured, but he did his best to define it and arrange those phrases that Helena had found to be meaningful. It wasn't difficult, and despite himself, he found it interesting. He modified an existing software program to help convert some of the sounds directly to musical notation, speeding up the process considerably. Hannah was able to catalogue the output and give sense to the notations, creating a reference library of sorts. They made a good team.

Zeke's enthusiasm increased dramatically when, out of boredom, he donned one of the skullcap electrode arrays and began noodling around with the console in the lab. The next day, Zeke brought in a bunch of equipment from his own studio, including several loop pedals, a guitar, and his laptop computer. Helena walked into the lab one afternoon to hear Zeke playing his "Music Straight From My Mind" symphony, opus number one, for his sister. Helena could only applaud, amazed. She thought it was the best thing he had ever done, in her opinion. Especially since she could hardly get herself to listen to most of his previous work. Zeke was thinking of trashing his PhD project and starting over with this new compositional concept. Since he was pulling down a nice salary from the lab, he figured he could afford an extra few years getting the degree. Of course, his advisor would go ballistic.

The lab settled into a productive routine. Helena ran the research side of the lab with her two young musical associates. Gabriel and Chuck ran the business side for Insight Technologies, attending to the increasing volume of work generated by Arthur's marketing arm. As the algorithms became more sophisticated, Gabriel and Chuck were able to free up more and more time for themselves. They trained junior associates in the daily running of the business, each taking turns at reviewing the interpretations for quality control. It settled into a nice, and highly profitable, routine for all involved. Arthur was particularly pleased.

They met at least weekly in Gabriel's office. Zeke and Hannah attended on occasion, but had their own responsibilities to attend to back at their respective music schools. Gabriel, Hannah, and Arthur sat once again in Gabriel's office, bouncing ideas about where to take the company next. Chuck hadn't made his appearance yet, still showering in Gabriel's adjoining overnight accommodation.

"Who takes a shower at 4:30 in the afternoon?" Arthur asked.

"Evidently, he has a date," Gabriel said from behind his desk. He was trying to find a printout of case production for the past month he had somewhere amidst the piles of paper on his desk. He groaned in frustration.

"Ever hear of a computer?" Arthur asked. "Why do you bother with printing out all that shit just so you can lose it or throw it out?"

"Fine, fine. I'll bring it back up on the screen. But I had printed out copies for all of you to look at while we talked."

"Ooh, that would've been great, Gabe," Helena said. Gabriel gave her his evil stare, and then went back to his computer. Chuck walked in wearing a towel and streaming water from his ponytail. He held the towel closed with one hand and handed a pile of wet paper to Helena with the other.

"Sorry, Gabriel. Here are those production reports we printed out. They got wet." Chuck exited again for the shower, which was still running.

Helena looked at the wad of soaked pages she held, dripping onto the carpet. She shook her head and tossed them at her husband, landing on his keyboard. Gabriel stood up and calmly distributed a copy of each soggy sheet to his partners. The printing was illegible. Gabriel sat back down at his desk.

"Do other Fortune 500 companies work like this?" he asked the other two.

"Most don't have a Chuck, I don't think," Helena said.

"They all have a Chuck," Arthur added. "But they don't let him touch anything. And they don't use paper anymore, either." They all tried to read the report for a bit, each giving up in turn and throwing the wet paper back at Gabriel. "By the way, Gabe. I'm the one who sent you those numbers in the first place, you know."

"Yeah, I guess you did." Gabriel looked sheepish.

"And I really don't give a shit," Helena added brightly.

"Just trying to add a little decorum to this organization," Gabriel said.

"So, is the meeting over then?" Arthur asked.

"We haven't talked about anything yet, Arthur," Gabriel pointed out.

"Is that a problem?" Arthur asked.

"We should talk about something. I don't think we talked about anything last week, either," Gabriel said.

"Last week Zeke brought doughnuts, so we had a party instead," Helena said.

"That's right, I remember," Gabriel said. "We decided to table everything until this week."

"Did anybody bring doughnuts?" Arthur asked. The other two shook their heads. "I guess then we should have the meeting. Gabriel, you start."

"I got nothing," Gabriel said.

"Okay, then," Arthur said. "Helena?"

"I got something to bring up," Helena said, looking back and forth between the other two.

"Seriously?" Arthur asked. "Because if we adjourn now we could probably beat the traffic on the way out."

"No, really. I have something I think we should talk about."

"Can it wait till next week? I can bring doughnuts," Arthur said.

"What is it, Leena?" Gabriel said. "The chair recognizes the Senior Vice President of Research."

"Thank you, Mr. Chairman," Helena began, leaning forward from her seat on the couch. "As I have reported to this august body in the recent past, the department of research has made great strides in the documentation and cataloguing of the audiometric representation of subject mentation. I believe all the employees of the department are to be commended for their tireless devotion to the efforts of this company."

"Where are Zeke and Hannah, anyway? They were supposed to bring the doughnuts," Arthur asked.

"They had to go to their real jobs," Helena explained.

"Well, the chair recognizes the employees of the department of research for their invaluable dedication and service. Each will receive one day in the 'Employee of the Month' parking space. Let the minutes reflect my decree," Gabriel intoned.

"They don't drive here, either one. Nice gesture though, commander. My minions, however, ask nothing in return for their service. They live to serve. That's not why I bring this up."

"Don't we pay them some crazy salary?" Arthur asked.

"Yeah," Gabriel answered. "They pull down more than the rest of the techs combined. Plus benefits."

"Silence! I have the floor," Helena yelled. "And they're worth every penny. We should give them a raise, next month. That's not why I bring this up, anyway."

"I think we have to vote on any proposed raises," Arthur interjected.

"I'll consult the bylaws," Gabriel said. "I'm sure I have them here on my desk somewhere." He began to go through the piles of paper on his desk again.

"You guys are pissing me off," Helena fumed. "I bring this up in order for you to understand that that my department is ready to begin a new project. To head in a brave new direction, as it were." She smiled at each of them in turn.

They each stared back balefully. Arthur stifled a yawn. Her smile melted. "Seriously, guys."

"Yes?" Gabriel asked.

"Yes, yes?" asked Arthur.

Helena moved to the edge of the couch. "I propose to begin the investigation of mental illness utilizing the knowledge and techniques which we have developed." She looked back and forth to each of them again, waiting.

They each stared back. "Really?" Gabriel asked.

"Seriously?" Arthur asked. "Mental illness? Like depression and schizophrenia and stuff like that?" Helena nodded.

"You talked about this before, Leena. Do you think you're ready?" Gabriel asked.

"Yeah," Helena said, nodding. "I think we are. I think we have the potential to really contribute."

"Seriously? Contribute? Hell, Leena, I don't know," Arthur said. "A bunch of crazies parading through the lab? I don't see much profit in it, gotta tell you."

Helena leaned forward and, without warning, slapped Arthur hard across his face. Gabriel froze, his eyes wide.

Arthur's hand went to his face as he almost fell off his chair. His cheek was already reddening. "Holy shit, Helena!" Arthur exclaimed. "What was that for?"

Chuck came flying through the door, shirt unbuttoned but otherwise dressed. "I heard a slap! What'd I miss?" He saw Arthur holding his face. "Damn, I missed something, didn't I?"

Helena was still leaning towards Arthur, glowering. "Stick around, Chuck. Depending on what Arthur says next, you might just see me squeeze his throat until his tongue turns black and his eyes bug out," she said with soft menace in her voice.

Gabriel stood up, looked at his wife, and then sat back down. Arthur was staring back at Helena, now leaning as far back in his chair as he could. He waggled his jaw and winced.

"I'm sorry, Helena. I know what I said. I take it back. I'm sorry," Arthur said. Helena leaned back, nodding. "I don't think I deserved that, though."

"I think you did, Arthur," Helena said, matter of factly. "Chuck, get Arthur some ice for his face, okay?"

Chuck turned to go. "Damn, I missed it. I always miss the good stuff."

The room was silent for a bit.

"What will you need, Leena?" Gabriel asked softly.

Helena turned to her husband. "In answer to our partner's concern, I don't plan to bring the subjects here. I don't think that's practical, and obviously raises some fear on the part of the unenlightened. I propose enlisting the technicians to do the subject recording in the field."

"Your technicians or mine?" Arthur asked, raising his hands defensively before him.

Helena gave him a smile. "Yours, I think. You got a problem with that, Arthur?"

By this time, Insight Technologies employed a small army of technicians nationally. It wasn't difficult to task each team with the occasional foray into various group homes and inpatient psychiatric facilities to perform the monitored interviews. Helena formed a national mental health company to identify and sign up volunteer patients who would consent to being subjects. Their treating psychiatrists or psychologists—after forwarding a summary of the subject's history, diagnoses, and treatment—conducted the interviews. Within six weeks, Helena and her small team were analyzing a steady stream of material.

Helena and her team maintained their every other day schedule for studying the recordings. Helena used the off days by herself to cull through the material, edit out the tedious and useless parts, and put together a day's worth of material for analysis. The next day the three of them would sit in Helena's lab, watching the videotaped session on the monitor, surrounded by the tracings and a crawl of subtitled dialogue. The room was filled with the sound of the mentation recordings, now enhanced and broadened into a veritable symphony by her musician colleagues. Each session was preceded by Helena presenting a brief summary of the subject, his history both personal and medical, his current state of well-being and treatment. Occasionally during the session, one of them would lean forward to switch from the orchestrations to the actual sound of the subject speaking during the interview, then back to the mentation audio signal. They would often listen to a particular subject or passage over and over again, saying little but each making notes on a yellow legal pad in the semidarkness. At the conclusion of each session, they brought up the lights and talked about their impressions.

"Thoughts?" Helena said, snapping on the lights as she stopped the video on the monitor with a stab at the keyboard before her.

Zeke rolled his eyes. "He's nuts."

"Glad he doesn't live down the block," Hannah said.

"Not helpful, guys," Helena replied.

"You're sitting here with a couple of musicians, Helena," Zeke said. "We're not gonna give you Freudian analysis, you know."

"That's not what I'm asking," Helena said. "Just focus on the sound, the waveform he's thinking. You're both the world experts on that."

"Well," Hannah began, "it's definitely different from what we heard with the normals." Zeke nodded.

"How? How is it different?" Helena asked.

"Like we talked about with the last few," Zeke said. "Multiple levels. The sickest of the patients, like this guy, have an overall different tempo. It's both faster and more variable."

"Yeah," Hannah added, "not faster so much as faster in changing tempo. And I think the swings in tempo are wider." Zeke nodded again.

"Can we quantitate that?" Helena asked.

Hannah thought for a moment. "I don't know if we can quantitate it, not give a percentage change from a norm or anything statistical like that. But we can characterize it, maybe develop a threshold definition or something."

"I'm not so sure it's that clear cut," Zeke added. "We would have to narrow the subjects into better groups to do that. It's pretty subjective."

"What else?" Helena asked. "I'm hearing a lot of stuff I never heard in the normal population."

Zeke looked at his notes. "Yeah, there's this one thing I noticed on this guy and a couple of others last week. That almost subsonic recurring pattern, pretty scary sounding." The other two looked at him quizzically. "What?" he asked. "You didn't hear that?" They both shook their heads. "You're kidding, right?" He leaned back to the console and punched the recording back to the middle of the playback. He lowered the lights so he could find the place he wanted, bringing up the sound again as he scrubbed the playback back and forth until he found the spot. "Here," he pronounced as he looked at their faces.

Helena and Hannah listened closely, each shaking their heads in turn. "Really?" Zeke asked.

"No clue," Helena said.

"Here," Zeke said, attacking the keyboard again. "It's just not in a good voice. Listen to this." Zeke scrubbed the recording back again, and then hit play. This time the room was filled by a loud, haunting low warble; the sound of a loon plaintively calling at dawn from the mists of a remote lake in the Canadian wilderness.

"Christ," Helena said. "That's been there all along?" Zeke nodded.

"That's the saddest thing I've ever heard," Hannah said.

"It's on a lot of these," Zeke said. "But I never heard it with the others, before."

"You're sure?" Helena asked.

Zeke shrugged. "Pretty sure, yeah. I'm not going to go back through all the others, though, if that's what you're thinking."

"It's not in the catalogue," Hannah said. "But I didn't know what to even look for before this, so I'm not sure."

"Can we run your software, as a screen?" Helena asked Zeke.

"Sure, you can try. But if it comes up zero, you won't know if it's because it wasn't there, or because the software wasn't good enough to pick it up."

"Run the program on this recording, see if it can pick it up and put it in the catalogue. Then run it on the previous batch."

"What should we call it?" Hannah asked.

"Call it 'Crazy as a Loon'," Zeke said.

"Loonie Tunes," Hannah said.

Helena killed the recording and leaned back in her chair, blowing a loop of hair off her forehead. "You guys make jokes about paraplegics, too? Just run the program. Let me know what turns up." She left the lab to find her husband.

CHAPTER 18

Helena found her husband sitting with Arthur and Chuck in his office.

"Hey, boys. What's up?" Helena asked, dropping onto the couch.

"Hey, Leena," Gabriel said, not looking up from what he was reading on his desk.

"Hey," Arthur said.

"How's the face?" Helena asked him.

"The face is fine, thank you. Though Sam still thinks you did it because I made a pass at you."

"That's what she wants to believe. Easier than admitting that she's married to an insensitive lout," Helena said, smiling at him.

"Think she probably knew that," Chuck interjected.

"Shut up, Chuck," both Arthur and Helena said together.

"Hey, I found the article. Be nice," Chuck said.

"What article?" Helena asked the group.

Gabriel kept reading. "Chuck found a research article coming out next month in Annals of Criminology. Our technology compared to standard lie detector evaluation," Arthur said, filling in the silence.

"He found it, or you pointed him to it? You planted this, didn't you, Arthur?" Helena asked. Arthur couldn't meet her gaze.

"You better not hit me again, Helena," he said, moving behind Gabriel.

"It had to happen at some point anyway," Helena said. "I'm assuming that we blew them away."

Chuck nodded enthusiastically. "Totally. They're going to have an editorial attached, essentially saying that the justice community needs to come into the twenty-first century and switch to our technology. They compare standard lie detection to dunking witches to see if they drown."

"About time," Arthur said. "Justice has been pretending we don't exist for almost a year. Now we should see some movement."

"We're totally fucked," Helena said. Gabriel looked up at her.

"Exactly what I was thinking," Gabriel said, smiling at his wife.

"No, it'll be great," Arthur said, looking from one to the other.

"No, it won't," Gabriel said. "It'll be a royal pain in the ass. Once this gets going, every ten cent police precinct will want to own it."

"Well, we won't sell it to them. They'll have to go through us, just like it is now," Arthur said. "We'll just have to increase capacity, that's all. Nothing wrong with increasing capacity, you know."

"That'll work for a while, Arthur," Helena said. "Right up until the Feds get interested."

"What do you hear from your end, Chuck?" Gabriel asked.

"Nothing yet. NSA thinks it's too immature to invest in right now. They're pretty much deleting all my reports without reading them, I think."

"Great. At least it shows some judgment on their part," Helena said. "What about the FBI?"

"Don't know," Chuck said. "But they got burned so badly by our first little interaction, I don't think anybody over there has the balls to even bring up the subject."

"That's essentially what my bridge partner says," Arthur interjected.

"For now," Gabriel said.

"Not for much longer," Helena said. "Let us know when the black Suburbans are heading our way, Chuck."

"No problem, Helena. If they tell me first."

Helena had a revolt on her hands. Her team was on strike.

"Sorry, Helena," Hannah said. "I've got classes starting in two weeks. I've got to get back to my real job."

"And my advisor comes back in town next week," Zeke added. "When he sees I haven't done shit since last spring—"

"Screw that shit, both of you," Helena said, pacing up and down in front of them. "This is your real job now. This is more important." She stopped in front of them, glaring.

"Helena, come on," Hannah pleaded. "We're musicians, not neuroscientists."

"You're an ethnomusicologist and a hulluva scientist, Hannah," Helena countered. "And you," she continued, turning to Zeke. "Well, you're doing a great job here, whatever you are. That composing thing is a dead end, I think."

"Gee, thanks, Helena," Zeke answered.

"I didn't mean it like that," Helena said. "Well, yeah, I actually did. But you've invented something here, something important. You can't abandon all this."

"But we're musicians, Helena. You need to get some really smart people, some scientists involved. You know, like neuropsychiatric research types, or whatever. Scientists like yourself, you know?" Hannah said.

"That's the last thing I need," Helena said. "Scientists will fuck this up royally and immediately."

"How can you say that?" Hannah asked. "This is research, this is what they do."

"What they do," Helena said, wheeling on her, "is cheat, steal, and lie. Anybody in the field with half a reputation will see what we've done so far and walk through the door with an agenda. Within one week they'd have a grant proposal started with their name on top."

"What's wrong with that?"

"That's just where it starts. And we don't need the grant, they do. To build their reputation. Then the real games begin. They'll have the paper written and the abstracts submitted to all the national meetings before they've even looked at the data. It's bullshit, all bullshit."

"Sounding a little cynical there, Helena," Zeke said.

"Hey, I've lived this life. I've been in it up to my neck. Gabe's the first nonasshole researcher I ever met that I have any respect for. Most of them just make it up as they go along. 'Torture the data enough and it'll admit to anything.' That's their approach."

"So you're going with musicians?" Hannah asked.

"Hey, you guys have done some important work here. Listen, Ligiti," Helena said, stabbing a finger at Zeke, "you discovered something important a couple of weeks ago. That loon tone is going to change the way we identify mental illness. That's your mark on the world. Your music—not so much. Sorry. No offense."

"You're really serious about us sticking around?" Zeke asked. Helena nodded. "What do you think, sis?"

"Can't do it, guys. Maybe next semester, probably more like next summer. But I have to get back to my department, there's only four of us."

"Take a sabbatical," Helena said.

"Yeah, right. In my dreams, maybe. And then only to do further research."

"This is research," Helena said.

"It's not ethnomusicology, Helena. Sorry. I'm thinking maybe I can come by once a month. I'll try."

"How about you, John Cage? You can rewrite 'Four Minutes Thirty-Three Seconds'. Call it 'Four Months Thirty-Three Days," Helena asked Zeke.

He smiled at her. "Let me talk to my advisor. I'm sure I can work something out in a couple of weeks. Maybe I'll change my project after all."

"Music straight from your crazy mind, bro?" Hannah asked.

"Maybe. I'll work it out."

And with that, Helena was back to working alone.

Helena was not good at working alone. The patient recordings kept coming in. Helena tried to maintain a regimen, but found her backlog building. She was missing hours out of the day. Her output slowed to a crawl. Zeke stopped by once and thought he woke her out of a trance as she sat behind the console of the lab. He didn't like the way she looked, but he only had a minute to let her know it would take a couple of more weeks to get back. At Helena's insistence, he stuck around long enough to help her set up a computer routine to automate screening of the incoming recordings. He left feeling worried about her.

The article appeared in the criminology journal. It was picked up in a dozen other journals and then in the national lay press. As predicted, the previously blind eye of justice slowly turned its gimlet gaze on their already burgeoning company. The snowball began to roll downhill.

Initially, Arthur was able to field all the police department requests to license and trial the technology. He became very efficient at saying no. The technology was not for sale. If the police were interested, they would have to work through established channels. They were not pleased. The unforeseen result of this approach was the sudden increase in the number of private citizens utilizing Insight Technologies to establish their innocence. Before long, a wave of defense attorneys felt that the first step in making their case was to produce an Insight scan of their client. Since they carefully conducted the interview, the scan produced was usually a picture of purity and innocence. If it wasn't, they ditched the result.

Prosecutors soon found that they had to fight fire with fire. Though they couldn't license the technology, they demanded budgets to hire Insight Technologies so that they could conduct their own interviews. At first, defense attorneys refused to allow their clients to be subjected to these interviews. Within months, however, most states had established judicial precedent that if the subject refused the prosecutor's interview, his own Insight Technologies interview was disallowed as evidence. The resulting caseload rapidly escalated at the offices of Insight Technologies. Gabriel and Chuck were kept busy training and supervising a cadre of associates charged with analysis and report output. The only one happy was Arthur.

Gabriel was unable to get away enough to keep tabs on Helena. His attempts at hiring her an assistant resulted in either outright rejection or noisy eviction within two or three days. His own work kept him out of her lab, sometimes working until nighttime. When Gabriel finally managed to meet his wife for dinner, often late, his concerns were magnified. Helena was often distant, answering his questions about her research with vague generalities. She displayed little interest in his own activities. He thought she had lost weight, though she dismissed this as well. Gabriel finally got Zeke on the phone and begged him to come back at least part time, explaining his concerns. Zeke agreed, promising to be at the lab next Monday. And then the black Suburbans showed up.

Gabriel was working alone in his office on Saturday morning, trying to catch up a backlog of cases from the last week. He didn't hear the man come in. He looked up to the knock on his doorframe to see a slight, balding man in his late fifties leaning against the open door of his office.

"Dr. Sheehan?" the man asked politely.

Gabriel startled and looked at the man suspiciously. "Hey—who the hell are you?"

"I'm sorry, Dr. Sheehan. I didn't mean to startle you."

"How did you get in here? This is a private office, we're closed. And locked, I thought."

"I know, Dr. Sheehan," the man said, crossing the room to offer his hand to Gabriel. "My name is Arnie Duncan."

Gabriel just stared at the man until he dropped his hand and shrugged.

"May I sit down?" Duncan asked.

"No," Gabriel said, leaning back in his chair. "What you can do is leave. You can call on Monday and make an appointment, like everyone else, Mr. Duncan."

"Please call me Arnie."

"Goodbye, Arnie."

"Monday's not good, Dr. Sheehan. I'm sorry, I know you're busy, and I don't want to take up too much of your time on the weekend."

"Then don't."

"I think it best that we talk privately."

"You're not leaving, are you?" Duncan shook his head. "Fine. Talk." Gabriel glanced out his window to see two Suburbans parked at the curb with two men sitting inside each. "Are you NSA?"

"No, Dr. Sheehan, I'm not with the NSA. You are somewhat correct, however. I do work for the government."

"No shit."

Duncan smiled. "It won't surprise you that the government has been closely monitoring the maturation of your work. Very impressive, Dr. Sheehan. You've made great strides of late."

"It's Saturday, Arnie. Cut the crap. What do you want?"

"Your help, obviously, Dr. Sheehan."

"Not interested. Thanks for stopping by. Please lock the door again on your way out."

"Please, Dr. Sheehan. A few more minutes of your time. I hope to convince you to reconsider."

"Of course you do. Don't get your hopes up, Arnie. I'm pretty busy here."

"To be brief then. We believe that your technology would be very helpful in resolving a situation. It is critically important to national security."

"Of course it is."

Duncan smiled indulgently. "I don't blame you for being cynical, Dr. Sheehan. The truth is, though, that your assistance would quite possibly be instrumental in resolving an issue of great concern to us."

"Life and death, eh?"

"I'm not at liberty to say, I'm afraid. Rest assured that the matter is of the gravest importance. Otherwise, we wouldn't be bothering you."

"My assistance, you say. Not my technology?"

"That's correct, Dr. Sheehan. That would be our preference. Due to time constraints and certain other factors, we feel that your personal participation, though burdensome I know, is preferable to simply allowing us access to your technology."

"You can't have access to my technology."

"So you say."

"What does that mean, exactly?"

"It's not important, Dr. Sheehan. We need you, not just your technology."

Gabriel sat thinking for a few minutes. Duncan said nothing.

"What do you need from me?" Gabriel finally asked, sighing.

Duncan leaned forward, smiling. "Two days."

Gabriel threw up his hands. "Fine, Arnie. Since you ask so nicely, I'll try to clear a couple of days next week, though it's been crazy—"

"I'm afraid that won't be acceptable, Dr. Sheehan."

"What won't be acceptable?"

"The matter is more urgent than that."

"When?"

"Now."

"Fuck that, Arnie. I'm not taking off for a couple of days with you just like that. It wouldn't work anyway. I have to get together some equipment, pack up some stuff."

"That won't be necessary."

Gabriel raised his eyebrows. "It won't?" Duncan shook his head. "Well, Arnie, I still must decline your offer. No, thanks. Maybe some other time."

"Dr. Sheehan, with all due respect, that is just not possible."

"What's not possible?"

"Declining my offer."

"No? What are you going to do, call those guys," Gabriel said, gesturing out the window, "to drag me out of here kicking and screaming?"

"Of course not, Dr. Sheehan. That's not the way it works."

"Really? So how does it work, then?"

"You reconsider and agree to leave with me now."

"No."

Duncan sighed. "Dr. Sheehan, we are wasting valuable time. It would be in your best interest, I assure you, to simply join me. We just need your help for one or two days. Realistically, two. Nothing bad will happen to you. There is no danger, I assure you."

"I can't just take off like that. My wife—"

"You can call your wife. Tell her what's happening."

"I don't know what's happening."

"You can tell her what you know, Dr. Sheehan."

"This is not a good time, Arnie," Gabriel said, shaking his head. "My wife is not well."

"I'm sorry to hear that, Dr. Sheehan. I think overall, however, she would be better off if you joined us. In the long run."

Gabriel looked at the other man sharply. "What the hell does that mean?" Duncan just stared back. "Keep talking or get out of my office, Arnie."

"I just mean to say that you are correct to be concerned about your wife's well being. Given her past, and certain activities of which the government is aware, I believe that your worries about her are quite justified."

"What activities? What past are you talking about?" The other man remained silent. "This sounds like you're accusing my wife of something, Arnie? Is that what you're doing?"

Duncan shook his head. He said, frowning, "No, Dr. Sheehan. Accusations imply evidence of wrongdoing. I assure you that we have no such evidence."

"Good."

"What I'm doing is threatening, Dr. Sheehan. I am threatening your wife. Threats, you see, don't require evidence."

Gabriel glared at the other man. "Exactly what are you threatening?"

The other man shrugged. "I don't think it's useful to go into specifics, Dr. Sheehan. Suffice to say that your wife's prior activities, both here and abroad, are sufficient to justify an extensive, and very personal, investigation. An investigation that, given someone of your wife's temperament and sense of personal privacy, I'm sure she would rather avoid. As I'm sure that you would rather avoid subjecting her to, as well." Duncan inspected his fingernails, appearing almost embarrassed.

Gabriel stared at the man. He picked up his cellphone. "There's no signal," he noted.

Duncan looked up at him. "Your desk phone will work fine, I'm sure."

Gabriel picked up the desk phone and dialed his home. Helena answered. "Hey, hon. It's me. Listen, there's a man here from the government. Ours, I think. He says that I'll be leaving with him for one or two days. Now. Yeah, I told him this wasn't a good time, but he's not really giving me any choice. I can't say much more than that, okay? Great, tell Arthur and Chuck to keep the ship afloat. Zeke said he should be coming by on Monday. Love you, Leena. Yeah, you too." He hung up. "What now?"

Duncan smiled. "Now, we leave. You can leave your cell phone here, Dr. Sheehan."

"I'll need to bring my laptop. I'm not going to be doing much work without it."

"If you wish. Just keep it shut down. And I'm afraid I'll have to carry it." He produced an attaché case from beside his chair that Gabriel hadn't noticed. "You can put it in here, for safe keeping."

Gabriel hefted the case. "Pretty heavy. Lead lined?" Duncan nodded. Gabriel shrugged and put the laptop in the case, handed it over to Duncan. "Lead on, Macduff."

"I believe the actual quote is 'Lay on, Macduff'. Changes the meaning entirely."

"It does, doesn't it, Arnie?"

Duncan led Gabriel to the lead Suburban. They climbed into the back seat, the other two men remaining in front.

"I hope this isn't where you put the burlap bag over my head," Gabriel said, only half joking. The side windows were tinted to the point of near opacity, but Gabriel could see out the windshield.

"I'm sure that won't be necessary," Duncan replied, smiling. An opaque barrier slid silently up in front of them, separating them from the front seats and eliminating the view outside. "We do ask that you don't discuss any aspects of our trip with anyone, though, Dr. Sheehan."

"Of course," Gabriel replied. "And you might as well start calling me Gabriel. That 'Dr. Sheehan' shtick is getting rather tedious."

"Thank you, Gabriel."

"So where are we going?" Gabriel asked.

"To the airport."

That was the end of the conversation. Gabriel could sense that the car made a complete circle around the block. He lost track of where they were soon after they got on the expressway. Thirty minutes later, the car came to a stop.

"Here we go," Duncan said. He got out of the car, carrying the brief case. Gabriel got out and noted the small business jet in front of him. He was at a small business airport, but not one he recognized. Duncan gestured him up the air stair. Duncan handed the briefcase to a crewman at the base of the stairway and took a seat next to Gabriel.

"Hold it," Gabriel said, standing back up and going back out the cabin door. He ran into the crewman coming up the stair with the briefcase in hand. "I'll take that," Gabriel said to the man, holding out his hand for the case. The crewman looked past Gabriel to Duncan, who was standing in the doorway. Duncan nodded and the man handed the case to Gabriel. Gabriel and Duncan retook their seats. Gabriel laid the briefcase in the seat across from them. "Not that I don't trust you, Arnie." Duncan just smiled and fastened his seatbelt. "How far?" Gabriel asked.

"Not far. Couple of hours," Duncan answered. "Want something to drink?"

"You mean like scotch or something? It's a little early."

"I mean like coke or water."

"Oh. No, thanks."

"We really appreciate your help, Gabriel."

"Yeah, I'm sure."

"You asked if I was with NSA before, in your office," Duncan said. "Why did you pick that organization?"

"I just assumed, because of Chuck and all."

"Chuck?" Duncan looked at a loss.

"Yeah, Chuck Parnell. He works with us. You don't know him?"

"Should I?" Duncan asked.

"He's with the NSA."

"Really? That's interesting," Duncan said.

"You'd think you guys would know about an NSA guy working in our office for over a year," Gabriel said, looking at Duncan sideways.

"You'd think," Duncan agreed.

"But you don't," Gabriel said.

"Nope." They sat, each thinking silently for a minute.

"Maybe you're not really from the government," Gabriel said, thinking aloud.

"Maybe he's not really from the NSA," Duncan said.

"He showed me his government ID," Gabriel said.

"Not hard to fake an ID."

"You never showed me your ID," Gabriel said.

"No, I didn't," Duncan said, smiling again.

"Not even a fake one," Gabriel said. The plane began to accelerate down the runway and lifted into the air.

"I think I will take that drink, after all," Gabriel said.

Zeke showed up at the lab at just after eleven. He walked into the semidarkness to see Helena sitting stiffly in front of the console. The sound and tracings of a subject recording came to an end as he entered.

"Hey, Helena," he said, and then stopped as he noticed something in her posture that wasn't quite right. "Helena?" She made no response as he came closer. She sat stiffly in her chair, eyes open but staring vacantly ahead. "Hey," he said more loudly, gently shaking her arm. Then he noticed the tiny line of spittle running from the corner of her mouth. Zeke ran from the lab toward Gabriel's office.

"Hey, we need some help," he yelled, sliding around the corner into the empty office. "Hey, hello! Help!" He stared around desperately. "Where is everyone?" he called more loudly.

Chuck came into the office from the other door.

"Hey, Zeke. What's wrong, buddy?" Parnell asked the other man.

"It's Helena. Where's Gabriel, we need him."

"Gabriel's been abducted by the government. Why, what's up?" Parnell asked again, more concerned.

"I think Helena's having a seizure. We need to call 911 or something."

"Show me," Parnell said. They both ran back to Helena's lab. She still sat stiffly, the room quiet. "Helena," Parnell called to her, without response. He passed his hands before her eyes, without eliciting a blink.

"Should I call 911?" Zeke asked.

"She'll kill us if she wakes up with a bunch of paramedics all over her," Parnell said.

"Well, Gabriel will kill us if we let her die or anything," Zeke said with concern.

"Good point," Parnell said. "I think she's done this before, though. Gabriel told me about something like this. I don't think it's a seizure or anything."

"What do you think it is, then?"

"Not sure."

"Then I'm calling 911," Zeke said, pulling out his cellphone from his pocket. He started dialing. Parnell looked around the lab; saw the recording skullcap that Zeke had been using lying on the back console. Parnell picked it up and began to flip switches on the front recording console. Zeke gave him a puzzled look as he began to give information to the 911 operator, explaining that he needed an ambulance right away. Parnell started to pull the recording device onto Helena's head. She gave no resistance, continuing to sit bolt upright. He flipped another switch and tracings began to track across the monitors. Zeke hung up the phone.

"What the hell are you doing?" Zeke asked.

"Nothing."

"What if she wakes up?" Zeke asked.

"Then we won't need the paramedics," Parnell answered. He watched the tracings appear on the monitors. "Shit, that's fucked up."

"What?" Zeke asked. He couldn't make heads or tails of the tracings. Parnell snapped another switch and the lab filled with the loud sound of a hundred loons calling.

"Oh, shit," Zeke said softly.

Two paramedics appeared at the door of the lab. "Where's the victim?" the lead paramedic asked. Both Zeke and Parnell pointed to Helena, still seated in her chair, unaware.

The small jet landed and rolled to a stop. Gabriel had no idea where they were. For most of the four and a half hours of the flight, all he could see out the window was the top of clouds. Now, the landscape looked somewhat southwestern, though Gabe thought it could've been anywhere from Texas to Utah. He didn't think they had flown long enough to have left the country, certainly not long enough to be at Guantanamo, though he had left expecting that destination.

"Where are we?" Gabriel asked Duncan. Duncan had seemed asleep for almost the entire flight but was now pulling off his seatbelt and standing.

"Here," Duncan said. He gestured to the briefcase. "You want to carry it?"

"Sure," Gabriel said, picking up the heavy case. He followed Duncan down the stairway. It was bright sunshine, and hot. Gabriel thought it must be over ninety. He saw a pair of black Suburbans waiting at the foot of the steps, identical to the last pair. This time though, there was an ambulance between them. "Somebody have an accident?" Gabriel asked.

"That would be us," Duncan said. "We're in the back." He led Gabriel to the back of the ambulance. The doors were open and the compartment empty except for a stretcher and two jump seats.

Gabriel stared into the cavity, reluctant to go in. "I've never been in an ambulance," he said.

"Well, you'll never be able to say that again," Duncan said, giving Gabriel a little push in the back toward the step up. Gabriel got in, sat down in a jump seat.

"Is this where you inject me with a tranquilizer?" Gabriel asked Duncan as the other man took the remaining seat.

"Don't give me any ideas, Gabriel." The large doors were slammed closed and the ambulance took off with a lurch.

Twenty minutes later, the ambulance backed to the sound of its warning tone. They stopped and the doors opened. Gabriel was given a hand down by a guy in a paramedic jumpsuit and gently hustled into a loading dock. Duncan followed as they walked quickly down a hospital corridor. The paramedic led them to a door marked "On Call" and unlocked it, holding the door for Gabriel and Duncan to enter. The room held a bed and a small desk. No window. Another door led to the bathroom.

"You want to take a shower or rest up?" Duncan asked.

Gabriel shook his head. "Lunch would be nice."

"I'll have room service sent over." He left, the door clicking shut behind him. Gabriel tried the door, which was also locked from his side.

Duncan returned twenty minutes later with a bucket of fried chicken and a couple of bottles of coke.

"Gee," Gabriel said. "I hope I didn't put you out or anything."

"Not a problem," Duncan said as he dropped onto the bed and took a leg of chicken. "I think they stole it from the ER nurses."

"For god and country, eh?" Gabriel sat down in the desk chair and began to eat. "What happens after lunch? Movie or naptime?"

Duncan grabbed some paper towels from the bathroom for napkins. "After lunch," he said, sitting back down on the side of the bed, "I'm going to introduce you to your patient."

"Patient? You mean subject. I'm not that kind of doctor, you know."

"No, I know. But in this case, he's a patient. And you're going to pretend to be a doctor."

"I can't do that. I don't know anything—"

"Don't worry about that part. It's not important."

"Oh, good." Gabriel finished his coke and wiped the grease from his hands. He watched Duncan do the same and pull a pair of surgical scrubs from the closet.

"You'll need to change into these."

Now also changed into scrubs, Duncan unlocked the door and led Gabriel down a short hall to the Intensive Care Unit. They were both wearing badges with their pictures and names, beneath which it said 'Neurology'. Several nurses and doctors bustled about the unit, not giving them a glance. Duncan carried a doctor's bag, Gabriel his briefcase.

Gabriel looked about the unit. He hadn't spent much time in hospitals before. Actually, he hated hospitals. "This is a real hospital," Gabriel said to Duncan, standing next to him.

"Yeah, how about that," Duncan said. "This way." Duncan led him to one of the glass-enclosed rooms. A nurse was writing on a clipboard at the foot of the bed. "Would you mind excusing us for a few minutes, nurse?" Duncan asked the man. The nurse gave him a smile and stepped out, closing the glass sliding door behind him.

Gabriel looked at the patient. The man lying in the bed appeared to be in his twenties or thirties, with short, black hair. He had a tube in his mouth through which he was connected to the ventilator beside the bed. A small feeding tube snaked from the man's nose. On the wall beside the bed, Gabriel noted the monitor tracing the man's vital signs. There were various soft beeping and ventilator noises. Gabriel gave a slight, involuntary shudder.

"Who is he?" Gabriel asked.

"Your patient, Dr. Sheehan," Duncan said.

"Oh, so now I'm Dr. Sheehan again."

"The patient is in a medically induced coma, Dr. Sheehan." Duncan pointed to a milk colored intravenous infusion entering the patient's arm. "It's standard treatment for a traumatic head injury."

"He had a traumatic head injury? I don't see any—"

"That's not what I said. He's in a medically induced coma. We would like you to do a brain scan on this patient."

Gabriel shook his head. "I didn't bring any equipment and besides—"

Duncan cut him off with a raise of his hand. He slid open the door to admit two men, wheeling a small medical cart with supplies. A briefcase was on the lower shelf of the cart. Both guys were bald. Duncan nodded to them and one began to arrange the equipment on the bed. The other took the case and set it up on top on the cart.

"These guys are Insight technicians!" Gabriel said. One of the men blushed but both kept working. The other technician began applying the skullcap electrodes to the patient. "These guys work for me," Gabriel said angrily.

"Yeah, that's true. You could say they're kind of freelancing for us," Duncan said.

"Not any more. You two clowns are fired," Gabriel snapped. They looked at him, than at Duncan.

"Don't be melodramatic, Dr. Sheehan. I'm sure that they were hired through a standard government contract with your company. They're just doing the job you trained them for." Duncan gestured for the men to continue, which they did, though with the occasional glance towards Gabriel. Gabriel watched them, fuming. The briefcase opened to reveal the standard Insight Technologies laptop, to which the monitoring devices were attached. Tracings appeared on the screen.

"This still isn't going to work, Arnie," Gabriel said, rounding on Duncan. "We study awake, voluntary subjects," he said, with an emphasis on voluntary towards the technicians. "We have no template for this."

Duncan gestured placatingly. "I know, Dr. Sheehan. That's why we thought it best that you were here, personally. This isn't the standard Insight interview, obviously."

"I can't interview somebody who's in a coma."

"Are you sure?" Duncan asked.

"Yeah, I'm sure," Gabriel spluttered. "He's in a coma, Arnie."

"Have you tried?"

Gabriel paced about the small room. The technicians just stood, watching the monitors. One adjusted the electrodes on the patient's head slightly.

"No, Arnie. I haven't tried. But it's not going to work."

"How do you know if you haven't tried?"

"Because even if we get a result, I won't know what it means. This is the argument I've been making all along. Even if you shout questions into his ear or something, I don't know if his thoughts are dreams, or memories, or actual responses to the questions. How could I tell?"

"I don't know, Dr. Sheehan, but I would like you to try. It's very important."

"Why is it important, Arnie?"

"I can't tell you that." Gabriel just stood across the bed from Duncan, arms folded and shaking his head slightly. Duncan gazed back across the bed. "How about this? What if we do a baseline recording, just like this? Then we do the interview, under coma. If you can't interpret anything in the difference, we'll have to try something else."

"That's all?" Gabriel asked angrily. "Why don't you just wake him up, then? Why the coma at all?"

"I can't tell you that, Gabriel. Can we try the baseline, then the interview under coma?"

Gabriel was shaking his head again. "He's not a voluntary subject."

"No, Dr. Sheehan. He is not a voluntary subject."

Gabriel sighed, shaking his head in thought. "We're crossing a line here." He paused, considering.

"It's important," Duncan said softly.

"So you keep saying," Gabriel fumed. "This is going to take a while." He stared at the patient's face.

Duncan looked at his watch. "Looks like we have about thirty more hours before I promised to have you home."

"Whatever. I'm going back to my cell. Come and get me when you have a baseline recording." He turned to the technician at the laptop. "Don't transmit the session and don't delete it either, asshole. Give me thirty minutes of clean recording. Find a way to filter out all this shit," he said, gesturing to the machinery surrounding the patient. "I'll be back." Gabriel slid the door open and walked out. A large man, dressed in orderly garb, walked Gabriel back to the on call room and let him in. Gabriel dropped onto the bed and waited.

He waited almost three hours. While he was waiting, he tried to retrieve his laptop from Duncan's briefcase, but it was locked. He fell asleep on the bed. Finally, he was awakened by a knock on the door. It opened and Duncan walked in, still in scrubs.

"The technicians think they have something for you," he said. "What now?"

Gabriel sat up. "I'll need a conference room or something. Someplace to work. Someplace bigger than this."

"Okay."

"Bring me the technician's laptop. Tell him to unhook everything from the laptop but not to disturb his setup, not a bit. Otherwise, the baseline isn't worth shit." Duncan nodded, turning to go. "And we'll need snacks."

"I'll be back in a minute," Duncan said.

Duncan returned and brought Gabriel into a conference room. One of the technicians, looking distinctly uncomfortable, was seated at the table with his laptop. Gabriel set up his own laptop across the table and hooked up a cable between. The technician transferred the recording to Gabriel's machine and returned to looking uncomfortable. Gabriel watched the screen as his computer processed the recording.

"This is slower than what we have back at the lab, but the results should end up about the same," he said to Duncan, who was staring at the screen over his shoulder. After a few minutes, a trail of words and phrases joined the waveforms. It was punctuated by long intervals labeled 'uninterpretable' and nonsense phrases. Gabriel was shaking his head. "This is why we don't study people in a coma," he announced.

"Anything?" Duncan asked.

"Nothing worth a damn, probably. I'll have to rescan it a couple of times when I get back to the lab, but I don't think anything intelligible will come out of it."

"Yeah, well. We'll have to talk about that later," Duncan said.

"Hey, Arnie, you are not making me wipe my laptop at the end of this," Gabriel said.

"We'll talk about it later, Gabriel," Duncan repeated. "Let's do an interview."

"Exactly how do you plan to do that, Arnie?" Gabriel asked.

Duncan shrugged. "Hook him back up to the machine and start asking questions, I guess. Isn't that the way it's done? You got any hints for me?"

"Hard to say, but based on the little bit I'm seeing here, I don't think you're going to get much in his drugged state. If you really want to try, I'd keep the questions simple. Don't look for a lot of open-ended information. None of that 'where were you on the night of the murder' stuff. Ask true-false, yes-no stuff, maybe I can look for some sort of verifiable response. Ask the same questions multiple times but mix them up, change up the wording, that sort of thing. Don't get your hopes up, though. This looks like a recording of a rock, almost."

"You want to help?" Arnie asked.

"Nope. I'm not even going back in that room. Going back to my cell now. Let me know when you want me to look at something. And what happened to my snacks?"

Arnie produced a flattened bag of chips from his back pocket and tossed them to Gabriel.

The paramedics had laid Helena gently on the floor of the lab. They made Chuck bring up the lights and turn off the sound from the recording. She still had the skullcap array in place.

"Was this thing on her when she went out?" the leader of the paramedic team asked.

"No," Chuck responded. "We were checking to see if she was having a seizure."

"Well, get it off her, then," the paramedic said. "She's not having a seizure. At least, I don't think so."

"Filling me with confidence," Chuck said. The man gave him a reproving look.

"Pressure's fine," the other paramedic announced, ripping off the blood pressure cuff from Helena's arm. "Pulse one twenty four, though." He wrote the data on his clipboard. Chuck removed the electrode cap and the monitors went flatline. Helena's eyelids fluttered and she took a deep, sighing inspiration.

"Here we go," the lead paramedic said. He sat back on his haunches. "Hey lady. Can you hear me?"

Helena turned her head to his voice and her gaze gained focus.

"Hey, Helena," Parnell said. "It's Chuck. You okay?"

Helena swallowed, nodded. She tried to sit up. The paramedics gently restrained her. "Not so fast, honey," the paramedic said.

"Fuck you, honey," Helena said, sitting up on her elbows.

The paramedics both smiled. "Seems okay," the leader said.

"Seems okay to me, too," the other said. He started to stow his equipment.

"What happened?" Helena asked, slowly trying to stand. Zeke helped her into the chair she had been in.

"We don't know," Chuck said. "Zeke found you when he came in a little while ago. You passed out, I guess."

"Yeah, with your eyes wide open," the paramedic said. "Weird."

"Thanks for coming, boys," Helena said. "Don't let the door—"

"Yeah, yeah. We get it, lady. You're welcome. Don't bother to get up. We'll let ourselves out." They spent a few more minutes filling out the paperwork. Helena let them recheck her vitals and thanked them as they left.

"Where's Gabe?" Helena asked, looking between Zeke and Parnell.

"He's gone, Helena," Chuck said. "Remember? The government took him away on Saturday, you said."

"I remember. Not back then?" Helena asked. Zeke and Chuck shook their heads. "He was supposed to be back by now. One or two days, he said." She put her elbows on the console and her head in her hands. "Find him, Chuck. Please. I need him to come home."

Gabriel waited in his room almost four hours this time before being brought back to the conference room. He transferred the new file and processed it through his computer. Duncan again stood behind him, looking over his shoulder. He was starting to look tired.

Gabriel listened to the audio of the interview as he reviewed the results appearing on his screen. Someone other than Duncan asked the questions. They were insistent, repetitive, and closed ended, as Gabriel had recommended. Listening to the questions, it was quickly apparent to Gabriel that the subject was suspected of being a terrorist in a sleeper cell planning an attack in the United States, somewhere in the Midwest and possibly on a transportation hub or sporting venue. It all seemed rather vague.

The results were rather vague as well. Gabriel was shaking his head as he watched the tracings. The software trailer was again a train of 'uninterpretable' and long pauses. The tracings themselves showed blunted spikes in response to many of the questions, but Gabriel couldn't interpret the spikes with any accuracy.

"You're shaking your head a lot, Dr. Sheehan," Duncan said from behind his shoulder.

Gabriel turned to face him. "Like I said, Arnie. I can't do it. There are some definite responses to the questions, but the signal isn't good enough for interpretation. Unless..." he trailed off.

"Unless what, Gabriel?" Duncan urged.

Gabriel shook his head again. "Just a thought. I couldn't do it here, anyway."

"Do what?"

"I was just thinking that, if the technician didn't screw up anything and the baseline was really unchanged, I could try some kind of subtraction analysis to clean up the responses to the interview. Might make it crisper, maybe allow some interpretation. I don't know." He leaned back in the chair.

"Try it," Duncan insisted.

"Can't do it, Arnie. Not on a laptop. I'd need to take this back to the lab, use our full facility. I've never even tried anything like it. It'd take a week of experimenting to even try a first pass."

"We don't have a week," Arnie said, dropping into a chair next to Gabriel.

"Yeah, well, I'm not exactly excited to try it anyway." Gabriel snapped his laptop closed. "Are we done here, then?"

"No, we are not done here, Gabriel. Not by a long shot."

"I can't help you, Arnie. It's not going to work."

"It'll work. We just have to go to plan B," Duncan said, rubbing his eyes with the heels of his hands.

"What's plan B?" Gabriel asked. "As if I want to know."

"We wake him up," Duncan said, standing.

"I'm not participating in the forced interview of your prisoner. I'm not going to be party to torture, or compulsion."

"Believe me, Dr. Sheehan," Duncan said, smiling. "This isn't torture. Not by a long shot. No, this is much better. You may have made torture obsolete. At least, I hope so."

"I'm not doing it. I'm not going there," Gabriel insisted. "Get me home. Two days, you said."

"You're already here, Gabriel," Duncan answered. "You might get home a little late."

"You can't make me do this," Gabriel said indignantly.

"No. But I don't have to let you use my little jet, either. And it'll take you a long time to get home your way, believe me."

"Why? Where are we, anyway?"

"A long way from home, brother. A very long way."

Chuck found Helena sitting in her lab. Zeke wasn't coming in today. He sat down at the console beside her.

"Whatcha doing?" he asked, smiling.

She tried to smile back, but shook her head instead. "Not much at the moment, Chuck," she said.

"Why don't you go home, then? Nothing doing here."

Helena shook her head again. "Nobody's home," she said. "Find out anything?"

It was Chuck's turn to shake his head. "Not a thing, Helena. Sorry."

"It's a big government," she said ruefully.

"If it was the government, I'm sure he'll be back soon," Chuck said. She nodded but said nothing. "How's the research going?"

"Pretty well, I think. You'd have to ask Zeke to get a straight answer, though."

"Too invested, huh?" Chuck asked.

"Something like that," Helena said. She didn't meet his gaze.

"I finally got you figured out, you know that?" Chuck said.

At that, she turned to look at him. "You think so, Chuck?" He nodded, smiling at her. "A few other folks thought the same thing, back in the day. Don't be so sure."

"She talks to you, doesn't she?" he asked softly, his smile disappearing. Chuck saw Helena stiffen slightly, her hands tightening on the armrests of her chair. She kept looking at him, quiet. "Your sister, right?"

Helena gave an almost imperceptible nod. He nodded back, smiling again. "It bothered me so much, you know? I told Gabriel a dozen times, even before I met you, that it didn't make any sense. A woman so obsessed with keeping private, with going unnoticed—why would a person like that help invent a way to invade a person's thoughts, something that violates a person's privacy? It didn't make any sense, I told him. I told him I thought you were setting him up, trying to sabotage him somehow."

"You were wrong, Chuck," she said quietly.

"I can see that now, Helena. I see that. You were working with him the whole time, helping. Just for a completely different reason. I see that now."

"I'm not crazy," Helena said. She looked pained, almost stricken as she said it.

"Of course not, Helena. That's what this," he gestured around them at the lab, "is really all about for you, isn't it?" Helena nodded again. Chuck thought of the recording he and Zeke had made while Helena was unconscious. "But what if you are, Helena?"

Helena looked at him then, her eyes filling with tears. "Then I'll have to find a way to fix it."

Gabriel was sent back to the on-call room and told to get some sleep. It would take until morning before they were ready to reverse the subject's coma and try again. Gabriel offered to continue working on the recordings in his room. Arnie only smiled and shook his head, keeping Gabriel's laptop locked in the case. Gabriel, for his part, insisted that the case stay in his possession. He knew Duncan couldn't access it, but he was afraid Duncan might try to have someone clone his computer's hard drive if he left it out of his sight for too long; that might be disastrous on multiple levels. If Duncan failed, Gabriel would be left without a computer and kidnapped for nothing, unable to work. If he succeeded, that would be much worse.

Gabriel was awakened early the next morning by a knock that announced breakfast. He had eaten and showered by the time Duncan arrived to collect him.

"Showtime," Duncan announced, gesturing to the hallway.

"Listen, Arnie," Gabriel protested. "I wasn't kidding last night. I know I agreed to help you, and I will. I'll interpret the recordings, same as I would for any other subject. But I'm not going to help you interrogate him. I'm not going back in that room."

"Yes, Gabriel, you are," Duncan replied. "This isn't like any other subject. It's no use standing outside the door so that you can pretend you're not part of it. You're in this and I need you in there. I'm not going back and forth between rooms just so you can live your little charade and feel better about yourself. I need to get this over with."

Gabriel just stood, considering.

"You want to go lock yourself in the bathroom, Dr. Sheehan?" Duncan asked. "Seriously, I don't give a shit at this point. I've got your laptop, and to be honest, it doesn't look that tough to hook the thing up and read off the results. Suit yourself."

"It's not that easy."

"So you say."

"You can't have my technology, Duncan," Gabriel said.

"I've already got it, Gabriel," Duncan said, gesturing with the heavy briefcase. "The question is, am I giving it back?" He paused, waiting.

"Let's go, then. I want to get home to my wife."

"Not as much as me, Gabriel," Duncan said, leading Gabriel back down the hall to the ICU.

The subject had been moved to a larger room. He was still connected to the ventilator. The monitors still reflected his vital signs. The same nurse busied himself adjusting an intravenous pump. The same two Insight technicians were present, now seated at a bedside hospital table, which held their equipment. They had already applied the electrode skullcap to the subject and were calibrating their input. As Gabriel and Duncan entered, a doctor in a lab coat, stethoscope draped around his neck, stood up from a chair in the corner.

"This is Dr. Ramirez," Duncan said to Gabriel, gesturing to the man. "Dr. Ramirez is the intensivist working with us. Dr. Ramirez, this is Dr. Sheehan."

Ramirez moved forward and offered his hand to Gabriel, who ignored it. "I'm not a doctor, Arnie. Quit calling me that," Gabriel said as he moved past the physician to take the seat the man had vacated. Duncan just shook his head.

"Doctor," Duncan said, addressing the intensivist, "where do we stand?"

The intensivist quit staring angrily at Gabriel and turned to Duncan. "We have two infusions running into the patient," the doctor said, indicating two intravenous drips mounted on infusion pumps. "One is a muscle relaxant, a paralytic agent. This prevents all voluntary movement at its current dose. His respirations are therefore dependent on the ventilator. The other agent," he now indicated a milky fluid infusing from another pump, "is a sedative. At the current dosage, the patient is being maintained in a deeply unconscious state."

"How do you know he's unconscious?" Duncan asked.

"We can monitor brainwaves, too," the physician said, smiling. "It's a crude device compared to their setup, of course, but it gives us a numerical reading of the patient's level of consciousness. Right now," he pointed to the monitor, "the number is less than fifteen, indicating the patient is completely unconscious."

"He's not a patient," Gabriel said from his chair in the corner.

"He's my patient," the physician said testily. "He's in my ICU."

"If they can make you believe absurdities, they can make you commit atrocities," Gabriel said.

"Please, Gabriel," Duncan said wearily, "Spare us the Voltaire. Let's just get what we need. Doctor, what next?"

The physician fumed for a moment, then continued with his back to Gabriel. "I plan to maintain the paralytic infusion at its current rate, but decrease the sedative. His level of consciousness will quickly rise. At some point, you can go ahead and conduct your interview—"

"Interrogation," Gabriel interjected.

"Gabriel, don't make me stuff a sock in your mouth," Duncan said.

The physician continued, "He won't be able to speak, of course. It's my understanding that it won't be necessary for the patient to actually speak."

"That's correct, doctor," Duncan said. "That's why we have Gabriel here. He'll interpret the subject's responses during the interview. How does that sound to you, Gabriel?"

"Awake but paralyzed? Sounds like torture," Gabriel said.

Duncan rolled his eyes. "Let's just do this, gentlemen. Go ahead, Doctor."

The physician nodded to the nurse, who in turn discontinued the sedative infusion. They waited. Within five minutes, the numbers on the consciousness monitor on the wall above his head began to climb. Shortly thereafter, the beeping of the subject's heart rate began to climb with it. Gabriel moved his chair to sit at the table next to the technicians monitoring the brain tracings. He said nothing.

Duncan leaned over his shoulder and handed Gabriel his laptop computer.

"You'll need this," he said. Gabriel took it and connected the laptop again to that of the Insight technicians.

"He's awake," Gabriel said.

"Not quite," the intensivist said. "The monitor still shows significant depression."

"Your monitor isn't worth shit, Doctor," Gabriel said. "Maybe that's why his heart rate is going through the roof." The intensivist stood with arms folded across his chest and said nothing. "Start talking, Arnie."

Duncan stepped to the bedside but turned to the others in the room. "Doctor, I'll need you standing by just outside this room, with the nurse. You two," he said, indicating the technicians, "go grab some coffee or something. Close the door behind you, please."

"How about me, Arnie?" Gabriel asked.

"You get to stay, Gabriel."

"You trust me that much, Arnie?" Gabriel asked, smiling.

"I can always shoot you later, Gabriel. I know where you live," Duncan said, smiling back. "Can we start?" Gabriel nodded, adjusted the recording on the laptop before him. Duncan bent down to speak softly into the subject's ear. Gabriel couldn't hear what he said.

"He hears you," Gabriel said. Duncan resumed speaking softly directly into the man's ear. Gabriel could only hear the occasional word or phrase. He watched as the tracings made their intricate dance across the screen. He started the program for interpretation.

Duncan straightened and turned to Gabriel. "Anything?"

Gabriel nodded. "He's definitely responding. He hears you, he understands."

"Can I ask him questions?"

"Sure."

"When will you know the answers?" Duncan asked. "How fast?"

"I'm not sure. There will be a lag, but probably not long. Go ahead."

Duncan bent close and began his interrogation. He spoke softly, in a measured pace. He seemed to be pausing between questions, but Gabriel couldn't hear specifics. He got the general drift, though; the occasional phrase and word he did hear confirmed his suspicions from the night before that this man was suspected to be a member of a terrorist plot of some sort. Suddenly, Gabriel's program began to stream words across the screen.

"Got it, Arnie," Gabriel said. "We're getting an interpretable response."

Duncan didn't straighten up, just nodded. He continued his interrogation. After an additional ten minutes, there was a knock at the door. Duncan straightened and swore softly. He crossed the room and opened the door halfway. The doctor was at the door.

"What?" Duncan asked him.

"The patient's heart rate," the doctor said. "I'm watching at the monitor out here. It's getting very high, I'm afraid."

"Is he in danger of dying?" Duncan asked.

"Well, no. I don't think that—"

"Let me know if he is," Duncan said, shutting the door in the man's face. Gabriel heard Duncan mutter a curse as he returned. Duncan looked over Gabriel's shoulder. "What are we getting?"

"All of it, multiple levels. Fear, panic. This here," he pointed to a tracing, "is a verbal track. If he were able to speak, this is what he'd be saying. But this," he said, pointing to another line, "is what he's thinking at a deeper level. I think this reflects the answers to your questions. He can't hide this."

Duncan pointed to the words crawling across the bottom of the screen. "Which is this, then? What he's saying or what he's thinking?"

"The program's default is to subtitle what he's saying. That's the trailer."

"Can you switch it?"

Gabriel nodded, made the necessary keystrokes on the laptop. Duncan watched as the subtitles switched to reflect the thought tracing.

"Rewind it to my first question. I want to see his answers."

"I can't do that. I'll lose the sync with the input," Gabriel said.

Duncan looked at him and leaned close to whisper into Gabriel's ear.

"You better not be fucking with me, Gabriel," Duncan whispered. He sat down next to Gabriel. The monitors indicated that the subject's heart rate was now almost two hundred. More knocking at the door, which Duncan ignored. Duncan remained sitting next to Gabriel, watching the monitor. He began to speak a little more loudly; to be sure the subject could hear him from his seat over the sound of the ventilator.

"I'm going to ask you again, Mr. Moussa. What is your real name?" Duncan asked, conversationally. They both watched as a name trailed across the screen, repeating itself four times: Ali ben Ali Moussef. Duncan whistled softly. "Okay, Ali. I'd like you to tell me the names of the other individuals involved in your activities." Within seconds, names appeared, repeating, mixing, and repeating again. Duncan smiled. He whispered, half to himself and half to Gabriel: "This is fucking marvelous."

The interview continued for another hour and a half. Duncan ignored the repeated bouts of knocking at the door. Once, when the door opened slightly, Duncan reached his leg out to kick it closed, yelling to stay out. After that, there was no more knocking. He finally finished his questioning and stood, smiling broadly at Gabriel.

"That's amazing," was all he said to Gabriel. He walked over and opened the door. The physician and the nurse were sitting at the main nursing station. Duncan waved them over. "Okay, Doctor. You can sedate him again. Thank you." The intensivist looked upset but gave the necessary orders to the nurse who had reentered the room as well. He made a show of examining the subject. "Will he live?" Arnie asked him. The intensivist nodded. "What a relief," Arnie said, smiling broadly.

Duncan turned to Gabriel, pointing to the Insight technician's laptop, still connected to the subject. "Is there anything recorded on that one?" he asked.

"Probably," Gabriel said. "Unless they specifically changed the standard settings."

"Then we take that with us. Do you need the technicians back or can you break this down?"

Gabriel shrugged. "I can do it."

"Then do it," Duncan said. "Let's pack up and get the hell out of Dodge."

"Where are we going now?" Gabriel asked, starting to shut down the computers.

"Home, Gabriel. I'm taking you home."

On the flight back, Duncan sat next to Gabriel with the laptop perched on a table in front of them. They reviewed the interrogation session over and over again. Gabriel set up the system so the verbal track was audible as the deeper thought track trailed as subtitles across the bottom of the screen. It was obvious that the subject had tried every manner of lie, but had no defense against his own thoughts. Duncan made copious notes on a pad, frequently asking Gabriel to pause the recording. Gabriel pointed out more subtleties in the tracings, indicating the signs of stress and, at some points, panic states.

"Don't give a shit about that," Duncan said. "Believe me, this guy got off easy. It ain't waterboarding, that's a fact."

"You should give a shit, Arnie. And not just because it makes you a sadistic bastard." He frowned at Duncan. "It affects the interpretation. Like I said back wherever we were, it's not just a matter of reading what the computer scrawls across the screen. There's a lot more to it."

"Doesn't look like it. I think you're bullshittin' me, Dr. Sheehan," Duncan said with a wry smile. "You don't want me appropriating this and cutting you out of the loop, that's what I think."

"Think what you want, Arnie. You'll be chasing shadows for the next few years."

Duncan pointed to the laptop. "So you're saying I can't believe this? Any of it? Some of it? What?"

"This? You can trust all of it. I've tweaked the input, adjusted the algorithm for the subject's emotional state, a dozen other things that even I'm not sure why they help. I was there, I could see what worked. If you had just hooked him up with those technicians and ran with it, it would've looked okay, probably. But it would've been mostly bullshit. And no way to tell what was real and what wasn't."

Duncan considered this, finally shook his head. "Still think you're trying to play me, Gabriel."

Gabriel shrugged. "Whatever. I don't really care what you believe, Duncan. You're not getting my technology, either way. And you're sure as shit not getting me to go on any more of your little excursions, either." He leaned back in the leather seat and closed his eyes.

"And here I thought we made such a great team, Gabriel," Duncan said. He looked at his watch. "Should be home in less than an hour, depending on traffic."

The Suburban pulled up outside the lab just after five. Gabriel turned to Duncan, seated beside him.

"Is this where you flash me with the memory wipe thingamajig?" Gabriel asked him.

"I wish. It'd make things a hell of a lot easier. No, this is the part where I ask you not to discuss anything that you've seen or heard under penalty of prosecution for violation of federal security. Do you agree?"

"What if I say no?"

"The car starts up and we take you into custody."

"Then I agree. What about my computer?"

"You'll get it back tomorrow."

"That's not acceptable, Arnie."

Duncan smiled at him. "You're a funny guy, Gabriel. You can get out of the car now. Thanks for your help."

"It won't do you any good, Arnie. You can't get into it." Duncan just gave Gabriel his wry smile, not saying anything. "No, really, Arnie. Anybody tries, they might get hurt. Really." They stared at one another for a minute. Gabriel shrugged and got out of the car.

Gabriel walked into his office to find Chuck at his desk, typing on his computer. Helena was curled up asleep on the couch.

"Hey, boss," Chuck said, smiling as he looked up at Gabriel. "Nice of you to show up for work."

"Just keeping the chair warm for me, Chuck?" Gabriel asked.

"Better for my back than working from my bed."

"My bed, you mean." Gabriel watched his wife sleeping on the couch, snoring softly.

"She missed you," Chuck said, pushing back from the screen and putting his feet up on the desk. "Hasn't really left here since you were kidnapped."

"Is she okay?" Gabriel asked softly.

"Nope."

Gabriel knelt down in front of the couch and gently touched his wife's cheek.

"Hey, Lena," he said softly. Her eyes fluttered open and she smiled.

"Am I still dreaming?" she asked him, smiling. She caught sight of Chuck smiling at them from the desk. "No, I guess not." She wrapped her arms around her husband and gave him a fierce hug. "Missed you lots. I don't think we should be taking separate vacations."

"I'll remember to tell that to whoever tries to abduct me in the future." He helped pull her up to sit on the couch. "Want to go home, beautiful?"

"Sure, why not?" she answered, rubbing the sleep from her eyes. "I'll make us some breakfast."

"It's after five in the afternoon," Gabriel pointed out.

"Whatever. Breakfast for dinner, my favorite. Pancakes!"

"How about me?" Chuck asked, almost springing out of the chair. "I love breakfast for dinner."

"Not invited," both Gabriel and Helena said simultaneously. They walked out holding hands.

Chuck leaned back in the chair. "No problem, guys. Really, not offended. See you in the morning."

"Maybe," Gabriel said over his shoulder as he walked with his wife out the door.

Gabriel and Helena walked back in the next morning, still holding hands. They stopped at the door when they saw Arnie Duncan sitting on the couch. Arthur and Chuck were also seated in the office. Nobody was saying a thing.

"Morning, guys," Helena said brightly. "Who's the suit?"

Duncan stood as Gabriel introduced him to his wife. "This is Arnie. Arnie, my wife, Helena. Arnie is my kidnapper."

Duncan shook his head, smiling. He shook Helena's hand. "Nice to meet you, Mrs. Sheehan. I'm sorry I had to abduct your husband. I'm sure you understand."

Helena dropped his hand and dropped onto the couch. "I'm sure I don't, Mr. Duncan. Since my name isn't Mrs. Sheehan, just call me Helena. What do you want now, Arnie? You can't take my husband any more. I get him now."

Duncan produced his briefcase and set it on the coffee table in front of the couch. "I promised Gabriel I'd return his laptop," he explained, clicking open the case. He took out the laptop and set it down on the table. It was twisted, charred, and mostly melted.

Chuck raised his eyebrows. "I guess you didn't teach him the magic chant, Gabe."

"I hope nobody was hurt," Gabriel said.

Duncan sat on the couch next to Helena. "Actually, our technician is still hospitalized with burns to her face and hands. We're considering pressing charges."

"Pressing charges?" Gabriel was incredulous. "I warned you last night, when you took it from me."

"So you claim. Truth is, that thing was a concealed weapon, which you conspired to have introduced into a federal facility. Kind of like rigging a shotgun to your front door—just because it's your front door, you still can't blow away an intruder, you know? Kind of like attempted murder. Kind of like."

"You really must work for the government," Helena said.

"Oh, I'm sure he works for the government," Gabriel said, disgusted. "Nobody else would have the balls to try that after I warned you what would happen."

"Hey," Chuck said. "I'm offended."

Duncan looked at him. "You must be the guy who claims to work for the NSA."

"No," Chuck said, blushing. "I'm the guy who really does work for the NSA. Who the hell are you? I'm looking at over two hundred Arnold Duncans in the federal employee database and I'm willing to bet my ass none of them are you." Duncan only looked at him, not smiling now. "Don't bother, Arnie. I can guess." Chuck pulled out his cellphone and pointed it at Duncan. "Smile," Chuck said. Duncan ducked his head. "Just kidding. Already got you when you sat down." Chuck plugged the phone into the computer on Gabriel's desk.

"Where to start?" Chuck asked wistfully, typing on the computer keyboard. "You know what I'm thinking, Arnie? I'm betting FBI. Twenty bucks says FBI." Duncan just looked at him, saying nothing. "Not a betting man, Arnie? How about this, double or nothing says you're Operational Technology Division. What do you say, Arnie? Come visit us all the way from Quantico?" Chuck continued to type at the keyboard, Duncan looking distinctly uncomfortable. "I hope I'm right," Chuck continued. "Sure would be embarrassing to find out a CIA spook was operating on US soil. That would be against the law, you know." Chuck slapped his palm down on Gabriel's desk. "Bingo!" he announced. Chuck turned the monitor around so the others could see Duncan's FBI employee badge photograph filling the screen.

"Enough of this shit," Duncan said, bright red with anger.

"I think somebody owes me forty bucks," Chuck said, "that's what I think." He turned the monitor back to read the details. "Yeah, Felix. Senior Field Agent Felix Arnold of the FBI, OTD, out of Quantico, Virginia. I think you owe me forty bucks. How long did that take, guys? I think that was less than a minute, that's what I think." He leaned back, gloating.

"Does this asshole ever shut up?" Felix, aka Arnold, asked.

"No," the rest of them answered in chorus.

"So, Felix," Gabriel said. "Let's move past the whole 'attempted murder' thing, shall we? Why don't you just answer my wife's question: What do you want? Now, I should add. What do want now? Because I think I've done quite a bit already, you know." They all stared at the FBI agent, waiting.

"We need to speak privately, Dr. Sheehan," Arnold said.

"Not going to happen, Felix," Gabriel said. "You want to talk, go ahead and talk. Or leave. I don't really care either way at this point. Somehow I doubt I'm getting reimbursed for my laptop, anyway."

Arnold sat, considering. "Fine, Gabriel. We'll do this your way." He looked around the office to the others in the room. "You guys know the rules, I'm sure. Nothing we talk about leaves this room."

"No problem," Chuck said, laying his cellphone down on the front of the desk. "I'm recording the whole thing." He smiled and leaned his chin on his hands.

Arnold just shook his head and turned back to Gabriel. "That project that you helped us with turned out well. Well enough, anyway. The information we obtained allowed us to roll up the entire cell last night. We—I appreciate your help. You saved a lot of lives, potentially."

"You're welcome," Gabriel said.

"I don't think you came back here to thank my husband, Agent Arnold," Helena said.

"You're right, Helena. But I'm not kidding when I say I appreciate what he did. Your technology is truly amazing, a breakthrough of extraordinary significance—"

"That the FBI would like to possess," Helena interjected. "Not for sale. Thanks for stopping by, you can put my husband's medal in the mail. See you, Felix."

"Gabriel made that clear, Helena," Arnold continued. "I'm in no position to negotiate anything, anyway. Not at my pay grade. I'm a field agent, not management."

"Great," Arthur said. "Then you can have management contact my office. We can work something out as a government contract."

Helena slapped her forehead loudly and buried her face in her hands.

"I'm sure you'll be contacted very soon," Arnold said. "Like I said, that's not why I'm here."

"Okay, Felix. I'm getting bored now," Gabriel said. "What is it?"

"We had to roll up the entire network because of the difficulty we experienced in the interview," Arnold explained.

"Interrogation," Gabriel said. Arnold rolled his eyes.

"Whatever, Gabriel," Arnold continued. "We had to act immediately because the subject was aware he had been interviewed."

"Of course he was aware," Chuck said. "He was still alive at the end, wasn't he?"

"Can we get him not to talk any more until I leave?" Arnold asked Gabriel.

"I wish," Gabriel said. "I'd keep you around for lunch, at least."

"You know what I'm referring to, Gabriel. You mentioned at one point that when you got back to your lab you might be able to do some further investigation into interpreting the more subtle recording we made."

"You mean the one while the guy was still under sedation," Gabriel said.

"Really, sedation?" Chuck asked. "Cool."

"Cool, Chuck? I don't think so," Arthur said, obviously disturbed. "That's not what we do. Voluntary subjects, freely submitting—"

"Could we get him to stop talking, too?" Arnold asked Gabriel. "My associates and I would like you to further explore the possibility of analyzing the sedated data set. You could work here, of course. No more abductions," Arnold said, smiling.

"Well, that's a relief, Felix," Gabriel said. "Problem is, you melted my machine. Not much to work with."

"Actually, your machine pretty much burst into flames when we stared at it funny. No matter, we still have the recording from the technician's laptop," Arnold said. "I could have it sent over."

Gabriel was considering this when his wife interrupted. "I don't mean to pry, Felix," she said, leaning forward, elbows on knees. "Let me just see if I got this straight. My husband, whom you abducted, was good enough to help you with your little waterboarding project, which ended up nabbing the bad guys, right?" Arnold said nothing, just looked at her with a neutral expression. "But that wasn't good enough? Why not?"

Arnold sighed. "It was our hope that we could gain the information we needed in a manner that wasn't apparent to the subject. In that way, it would be safe to release him and—"

"Oh, I get it," Chuck said with sincere excitement. "That would be great."

"No, Chuck," Helena said, looking at him with disgust. "That would be the opposite of great. That would mean that the government would have the capability of interrogating citizens—"

"—Terrorists," Arnold corrected, emphatically.

"Citizens," Helena retorted. "The government would be able to interrogate citizens and they—we—wouldn't even know it had happened.

That really, really sucks, Agent Felix. Really." Helena leaned back on the couch.

"Gabriel?" Arnold asked.

"We're not going to do it," Helena said from the couch.

"Gabriel?" Arnold asked again.

Gabriel shrugged. "You heard the lady, Felix. Doesn't sound like something we want to get involved in."

"Is he giving us a choice?" Arthur asked.

"I'm trying to," Arnold said, still looking at Gabriel.

"Then we choose not to," Gabriel said. "Thanks for bringing back my laptop, Felix. Bye."

"Thanks again for your help," Arnold said, standing. He shook Gabriel's hand. "I wish I could tell you this was over."

"I wish I could believe a fucking thing you were saying," Helena said from the couch. "Bye, Felix."

"Good bye, Mrs. Sheehan. Pleasure to meet you." Arnold picked up his briefcase and left.

Chuck waited until he heard the outside door close. "Boy, he's kind of a dick," he said.

"You think?" Helena asked.

"Gee," Arthur said, "I don't know. Seemed like a reasonable guy to me."

They all looked at him.

"Are you shittin' me?" Helena asked him finally. "The guy just spent that entire conversation threatening us. Repeatedly, and like in six different ways."

Arthur shrugged. "You hear threats, I hear business opportunities."

"I hear you being a meshuggenah schmuck," Helena said.

"I love when you swear in Yiddish with that lilting Irish brogue," Arthur said.

"Yeah, well brogue this up your ass," Helena said, throwing the melted laptop at Arthur's head. It missed and clattered off the wall behind him.

"Children," Gabriel said, alarmed at how close the laptop had come to his friend's head. He shook his head at the dent it had left in his office wall. "Some decorum, please."

"She started it," Arthur said.

"He's a dick," Helena replied.

"That's what I said," Chuck added. "Or were you talking about Arthur? I'm getting confused."

That surprised none of them but brought a moment's silence. Helena finally sighed and sat forward again, saying, "We have to deep six this thing. They're not going to stop until they get it."

"Deep six what thing?" Arthur asked. "The FBI contract?"

"No, Arthur, not your FBI contract," Helena answered. "The whole damn thing. Insight Technologies. We have to pull the plug."

Arthur looked at her aghast. He finally found his voice enough to say, "It can't be done, Helena. You can't pull the plug on this. I told Gabriel when we started."

"Told him what, Arthur?"

"There is no exit strategy on this. You know it as well as I do. You won't let us sell the intellectual property off, you said so a thousand times. And we can't just shut it down."

"Why not?" Chuck asked. "You ask me, it's getting kind of tedious anyway. Shut the thing down if you ask me. I'm with Helena."

"I'm telling you guys, it can't be done. If we don't produce it, it'll spring back up like a weed, in a hundred other companies. The genie can't be killed; it's out of his bottle. It's part of society now. You can't put it back in the box."

"Geez, Arthur," Gabriel interjected, "could you mix in any more metaphors there?" He turned to his wife. "I don't get it either, hon. What exactly did you have in mind?"

Helena leaned back on the cushions and spoke up at the ceiling. "The government isn't going to stop now until they own this. It's too important to them; they finally got around to figuring out what it can do. Time to bury it as deeply as possible or they'll take it, one way or another."

"I don't really think we should assume that's a bad thing," Chuck added, hopefully.

"I think, Chuck, that we can pretty much assume that's a bad thing," Gabriel said. "I wish I could tell you the story of my recent lost weekend. You'd realize just how bad an idea that is. But I agree with Arthur; I don't see how we make this disappear."

"It'll take some time. And a lot of money, no doubt. But we can make it go away," Helena said.

"Can we go back to the part where we talk about whether it's a good idea to make it go away?" Chuck asked from behind the desk.

"How?" Arthur asked.

"Just by going back and talking about it, I guess," Chuck said.

"Shut up, Chuck," Arthur said. "How, Helena? Short of paying someone to burn this all down. Which, as I said, I don't think would accomplish much, anyways."

"It would probably help, but that won't be necessary. No, I think we need that marketing savant you got for us when we first started this thing, remember her? She was brilliant," Helena said.

"Yeah, brilliant all right. We made her a billionaire. And by the way, a Senator now," Arthur added.

"No shit?" Helena asked. "State?"

"No," Arthur replied, "a real live US Senator. You should know, we've sponsored a fund raiser for her every year since she first ran for office seven years ago."

"No, we don't. We don't do political," Helena said, raising up from the couch indignantly.

"Yes, we do," Arthur replied. "You'd know that if you ever showed up for a board meeting."

"We have a board?" Helena asked.

"Yeah, we have a board. You're on it, you know."

"I am? I didn't know," she answered sheepishly.

"That explains your consistent lack of attendance, I guess," Arthur said.

"Are you on the board?" Helena asked Gabriel. He nodded.

"I'm kind of the chairman," Gabriel said, embarrassed.

"Am I on the board, too?" Chuck asked.

"You're not even an employee," Arthur said.

"Well, even better," Helena said. "We need to talk to her. And we'll need someone who knows something about civil rights law. And we'll need a judge, a federal judge. Probably one of the smarter, older ones. Salt and pepper hair, you know the kind. You can do that, right Arthur?"

"I'm sure there must be a doddering federal jurist or two hanging around the bridge club," Arthur mused. "It's not like they have a real job or anything. Anything else? I hardly feel challenged at this point."

Helena flopped back on the couch. "Like I said, this is going to take a while. Maybe a year or more. So, yeah, Arthur, you get your wish. Start the government-contracting gambit, have a ball. It'll probably take them close to a year to come up with a contract, given all the super secret bullshit and clearances you'll have to wade through."

"At least," Chuck agreed. "While we're waiting, can I quit?"

"No way," Gabriel said. "I'm quitting first. I'm promoting you to chief of daily operations."

"But I can't be promoted," Chuck complained. "Arthur said I'm not even an employee."

"Fine," Gabriel said. "First we'll hire you, then we'll promote you. Send me your CV by this afternoon or you're fired."

"No way. Promote one of the lackeys you already hired to help us with the readings. They're already real employees. I quit. I'm going to work with Helena," Chuck said.

"You can't quit, you're not an employee. And you don't even know what I'm doing," Helena said to the ceiling.

"I know it's gotta be more interesting than what I'm doing now," Chuck said. "What are we doing?"

"Researching mental illness," Helena said, sighing.

"Of course," Chuck said, also sighing.

"You guys'll be great together," Arthur said. "See who drives who crazy first."

"Whom," Gabriel said.

"Probably Helena, my bet—pretty much a tossup, though."

"I guess that leaves you and me to battle the beast, Arthur," Gabriel said. "You baffle them with the legal bullshit and I'll confound them with the power of science."

"Sounds like a plan."

Chuck moved into Helena's lab that afternoon. He sat next to her at the console, legal pad and pen in hand.

"Okay, boss. I'm ready. What do we do?" Chuck asked.

"You really want to work here, on this? Why?" Helena asked.

"I have my reasons," he said.

"Yeah, I figured. That's why I'm asking."

"I want to help the crazy people."

"Bullshit. And quit calling them crazy people. It's impolite."

"Fine, whatever. I'm not doing that commercial shit anymore, that's all. I'm tired of it."

"Why pretend to help me? What are you playing at, Chuck?" Helena asked. She stared at him, waiting.

"I just want to help, Helena. I'm worried about you."

"Bullshit."

"You say that a lot, you know that?" They looked at each other.

"Why play games, Chuck? Just make your move, be on your way."

"Maybe I don't have a move, Helena."

"You're a lousy liar, Chuck. You've been here a long time. You waiting for me to grow old and die, or get tired of watching you, or what?"

"Maybe I'll just wait for you to go catatonic again, Helena. Maybe then I'll make this move you say I'm waiting for. How about them apples, huh?"

She didn't have an answer for that.

"When are you going to tell Gabriel?" Chuck asked her.

"Tell him what, Chuck?"

"I may be a lousy liar, Helena, but you're a lousy lunatic, you know that? About the voices you hear. When are you going to tell your husband?"

"I don't hear voices, Chuck."

"Voice, then. Excuse me. I didn't mean to imply you were crazy or anything."

"I'm not crazy."

"Well, let's just say you're not the sanest one in the room. Ever."

"Sanity is overrated."

"Maybe. But paranoid schizophrenia doesn't look like a barrel of laughs, either."

"Is that what you think I am? In your professional opinion?"

"You tell me," he said, bending down to switch on the console before them. He started a recording and the sound of a thousand loons, of a roomful of reverberating oboes, filled the lab.

Helena stared around the lab, listening as the sound rose and fell, throbbing more and more loudly. "Who is that?" she yelled over the sound.

Chuck leaned back over and switched it off, the sudden silence bouncing off the walls. "That's you, Helena. That's you during that last little spell, before the paramedics showed up."

Helena said nothing. She shook her head slowly, and then looked at her friend.

"What am I going to do?" she asked him.

"Tell Gabriel," he answered.

"Tell Gabriel what? That his wife is a nut case? I don't even know what's going on, what to tell him."

"Tell him the truth."

She shook her head. "No, not a good idea, Chuck."

"You know what the say about the truth, Helena. It'll set you free."

"No, Chuck, the truth will not set you free. The truth will get you killed."

"Somebody said that, right?"

She nodded. "Screamin' Jay Hawkins."

"Yeah, he sounds like a role model for your situation. Tell Gabe anyway, Helena. He can help you."

She shook her head vigorously at that. "No. We don't say a thing to Gabriel about this. Promise me, Chuck." She looked at him, her eyes desperate.

"He can help you, Helena."

"No. You can help me. Promise me. Promise me or I'll throw you out of here. I'll send you back to Washington. I'll kill you in your sleep. Don't say anything to Gabriel. Please, Chuck." She grabbed his wrist.

Chuck looked at where she was squeezing his wrist. "If I promise, will you not break my wrist?" She nodded and let go of him.

"Sorry."

"Hey, no problem," he said, gingerly flexing his wrist. "So we don't tell Gabriel. What do we do?"

"We need to figure this out," Helena said.

"Yeah, so you're going to get back to me on this, is that what you're saying? Reconsider the whole 'kill me in my sleep'?"

"It's just a phrase, Chuck," Helena said.

"No, Helena. It's not just a phrase. 'It is what it is.' That's a phrase. It doesn't mean anything, just a phrase. 'I'll kill you in your sleep' is what most people consider a threat. It's the kind of thing that if I were to write it down, say, and put quotation marks around it, and show it to a judge—probably get you put away for ninety days. Just saying."

"I like that phrase."

"'I'll kill you in your sleep?' I noticed. You say it a lot."

"Just saying."

"Yeah, well, quit saying it. You're making me nervous."

"No, that's not what I meant. Pay attention here, Chuck. I'm going to need your help."

"That's what they don't pay me for."

She nodded. "I need my musicians. Both of them. Can you get them back here for me? To help us?"

"I can try."

"I think they're avoiding me. They promised they'd come over, but they haven't. Zeke came by for a bit but left again. He's the one who figured out the loons, you know."

"Yeah, Helena, I know. He was there when we made that recording of you."

"Shit."

"Yeah, well. I guess that does explain why he's been too busy to stop by, huh?"

"Talk to him, Chuck. We need their help."

"Check. What else?"

"Talk to the field techs, the ones doing my research recordings. Tell them I only want recordings of schizophrenics now, that's all. No more depressives or manics or bipolar or those other crazies, okay?" Chuck nodded, writing on his pad.

"Check. None of those other crazies. Got it."

"And this is the important part; listen, Chuck. Tell them I need recordings of when the subjects are hearing voices, especially when they're hearing voices."

"How are they going to do that, exactly?"

"I don't know, Chuck. Don't give me more problems here; I'm trying to work. Just help me, okay?" He nodded again. "This is important; tell them the recordings need to be marked for the periods when the subjects are actually hearing the voices."

"Got it."

"But that's not all of it. Whenever they get a recording of the subject during the voices, they also have to record him when he's not hearing the voices, too. Do you understand?"

"Got it."

"No, really, Chuck. This is important. Recordings hearing voices, recordings without voices. It would be best if we could get them recorded before they start hearing the voices, then during the voices, then again after the voices, you see?"

"Yeah, Helena, I get it. Not that complicated. I don't see how the techs are going to do it, though. Might as well have a couple of schizo's live here for a while."

"You think we should?"

Chuck looked up at her, abashed. "No, Helena, I don't. One's enough." He returned her scowl with a smile. "I was just kidding. Shit, maybe we should just hook you back up and record you twenty-four, seven for a while—"

"No! You don't ever do that to me again! Do you hear me, Chuck? I mean it—"

"Yeah, yeah. I get it, Helena. Or you'll kill me in my sleep." He smiled at her.

She softened and smiled back. "I'm just saying."

"It is what it is."

CHAPTER 19

Arthur and Gabriel set up their war room in Arthur's Transamerica Building offices. They established a two front campaign for themselves. One group was enlisted to begin Helena's "Operation Deep Six", the mission statement being written out by Helena in a scrawl on several napkins from the lab. The napkins were scanned, blown up to poster size, and mounted on the white board of conference room number one. A group of fifteen consultants met daily to bring the napkin's simple plan to fruition. Arthur and Gabriel sat in on weekly progress meetings, though they had little to offer beyond encouragement. Actually, Arthur was somewhat less than encouraging since, if successful, Operation Deep Six would result in the loss of Insight Technologies highly lucrative revenue stream.

It was in conference room two that Arthur and Gabriel spent the greatest part of their efforts. Here they assembled a group of senior and middle management to pursue Insight Technologies new focus, government contracting. Several sections were created to establish liaisons with the Department of Defense, the FBI Office of Technological Development, and the Homeland Security Agency. Each working group was charged to work independently and through standard governmental procurement channels. Each group was required to establish its own projects and proposals. Groups were forbidden from collaborating, ostensibly to encourage a broad range of original thinking. It was slow and deliberate, perfect for government contracting.

After three weeks, Chuck appeared in Arthur's office. He collapsed into the deeply cushioned couch, interrupting a brainstorming session between Arthur and Gabriel. They stared at him for a while, waiting for him to speak. He didn't.

"Hi, Chuck," Arthur said, finally. "We saw you come in, you know."

"What's up, Chuck?" Gabriel added.

Chuck stirred dramatically to a semi erect posture. He sat with arms outstretched, feigning a crucifixion pose. "You guys have to take me in. I need to be here, with you. I can help. Please."

"What's wrong, guy? Don't like working with my wife?"

"Hey, buddy, it was your choice, remember?" Arthur chipped in. "You needed a transfer, you said."

"Please, I'm not kidding. She's killing me down there. I need to be here, with the nice people."

"Gee, Chuck. I don't think so," Arthur said, shaking his head and trying to hide a smile. "We're just doing really boring contracting stuff here."

"No, no," Chuck said, sounding desperate. "That's what I need to be doing. I know the system, I can help. I can get us in with these agency guys, like that." He snapped his fingers.

"Yeah, Chuck," Gabriel started to say, "That's really not the tack we're pursuing just yet—"

"But they're all crazy, Gabriel," Chuck said, sitting up to look earnestly from face to face. "All of them. I can't work with them—no offense, Gabriel, I mean Helena is a nice person and all, but I can't work with her anymore. And the other guys; they're musicians, you know? I can't work with musicians. We made such a great team, before. Remember? Please, Gabe? Arthur?"

Arthur had to look away, the man looked so pathetic. He turned to Gabriel, saying, "Did he just say Helena is a nice person?"

"Yeah, I think he did," Gabriel answered. "Maybe we should get him out of there, you think?"

"Yes! Yes!" Chuck enthused. He started to fumble with the laptop from his satchel. "Look at this, Gabriel. When they weren't sending me for food and stuff, I was able to work a little on your problem..."

"What problem was that, Chuck?" Gabriel asked, only mildly interested.

"You remember, the problem you had with Duncan, from the FBI interrogation. The problem extracting information from the sedated subject. I've been working on it."

Gabriel suddenly became very concerned. "Why did you do that, Chuck?" he asked, coming around the desk to sit next to him and look at his laptop screen as it started up.

"Well, you know, it sounded like an interesting problem, something I might be able to help with, but—"

"Where did you get the recording?" Gabriel asked, sharply.

"Duncan dropped by at the lab last week, I think it was. But, listen—"

"Duncan came by the lab," Gabriel fumed, "and you didn't tell me?"

"What? Yeah. No, I guess I didn't. We just got to talking, and he let me have a copy of the interrogation—"

Gabriel began to seethe. "Chuck. Stop. That recording was taken from a subject in a medically induced coma. You realize that, right? Medically induced, by Duncan and the FBI. You don't have a problem with that?" Gabriel asked.

Chuck looked at him sideways. "No, Gabriel, of course I do, that's what I was about to say—"

Gabriel relaxed a little. "Good. Because, Chuck, I gotta say, I was a little concerned that you—"

"—I've got a real problem with what you were thinking, because I don't mean to be insulting, Gabriel, but you were completely off base when you told Duncan you could analyze that recording back at the lab and get something out of it. I mean, look at this mess," Chuck said, pointing to the computer screen between them. "No way you can get anything meaningful from this. I mean, I heard you talking about running a differential analysis between the two recordings, but Hell's bells, Gabriel, it's not going to work."

Arthur and Gabriel sat staring at Chuck. Finally, Arthur asked, "That's it, Chuck? That's your problem with the whole concept?" Chuck stared back at them, blinking.

"Well, yeah, Arthur. That's my problem, all right. I don't think it can be done, to be honest. I mean, a coma's a coma, right? If the dude's not mentating, then what's to interpret? Blood from a stone; garbage in, garbage out."

"Are you done now?" Gabriel asked.

"Well, yeah. I guess. Sorry, I know you're disappointed and all," Chuck said. He closed up his laptop and began to put it back in his messenger bag.

"You have no idea, Chuck," Gabriel said.

Chuck looked back up at them and brightened. "So, what do you say, guys? Can I stay and work with you guys? Huh? Can I?"

Gabriel and Arthur exchanged a glance.

"Sure, Chuck. Why don't you set up in there with the group in conference two, see if you can give them some of your governmental insight."

"Great," Chuck said, smiling and heading to the door of the conference room. "Let's get together for lunch, whaddya say?"

"They do a working lunch in there, Chuck. Today's pizza, I think. Catch you later." Arthur waited until the conference door closed behind him. "You should've let Helena kill him in his sleep."

Gabriel told his wife the story, as they lay in bed that night side-by-side, staring up through the skylight at the little square of stars above them.

"Well," Helena answered quietly in the dark, "that explains why he never came back with our lunch."

"Arthur says you should have killed him in his sleep," Arthur replied, squeezing her hand in his.

"That's just a saying, you know."

"You say it a lot."

"Just an expression."

"How about 'I'm going to rip your leg off and bludgeon you to death with it'? Is that just an expression, too?"

"Who says that?"

"You did, last week. When I forgot to run the dishwasher." He tried to see her face next to him, but it was too dark.

"Oh, yeah. I remember. Actually, I meant that, but not literally."

"Oh, good. I think."

"You'll know when I'm really serious, don't worry."

"How will I know?"

"If I start cursing in Croatian, you're in serious shit, Gabriel."

"Oh, good to know. Like what should I be listening for, exactly?"

"Ja cu ischpati iz vase oci i koristiti ih da vam pokazati kako ruzan si."

"Sounds sexy. What's it mean?"

"Roughly, 'I am going to pluck out your eyes and use them to show you how ugly you are.' But the real malevolence of it is kinda watered down in the translation."

"Oh."

"I dated a Croatian for a while. Didn't work out."

"Shame. He sounds fun."

They lay like that, quietly for a time. Helena waited for the snoring to begin. When it didn't, she asked, "What are we going to do about Chuck?"

She heard him shrug beside her. "I guess we could go all Croatian on him. Arthur and I just threw him in with the workerbees, didn't think he could cause much harm in there."

"He denies it, but I think he's getting close to making his move."

"Listen closely to the sound of my eyebrows raising."

"Go for it."

"I already did, you missed it. What move might that be, exactly? Stealing more of your lunch money? Making another pass at the ethnomusicologist?"

"No, cloning the program so he can take it back to NSA. He's been biding his time while we matured the technology, but he's got a vision. I'm sure of it."

"A guy's got to dream."

"Yeah, well, his dream is to save the world and fuck us royally, Gabriel."

"You really think the nebbish would try that? He seems so nice."

"He is nice. Everyone loves Chuck. But he has a vision and he has the purity of a zealot. Quis custodiet ipsos custodes?"

"Latin, right?"

She nodded in the dark. "Who will guard the guards, themselves?"

"Now I'm confused—is that like a bumper sticker? You're right, though; Chuck does seem to have an unhealthy respect for Duncan, or Felix, or whoever he is. But he told me today it couldn't be done."

"No, he said what you were talking about couldn't be done. You knew as much already."

"Yeah, it's true. I was just blowing smoke up Duncan's ass to try to get him to let me get back to the lab. It didn't work at that level, either."

"I still don't understand why you ever agreed to help him."

"More like an abduction than an agreement, Lena."

"Was he holding a gun to your head, or what?"

"Something like that."

"Something like a gun? A big salami? What? Why didn't you just throw him out on his ass?"

"It's over, Lena. Let's move on."

"I don't think it's over, Gabe. They know they can get to you, whatever they did. They'll come for you again. Bet on it."

"Boy, you're in a happy place tonight, aren't you?"

'I'm just saying."

"You know what the Hungarians say."

"No, I never dated any Hungarians."

"Don't look for the shadow of the devil on the wall, he may be behind you."

"Is that what they say in Hungary? Because it doesn't make much sense."

"Loses a little in translation."

"It is what it is."

"Just saying."

The team in conference room one was making amazing progress. From concept to courtroom, Helena and her associates had anticipated at least twelve months. Remarkably, the consulting team identified and dressed their candidate in less than three. Once the team found Maria Garcia-Rojas, a migrant farm worker in jail in Arizona, their plan crystallized. A pleasant looking woman of thirty-two, they found her incarcerated on charges of attempted murder when she fought off the alleged attack of her white supervisor. The man ended up with a severe head injury after she struck him with a baseball bat, an act that she said was needed to prevent his attempted rape. She was an undocumented worker, downtrodden, but sympathetic as the widowed mother of three small children. She also interviewed well, speaking accented English in a voice that sounded of stoicism in the face of a life of hardship and misery.

Arizona remained one of only six states that provided no public support for Insight Technology interviewing to those without the financial means to hire the company on their own. The accused supervisor, in contrast, had undergone no less than three IT mental interviews at the behest of his legal team. These readings were inconclusive due to the subject's traumatic brain injury, creating enough ambiguity to make a mental interview of Maria seem all the more important for the cause of justice.

The conference room one team arrived en masse to Maria's cause, but only sub rosa. When the local ACLU chapter began to get involved, the team quietly convinced them that their participation would not be necessary. As publicity grew, a wealthy farmer in the area began a defense fund for Maria to allow her to afford the mental interview that hopefully would aid her defense. In a stirring jailhouse speech, however, Maria thanked her would-be supporter, but felt it wasn't right to take the money when she had already met so many others in jail like herself who would have no such benefit. The story, with the surreptitious urging of a small army of media consultants, went national.

Maria's defense was led by a world famous, elegantly coiffed, criminal defense attorney who declared that he would take up her cause because of his deep-seated belief in justice for the downtrodden. He didn't mention the full financial support of Arthur's team that he was to receive at the conclusion of the proceedings. What the steely-eyed attorney with movie star looks did say, however, to every syndicated interviewer and talk show host in the country, was that Maria's was a case that exemplified the twisted state that American justice had reached. A state where only the privileged could afford the tests that could potentially prove a person's innocence. This wasn't just about money, he pointed out more emphatically. This was about the new standard of innocence in America, a standard that had arisen de facto, that said anyone that didn't have an Insight Technology mindreading interview was probably guilty. A standard that presumed that any citizen, rich or poor, now felt compelled to prove his innocence, not in court, but at the technological altar of a strange cabal of scientists. That was his favorite phrase, 'strange cabal of scientists'.

With careful timing of interviews, interest pieces, and the manipulation of the judicial docket, the case of Maria Garcia-Rojas held the country's attention for a solid month. At the conclusion of the trial, the jury found Maria innocent of all charges. The judge, in announcing the jury's verdict on live national television, felt compelled to pontificate on how this case wasn't just about one individual, but should serve as a precedent and warning that the dark science exemplified by Insight Technologies was antithetical to the system of American justice as formulated by our founders. Conference room one exploded into cheers and high-fives all around. If Insight Technologies had ever been a public corporation, its stock would have turned to ashes overnight. Gabriel and Helena were ecstatic; Arthur not so much. Every pundit predicted the verdict would be the basis of an eventual Supreme Court ruling that would eliminate mind reading nationally as acceptable courtroom evidence.

The principals of Insight Technology were together again at Arthur's house the week after the verdict. Arthur was trying to drink heavily, but his heart wasn't in it. Chuck, Helena, Gabriel, and Sam sat with Arthur on his deck, watching as the sun dropped redly into the Pacific. They had progressed from champagne to beer, and now were starting on coffee. Bottles of various liquors were scattered about to add to the coffee.

Arthur tried to sound depressed. "We've had over two hundred cancellations since the verdict," he said, shaking his head.

"That's great, Arthur," Helena said, smiling at him.

"I'm going to have to start laying off technicians, you know," he said, still wagging his head like a sheepdog.

"The actors guild will have to go back to acting," Gabriel replied.

"We'll finally have the good looking waiters and waitresses back," Chuck added.

"I can't believe you guys aren't even a little sad about this. Come on, this was a big deal," Arthur said.

"Was, done, over it. Exit strategy, Arthur. You said it couldn't be done, but it's done. Moving on," Gabriel added. "Time to do some honest work again."

"What we did was honest," Arthur replied, offended.

"I don't know, Arthur," Gabriel said. "It felt just honest enough, you know? I never felt really good about it."

Samantha leaned over and gave her husband a hug. "You did good, Artie. You wanted out too, remember." Arthur nodded. "Maybe you could write a book about it or something," she continued, trying to soothe him.

"Yeah, that'd sell in the dozens, I'm sure," Helena said.

"Unless we made it a tell-all, you know, like an exposé," Chuck said. "We've got a ton of dirt on all sorts of famous people, Arthur. You could become like a high tech LA gossip queen. How cool would that be?"

"Thanks, Chuck," Arthur said. "I hadn't realized. Something to consider, I'm sure." He took a deep swig of something alcoholic from his glass.

Chuck, however, was almost manic. Grandly addressing the group, he said, "Well, I've got some news, too. I haven't just been wasting all that time in the other conference room, you know."

Actually, that's exactly what the other three had assumed Chuck was doing all that time. Arthur and Gabriel had spent the past several months pretty much ignoring the activities of the other working group. They had stopped attending the weekly summary meetings months ago. Helena had been earnestly pursuing her mental health research in the lab. The three of them suddenly realized that they had left Chuck unsupervised and unmonitored for quite a while. They exchanged nervous glances. Helena added a large dollop of rum to her mug of coffee.

"Actually, Chuck, I think I speak for the group when I say we assumed you were just wasting time in the other conference room," Helena said. She polished off the coffee and poured three fingers of Kahlua into the mug. She took a large swig. "Hoping, actually."

"You're funny, Helena. I think you're a little drunk, too, darling. You might want to slow down a little. Gabriel, you might want to slow down your wife a little, you know."

"Yeah, that's a great suggestion, Chuck. Why don't you just give us the short version of what you've been up to."

Chuck sat up straighter, coming to the edge of his seat. "Well, it gives me great pleasure to announce that my working group, just today, received approval and certification of full funding for our pilot project." He stared around the group, smiling like a first time father.

"Well, congratulations, Chuck," Helena said thickly. "Tell us your little project, Chuckie."

"Don't call me that, Helena. You know I don't like that, but you're drunk, so I won't blame you." He smiled more broadly. "The project is a joint collaboration of my parent agency, the NSA," at this point Chuck did a fluttering jazz hands, "DARPA, and Homeland Security."

"Seriously?" Arthur said, taking interest despite himself. "DARPA? That's great, Chuck. That must be some serious funding."

"It is. Thank you, Arthur. Two point six for the first year, guys. Isn't that great?"

"Two point six million?" Gabriel asked, incredulous. Chuck nodded enthusiastically.

"With the option to renew annually for five years, too," Chuck said. Arthur whistled softly.

"What the Chuck for, Fruck?" Helena asked, trying to sit forward and spilling her drink slightly.

"Oh, you are too funny," Chuck said. "You know, the project Gabriel started with Felix, the FBI stud."

"Hold it. Back the truck up, Chuck," Gabriel said. "What project? I never had any project with that asshole."

"Yes, you did, Gabriel," Chuck said, annoyed. "You just weren't very smart about it, remember? They needed a way to do mental readings on subjects without their being aware they were being studied. The coma thing."

"Yeah, Chuck, I remember that," Gabe said. "But it wasn't possible. You said so yourself, as I recall."

"Yes, no, you're right," Chuck said. "The coma thing couldn't work. But we have a new approach that I'm sure will work. It's genius, really. And now we have the money and support to pursue it."

"You're losing me, Chuck," Arthur said. "What's genius? Yes, no? What project?"

"Remote sensing and interpretation," Chuck said, smiling proudly again. "The ability to read mental waveforms without applying electrodes directly to the subject. Can you believe it? Genius, right?"

"Call it genius or whatever you want, Chuck," Gabriel said, somewhat relieved. "Won't work, so call it done and stick a fork in it. Time to mail back the check, Chuck."

"Don't be a jerk, Gabriel, just because you didn't think of it. You're not the only genius in this field, you know. It can be done. It has been done. That's why I have DARPA involved, if you must know. They have a couple of guys who are the world's gurus on focused remote sensing. Way advanced stuff, you wouldn't believe the resolution."

"You're serious?" Gabriel asked, suddenly very worried again. He took the drink from Helena and stole a gulp.

Chuck was back to nodding enthusiastically. "We've already done some prototyping, of course. Homeland wouldn't fund without some preliminary data. We've got this antenna that I can aim at you from over thirty meters away and get a signal good enough for basic interpretation. With some computer algorithms I'm writing, it's getting better and better. It's phenomenal. Are you impressed? You look impressed."

Gabriel's mouth was open. He took another drink and Arthur started to look around for another bottle of scotch. Helena was speechless.

Samantha seemed unphased. "I don't understand something, Chuck. You keep talking about Homeland Security being involved. Not the FBI? I thought the FBI were the ones who wanted to do the interrogations without being detected."

"No, you're right, Sam. FBI is interested, but they're not deeply involved yet. But you got the best part, why Homeland is so enthusiastic about this. They're giving us the majority of the funding."

"Why, Chuck?" Gabriel asked, recovering but almost afraid to ask. "Why is Homeland so interested?"

"They want us to work up a way to use field antennas, combined with large scale computer analysis to scan entire crowds. Can you believe it? What a great concept, huh? It's like how you started the whole field of mental imaging so many years ago, Gabriel, but expanded to entire populations! Is that exciting or what? No more stupid lines at the airport, no more bag searches at the football stadium or anything. Continuously monitor everyone on the subway. Or just have a portal scan of the thoughts of everyone getting on the plane. It's an NSA agent's dream, that's what it is. 'Population based mental monitoring,' I call it. I've found my Holy Grail, Gabriel."

There was silence for a minute. Chuck smiled at his stunned companions. Finally, Helena quietly slurred, "I'm not gonna wait until you're asleep, you Orwellian motherfucker! I'm going to fucking kill you now!" She launched herself from her couch, arms outstretched to choke the life from Chuck seated across from her. She missed him cleanly and sailed off the side of the balcony.

CHAPTER 20

Helena was screaming a continuous stream of curses in a variety of languages. Gabriel was partially relieved that he could understand only a fraction of what she was calling him, but that part was still quite disturbing. She was naked, seated on the side of the bathtub in their bathroom and covered from head to toe in a thousand superficial cuts and bruises. Gabriel was trying to apply antiseptic solution as he knelt on the floor in front of her, with only limited success.

"Hold still, dammit, Lena," Gabriel finally yelled back at her in frustration. "Do you want me to do this or not?"

"Are you yelling at me? Why you sadistic little bastard! Here you're pouring this acid all over my open wounds, which stings like a sonofabitch, by the way, and now you have the heartlessness, the baseness, to scream at your wife when she has the hangover from Hell, and in here, with these acoustics! I feel like I'm in the middle of one of those Hieronymus Bosch paintings." She whimpered pathetically.

Gabriel leaned back on his haunches in front of her, feeling chastened. "I'm sorry, babe," he said softly. He looked at the bottle of antiseptic. "It says it's no-sting."

Helena grabbed the bottle from him and took several deep swallows. She threw the bottle in the bathtub.

"Ugh. Tastes worse than it feels."

He looked at her aghast. "It says it causes blindness if ingested."

"Yeah, well," she said, standing up with a grimace, "it says it's no-sting, too. I'm not impressed with their labeling. I'm going back to bed." She hobbled back to their bedroom and flopped facedown onto the bed. Gabriel followed and sat on the bed next to her. Her back and thighs were a plaid of scrapes and cuts. It had taken the four of them almost half an hour in the dark to find her. Helena had come to rest in a nest of brambles, after rolling down the thirty-foot bluff between Arthur's deck and the shore. Since they discovered that Samantha and Arthur didn't own a single flashlight, the group had only found her by following the sound of Croatian cursing in the bushes.

"Is he dead? Did I slay the beast?" she muffled into the pillow top mattress.

"Who? What beast?"

"The Judas Bastard! Chuck Parnell, is he dead?"

"No, but he did get a nasty pricker from a thornbush in his butt. When we were looking for you. I think he's still in the emergency room. He made Sam drive him over."

"The beast must be killed. He is the Antichrist."

"So you told him last night. I think you might've hurt his feelings."

"That's not all I'm going to hurt." She moaned pitifully into the pillow. "I don't feel well. I might barf." She rolled over onto her back. "Shit, Gabriel, turn off the light!"

"That's the skylight, hon. That's the sun."

"Make it stop."

"I can't."

"You don't love me. You don't love me and you don't care that I don't feel good. I'm going to throw up on your side of the bed."

"I've never seen you drunk like that before."

"I've never been told that the Apocalypse was here before, either. He walks the earth and chaos reigns in his wake."

"I think that makes us the four horsemen, three Jews and a drunken Irish girl. And you were way drunk before Chuck made his little announcement."

"It's the end of the world."

"As we know it."

"Seriously." She gave another little moan. She tried to raise up on her elbows but gave up and flopped back. "We are the horsemen, babe. We made it all possible."

"I was thinking the same thing, all last night. Do you have any idea what's going to happen?"

"1984 on steroids, yeah," she said. " I can see it all. A world made safe for despots and fascists. At least in the book, you had to be in front of a TV screen to be under surveillance."

"That's not the worst part—"

"No, the worst part was the rats, but I don't think Chuck has the funding—"

"No, not that. I was thinking of what the world will be like, you know? I couldn't sleep at all, what with you screaming and moaning all night—"

"Oh, sorry I disturbed you. It's just that I had fucking vaulted off Arthur's fucking deck, which, by the way, I now can't help but notice has no fucking railings! How can that be up to code? You just know the Jew bastard paid off some inspector so he could have an unobstructed view."

"So now we're going off on the anti-Semitic tangent, are we? Hello, your husband is sitting next to you."

"Sorry, I digress. Blame the alcohol. Please, continue to tell me of your dystopian vision of our future."

"Right. I was thinking, wait until the advertising agencies get hold of Chuck's technology. You know they will, they'll be right behind the government on this. Marketing to the masses using the Parnell mental screening devices. It'll be everywhere, in the TV's—"

"Like in the book!"

"—in the subways, built into our cellphones, we'll be under constant bombardment. 'Hi, there, you're thirsty.' 'Hey there, you thinking of a new car, aren't you? We've got one right here.' Hell, Lena, they could point their antennas at us right now, hearing our thoughts as we lie in bed. Who's to say it can't be tuned to see through walls?"

"Shit, Gabe. I'm the paranoid here, remember? You're freaking me out."

"Sorry. But it's true. This is not good. Not good at all."

"Yeah, you're right. And it's all our fault. You made it all possible, Gabriel. Your life's work."

Gabriel looked stricken. "You helped. It's your fault, too."

"I tried to stop you. I knew you were Frankenstein the moment I met you. I only married you to try to save the world from your evil."

"That explains so much." Gabriel lay on his back next to his wife, staring with her out the skylight. A cloud shaped like a duck passed overhead.

"That cloud looks like Chuck," Helena said, pulling the covers up to her neck.

"We have to stop this, Lena. Somehow."

"He must be killed."

"No, seriously. We have to do something."

"I am serious. Chuck Parnell must die. Look," she said, pointing to the sky. "That one looks like a handgun."

"Be serious. We can't kill Chuck."

"Yes, I can. I was just too drunk last night. I can kill him, easy. He's thin, and he's weak. I know lots of ways. I used to teach Krav Maga to the Mossad, to their katsas."

"What's a katsa?"

"Their field agents. I used to date an Israeli colonel who was in charge of their training. He thought it was funny to have the shit kicked out of his guys by his 'little tiger'. That's what he called me. He was funny, but it didn't last."

"Was he the Croatian guy who taught you to swear?"

"No, silly," she said, punching his arm and then pulling the sheet back up around her neck. "Why would the Israelis let a Croatian be in charge of anything? The Croatian was in Boston, way later."

"You had a lot of boyfriends."

"What, after over twenty years of marriage, now you're worried that I was sleeping around? A little late."

"On our wedding night you said you were a virgin."

"I said a lot of things. I lie all the time, you know that. But it's okay, because we love each other."

Gabriel considered this statement carefully. More clouds passed by, but they were mostly plain and shapeless.

"I would just grab the bastard's stupid ponytail, that's what I'll do," Helena continued. "I hate that stupid ponytail. What grown man has a ponytail? I mean, has a ponytail but not a Harley? I knew he was evil, I said so every day since he joined us. I'd grab that ponytail and I'd start swinging him around, you know? Just start slowly swinging him around and around and around and go faster and faster and faster and then—"

"Hey!"

"What?"

"Enough with the swinging crap already. You can't swing him around by his ponytail. That's not physically possible."

She considered. "You may be right. You know what, though? Listen, this is better. I'll take the anchor from Arthur's stupid boat. He's used that boat like, what, three times since he bought it? He'd never notice the anchor's missing, probably doesn't even know how to use an anchor. You could distract Chuck, pretend like you're going to help him with the project, okay?"

"I don't want to help Chuck destroy the world."

"I know, you'd just be pretending to help him destroy the world, just to keep his attention while I quietly tie his ponytail to the anchor. You got it?"

"Can you quietly tie an anchor onto somebody? Aren't anchors really noisy?"

"No, stupid. Why do Jews know nothing about boats, every one of you? Anchors are really heavy. They're made not to be noisy, so they don't scare all the fish. Everyone uses their boats to fish, so they make the anchors really quiet. This will work, I'm sure. I'll tie his ponytail to the anchor and then throw the anchor off Arthur's dock. It'll be great; it'll drag him straight down to the bottom. How deep is the water there? Doesn't matter, I'm sure it's deep enough, what with the anchor holding him down. His ponytail is really long though. How long is Chuck's ponytail?"

"I'm not sure."

"Can you measure it? Surreptitiously, like? So he doesn't know you're measuring his ponytail?" Gabriel nodded solemnly. "This will work," she said confidently. "We should do this today, it looks like a nice beach day. Chuck will never suspect, he thinks we're happy for him. It'll be great. The water is really clear, too. I hope I can see his face. I hope I can see his expression, down there lying on the bottom of the ocean, being held down by that stupid affected ponytail of his, trying so hard not to let that last breath of air out of his lungs but he can't and he's got to let it out and his eyes get real big as the great big bubbles come out of his mouth and—"

"Helena!"

"What?"

"You're starting to sound a little creepy. Just saying."

"Sorry. It's important to visualize, though. It helps in the planning."

"We're not going to kill Chuck."

"Why not? I can do it. No joke."

"I know you can. I'm so proud you're my little tiger. But it won't help. Chuck is just the tip of the iceberg, the straw that stirs the drink, the keystone of the arch."

"Yeah, exactly. Take him out and the whole evil plan falls apart. Let's kill him. With the anchor thing."

"No, it won't stop this. It's going to happen. We've ruined the world."

"You ruined the world. It was all you. I tried to stop you."

"Thank god we never had children."

"Yeah, that was fortunate, on so many levels. Especially now that you've pretty much fucked up the world for all children, everywhere. Forever. But at least they're not our children. Thank god for small favors, huh?"

"I've got to make this right, Lena. For the children. We can't let this come to pass."

"Fine. If you really want to, we can fix this."

"I won't kill to do it."

"Fine, be that way. We won't kill anybody. Don't worry."

"Then how? How do we stop this without killing? How?"

"If you'll stop asking how, how, how, I'll tell you. It's not that hard."

"What?"

"We fry the salmon."

"Food analogy, lost me there."

"The entire program. Destroy it."

"We can't do that."

"Yeah, we can. As a matter of fact, we designed the whole system just to make that possible. That was the point. That's the real keystone. Destroy the program, and the government has nothing to attach to their supersensitive antennas. Problem solved. And the crowd goes wild. Thank you."

"The entire program? Everything?" She nodded. "They'll find a copy, they'll seize it. It's not that easy. Is it?"

"It is that easy. We knew this could happen, Gabe. We knew it was dangerous, that one day the government or somebody would try to take it from us. Don't worry, we're prepared. Melt it down. And melt it down soon, because they will come and take it. As soon as we let on that we're not going to play their game, they'll come in with the SWAT guys to take the ball. The salmon, I mean. Guaranteed."

"It's our whole life's work, Lena."

"You mean the life's work that two seconds ago you were lamenting was the cause of the end of civilization? The life work that'll destroy Christmas for children forever? That life's work, right?"

"I see your point. I don't know if I can do it. What about you? What about your research? Just burn it all down?"

"I don't need the program. We've moved past it. I think I've made some little breakthroughs of my own, if you really must know. I don't need the program, but even if I did, doesn't matter. Too dangerous. Burn it down. It served its purpose."

"I'm not sure, hon. Thirty years, you and me. And Arthur, Arthur will be pissed."

"Arthur will be fine. He might want to save the world, too. Might find a way to recapitalize the future or something profitable like that. Listen, Gabe. You and I are Einstein and Oppenheimer and we just discovered the atomic bomb—"

"Who's Einstein and who's Oppenheimer? I want to be Einstein."

"Fine, I can be Oppenheimer. No problem there, he was infinitely cuter. We just discovered the atomic bomb. We built one bomb so Truman can blast the Japs into surrender, got it?" He nodded. "One bomb, stop the war. But we have this hard drive with everything that's known about how to build nuclear weapons. The entire knowledge of the world about the bomb, right there in our hands. What would you do?"

"I'm Einstein, right? What would Einstein do or what would I do?"

"What would you do? Jesus, Gabriel, it's not rocket science we're talking about."

"What would Jesus do? Is that what you're asking now?"

"No, Gabriel. What should we do? What do you want to do? Really?"

"I want to smash it and save the world. At least until someone else invents it again."

"It'll take them fifty years."

"Let's go to the lab."

"I'll get dressed."

They borrowed Arthur's car. They lied and told Arthur that they wanted to go to Sausalito but were vague as to their reasons. Arthur just shrugged and tossed them the keys to the Porsche. He was still in his pajamas.

Gabriel insisted on driving. He felt it would just be too ironic if Helena got them killed with her driving while they were on their way to save the world. Helena agreed, being deathly afraid of irony. It had started to rain anyway. Helena couldn't drive the Porsche unless the top was down.

Gabriel drove slowly and consistently in the wrong gear. They lurched up the coast to San Francisco in the rain, being repeatedly passed by elderly Sunday morning drivers who gave them the finger. Gabriel just smiled and turned to admire his lovely wife sitting next to him.

"You said you made a breakthrough. In your research." Helena nodded, gritting her teeth as Gabriel gnashed the shifter into sixth gear doing thirty-four miles per hour. The engine behind them made a sad sound. "You want to tell me about it?"

"Maybe later. This isn't the time."

"Fine, no problem. Big secret, huh? Mind if I turn on NPR?"

"Do you believe in god, Gabriel?"

"It's just NPR, Lena."

"No, I'm serious. Do you believe in god?"

"Sometimes. Occasionally. Mostly when I think I felt a lump in my testicle in the shower. How about you?"

"No."

"That's it? One big no? Not at all, ever? Come on, you were raised a Catholic, right? You must've been in church a lot growing up."

"Almost every day. Pretty much every day. That's church, that's not what we're talking about. They can't make you believe, Gabriel."

"Don't you have to believe, though, just because you're exposed to it so much? Especially as a child, I would think. You're so impressionable."

"Especially as a child. They can make you so sure—so sure there's no such thing as god."

"Sorry. Chuck once tried to tell me about the Catholic orphanages in Ireland. I made him stop."

"Just as well. Chuck doesn't know shit."

"Why are we talking about this? You're not dying or anything, are you?"

"No, I'm not dying. You asked about my research, that's all."

"You discovered god? While doing pattern analysis of schizophrenics?"

"Something like that. Not exactly."

"An epiphany, huh? Born again while sitting in the dark back there in the lab?"

"No, that's not it all. You're making fun. It's just, when you discover something, when things fit together. It makes so much sense, it makes me wonder if maybe I was wrong."

Gabriel nodded as he looked through the windshield. "I know exactly what you mean. I felt like that a lot, when the research went well. Like I was supposed to be finding stuff out, you know."

"Exactly."

"It's been a long time, though. I haven't felt that way since we left Ann Arbor. How about you?"

"Last week."

"Really? Just last week? Wow."

"Yeah. Wow."

"That's great. I'm happy for you. God is good." He nodded in her direction.

"I'll let you know."

They drove on in the rain.

"How about time travel?" Helena asked matter of factly.

"I'm sorry. Come again?"

"Time travel. Do you believe in time travel?"

"No, definitely not. God, probably, depending on the circumstances. But time travel, I'm definitely going with your answer. No."

"You sound quite sure."

"I am."

"Why are you so sure? You seem pretty ambivalent about this stuff, in general."

"Not time travel. Never happen and that's a fact."

"Why?"

"Two irrefutable proofs. First, everybody knows that you can't travel back in time because it would change everything and then everything would be so screwed up you would've never existed in the first place. Like if you went back in time and killed your grandmother. Can't be done."

"Actually, that's not true, Gabe."

"Yes, it is. It's the contradiction that proves it's impossible."

"No, they've already gotten around that one. Cosmology, the multiverse. All the modern theories make time travel possible. If you touch something you weren't supposed to, you just cease to exist in this universe and switch to another."

"Another universe? I thought the universe was everything."

"That's last century. Now we have the multiverse. Infinite number of universes."

"I forgot you were doing grad work in the astronomy department when we met. I'm not sure I buy it. I don't remember it coming up in Star Trek."

"Trust me, it's true."

"I don't think I've ever seen anybody just wink out of existence. Have you?"

"Happens all the time. Thousands of time every day."

"Really? I hadn't noticed."

Helena nodded. "Sure you have. It's called dying."

"Hold it. You're saying the reason people die is that they traveled in time and tried changing something that changed their reality, so they wink out of existence here and reappear in another universe? Is that what you're saying?"

Helena shrugged. "Just a theory."

Gabriel guffawed. "No, Lena. That's not a theory. A theory is a hypothesis, supported by scientific observation. You know, like Einstein's theory of relativity, say, or string theory. Those are theories. What you're saying is more what I would call magical thinking."

"So you say."

He looked at her. "You're serious? Do you have one scrap of evidence? Any proof at all about what you're talking about?"

She shook her head. "Don't think so."

He smiled smugly as he drove. "Well, you get back to me on that, will you?"

"I'll do my best, Gabe."

He thought about that for a while. He was uncomfortable. His wife had never talked like this before. "And you know," Gabriel continued, "That's not the only thing, either."

Helena looked sad. She sighed. "Really, Gabriel? What's the other thing?"

"Well, the really incontrovertible proof that time travel will never, ever be accomplished is that we've never met someone from the future. I mean, if we ever invent time travel, certainly someone, sometime is going to want to come back. I mean, we'd notice."

"Yeah, I thought that was a good point, too."

"It is a good point."

"What if people do come back, by we don't notice?"

"What, they come back secretly and leave? Or live amongst us and just pretend to be impressed by the new cellphones every year?"

"Maybe they don't know. Maybe they don't remember, or they're too crazy to realize."

"Oh, yeah. I see, now. So that's your discovery, back in the lab? You found out that the crazy people are all from the future? Cool."

"You're making fun of me."

"Hey, it's your theory, not mine. I just know how to read minds. I think it's great that you discovered the existence of god and how to travel through time. And so fast, too. That took you all of, what, five or six months?"

"That's not my discovery. Not even close. I was just wondering what you thought, that's all. We're married, we should talk about these things more."

"You're right, Lena. We should talk about this stuff more often. And drink more. We should definitely be drinking more. Life's short, then we wink out and travel to another universe. What if the alternate universe doesn't have alcohol?"

"Now I'm sorry I even brought it up."

It was raining harder in the city.

"So how about life on other planets?" Gabriel asked. "Where do you stand on that issue?"

"Of course there is. No doubt in my mind. I was almost an astronomer, you know."

"All astronomers believe in extraterrestrials?"

She nodded. "They won't admit it out loud, it's unprofessional. But we all know it must be true. Why spend all that time studying this shit, otherwise? It's all really boring."

"Have they visited Earth?"

"I don't think so. There's no good evidence."

"Maybe that's because the government locked them up with the time travelers. Ever think of that?"

"I'm afraid you're not being serious now, Gabriel. Obviously, time travelers would help the extraterrestrials escape, they'd just travel to a time when the door was unlocked."

"Good point. So if it's not god or time travel, what did you find?" Gabriel asked as he navigated through the nearly empty streets.

"It's not a big deal. I didn't mean to build it up like that."

"So? Tell me. We can draw a picture of it and put it up on the refrigerator when we get home."

"Zeke, the musician, found it first. It's a sound, a pattern that some people have in their thinking."

"Crazy people, you mean?"

"Yeah, but you're going to have to stopping calling them that. It's not all mentally disturbed people. Just certain types. A very unique pattern, like a leitmotif in an opera, Zeke says."

"Well, Lena, that's great. Congratulations on that. You should present it to a psychiatric conference or something."

"No, it's not just that. It's not just that certain types of mentally ill people have this pattern. The pattern only occurs at certain times."

"Oh. Like when? Have you figured that out?"

"Yeah, that's what I figured out last week. Or at least I finally convinced myself of it last week."

"So when does this leitmotif occur?"

"When they're hearing voices. Only in schizophrenics, and then only when they're hearing voices."

"You mean, not real voices, right? Like voices in their head?"

"Yeah, that's what I mean. Weird, huh?"

"Yeah, crazy. So what does that have to do with god and time travel?"

"Nothing. I told you."

"Extraterrestrials? Ghosts from the great beyond? Holistic medicine?"

"True, true, and unrelated. I don't know what it means."

"Hey, I just gave myself an idea. Our next research project: paranormal activity. We could do readings on psychics and telepaths. It'd be perfect."

"Arthur would jump all over it, I'm sure."

"Yeah, and he needs something. Badly. He's still pretty broken up that we destroyed our multibillion dollar company."

"He'll bounce back."

"I'm sure I can fiddle with the electrodes to detect psychic auras. Don't you think?"

"Sounds brilliant, Gabriel. Maybe Chuck could help us get some funding."

"Oh my god, Chuck!"

"What? Where?" Helena asked, looking around frantically. Gabriel had been trying to parallel park in front of the lab for several minutes now, but paused in sudden thought.

"What if he's here? He lives here, you know."

"Let's hope he's not home. Shit, Gabe," she said in exasperation. "Just stop the fucking car. We can walk to the curb from here."

They let themselves in and turned on the lights. Chuck appeared out of the darkness. Helena screamed.

"What?" Chuck screamed back. "What is it?"

"Hi, Chuck," Gabriel said, shaking his hand. "You're here."

Chuck looked at Gabriel, puzzled as he retrieved his hand. "I live here. What are you guys doing here? I figured you'd have the hangover from hell," he said to Helena.

Helena seized Chuck in a violent hug and kissed him. He pulled away.

"What the hell?" Chuck asked, scared.

"We just had to come up here and tell you how proud of you we are," Helena said, wiping her mouth with the back of her hand. She spat.

"For what?" Chuck asked.

"The research. The work. The grant. We're so proud of you."

"Last night you called me the antichrist."

"I was just kidding."

"Like six times, you said it. You kept trying to choke me."

"I was really sloshed last night. Wasn't I, Gabe?" Gabriel nodded.

"You pushed me down in the pricker bush. After I helped find you. I got a pricker in my ass. It really hurt, Helena."

"I'm sorry, Chuck."

"Samantha took me to the ER. We just got back. Sam's nice."

"Yeah, Sam's a princess all right," Helena said. "Listen, Chuck. While we're here, Gabriel and I were talking in the car. You know, on the ride up—"

"About god and time travel and stuff," Gabriel said, hoping to help.

Helena shot him a look. "Yeah, that too. Mostly though, we were talking about how we could help you. I mean, you have spent so many years helping with all of our projects—"

"Without any pay," Chuck pointed out.

"Right, exactly. Selfless devotion, all this time. So we'd like to do a little bit to help with your project."

"Really? What do you guys want to do?" Chuck asked. Gabriel shrugged. "I was actually afraid to ask last night, but they are going to want to meet with Gabriel in DC. That would be a big help."

"I'm sure Gabriel would be happy to go to DC with you. He was saying in the car how he wished there was something just like that he could do to help you. But here's another thing. We thought it would be great if we updated the program, so that it would work better for your government project," Helena explained.

"Really?" Chuck asked. "Because I was afraid you guys would be so pissed off that you'd like, fry the whole thing just to screw me." Gabriel and Helena laughed. "No, really, I thought that."

"Chuck, come on," Gabriel said. "Why would you think such a thing? We've worked together for so long."

"Yeah, and you're always saying that the program can't interpret what people are thinking, it's just a tool. We fight about it all the time, Gabriel."

"No, we don't fight about it. It's just like a running difference in approach, that's all, Chuck," Gabriel said, reddening.

"Yeah, well. Whatever," Chuck said. "I was thinking about that, too. I was going to ask you, Helena, if it would be okay to clone the drive with the program on it, for my project. I know you feel strongly about—"

"No, don't be crazy, Chuck," Helena interrupted as she led the three of them back to the lab's inner sanctum where the central processor was kept. "Of course we'll get you a copy of the program. That's why we're here." She keyed the pad and the security door opened for them.

"Wow, Helena. That's great," Chuck said. "I'm genuinely surprised. I really was afraid you were going to give me a hard time about this. I thought I was going to have to actually steal it—"

Helena and Gabriel stopped and stared at Chuck.

"No, of course I'd never actually steal it. I'd ask you guys for it, nicely. I mean, I didn't think—"

"That's okay, Chuck," Helena said. "You just didn't think. I know." She started to disconnect the hard drive unit from the server.

"Whoa, Helena," Chuck said, putting a hand on her arm. "What are you doing?"

"I'm disconnecting the hard drive," she said, looking at his hand on her arm. "Why are you touching me?"

Chuck let his hand drop and smiled sheepishly. "But you said you were going to clone me a copy. You don't have to take it out to make a copy, we can do it from the console."

Helena continued to disconnect the unit. An alarm tone started to buzz softly and she quickly keyed a code into the keypad next to the drive to silence it. "Of course we need to remove it. We can't just give you a copy of the drive, you know."

"Why not?"

"Chuck, this is the entire Insight Technology shit. You said yourself last night, there's a ton of confidential stuff on here, all the client files and everything. We can't just give you a clone."

"Sure you can. We could just—"

Helena rounded on him. "No, Chuck, we can't. Now do you want a copy of the program or not? Gabriel and I drove all the way up here on a Sunday morning, in the rain, and I'm really, really not feeling too well, but we're trying to do something nice for you here and you're giving us nothing but grief about it." She looked at him. Chuck couldn't meet her gaze so he looked at Gabriel instead. Gabriel tried to look both disappointed and supportive. He ended up with a half shrug and a stifled yawn.

Chuck finally forced himself to look back at Helena. "Sure, Helena. I'm sorry, I know you're trying to help, but—"

"Fine, then," she snapped as she released the last restraints on the drive and lifted it out. She tossed it to Gabriel. She spun on her heel and started out the door. Gabriel followed and Chuck hurried behind to catch up.

"I still don't understand," Chuck called to her as he followed back up the hallway to the front office. "Where are you going with it?"

"To make you your copy, that's where," she called back to him. "I'm telling you, Chuck, don't keep trying to piss me off or I'll toss the fucking thing in the ocean."

Chuck blanched and stopped dead in his tracks. "Please, don't. I didn't mean it," he squeaked after them. Helena and Gabriel strode right out the front door to the street without breaking stride. Helena climbed in the driver's seat of the Porsche and slammed the door.

"Keys," she commanded as Gabriel got in alongside her with the hard drive. Chuck stared at them from the window in the front lobby, his palms and forehead pressed against the glass. Gabriel handed her the keys.

Helena started the car and squealed into the street with a force that snapped Gabriel's head back into the seat. "Where are we going?" he yelled as he struggled to fasten his seatbelt.

"To toss the fucking thing in the ocean."

CHAPTER 21

Helena never slowed below fifty until they got onto the Golden Gate Bridge. Gabriel almost threw up as they nearly became airborne once cresting a hill. They finally swerved onto the bridge, fishtailing in the pouring rain. In the middle of the span, Helena brought the car to a screeching halt halfway up onto the right curb and yanked the hand-brake. She hit the emergency flashers, then she mashed the switch to lower the convertible top. The rain poured in on them.

"Shit, Lena," Gabriel said, looking up at the steel gray sky and the rain pouring down. "What the hell are we doing?"

"Toss it in the ocean!"

"You're not serious!" They looked around as they heard a siren approaching rapidly from behind them. "Shit, Lena. We can't stop here!"

"Throw the fucking thing in the ocean, Gabe!"

Gabriel shook his head "Helena, it's our whole life's work. Come on. I've been thinking maybe we should—"

"You're right, Gabe. Here, let me see that for a second." Gabriel handed her the drive. Helena flung it over the guardrail into the ocean.

"Shit, Lena. I cannot believe you just did that."

"Did what?"

They heard the police cruiser come to a screeching stop behind them. The siren died as they were painted with the flashing red strobes. "DON'T MOVE. BOTH OF YOU RAISE YOUR HANDS AND DO NOT ATTEMPT TO LEAVE THE VEHICLE."

"Shit, we are so fucked," Gabriel said. "He saw us throw it."

"You think?" Helena asked, raising her hands. Gabriel watched her and did the same. The police officers slowly approached from either side with pistols drawn. "Morning, officer," Helena said to the one on her side.

"Shut the fuck up," the officer replied. He opened the door with his free hand. "Slowly get out of the car and lie face down on the ground. Now. Slowly!" Gabriel and Helena did as they were asked. One officer handcuffed them as the other kept his gun aimed at Gabriel. "Now slowly stand up and move back to the police car." They did this too.

"Thanks for stopping to help, Officer," Helena said. "We're having trouble with the convertible top. It just started to—"

"Shut up! What did you throw off the bridge?" the officer demanded.

"Oh, you saw that?" Helena asked.

"Yeah, lady. We saw that," the officer said with a sardonic smile. "So how about you tell us what you threw over."

Helena looked over at her husband. Gabriel was white as a sheet and looked about to faint. "It's your fault," she said to him. "I'm not sorry." Gabriel looked at her, confused.

"What's his fault, lady?" the officer asked with irritation. "What did you throw?"

"A gun. I had to throw the gun in the ocean, officer. He said I'd be sorry, but I'm not."

"I knew it," the officer said, turning to his partner. "Freddie, call for backup and transport."

"Transport?" Helena asked plaintively. "Why? Are you arresting us, officer?"

"Yeah, lady, I'm arresting you. You just told me you threw a gun into the ocean."

"Is that illegal?" Helena asked.

The policeman looked puzzled. "Yeah, lady. It's illegal. You're under arrest."

"For littering? You arrest people for throwing something out of a car?" Helena asked, then fell to her knees and started to cry.

"Stand up, lady," the policeman said, gesturing with his gun. Helena ignored him and started to sob loudly. "I don't care, Gabriel," she said between loud, dramatic sobs. "I'm glad I did it! I'm not going to live with you and that gun! Arrest me, I don't care. I'm glad I did it!" She started to sob more loudly and allowed herself to collapse fully onto the pavement.

The other officer returned from the squad car. "Transport's on the way, be about ten minutes. Not so sure about backup. They didn't sound too impressed." He looked at Helena on the ground, still sobbing loudly. "What the fuck?"

The other officer just shook his head and looked at Gabriel. Gabriel tried to look the rational one. "I'm sorry, officer," Gabriel said. "My wife's very emotional."

"That's your wife?" the officer said, gesturing with his gun toward Helena. Helena screamed and scrunched up under the front bumper of the police cruiser. "Hey!" he yelled at her. She was almost under his car.

"I'm sorry, officer," Gabriel continued. "She hates guns, she's deathly afraid of them. If you could not point that at her?" The policeman realized that he was still holding his firearm and holstered it.

"What the fuck is going on here?" the officer demanded of Gabriel.

"I'm sorry, officer. My wife is very emotional. She hates having the gun in the house, it was just an old gun—"

"You got a license for the gun?" the police officer demanded.

"No," Gabriel stammered, "It wasn't much of a gun. It was old; my dad left it to me. I had it for years and years, don't even have any bullets for it or anything. But the wife and I were arguing, you know how it is when you're married, and I started waving it around, you know. She went crazy, said she would throw the thing in the ocean. She lost a sister, you know how it is—"

"Hold it," the policeman said, holding up his hand. "You were threatening your wife with a gun? Is that what you're telling me here, jackoff?"

"I'm sorry, officer. It's just that—"

"Shut up, asshole," the policeman barked. He got down on his knees to gently coax Helena from under his car. "Lady, sorry. Come on, lady, you can't stay there." He helped Helena up. Helena stood up and the officer unfastened her handcuffs. Helena wiped at her tears rather ineffectually; she was soaked and streaming with rain. She smiled appreciatively at the policeman. "Did he hit you, ma'am?" the officer asked, gesturing to Gabriel.

"Oh no, officer. My Gabriel never hit me, no. It's just that I was afraid of the gun, is all. My Gabriel never hit me, ever. Oh, no." She smiled at the other officer, too.

"Do you want to come with us, ma'am?" the other officer asked. "We can take you someplace safe, if you'd like."

"Now hold on—" Gabriel started.

"Shut up, asshole," the first officer snapped. He looked warmly at Helena, her red hair sticking wetly to her face. He tried an endearing smile with partial success. "You want we should take you to meet with the social worker back at the station, lady? Wouldn't be any trouble." Helena shook her head meekly. "You can press charges for threatening you with a gun. We can take him in if you feel threatened. Couple days in jail might set him straight." He looked at Gabriel, daring him to speak. Gabriel just looked down at the puddle that had formed around his shoes. He was soaked.

"No, thank you, officers, both of you," Helena said. "You've been too kind already. Real gentlemen. It's so good to know that a woman in this city can be protected that way. But the gun's gone now, forever."

"You sure, lady?" the other officer asked. Helena nodded and shuffled her feet. The policeman looked at the other officer questioningly. The other man shrugged. "Gun's gone now," the second cop repeated.

"Okay, lady." The first cop turned to Gabriel and stabbed a finger in his chest. "You, asshole," he spat, "you are a lowlife scumbag. She doesn't deserve you. Next time she calls, you'll wish we locked you up. Count on it." The two officers returned to their cruiser. Helena got back into the Porsche, this time on the passenger side. Gabriel got into the driver's seat and started the car.

"Oh," Gabriel said, fiddling with the switch to raise the roof, "so now you want me to drive?"

They drove towards home slowly, quiet save the sound of the water sloshing around the floor of the car. Eventually, Gabriel couldn't stand it any longer. He asked, looking sideways at his wife, "Can you tell me why you said it was a gun?" Helena shrugged. "No, really. I want to know what was the thinking behind that. I'm fascinated."

"Oh, you know," Helena said, still staring straight out the windshield, "you know how it is when you're married." She gave him an icy sidelong stare.

Gabriel reddened and looked forward. "Don't give me a hard time about that, Lena. I was dancing as fast as I could back there. Sorry if my stream of consciousness lying offended you, but I still want to know. A gun, for shit's sake, Lena?"

"It's what they wanted to hear. Rule number one when you're dealing with cops, Gabriel. Tell 'em what they want to hear."

"I'm not getting it."

"Why do you think they came flying at us like that, guns drawn and with the bullhorn thing? Did that feel like a traffic stop to you?"

"No, but shit, we were stopped in the middle of the fucking bridge in a black Porsche with the top down in the rain—"

"Yeah. Pretty fuckin' suspicious. And then a black metal object goes flying out of the car into the ocean. What do you think they were thinking?"

Gabriel nodded. "Yeah, I get it. Probably looked pretty criminal."

"Damn right," Helena said. "Try to tell them anything else, we'd spend the next two or three nights waiting for Arthur to get us out of jail. I hate jail."

"Yeah, jail sucks. I'm not sure Arthur would even bail us out, not once he finds out what we've done to his car." Helena just nodded. "I don't know, though. I was just going to tell them the truth."

Helena looked at her husband. "Seriously, Gabe? The truth? The truth, Gabriel, will not set you free. The truth will get you killed. Remember that, love."

"Screamin' Jay Hawkins. Do you know he had seventy-five children?"

"I did not know that."

"It's true."

They drove on for a bit. The rain had finally let up, leaving behind a light fog that merged with the steel gray sky above. Gabriel made a squishing sound as he moved in his seat.

"Gabriel?" Helena asked softly from beside him.

"Yeah, hon?"

"Why did you tell the cop I lost my sister?" Her voice was soft, but Gabriel heard a painful inflection that he hadn't ever heard before. He glanced sideways at his wife, but she was still looking ahead, her profile revealing no expression.

"Same as the marriage comment, I guess," he said, trying to sound lighthearted. "I'm not a very good liar, you know."

"No, Gabriel, you're not. It's one of the things I love about you."

Gabriel just nodded.

"I don't want you to speak of her again, Gabriel. I don't care what Chuck dredged up and told you. Don't speak of her, ever again."

Gabriel frowned at the oncoming traffic, confused. "Chuck never told me anything, Lena. I'm the one who told Chuck. I'm sorry."

"You told Chuck? How? How do you know about my sister, Gabriel?" She sounded wounded, painfully so.

"I don't know, not really. I just know what you said, that's all."

"I've never said anything to you about my sister, Gabriel."

"Not consciously, no. But during your seizures, you say—"

"I never said anything during a seizure, Gabriel. People don't talk during a seizure. What the hell are you talking about?"

"Not a seizure, then. Shit, Lena, I'm not a doctor. Your spells, whatever they are. Like what happened in the museum that time. Like happened a few times." He kept his eyes fixed on the road ahead, afraid to look at her.

Helena considered, asked softly, "What did I say?"

Gabriel sighed. He was afraid he was hurting her. They had never spoken of any of this before. Helena had always pretended the spells never happened, and he had never had the nerve to broach the issue, not after he had tried to have her seen by the doctor that first time.

"It's hard to understand most of it. But I recorded you once, and I asked Chuck to help interpret it. He understands—"

"What does he understand?"

"He understands some Irish. And he had the tape enhanced, using some NSA technique or something. You were talking in Irish, like you were having a conversation. With your sister."

Helena had drawn her feet up onto the seat and was hugging her knees to her chest. Gabriel stole a look at her, but she was still just looking straight ahead.

"You okay, babe?" he asked her. He saw her nod.

"Every time?" she asked. "Every time I go out, I talk to her?"

"I don't know, Lena," he said softly back. "Most times, I can't make out what you're saying. But I think so, yeah."

She was quiet then. Gabriel grew more concerned.

"What does it mean, Lena?" he asked finally.

"I don't know, Gabe. Let me think for a bit."

They drove on in silence down the coast, watching the fog lift and the sunset paint the underside of the leaden clouds with deepening hues of orange and red.

The sky was almost dark and they were almost back to Half Moon Bay when Helena stirred. "Gabriel," she began, "do you believe in ghosts?"

"No, I don't think so. You mean like the dead still walking among us? Why, you think so?"

"I don't know. I don't know, Gabriel. I don't know about ghosts, and I don't know about god."

"How about time travel? Or aliens?"

"I don't know, Gabe. I wish we were home."

"Home soon, hon. Real soon." He gave her a smile and was thrilled when she smiled back at him. "I don't know what we're going to tell Arthur, though. When we bring back the car."

"We're not going to bring it back. I'm taking it."

"What? Where? Where are you going?"

"Michigan. I'll drop you home and then I'm going to Michigan."

Gabriel was flabbergasted. He tried to recover his balance as he downshifted off the expressway. "You're driving? Why?"

"I've got to get to Ypsilanti. To the backup. I have to destroy the program backup."

"Why, Lena? You think Chuck will try—"

"Of course he will. I just don't know how long it'll take him to figure out that he's just taken it in the ass, big time. Once he figures it out, though, that we destroyed the salmon, he's got to go after the backup. His whole project depends on it now."

"But he can't," Gabriel protested. "He doesn't even have an access key. Just the three of us."

"He'll try. He's a smart guy; he'll figure something out. I have to get to the garage first. I'll destroy the backup tracking numbers."

"But then it'll be gone. For real and forever gone. All of it."

"No, Gabe. Not gone, not really. It'll still be out there. It'll be a lot harder to piece together, that's all. Nothing ever goes away. You can't destroy anything. All you can do is try to bury it as deep as you can."

"Is that what you believe? Nothing ever disappears?" She nodded. "Souls, too? Is this the ghosts thing? When we die, the soul lives on, huh? That what you believe?"

"I don't know what I believe, Gabe. It's what I hope."

Gabriel pulled onto their driveway and turned off the engine. Neither moved to get out of the car. They stared ahead at the livid sky, now a purplish bruise pressing low over their heads.

"Do you really think Chuck will try for the backup?"

"I'm sure of it."

"Then we should fly there, make sure we get there first. You're right. We need to finish this while we can."

"No, I can't fly there. Chuck will know immediately where I'm going. It won't work. He's pretty well connected."

"Have Arthur arrange for a jet. Like before."

"No, Chuck will know two minutes later. Don't tell Arthur."

"I've got to tell Arthur. He's going to wonder where you are. Shit, he's going to wonder where his car is."

"Make something up. Tell him I took the car on a joyride or something, to air it out. Tell him it got a little wet or I threw up in it, I don't care. Give the same song to Chuck, try to stall him as long as you can. This may take a few days. Come on, I've got to pack a bag." They went in the house, now dark.

When they walked into the kitchen, Gabriel saw the red light on the answering machine winking insistently. He clicked on the lights and saw that there were twenty-one messages on the machine. Gabriel pushed play. Chuck's voice sounded frantic, saying "Hey, guys! Where are you? Gabriel, I left like fifty voice messages on your cell! Call me!" Gabriel fished his cellphone out of his pocket and saw that, indeed, he had fifty-three messages, all from Chuck. He hadn't noticed. Next message, "Gabriel! Helena! Don't take the hard drive anywhere, please! We need to talk about this. Call me!" Gabriel stopped the machine.

"I don't think we need to listen to the rest. I'm detecting a theme," Gabriel said.

Helena shook her head. "He'll be here pretty soon, I'm sure. If's he's not already hiding upstairs, under the bed."

Gabriel looked up involuntarily. "You don't think really think—"

Helena started up the steps. "I've got to pack and get out of here before he arrives. He'll want to see the drive. If we're both here without it, he'll know. If it's just you, you can tell him I took it to be split and copied." She went up the steps two at a time. Suddenly there was pounding on the front door. Gabriel glanced out the window.

"Shit," he called up the steps. "It's him. He's here."

Helena called down from the bedroom. "Stall him, get rid of him. Don't let him upstairs. Tell him I took the drive to Arthur's." Gabriel heard the bedroom door slam.

Gabriel opened the front door and Chuck burst in like he was pressurized. He grabbed onto Gabriel's lapel to steady himself. "Thank god," Chuck said. "I was calling. Why didn't you answer?"

Gabriel tried to remove Chuck's grasp. "I just got in two seconds ago, Chuck. What's wrong?"

Chuck looked around for Helena. "Wrong? Nothing. Nothing, except you won't answer your phone. Why won't you answer your phone? Where's Helena?"

"Geez, Chuck, take it down a notch, will you?" Gabriel replied. He tried to act nonchalant. "I told you, I just walked in. I just got your message."

"What about your cell? I called like fifty-two times."

"Yeah, I noticed. I was driving. In the rain. I didn't think it was a good time."

Chuck kept looking around. 'Where's the drive? Where's Helena?"

"She's not here."

"Where is she? Does she have the drive?"

"She's at Arthur's, like she told you. Yes, she has the drive, she's going—"

"You're lying, Gabriel. You're a lousy liar, you know that?" Chuck asked.

"Actually, yes, I do know that. Helena tells me that all the time."

"Yeah, well, you should listen to her. She's upstairs." Chuck started in the direction of the steps but Gabriel took a step to block him.

"I told you, Chuck, she's not here. I dropped her at Arthur's place, with the drive."

"I don't believe you. There's muddy footsteps going up the stairs."

Gabriel looked at the trail left on every other step by his wife. "Yeah, Chuck. Thanks for pointing out our housekeeping inadequacies. But she's still not here. Now listen, I'm soaking wet here and—"

Chuck eyed him suspiciously and seemed to notice the puddle forming on the floor around them for the first time. "Yeah, why are you wet?"

"We had the top down."

"What? Why? It's been raining."

"Yeah, Chuck, we kinda noticed that after a while. We had to pull over to get the top up."

"So? That takes like two seconds."

"Not when you're in the middle of the bridge, it doesn't. And guess what? The police really don't like it when you stop in the middle of the bridge to put it up."

"The police? You were stopped by the police?"

"Yeah, Chuck, we were stopped by the police. They helped us get the top up. No ticket or anything."

"Really? Because those guys are usually real dicks, you know?"

"Yeah, I know. But Helena sweet-talked us out of a ticket and they let us off. You know how she can be. Now, Chuck, listen, this has been fun talking and all, but I want to get out of these clothes and—"

"Fine," Chuck said, waving him off and heading in the direction of the kitchen. "I'll get something to eat."

"No, Chuck, no. You gotta go, really. I have to get changed and then pick up Helena."

"That's fine, no problem. Get changed, you're all wet and making a mess. I'll wait and we'll go get Helena."

"Chuck, no. It might be a while before she calls. I'll talk to you tomorrow." He tried to gently usher Chuck in the direction of the door.

"No, no, Gabriel. We gotta go tomorrow, first thing. We need to get the drive from Helena now."

"Go? Go where?"

"To DC. I told you in the lab. I need your help presenting to the committee. You promised you'd help."

"You didn't say anything about going to DC tomorrow. I can't just—"

"I did say. And you promised, you promised to help." He looked at Gabriel, stricken.

"Fine, Chuck, whatever. But right now, I need you to leave. Go back to the lab. I'll call you later and talk about DC."

"You'll come with me, right?"

"We'll talk about it, I said."

"I'm not going to leave unless you promise to come with me." Chuck was looking at the footprints on the steps again. Gabriel watched his eyes trace up the stairs.

"Fine, Chuck. I promise. Now go. Please." Chuck gave a last look up at the bedroom and allowed himself to be shepherded out the door. Gabriel locked it and leaned his back against the door, sighing. Helena appeared in front of him with a duffle bag in hand. She had changed into jeans and a dry sweatshirt that said 'Spartans' across the front. Her hair was still wet but pulled back in an Aboriginal ponytail. "He suspects something," Gabriel said to her.

"Yeah, you might be right. You're about the worst excuse for a liar in the world. I've told you that, right?" Gabriel nodded sheepishly. "Nice move, Bozo, telling him we were stopped by the cops."

"I needed to say something, I—"

"Yeah, except Chuck is really good at accessing all kinds of official records. Pretty soon now, he's going to read a police report about a couple who look a lot like us tossing a gun off the Golden Gate bridge. Only he'll know it wasn't a gun."

"Shit, you're right. I screwed up. I'm sorry." He looked embarrassed.

"Whatever. He would've figured it out at some point anyway. Only now he'll be sure. You can tell him the drive's at Arthur's till you're blue in the face, he'll know it's gone."

"What are we going to do? He can just fly to Michigan before you—"

"No, you're not going to let him. You're going to go with him to DC. Keep him there, go to all those meetings with him. Take him for sushi, I don't care what you do with him, but don't let him get on a plane."

"Well, at least you might as well fly now."

"No, by the time Arthur can arrange a flight I'll just about be there anyway. And this way, at least you can pretend."

"Then just take a commercial flight. There's probably something out of SFO tonight, a redeye will have you there in the morning."

"Gabriel, what's wrong with you? You know I don't fly commercial."

"But you said yourself, Chuck probably already knows where you're going."

"It's not just Chuck. It's never just been Chuck. Now shut up and give me a kiss, I gotta go." He gave her a quick kiss and carried her duffle out to the car. There was no sign of Chuck.

"The seat's really wet, hon," he said as she got in.

"Yeah, don't worry. I'll probably have to ditch the car anyway." She leaned out and gave her husband another kiss. "Bye. Love you."

He stood up. "Love you, too. What do mean, ditch the car? It's Arthur's car."

"Yeah, but it's really wet. We'll see, don't worry. Just don't mention anything to Arthur."

"When will you be back, do you think?"

"Less than two days to get to Michigan, two days back. Maybe I'll spend a couple of days in Ann Arbor, visit your folks."

"I don't think my folks would even recognize you. You know which nursing home they're in?"

"Yeah, I know. And they'll recognize me. They love me, always did, you know."

"Yeah, I know. My Dad always said I was lucky to have you."

"Your dad is a smart guy. I'll be back in five or six days. A week, tops."

"If you're not, I'm going to come looking for you. Like Boston."

"If I'm not, I don't think you'll find me, Gabe. Not like Boston, this." She gave him another kiss and held him by the back of the neck for an extra second, kissing him two or three beats longer than was her usual goodbye. He straightened up as Helena dropped the shifter into reverse and accelerated out of the driveway at her accustomed breakneck speed, missing his toes by a couple of inches. As she sped down their street, she waved out the window at him with the hand that should've been on the steering wheel, rapidly shifting through the gears on her way.

Gabriel stood in their driveway, worried about the sudden feeling that haunted him; the feeling that he had just watched his wife disappear from his life. He had no idea where the thought had come from, unbidden. He stood, watching the empty street after she had squealed around the corner and disappeared from view. The kiss, he realized. It must've been the kiss. Yes, he decided. It was definitely the kiss. That, he thought to himself, was a kiss goodbye. He went in the house to call Chuck.

Helena went screaming across the Bay Bridge, heading for I-80 east. She had already passed through one tollbooth, which was potentially a mistake, she knew. She had paid cash, having ripped Arthur's Fastpass transponder off the dash and tossed it out the window two miles back. She didn't want to take the chance that Chuck was already hunting for her. Helena felt the wet starting to seep into her jeans from the seat. She had to ditch the car. The problem was, she couldn't just pull into a parking lot to try for another ride. She had to assume that Chuck would be monitoring for any reports of an abandoned black Porsche. He'd probably monitor any stolen car reports along I-80 between here and Ann Arbor.

She continued to weave between traffic as she considered her problem. She knew she was going about this all wrong. Years of running had taught her hard lessons. Lessons like, always have a plan. She didn't have a plan right now, not really. She had a goal, a destination, but that wasn't enough. She was up against a formidable foe, she thought. Her opponent was bright, and he had considerable resources at his disposal, many of which she couldn't begin to guess at. The worst part, she knew, was that her adversary was very highly motivated right about now. Motivated, and very, very pissed off.

She cut off some twenty-something in a BMW roadster that honked at her as she shot past him. She saw in the mirror that he was trying to catch up to her, probably to give her the finger. Not much chance of that. She was running out of time, however. She really should ditch the car pretty soon. Getting rid of a late model Porsche with California plates without anyone taking notice was going to be harder and harder the farther east she traveled. People notice out of state plates, and nobody east of Nevada can stand a rich girl from California, even if she was short, redheaded, and getting up in years. She shifted in her seat, cursing the discomfort of wet panties. That's when she got her idea.

Helena pulled off the expressway in Reno and pulled into the first big shopping mall she came to. It didn't take long. She found what she was looking for right away, a sporting goods store. It was one of the huge chain store variety, the kind so large they have a pond inside to try out the fishing equipment. She headed that way. Helena bought a spool of high test fishing line, making sure it was clear and just strong enough for what she planned. Light weight was just as important as strength for this. She also bought a heavy dressing needle, the kind hunters used to sew up a deer carcass after gutting it. At the register, she saw a flashlight and thought that might be a good idea, too. She might have to sleep in the car one or two nights. She might have to hit someone over the head, too, she thought. She paid cash and went back out to the car.

It was dark and nobody would really see anything of what she was doing, she figured. She sat in the car and threaded one end of the fishing line onto the dressing needle. She jabbed the needle up through the fabric roof of the convertible. Back outside, she threaded the line along the passenger side of the car and stuck the dressing needle into the trunk and closed the trunk. Back inside the car, she took the other end of the line from the spool and tied a small loop. She was careful with this part, the loop had to be just the right size to do its job, and then pull off. She reworked it twice before she felt it was right. She hid the rest of the spooled line under the passenger seat.

Helena started the car and headed back to the highway. She stopped to fill the tank before resuming her run eastward. This just might work, she thought. She ate the chips, bottled tea, candy bars, and beef jerky she had bought at the gas station. Finger food, for when you have to eat and drive a six speed manual transmission at the same time. It was the timing that bothered her. Her whole goal was to ditch this car and get a new one without risking any notice. She would like to pull it off in Nevada rather than farther eastward, but her plan required the sting to be done during regular business hours. That wouldn't be for at least twelve hours and she couldn't afford to stop that long. Oh well, she thought, no plan's perfect. Particularly when you're making it up as you go. She slowed done to ten over the limit, trying to make a mental calculation of speed and distance. It would have to do, she thought.

Helena pulled off the expressway in Salt Lake City. The sun had been in her eyes for over two hours and she had a splitting headache as a result. Morning rush hour traffic was at a crawl. She began to look for a car wash. She drove past two, not thinking them suitable. When she hadn't passed another in fifteen minutes, however, she decided to double back to the last one. Some plan, she thought to herself, driving back the way she came.

Helena waited a few minutes until the car wash was empty, then pulled in. It was early enough so that the housewives weren't out yet, but after the crazy car fanatics got their sport cars washed on the way to work or their tee time. She stopped at the appointed line outside the wash. A big, blond haired man with a beer belly and a crisp white shirt approached her car. A Hispanic looking youth was holding a sprayer at the entrance, waiting.

Helena lowered the window as the man approached. He leaned in, looking at her and smiling. "Morning, ma'am. Like a wash today? Pretty car."

Helena gave the man her demure smile. "Yes, sir. Thank you. Actually, it's my husband's. I swear, I think he loves this car more than me." The man laughed appreciatively.

"Well, nice of you to wash it for him. What kind of wash do you want?"

"The supreme, I'm sure. But wait a moment. Are you the manager?"

"Why, yes I am, ma'am." The big man indicated the nametag on his shirt, which did, indeed, announce that his name was Ed and he was the manager. "Manager and owner."

"Oh, great," Helena said, looking at the man seriously. "Then you're the man I need to talk to. I have to know that this is a good car wash. I don't want any scratches on my husband's car, Ed. He would know in a second and I have to tell you, he would skin me alive and gut me to boot. He would, I swear."

Ed laughed again. "Don't worry about that, ma'am. It's touchless, see," he said, pointing at the sign.

"Okay, then, Ed, if you say so," Helena said. "Is this where I get out?"

"Just pull up a little further, ma'am," Ed said, writing on the windshield with his marker. "Jesus will take it from there."

Helena gave Ed an endearing smile and pulled the Porsche up to just short of where Ed had indicated. She got out and went to the trunk. She pretended to take something out but palmed the needle instead, closing the trunk and stepping to the passenger side as the Hispanic guy got into the driver's seat. The guy gunned the throttle and brought the car into the wash bay, lining up the front wheel with the tow track expertly. Helena gave him a smile, too. He winked at her. Helena stuffed a ten-dollar bill into the tips box outside the entrance to the wash. Jesus gave her an appreciative nod and began to spray the car. Helena waited until the man had turned his back as he worked. She went to one knee and pretended to be tying her shoes as she stared into the carwash. She made a rough calculation and waited until Jesus stepped away from the car to hit the button that would send the car into the automated wash. Then she quickly pulled and coiled a length of the fishing line around her hand and knotted it off like a miniature climber's coil. She wedged the large needle and coiled line in the doorframe. Satisfied, she stood and went inside.

Helena stood in the narrow hallway, watching through the large plate glass windows as the car progressed through the stages of the wash. Neon lights flashed and announced the various miraculous solutions being applied to Arthur's Porsche. Helena was beginning to think that she may have miscalculated the length, or maybe the loop on the switch had slipped off prematurely. She frowned, wondering if she could retrieve the needle and line to try again at the other carwash. Then she saw it. She suppressed a smile as she saw the convertible top begin to open. She waited until it was almost halfway open and high-pressure jets of water and suds were streaming into the open cockpit, and then started screaming.

"Oh, no, oh no! Holy shit! Somebody help! Stop it! Stop the wash!" She pounded frantically on the glass. Ed came running up to her.

"What is it, ma'am?" he asked. "What's wrong?" Helena pointed through the glass at the car, the top now near completely open. Ed looked and the color drained from his face. "Oh, my god!" he said. He ran into the wash way and hit the emergency cutoff switch.

"My husband is going to kill me," Helena wailed, holding her hands to the sides of her head and rocking back and forth. She was in Ed's office, sitting in the cheap office chair that the manager had directed her to as he pulled the car out of the wash. Ed now sat behind the little desk, looking like he had just lost his best friend.

"No, ma'am. Don't talk like that," Ed said, trying to sound reassuring.

"Yes, yes he will," Helena said defiantly, looking the man straight in the eye. "You don't know my Frank. He's a very physical person, and very passionate. That car is so important to him. How could this happen? You said nothing would happen, Ed."

Ed looked at her, suspiciously for an instant. Helena gulped, feeling that last bit was a little overplayed. "I don't know," Ed said slowly. "I've never seen anything like it in twenty years. What do you think, ma'am? Any idea how that top could've started going down like that?"

"What are saying, Ed? You think I did that, on purpose?" Helena sobbed loudly into her lap, then looked at him angrily. "I don't know how you can even imply such a thing. I wasn't even near the car. You know that. 'Give it to Jesus', you said, and that's just what I did. You are a very insulting person, Ed. Very insulting. My Frank is going to be upset you ruined his car and then blamed his wife for it, let me tell you."

Ed rapidly reconsidered his position. 'No, ma'am, not at all. That's not at all what I meant."

"It's what you said. I'm going to tell my husband what you said, that I did this on purpose. What sense does that make, anyway? It's a brand new car."

"No, ma'am, no sense at all. It's not what I meant at all. I am going to take care of this, don't worry." He tried to smile. "This is what we have insurance for, after all. Please, ma'am, don't worry. I'm going to make this right."

"You're going to fix Frank's car? Make it just like new?" Ed nodded.

"Yes, ma'am. I'll call the Porsche dealer, here in town. I'll have him pick it up today and start working on it. I promise."

Helena started to bawl again. "But that'll take days. What will Frank do for a car? He's going to kill me, I tell you. I shouldn't have tried to do something nice—"

"Don't worry about that, either," Ed said, picking up his phone. "I'm going to arrange for a rental. They'll bring it right over."

"In your name, Ed? I don't want my Frank to see any bills about this, he'll gut me, I tell you. Gut me like an elk."

"Oh, no. I'll take care of the paperwork. It's just insurance, that's all. I'll just need to make a copy of your driver's license, that's all."

"It'll have to be a sports car, Ed. With a manual transmission. If my Frank is gonna drive it for a couple of days, he'll gut me if it isn't some kind of fancy sports car. Bet on it. He'll beat me silly."

Helena let the man make a copy of one of her six driver's licenses, this one naming her as Ana Livia of Cambridge, Massachusetts. Less than thirty minutes later, Helena had the keys in hand to a canary yellow Corvette ZO6, and had transferred the duffle from the inundated Porsche. Helena gave Arthur's cellphone number to Ed to let him know when the car was ready to be picked up. She wished she could listen in on that conversation. Arthur loved that car almost as much as Frank.

She stared at the Corvette with disdain. Why were they always this putrid yellow, she thought, preparing to get in and drive away. "Lady, wait," she heard. She turned to see the Hispanic guy walking toward her, definitely with a purpose. She didn't like his body language, not one bit. She got in the car but the man got to the door and held it before she could close it. "Please, lady. Don't go."

Helena looked at him. The young man looked about twenty-five, tough and wiry. His expression looked determined. "It's Jesus, right?" she asked him. The man nodded. "You want something, Jesus? Something from me?" He nodded again. "I see. Why should I give you something, Jesus?"

The man looked at her, still holding the door. "He fired me. Just now. He says your top opening is my fault."

"Well, Jesus, I'm sorry to hear about you being fired and all, but you were the last one in the car. Maybe you hit the switch accidentally, without knowing it when you got out."

Jesus shook his head. "It's your fault I get fired, lady. It's your fault."

"Jesus," Helena started, "I don't think you can blame me for—" She stopped as she saw the item in Jesus's other hand. In his palm he held out the dresser's needle and coiled line. She looked into his eyes and asked, "How did you know, Jesus?"

"Your ass is wet, lady." He held the door and looked at her, waiting.

"You are a very perceptive young man, Jesus. How much?" Helena asked.

"What do you mean?"

"How much money do you want me to give you?" She waited. Jesus appeared to be considering this feverishly.

"You take me with you," he said finally. "You got me fired, it's only fair. Take me with you."

"Take you? You don't even know where I'm going."

"I don't care. I hate it here. I hate Salt Lake City. I have no job now. I'll go with you."

Helena considered this. No matter how much money she gave him, she realized, he'd still turn her in before she made it ten miles, maybe get a reward or his job back. She took the needle and line gently from the young man's hand.

"Fine. No problem, Jesus. I'll take you as far as Chicago. If you hate Salt Lake City, you'll love Chicago." He smiled and started to go to the passenger side to get in. "Whoa, there, Tonto," Helena said, grabbing his arm. "Might look a little fishy, you just getting in and driving away with the cute chica, don't you think? Makes it look like we were in this together from the beginning, like maybe you did mess with that switch after all."

"What are you saying? You said you'd take me to Chicago."

"Go tell your boss you want to be paid for the rest of the day. Make a fuss."

"He's not going to pay me anything. I'm fired."

"Fine, maybe he will and probably he won't. Argue with him for a while, at least. Swear at him in Spanish, Mormons hate that. Then start walking home. Which way is home?" Jesus pointed straight ahead. "Fine. You start walking home and I'll come around and pick you up a couple of blocks down, where they can't see us."

"You're going to take off. You won't come back."

"I'm a little hurt, Jesus. You have trust issues."

"Why I should trust you, lady? You're a thief."

"Here," she said, handing him back the needle and line. "If I don't pick you up, give this to your old boss. Tell him you want your job back, with a big raise."

Thirty minutes later, the two of them were driving east on I-80 at ninety-five miles per hour. Jesus looked at her admiringly.

"You drive angry, lady."

"Yeah, Jesus. I guess I do." She glanced at him, watching her. "What's your real name, hombre?"

"Real name? My real name is Jesus. Jesus De la Corazon."

"Really?" Helena asked, incredulous. "You use your real name? Interesting approach."

"What do you mean? What approach?"

"Well, maybe I'm just being a bit prejudiced here, or something, but I assumed you were here in Salt Lake illegally. Sorry, I just assumed. That was rude of me."

"That's right. I come here from Mexico, six weeks ago."

"Six weeks? Wow, welcome to America, Jesus. Six weeks, and already working, living the dream."

"Not no more. You fixed that, lady," he said. He looked at her. "You think I should change my name?"

"No, I was just talking. Doesn't matter. If they want you gone, they'll throw your ass back to Mexico no matter what you say your name is."

"True that, lady." They drove on for a bit, both looking ahead. "So, lady. What is your name?"

Helena looked over at him. "What, you don't like calling me 'lady'?" He shook his head. "What's your mother's name, Jesus?"

"Why do you want to know my mother's name?"

"What is it?"

"Mariangela," he said.

"Mariangela," Helena said. "That's a beautiful name. Is your mother still alive?"

Jesus nodded. "Why are we talking about my mother?"

She looked over at him again. "You can call me Mariangela. If you don't like 'lady', you can call me Mariangela."

"Why should I call you by my mother's name?"

"Well, Jesus," Helena explained, "I figure if you and I pretend that I'm like your mother, maybe you won't stick me with that knife you got. Maybe," she smiled at him, "If you call me Mariangela, you won't try to rape and kill me tonight when we stop. Because I have to be honest, Jesus. I see you looking at me, and I see a young man who's expression says, 'I can own that, and take that little chica's money, and drive away in her piss yellow Corvette.'"

Jesus laughed. "You read my mind, lady? I think this is a piss yellow Corvette."

"Yeah, Jesus, I read your mind. It's my job. Was my job."

"How you know I have a knife?" He pulled a wicked looking switchblade from his pocket and spun it, then flipped it open and closed several times in an obviously well practiced move.

"I don't have to read your mind to know you have a knife, Jesus. Give me a break."

"I can use it, too." He looked at her with his best menacing expression, pointing the blade at her nose.

"I'm sure you can, Jesus. I'm sure you're one mean mofo hombre. Well, not motherfucking. At least, I hope not, since that would sort of defeat the purpose of calling me Mariangela." She smiled at him. "I just want to be clear, Jesus. I feel bad you got caught up in my play back there. I promised to give you a ride to Chicago. I won't try to ditch you or kill you or anything." He snorted derisively at this. "Yeah, you laugh, asshole. I won't kill you, but you try coming at me, Jesus, and I'll use your little penknife there to cut off your balls. I'll cut off your balls and make you swallow them. Both of them. Am I making myself clear?"

Jesus looked at her, appraisingly. Finally, he said, "You want, lady, I'll call you Mariangela. Fine. But you ain't anything like my mother."

CHAPTER 22

Arthur found himself wedged in the center seat between Gabriel and Chuck. He tried to position his laptop on the fold down table so that he could do some work without spilling his drink. He thought he had found a workable position when the football lineman in the seat in front of him reclined his seat with a force that sent the computer and his coke jetting into his lap.

"God Damn it all!" Arthur exclaimed. The man in front twisted in his seat and muttered an apology. "Hey, no problem. Tell me again what I'm doing on a goddam commercial redeye and not even in first class," Arthur inquired of his seatmates, surreptitiously using the corner of Chuck's jacket to soak up the spilled drink from his lap.

Chuck pulled his coat back. "I work for the government, Arthur. I'm not allowed to fly first class. Sorry."

"Yeah, that's you. Doesn't explain why Gabriel and I have to suffer."

"I just assumed my friends would like to sit with me when I booked the tickets. I'm sorry if I was wrong," Chuck said petulantly.

"You were wrong," Gabriel replied.

Chuck had begged both to join him for a series of meetings in DC to help finalize his proposal. As it happened, Chuck was forced to admit that he had used Insight Technology and the working group he had commandeered as the entire basis of his proposal. Arthur was upset that, not only had Chuck finagled his company, but that he would be made to suffer through a series of governmental committee meetings. He had vehemently refused until Gabriel had secretly told Arthur that it was important that they cooperate with Chuck to buy Helena time to get to Michigan. Arthur had reluctantly agreed.

Gabriel was surprised when Chuck's initial impatience to get them to DC suddenly waned. When Gabriel first called Chuck, he had talked about leaving as soon as they could get packed. Chuck let the timetable slip, however, not pestering Gabriel and Arthur for two more days before shepherding them onto the redeye flight to Washington. Gabriel was clueless as to what had caused the change in Chuck's attitude, but it made it easier to achieve his given assignment of keeping Chuck away from Helena for at least a week.

"I can't read the stupid position paper you wrote under my name," Arthur complained. "I'm like a pretzel in a sardine can here. I'm not going to be ready for the meeting."

"Don't worry, Arthur. The meetings don't start until tomorrow. You'll have plenty of time. I really appreciate you doing this, Arthur," Chuck said.

"Well, since you fabricated your whole project on the basis of pirating our company's resources, it's not like I have a lot of choice here," Arthur replied. He twisted in his seat, trying to find a way to reopen his laptop, but without much success. The linebacker, semi-reclined in Arthur's lap, began to snore loudly. "That's it!" Arthur announced, slamming his laptop shut and struggling to unhook his seatbelt. He twisted in his seat again and dug the wallet from his back pocket. Arthur began to count money. "How much cash do you have on you?" he demanded of Gabriel.

"I don't know," Gabriel replied, "one fifty, two hundred. Why?"

"Give it to me. Give me all of it," Arthur demanded.

"Why?" Gabriel repeated. Arthur was struggling to climb over Gabriel into the aisle. "Where are you going?"

"Give me the fucking money, Gabriel," Arthur hissed. "I'm going up there," he pointed to the curtain separating them from the first class cabin, "and I'm going to pay some flight attendant whatever it takes to let me sit someplace where I won't get myself killed by trying to strangle a three hundred pound linebacker with his head in my lap." He held out his hand and Gabriel gave him the money. "Is that all of if?" he asked, counting.

"Arthur, they may not have an empty seat up there," Gabriel said.

Arthur looked at him wild-eyed. "Then I'll pay some fucking vice president of Butfuck Bank riding up there on his expense account," he counted the money in his hand, "six hundred and eighty six dollars to switch seats. I'm betting he takes it, because if somebody doesn't take it, this plane is going down. See you." Arthur strode through the curtain and Gabriel could hear him being challenged by the flight attendant. He didn't return.

Gabriel looked across the empty middle seat at Chuck, who rolled his eyes. "Arthur likes his space," Gabriel explained.

"He seems upset," Chuck said.

"Yeah, a little," Gabriel agreed. "I think he's a little offended. You know, the whole thing about you getting us involved in a five year, multi-million dollar government contract without mentioning anything to the actual owners of the company—us."

Chuck looked sheepish. "You guys were always so busy. You hardly ever showed up for our meetings. We felt pretty neglected, I got to tell you."

"We?"

"My working group. You guys were always working with the other group, the group in charge of destroying the company. The company that everyone in those groups worked for, by the way. It was hurtful."

"Yeah, whatever. Had to be done."

"So you say." Chuck brightened. "So, did you have a chance to review the materials I sent you? Or were you planning on waiting until the last moment, like Arthur?"

"Actually, I haven't looked at anything. You sent me something?"

Chuck was crestfallen. "Well, yeah. I sent you a copy of the entire proposal and your position paper, the stuff I think you should say in the meetings."

"Really? That's nice of you. Why don't you just say it, go ahead and do all the talking? I can just nod a lot."

"No, I think it's important that you appear to take the lead on this, Gabriel. You're kind of a big deal, you know. It'll be more impressive that way."

"What do you mean, Chuck?"

"Well, you know. You're famous. The inventor of the technology that changed the world, that allowed mankind to read each other's mind. Face on the cover of Time and all that."

"That picture made me look like a pedophile."

"Yeah, I thought so, too. Why did you let them run that picture? That was a weird smile."

"They never even showed it to me. First time I saw it was in the drugstore."

"Shame. But everyone in Washington will want to hear your proposal. You're the face of the project, Gabriel."

"I don't want to be the face of the project, Chuck. It's not my project."

"Well, technically it is. You and Arthur are principals on all the paperwork."

"Great."

"You're upset, aren't you? Like Arthur."

"Different reasons, Chuck. But yes, to be honest, I am upset."

"I should have discussed it with you, I know, Gabriel." Chuck tried to sound remorseful. "But I knew you'd have issues with it."

"Damn right. Issues."

"I know that you used to be considered, like the world's leading authority on sensing technology for a while there, Gabriel. It must've been hard to realize that the DARPA guys had invented that remote sensing stuff. You didn't even see that coming."

"I was a bit taken aback, I will admit that, Chuck. When you're not actively researching in the field—"

"Things can really pass you by, that's for sure. If you're not driving the train, you'll probably get run over, huh?"

Gabriel shrugged. "Progress marches on, I get it. That's not really my issue, you know."

Chuck nodded. "I know, but it's gotta hurt, knowing that you're not a player anymore."

"I'm okay with it, really, Chuck. Thanks for caring. Like I said, that's not really my problem with this whole thing."

"You don't think we should be scanning people without their knowledge, right?" Chuck asked.

"Without their knowledge, without their permission, against their will; yeah, that's my problem with it, in a nutshell."

"You've always been such a purist, Gabriel." Chuck smiled at him.

"That's not what I'm talking about, Chuck," Gabriel said, twisting in his seat to face him. "This isn't about the whole interpretation thing you and I go round and round about. You're wrong about that too, by the way."

"Such a purist," Chuck sighed.

"Yeah, fuck you too, Chuck. That's not what we're talking about here."

"So what are we talking about? What else do you have a problem with?" The linebacker gave a loud, stuttering snore. "Hey!" Chuck told him, smacking the man's shoulder. The snoring continued.

"Chuck, you're proposing scanning the thoughts of whole populations of people without their knowledge. You don't have a problem with that?" Chuck shrugged and shook his head.

"Nope. Should I?"

Gabriel pounded the back of the linebacker's seat without effect. "Yeah, Chuck, I think you should. You never read '1984'? Never saw 'V for Vendetta'? You're making it possible to create a police state."

"As a lifelong, dedicated civil servant, Gabriel, I'm offended. I swore an oath, you know. When you join the NSA, they make you swear an oath."

"Yeah, I think you mentioned it once before. A long time ago. Something about being the very best you that you can be, right?"

"No, to preserve and protect, Gabe. The Constitution of the United States of America. Did you swear an oath?" Gabriel shook his head. "I didn't think so. You shouldn't be so high and mighty. Your motivations aren't so pure, mister. You created this technology. What were you thinking?"

This gave Gabriel pause. He didn't really have a good answer to that question. "I know what I wasn't thinking. I wasn't thinking of creating a technology to make the world safe for dictators and the thought police."

"No, I'm sure you weren't. And you haven't. You wanted to change the world for the better. Everybody does. Well, we have. We did it. We didn't make it any easier to be a dictator. Dictators will always find a way, they always have. Before this technology, they just rounded up all the people they thought might be conspiring against them and threw them in prison, or killed them all, or tortured them until they confessed and gave up the names of all their co-conspirators. Been going on since the middle ages."

"Yeah, well, this will make it a lot easier. At least before, you had to actually be a conspirator. Now, you'll be arrested if you walk past an antenna in Times Square while you're thinking about how much the government sucks. I see a problem."

"The problem you see isn't the technology, Gabriel, it's the implementation. You can't control that."

"Exactly."

"But why do you immediately assume that the government will screw this up? We are the government, we do shit like this every day, just not as well."

"The government isn't surveilling our thoughts. At least not until this plane lands."

"It's just a matter of degree. We do everything just short of that already. I can open my laptop, if I had any damn room here in this seat, and I can find out what anybody, anywhere, is doing—or just about. We have that. We put that in legislation. We wanted to be able to find people, so we put GPS in everybody's cars."

"You did not. What are you talking about?"

"Sure we did. It was going to happen anyway. Everyone wanted a GPS device in their car, to find where they were going and how to get somewhere. Well, how do you think that little dot gets on the screen to show you where you are? It's receiving a signal from a satellite, of course. But that wasn't good enough for us, we wanted to find everyone. So for the public good, we said, we'll require a locator in every car, just in case. You know, if you're in an accident, we said, it would be great if the airbags going off triggered the locator so 911 would know where you are and come help. That's what we told Congress, that's what the bill said when we wrote it. We just didn't advertise the fact that NSA could trip that little switch on the chip, just like the airbags, any time we want."

"You're making this up."

"No, I'm not. We do it all the time. If I have a car's VIN number, say of Arthur's convertible Porsche, I can sit at my computer and punch a button and just watch that little automobile move straight across the country. It's amazing. I'll have it on my phone pretty soon."

Chuck watched Gabriel, smiling. Gabriel wasn't smiling. Now he realized why Chuck had changed his mind about rushing them to Washington. He knew how much time he had. Chuck knew he could get to the backup before Helena any time.

"You don't really know what's going on, who's driving, or what they're thinking," Gabriel ventured cautiously.

"No, I guess technically you're right about that. But when I see that little dot moving across state lines like a freaking bat out of hell, makes me think of only one person I know who drives like that, I tell you." Gabriel said nothing, his expression neutral. "Hey, Gabriel," Chuck asked, "Who does Helena know in Salt Lake City? She's been visiting someone for a couple of days, did you know that? Probably not, she never calls, does she? She's still the one person without a cellphone, right?"

"What's your point, Chuck?"

"My point? Oh, right. Anyways, I was on a conference call with the engineers from DARPA yesterday, the antenna geeks I was talking about. This one guy was actually reading from one of your early papers about electrode design, one of the old ones from Michigan. They're all really big on your early work. I mean, you used to be wicked smart, I guess. It got really tedious, though, listening to this guy read out loud over the conference call, those things are all echoey, it makes me nuts. I kind of tuned him out after a while, but it got me thinking about that stuff you did when you first came out to California, when you designed that ear bud antenna thing, remember?"

"Yeah, Chuck, I remember."

"So, I was thinking how easy it would be to incorporate an antenna in the standard cellphone chipset, make it capable of monitoring brain-waves like you did."

"Phones already have nearfield antennas, Chuck. Most of them, anyway."

"Yeah, of course they do. Well, that's great, we're halfway there, then. So I'm thinking that we could standardize the chipset to monitor brainwave patterns. Legislate as a public health benefit, detecting impending strokes or some such. Then if certain thoughts are detected, it would send a burst transmission or something."

"Send a transmission where, Chuck?"

"I don't know, the FBI probably. NSA could set it up as an overseas thing, but FBI would have to run the domestic side, long-term. And here, this is great, too. I thought of this last night. If the chip was sophisticated enough, we could push from our end to the chip, to update it, you know?"

"You lost me. Which is okay, really. I'm okay with being lost at this point."

"No, listen. Say the FBI gets a tip that someone named Mohammed—"

"Really, Chuck? Mohammed?"

"Or Teddy, it's just an example. The FBI gets a tip that some dude named Teddy, no last name known, is planning a terrorist attack on a bridge in New York. But you know how it is, we don't know if Teddy is a real name or a codename, we don't know if the attack is imminent or still in the planning stages. All the stuff that keeps us from doing anything."

"I think in that case we just round up all the Muslims wearing teddies."

"I don't get it."

"That's okay."

"Quit interrupting, this is important. I'm thinking, with my system, the FBI or NSA could push instructions to all the cellphones, telling them to monitor for thoughts of 'Teddy' and 'New York', and 'bridge'. If the phone detected that combination, it would notify the FBI. And we would know exactly who was planning the attack. Isn't that brilliant?"

Gabriel stared at him in disbelief. "Helena was right," Gabriel finally announced. "You're evil."

"I am not evil. Quit saying that."

"You are. You are the antichrist. Helena was right."

"Helena was drunk. She said she didn't mean it."

"She meant it. And I agree with her."

"I don't get your problem, Gabriel."

"That's the really scary part, Chuck."

"Why do you hate me? I don't get it. We're the good guys." Gabriel just shook his head and reclined his seat, closing his eyes. "So you don't think the government should do this, is that what you're saying? Just scrap the whole idea, the whole proposal?"

"Exactly," Gabriel said with eyes closed.

"So, if snoring linebacker dude here is dreaming of blowing up the Statue of Liberty and we had the technology to read his mind, right now, you don't think we should do that? Just wait till Lady Liberty goes boom?"

"Let him dream, I say. Everybody's got a dream, Chuck."

"And if that smelly guy next to him is thinking right now about a nuclear bomb he's picking up in New York, and how he's going to plant it right next to you and Helena at your next anniversary, and blow half the country to kingdom come, you don't want to know about that, either? Everybody's got a dream; how about the ones who have a plan, a bomb, and the will to use it?"

"Not my call, Chuck. Not yours, either."

"You know why you don't care, Gabriel? Because you don't have kids, that's why. You really don't care about our security, or the future, or anything, because you and Helena don't have any children."

"You don't have any kids either, Chuck."

"Not now, but maybe someday. I could still have kids, I care about the world being safe for the children I might have someday. Not you. You've given up. You guys had your fun, let it all blow up. That's what you're saying."

"No, Chuck. I'm saying you're misguided, you're dangerous, and you're evil."

"You're an idiot, Gabriel. I never thought I'd say that, but you are."

"I'd rather be an idiot than the antichrist, Chuck."

"I'm not the antichrist."

"So you say. It doesn't matter. I'm taking a nap."

"What do you mean, it doesn't matter?"

"I'm taking a nap now, Chuck."

"Why did you say it doesn't matter?"

Gabriel opened his eyes reluctantly and looked at his companion. "Because," Gabriel began, "your supersensitive mind monitoring cellphones are never going to report in to the federal thought police, Chuck. Not going to happen."

"Why not?"

"I'm taking a nap." He closed his eyes again.

"I know what you're talking about. I know what you two did with the drive from the lab, Gabriel. Helena lied to me." Gabriel said nothing as he envied the linebacker's sonorous breathing just in front of him. "She said she was going to make me a copy, you heard her. She lied. But there is a copy, Gabriel. It's not a problem. We can make this work."

"I don't think so, Chuck."

"I know where Helena is going," Chuck replied. "I know she's going to lock down the backup, wherever that is."

Gabriel opened his eyes and looked at Chuck with a sense of pity. "Not lock it down, Chuck. Fry it. Get rid of it."

Chuck looked horrified, his jaw slack. "She wouldn't do that. Your whole life's work, Gabriel! Thirty years, both of you guys. She couldn't do that."

"Then you don't know my wife. She's going to burn it down."

"But it's too important," he implored. "It's one of the great discoveries of all time. She can't do that. My project depends on that program. The defense of the free world depends on that program."

"She can. She will. I'm sure of it, Chuck. Don't look so upset. She says it won't ever really be gone, anyway. She said you can't destroy it, just make it harder to find."

Chuck had his head in his hands. "Your wife is nuts, Gabriel. No offense, but she's certifiably crazy. No joke."

"Yeah," Gabriel said, closing his eyes again, "nobody's laughing."

Helena drove on in the gathering darkness, getting progressively drowsier. It had been a very long day. Her eyelids heavy, she managed to maintain an excessive rate of speed as they progressed eastward, approaching Lincoln, Nebraska. Jesus had been slumped against the door, sleeping, for the past two hours.

Helena snapped alert to the staccato warning sound of the Corvette rocketing along at over a hundred with two wheels off on the left shoulder. She snapped the car back onto the roadway, Jesus's head lifting in its sleep from his perch on the passenger side window and gently sailing across the cabin to land on Helena's shoulder. He schnorgled and continued to sleep.

Helena could tolerate this for about a minute. "Jesus," she called, "you're taking this mom thing a little far. Get off of me." When he failed to awaken, she licked the end of her index finger and stuck it in his ear. He scrambled off her shoulder, awake.

He scrubbed at his ear. "What the hell?" he asked, wiping at his ear again. "What happened, chica?

"That what you call su madre, mi macho hijo?"

"Mariangela. Que paso?"

"I'm tired and I'm going to get us killed if we don't stop for the night."

"I can drive."

"No, you can't."

"I'm a good driver. Not angry, like you."

"You can't drive because you're sitting over there and I'm sitting over here. And since you are not ever going to be sitting over here, you can't drive."

"Fine. You didn't have to wake me up then."

"If you don't engage me in scintillating conversation, I'm going to put us in the ditch."

"I don't get you."

"Start talking or die screaming."

"What do you want to talk about?"

"Don't much care."

"Why did you trash your husband's car?"

"It wasn't my husband's car."

"You said it was your husband's car. "

"I lied."

"Whose car was it?"

"A friend's. It's a long story. I don't want to talk about it."

"Some friend you are. Fine, what do you want to talk about?"

"Don't care."

"I can tell you about my mom's cooking."

"Let's pretend we already talked about that. What do you want to talk about now?" Jesus shrugged. "Tell me about you, Jesus. Why did you come to America, Jesus?"

"Things are better here. Everybody at home says so."

"Well, you're the expert now. What do you think; things better here?"

"Yeah, it's better. I can do stuff here, lots of things to do. I can wash cars that cost enough money to feed my whole family for ten years. Lots of fun things like that."

"No car washing jobs at home?"

"No nothing at home. Just sit, every day, just sit."

"You don't like to sit, huh?" He shook his head. "So, Jesus," Helena continued as she swooped the car around a truck in the left lane, "where do you see yourself in five years?"

"What do you mean?"

"Your plans. What do you plan to be doing with your life, five years from now?" Helena glanced over at him. He shrugged again.

"Don't know. Probably be in jail, or deported back home by then, you know?"

"Why in jail? If you don't get deported, why would you be in jail?"

"I don't know. Probably for stealing. For being a Mexican."

"I can understand your reasoning there. But why steal? You already had a job, six weeks here and you were working."

"That job sucks. I was gonna quit soon, anyway." Helena nodded. "Salt Lake City sucks."

"Never spent any time there, myself. Looked pretty," she said.

"Too cold."

"You're going to love Chicago, Jesus."

"You think so?"

"I'm sure of it. You have any skills?"

"What do you mean?"

"Talents, training? Are you a carpenter? Do you play accordion?"

"Not really. I wash cars."

"That's not a skill, Jesus. That's survival, and there's no shame in that. Sometimes, you just gotta survive. But you can do better, mi hijo."

Jesus smiled. "Yeah, momma Mariangela, like you know me."

"Yo te conozco, mi pequeno." She smiled at him.

"You know some Spanish, that's good," he said, smiling back.

"Used to date a guy from Barcelona."

"Was he as good looking as me?" Jesus asked, dramatically sweeping the hair from his forehead.

"No, not as good looking as you, Jesus. But he had a lot of money. At the time, that looked pretty damn fine, I'll tell you."

"What did he do for all his money? He steals cars like you?"

"No, we never stole any cars, Jesus. He rode bikes, very fast."

"Bicycles?"

"No, motorcycles. He was very good, very successful."

"What happened? How come you didn't marry him if he was so good?"

"Oh, I wouldn't have married him or anyone else back then. I was young, younger than you. Anyway, he snapped a strut doing about one eighty. Not much left to love after that."

"Maybe someone didn't like how good he raced."

"Maybe." Helena nodded at that. "So what are you the best at, Jesus?"

"Washing cars, I guess."

"I don't believe that, Jesus. You're too smart for that."

"How do you know how smart I am?"

"You spotted my con, that's how I know."

"Wet ass lady." They both laughed at that.

Helena looked for signs of a place to rest for the night. She found a motel just short of Lincoln right off the highway. Helena paid for two rooms with cash, letting the clerk make a copy of her fake driver's license. They ate a late dinner at a 24-hour diner a walk from the motel and headed back to the motel. The night was crisp and clear, Helena walking with her arms wrapped around herself for warmth.

"Thank you for dinner, Mariangela."

Helena nodded. "No problem. You're welcome." They walked along the roadside towards the motel. "What will you do when you get to Chicago, Jesus?" she asked him as they walked, gravel crunching beneath them.

"I don't know, Mariangela. You keep asking what I will do. What will I do in five years, what will I do in five days. How can I know?"

"Well, what are your plans? What do you want to do?"

"These are stupid questions, Mariangela. What does it matter what I want to do? What does it matter what plans I make now?

"You don't think about what you're going to do, try to plan ahead?"

Jesus shrugged in the darkness. "You will stop the car. I plan on getting out. Then, who knows?"

"I think you can do better than that, Jesus. Show a little motivation."

"I don't understand what you mean. If I say I will walk to the nearest diner and ask for work, will that please you? Will I impress you with my plan?"

"That's a start, sure. Better than nothing."

"No, Mariangela, it is less than nothing. It is a fool's dream, to think like that."

"It's not foolish to have some sort of plan."

"It is. I tell you that I will walk to the diner and get a job. Maybe. But maybe it's raining so hard when I get out of your piss yellow Corvette that when I walk into the diner, I look so bad they throw me out. Maybe there are police in the diner; that would be a bad plan. Maybe you'll feel bad and give me some money, and I can sit and buy food. But maybe you won't feel bad enough to give me any money. Maybe you get out of the car and I drive away in the Corvette with all your money. Are you going to walk to the diner in the rain? What is your plan, Mariangela?"

"I don't plan on being the one getting out of the car, that's for sure."

"You don't know. It is stupid to think you know. When you say, 'for sure', you are being stupid."

"Great, I picked up Camus at the car wash."

"I like Borges better. He was a better writer than Camus, and from Argentina."

"I don't know Borges."

"Of course you don't. Like I say, he was Argentinian. Jorge Luis Borges. Greatest writer ever, but from Argentina. No Nobel Prize if you're from Argentina. You should read him."

"Don't think I'll have the opportunity, to be honest. Give me the short version."

Jesus looked at her quizzically. "He wrote many fantastic stories. And poems, too. He wrote a famous essay that there was no such thing as time. Famous in my country, I mean. You never heard of him."

"I think someone is a little defensive about Latin American literature. He didn't believe in time? Did he write about time travel?"

"No, not travel. He wrote an essay, 'A New Refutation of Time'. Get it? If there is no time, how can anything be new? Get it?"

"Yeah, that's deep."

"No, it's ironic; *contradictio in adjecto*. He wrote: 'Every instant is autonomous. Not vengeance nor pardon nor jails nor even oblivion can modify the invulnerable past. No less vain to my mind are hope and fear, for they always refer to future events, that is, to events which will not happen to us, who are the diminutive present.'"

"You memorized that?"

"Yes, for school. But I won't forget it, ever. Because it is true."

"I hope your Borges was wrong, at least about the invulnerable past."

"I think he was right, about everything. You would like his writing."

"Doesn't sound like it."

"That's just because he wrote in Spanish."

"Doesn't help, that's a fact. Tell me how you got to America. You must've had a plan then."

"Oh, yeah, some plan. I hate my life, I hate sitting. So I started walking north. Here I am. Some plan."

"You walked north, not south."

"North was downhill, south was a garbage heap." Jesus scooped up a rock from the roadside as they walked. He threw it and Helena heard a squeal from the darkness ahead. She couldn't see what had made the sound.

"So, you're just moving through this life, leaving it all up to God, eh?"

He looked at her in the dark, seeing little but her profile. "I didn't say anything about God. It would be stupid to leave anything to God."

"You don't believe in God?"

"I believe in God, of course. It is stupid not to believe in God. I don't believe he likes my plans very much, though. He makes fun of my plans."

"Man tracht un Got lacht," Helena said.

"What did you say?"

"It's Yiddish. 'Man plans and God laughs.'"

"Borges wrote some of Yiddish. You dated a Jew once, right?" Jesus asked, smiling.

"Married him, actually." They walked along for a bit, Helena thinking of her husband. She tried to picture what he was doing, but realized she didn't even know where he was. She fingered the little worn piece of paper in her pocket. "I miss him."

"Then why did you leave him?" Jesus asked, smiling. "To have a wild trip across the country with a young, handsome Mexicano, si?"

"No, Jesus, that wasn't the plan. Not at all."

"You see my point then." Helena was forced to agree. "If you miss him, why are you wrecking his friend's car and driving so fast to get away from him?"

"Had to. I have a job I have to do."

"You should pay someone else to do this job. Then you could go back to the husband you love so much."

"I can't."

"You won't. It is different than 'can't'. So, then, Mariangela, when will this job be done? When will you see your husband again?"

Helena shook her head in the darkness. "I won't."

They had arrived back at the motel and stood outside the doors of the adjoining rooms.

"Maybe you would like to keep talking, in there," Jesus said.

"No, I think not, Jesus. We can talk in the morning. Lots more driving to do." Jesus shrugged his shoulders. He turned to the door of his room. "Jesus?" He turned back to her, smiling broadly. "If I hear anybody even trying my door tonight, I'll leave you in my dust. You'll spend the rest of your life in Lincoln, Nebraska. Think Salt Lake City without the pretty mountains." His smile disappeared. "Good night, Jesus."

"Hasta manana, momma Mariangela."

Chuck signed the three of them in to the hotel. Two rooms, Chuck in his own. Gabriel lobbied to change the assignments, trying for some way to keep closer tabs on Chuck's activities, but to no avail.

The next day was spent in a succession of meetings of various sizes and durations, punctuated by short cab rides between governmental buildings. Arthur disappeared after the second meeting and wasn't seen again until the other two returned to the hotel for dinner.

"How'd it go?" Arthur asked when they came back.

"Great," Chuck answered.

"Horrifying," Gabriel said. He collapsed onto the bed.

"Sorry I missed it," Arthur said.

"You can come with us tomorrow," Chuck volunteered.

"Instead of me," Gabriel added.

"Let's get dinner," Arthur said. "I made reservations."

"Two minutes," Chuck said. "I've got to check my mail." He left for his room down the hall.

"You think he went to check on Helena?" Arthur asked, after the door had closed.

"I'm sure of it."

"What should we do?"

"Nothing to do. As long as he's here, he's not there. That's all we can do."

They waited for Chuck to return. After twenty minutes, they went down the hall and pounded on his door. There was no response.

"Shit."

Helena and Jesus were back in the car at seven the next morning, both wearing the same clothes they had on the day before. They drove to the diner for breakfast.

They ate huge mounds of pancakes and eggs and sausages, swimming in butter and syrup. Large volumes of coffee and juice were consumed. Helena watched as the young man started a second stack of pancakes.

"Expecting a famine soon?" she asked him.

"No. Expect to be paying for my own food soon." He ate some more. "Here," he said, pausing to fish his cellphone from his pocket. "I got something for you. I downloaded you a story by Borges, 'The Garden of Forking Paths'." He pushed the phone over to her.

"Wow, how sweet of you," she said, looking at the phone sitting on the table before her. "Is this your phone?" He nodded and went back to eating. "And you downloaded the story, on the phone? For me?"

He nodded, smiling. "You should read it now, it's not long. It talks about time travel—"

Helena read the first line of the story as she drained the coffee from her mug. Then she brought the mug crashing down on the phone, smashing it into pieces. The other diners in the restaurant looked over at the sudden noise.

Jesus stared at her in disbelief. "Why the fuck? That was mine," Jesus said, angry. "That was my phone."

"I know, I'm sorry, Jesus," Helena said calmly, sweeping the fragments off the side of the table into the mug. "It was an accident."

"Why did you break my phone, Mariangela?"

"I'll buy you a new one, Jesus. Promise."

"I don't want a new phone. I want my phone."

"Believe me, you don't want that phone. It doesn't work."

"I mean, I wanted my own phone. You shouldn't do things like that."

"I know. I'm sorry. Thank you for getting me the story. I liked the way it starts."

"Fuck you, Mariangela. Why did you smash my phone?"

Helena sighed. "I'm sorry, really. It's just that phones can be tracked, that's all. It was risky."

"Nobody track my phone. I'm nobody. Why would somebody track my phone, Mariangela? It doesn't make sense." He pushed his plates away.

"It does, actually. You and I disappeared from Salt Lake on the same day. We can be put together—by the carwash guy, the insurance adjuster, the rental agent. It's a chain of events. Everything went into the computer."

"All those things were you. Not me, you. Smash your own phone."

"I don't have a phone."

"No phone?" She shook her head. "Why didn't you just ask me to turn it off?"

"Doesn't help. I'm sorry, Jesus. I'll buy you a better one, promise."

"Like hell you will, Mariangela. Or whatever your real name is. You're going to push me out the door of the car in Chicago. Maybe you don't even slow down."

Helena pushed the unfinished plate of pancakes back to him. "Tell me about the story. I didn't get a chance to read the whole thing."

"It's not important. Not like Camus. Camus won the Nobel Prize, you know. 1957." He sulked.

"What was the name of the story, again?"

"'El Jardin de Senderos Que Se Bifurcan'. 'The Garden of Forking Paths'."

"It's a good story?"

"It's an amazing story. It is a story that Borges made to be read in many different ways, like branches."

"Yeah, I've heard of that, lots of times. It's called hypertext. Lots of stories are like that, Jesus."

"Yeah, I know. Now they are. But Borges wrote it in 1941. Before the invention of the computer."

"Really?"

"Yeah, really. He was genius, I told you."

"But never won a Nobel. How genius could he be?" Jesus looked up from his plate in anger but saw Helena smiling at him, teasing.

"I'm sorry, Mariangela, I'm still pissed about my phone. I think you're a little crazy, Mariangela."

"Yeah, can't blame you there. Tell me about the story."

"You can read it yourself. When you finish your job."

Helena shook her head. She caught the attention of the waitress and made a gesture for the check. "Like I told you, no time."

Jesus pushed the empty plates away and drained his coffee. "You keep talking like you're dying."

"Everybody's dying, Jesus."

"Are you sick?" The waitress brought the check.

"Not sick, Jesus," Helena said, fishing a twenty from her pocket and placing it under a glass with the check. "Just crazy." They walked out to the car. Helena spewed gravel from the lot as she fishtailed the sports car onto the road and headed back to the highway.

"If you're not sick, how do you know you're dying?" Jesus asked, buckling his seatbelt as they merged into the morning rush hour traffic.

"You read any Hemingway down there in Mexico?"

"Sure. We don't just read Latino authors, you know."

"Gotta let it go, Jesus. Hemingway said, 'All true stories end in death.'"

Jesus looked at her. "Jesus didn't die. He came back to life."

"My point, exactly."

"You don't believe in Jesus?"

"Ask me again next week."

"You still be alive next week, Mariangela?"

"No."

Gabriel and Arthur sat on the beds of their hotel room, staring at one another.

"What should we do?" Arthur asked.

"I'm not sure."

"We could follow him. To Michigan. Or go back home."

"I'm not sure. Let me think for a second."

The phone rang. They both looked at it, ringing. Arthur picked it up.

"Hello?"

He listened, saying nothing. After a minute, he hung up the phone.

"Well?" Gabriel asked.

"It was Chuck. He says hi."

"And?"

"And he's emailing us a list of meetings for tomorrow. Sorry he missed dinner. Sorry he can't be at the meetings tomorrow. He'll meet us tomorrow night, back here in the hotel."

"Asshole. Judas. Antichrist."

"What should we do?" Arthur asked. "I say we just go back home. Fuck him and his meetings."

"No, we stay put, for now. I don't know about the meetings, we'll see. It's not important. But we gotta find a way to give Helena a head's up."

"You don't think Chuck would try to hurt her, do you? Come on, it's Chuck we're talking about here."

"No, I don't think he would. But I told him that Helena was going to torch the whole thing. Probably shouldn't have said that."

"Shit no, Gabriel. Why in hell did you tell him that? Now he really is desperate."

"I don't know. I'm a lousy liar."

"Still can't see Chuck doing anything too crazy. Helena can be a lot crazier than Chuck could ever be. Crazy match, I'd put my money on your wife."

"Yeah, I hope you're right. But Chuck knows a lot of people. Some of them might be just as crazy as Helena."

"Maybe crazier, with guns."

"Thanks, Arthur. I feel much better now."

Arthur looked at his watch. "Shit," he said. "We missed our reservation."

The traffic was stop and go through Lincoln. Helena kept shifting through the gears and revving the engine, though she held the clutch in and they weren't moving.

"You should stop doing that," Jesus admonished. "You're going to break the car."

"Hate traffic."

"Do you have any medicine to take?"

"For what?"

"Forget it."

"Tell me about the story. The garden thing."

"'The Garden of Forking Paths'. I told you, it was a hypertext, with many possible endings. The forking paths are networks of time, none of which is the same, but all of which are equal. Borges called it 'a labyrinth that folds back upon itself in infinite regression so we become aware of all the possible choices we might make.'"

"I'm liking him a little more."

"You are? Why?"

"Did he feel then that we could go back on the forking paths, go back in time? Make another possibility?"

"I don't think so. At least, I don't remember that being in the story. He treats it like a maze, a labyrinth that is in time, though, not space."

"But you can go backwards in a labyrinth, retrace your steps and then take another path. Is that what he was saying?"

"No, I don't think so, Mariangela. He was saying that a man's search for the true path is fruitless, that there are so many paths in an infinite universe that if we think of all the possibilities, we must go mad."

"I don't think that was what he was saying. I think Borges meant that there were an infinite number of universes, where everything can happen. And the forking paths mean that we can go back. Go back in time and take another path, a path to another possible universe."

Jesus looked across at his companion. He said softly, "You never read the story, Mariangela." She was quiet then, but went back to futilely shifting through the gears.

They drove in silence for the next hour. The traffic thinned out and Helena brought the car up to speed as they headed east for Chicago. Helena cleared her throat dramatically.

"Listen, Jesus. I'm sorry about your phone."

"It's okay, Mariangela. You'll give me all your money when you drop me off in Chicago, because you feel so bad for me. I'll buy a new phone."

"Yeah, maybe. Something like that. Listen, Jesus. I was thinking, last night. I couldn't sleep, I—"

"Because you wanted me to come to your room, si?"

"No. That's not why. I was thinking a lot, about Borges and a lot of other stuff. About this job I have to do."

"And about dying? Surely you thought about dying, too? In the dark, all alone?"

"Yeah, dying too. Thanks for reminding me, Jesus. Just shut the fuck up for a while and let me talk, okay?"

"Hey, excuse me. You talk, I'll listen."

"Good. I'm figuring some stuff out here. It's all starting to fit together, you know? It fits with my research, my work. The job." Jesus sat impassively, listening. "You can make those little noises that people make, to make it seem like you're paying attention."

"Oh, yeah. Sure. Do go on, please."

"Don't get sarcastic with me, Jesus. This is really, fucking important. I'm going to change your life now. I'm going to rock your world."

"You weren't much interested in rocking my world last night, chica."

"Okay, you need to shut up again. Just listen. I am really, really rich."

"Yeah, right, Mariangela. In your dreams, maybe."

"No, really. Really, really wealthy. Have you ever heard of Insight Technology?"

"Of course, the mind readers? Everybody knows that company. We have them, even in our backward little Mexico City."

"Yeah, great. I get it. Anyway, that's my company."

"No shit? You're married to the guy who owns the company?"

"No, asshole. I own the company. And my husband. And our friend."

"Your friend who owns the Porsche you trashed?"

"Yeah. We're partners."

"You see that blue sign with the 'H' on it up there? Why don't you follow those signs, Mariangela?"

"I'm not playing with you, Jesus. It's true. I've got more money than God."

"Fine, I'm going to pretend to believe you now. Mostly, because you're driving. I believe you, Mariangela."

"My name's Helena. Helena Sheehan. We own Insight Technology. And I'm really, really rich."

"Okay. I'm listening."

"Good. Here's the good part. We're going to stop at a bank in Chicago and I'm going to give you half a million dollars."

"You mean, we're going to rob a bank?"

"No, Jesus. That won't be necessary. I'm going to wire transfer $500,000 into an account with your name on it. It will be your money. Nothing illegal."

"That's great, Mariangela."

"Helena."

"Yes, right. Thank you, Helena. In advance. You are very kind. I can buy a new phone."

"I'm not kidding, Jesus."

"Why would you give me $500,000?"

"I'm not entirely sure, to be honest. It came to me last night, while I was thinking. I believe in you, Jesus."

"I'm not trying to talk you out of this, Helena. I just don't know what you expect me to do with all that money. What do you want me to do?"

"Nothing. I don't want anything. I don't know what you should do. Just do your best, that's all."

"I can do that, Helena."

"There is one thing."

"Okay, here we go. What is the one thing, Helena?"

"Do you still have your knife, Jesus?"

"You didn't smash it, not yet. Why?"

"Are you good with your knife, Jesus?"

"Why are you asking, Helena? Because if you're talking about me killing someone, half a million dollars is not enough."

"I don't want you to kill anyone, Jesus."

"Actually, I was just bullshitting. I'd kill someone for half a million dollars. If they were a bad person. I don't want to sound greedy. Not a child, though. Or a woman. Or a priest. Or—"

"I'm not asking you to kill anyone, Jesus. Just listen. This is important. I'm going to tell you where to find a tree."

"A tree?"

"Yes. A tree in upstate New York. It will be hard to find, so listen carefully. Have you ever been camping?"

"You mean, sleep outside? My family's not that poor, we don't camp."

"Well, you're going to have to camp, but probably just one night. I'm going to give you directions. You have to remember this, it's really important. I'm going to make you repeat everything. Ready?"

"Sure, Helena. Tell me where to find your tree."

"There's something else."

"You said there was just one thing."

"I lied. I do that a lot."

"I'm beginning to think that."

"Not about the money. I didn't lie about that. Don't worry, you'll see. But there's something else. You'll have to go to the tree right away, and do exactly what I say. I'll draw you a map and a picture. A picture of what you have to do."

"A picture?"

"Yes, a picture. Right away, as soon as you can after I leave. But later, I don't know when, you'll have to do something else."

"Kill a man."

"No, you won't have to kill anyone. I don't know when it will happen, but a package will come for you. Probably in a few months, but I'm not sure yet."

"How will a package come for me? I don't even know where I'll be living in a couple of months."

"I'll show you. The package will come in a few months and you will find out when it arrives. It might be really heavy, though. I don't know."

"Is it a bomb? Are you a terrorist?"

"No, it's not a bomb. I'm not a terrorist. Shut up. You're going to have to take the package to the tree."

"The same tree?"

"Yeah, the same tree."

"In upstate New York?"

"Yes, the same tree in upstate New York."

"Why do you want to blow up a tree in upstate New York?"

"It's not a bomb, Jesus."

"What is it then?"

"I can't tell you. You can't open it. Promise me you won't open it."

"Because it's a fucking bomb."

"No, I swear it's not a bomb. It's not anything dangerous, I swear."

"You said you lie a lot."

"I was lying then. Not now."

"You mean when you said you were lying?"

"No, before. Can we continue now?" He shrugged. "When the package comes, you'll have to find a way to get it to the tree. It might be heavy, I don't know. But you'll have to bury it beside the tree."

"Bury the package next to the tree?"

"That's right."

"I'm thinking this is a lot of work for only half a million dollars."

They made it to downtown Chicago before evening rush hour. Jesus liked what he saw of the city—it was warm, and the lake sparkled with sailboats. They parked and went into the downtown bank, a branch of a large international firm with which Insight Technology maintained several accounts. Helena had $550,000 wired from San Francisco. She had the bank manager count out eight thousand dollars in cash to Jesus. At this point, Jesus stopped worrying that Helena was about to produce a gun at any minute and try to rob the place. They signed the papers to open an account in Jesus's name and deposited $500,000. Helena took the balance for herself, as cash. Finally, they rented a large safety deposit box, paying in advance for one year. The bank manager was happy to arrange for Jesus to be notified whenever a package arrived in his name at the bank. It would be kept in the vault until Jesus could transfer it to his box.

They drove then to get a new cellphone for Jesus. He bought two, though he wouldn't explain to Helena why he wanted two. He actually wanted a spare in case Helena tried to smash one again. Helena listened as he called the bank and spoke with the manager himself, giving him the new phone number to be called when a package should arrive in his name. Then she listened as Jesus called his mother in Mexico and explained that he was rich, that America was great, and that he lived in Chicago now. No, he explained, he had decided to quit the job in Salt Lake City. He promised to send money by the end of the week. First, he had to go visit New York.

They stood then on a corner in downtown Chicago. It had started to rain.

"I think I should find a diner now," Jesus said, smiling broadly at Helena.

She smiled back at him. "What will you do?" she asked.

"I will eat dinner. Maybe buy the diner, if it is nice. Maybe make it into a Mexican diner. I don't know."

"I'm sure you'll figure something out, Jesus."

"I'm sure I will, Senora Helena. I will do my best."

"Do you have the picture? And the map?" He nodded solemnly, patting his breast pocket. "You won't forget? You won't let me down?" He shook his head.

"I don't think you should die next week, Helena," he said.

"Maybe I shouldn't, Jesus." She gave him a hug and a kiss on the cheek. It was starting to rain harder.

"God bless you, Helena."

"And you, Jesus. Goodbye."

"Goodbye, Helena. Vaya con dios." He turned away then, and walked quickly towards the diner. Helena got back in the car. She continued her drive to Michigan alone.

CHAPTER 23

Helena drove through the streets of Ann Arbor like a yellow pinball, ricocheting from place to place as fast as she could. She didn't want to stay very long, hoping to accomplish her tasks and get back on the road by the end of the day, or sooner. She would have to be a little lucky; hardly ever her strong suit.

Helena nearly bolted from the stationary store, promising to return that afternoon to pick up her package. She found a place to park in the faculty lot outside the Mathematics Building. She hoped the professor would be in his office. She had called him from a public library in Kalamazoo to arrange the appointment, having sought him out with a search of the University of Michigan's online faculty directory. Helena hoped he wouldn't mind that she was over an hour early for their appointment.

The professor had indeed been in his office, and thrilled that Helena was early. More time for his photography hike in the arboretum that afternoon, he explained. He was old and looked like a professor of mathematics should look, Helena thought, with bushy white eyebrows and a shock of unruly white hair. She was mildly disappointed that he didn't smoke a big old Meerschaum pipe. But then, she didn't think anybody smoked pipes anymore. They had a conversation for over an hour, much longer than Helena had anticipated. The man had proven charming, and knowledgeable, and surprisingly interested. She thanked him for his time and left with his card. Helena was forced to decline his offer to stay in touch. She pulled the parking ticket from the windshield and tossed it behind the seats as she got back in the car.

She stopped next to visit Gabriel's parents. They were roommates at the nursing home, just outside Ann Arbor. It was a pleasant enough place, with lots of active younger seniors occupying the assisted living apartments attached to the nursing home itself. Gabriel's parents were in the full care section now, both asleep in the big hospital bed when she arrived. Helena wasn't surprised to see the envelope on the nightstand next to the bed with her name on it. She quietly picked it up and broke the seal. It was from Gabriel, of course, probably sent overnight express. A very short note in her husband's scrawl hoped she was well, sent his love, and warned her that Chuck had disappeared from DC last night. No surprise there, she thought. At least her ruse had slowed him down that much. Helena replaced the note in its envelope and added the professor's card before resealing it as best she could. She carefully placed it back on the nightstand.

Helena sat for a few minutes in the chair at the foot of the bed, watching the old couple sleep. They looked ancient to her, but happy enough; not so much happy, she thought, as content. Eventually, she decided to wake them. They were surprised and seemed genuinely delighted to see her. They asked after Gabriel, of course. Helena promised that he would be visiting them very soon. She stayed for half an hour, talking about their work and how wonderful it was to live in California. The older couple had great insight into the weather, holding forth on Michigan's lack of sunny days vis-a-vis California, and the difficulty they expected from the coming Michigan winter. After that, they said they were sorry, but were very tired, so Helena kissed them both goodbye, gave them her love, and left.

She wished she could stop in at the old condo, to wash and change clothes. They had finally sold the unit over a decade ago, however. She'd have to wait until she found a discount store and a motel on the road tonight. She returned to the stationary store and picked up her order, paying cash of course, and complimenting the owner on the quality and speed of her work. Probably took all of an hour, Helena thought to herself.

Unable to delay it any longer, Helena drove to the garage in Ypsilanti. She drove in a circuit around the area, doubling back on her route twice as her old Mossad boyfriend used to do, to make sure she wasn't being followed. She pulled the car up close to the garage. Helena was a little disappointed not to see the building surrounded by black Suburbans. Except for a new layer of graffiti and gang tags, the place hadn't changed a bit. Helena checked the tell next to the door—it was off its mark. Somebody had been here.

Helena pulled up the heavy garage door with a squeaky rumble and stepped inside. Sunlight spilled into the cluttered space. It looked unchanged from her last visit. She turned to pull down the big door.

"Hello, Helena." Helena froze, recognizing Chuck's nasal twang at once. His voice, however, had a more serious note than usual, she thought. Maybe desperate was more accurate. Not the usual twist of amusement. She could see him in her mind's eye, a glint to his stare as he pointed some small, effeminate handgun at the small of her back.

"Hello, Chuck. You found me." She stayed frozen, back to her assailant, hands still raised on the door above her. She remembered back to another visit she had made to this garage, when she was running from this same provocateur, many years ago. She remembered almost leaving, then deciding to tape a package to the door, this door she was holding. Why had she done that? Helena thought again. At the time, she hadn't been certain. Had she'd just been manifesting her usual paranoia? Or had her little sister told her to do it, in one of her "spells"? She didn't know. She could never remember what happened during those episodes. Helena slid her right hand slightly to the side and there it was, right where she left it years ago.

"Took you long enough to get here. I've been sitting here for like, three hours. And there are spiders," Chuck said from behind her.

"Nobody likes spiders," Helena agreed. Swiftly, and with the practiced speed and grace reminiscent of her youth, she swept the package from its perch on the door, falling and twisting in the air as she did so, pulling the gun from its oilcloth with her free hand. She forced herself to fully exhale as she landed prone on the ground with a grunt, breath held, arms slightly bent at the elbows, the gun held like a rapier between both hands, it's sight rock steady at the target's midchest, framed in the sunlight from the doorway behind her. Shlomo would be so proud of his 'little tiger', she thought briefly, then fired.

"Holy Shit!" Chuck screamed, falling to the cement floor and covering his head with his hands. "Why the FUCK did you do that?" Helena stared at the man over the top of the gun, warm in her hand.

"Do what?"

"Try to kill me, that's what! Are you fucking crazy? Don't answer that. We both know the answer." He sat up and cradled his knees, rocking a little.

Helena stood, looking at the gun. She tossed it away, clattering to the floor behind her. "I did not."

Chuck looked at her with an unbelieving gape. "You sure as hell did. You fucking tried to shoot me. How can you stand there and deny it?"

She walked over to him and offered her hand to help him up. "If I had wanted to shoot you, don't you think I would've? Come on."

Chuck ignored her hand and straightened himself up, standing. He carefully brushed dirt from his slacks. "You can't shoot worth shit. I think you hit the ceiling or something. What kind of person tries to shoot an unarmed man, just for saying hello?"

"Sorry," she said. She hopped up to sit on a pile of boxes. "I thought you had a gun. My bad."

"You thought I had a gun? I hate guns. Why would I have a gun?"

"A girl can't be too careful, Chuck. Let it go, okay? You're starting to whine."

Chuck pulled a handkerchief from his back pocket and dusted off the seat of the old desk chair next to him. He sat and took a deep breath.

"Gabriel said you were going to burn the backup. I am praying that he was just being dramatic."

Helena pointed across the garage to a metal wastebasket, blackened with soot. "Gabriel is many things, Chuck, but I wouldn't call him dramatic. How did you find me?"

Chuck stared at the basket and looked sad. "I didn't. I couldn't. NSA tracking still has you visiting a Porsche dealership in Salt Lake City. Don't tell me, I don't even want to know."

"Then how did you find this place?"

"Computers, Helena. UPS has a lot of them. Not a great security system, though. Leaky."

"You found the tracking numbers?"

"No, they're not that incompetent. But I had the office do a big pattern search on UPS shipments, looking for that randomization algorithm you had the crazy Israelis design."

"No way."

Chuck smiled. "Wasn't easy, I grant you. Guys at the office had to buy a lot of time on the old Cray supercomputer, like almost ten minutes of actual computation. Crazy, huh?"

"If you say so. I'll have to take your word for it. So that pointed you here?"

"Yeah. Your plan was pretty good, using random offices as the sender. But the addressee was fixed, you see? Completely random pattern except for one fixed point. Once I had enough data, the pin dropped right on this place. And such a lovely place it is. You couldn't pick a post office box or some apartment in Paris?"

Helena shrugged. "This place has sentimental value. Listen, Chuck. I need a favor."

"You're kidding, right?"

"No, why?"

"You tried to kill me, for one thing."

"We've moved past that."

"I haven't."

"Get over it. Believe me, if I'm any judge, it won't be the last time a girl tries to kill you. What's the other thing?"

"I want the tracking number. I want access to the backup."

"I told you. I burned it."

"No, you didn't say that. You just pointed at the trashcan. I think you burned something, probably the mountain of old tracking slips that should've been here when I came in. But I can't believe you burned the real one, the last one."

"Can't believe it or don't want to believe it?"

"Where is it, Helena? I know you have it. You couldn't burn it. You of all people, you wouldn't let your salmon get cooked."

Helena hung her head for a moment. "Yeah, you're right, Chuck. I have it."

"Give it to me."

"No."

"You have to. I need it for the project. You know that."

"Not going to happen."

"I can take it from you, Helena."

She almost snorted. "Yeah, right."

"Not me personally. I know people. I'll get it, I promise. This is important."

"You're right," Helena answered, starting to look about the garage. "Where did I put that gun?"

"Stop with the gun, already."

Helena hopped back on her box. "Stop threatening me. I have the tracking number, you don't. You're not going to get it. Wouldn't do you any good anyway, Chuck."

"Why not?"

"Because you don't have an access code, that's why. It's part of the setup, remember? Unless you have a key number, you can't even access the algorithm, even if you got your hands on the tracking number, which you won't, by the way."

"I have an access number."

"No you don't. Just me, Gabriel, and Arthur. No one else in the world. And I didn't let either one of those guys write it down, either. I made them memorize it."

"Yeah, that was smart. Especially the part where Arthur asked me what a good twelve digit number would be to use for his code."

"No fucking way! He didn't."

"You expect Arthur to be able to memorize a twelve digit number? Give me a break. You know, there's a reason they made phone numbers seven digits long, back when they set up the system."

"Really, why?"

"Because normal people can only remember seven digits, that's why. They did all sorts of studies. Then area codes screwed us all up."

"Huh. I didn't know that. What number did you give him? Let me guess: Pi? 3.14159265358?"

"Yeah, of course. The guy has no head for numbers, couldn't memorize anything past seven digits if his life depended on it. He was panic stricken, he was so afraid of telling you. It was one of your blue periods, remember? So I taught him a piem, the one by Sir James Jeans. You know: 'How I want a drink, alcoholic of course, after the heavy lectures involving quantum mechanics.'"

"Huh. Did you plan on stealing the salmon then?"

"Yeah, thought I might have to. You two are so antigovernment and all, such hippies."

"Ann Arbor, home of the SDS."

"Yeah, lovely roots of anarchy, here."

"I told Gabe you'd try to take it."

"You're a deeply gifted judge of character. I commend you."

"You're still not getting the tracking number, not yet."

"What do you mean, not yet?"

"If I promise to give it to you, will you do me a small favor?"

"Last time I saw you, you promised to make me a copy of the hard drive. You lied."

"No, I said if you kept pissing me off, I was going to throw it in the ocean. And here we are. And I'm really, really, pissed off at you, Chuck."

"What do you need? You want me to kill somebody, right?"

"Why do people keep asking me that?"

"Because you're fucking crazy, that's why."

"Don't be hateful, Chuck."

"What then?"

"Nothing much. When we're done here, I need you to keep Gabriel and Arthur busy for a day or two. Not long."

"That's it?"

"Not entirely."

"Here we go. Who's gotta die?"

"Then you have to tell him to go visit his parents, in the nursing home."

"That'll sound weird, coming from me. I'm not much of a family guy."

"Well, you should be. When's the last time you called your mother?"

"My mother died years ago, remember? Thanks for asking."

"Right, you're a bastard and all that. That was rude of me."

"Damn right. Fucking insensitive, that."

"Don't worry, though. Just tell Gabriel you met me here, I send my love, yada yada, that I said it was important that he go straight from DC to visit his mother. But keep him in DC a day or two first. And get Arthur to go with him, to visit his parents."

"Why should Arthur visit Gabriel's parents?"

"It's complicated, okay? Just do me this little favor."

"I don't know. Arthur's getting a little testy."

"Buy him something. Bring him back a wolverine tee shirt or something. He loves souvenirs."

"And then you'll give me the tracking number?"

"No."

"I knew it."

"Then I'll tell you how to get the tracking number. Next week."

"Next week? Why next week?"

"Because I said so, that's why. Do we have a deal or not, Chuck? There are spiders everywhere in here. Big furry ones that bite."

Chuck jumped out his chair and brushed at his pants violently. "Fine, deal. I'll go back to DC and drive those two crazy for a couple of days, then send them to the nursing home. I expect to hear from you next week, right? You're not playing me again, are you, Helena?"

"If I'm lying, I'm dying, Chuck. Travel safe, mon frere." She hopped off the box and strode towards the door and her car. "Fucking Judas Antichrist," she muttered under her breath as she left.

"I heard that," he called after her.

Helena immediately started driving, west now on I-94. She thought about actually flying. She felt the press of time on her, like she was in a box and the sides were slowly pressing in. She had set many plates spinning, but now she had to keep moving quickly to keep them from crashing down. And she had several more to start up, some of them really big platters, with only a little time left to her. Shit, she thought to herself, I feel like the clown in a goat rodeo.

Flying to Salt Lake City would alleviate all of her worries about the schedule, buying her at least a day and a half. She had never been on a commercial airplane in her life, she realized. She was probably being overcautious, she thought. Helena didn't think any of her false driver's licenses would pass scrutiny at airport security, they were old and the technology had improved so much since she had invested in her alter egos. She could use her real license, though, her California driver's license without a problem. That, however, would bring her name back onto the grid in a heartbeat. Maybe that wasn't a problem, she thought. She had cut a deal with Chuck, who else was looking for her?

Probably no one, she thought to herself. Maybe everyone, something in her mind replied. She continued to drive.

Driving alone cross-country is a uniquely personal experience. Many people, truck drivers for instance, enjoy the solitude and opportunity for introspection. Helena was no fan of introspection. "I should have taken the plane," Helena said aloud to herself. She had the roof off the Corvette and her hair was a tangled pennant streaming behind her. "No one is looking for me. No one cares that much to look. Except Gabe. And he knows where to find me. But I don't want him to find me. Not yet. I'm talking to myself. I'm paranoid and I'm talking to myself. Great.

"I've got the time. It's going to be tight but it'll work, you'll see. It's too late, anyway, I'm already driving. I could go straight to Midway and grab the next flight to Salt Lake City, there's probably like two more flights tonight, at least. They'll have empty seats; no one flies to Salt Lake City except to ski, anyway. I don't think I can even face airport security, no way. Let those guys X-ray me and pat me down? No fucking way." She shuddered at the vision. She pushed the car over a hundred, the traffic being sparse.

"What do you think, sis?" she said to the wind. "Keep driving or start flying?" She paused, listening to the rushing hundred mile per hour wind in her ears. "What, no opinion? Nothing to say? Probably just as well. High-speed catatonia probably not a great concept. Great name for a punk band, though.

"O—kay," she said slowly, "the delusional paranoid schizophrenic girl is hungry. And I stink. Someplace west of Chicago that isn't Lincoln, Nebraska. Someplace with a classy mall where I can get a beer and a steak and buy something pretty. Something expensive and pretty. And comfortable, it's still over a thousand miles of driving to get home. Expensive, pretty, and comfortable." She pictured the map in her mind, herself as a little redheaded Barbie in the pink Barbie Corvette, speeding west across the map of the country on I-80. "Des Moines," she announced to herself. "Stopping in Des Moines. Mall, steak, sleep. Sounds like a plan. Now shut up and let me drive." This last made her think of her friend, Jesus. She wondered what he was doing with his half million dollars. She hoped he was happy. Not so happy, though, that he would blow off what he promised to do for her. He could be happy after. Maybe she would send him an invitation, too.

Helena came over a rise at one twenty, felt the weight come off the car and carefully steered past a semi, hoping this 'Vette didn't share the earlier models proclivity for becoming airborne at speed. That would be embarrassing. In a split second, as she passed the truck, she saw the Illinois state trooper with his big hat, standing next to a car he had pulled over, his trooper lights still flashing red. As she rocketed past, Helena saw his head snap around, watching her tail as she disappeared down the road. "How fast can you write that ticket, asshole?" she said out loud to him. She started a mental calculation. She assumed a worst case scenario wherein he had just completed the ticket and now had tossed it at the hapless busted motorist and sprinted back to his cruiser, his rate of acceleration to match her (here she stole a glance at the speedometer) one hundred thirty five miles per hour at best rate for his big V-8, and the current approximate distance to the Iowa state line. She knew the trooper could call ahead to have someone stop her, but she was (picturing the Barbie car on the map again) just short of fifty miles from the state line. In these economically challenged times, that meant that the trooper she had just passed was probably covering all the way to the border. Unless he was at the western limit of his patrol area, in which case she was about to meet his little friend at a rate of speed that would land her skinny butt in jail. She ran the math in her head. Postulating no other trooper between her and the state border, she'd cross into the Iowa state line about three minutes before Tommy the Really Pissed Off Illinois State Trooper came within hailing distance. She ran the math again, tried to tighten up the confidence limits. She smiled to herself and pushed the accelerator further down. I love to drive, she thought. Wish I still had Arthur's Porsche, though. Wonder if it was fixed yet?

Arthur's cellphone rang. He and Gabriel were back in the hotel room, waiting for Chuck again. Chuck had called to announce he was flying back that night. They could all be together for tomorrow's meetings. They were not excited at the prospect.

"Hello," Arthur said, not recognizing the number. He listened for a few minutes. "What?" A pause. Gabriel couldn't make out what the other party was saying, but couldn't help but notice his friend's face turning beet red. "When? How much? Fine. Great. Thanks. Yeah, I'll be at this number."

"What?" Gabriel asked him after Arthur had hung up.

"That was the Porsche dealership in Salt Lake City. My car's not going to be ready for a while because they had to order a whole new interior." He looked at Gabriel suspiciously. "Why would my car need a whole new interior? It's less than three months old."

"A whole new interior? Really?"

"Yeah, that's what the guy said. Whole new interior. Really expensive, he said. Insurance adjuster is still trying to decide if it's covered, can't really decide if it's an accident, he said."

"Weird."

"Yeah. Weird. Where the hell is Helena?"

Gabriel shrugged. "Haven't a clue," he said.

There was a musical knock at the door. Gabriel got up off the bed to open the door and let Chuck in.

"Hey, guys," Chuck said.

"Hi, Chuck," they replied in morose syncopation. Gabriel flopped back down on the bed.

"Hey, why so glum? What's the problem?" Chuck asked.

"Fuck you, Chuck," Gabriel said to the ceiling.

"Hey, Arthur," Chuck said, tossing a bag at Arthur. "I got you a present."

Arthur let the bag sail past him onto the floor. "Fuck you, Chuck," Arthur said.

"I saw Helena today," Chuck beamed. Gabriel sat up on his elbows to look at him. "Yeah, she's good. Really good. Sends her love and all."

Helena slept great in Des Moines. She had one of the best steak dinners she had ever had in the most ridiculously expensive steakhouse she'd ever been in. Well, she supposed it was the most expensive but, truth be told, she never paid much attention to the prices on the menu, so it might not have been the most expensive; that place they went to in New York City for their anniversary seven or eight years back was probably way more expensive, now that she thought about it. She had two glasses of a local craft beer they had on tap and it was great with the steak and the huge sides of spinach and sweet potato fries. Normally, she would never have consumed such an enormous amount of calories, not at her age with a figure to worry about. She had just stopped worrying about that.

It was five in the morning, with only a hint on the horizon outside her hotel window of the sunrise to come. She had found the best hotel in Des Moines, which, luck would have it, had a vacancy for the night. She allowed herself to be talked into taking the Presidential Suite for a substantial upcharge, it being on the top floor with a beautiful view of Iowa. Besides, it had the most fantastic Japanese soaking tub. She had luxuriated in it until her toes were wrinkled like tiny pink prunes. She sat now on the edge of the huge, rumpled bed, showered and rested. She was dressed in an extremely flattering new pair of jeans and top that had cost over five hundred dollars each at the upscale mall she cruised into straight off the highway. Helena was staring at the other new outfit she had bought, hanging on the doorknob of the walk-in closet, next to the embarrassingly huge bathroom suite. She didn't know a hotel room could have a walk-in closet; a concept that was new to her. It was an elegant black cocktail dress which had cost almost two thousand dollars but, the sales lady had to admit, made her look drop dead gorgeous. Helena regretted the woman's choice of words, but she felt compelled to agree with the sales lady, especially when she insisted that the dress would be ruined without the perfect pair of heels with which she matched it. The shoes were positioned now on the floor, just beneath the dress, just so. She tried to picture her inert corpse lying elegantly in the dress, the left shoe dangling provocatively. Drop dead gorgeous, she thought.

She shouldn't be so happy, she thought. It wasn't the dress, or the shoes, or how great her butt looked in these jeans. These things helped, she realized. The real crux, however, was that she felt she was doing the right thing, finally. Up until last night, she had been constantly pricked by a thousand doubts. What if she was wrong? What if this didn't work? Why was she going to hurt the only person she ever truly cared about? All the doubts and fears had dissolved in a great night's sleep. She remembered dreaming a little, a vague but pleasant image of thousands of plates spinning in harmony atop a field of thin poles, bending together like sunflowers in a breeze. None of the plates fell. And she had awakened with a vision of Gabriel's face floating in front of her. He had looked a little sad, maybe a little sadder than usual, but not too bad—not destroyed or anything. She thought he was going to be okay, and this last and greatest doubt disappeared like smoke.

Helena slapped her thighs and bounced up off the bed. "Time to pack up and get on the road," she enthused out loud. She thought about singing that country song, but felt that might be pushing the mood a bit too far.

CHAPTER 24

Helena navigated the downtown streets of Salt Lake City in the late afternoon. She had driven all day without pause, making great time. It was as if the traffic parted before her speeding yellow chariot and she refused to spoil the blessing by stopping for anything. She knew exactly where she was going. She had found the jeweler's website while using the computer in the Kalamazoo library. What a great concept, she reflected, and not for the first time. The presentation of any old, forged identification card granted unlimited, free public access to the Internet with complete anonymity. Even Chuck and his NSA stormtroopers couldn't backtrack that session to her, no way. What a great country.

She needn't have hurried. The web site had promised the store stayed open until seven, and here she was pulling into the parking lot at half past five. A miracle. The building was in an interesting southwest modern motif. Light glowed from the large front windows, jewelry glittering from within. She went in. A bell tinkled as the door closed behind her.

A pleasant looking man wore a jeweler's magnifying glass as he sat working at his bench behind the display cases at the rear of the store. He didn't look up as Helena approach. He seemed engrossed in what he was doing, something intricate to a gold ring mounted in a pinvise on the bench.

"Hello," Helena called to him, crossing the length of the store to stand across the display case closest to him. "Are you Charley?"

The man, blond and with those watery blue eyes you sometimes see, Helena noticed, his eyes magnified tenfold in the glasses as he straightened to look at his visitor. He raised his hands in mock surrender, still holding small tools in each.

"You found me," he laughed, smiling. He pulled off the glasses to get a better look at Helena. "Can I help you in some way, Miss?"

"Oh, you flatterer," Helena blushed. "I'm no miss, Charley."

He pointed to her left hand. "You're not wearing a ring."

"No, I'm not," she agreed. She pointed to his hand. "But either are you, Charley."

"I'm not married, ma'am."

"Well, I am, and happily."

"Then you're one in a hundred, I'd say. How come you're not wearing a wedding ring?"

"He never gave me one."

"Well, your husband's no friend of mine, I must say. No offense, ma'am."

"Please, call me Helena," she said, offering her hand. The jeweler shook it.

"What can I help you with Helena?"

"Charley, this may sound forward, but I would feel more comfortable discussing this matter in private. Do you have a small office on the premises? Somewhere we can talk briefly?" He nodded, but looked at her suspiciously.

"We can sit in there, if you'd prefer," he said, nodding to the office behind him. "But I'll have to keep the door open. I'm open for business still, customers might walk in."

"Of course, Charley. Wouldn't be proper, otherwise." She followed him into the office, sitting across from his small desk. He sat, his head appearing to bob above the sea of papers stacked in front of him.

"Sorry," he said. "This won't do, I can't even see you sitting there." He proceeded to clear away several piles. "There, now. What is this matter you wish to discuss in private, Helena?"

Helena paused and tried to look demure. Finally, she looked him in the eye and said, "Charley, are you of the church?"

The man, usually pale, blushed brightly. "Why, yes ma'am. If by the church, you mean the Church of Latter Day Saints. A proud member, all my life. Third generation." He beamed.

"Well, that is a relief," Helena sighed. "I couldn't be sure from your website. It didn't say."

"No, I guess it doesn't," he admitted. "Never really thought about that before. Do you think that would be proper?"

"Maybe not, I'm not sure," Helena said. She took a deep breath and appeared to gather her strength. "Charley, do you believe that a person can be called upon by God?"

"Why, yes ma'am. I certainly do, indeed. I myself have been on three missions, if you don't mind me mentioning. I'm not bragging, mind you. I just mention it in way of agreeing with you."

She smiled nervously at the jeweler. "I believe, Charley, that I myself have been called."

"That's a great thing, ma'am," Charley heartened. "What type of mission have you been called upon to do, may I ask?"

"Please, Charley. Call me Helena." He nodded and blushed again. "Well, here's the embarrassing part."

"No need to be embarrassed, Helena. We all serve as God sees fit."

"Yes. Yes, indeed, Charley. That's very well said." He visibly swelled with pride at this.

"I am an elder, did I mention that?" he said.

"Are you really? I'm not surprised, a fine upstanding professional such as yourself."

There was a moment's uncomfortable silence. 'Way too thick,' she thought to herself.

"Your mission, Helena? You were saying?"

"Oh, yes. Well, just out with it I guess. Ready?" He nodded encouragingly. "You won't laugh at me, you promise?"

"I promise."

"I have traveled a long way to see you, Charley. God told me to find you."

"Me? Why me, Helena?"

"I was told that you are the only jeweler, goldsmith I mean, the only one to take up my project. The project that I have been given, as my mission."

Charley looked deeply concerned. "What type of project would this be, if I may be so bold?"

Helena sat up straight, hands folded primly in her lap. "Charley, I charge you with the creation of the golden book, the holy Book of Mormon." She paused. "There, I said it."

"That's it? That's your mission?" She nodded. Charley exhaled in relief. "Well, Helena, that's fine. No problem at all."

"You'll do it then? Really?"

"Helena, of course. This is Salt Lake City. I get asked to make a replica of The Book six or seven times a year. Have every year since I opened the shop. Actually," he began, rising from his chair, "I just might have a small one in the case in front. Just give me a sec."

"No, Charley," she said sternly. He stopped halfway to standing. "You're not understanding me. I don't want you to just make another replica."

He sat back down. "I don't follow."

"I want you to make the real book. Page for page, word for word. The actual Book of Mormon. In gold."

Charley blanched. "What do you mean, exactly? A real book, with gold pages, like?" She nodded vigorously. "With the scripture actually written on each page?" She nodded again. "Not just a replica, like I have out front?" She shook her head. He was quiet, considering.

"We have to, Charley. It's our calling. It's our mission."

He looked up at her from his reverie, displeased. "Your mission, you mean."

"No, Charley. God sent me to you. I'm sure of it." She looked determined. Proper, but determined.

"You don't understand what you're describing. The real book? With the actual scripture? Not just the boilerplate print we usually put on; we have decals, you know?"

Helena shook her head. "No, not boilerplate. And not decals. Engraved."

He looked shocked. "Engraved? You're joking."

Helena shook her head. "It is my vision, Charley. My vision had the words actually engraved. The pages magically turned, and every page was beautifully engraved in a glowing script."

Charley looked stricken. "But, ma'am—"

"Helena."

"Helena, whatever." He was clearly flustered. "To engrave the entire text onto gold pages by hand! That would take years, maybe a lifetime."

Helena laughed heartily, actually wiping away a tear of mirth at last before gathering herself to speak. "Charley, Charley, Charley. You are too funny. How is it that you are not married? You are too cute." She made to pinch him.

The jeweler pulled away involuntarily. "I don't understand you, ma'am."

"There you go 'ma'aming' me again, Charley." She wagged her finger at him playfully. "Charley! With modern computerized laser engraving techniques, I'm sure you can knock this bad boy out in a couple of weeks. What do you say?"

"Modern computerized laser engraving techniques?" She nodded at him, smiling. "Not by hand, then?" She giggled and shook her head.

"Charley," Helena offered. "This is a replica, you know. Only our lord could inscribe the actual scripture, I'm sure. You're not the Lord, are you, Charley?" The man blushed, shaking his head. "Then I guess computerized laser engraving techniques will do just fine, don't you think?"

They both looked through the door as they heard the little bell tinkle. An elderly woman had entered and was looking at the display.

Charley looked relieved. "I'll see to my customer. Just one minute, Helena." He started to rise again from his chair.

Helena nearly panicked. She almost had him. "Oh, Charley," she said pleasantly, "That's not a customer. That's just Sheila, a friend of mine. She's looking to meet me, but bless her, she's so early. I'll go talk to her and ask her to come back in a little bit." She desperately hoped that the lady wasn't one of his regular customers. She quickly rose and strode out into the store. Charley didn't stop her.

Helena smiled at the woman and took her elbow, steering her to the front of the store. "Good afternoon, dear lady," Helena said. "I'm sorry, but the store is closed."

The woman looked confused, pointing at the sign in the door. "But it says, you're open till seven."

"I know and I apologize. Charley has to close up a little early tonight, I'm sorry."

"Is he not well?"

"Oh, you know our Charley," Helena said, gesturing with her thumb to her mouth, as if she were tippling.

"No, really?" Helena nodded, ushering the woman to the door. "I didn't know. I thought he was an elder and all…"

"Oh, you know how it is. God tests all of us, each in his own way."

The woman stood fast at the doorway, turning. "But when will he be open? Can I come back tomorrow?"

"Oh, no, ma'am. I'm afraid not. Charley is closing the store, I'm afraid"

"For how long?"

"I think he said indefinitely. I'm not sure what he meant by that."

"That's a long time. Tell him that he'll be in my prayers."

"I will, ma'am. God bless you."

Helena returned to the office and sat down in the chair again. "I'm sorry, Charley. Sheila is such a ditz, sometimes." Charley was writing on a pad. He looked up. He had his personal copy, well worn, of the Book on the desk.

"I've been making some calculations," he said. He seemed distracted. "It's a big book, you know. If you're talking about the entire book. Every page?" Helena nodded emphatically. "In real gold?" She nodded again. "Even using gold foil—"

"Oh, no, Mister," Helena interrupted. "No foil."

"Solid gold pages?" he asked in wonder. She nodded again. "The material alone, Helena. This is going to be very expensive."

"In my vision, Charley, God didn't say it would be cheap. What are we talking here?"

"Well, that depends. How thick a page are we talking here?"

"Well, I think it should be substantial, but not ostentatious. The scriptures say gold plates—not too flimsy." He nodded and returned to calculating on the small pad.

He looked up at her with concern. "Helena, I'm sorry. But at today's market costs for gold, just the materials alone will cost almost three hundred thousand dollars."

"Really?"

"Yes. I'm sorry." He looked pained.

"Well, that is a relief. I was afraid you were going to tell me some outrageous number."

"You're okay with three hundred thousand?"

"Oh yes, Charley. In my vision, God told me to budget five hundred thousand dollars, including shipping and insurance, of course." She smiled at him.

"Five hundred thousand?" She nodded.

"I have to know, Charley. I have to know right this second. Will you do it? Will you help me fulfill God's holy plan for me? I pray you will, Charley, I pray you will." Helena dropped from the chair to kneel in front of the desk, praying.

Charley turned red again. "No need for that, Helena. Please, get up. Up in the chair, please." He glanced nervously towards the storefront, concerned a customer might see. He didn't realize Helena had flipped the 'Closed' sign and locked the door behind the last customer.

Helena looked up at him imploringly. She fought the urge to grab his pant leg, not wanting to overplay this. She always overplayed the endgame, she thought. "You'll do it then, Charley? You'll do it?"

Charley stood and pulled her gently to her feet, nodding. "Yes, Helena," he said solemnly. "I'll do it. It is a very righteous thing that you are doing. I believe it is a very righteous mission."

"Bless you, Charley. Bless you." She shook the man's hand vigorously. "My prayers have been answered." They stood awkwardly like that for a minute, then both sat back down.

Charley did more calculating on his pad. "There is a problem with the material, however—"

"Oh, that's no problem at all," Helena said. She peeled off forty thousand dollars from her wallet and placed the neat pile of money on the desk in front of Charley. He gaped at it.

"No, that's not what I meant."

"Oh, don't be embarrassed, Charley. You'll have expenses, to get started. That's just a small down payment, I realize. I'll send the rest as soon as I get home."

"No, that's fine. Really. But that's not what I was going to say. The book, the gold book. This is going to be really, really heavy."

"That's okay, Charley. It's not like I'm going to hold it in my lap and read it or anything. How heavy do you think? I mean, are we talking about something that a young, strong man could strap to his back and carry into the woods? Or are we talking about something that's going to need a forklift? What exactly are we talking here?"

He looked at her, bewildered. "I'm not sure. It depends on the thickness of the pages, of course."

"Because, let's think about this, Charley. I mean, you do believe the story, don't you? The story?"

"What story?"

"That Jesus, after he was crucified, spent those three days he was missing from the cave in upstate New York and buried the Golden Book. And in 1827, a dead guy—"

"—the Angel Moroni—"

"Yeah, him. He helped Joseph Smith discover the book and Joseph Smith dug it up. That story."

"Well, that's not exactly—"

"It's a funny story, don't you think? I mean, finding a solid gold book in 1827, that's a modern day miracle, right? I mean, that's when we had newspapers, and telegraphs, and stuff. And a miracle happens like that, right in the middle of rural New York. You'd think it would be in the papers, 'Neighbor Smith Hits the Lottery', or some such. I mean, Smith could've used that much gold to buy like half of Texas, become an oil baron or something. You believe that happened, though? Don't you?"

"I believe the Scriptures, sure. You believe the story, surely?"

"You have to admit, it's a funny story."

"If you're a Mormon, surely you believe the scriptures as written. You are a Mormon, aren't you, Helena?"

She looked at him, weighing her answer. "I'm not sure, actually."

"Most people know whether or not they are Mormon, Helena."

"I'm an orphan. I'm not sure what I am, religiously and ancestrally speaking."

"Oh, I'm sorry. I didn't know."

"Don't feel bad, it's been a while. I'm pretty much over it now."

"That's good. We must accept our lot in life."

"Yeah, whatever. So what's this thing going to weigh? Because when you consider the story, the story of Joseph Smith lifting it from a hole in the ground and all, I mean, I can see him getting a couple of guys with ropes to help, maybe some kind of ropes and pullies, they had that back then. But if we're talking forklift, Charley, well, I just don't see how that jives with Scripture, as we know it. Do you?" Charley didn't answer, but went back to his calculations. Helena patiently watched him work. Finally, he straightened and smiled at her. "I don't think it's a problem, Helena. Even with fairly solid pages, but making the pages bigger—"

"It's gotta seem like plates, Charley. The scripture says golden plates. No foil for my God, Charley. Not gold plated, either."

"No, of course not. Solid gold. It looks heavy, but not too bad." He looked up at her hopefully. "Just over six hundred seventy ounces."

"Really? Over forty pounds? Of gold?" He nodded. "An impressive book." He nodded again. "Let's do this, Charley!" She sprang from her chair and gave him an inspiring hug.

Charley escorted her towards the front of the store. She stopped and turned, smiling at him.

"Charley, there is one more thing."

"Sure, Helena. What is it?" He was holding the thick wad of thousand dollar bills.

"If we wanted to change the text, in the book I mean. I mean, it is just a replica and all."

Charley looked puzzled. "Change the text? What do you mean?"

"Nothing too big, mind you. I was thinking maybe we could insert just a short series of numbers somewhere, maybe a letter or two. Nothing that would change the storyline or anything."

"Gee, Helena. I don't know. How many numbers are we talking about here?"

"Twelve, that's all. And a couple of letters, all together in a row. Why, do you think that might be sacrilegious?"

"It might be, yeah, Helena. I'm not comfortable with changing the text like that. Was that in your vision, some sort of numerology?"

"No, no, you might be right, Charley. Let me think about it. I mean, we don't want to do something that might make your whole religion just wink out of existence, do we?" She winked at him.

"No," Charley agreed, looking lost again. "We sure don't want to do that."

"I'll send more money in a couple of days, Charley."

"God bless you, Helena."

Helena climbed back in the car. She stopped to fill up the tank and piled the passenger seat with her usual array of cross-country driving junk food. No more stops until she pulled up in her driveway in Half Moon Bay.

"Sorry, Chuck," she said aloud as she accelerated back on I-80. "Maybe it can't be done. I might've lied, after all. Again." She set the cruise control to an even one hundred and stretched. Her bones creaked. She felt ancient. She had done a lot of driving.

"Ladies and gentlemen," Helena intoned in a mock announcer's voice, "the final lap, final lap coming up. Sheehan leads as the white flag comes out and, yes, there she is, with a good two second lead going into the first turn of this, the very—final—lap—ever!" She snapped off the cruise control and smoothly slalomed the car between the sparse traffic; right, left, right, then again into the left lane. A car from the right started to move into the lane in front of her but was scared out of it with a long, angry blast of the Corvette's horn. She was past the guy before he had a chance to give her the finger, a piss yellow blur heading west.

"What the hell are you thinking?" she asked out loud. "Not sure. Not really sure at all," she answered herself. She had felt so confident when she awoke that morning, but doubts were seeping back in. It all seemed too crazy, even to her, when she made herself stop to think about it. The research was real, though. She was sure of that part; she wasn't even the one who had made the original discovery; that was Zeke. That counted for something, right? How could all this be the construct of a sick mind if it was started by someone else? Maybe, though, she'd just twisted what Zeke had found to fit what she wanted to believe. She was pretty sure that that's just what a high functioning schizophrenic would do.

She would be completely confident if she were sure about her sister. The evidence, she had to admit to herself, was pretty circumstantial. Less than circumstantial, actually. She couldn't remember ever talking to her sister, or hearing her voice. But Gabriel had it on tape, and Chuck had said the same thing. He had the tape analyzed, Gabe said. But what did that prove? One side of a conversation with a dead girl, big deal. The wrong side, really. Maybe I was just hallucinating the other voice, during my catatonia. Maybe my sister's voice is just my sick brain activity again, rearing up in my later years despite the shock therapy and the drugs and all the rest. Or maybe because of all that stuff. She didn't know.

"What I do know," she said to the wind, "is I'm going to take my shot. If I'm nuts, and this is all an incredibly complex stupid fabrication of my diseased mind, then Gabriel is better off anyways, before I really do something crazy. And if I'm right, and there's even a chance of this working, well..." She thought hard about that. That part, she realized, if she was right, and the whole complex mechanism miraculously worked, led to what? She didn't have a clue. Funny, that. To think that's the best thing she could hope for.

It was the middle of the night when she pulled into her driveway. The house was dark. She walked in, stripping off her clothes as she went upstairs. Her whole body felt like a giant cramp. She took a long, hot shower to relax the kinks from her muscles. Relieved and exhausted, she put on her favorite flannel pajamas and went to bed, alone in the big bed for the last time.

The next morning, she woke up early. She did her nails, and her hair, and her makeup, like she was going to the Inaugural Ball. She dressed in the new black dress, and the new shoes. They pinched a little, of course. No matter. She studied herself in the mirror. She had to admit, she was impressive for an old girl. "Drop dead gorgeous," the woman in the mirror told her. "Damn straight."

She drove up to the lab, driving in her bare feet. She parked the Corvette in front. The offices were open. She breezed into the main office like it was just another workday.

"Helena!" the secretary exclaimed as she strode in.

"Hey, Faith. How's it going?" she said, trying to sound nonchalant.

"How's it going? You're the first person I've seen in over a week! Is Gabriel with you?"

"Nope."

"Chuck? Arthur?"

"Don't think so. Just me, sugar." Helena tried to move past her towards the labs.

"I don't know what's going on, Helena. Hold up a second." Helena stopped. "Damn, girl!" Faith exclaimed. "You look good. What's up with you?"

"Just another day at the office, Faith. Listen, I'm going to go back in the lab for a while. Is anybody in there? Zeke, Hannah? The techies? Anyone?"

"I told you, Helena, you're the first one I've seen in like, forever. Look at these messages." She indicated stacks of small pink slips on her desk. "There's like a hundred of them. It's out of control here. When is everyone coming back?"

"Soon, Faith. Couple of days, tops. We'll take care of the messages later, okay? Gabriel is really good at that stuff. Don't put any calls through to the back, though. Okay? 'Hold my calls', isn't that what they say?" Faith nodded, concerned. Her boss didn't sound herself, not that she ever was all that normal.

"Better idea," Helena said, turning back to Faith. "Why don't you take the rest of day."

"What, just leave? It's like nine o'clock in the morning, Helena."

"No problem, Faith. You've been working way too hard, while we've been gone, having fun. Go ahead and lock up. As a matter of fact, what day is today?"

"Thursday. You okay, Helena?"

"Fine, fine. Thursday's good. Take the rest of the week, take a nice long weekend. Gabriel and Chuck will be back when you come back on Monday. Have a great weekend."

"What about you?"

"No, I'm going into the lab. I've got work to do."

"I meant, will I see you on Monday?"

"Maybe. Depends, really. Before you go, though, can you do something with the phones?"

"Like what?"

"You know, forward them or put them on voicemail or whatever. So they don't ring. Drives me nuts."

"Sure, Helena. I'll do it before I go. Thanks. I'll see you Monday, then."

"Yeah, Faith. Thanks, great." Helena walked quickly through the security doors to the labs. She came back a second later. "Almost forgot," Helena said, fishing a stack of square, sealed envelopes from her bag and handing them to Faith. "Could you mail these for me?"

Faith looked at the letters. "There's no addresses on them."

"Oh, yeah," Helena said, embarrassed. "I'll leave a list of addresses on your desk. Can you try to get them out on Monday?"

"I can come in over the weekend, if you like."

"No, no. There's no hurry. But here," she said, fishing a tattered piece of yellowed paper from her bag. "I don't have this guy's address. You'll have to call him and get his mailing address, okay?"

"Sure, Helena. No problem. Are you sure you don't want me to stick around, maybe start working on this now?"

"No, go. Go see that boyfriend of yours."

"That was Chuck. We broke up like seven months ago."

"Yeah, of course. Smart move, Faith. He's the Antichrist. Well, have a good weekend. Bye, now." Helena left through the door of the lab again, this time for good. Faith packed up her things and put the phones on forward. She locked the door behind her on the way out.

Gabriel landed in Detroit harried, tired, and totally ticked off. Chuck had done everything short of clubbing him over the head to keep him from going back to San Francisco two days ago. Initially, he had cajoled Arthur and Gabriel to attend "just two more really short meetings." Not even really meetings, Chuck insisted, just a "quick Q and A, to fill in the blanks," whatever that meant. But both meetings had been delayed, and when they finally arrived for the last one, no one else showed. Chuck insisted that he had just screwed up the date and that it was definitely on for first thing the next morning, but by then Gabriel and Arthur had had more than enough. They both announced that they were getting on a plane first thing the next day.

It was then that Chuck remembered his conversation with Helena, wherein she had told him to tell Gabriel that it was very important that he visit his folks as soon as possible, implying that Helena was hinting that both had one foot in the grave and could go at any time. Gabriel almost lost it at that point, demanding whether Chuck had chosen to delay the message until all his precious meetings were done. Chuck was contrite, even helping Gabriel book flights for the next day to Detroit. He relayed Helena's recommendation that Arthur accompany Gabriel to see his parents, but this made no sense to either of them, seeing as Arthur had never met Gabe's parents before, and this probably wasn't a good time to strike up a new friendship, seeing as how most of the time they didn't even know their own son. Chuck volunteered, however, that Gabriel might want his best friend along for moral support, you know, in case the worst were to occur. Or already occurred. Gabriel almost punched Chuck at that point, but settled for pushing him backwards into the closet and wedging the door shut for two hours while he and Arthur got dinner. Arthur grabbed a redeye that night for San Francisco, first class.

Gabriel would've landed in Detroit a whole day earlier if further delays hadn't occurred. He had made the mistake of accepting Chuck's offer to drive him to the airport in his government rental car, believing Chuck's argument that it would take almost an hour less than the shuttle. But Chuck had insisted on a brief stop in Adams Morgan to buy something he ended up at the last minute deciding he really didn't need, and then proceeded to get hopelessly lost trying to find the Belt Expressway, which, once found, turned out to be snarled with the worst rush hour traffic Gabriel had ever witnessed. By the time Chuck pulled up to the curbside check-in, Gabriel was late to the point of panic stricken. He tore through the airport, stood interminably in the security line, and ran pell-mell down the concourse to fling himself at the gate just in time to see the plane backing away. He waited another two hours for Chuck to come back and pick him up. The next morning, this morning, he insisted on getting to the airport on his own.

Once landed in Detroit, of course, they had lost his reservation at the rental car desk and had no car available. He would have throttled the clerk, except he realized at the moment just before he launched himself over the counter that it was actually his own fault, seeing as the car had been rented for the day before and Gabriel hadn't remembered to change it. Eventually, having secured "the very last car on the lot" from another agency, he sat in bumper-to-bumper traffic northbound on I-275. If he had a gun, many would have died that day.

Gabriel's visit with his parents wasn't quite the familial bliss expected of the prodigal son's return, either. Just as the last time Gabriel had visited, his parents spent the first ten minutes thinking he was the orderly and berating him for removing their lunch trays before they were finished. Once he had secured them late trays (they had both slept through lunch), their moods improved to the point where he was able to convince them that he was, indeed, their son. Yes, indeed, he still lived all the way away in California and no, he didn't have any immediate plans of moving back to Ann Arbor even though, yes, he did realize that they were all the family he had in the world.

The rest of the visit was spent listening to his parents sing the praises of Helena, who, according to his parents, he had just missed, as she left only like two hours ago. This piqued Gabriel's interest for a bit, briefly hoping that he might actually be in the same city as his wife. He was quickly disabused of this hope, however, when the real orderly came for the trays and explained that Helena had given him a hundred dollar tip for taking such good care of her in-laws, a full two days ago. At that, Gabriel heaved his fiftieth soul-cleansing sigh of the last forty-eight hours and said his goodbyes to his mom and dad, promising to visit again soon if they didn't die first.

As he was bending to give his dad a kiss, however, Gabriel noticed the letter on the nightstand, the letter he had overnighted for his wife. He picked it up and saw it had been opened. Obviously, Helena had read it, but it puzzled him that she would just leave it there on the stand. He took out the card he had written. In the envelope, he saw, was a business card that he knew he hadn't put in there. It was a card of a professor of mathematics here at the University of Michigan. Helena had left it, but why? Gabriel sighed once again and pocketed the card. His parents were already asleep as he left.

Gabriel felt in no mood for any more games. What he wanted, the only thing he wanted, was to be home with his wife. The card bothered him, though. He was only ten minutes from the man's office. Besides, his flight to San Francisco wasn't until tomorrow morning. He decided it wouldn't hurt to at least pay the professor a visit.

The professor proved to be in his office, a well-worn academic space filled with stacks of articles and dark wooden bookshelves lined with arcane texts. Gabriel bent over the desk to shake the man's hand. He noticed an ornate, carved ivory pipe sitting in an immaculate ashtray on the professor's desk.

"You smoke?" Gabriel asked the older man, gesturing to the pipe.

"I don't think so," the Professor answered. "Not yet, anyway. A young woman thought I should take it up. She was so pretty, I thought she might be right." He blushed.

"Kind of strange that some pretty woman thought it would be a good idea if you got throat cancer," Gabriel said. "Nice pipe, though. My grandfather used to have one. Smelled great."

"Really? I can't find tobacco for it yet."

"Don't. He died breathing through a tube. It was horrible."

"Oh. Thanks for that." He moved the ashtray to the side of the desk.

"Thank you for seeing me without an appointment, Professor. I know you must be busy," Gabriel said.

"Must I? I'm a mathematics professor. I wouldn't call my schedule hectic."

"You don't have to teach a class soon or anything, do you? I'm not imposing?"

"You obviously never went to this university, if you think a professor of mathematics teaches class."

"Actually, Professor, I did. I got my PhD here."

"Really? In math? I don't remember you, I'm afraid."

"Oh no, we've never met, Professor. I was in the biophysics department. No reason why you should remember me."

"Oh, good. Because I don't. What is it I can do for you, Mr. Sheehan?"

"I'm not sure, Professor. This may be something of a wild goose chase, I'm afraid. I found your card in a letter I sent to my wife."

"And now you suspect that we are having an affair," the elderly man said, smiling.

Gabriel smiled back. "No, that wasn't the first thing that occurred to me, Professor. But I'll keep that in mind, just in case. No, I was wondering if—"

"Oh, oh!" the professor interjected. "I know who you are! You must be Gabriel. You're the husband of the pretty redhead who came to visit me a couple of days ago."

"Yes, I guess I am. That would be my wife, Helena. She was here?"

"Helena, you say? I don't think she ever told me her name. But she said that you'd be stopping by to see me. I didn't expect you so soon. We had a very pleasant conversation. She's a very knowledgeable young lady, a very insightful mind. Is she a mathematician?"

"No," Gabriel said, and then on further consideration, "at least, I don't think so."

"You're married recently, then?"

"Something over twenty years, actually."

"Oh."

"Did she say why I would be stopping by?" Gabriel asked.

"Why, no she didn't. I guess she assumed that you would know why you would be stopping by. You know, since you're the one doing the stopping by. You don't know?"

"No, I don't think so." This led to an uncomfortable silence.

"She is quite lovely, your wife. Charming, really. You are a lucky man, Mr. Sheehan," the professor ventured, attempting to rescue the conversation. "She's the one who thought I'd look good holding a Meerschaum."

Gabriel was a bit adrift. "I'm sorry, a what?"

"The pipe. She though it would make me look more professorial."

"I'm sure it does. Just don't light it."

"She said she wished she had the time to mail me some tobacco, from Ireland she said. She said they had the best leaf in Ireland, Peterson's I think she called it. She seemed genuinely sad that she wouldn't be able to send me some. Lovely girl, very thoughtful."

Gabriel wasn't really following, lost in thought. He looked around the small office. "What type of mathematician are you, professor?"

"Old and doddering, I'm afraid." He was playing with the pipe.

"No, I mean what field is your specialty?" Gabriel asked, frowning at the man.

"Oh, you wouldn't understand."

"Maybe if you just give me the general idea."

"My interest is in an area of topology. You know topology?"

"Yes, sure. Mathematics of shapes, right?"

"Yes, I suppose that that's the high school definition. It's a little more involved than that, but no matter. Anyway, my research concerns the dynamics on Teichmuller spaces. Got that?"

"Never heard of it."

"Didn't think so."

"Why would I want to meet with you if I don't even understand what it is you do?"

"I think that's the question I asked you when you came in, as I recall. Why don't you ask your wife? She seems very knowledgeable."

"I'd like to. Do you know where she is?"

"You give me too much credit, I'm afraid."

"I mean, did she mention where she was going? When she left?"

"I don't think so. Oh, I think she mentioned that she had to get home. Something like that. That she had to be going, she had a very long drive home, she said."

Gabriel thanked the man for his time and said goodbye. He kept the card. Sitting in his rental car outside the mathematics building, he tried calling his home. No answer. He called the lab next, but it went straight to voicemail. Voicemail in the middle of the day, on a Thursday? What the hell was going on? He didn't have a clue. He just had to get home, he thought. He was sure that Helena would have some answers when he got home.

CHAPTER 25

Helena sat down at Gabriel's desk and started his computer. She typed in his password, "Penny4"; he hadn't changed it in twenty years. She spent a half hour creating an address list for Faith. Most of the addresses she either had in her address book or could find easily by searching online. A few she had to leave for Faith, but she was confident the secretary would find them; she was tenacious with projects like that. She printed out the list and left it on Faith's desk. She returned to Gabriel's computer and arranged to have three hundred fifty thousand dollars wired to Charley the jeweler in Salt Lake City. Helena figured that that was an amount of money that should guarantee that the man didn't abandon her project, maybe even shame him into working extra hard. She emailed Charley the instructions on where to ship the finished book. Gabriel would flip, she thought. She had drained the better part of a million dollars from their joint account in the last twenty-four hours. Well, she thought, that's how you keep a marriage exciting.

Next, she made her signs. Nothing fancy, just the biggest font she could fit on the page. She printed out six copies and took them from the printer. On a whim, she added a large skull and crossbones to each, the only thing she was ever really good at drawing. On a couple, she added a few X's and O's, as well as some pink hearts. These she taped securely in various strategic locations around the lab.

Helena checked the time and thought she was doing fine. She shut down Gabriel's computer and walked back to her own lab, now dark and empty. She clicked on the lights in the control room and sat down at her own computer, turning it on and typing in her password, "YourThoughts". She pulled up the movie file she had made several weeks ago. It had taken her almost a full day's study to learn how to do it and get it right. She ran it again just to make sure. It was perfect, she hoped. She couldn't really be sure. She ported it over to the other computer in the lab, the one used to collect the recordings from subjects. Helena then erased the original file from the computer she was sitting at. She reached under the console and pulled all the connections to the computer, then pulled the computer itself out from its niche. She popped the case and removed the hard drive. Closing the case, she put the computer back in its place.

Helena carried the drive to the break room and placed it in a shallow bowl of water in the microwave. She set the oven to one hour and scurried out of the room to escape the crackling sparks emanating from the machine. From here, she went to the utility closet and got the coil of black plastic tubing she had bought at the hardware store three weeks ago, hoisting it on her shoulder, and grabbed the roll of duct tape in her free hand. She carried all this back to the lab, where she secured one end of the hose to the console with duct tape. She opened the window and tossed the rest of the coil outside. She closed the window again as far as she could, then sealed the gap with more duct tape. Love this stuff, she thought.

On her way back to the front of the lab, she stopped back at the utility closet and opened the alarm panel. She wasn't completely certain that this step was necessary, but she didn't want the whole deal ruined by some ill-timed siren going off or an automatic call to the fire department. This was California, after all, she thought. The building code probably required alarms for anything even mildly annoying, like more than three libertarians in the building at once. She disarmed everything she could find and closed the box.

On her way out the back door, she had a brief instant of panic as she started to let the door close behind her. She realized in that moment that she was about to lock herself out, and leapt back to grab the door, breaking a nail in the process. She stared at the ruined nail and fought back tears. She then wedged the door open with a nearby rock. Making her way around the building, Helena found the coil of tubing and dragged the end to the generator. She attached the end to the generator's exhaust manifold, sealing the connection with a copious amount of duct tape. Love this stuff, she thought.

Back inside, she sucked at her finger and mourned her flawed manicure. She willed herself to move on, emotionally. At this point, she had planned to kill the power, but now thought better of it. Better check first, she thought. She went back to her lab and set up the subject chair in front of the white board, just so. She adjusted the camera, watching herself on the monitors to be sure everything was perfectly aligned. Test run, she thought. She cued the recorders, smiled at the camera, and waited. Nothing. She cued the camera again, waited again, and again, nothing. "Well, fuck me sideways," she cursed aloud. It took her over an hour of troubleshooting to realize that the system wouldn't record without a hard drive either in the lab computer or the main—one she had fried and the other tossed in the ocean. "Fucking Sabras!" she screamed to the lab, realizing the crazy Israeli brothers had set up the system so that no data would accidentally go unbacked up. She checked the time again—this was starting to take too long. At some point, she realized, either Gabriel, or Chuck, maybe both, would come strolling in. If they returned too soon, she'd have a little difficulty explaining the changes she'd made to the lab.

She thought about driving over to the computer store to buy another drive, but rejected this as just too awful to think about; braving rush hour traffic to face some computer nerds dressed like this was not in the cards. She opted for plan B, cannibalizing Gabriel's computer for its hard drive. He'd figure it out eventually, she thought. She repaired the computer in her lab and tried again. This time, the little red light came on and she could see her image on the monitors. Finally, she thought. She checked the time again and cursed. Deep, relaxing breaths. There was still so much to do.

Helena pulled two amplifiers from the console in the spare lab and wired them with jumpers into the console of her own. Time to test the brainwave recordings. She would use the supersensitive full skull electrode array, wired through the extra amplification system and cranked to the max. This was not time for halfway measures, she thought. Not like I'm likely to try this again if Gabriel doesn't get a clean recording the first time. The lab hummed as she lit up the power across the console and cranked the gain across the dozen sliders to ten. Next time, we get the amps that go to eleven, she thought, smiling. She watched the waves parade in lockstep across the multiple monitors in the lab, adjusting the filter sliders to clean the baseline signal. She'd done all this several hundred times before, but still kept worrying that it wasn't quite right. After ten minutes, however, she was convinced the recording equipment was functioning perfectly.

Time to kill the power? she wondered. One more test, she thought. She sat in the subject chair and started to pull on the electrode skullcap. "Holy shit," she said aloud. It didn't fit. She looked at her image on the monitors. The skullcap array stretched over her mountain of red hair, looking like a campy Martian beehive from some fifties sci-fi movie. She watched the tracings on the monitor, squishing her mountain of hair against her scalp. The tracings jumped and jiggled. "No fucking way," she lamented. She pulled off the skullcap and stared at it. Helena dropped the skullcap on the floor and sighed deeply. She looked up at the camera and triggered the recording.

"Hi, guys," she said brightly. I have to do a little something with my hair in a bit, for the recording. I thought it would be a good idea, though, for everyone to see just how great I look, you know, before I start this whole thing." She stood, curtsied slightly to the camera, and gave a model's half turn. She looked coquettishly over her shoulder at the camera. "Not bad, huh? Damn straight. Just so you know what you're missing, honey. I'll be right back." She killed the recorder and sat, sighing again heavily.

With resigned steps, Helena made her way back to the living quarters behind Gabriel's office, Chuck's little home. She went in the bathroom and marveled at how clean and neat the man kept it. She pawed through his toiletries to find what she needed and finally sat heavily on the small stool in front of the mirror. Helena stared at herself in the mirror for a full minute, gathering her courage. Then she took the scissors and began to cut. After twenty minutes of heartbreaking cutting and shaving, she sat in the middle of a corona of bright red curls surrounding her on the floor about the stool. Her scalp was pink, and shiny, and bald. She threw the razor into the sink and stared in the mirror. "If you start crying," she said to herself, "you'll just have to redo your mascara." She did anyway.

It was finally time. Helena thought that she would be scared, but she wasn't at all. Actually, she was excited about what she was about to do. She was a little sad, of course. She felt bad for Gabriel. He would be fine, she told herself. He would be busy with the work, that would get him through. It always had before. He would be fine. She hoped he would be fine. If not fine, she hoped he would at least understand. She really thought he would at least understand. Eventually.

Helena went back to the utility room and opened the electrical panel. She pulled the main breakers and waited. The lights went off, the room went black. She listened, but only heard the sound of her own breathing. It seemed much longer, but twenty seconds later Helena heard the generator fire up. The lights flickered back to life. "Showtime," she said aloud.

Helena returned to her lab and closed the door. She sealed the cracks with duct tape. I love this stuff, she thought. She checked the console, then the monitors. The lights were all lit, the tracings straight and rock steady. All was ready. Helena took her seat in the subject's cubicle, carefully positioning herself in the monitor. She saw herself, bald and frail looking, in the monitor. Helena had a fleeting image of herself lying in a casket, surrounded by white silk padding. She thought she looked like a little dead bird, fallen from the nest. She scrunched her eyes shut tightly and willed the image away. When she opened her eyes again, she avoided looking back at the monitor. She picked up the electrode array and carefully donned the skullcap, checking the tracings. They immediately began to dance and jump across the screens arrayed around the lab. She caught sight of herself in the monitors and pulled the cap off again, shuddering.

Helena took the small piece of paper from her bag. She had carried it with her every day since her wedding night. Now it was so old and worn that the writing was almost illegible. It didn't matter; she had long ago committed the lines to memory. She remembered the moment when Gabriel had given it to her as his wedding gift, the worried and expectant expression he had worn, watching her face as she read his poem for the first time. She had loved it, straight off. Her second thought, she was ashamed to admit, had been to wonder if he wrote it himself. He was, after all, an engineer. As best she knew, the only other thing Gabriel had ever written were grant proposals and research papers. She felt a little guilty, thinking back over the years to how many times she had asked him if he really had written it himself. Pretty much every anniversary, actually. Was it in a fortune cookie you found? she'd asked one year. Every time she asked, no matter how kindly, he looked a little hurt. Helena had gone so far as to do a computer search for the poem, but no, it seemed to be original. She looked at his writing, now faded. He didn't even know it was a haiku, probably still didn't know what a haiku was. He had the arrangement all wrong. She kissed the little piece of paper lightly. She sat up straight, took a deep breath, then another. It was time. She squeezed the paper tight in her fist. She missed him already. "Showtime," she whispered to herself. She triggered the recorder, and smiled.

CHAPTER 26

Gabriel dragged himself up the walk to his home. He had fallen asleep in the taxi from the airport, awaking with a start from some nightmare that he couldn't remember. He opened the door and stepped inside, calling his wife's name. There was no reply. He noticed, then, the trail of clothes leading up the stairway. His heart leapt as he realized that Helena and he were finally back together. He dropped his bags and followed the trail upstairs, picturing his wife waiting for him in their bed. Instead, he was crestfallen to see the trail end in a pile of damp towels on the bathroom floor, the bed rumpled but empty. It wasn't the first time he had been so disappointed; it would be the last.

He went to the kitchen and started to make himself a sandwich. As he cobbled together stale bread and old pastrami, he cradled the phone on his shoulder. He called the lab, again without success; straight to voicemail. He called Arthur's house. Arthur answered, welcomed him back from the purgatory they had endured with Chuck. No, he answered, he hadn't seen Helena or Chuck, yet. But he hadn't been by the office or the lab, deathly afraid that he might run into Chuck. He wasn't ready for that, not for a couple more days. He was planning to stop by on Monday. Was everything okay?

Gabriel thought it was, and told his friend so. He told him that he'd see him Monday at the lab, give his best to Sam. He hung up and walked around the empty house, finishing the sandwich. He dropped onto the couch and fell asleep again, mentally cursing his jetlag.

When Gabriel awoke, the house was dark. He had a vague impression of another nightmare, or the same nightmare again, but it was only the impression and he could recall no specifics. His legs were cramping and his neck in spasm. He stretched as he walked around the house, turning on lights. He looked at his watch and was shocked to see he had slept almost six hours. Damn westbound jetlag, he cursed again. Gabriel walked around the house, looking to see if his wife had come home, but found no sign of her. For the ten thousandth time since he had met her, he pulled out his cellphone with the intention of calling to find out where she was, cursed himself for an idiot, and put it back in his pocket. He dropped back onto the couch and tried to imagine where his wife might be. He drew a complete blank.

He couldn't just sit and wait for her. He had a pain in the pit of his stomach, a feeling he hadn't known for many years. It was the physical ache he got when he and Helena had fought, or were apart, or he feared for his partner's well being. He had that feeling now, and he was sick with worry. He pulled on a jacket and got in the car.

Gabriel headed for San Francisco. He knew where she wasn't, no sense dropping by at Arthur's. He was certain that Arthur would've called to bring him over if she had shown up at their place. He could think of only one other possibility, and though he couldn't come up with any reason for her to be there, he headed for the lab on Embarcadero.

Gabriel parked behind a yellow Corvette he had never seen before and looked at the lab building. Lights were on inside, but there was something different about them that he couldn't quite identify. His unease grew, and he felt like someone was standing on his chest. He tried the door, found it locked. Gabriel fumbled with his keys, unlocked the door and went inside. The front office looked fine, Faith's desk piled with letters and messages. An unusual smell, he noticed. Gabriel headed for the door leading back to his office and stopped dead, staring at a crude sign on the door; a skull and crossbones. Obviously, Helena's skull and crossbones; the vision of his wife drawing the same image on a bag of unsafe rope came to him in that moment. The sign made no sense to him: DANGER! POISON GAS! STAY OUT!

Gabriel opened the door and immediately sensed the smell was stronger. Not overwhelming, but definitely the smell of exhaust. He still couldn't make any sense of the situation, turning on more lights as he headed back to his office. His office door was shut, the same sign on the door but this one adorned with pink hearts and scrawled in marker: "Hey DUMBSHIT, didn't you read the first sign?" He opened the door, sat at his desk. No Helena, no notes. He tried to turn on his computer, see if there was some sort of message, but it wouldn't even turn on. What the hell? he thought. Suddenly, his head swam and his vision grayed out. Holy shit, he thought, I'm passing out. He hadn't felt like this since he passed out in the shower many years ago, when he had had pneumonia. Helena had found him slumped in the shower that time, turned the water on full cold and nearly given him a heart attack. Heart attack, he thought, and suddenly the signs made sense to him, or some kind of sense. He wasn't sure exactly what was happening, but now knew he was in trouble. He had an intense pain in his chest, he couldn't breathe. He thought he was probably dying. "Helena's gonna kill me," he said aloud, stumbling to the door, pulling his phone from his pocket. He dialed 911, and passed out.

Gabriel awoke on the sidewalk with a headache that felt like he had been hit on the head with an axe. He was wearing an oxygen mask. He turned his head and nearly threw up.

"Whoa there, cowboy," a strange voice said. "Just relax and suck on the oxygen. In with the good, out with the evil carbon monoxide gas, amigo." Gabriel looked into the eyes of the EMT bending over him. Gabriel was utterly confused. She gave him a sad smile.

Gabriel was having a hard time putting the pieces together. At first, he couldn't remember where he was. He looked around at all the flashing red lights, at what looked like an army of firemen and paramedics milling about. Had there been a fire at the lab? he wondered. His head was clearing rapidly now, the intense pain between his eyes subsiding to the worst headache he'd ever had in his life. He was remembering now; he had been sitting in his office. He remembered the signs, Helena's scrawl:

'Hey, DUMBSHIT,' he remembered. "Helena?" he said to no one in particular, but now Arthur was at his side, holding his hand. He looked so sad, stricken.

"She's inside, Gabriel," Arthur said. "She's gone."

Gabriel looked into the eyes of his friend, not comprehending but sensing his friend's pain, bile rising into the back of his throat. "What do you mean?" he managed to ask. Arthur could only shake his head and squeeze harder on Gabriel's hand. Gabriel closed his eyes. He let his head fall back on the sidewalk, felt the tears spilling down the sides of his head, and wished he were dead.

It was two hours before the firemen let him in to see her. They hadn't moved her. She still sat slumped in the chair in the little booth, the monitors still alive around her. The monitors were alive, but they bore cruel witness to the fact that Helena was not, tracing a steady flatline across their screens. Gabriel sat on the floor, looking at her face. She had shaved her head, he saw. Why would she shave her head? he wondered. She looked peaceful, he thought. No, not peaceful, something better: happy. Or relieved. She looked the way he remembered her looking when she had discovered something important, when things had fallen into place. She looked, he thought, seeing her face clearly now, exactly like that moment on our wedding night, that moment when she had finished reading his poem for the first time, and looked up at him with such pride, and love, and hope for the future. That was how she looked now, he thought. And then he started to cry again.

His friend Arthur was there, his hand on Gabriel's shoulder, squeezing. Gabriel blinked back tears, made an effort to compose himself. For the briefest moment the thought occurred to him that they were all wrong, that his wife wasn't dead—it was one of her spells. They didn't know about her spells, only he did. He was going to say this, explain it to the EMT's milling about, tell them to check her vital signs. But then Gabriel looked again at the monitors, and a lifetime of work brought his world crashing back down, convincing him utterly that his Helena had really left him.

He stood and walked over to her, touched her cheek. He pulled off the monitor skullcap and marveled again that she was bald. For the first time in his life, he saw the scars at each temple, the spots where, as a child, the electrodes had been applied over and over again. In life, Helena never wore her hair short.

He touched her hand. Her left hand was clenched so tightly that she had drawn a small drop of blood, where a broken nail had pierced her palm. He gently uncurled her fingers and saw the little piece of paper escape and flutter to the floor. He kissed her on the forehead and said goodbye.

The invitations began to arrive the following week. Gabriel sat at his kitchen table, his mouth open in disbelief as he read it. "A Wake for our Dear, Beloved Wife and Friend, Helena" it said. The date was in ten days time, the location her adopted father's bar in Boston. Gabriel managed to close his mouth and shake his head in wonder. He realized that the phone was ringing, and stood to answer it.

"This betta be one of 'er sick, fucking jokes, Gabriel," the gruff voice said on the other end, before Gabriel even had the chance to say hello. Gabriel recognized the voice immediately. He couldn't speak. "Gabriel? Are you there?"

"I'm here, Dad. I'm sorry, it's no joke. We lost her, last week. I'm sorry I didn't call you. I haven't really called anybody, yet."

"Oh, dear Jesus," the old man on the phone said softly in reply. They were both silent for several minutes. Finally, the voice said, "I'll get ready, Gabriel. You don't worry about a thing; I'll take care of this. I don't know how I'll tell my missus. This'll near to kill her." He paused again. "You take care of yourself, Gabriel. I'll see you at the wake. Dear, sweet Jesus." He hung up.

The phone kept ringing but after a few subdued conversations, Gabriel had to stop answering. He didn't have the strength. The funeral had been simple, and brief. The only attendants had been Gabriel, Arthur's immediate family, Chuck, and the people from the lab; less than twenty in all. Little was said. Chuck had tried to speak to him on several occasions, at the funeral and since, but Gabriel couldn't face the man. Gabriel knew it was unfair, but in his heart he felt that it was partly Chuck's fault that his wife was dead. He felt that if Chuck hadn't manipulated him so in DC, he would have been home to save his wife. He knew this was unfair, that Helena was as much to blame as Chuck, probably more so. He stilled blamed him, nonetheless.

Insistent knocking at the front door roused Gabriel from his quiet spot at the kitchen table. He opened the door to Chuck, tried to slam it in the man's face. Arthur's hand stopped it from hitting Chuck in the nose.

"What is it, Arthur?" Gabriel asked, ignoring the other man.

Arthur and Chuck came in and settled themselves on the couch. Gabriel sat resignedly across from them. "What?" he asked again.

Chuck fidgeted, finally gathering the nerve to speak. "You have to come to the lab, Gabriel. She left a recording."

Gabriel hadn't been back to the lab since his wife's death. Actually, except for the funeral, he hadn't left the house. He allowed himself to be led back to her lab, in a daze. Chuck sat him down in front of the console. Chuck had removed all evidence of that night, returning the lab to its prior state as much as he could. He had found Gabriel's hard drive in the lab computer and returned it to its proper place, wondering why Helena had switched it. Chuck had done some experimenting, discovered what Helena had found regarding the backup system, and replaced the lab computer's hard drive with a new one.

"It took me a couple of days to figure it all out," Chuck explained to Arthur and Gabriel as they all sat in the lab control room. "She did some weird shit with the amps. Look at this," he said, showing them the additional equipment Helena had wired into the system. "Who knew the chick knew anything about high fidelity recording, huh?" He looked at them both, but Arthur only winced and Gabriel looked lost. "Anyways, the changes were pretty sophisticated. She was going for a super clean recording. That's why she shaved her head, used the skullcap and all."

"What recording?" Gabriel asked, seeming to come awake.

"The whole thing seems like some sort of twisted experiment," Chuck said. "Or maybe just a crazy suicide note, I'm not sure. I tried to tell you at the funeral, and like thirty times since. She made a recording."

"Show me," Gabriel said flatly.

"Gabe," Arthur said, "I've seen the first part. I gotta tell you, it's pretty disturbing. Are you sure this is the time? We can do this—"

"I'm here, aren't I?" Gabriel snapped. "Let's see it."

Chuck dimmed the lights and started the recording. Helena's smiling face, crowned with her full head of fiery red hair, filled the half dozen monitors around them. Chuck killed all except the large main screen in front of them.

She looked happy. She looked great, actually. "Hi, guys," she said brightly. " I have to do a little something with my hair in a bit, for the recording. I thought it would be a good idea, though, for everyone to see just how great I look, you know, before I start this whole thing. Not bad, huh? Damn straight. Just so you know what you're missing, honey. I'll be right back."

There was a jump and then she was back, her head now shaved. She smiled into the camera weakly.

"Oh, my god!" Chuck exclaimed. "She has cancer! Oh, I didn't even know. The poor, brave girl." Without a word, Gabriel smacked Chuck solidly upside the back of his head. "Ow! What?" Chuck complained. "She looks like a dying little bird. No wonder she couldn't go on." Gabriel hit him again. "Ow, stop doing that!" Chuck insisted.

"Then shut the fuck up," Gabriel replied, still not taking his eyes from the screen. Gabriel thought Helena looked like she was gathering her strength, as if to start a leap across some yawning chasm.

"Actually," Chuck continued more quietly, "she looks pretty hot bald, don't you think, Arthur?" Arthur smacked him this time.

"Okay, guys, I'm back. It's showtime. I'm sorry, Gabriel. I truly am. I love you and miss you more than life itself." She gave a little pouty smile at this. "I have to do this. Believe me, honey, if there were any other way, I would've killed off Chuck instead." She smiled again, this time her characteristic impish grin. "Hi, Chuck." She gave a little wave. Chuck gave a little involuntary wave back and then, embarrassed, dropped his hand back in his lap.

"It is truly fortuitous that you're here with your friends, Gabriel. Truly fortuitous. We are lucky to have a friend like Arthur. Arthur, you're a dear. Give my love to Sam and stay well. I know you'll get my Gabriel through this. You remember to take care of yourself, too.

"I hope Faith mailed the invitations. I know things have been a little hectic over there the past few days, but if she didn't send them yet, tell her to get her skinny little ass in gear. And she better not open them! Chuck, you screwed up big time with her, let me tell you. Too late now, though. Anyways, it's going to be a hell of a party. I wish I could be there, really."

Chuck paused the recording. "Party? What party? What is she talking about?"

"I think she's talking about how badly you played Faith," Arthur said.

"Not that, idiot. What party?" Chuck asked again.

"Shut up and restart the thing," Gabriel said gravely. Chuck hit the play switch and Helena came back to life.

"Don't worry, Chuck, you're invited. I just hid your invitation under your bed, just to screw with you. Even in death, what a card, huh?"

"Your wife has a sick sense of humor," Chuck whispered.

"Had," Gabriel said. "And shut up."

"Damn, boys," Helena continued. "I gotta tell you, I'm not feeling the least bit sleepy yet. I thought I'd be halfway gone by now," she said, turning her head to check the lab clock. "Didn't really plan a whole show, to tell you the truth. Gotta kill some time here...let me think.

"Okay, how about a song? Here's a lovely old Irish tune I'm sure you'll remember from those happy childhood days spent having the crap smacked out of you during chorus time. Here goes." Helena took a deep breath and, with hands folded primly in her lap, launched into an acapella rendition of Amazing Grace, the acoustics of the studio perfectly reflecting her pure, sweet alto. The three of them listened intently, all three on the verge of crying.

"Shit, Gabriel," Chuck squeaked, "your wife could sing."

"Like the fucking angel of death," Gabriel said softly.

On the screen, Helena took a deep breath and said, "Now listen carefully, this is my very favorite verse:

T'was Grace that taught...
My heart to fear.
And Grace, my fears relieved.
How precious did that Grace appear...
the hour I first believed."

Onscreen, Helena paused. She looked over at the clock. "Oh, Jesus, Mary, and Joseph," she swore in her brogue. "I don't feel a bit like dyin' yet. Okay, same song again, but it's so much prettier, I think, in Irish." She then started the song again, this time singing in her native tongue. It was much prettier, Gabriel thought. Chuck was sobbing and searched for tissues. He blew his nose noisily.

They watched as Helena took a deep, shuddering breath. "Okay, that's more like it. I definitely feel a touch of carbon monoxide poisoning coming on." They saw her don the skullcap, then check the monitors. "Looks good, Gabriel. I think this is going to work. It better, because I'm going to have a heckuva time arranging a do-over." She took another deep breath. "Okay, Chuck, I better get this out of the way first. I know I promised, and I tried, I really and truly did. I don't know for sure if I got it done, though. If not—your problem, not mine, I guess. Just listen carefully, because here it is: Have faith, and don't be a fucking moron. Got that? I'm getting a little dizzy here, so I'm not sure if that came out right. I just hope you got it. Chuck? It's fortuitously in the golden book, too. You got that, you moron? I hope so, because I can't make it any plainer than that, partner. I wanted to put it in chapter 666, that would've been just so poetic, you know? Couldn't get it to work, though; wrong book, would've changed the whole thing and then who knows what would happen. I sure as hell don't, I tell you. Charley would've had a conniption. Anyway, if you want it, it's there waiting for you. I hope. Unless Jesus really fucked it up, in which case, I lied. I tried. If it didn't work, blame Jesus, not me."

"Why is she using a Spanish accent?" Chuck asked, then ducked just in time to avoid the attempted dope slaps of both Arthur and Gabriel.

Helena's usually alabaster complexion was becoming noticeably cherry red on the screen. "Okay, guys, I think it's time for me to die now. I love you, Gabe. Every day; then, now, and forever. I love you. I pray this works."

Onscreen, Helena closed her eyes and let her head lay back against the study chair. She looked calm, and peaceful, and happy. Suddenly, her eyes snapped open and she raised her head to look straight at the camera. "Gabe," she said, slurring her words slightly, "Don't forget about the party. It's really important, babe. Don't be la—" And then her eyes closed again and she let her head fall softly back against the headrest.

She was smiling. She was moving her lips, saying something that they couldn't hear. The tracings on the monitor danced. They watched her as she breathed deeply, then less deeply, and then, finally, not at all. After a few minutes, Chuck stopped the recording.

Finally, Arthur asked, "What did she pray would work?"

"I don't know," Gabriel said.

"Why did she keep calling me a fucking moron?" Chuck asked, visibly hurt.

"Probably because you're a fucking moron," Arthur said.

"Maybe. Maybe not," Gabriel said cryptically. "Play it again, Chuck."

"What?" Arthur said. "Why? I don't want—"

"Then leave, Arthur," Gabriel snapped. "Play it again."

Chuck shrugged and restarted the recording. "From the beginning?"

"Yeah," Gabriel said, watching with his head in his hands. They watched and listened from the beginning. At the point where Helena returned with her head shaved, Gabriel grabbed Chuck's arm, saying, "Freeze it."

"What?" Chuck asked. "Why?"

"Just freeze it. Can you do that for me?" Gabriel asked.

"Sure," Chuck said, tapping a button on the console. The image of Helena froze on the monitor. Gabriel got up out of his chair and walked into the subject recording studio. He came back a minute later, visibly angry. "Chuck," he barked. "Why did you erase the board?"

"What board? What are you talking about, Gabe?" Chuck asked.

"Look," Gabriel said harshly, stabbing a finger at the monitor. "Behind her."

They all leaned forward to stare closely at the screen. Behind Helena, on the whiteboard, was clearly written a lengthy and complex mathematical formula.

"Shit, Gabriel," Chuck said. "I didn't see that." Chuck stood and began to walk over to the studio.

"It's not there," Gabriel said, grabbing Chuck's arm. "Someone erased it. Who would do that, Chuck? Who else was in here, besides you?"

Chuck yanked his arm away and went into the studio. He returned a few minutes later.

"Well?" Gabriel demanded.

"It was never there, Gabriel," Chuck answered. "I just checked. There's no erasure marks or anything. It was never there."

Gabriel stabbed his finger into the monitor. "Look! It's right there. You erased it. Why?"

Chuck raised his voice back, saying "It was never there, Gabe. I didn't erase anything. She green-screened it. It's just a video trick."

This brought silence. "You're sure?" Arthur asked. Gabriel stared at the screen, fuming.

"Yeah," Chuck continued. "I missed it before, but I'm sure that's what she did. That's why she did the recording in front of the screen. It was never really there."

"Why?" Arthur asked.

"No clue," Chuck answered.

"Start the recording. I want to watch it all the way through."

They watched the entire recording twice more. Throughout the recording, Helena's head obscured the central portion of the equation. "Damn," Arthur said.

"No, she did it on purpose," Gabriel said. "For some reason, she didn't want us to see that part of the equation."

"Why would she bother to project the equation and then carefully block part of it? It makes no sense," Arthur said.

"Hold it," Chuck said. "I have an idea. If she used the lab computer to generate the effect, the equation might be on the hard drive. I just need to—oh. Oh, shit."

"What?" Gabriel asked. "What's wrong?"

"I just figured out why there's a molten heap of metal in the microwave," Chuck said.

"Shit," Arthur said.

They sat through the recording six more times, but found nothing new. Arthur was shaken, and said he had to get home, promising to call Gabriel in the morning. Chuck eventually drifted to his room behind Gabriel's office. Gabriel sat at the console, watching his wife's last moments on earth, over and over again.

CHAPTER 27

Chuck couldn't sleep. He tossed and turned in his bed, hearing and seeing Helena's recording in his head. He finally threw aside his covers and shuffled back to Helena's old lab. The lights were still on, the console lit. Gabriel was asleep at the console, head resting on his arms, nearly touching the image of his wife, frozen in death on the monitor by his head. How touching, he thought, and then shook Gabriel until he was awake.

"Gabriel, wake up," he yelled at him. Gabriel came awake slowly, stretching his twisted neck this way and that. He looked at Chuck, standing there in flannel pajamas and fuzzy slippers. "You look like hell," Chuck told him.

"What are you, at sleep-away camp or something?" Gabriel asked, rubbing his eyes.

"It's really cold in here at night. Not that you would know."

"Sorry, I have a home, and a family." He paused. "Had a family. What do want, Chuck? I'm sleeping."

"I figured it out."

"You figured out what, Mr. Fuzzy-Wuzzy?"

"Helena's recording. It's a message. It's in code."

"Really, you think so? What was your first clue, when she says 'Listen closely, here's the part that's a coded message'? The whole damn speech means something."

"You knew that? Already?"

"Yeah, Chuck, I knew that. Like two minutes into it. That's why I'm still here."

"I knew it, too. I've been thinking, you know? Helena never says 'fortuitously', never heard her talk like that. That's a clue, no doubt about it. You think?"

"Yeah, I think. She says it three times on the recording. She never said that word before in her life." Gabriel gave a jaw-cracking yawn.

"What does it mean?"

"What do you think, Sherlock? 'Fortuitously'; what does that sound like to you, clue like?"

Chuck thought, then gave himself a dope slap on the forehead. "Forty-two!" he proclaimed, smiling. "Her tattoo."

"Yeah, quit thinking about my dead wife's thighs, pervert. Have a little respect. But yeah, forty-two. Forty-two three times, maybe."

"One hundred twenty six? What does that mean?" Gabriel shrugged.

"Not a fucking clue, Clouseau. But that's not the part that's got me. Listen to this." Gabriel restarted the recording from the beginning. He turned the volume way down. They had watched the recording so many times by now, they almost had the soliloquy memorized. "The first part, I think, is for both of us, mostly just an introduction to get us through the trauma, you know? Though I'm not sure and I don't know what the forty-two refers to.

"I'm sure here she's really just dancing to fill time. Those are the actual lyrics, I checked. It really seems like she's just killing time to get the timing right. Here, where she says, 'this part's for Chuck', I'm thinking is probably for you. Obviously it's a string of clues to something, what I don't know. Do you?"

"Yeah, I think so. When I saw her in Michigan, we kinda cut a deal."

"What kind of deal?"

"She agreed to stop trying to kill me, I agreed not to release the hounds. And she promised, she promised, to give me the tracking number."

Gabriel paused the recording at this point. "She didn't burn it? I don't believe you."

"I'm not sure. I don't think so. She never really said, exactly. She did promise to give me the tracking number this week, so that someday I could get the program back. I think that's what she meant. I think."

Gabriel restarted the program. "Well, that sounds definitive. Anyway, that part's your problem, not mine. I don't give a shit whether you figure it out or not. This last part, this is for me, I'm sure. It's weird. I keep listening to it, but I don't have it yet. Listen to this."

Gabriel turned the volume back up and Helena's voice filled the lab: "Don't forget about the party. It's really important. Don't be la—" He stopped the recording and replayed the last part: "Don't be la—"

Chuck frowned at Gabriel, not understanding. "What's the mystery? 'Don't delay'.

"No, Chuck, that's not what she's saying. Look at her mouth." Gabriel twisted a knob on the console and scrubbed the 'Don't be la—" back and forth several times. "See? She's making a 'b' there, not a 'd'. I'm sure of it." He sat back in his chair.

"Fine, then. 'Don't be late.' Makes more sense that way, you're right. Not much mystery there, Gabriel."

Gabriel slapped the console, startling the other man. "That's not what she says either, dammit." He scrubbed the last syllable back and forth violently: "Lay—, Lay—, Lay—, Lay—"

"Enough already," Chuck said, pulling Gabriel's hand from the controls. "I get it. She never pronounces the 't'. It's just a bad edit, Gabriel. An early jump cut, like in the beginning."

"How? In the beginning, she's not dying, Chuck. Who did the edit? Her? She's like—" he looked at the time counter in the corner of the screen, "thirty four seconds from lights out. How did she do a sloppy edit when she's lying there dead?"

Chuck considered this. "Maybe not, Gabriel. If she did an edit there, maybe she wasn't so near death as it seems. Maybe she stops the camera, jumps up, fries the hard drive in the microwave or something, or goes to the bathroom. I know I would, I'd be afraid I'd lose control of my bowels or something, you know? That would be so humiliating. Then she comes back and does the rest. Maybe that's what happened."

Gabriel leaned on the console, staring at the monitor. "You could be right," he said, staring at his wife's face. He began to scrub the last words of the recording back and forth again, more slowly: "Be lay—, Be lay—, Be lay—"

"Gabriel!" Chuck said in exasperation, "stop that. You're killing me here."

Gabriel didn't hear him. He kept scrubbing the last two words, finally realizing what Helena's last words to him meant. Not 'Don't be la—'; she said, "Don't belay." Belay. It wasn't meant to make sense, it was meant as a code, a signal. It was a signal to only one person in the whole world; no matter how many people viewed this recording, no matter how long anyone analyzed her every nuance and inflection, only Gabriel knew what she was talking about. He was certain of it. Suddenly and clearly, the memory of that day so many years ago crystalized into his consciousness: the day she had taught him how to climb. He had learned a new word that day; belay. He remembered then, something more, something that seemed so strange to him at the time it had happened. He remembered how Helena had gone on and on about that stupid tree, the one she'd tied the rope to. 'Big tree, strong tree': even though he was scared out of his wits at the time at his impending first attempt at jumping off a cliff, he felt she was being maudlin. Maudlin, he remembered thinking, was way out of character for his wife. That big, stupid tree.

"Gabriel? You still in there?" Chuck asked, tapping the other man on the forehead. "You okay, buddy?"

Gabriel emerged from his fugue and nodded his head. He had figured out something important, he knew. He had no idea what it was, but it felt important. He had to find that tree. Could he find that tree again? He'd have to, that's all.

"I gotta go to New York," Gabriel announced, standing.

"What? When? Why?"

"Now. I have to leave now."

"It's almost four in the morning, buddy. Hold your horses."

"Do you have any camping gear? Tents, sleeping bag, that sort of thing? Here in the lab?"

"Are you crazy? You're asking me if I have a tent? You're talking to a guy whose idea of roughing it is a two star hotel instead of a four. Sit down, Gabriel. You're starting to scare me."

Gabriel dropped weakly back in the chair. "I gotta get to New York."

"Later, okay? I want to finish this." He restarted the recording.

"That's it, Chuck. She doesn't say anything else."

"Yes, yes she does. Look." They both watched her dying form closely and Gabriel noticed her lips mouthing nearly silent words.

"What is she saying?" Gabriel asked. "I can't hear it." He cranked the gain to full. The only sound was the hiss of background static.

"That won't work. You're just increasing everything that way, it gets drowned out in the electronics."

Suddenly, a thought returned to Gabriel from that horrific night. "Is she having one of her spells? Is she talking to her sister again?"

"It's possible," Chuck said. "I didn't think of that. Hold it, we can check. She hooked herself up to the world's best encephalography. We can run a level one on the tracing, get a speech analysis from the program." He bent to the keyboard.

"What program? There is no program, Chuck. It's gone." Chuck stopped tapping on the keyboard and looked at Gabriel.

"Shit, you're right. We're screwed."

They sat, mutually considering the perfect shitstorm they were sitting in the middle of.

Chuck came to life, spinning his chair to switch on the audio processors behind them. "No, we can check this. If she's having one of her crazy spells, one of her catatonic episodes, we can hear it. Her brainwaves should do that loon tune thing, like before."

"Check it. Is it? Is that it?" Chuck brought up the power on the audio system and they listened for a minute.

"No, it isn't there. No loony tune thing. Believe me, when it's there, you know it. I have that band all the way up, no loons. She's not talking to the dead. At least, not yet."

Gabriel let this pass. "Then what is she saying? We have to know." Actually, he thought he had a pretty good idea already, but felt it was important to be sure.

"If you're not against calling in the fascist forces of the government, I can send the audio to NSA, have it selectively amplified and interpreted. It's what we're good at."

Gabriel considered this. Potentially, this was the worst thing in the world to allow. Potentially, but not certainly. He had to know what she was doing. He needed hard data from which to work; without it, he was lost. Helena had done this on purpose; what purpose, though, he still couldn't fathom. He had to know why his wife had done this.

"Not the whole tape, Chuck. Just this part, just send this section, and audio only. No images of Helena to the government. Promise?"

"Sure. Paranoid crazy by insemination, I get it. I can do that."

"How long?"

"Six hours, tops."

"Do it. I'm going to New York."

"You keep saying that."

"I'm going. I have to stop at home first, then I'm going to New York."

"Got it. You're going to New York. You're not going to miss the party, are you?"

"No, I'll be there. Of course I'll be there." Gabriel headed out the door.

"Hey, Gabriel," Chuck called after him. "Do we have to RSVP? The invitation didn't say."

Gabriel kept walking.

It took him two and a half days to find the tree. He remembered perfectly where they had camped, and found the trailhead with the help of a topo map and a ranger. The actual tree, however, was a bigger challenge. Eventually, he was standing on the same ridge where Helena had laughed at him as he crawled to her side. Now he stood unbent, staring out at the vista. He turned slowly in a circle, convincing himself that this was the place. He walked over to the tree. This, indeed, was the tree. He remembered Helena's silly speech and smiled inwardly. He bent and ran his fingers over the line in the bark where countless ropes had worn it smooth. The tree, indeed, was still here, still solid.

Gabriel walked slowly around the large, proud oak. He carefully stepped over its gnarled roots, staring at the ground for any sign of something buried beneath. The ground looked undisturbed. He stopped and stared at it, root to crown. Why was he here? he wondered. He was certain that this was the spot Helena had meant. But why?

He circled the tree again, this time studying its broad trunk, and as he came back to the side facing away from the cliff, he saw it. It was small, and if it hadn't been carved in that flat spot of the bark, the trunk worn smooth by the hundreds of encircling ropes placed over many decades, he would never have seen it. He knelt down in front of the spot, looking at the small carving lit by a shaft of sunlight through the canopy, no larger than the size of a quarter. It was a shallow carving of a heart. It looked fresh carved even to his naive eye, the edges sharp. Surrounding the heart on all three sides was a sunburst of short, straight lines. He ran his fingers across the carving, and in doing so noticed the small pieces of bark lying just beneath. Gabriel was no woodsman, but he couldn't imagine that this carving was much more than a few weeks old, maybe less. How could Helena know it was here? The last time either of them had seen this place was over twenty years ago.

Gabriel stared at the glyph for another minute, then sat down with his back against the trunk. He had done it, he was sure. He had sussed out his wife's cryptic comment, taken her clue, run here goaded by her coded suicide note. He had succeeded in discovering that which she wanted him to find. He just didn't know what the hell it meant. He looked at his watch and gulped water from his pack. If he started now, he thought he could make it back to his car before it got too dark to walk back down the difficult trail.

Gabriel drove the rental car towards Boston. He had managed to sleep for a few hours on the flight from San Francisco to New York. Other than that, he was pretty much running on fumes at this point. He still had two days before the wake, but it certainly made no sense to fly back at this point. Nothing there anyway. He guzzled truck stop coffee and called ahead to book a room at a hotel in Boston. He thought about Helena. The recording ran in an endless loop in his mind as he drove.

He kept coming back to one innocuous sentence: "I pray this works." Pray what works? She had certainly succeeded in killing herself, if that was her aim. But why? His wife was volatile, emotional; was probably capable of violence if pushed far enough. She was certainly troubled and, he had to admit to himself, possibly mentally ill in some clinical way since childhood. What she was not, he still felt despite recent events to the contrary, was depressed—or suicidal.

Gabriel remembered his wife's last weeks. Of course, he hadn't seen or spoken to her for days before her death, but she left him with a sense of purpose, not sadness. She was on a mission, not looking for a way out. It made no sense on the surface.

His wife had a reason to take her life like that, a purpose in dying and leaving him here alone, without the only partner in life he had ever had. He shook his head, still not completely believing she was gone. He couldn't remember all that stuff about the stages of grief, but was pretty sure he was stuck in the angry stage. Why had she done this?, he kept asking himself. Why did she leave me? Gabriel hoped that his wife had a reason to do what she had done. It had better be a damn good one. Until he figured out what it was, he was going to be really pissed off at her.

CHAPTER 28

Gabriel stayed in his hotel room almost the entire next day. He called no one. He slept, and dreamt fitfully about his late wife. He knew he should go over to the bar, pay his respects to the man Helena called, "My Da," her adopted father. Gabriel couldn't summon the strength to face the man. He had been okay calling him 'Dad' when he was with Helena, pretending the man was a kind of father-in-law. Now without Helena, it didn't feel right. Besides, it hurt too much to imagine the conversation. Gabriel remembered the pain in the old man's voice when he had told him on the phone that Helena was gone. He was in no mood.

Chuck had called a half dozen times since Gabriel left San Francisco, but each time Gabriel had allowed the call to go to phone mail. He hadn't bothered to listen to the messages to this point, but now checked. They all said the same thing: "Where are you? Call me." As Gabriel was listening to the last, his phone rang. It was Chuck.

"Why don't you answer your phone?" Chuck asked before he had the chance to say hello.

"I just did. What do you want, I'm busy."

"Busy? With what? The party's tonight."

"I know, Chuck. What do you want?"

"Are you in Boston? I'm here, at the hotel on the wharf. Do you want to get together? Dinner?"

"I'm not in Boston," Gabriel lied. "You'll have to buy your own dinner for once. What do you want?"

"I have the transcript of the recording, from NSA. I've had it since an hour after you left, but you never answer your phone. You're going to the party, right? I probably won't know anyone else there. You and Arthur are going, right?"

"Yeah, Chuck. I'm going to the party. Send the transcript to me, email it or something."

"Where are you? It would be easier if I knew where you were. Is Arthur with you? He wasn't on my flight."

"Just email it, Chuck. I'll see you tonight. Bye." He hung up the phone before the other man had a chance to say anything more. He crumbled back onto the bed. He was in no mood.

As he lay there, staring at the textures on the ceiling, his phone vibrated. He looked at the screen; saw that Chuck had already sent the transcript. The man had no life. Lying there, he pulled the message up on the small screen and scrolled through it. It was what Gabriel had suspected days ago. Helena had spent her last moments of consciousness reciting the lines of the little poem he had written for her when they were married, repeating it over and over again. Written out in black and white like that, repeated over and over, it looked ridiculous and pathetic, he thought. He shut down the phone and resumed his study of the ceiling. On a whim, he reopened the file and looked again, counting the repetitions. He knew before he started how many he would find. But no, he realized as he counted again; forty-one. Death took her too soon, he thought.

Gabriel delayed as long as could, then quite a bit longer. Eventually, he found himself dressed in his best, somber grey suit, a muted tie. He looked like he was going to a funeral, again. What did one wear to a wake, anyway? He wanted to ask Helena; he was sure she would know. The whole thing would've been much more fun with her there, he thought. This didn't bode well.

A line of taxis stood at the front of the hotel. As he hesitated, the doorman, dressed in an outrageous uniform of stark red with gold embroidery, asked if he'd need a cab. He just looked at the man, and then finally shook his head. He decided to walk. Unfortunately, it wasn't far and he knew the way. He eventually stood outside the door of the bar, listening. It sounded like a very big party. He could hear music, and laughter, occasional shouting. He suddenly felt very overdressed. He looked at his watch; he was an hour late. He was considering a walk around the block, just to gather his thoughts, when the door burst open before him. A large, stocky man staggered into Gabriel, nearly knocking him over, obviously drunk. He grabbed Gabriel's shoulder to steady himself.

"Sorry, mate," he slurred, and then, still holding onto Gabriel's shoulder, leaned his mouth close to Gabe's ear and whispered, "God bless the dead." His breath stank of whiskey. The man released his grip on Gabriel and staggered to the curb, where he proceeded to be sick. Some party, Gabriel thought to himself. He took a deep breath and went inside.

Gabriel stood two steps inside the bar, surveying the scene. He knew the bar, that was no surprise, but was amazed at the number of people; easily over two hundred, he guessed. The place was packed. There seemed to be a significant number of very large men, apparently football players. The rest, a very eclectic mix.

Gabriel was having a hard time making his feet move further into the bar. He stared about him like a child who's just misplaced his mother at a crowded mall. At that moment, however, he locked eyes with Dad, wading through the crowd like an overweight icebreaker in a starched white apron. The man looked like he had aged twenty years. The old man approached, and Gabriel saw his eyes were red-rimmed and clouded with the same sorrow he himself had been carrying for weeks.

"Hi, Dad," Gabriel said weakly as the man wrapped him in a silent bear hug.

"I'm sorry for your loss, Gabriel," Dad said softly to him as he released him. "Come over to the bar and let my boys and missus say their respects." He towed Gabriel by the wrist towards the bar where his family was pouring out a huge field of whiskey shots arrayed on the expansive dark wood. Each came out from behind the bar in turn to give Gabriel a hug and the same few words of empathy. Gee, that was great, Gabriel thought. Maybe I can go now.

Dad was saying something into his ear but Gabriel wasn't catching any of it. Someone had cranked the music too loud as the Dropkick Murphys began "The Legend of Finn MacCumhail."

"Billy!" Dad roared over the heads of the crowd at his son some twenty feet away, "Who's fucking with the sound system?" The younger man shrugged in response. "Well, take care of it. I'll not have that shit blasting at my daughter's wake, hear me there?" Billy nodded and disappeared behind the bar. The music was replaced by a brooding orchestral piece, receding into the sounds of the hundreds of conversations about them. Dad continued what he was saying to Gabriel, saying, "...keep it short. For God's sake, don't try to tell any jokes or stories about Fiona. Sorry, Helena. Whatever."

Gabriel had no idea what the man was talking about and wanted to explain that to him. He was horrified, however, when Dad reached behind the bar for a short baseball bat and began to pound it insistently on the tabletop of a nearby booth. The crowd quickly grew quiet, all looking their way.

Dad seemed to swell even taller than his usual imposing bulk. "Ladies and gentlemen," he boomed in a voice suited for hailing ships at sea, "I am sorry to bother you, but a moment if you please. I trust you all have something at hand to make a toast. We are joined by Dr. Gabriel Sheehan, husband of Fion—I mean, Hel—the dearly departed. He wishes to say a few words.

With that, all eyes turned to Gabriel. "No, I don't!" Gabriel hissed at the man in a stage whisper. "Where the hell did you get that idea?" Dad just looked at him sternly and somehow maneuvered Gabriel, unwillingly, to step from the seat of the booth onto the bar itself. He stood there, feeling naked. He scanned the crowd of upturned, expectant faces. For the first time in his life, he felt stage fright.

He cleared his throat and desperately tried to think of two words to put together. He looked down at Dad who shoved a shotglass of Irish whiskey into his hand and gave him a nod.

"Helena," Gabriel said, his voice cracking on her name. He shook his head, could say no more. His chin drooped onto his chest and a moment of silence ensued. After a minute, a strong voice from the back of the bar rang out "Helena!" and everyone raised their glass and drained their shot. A sound like the staccato report of gunfire rang out as a couple hundred shotglasses were smacked down on tables around the bar. Gabriel looked up and scanned the sad faces all about him. He raised his own glass and drained it, nearly choking but not. Another voice called out "Fiona!" and the process was repeated. Gabriel climbed down off the bar and Dad handed him another shot, which he downed; this one more easily. This is expensive whiskey, Gabriel thought inappropriately. As the shotglasses smacked down again, there came the sound of a glass smashing against the far brick wall of the bar.

"Hey!" Dad roared with fury. "No smashing my glasses, dammit! The next man breaking my glasses is drinking water the rest of the night."

"Issy!" someone called out, and everyone drank again.

"Issy?" Gabriel asked Dad, who just shrugged and downed his own shot.

"Mariangela!" a young voice called from the middle of crowd, and amid general laughter and the sound of shots being downed, half a dozen more women's names of general outlandishness were called out above the rebuilding noise of the crowd. Finally, Billy from behind the bar raised his own glass above his head and, in a voice laden with sadness but over-topping all the others in the bar, called out "God bless the dead!" This was echoed by all with a final salute of shot glasses hitting wood. One glass sailed over the crowd to crash into the wall behind Dad. General laughter and the sounds of the party resumed.

"Fucking Irish!" Dad whispered, shaking his head. He pulled up a chair at the end of the bar and sat. He waved Gabriel into the next. "That was well done, son, well done. Your wife is proud of you, I'm sure." He sipped his whiskey and stared at the bar.

"Dad," Gabriel said, now that the bar had resumed a reasonable buzz of noise, "was that for real or a joke? The names, I mean."

Dad reached down the bar and slid a full shot over to Gabriel. He looked at Gabriel in the eyes, seeming to see something that made him even sadder. "You didn't know your wife very well, did you, Gabriel?"

"What do you mean?" Gabriel said, feeling hurt. "Of course I did. We were married over twenty years." He sipped his own drink, more cautiously. He was already drunk, he knew.

"I didn't ask you how long you were married, son," Dad continued. He shook his head. "Your Helena, my Fiona. I get the feeling she didn't tell you a lot of things, Gabriel." Gabriel was forced to consider this fact. He remembered the early weeks of what passed for their courtship, when he had allowed her to move into his place before he even knew her last name. How he had kept trying to get her to tell him about herself, Helena repeatedly promising to do so but never actually getting around to it, until Gabriel had finally given up asking. "Your wife," Dad was continuing, "changed her name like I change my socks."

Gabriel laughed at this. "But why?"

"Because she was a fucking thief, that's why," Dad said, finishing his shot and smacking down the glass. He reached for another and slid another to Gabriel, who had not yet touched the one he had.

"A thief? What do you mean?" Gabriel asked, not understanding the man's meaning.

"I mean she stole things, lots of things. When she showed up here, that's what she did, for a job. And damn good at it, too. Wasn't she, Billy?" Gabriel noticed that the young man, now looking not so young, had joined them, leaning on the keeper's side of the bar as he took a break from pouring.

"She was the best, god bless her," Billy said, then raised a shot overhead and called out, "God bless the dead!" This was echoed around the crowded bar and shotglasses again rang out. None broke this time. Billy drained his own. "I remember the day she showed up here. You remember, Dad?"

"Of course I remember. Little red-haired girl dressed in that crazy leather biker suit of hers, strolls in like she owns the place, remember—"

"That was the only clothes she owned then, you know?" Billy interrupted. "Straight off the boat with that stolen bike of hers."

"Quit interrupting, Billy. I'm telling the story to Gabriel, here. Walks in the front door like she's the Queen of England. Goes straight to the back room without so much as a hello, and grabs an apron off the hook. She takes a pad in hand and goes into waiting tables like she'd been doing it all her life."

"Only she never had, that's for sure," Billy laughed. "She sucked as a waitress."

"In the beginning, sure. But she caught on fast."

"You just let her hire herself like that?" Gabriel asked.

"Didn't have any choice," Dad replied. "I remember like it was last week. She was so young, a tiny thing; but fierce, you know? Mean, actually. I walked up to her and asked what she thought she was doing. 'Are you daft?' she asked me. I just didn't know what to do with her. By the end of the day, she had figured out how to do the job well enough to make good money in tips. I wasn't going to pay here, that's for sure."

"It's not money she was looking for," Billy said. "She had no place back then, no people at all."

"That's a fact," Dad agreed. "Little girl all alone, she was. Mean as anything, too."

"So what happened?" Gabriel asked. He knew none of this.

"She moved in with us, upstairs." He gestured to their apartment above the bar. "She kind of adopted us, I guess. Her room's still waiting for her, untouched since when you guys were here last," Dad said. He looked sad, took another sip. "Missus and I loved her like our own. My wife always pined for a daughter. One day, one just shows up."

"But she was Fiona then?" Gabriel asked the two men. Both nodded back. "When did she change her name? When did she leave Boston?"

"Oh, I guess she changed her name when she left here, probably. Fiona was with us almost four years, right Billy?" Billy nodded. "But she used a lot of names while she was here, too. Has a shoebox filled with ID and passports and shit, up in her room still. Must be twenty different names, she used."

"Yeah," Billy laughed. "Most of them, crazy. She loved to use names from Joyce, mostly Finnegan's Wake, you know? Crazy strange names, like Issy. It was her way of making fun of us Boston Irish, said we weren't real Irishmen, didn't know our own culture." Someone in the back of the bar, a woman's voice that carried well, sang out "God bless the dead" and all echoed and drank. Gabriel drained his own shot and began on the other before him. Billy slid over another without a word.

"I still don't get all the names," Gabriel said with a slight slur. He was going to have to slow down if he was going to get back to his hotel tonight, he thought.

Dad's other son, Sean, had joined them. Billy asked who was covering the bar and Sean pointed to their mother, pouring shots at the other end.

"It's because of what Fiona did for a living," Sean explained. "Dad never paid her for waiting tables, you know."

"I fed her and gave her a place to sleep," Dad protested. "What do you mean I never paid her? She weren't a thief because of me, you know. She came to us thieving, from day one. You remember?"

"Remember what?" Gabriel encouraged.

"First night she was here," Billy explained, smiling at the memory. "We're all sitting at that booth over there," he pointed to the big booth at the back of the bar. "The way we do every night after closing, counting out and all."

"He means polishing off the nearly empties," Sean added with a wink.

"Quit interrupting, you're as bad as Dad. First night, we didn't know who in fuck this little girl was. I thought she was, like fourteen or fifteen, when she arrived."

"Wrong!" Sean said, drinking.

"Yeah, whatever," Billy continued. "We didn't know what we were dealing with then, that's a fact. So that first night, she says to me, 'Billy, I'll bet you a hundred bucks. Remember, Sean?" Sean nodded, smiling broadly.

"Bet what?" Gabriel asked. Billy pointed out the front window to the office building across Mass Ave, a nondescript twelve story building.

"I'm telling you. She points to that building and tells me that she can race up the stairs to the roof before I can make it up in the elevator. 'No fucking way,' I told her. Now you have to understand, we all know this girl don't have two cents to rub together, let alone a hundred dollars. But we didn't know what to think of her then, wanted to see what she was playing at." Gabriel stared out the window at the building, its windows lit up in the dark.

"No way she could do that," Gabriel said. Dad snorted at that.

"Yeah, that's what I thought, too, " Billy continued. "And I wanted to see how she'd get out of paying me, when she lost." He winked at Gabriel, then blushed as he immediately regretted the gesture. Gabriel pretended not to notice.

"So what happened?" Gabriel asked, moving past the moment.

"So I bet her," Billy said. "We raced first thing next day, soon as security unlocked the doors. To this day, I still don't fucking believe she beat me. It was something superhuman, I tell you." He shook his head. "Wouldn't even been close, except the elevator did a little hiccup thing, you know? Wouldn't move for a couple of minutes."

Sean looked like he was about to explode, turning beet red. They all looked at him.

"What is it, son?" his dad asked, concerned. "Go outside if you're going to sick up."

Sean laughed, spewing little drops of whiskey with gusts of laughter. When he finally composed himself, Sean said, "She never told, did she?"

"Told what?" Billy and Gabriel both asked.

"Nothin'," Sean replied weakly. He raised his glass and said mildly, "God bless the dead, gentlemen."

"Fuck that, Sean," Billy said, his color rising. "Told me what? You don't tell me and Dad's gonna need to get his bat."

"I shouldn't say, she made me promise," Sean said. He looked at his brother and reconsidered. "Okay, okay. I can't believe after all those years she didn't tell you. That elevator hiccup, you call it? That was me." He looked around, pretending the story was over.

"What do you mean, that was you?" Billy demanded.

Sean sighed. "She paid me fifty bucks to pull the breakers on the elevator for three minutes, she said. Then go ahead and turn 'em back on."

"No way, Sean. She didn't have fifty bucks," Billy protested.

"She did after you coughed up the hundred, brother," Sean replied, polishing off his whiskey and wiping his mouth on the back of his sleeve. "Gotta go help mum. I'm the good son, remember?" He scampered off down to the other end of the bar.

Billy looked at the two of them with wonder. "Well, fuck me."

"Sounds like she did," Gabriel said, laughing.

"Almost every day," Dad agreed.

The three of them held forth for the entire evening, occasionally being joined by Dad's wife and various others as the night wore on. Arthur and his wife, Samantha, came by with Chuck in tow. Gabriel made the necessary introductions, but the two groups were as disparate as the two coasts they represented; the California contingent left after a polite period of time, promising to see Gabriel as soon as he returned home.

A young Hispanic man came over and introduced himself to Gabriel.

"I am here to say thank you and pay you my respects," Jesus said respectfully to the three men after he had shaken hands all around.

"What are you thanking us for, Jesus?" Gabriel asked.

"Your wife was very kind to me, Dr. Sheehan—too kind," Jesus replied.

"Then count yourself one lucky man," Billy said under his breath.

"I want you to know that I will honor Mariangela's—Helena's—trust in me my whole life. Next week, my mother and brother and sister will join me in Chicago, because of your wife's generosity," Jesus said to Gabriel.

"That's great, Jesus. Helena was a very generous person, I agree. It helps me to know she helped you in some way. Thanks for coming to honor her," Gabriel said.

"I want you to know, Dr. Sheehan, that if you or your family is ever in Chicago, you will be welcome as my honored guests in our restaurant. It will be open in six weeks, on State Street. It is called Mariangela's Diner. Please come if you can." He shook hands all around and dissolved back into the crowded bar.

"What was that about?" Dad asked.

"Haven't a clue," Gabriel admitted. "Dad, you said Helena was a thief, before. It sounds like she played Billy pretty well, but that was a con, not stealing."

"Oh, no, Gabriel, she was a thief, plain and simple," Dad said. "Damn good one, too. Right, Billy?"

"The best, Dad. Best in Boston, that's for sure." He turned to Gabriel. "She knew her trade damn well when she showed up. Made a small fortune from the start."

"What are you talking about? Why would she steal?" Gabriel asked the two men.

"She had to, Gabriel," Dad said. "It was all she knew, other than racing motorcycles, of course. Couldn't do that anymore, after she ran to America."

"What do you mean, it's all she knew? Helena was a smart woman, she could've done anything she wanted," Gabriel argued, somewhat miffed at the man's low opinion of his late wife.

"Bullshit, Gabriel," Dad said, sensing the other man's indignation. "Your wife never had any schooling past eighth grade, you know. Catholic school did okay by her up to a point, but she spent her high school years in a mental hospital. Did you know that?"

Gabriel nodded, remembering his talk with his father. "A little. No details."

"Well, no one knows details, that's for sure," Chuck said. Gabriel hadn't noticed that he had drifted back to stand beside them. "The records from that time, in Ireland, suck."

Dad seemed not to have heard him. "Oh, Fiona had a great head for the numbers, I'll admit that. She was whip smart, in her way. Helped straighten our finances out right quick. But she had no schooling, she had no papers; no real name to put down on a job application or a school application. Not in the beginning."

"And there was the other thing," Billy added, passing pints of beer around the group. Thank god it's not more whiskey, Gabriel thought.

"What other thing?" Gabriel asked.

"She was on the run, that was clear from the start," Billy said. "Kept her head down, wouldn't go to certain places at all."

"Airports, yeah. I know," Gabriel said, sipping his beer.

"No way, airports. But a lot more than that, Gabriel. Stayed away from cameras, tourists, places she thought she might be photographed. Crazy paranoid, especially at first."

"What was she running from? Did she ever say?" Gabriel asked. Billy and Dad both shook their heads and drank.

"Wouldn't say. We asked plenty, though. She had her spells, you know. Nightmares, too. She was a very scared young woman when she came to us," Billy said. Dad nodded in agreement.

"Something about a sister, I think," Dad said. "There were hints, there was the one picture."

"What picture?" Chuck asked immediately.

Dad seemed to notice him then for the first time. His expression showed a bald dislike, the old Irishman being too drunk or too disinterested to disguise his feelings. He directed his answer to Gabriel. "There's one old picture in her shoebox. I'll show it to you later, Gabriel," he said pointedly. "Here, come walk with me. I'll show you some pictures Billy and Sean put around the place." He grabbed Gabriel's elbow and walked him away from the bar where Chuck remained with Billy. "I don't like that guy, Gabriel," Dad said. "Who is he, again?"

"That's Chuck. He works for the government, but has been with us at the company for a couple of years now. He's kind of a pain in the ass, but not entirely a bad guy."

"Don't like him," Dad repeated. They stopped in front of a table where the brothers had arranged a dozen framed photos of Helena. She was radiant in every one. Mostly, Helena with the boys. Helena dressed in black riding leathers, her hair spilling out beneath a black watch cap, her arms around the two brothers. One picture in particular caught Gabriel's attention. Gabriel pointed to it; a picture of Helena dressed in robes with a large church choir. She was beaming.

"I never knew Helena belonged to the church," Gabriel said, amazed. He picked up the picture to get a better look. Dad snatched the picture from Gabe's hands and set it back down on the table, face down.

"She didn't. I don't want to talk about that. Boys shouldn't have put that picture out. Dumb jackasses for boys, I've got." He picked up a picture of Helena in tight black jeans and turtleneck, stocking cap and with a rope slung over her shoulder. "This is what Fiona did for a living. She could go up the side of a building like a spider, day or night. Crazy. She could do that thing the Army Rangers do, you know, when they run face first down a rope."

"Rappelling," Gabriel said. "I know, she taught me. I wouldn't try facedown, though."

"You're not as nuts as her then. She could run straight down the side of a building faster than my boys could run down the street. Crazy." They walked back to the bar where Billy, Sean, and Chuck were talking quietly.

Gabriel looked at his watch and saw it was well after midnight. "I don't mean to offend, Dad, but this is my first wake. Is there going to be a priest or something stopping by to say some kind of prayer or something?" The expression that crossed his companions' faces gave Gabriel the impression that he had said something wrong. "I'm sorry, I just thought since she was in the church and all…"

"Fiona was never in no church, unless it was to steal something," Dad said bitterly. "You shouldn't have put out that picture, Billy. Gives the wrong impression."

"I'm sorry, Dad. You're right. I'll take it away," Billy said, embarrassed.

"Leave it, dumbshit," Dad said. "Too late now, anyway." Dad turned to Gabriel with a sigh. "I'm sorry, Gabriel, I mean no disrespect for your late wife. But Fiona hated the Roman Catholic Church with the passion of a thousand burning suns." He downed a shot, reached for another but thought better of it.

"But the choir picture," Gabriel said. "She loved to sing."

"She did that," Sean agreed, smiling despite the obvious discomfort of his father and brother. "But that picture, that's a great story—"

"Which you won't speak of in my presence!" Dad roared, slapping his palm down loudly against the bar. An awkward silence ensued, punctuated by drinking. Dad calmed himself with an effort. He pointed to the big booth in the back of the bar, saying to Gabriel, "She'd sit there every Saturday morning with all the papers. Doing her research, she called it. Checking all the estate sales, the gossip pages. Finding out what stars were in town, which of the rich folk would be hosting some fundraiser or ball so she could knock off their place while they danced across town somewheres. Bah." He shook his head, remembering.

"Bah, bullshit, Dad," Billy said, facing the old patriarch. "You didn't have a problem with what she did, don't pretend you did. You helped, you old bastard! You did all the casing with her, every weekend." He turned to Gabriel. "It's true. He'd take her to the auctions, the estate sales and all. I had to do up her disguise, before they left."

"Disguise?" Chuck asked.

"Yeah, her favorite was to be a little girl, used it a lot, particularly for the banks. She had me wrap her chest, you know, round and round with spandex so she'd look flat. When she did her hair like that, and dressed up, she'd walk into a bank holding my Dad's hand like she was a twelve year old. It was magic." He looked at his Dad, but his Dad was not meeting his gaze. "Tell Gabriel about the Liberty job, Dad." Billy stared at his father defiantly.

Dad puffed out his cheeks. "It was a good job, I won't say different now that she's gone." He paused, remembering. "Fiona heard somehow about the Liberty Bank, that the strong boxes held a lot of these special bonds, I don't remember the details—"

"Bearer bonds, Dad," Billy said. "She didn't like taking money," Billy added for Gabriel's benefit.

"Am I telling this story?" Dad said, irritated. "Fiona and I walk in hand in hand, father and daughter, you see?" he said, now smiling as he remembered. "Bright Saturday afternoon, just a regular family. Fiona's playing a little girl who's a little touched, you know? Talking too loud, making girlish talk and all. But she's got her head on a swivel, checking out the cameras and the guards, the whole thing. All of a sudden, when we're near the vault and I'm pretending to fill out the deposit form, she pulls away from me and goes running around the bank, then straight into the vault right behind a customer, when the gate's open. Oh, boy, the staff goes nuts at that. They make me come over to get her out, but I'm making out the forms, pretending I don't know where my little girl's got to, it was a beautiful thing. She had a good five, six minutes in there to check it out." He was smiling broadly now, remembering.

"She couldn't steal anything like that, right in broad daylight!" Chuck said.

"Oh, no. Of course not. We come back here to the bar and she lays out the job. She draws her schematics, she called them. Distances, camera angles, guard positions, lines of sight, the whole thing. She was careful, knew her stuff, like I said. She made us wait three months before pulling the job. She read the paper; the local business trades, and somehow knew there would be a lot of those bearer bonds in the safeboxes.

"So three months go by, I've forgotten all about Liberty Bank. I figured she had, too. One morning, she tells me she's hitting the bank next Saturday. She won't tell me anything else, just in case. That Saturday, two minutes before they're locking up, Fiona and I go back to the bank.

She's fourteen years old again, but very quiet this time. Very shy. She's wearing a 'Hello Kitty' pink backpack, I remember. I walk her to the spot she tells me, showed me on the schematic beforehand, you know? Just before they close the gate for the night, you know, the gate to the vault, I fall down with a heart attack, bang. Lots of 'Can't breathe, can't breathe,' call 911, ambulance, the whole thing. I had to spend the night in the hospital. She was gone, though, poof! Straight into the vault and gone."

"What do you mean, gone?" Gabriel asked. "They must've checked the vault before locking up for the night."

"You screwed up their usual routine," Chuck said, interjecting. "Broke their pattern."

"Yeah, but so what?" Gabriel asked. "She couldn't grab much before getting out, even if their routines were screwed up."

Billy took over. "That was all Fiona, that. When she cased the vault, she saw that the cabinets, the lockboxes, met in the corner." He drew a picture in the condensation on the bar, drawing a right angle corner. "Stupid, really stupid. There's this big dead space in the corner, where the cabinets come together. She had a minute to jump right in that blind corner and hide. Nobody knew she was there." He smiled and looked at Gabriel and Chuck to make sure they understood. "She had all day Sunday to go through the boxes. She loaded up her Hello Kitty backpack with bearer bonds and gold certificates."

"She picked all those locks?" Chuck asked. "There's two locks on every box, and those are not easy to pick, even if you're taking your time."

"Never saw Fiona pick any locks," Billy said. "She liked the direct approach. Hammer and punch—bang, bang, little door swings right open. She made everything nice and clean before Monday morning, just put the locks back in the holes so it looked nice for a bit. Monday morning came, she waited until the opening rush comes in and walks straight out with a lady and her daughter. Said she was afraid a man was following her, which there was. Sean and I watched from across the street, picked her up two blocks down."

"You're kidding me?" Gabriel asked. Billy and Sean just smiled and shook their heads.

"But the FBI must've been called in," Chuck said. "Any bank with deposit insurance is required to call in the FBI. They must've checked the tapes, seen you two had cased the place before."

"Oh, they probably checked," Dad said. "But Helena said they were on a three month cycle. That's why she waited. Must've worked, never heard boo about that job."

"How much?" Chuck asked.

Dad just looked at him narrowly. "Enough," was all he said.

"Two million," Sean said proudly. Dad gave him a winnowing stare.

Chuck whistled softly.

"That was her biggest," Billy said. "After that, she stuck mostly to estate sales and rich people's apartments."

"Was she ever caught?" Chuck asked.

"Fiona? Never," Billy said. "Too careful. Anybody home or any little thing unexpected, she'd bail. She bailed a lot, too. It wasn't the police she worried about."

"What did she worry about?" Gabriel asked.

"Those guys," Billy said, pointing over their heads into the back of the bar. Chuck and Gabriel turned to look where Billy was pointing.

"Holy shit," Chuck said, ducking his head behind his hands. "Gabriel, it's the Lonegan brothers. Don't look, don't look."

Gabriel looked anyway, and then turned angrily to Dad. "What are they doing here, Dad? Is this going to be a problem?" The Lonegans were walking over to where they sat at the bar. Before he got an answer, they stood in front of Gabriel.

"Very sorry for your loss, Dr. Sheehan. Fiona was a good 'un. She'll be missed," the older one said, the other nodding in agreement. Rory, the older brother, shook Gabriel's hand.

"Deepest sympathies," the other brother said. He shook Gabriel's hand in turn. They nodded to the others and disappeared back into the crowd.

"Well," Chuck said, recovering. "They seem civil enough."

"Damn well should be," Dad said.

"I thought Helena—er, Fiona, ripped them off for some godawful amount of money," Gabriel said.

"Yeah," Billy said, "but that's been taken care of, you know. They're happy as pigs in shit now. Been coming around quite a bit."

"You paid them back, Dad?" Gabriel asked. "I told Helena I was worried—"

"Me? No way I could come up with that kind of money, son," Dad said. "Your wife took care of it. It was hilarious." He smiled, as did his sons, thinking about it.

"What?" Gabriel asked. "What did she do?"

Dad looked at him archly. "She didn't say anything to you?" Gabriel shook his head. "What kind of marriage did you two have, anyway? Did you even live together?"

"Yeah, we lived together," Gabriel replied indignantly. "Helena kept a lot to herself, that's all." He thought about that for a minute, and added, "A lot, actually."

"Yeah, so it seems," Dad said.

"What was so funny?" Chuck asked.

Dad wasn't inclined to answer any questions from Chuck, but obviously couldn't resist the invitation to another favorite story. "It was almost two months after you guys booked out of here with your tails between your legs. The Lonegans were good and pissed off, as you can imagine. They were trying pretty hard to find where you and Fiona had got off to, felt it was well worth hiring out of town help to collect their debt."

"How much did Fiona take them for, Dad?" Gabriel asked.

"Oh, I can't be sure of the amount. Something north of a few hundred thousand, I'm sure. Enough to still matter after all those years, that's for sure."

"But Helena paid them back?" Gabriel asked.

The others laughed. Billy said, "Paid them back real good. Typical Fiona, it was." He finished his beer and slid the glass with a professional spin back down the length of the bar to where Sean scooped it up, gave it a triple flip, caught it behind his back and plopped it in with the growing pile of dirties.

"Like I said, about six, eight weeks after you guys left," Dad continued, "one of Boston's finest comes strolling into the bar, looking like he owns the place. 'What do you want?' I asked him, because it wasn't

Bobby, who usually does the collection, and it wasn't even close to the first of the month. I was ready to give him a hard time. He tells me to cool off; he just has a delivery to make. Me and the boys look outside and there's his cruiser with lights flashing and a big old armored car double-parked alongside. I couldn't figure out what was up, I'll tell you.

'Go ahead with your delivery,' I told him. I just wanted him out of here, you know? Before I can figure out what's going on, the guards carry this big strongbox into the bar, drop it right there in the middle of the place," he said, pointing to the spot. "Took the two of them to carry it, I'll tell you. Cop made me sign like twenty-six different pages that I took delivery. He actually had the nerve to have his hand out, too. Can you believe it?" He shook his head.

"What was the delivery?" Gabriel asked.

"Hey, Sean," Billy called down the bar to his brother. "Send down the brick." Sean gave a thumbs up and reached behind him into the display case where they kept the most expensive liquor, the kind in the impressive bottles that nobody in this neighborhood ever ordered. Sean pulled the brick from the shelf amid the bottles and gave it a shove back down the bar. Chuck made to catch it but Billy pulled his hand off the bar. "I wouldn't," Billy told him. Billy put both hands up on the bar and caught the thing like a baseball catcher. He handed it to Chuck, who almost dropped it.

"Holy shit," Chuck said, hefting the thing. "It's a solid ingot. How much?" Chuck asked, using two hands to pass the gold brick to Gabriel.

"How much today?" Billy called down to his brother.

Sean looked up from toweling off washed glasses. "That ingot's eighty ounces—today it's $33,600 at closing," Sean called back to him.

"Holy smokes," Gabriel said. "What is it doing here, just sitting on a shelf like that?"

Dad grinned at him. "Well, I don't think your wife was very accurate in her accounting on that one occasion," he said. "I'm sure with the vagaries of daily gold value fluctuations, she just meant to err on the safe side and all. There were twenty of those little bastards in the box, when it arrived. Came with the Lonegan brothers name on it, of course, but we felt we should open it up, you know, to check it. Anyway, it seemed reasonable to take one as our share, handling charges and all."

Gabriel carefully let the thing down on the bar with a thunk. "That's amazing."

"It was hilarious, that's what it was," Billy said. When we called the brothers to tell them to come and pick up their money, it was something out of a comedy. Do you know how hard it is to find somebody who'll convert one of those to cash? Pretty fucking hard, I'll tell you. And they had twenty—er, nineteen, to move."

"Eighteen, actually," Sean said. He had come back down the bar to retrieve the brick. "Fiona was way overpaying those bastards. I couldn't let it happen." Billy gave his brother a chuck in the shoulder and the other moved to replace the brick in its place of honor.

They went back to drinking beer for a bit.

"You said Helena was worried about them, Dad?" Gabriel asked, wanting to restart some kind of conversation, mostly to keep himself from remembering why he was here.

"Yeah, she kind of got herself into trouble, there in the beginning," Dad said. "She was good at what she did, like I said, and successful right off the bat. It wasn't long before word was on the street that some little redhead was making a killing. That got the Lonegan's attention, and not in a good way. They run most of the trade around this area, you know."

"Did they threaten her?" Gabriel asked. He was starting not to like these guys again.

"Threaten her? Naw, it was more like they were gonna kill her. That was their plan, anyway. Billy and Sean were there. You tell him, Billy."

"Scared the shit out of both of us," Billy said. "We were walking down Boylston with Fiona in the middle of the afternoon, broad daylight. Car pulls up with the Lonegans in the front and the headcase, Viktor, in the back. They grabbed Fiona right in front of us, gave Sean a couple of vicious kicks when he tried to stop him."

"You didn't try to stop them?" Gabriel said, obviously disappointed in the man.

"They have guns, Gabriel. Don't be an idiot. We just waved goodbye. Sean and I were pretty sure we'd never see her in one piece again, not with Viktor involved."

"Who is Viktor?" Chuck asked.

"Was Viktor, you mean. He left town pretty shortly after he got out of the hospital. Viktor the Croatian, he liked people to call him. Real nasty son of a bitch; he was the Lonegan's enforcer. Real sadist."

"Hold it," Gabriel interrupted. "Helena mentioned this guy, I think. She said he was her old Croatian boyfriend."

Billy laughed at that. "Yeah, some boyfriend. That was the worst part; he had a thing for Fiona. Kept coming around trying to get her to go out with him, have a drink with him, anything. He was smitten for a while, at least until the Lonegans told him to smitten her instead, big time. He would've enjoyed hurting her at that point, I'm afraid. A lot."

"So what happened?" Gabriel asked. "It doesn't sound like you and Sean came riding to her rescue."

"Fuck no—and fuck you, too, Gabriel. I told you, we don't play in the same league as these guys. We told Mom and Dad to light a candle, that was about it."

"So what happened? How'd she get away?"

Billy shrugged. "Never got the details," Billy said. "Fionna just joked about it a lot, especially around the Lonegans. She always said, 'Viktor should've worn his seatbelt'. Seems he somehow left the car when it was going about forty miles an hour. He spent a couple months in the hospital, then disappeared. Good riddance. Guy scared the shit out of me.

"After that, the Lonegans were in some trouble. They lost their muscle. Word got out that this little girl had snuffed Viktor. They lost respect. That's bad in their business, you know. Started costing them a lot of money. Fiona felt bad—not about Viktor, he was an animal. But she liked the brothers. They're decent guys, both of them. So she kinda took them on as a project, showed them how to run the racket without the muscle. They did even better than before. They both loved her, I'll tell you. She knew it, too. Played them both shamelessly. That's how she ended up with most of their money, in the end." He paused and surveyed the bar, and Gabriel noticed that Dad was checking his watch.

"Well, then. I think it's time we started winding this thing down, Billy," Dad said. Gabriel looked at his own watch and was startled to see it was after three in the morning. There were still twenty or thirty people in the bar. "I'll take care of the stragglers, Billy. You and Sean clean up before you go to bed. Tomorrow's a work day, you know." The old man stood up from his stool with difficulty, stretching his back. "Gabriel," he said, slapping him on the back, "you stay in Fiona's old room tonight, upstairs."

"Not necessary, Dad," Gabriel said. "I got a hotel just down the block. I'll be okay."

"Didn't say it was necessary," Dad said. "I said you'll stay upstairs tonight. See you in the morning." He shuffled off to the nearest clot of patrons.

Gabriel looked at Billy, who just shrugged. "He likes you," Billy said. "You're all he has left of Fiona now. This nearly killed him and mom, you know. Dad never asked how she passed, did he?"

"No, he didn't. I'd prefer if you didn't either, just yet. We'll talk about it tomorrow, okay?" Billy nodded. "But since the old man's out of earshot," Gabriel continued, "tell me about the picture. The one where she's in the choir."

Billy laughed. "I was wondering if you'd let that go." He gave a meaningful look to Gabriel and Chuck. "Some of it was my fault, I shouldn't laugh. That's what got her out of Boston, I think. Otherwise, mom and dad would never have let her go."

"What happened? What did she do?" Gabriel asked.

Billy settled back on his stool. "One Saturday morning, Fiona's doing her research in the booth, reading all the papers like Dad said. All of a sudden, she's all pissed off and excited, both. Never seen her so worked up. She's beet red, you know how she gets when she's really pissed."

"Oh, yeah," Gabriel agreed. "Looks like a firecracker about to explode."

"Yeah, I'm sure you know better than I do," Billy said, smiling. "Turns out, it's because the Bishop of Ireland is making a visit to Boston in a few months, the paper says. He's going to say a special Christmas mass. After a couple days of kicking at passing dogs and cursing out anyone who says hello, suddenly she's all calm and thoughtful, you know. That's when I knew there would be trouble."

"What?" Chuck asked. "What did she do?"

"Shut up," Billy said. "This is a long story. Fiona pulls me aside and makes me swear not to say a thing to Dad or Sean. She knows she can trust me, she said."

"So she played you and your brother just like she did the Lonegans," Chuck said.

"Yeah, all the time. Difference was, Sean and I knew her game. And she was our sister, kind of. Took away a lot of leverage, you know?" He winked at them. "Fiona asks if I've been going to church with mom and dad, though she knows I'm not religious like Sean and them. Then she asks me if I know what a Bishop would wear at a really special event, like Christmas mass. 'What are you talking about?' I asked her. 'You know,' she says, 'like the vestments and the tall hat and all. Do you think all that is real, gold and jewelry quality stones, or is it all costume stuff.' Shit, I don't know, and I told her."

"You have got to be shitting me," Gabriel said.

"She wouldn't," Chuck said.

"Shut up, both of you," Billy said in mock irritation. "So Fiona and I do a little research trip, take the T over to Boston College. She's all dressed up like a college student, and I'm in my suit. She made an appointment with this professor of religious studies; we met him in his office. 'We're doing research for our humanities class at BU, she says, never saying what class or anything. Real devious, my sister. Anything to help, he promises. After a little chitchat, we walk out with the complete list of what the Bishop will be attired in during his upcoming service, with a complete explanation of the history and religious significance of every doodad and device. Turns out, if you're a Bishop, you dress pretty fancy. No gold plated shit or costume jewels on your miter and vestments for you, no sir. Everything's real, the Vatican's best."

"I am so embarrassed," Chuck said. "She's going to hell."

"Then she's there already, brother," Billy said. "But I'm not too worried about my Fiona, I tell you. Devil himself wouldn't stand a chance. Stop interrupting. So her plan starts right then and there, on the T coming back from Chestnut Hill. I can see the gears turning. Two weeks later, she comes home with her choir robes. Mom and Dad are so proud; they make her stand for about fifty pictures. Best church choir in the city. Your wife could sing, you know."

"Like an angel, I know," Gabriel said.

"She's showing up for every rehearsal. Of course she is, she's casing the church. Learns the whole routine, finds out when the vestments are arriving, where they'll be kept until the service. Long story, short; she pinches the Bishop's raiments, jewelry, scepter; the whole works, and hides them in a box in the basement two hours before the service. Half an hour before mass, the whole family is in the pews, so proud and happy that our sister Fiona has finally found religion. We got there real early to get a good view of the choir, brought the video and everything. Everybody we knew was there.

"We're sitting there and it's getting more and more obvious that something is really wrong. Deacons and shit are running around like chickens, you wouldn't believe it. Yelling and arguing from the offices behind the sanctuary, everybody can hear all hell's breaking loose. And there's our Fiona, dressed like a fucking angel in her robes, sitting with the choir, smiling like that cat that ate the canary.

"It was a beautiful service, really was. Fiona had a solo and everything. The Bishop was a bit uninspiring, as I recall. Definitely underdressed for the occasion. Fiona stayed on with the choir, of course. We switched churches, just so we could hear her every Sunday. Mom and Dad were ecstatic. Never seen them prouder."

"So what happened? Why did Fiona have to leave?" Chuck asked. "They found out about the stuff?"

"Oh, no. Never. Fiona retrieved the box a couple of weeks later. I watched her hammer the stuff into unrecognizable crap; pull out all the stones and all. Seemed like she was taking an uncalled for amount of pleasure in that, I'll say. Fenced the whole thing someplace out of state. She made a killing on that stuff."

"I know what happened," Gabriel said, sadly. "No way Helena could keep up the act. Not with how she felt about the church."

Billy nodded sagely. "Exactly, brother. Exactly. You could see it in her face, towards the end. My sister was no hypocrite; I'll say that and more for her. She had to find a way out. So in confession one Sunday, she let's out that she's with child, and how scared she is that everybody can tell, right through the robes. Not three days go by before the music director calls her in to say how sorry he is that, for financial reasons, they've decided to downsize the choir. You know, because they pay the members so much, right? Well, last in, first out is only fair, so she's out of there."

"That works," Chuck says.

"No, it don't," Billy said. "Because my Dad was having none of it. He loved hearing his little girl singing every Sunday. Hell, he brought the recorder almost every week. Never even took the thing out of the box when Sean and me were growing up. Anyway, he charged into that music director's office like his hair was on fire, gave that man such a chewing out about what kind of bullshit did he think he was shoveling, 'financial considerations' his ass. You get the idea. I think he may have accused the man of liking boys too much at some point in there. Enough, anyway, to get the man to admit that he had to let Fiona go because she was pregnant. Well, that shut my Dad up, real quick. He came home looking like someone had punched him in the gut. His little girl, singing in the church choir one minute, knocked up the next.

"Give Fiona credit, though. She tried to tough it out, stuck to her story. She stood there and took the abuse from Dad, Mom, Sean, every night. Even I piled on, just for appearances, of course. Went on for almost two weeks, she never broke character."

"You knew better?" Gabriel asked.

"Sure, I knew better. Not in so many words, but you and I know our Fiona wasn't about to get knocked up by anybody, not unless it suited some grand plan of hers. No way. I kept my mouth shut, though. Didn't see as I was going to be any help, one way or the other."

"So she checked out, left Boston?" Chuck asked.

"No, that wasn't it. She was going to just ride it out, claim she lost the baby or something when the time came. But then things got messy. It wasn't her fault; she couldn't have seen it coming, really. Dad decided that it wasn't just Fiona to blame. He had an idea that the father was one of the Lonegan brothers, and he was pissed. He didn't know which one, but he didn't much care, either. He nearly started a war with them, and that was going to be very ugly for our family.

"Not only, but the Lonegans had their own suspicions. Like I told you, they both were hot after Fiona for years, each without any luck whatsoever. She played them both like a harp, year after year. Well, each of them knew he hadn't gotten into her pants, figured it must've been his brother. That's when things really started to get ugly around here. It came close to killing somebody, probably one of us, to start.

"So what happened?" Gabriel asked. He was getting way too tired for this story to go on much longer.

"Fiona stepped in. She had to. Made it clear to Dad, and then everyone else eventually, that she had made the whole story up, she wasn't with child at all. Of course, that lit Dad's fuse all over again, made him look like a fool. Dad, you may guess, doesn't play the fool well. He had to back down to the Lonegans, to the whole neighborhood. He had a hard time showing his face in the bar, that's how humiliated he was.

"What was killing him, he kept saying to all of us, at dinner, even to Fiona's face, was why? Why would she say such a thing? He couldn't understand it. Fiona kept telling him she just couldn't do the church thing anymore, didn't want to confront us with her disbelieving ways, thought this would get her out quietly, she said. She was sorry it had blown up the way it did.

"Your Dad didn't buy it, did he?" Gabriel asked. "The man's no fool."

"Exactly," Billy agreed. "He may never have graduated high school, but like I said, the man is nobody's fool, Gabriel. It took him a while, but he put it all together. I watched it happen, saw it on his face. Everyone knew about the robbery of the church stuff, of course. It had been in all the papers, played up large about 'What lowlife scum could steal such things from our holy church,' that sort of thing. Dad put it together once he worked out the timing. I could see it in his face, the way he looked at Fiona one night at dinner."

"Did he say anything? Anything to you?" Gabriel asked.

Billy shook his head. "Never said a word, to Fiona or me. He was sure about Fiona, but he only had a vague suspicion I might be in on it. Hell, all I had done was ride on the T with her, I didn't help her any. Dad chose to let any suspicions about me just fade away. But it was never the same between him and Fiona after that. She wasn't the perfect little red-haired angel—"

"—who happened to be a thief and a fugitive," Chuck interjected.

Billy shrugged. "That stuff never bothered him so much. God had dropped her into our family for a reason, that's what Mom and Dad thought. The little girl they never had. But for Dad, that went up in smoke. Mom never figured it out. I don't think so, anyway. But she could see the change; the way things were between Dad and Fiona. It wasn't long before Fiona set up her endgame with the Lonegans."

"Why did she screw them?" Chuck asked. "It doesn't sound like she needed the money."

"No, she could buy and sell them two twice a week for a year. No, she needed to save face, create a reason she had to leave town. Stealing a little wouldn't be convincing. Steal enough to bring the brothers back together in a common cause, to get Fiona. That was a good reason to book out of town, and at the same time eased her guilt about driving a wedge between the boys. Two birds, you know. One day, she and her bike were just gone. It hurt, I won't lie to you. Hurt us all."

Billy looked about, saw that the bar was empty save for them and Sean, who was still cleaning up. "Gotta clean up, boys," Billy said, smacking the bar with his palm as he rose from his stool. "Tomorrow's a working day."

"Can I help?" Gabriel asked, praying the answer was no.

"Thanks, no," Billy said, waving him off. "Go to bed. You know where the room is?"

"Think so," Gabriel said. "Thanks, Billy. See you in the morning. I'll see you back in California, Chuck. Good night."

"God bless."

CHAPTER 29

Gabriel wished he were dead. He lay in Helena's old bed, his feet hanging off the bottom and his head wedged amongst a collection of stuffed animals Gabriel was sure his wife had never had to sleep with. A stuffed monkey had its tail in Gabriel's ear. He didn't care. He didn't dare move his head in any direction for fear it would split like an overripe melon.

The last and only time he had felt this badly after drinking had been the first night he had spent with his wife. How poetic, he thought. It did nothing to ease the pain. He knew that at some point, he would have to get up and present himself downstairs. It seemed that it was daylight. The thought of moving anything more than his eyes made him afraid. Perhaps, if he could manage to smother himself quietly with the stuffed giraffe, he could die peacefully.

A knock on the door caused Gabriel to moan involuntarily. The door squealed open, eliciting another moan. It was Dad; dressed, sober, and amazingly pleasant for a man who had, at his advanced age, consumed at least his weight in alcohol, Gabriel thought.

"Breakfast is up," Dad announced in a voice that made Gabriel think of chewing on aluminum foil. "You'll want this." He put a fizzing glassful of something black and steaming hot in Gabriel's hand. "Take your time if you don't want to eat. Mom says she's only cooking another twenty or thirty minutes." Thankfully, he left without closing the door. Gabriel didn't think he could stand the sound.

Gabriel was proud he made it to the bottom step without falling down or vomiting. The drink had already helped to an amazing degree. He could make out vague, blurry people shapes seated at tables in the bar. He moved to the closest. Billy caught him by the shoulders and steered him to the big booth at the back to join Dad. Billy and Sean were waiting tables. Mom was doing the cooking this morning. Mercifully, the crowd was small and quiet. Gabriel sat across from his father-in-law; a plate full of eggs and sausages appeared in front of him.

"Morning, sunshine," Dad said, finishing a mug of coffee. "How'd you sleep?"

"Don't remember," Gabriel replied. He moved his head back and forth experimentally, and was pleased that he didn't see double anymore. His vision was getting sharper, as well. "Gee, that potion really works. What was it?"

"Secret family hangover cure. Boiling hot Coke, mixed with all those pills left over in the half open vials from Mom's medicine cabinet. And whiskey, of course. We put whiskey in everything, you know."

"Why Mom's? Why not yours?"

"Because you want to feel better, not get an erection, right? Or am I misjudging?"

"Well, it works. Thank you." Gabriel actually felt hungry. He tried the eggs with good result, digging into the rest of the plate with more enthusiasm.

"I know you weren't planning on sleeping over," Dad said. "Thank you for indulging an old man. It feels good to have family around, that's all."

"You were right to insist, Dad. I'm glad I'm here. I'm not looking forward to going back to the hotel room. Or home, for that matter."

"Well, you're certainly welcome to stay as long as you want, Gabriel. Which will probably be right after you finish your breakfast, I know. You don't owe us any more than that, son. Glad Fiona had the brains to put on this party, at least." Gabriel ate, waiting for the man to get to the question he was dancing around. "Seems strange," Dad continued, "that the girl knew when she was going to die to the point of arranging her own wake. Had she been ill very long? Couldn't have been any kind of accident."

Gabriel could think of no easy way to answer the man, so he didn't try. "No, it wasn't any kind of accident. Helena killed herself, Dad." He put down his knife and fork, looking the old man in the eye. He looked pained to the soul, shaking his head in disbelief.

"What a waste, my god," Dad said. "I knew she had a troubled heart, all her life. But it was a good, strong heart for all the time I knew her. I can't believe she'd do such a thing. You and she had marital troubles, I guess. You cheated on her, did you?"

"No, Dad. I didn't cheat on her. We had a great marriage."

"It was the sex then, huh?"

"What? What are you talking about?" Gabriel said, outraged. His head was starting to pound again.

"Making her do the crazy sex stuff, with the choke holds and all?" his Dad said seriously, looking Gabriel in the eye accusingly. "Regular Christian stuff not fun anymore for you, right?"

Gabriel was almost spluttering eggs at the man. "No, Dad, nothing like that. No crazy sex stuff—"

Dad's face split into a grin. "Just fucking with you, Gabriel. Just kidding. I know you were a good husband to my Fiona. Probably a damn sight better than she usually deserved, knowing her temper." Gabriel took a minute to recover himself and managed a weak smile in return. "You better finish those eggs or mom'll kill you. Eat."

Gabriel picked up his fork and resumed eating. "It's a damn strange thing, Dad. I still can't figure it. She wasn't depressed or anything."

"She had a troubled soul, Gabriel. I wish I could say I'm surprised, but her type burn bright and fast. Sad, but not entirely surprised. There was a deep, black hole in her heart; some horrible wound that never healed. Saw it when she first came into our lives."

"Her sister, you mean?"

"Something like that. Don't really know, for sure," Dad said, nodding. "She only made a couple of comments, in an unguarded moment, you know? And our Fiona wasn't unguarded very often."

"What did she say?"

"Just a phrase, here and there. If I'd come upon her on a rainy Sunday, you know. Ask what was troubling her, she once said she was remembering her 'poor, sainted kid sister'. She'd bust the chops of the boys if she thought they were fighting over something stupid, tell them they're lucky to have each other, some folks have no one on this earth. That sort of thing. Nothing special. Did you look at the picture, up in the room?"

"No, I don't think so. Where is it?"

Dad twisted in the booth to call over to his son at the bar.

"Sean, be a good boy and do your old man a favor, will you? Jump up to Fiona's room and bring down that shoebox of hers. Thank you, son." Sean left for the stairway.

Gabriel pushed the empty plate away. "The thing is, Dad, I don't think that's why she did it. I agree she was troubled, no arguing there. She'd been through hell; anyone who knew her could see that. And she had her spells, talking to her dead sister and all. She was troubled, all right. But not depressed, Dad. She's the last person in the world I would've expected to do this. The last."

"You're probably just fooling yourself, because you can't admit you were so depressing to be married to that she had no choice," Dad answered, shaking his head. Sean arrived and deposited the shoebox on the table between them. He leaned on his Dad's shoulder and pretended to get the old man in a headlock.

"Dad's only fucking with you, Gabe. It means he likes you. Like you should give a shit. You want some coffee?" he asked, releasing his dad and clearing the plate.

"That'd be great, Sean. Thanks." He struggled a smile for Dad. "You've got some fucked up sense of humor, old man."

"Yeah, I'm thinking of putting up a little stage and doing standup over there in the corner on Saturday nights," he said. "Really bring in the crowd." Sean arrived with the coffee and sat down in the booth next to Gabriel. He pushed the shoebox over to him. Gabriel took off the top and rummaged through its contents. About a dozen fake passports and driver's licenses, each with Helena's picture but with a different name. Gabriel muttered each aloud, amazed.

"Anna Plurabelle, Issy Earwicker, Livia Chimpden—she actually used these names?"

Sean nodded. "And with a straight face. Nobody ever took any notice at all, far as I saw."

"At least she never claimed to be Joyce James," Gabriel said. He took out the only remaining item, the photograph, and stared at it long and hard. It was a fading color photograph of two redheaded young girls dressed in matching pinafores, hugging each other tightly and both smiling like fools at the camera. They looked about twelve years old and identical. Gabriel couldn't make out which was his wife to be, they looked so alike. "My god," Gabriel finally said softly, "identical twins. I never knew."

"Nobody knew nothing, Gabriel," Dad said, taking the picture from him to look at it himself. He handed it back to Gabriel. "If there was a story to go with the picture, I'm afraid it died with your wife."

Gabriel took the photograph back and turned it over. There was nothing on the back. He held it out for his father in law.

"You keep it," Dad said. "You said, you didn't think she was depressed."

"No, she wasn't. At least, couple of days before, when she left me for her trip to Michigan, she seemed fine. Better than fine, it was like she was on a mission, had a real purpose. Chuck saw her in Michigan after that, said she wasn't depressed at all. Just the usual Helena, he said."

"Yeah, like I'd trust anything that joker had to say," Dad said, just about spitting on the floor as he said it.

"And she made a recording," Gabriel said.

"Like a suicide note sort of thing?" Sean asked.

"Not really. Partially. First part, she said she was sorry for what she was about to do, said goodbye, kind of. But you could tell, that's not why she made the recording."

"Who knows why people do that sort of thing," Dad said. "I hope you destroyed it."

"No, Dad. I watched the thing like fifty times."

"Bad idea," Sean said, and his father nodded in agreement.

"Maybe. The more I watch it though, the more certain I am that she was doing some sort of experiment." He shook his head and drank the black coffee. "I know it sounds a little crazy."

"She was a little crazy," Dad said. "What kind of experiment is killing yourself on camera?"

"I don't think I should show it to you, but—"

"No way I ever want to see it, Gabriel. Never," Dad said emphatically.

"No, you shouldn't. It's really disturbing. I see the whole thing in my head every night, I'll tell you. But I had to, because I'm sure it's a message. It has all sorts of hidden meanings to it." He shook his head again.

"What are you talking about? Hidden meanings? Like some sort of mystery clues?" Dad asked.

"You sure you're not just putting your own spin on it? You know, trying to read more into it than is really there," Sean said.

"No, not a mystery or anything like that. But I'm not just making it up, either. If you watched it, you'd see. I've been trying to work it out. I figured one part, an important part."

"And?" said Dad, sounding skeptical.

"And I'm kind of at a dead end. She left a particular clue that I'm sure was meant so that I'm the only one who could possibly figure it out. And I did figure it out. I just don't know what it means."

"So what is this clue that only you could figure out?" Sean asked.

"It's a figure that was carved in a tree. The tree was in the middle of a forest, in upstate New York. No way anyone else could've found that tree but me. But it looked like the carving was pretty new. Helena couldn't have made it—at least, I don't see how. She wouldn't have had the time. I know about when she left my parents in Michigan, then she set up back in California. I can't figure out how it got there or what it means. But I'm sure Helena wanted me to find it."

"What was the figure?" Sean asked. "Carved in the tree, what was it?"

"It was weird," Gabriel said. "I've never seen anything like it. Kind of a fuzzy heart."

"A fuzzy heart?" Sean echoed.

Dad looked at him quizzically. "Draw it," Dad commanded. The other two looked at him. "What are you, deaf? Draw a picture of this fuzzy heart you saw." Sean took his order pad and pen from his apron and handed them over to Gabriel. Gabriel drew the stylized heart shape as he remembered it, surrounded by many short, thick lines like the radiance of a cartoon sun. He pushed it over to Dad. Sean leaned over to look at it, too, then just shrugged.

Dad looked at it for about ten seconds before he said, "Well, son, that answers that."

"Answers what?" Gabriel asked, looking back and forth between Dad and the picture.

"That shows just why Fiona had to kill herself, that's what," Dad said.

"What? How?" Gabriel was incredulous. He turned the picture back to look at it more closely.

"Because it proves she couldn't stand being married to a fucking idiot no more, that's what," Dad announced. The other two just looked at him. "Now I've never been to your magic tree in upstate New York, Gabriel, but I'll bet you my right arm that that isn't no fuzzy heart carved into it." He grabbed the paper and pen from Gabriel. "Fuzzy heart, my ass. This is what you were looking at, right?" Dad redrew the picture next to Gabriel's. He drew the same heart, but this time with three short, thick lines coming out of the top. He drew four short, thick lines coming straight out of each side. He slid it back to Gabriel.

Sean looked over. "What the hell's the difference, Dad?" Sean asked. "Fewer lines, so what?"

"You," Dad said, pointing to his son, "I don't blame so much. You're no fancy professor with a PhD. You're just a bartender, like your old man. You—" he stabbed his finger at Gabriel, "are a fucking moron."

Gabriel looked back down at the new picture. "That's what Helena always said," Gabriel said, sadly. "I'm sorry, Dad. I just don't get it." He looked up at the man with sadness.

"How long you been puzzling over your leprechaun carving?" Dad asked.

"Couple of days now," Gabriel admitted.

"And how long you been wearing that gaudy thing on your hand there?" the old man asked, grabbing Gabriel's left hand and twisting it so that Gabriel could see the Claddagh ring he wore; two hands grasping a heart, topped with a crown.

"Since Helena and I—Holy Shit! Dad, you're a genius!" Gabriel exclaimed.

"Genius, my ass. You're a fucking moron, that's all. Fiona was right about you. You been staring at that thing for twenty years."

"More." Gabriel kept staring at his ring, smiling. "How could I not see that?"

"Fucking moron," Sean agreed. Gabriel didn't care. He grinned like an idiot at the two of them. "So why did she lead you on some goose chase, just to get you to look at the ring sitting there the whole time on your finger?" Sean asked.

Gabriel leaned back in the booth, his smile dissolving. "Well, you should know that, Dad. It's your ring. You gave it to her."

"Where you'd ever get that idea?" Dad asked. "It wasn't ever mine."

"Helena," Gabriel protested. "On our wedding night, when she gave it to me. She said it was a gift from her Dad."

"Well, that was another of her lies, plain and simple. It was never mine to give."

"But then who's was it? Who gave it to her?" Gabriel asked.

"It was stolen, like everything else she had," Sean said. Dad gave his son a withering look and Sean wilted noticeably. "Oh, sorry. Shouldn't have said that. God bless our dear departed sister," he muttered. He gathered the empty mugs and retreated into the kitchen.

They watched him go, Dad shaking his head.

"Was it, Dad?"

"Yeah, of course. Just look at the thing. You can't buy a ring like that, you know."

"You said I shouldn't wear it around while in Boston. You said some folks might take it wrong."

"Well, there's good advice for you. Suspect I was referring to the rightful owners, since it had been wrongly taken already, in a manner of speaking."

"Who'd she steal it from, Dad?" Gabriel looked at the thing on his finger with a different appreciation.

"Don't worry about it, Gabriel. They're not really going to want it back. I'm just sorry my son is such an idiot for opening his mouth."

"There's a reason she pointed me to that tree, why there's a carving of my ring on that tree. She had a reason."

"I'm sorry, Gabriel. I don't know her reasons. The Claddagh is a storied ring, lots of legends surround it. Most of them bullshit, I'm sure."

"No, I'm sure she meant this ring. This ring, in particular."

"Maybe she did. I don't know, Gabriel."

"So tell me then. Who'd she steal it from? I think it's important, Dad. I'm not offended that she gave me a stolen ring for a wedding present."

"You're not? My opinion, you should be."

"Stop dancing here, old man. What's the story?"

Dad sighed. "I was with her on that one, too. Very strange job. Completely out of character for Fiona."

"What do you mean?"

"She saw the announcement in the paper, like she usually found her marks. But the way she did it—not like Fiona at all. And the mark itself—it wasn't an estate sale or auction house, like she usually hit."

"What was it?"

"It was an exhibition at the university, in Cambridge I think."

"MIT?"

"Yeah, MIT. It was a visiting exhibit, like a museum show."

"About jewelry?"

"Nah, not the jewelry exactly. It was a show about some famous scientist. I'm sure Fiona took notice because he was from Ireland."

"So, that's what was different about it? That it was a museum?" Gabriel didn't say that for a girl willing to steal the vestments out of a church on Christmas, stealing from a museum didn't seem like much of a stretch.

"That was part of it, sure. But the real strange part was the job itself."

"What happened?"

"Well, like I was telling you last night, I usually joined Fiona on Saturdays for her little research visits—"

"You mean, when she cased the places she was going to rob."

"Yeah, exactly. It made it look more natural, two people together instead of one snooping around. Like a family just out having a good time."

"So you and Fiona went to MIT to check out the exhibit?"

"Yeah, just like always. She's checking everything, drawing pictures on her yellow pad like she sometimes does. All of a sudden, she pulls up short like she's just seen the face of the Blessed Mother in the glass case. She's looking at the ring."

"Whose ring was it?"

"I don't remember, Gabriel. Some Irish scientist, that's all I know. It was almost thirty years ago, more. She freezes there, staring at the thing. I was starting to think she was having one of her spells. Then she tells me to go stand over by the door. 'Why?' I asked her. You have to realize, Fiona never did anything rash. She always had her plans, her schematics and all. Every detail was in the plan. No drama, no noise. Not that day. She snapped at me, told me to get the hell over next to the door. 'What do you want me to do?' I asked her. 'You'll figure it out', she tells me, and gives me a look that's like to melt lead. I go stand by the door, watching her. I had no idea what was going on. Suddenly, Fiona's removing her top, right in the museum, with a big crowd around. I mean, she's wearing a bra and all, nothing too indecent, but people are noticing. The security guard who's standing next to me by the door gets one look and starts over, telling her she can't do that. Before I can blink, she's dropped the guard like a sack of potatoes. Don't know what she done to him, didn't kill him, but he was on the floor, out cold. She took his radio, then wraps her top around her hand and smashes the glass case. Takes the ring, nothing else, and goes tearing out like a banshee straight past me and out the door. The guard was up in a couple of minutes and trying to call on a radio he didn't have any more. When he finally tried to follow Fiona out the door, we kind of got all tangled up for a bit. Long enough, anyway."

"That's it? She just took off?"

"Yeah, pretty much. She was waiting here when I got back, calm as a cucumber. I asked her what the fuck that stunt was; she could've gotten both of us arrested, I told her. She just laughed. Never talked much about it after."

"Did she say why she wanted it?"

"No, and I asked; pretty emphatically, too. She scared me that day, with that stunt. But she never explained why she had to have that ring so badly."

"What did she do with it?"

"Nothing, as far as I know. Until she gave it to you. Just kept it with her other stuff, then it disappeared with her when she left."

"Any chance of remembering more about who the exhibit was about? Whose ring it was she stole?"

"I told you, Gabriel. It was a long time ago. I didn't take much notice at the time of the man's name, anyhow. Certainly don't have a clue now."

"Then I'm back at that brick wall."

"Sorry, Gabriel. You know, I'm not trying to tell you your business, but maybe your government friend can check it out."

"Chuck?" Gabriel considered this advice. "I'm not sure I want him to know about this. Helena went to a lot of trouble to make sure I'm the only one who could figure out this ring business, whatever it is."

"You may be right about that. Rubs me the wrong way, that one."

"Helena had a problem with him, too, some of the time. But I may not have a choice."

Gabriel said his goodbyes, and promised to get back to Boston as soon as he could. Dad let him keep the picture of the two sisters, though he wasn't even sure he wanted it.

"Hey," Dad said, just before he left. "What about Fiona's bike?"

"Her motorcycle? The Ducati?" Gabriel asked.

"Yeah, she left it. We kept it in the shed out back. You want we should ship it to California?"

"Wouldn't bother, Dad," Gabriel said. "I'm not about to start riding a stolen motorcycle. Let the boys figure it out."

"Oh, Billy will go crazy for that thing. I'll let his wife give it to him for his birthday, it's coming up in a month."

"Great. She can give it to him for his last birthday present, Dad. That machine has a history, you know."

"I'm sure it does. Everything that girl touched. Godspeed, Gabriel."

"And you, Dad. Whatever that means."

CHAPTER 30

Gabriel packed up and caught a plane out of Logan for Detroit. He knew he was probably looking for any destination other than San Francisco. He dreaded the thought of walking back into the house he had shared his entire adult life, now without his life's companion. He wasn't ready to start the 'after Helena' chapter.

He justified the change in destination with the rationalization that the ring clue was at a dead end, and therefore he should pursue Helena's other major clue—the formula. He could have just as easily sought out a mathematician at UCSF or Berkley, but felt that Professor Wells had been brought into the picture by Helena, and was therefore special. He also liked the man from their first meeting. And with Helena gone, maybe he should visit the only remaining family he had on this earth—even if they sometimes didn't know who he was.

The professor seemed genuinely pleased to hear from Gabriel, and encouraged him to stop by his office at whatever time was convenient. Gabriel reappeared in his oak-lined office the next day. Gabriel noticed that the man must have found some tobacco for his pipe after all, the unique aroma pleasantly greeting him as he shook the professor's hand again.

"Very happy to see you again, Dr. Sheehan," Professor Wells enthused, settling back in his old leather chair with a creak.

"Please, Professor. Call me Gabriel."

"Only if you'll call me Everson, then. How is your lovely wife, Helena?"

"She's passed, I'm afraid, Everson."

"Well, do give her my regards—I'm sorry, did you say she's passed?" Gabriel nodded. "My god, Gabriel. I am so sorry. She was so vivacious, so enthusiastic. I didn't realize that she had been ill. Was it sudden?"

"Yes, very. Thank you for your kind regards, Everson. Helena is actually why I'm here. You remember our last meeting, when I didn't know why I should see you?"

"Yes, yes." The man was obviously distraught by Gabriel's news. "And I remember being surprised to see you that soon. Something in what Helena had said implied that you'd be seeing me much later. And now here you are, again."

"Yes, and now here I am. It seems that Helena was involved in some research with which I'm not familiar. I'm trying to sort it out."

"It doesn't seem as if your's was a very close marriage, was it, Gabriel?"

Gabriel flushed. Why did so many people accuse him of that? "On the contrary, Professor. Helena and I enjoyed over twenty years of a very good marriage, thank you. Helena, however, was a very private person in some respects. She pursued an independent course in her research, towards the end."

"I am sorry, Gabriel. That was very rude of me to say. Your marriage is none of my business, least of all in your time of grief. I'm sorry." Gabriel nodded. "Please, how can I be of help?"

Gabriel produced a small thumb drive from his pocket. "Helena made a recording, just before she died. If you don't mind, I'd like to play it for you."

"Certainly, by all means." He pushed his chair away so Gabriel could plug the drive into his computer. Gabriel stood to watch over the man's shoulder as the recording began. Gabriel muted the sound and advanced the playback to the point where Helena is seated in front of the formula, and then let it run, in silence. "What is she saying?" the professor asked, looking up at Gabriel.

"I don't think that's important just now," Gabriel said defensively. "I'm more interested in your opinion regarding the formula behind her."

"Oh, I see. Can you make the image bigger? I'm not good with these things." Gabriel leaned over and adjusted the image so that it filled the screen. "Interesting. When does she move out of the way?"

"She doesn't."

"Oh. Well, that does make it more difficult, Gabriel. The whole middle portion of the equation is obscured."

"I know. That's why I'm here. Can you tell me anything from what you see?"

"Could you freeze it? Thank you. Let me see." He studied the image for a few minutes. "No."

Gabriel was taken aback. "What do you mean, no? Surely it has some meaning to you, the part you can see?"

Wells studied the image some more. "It does, of course. It's a complex equation, obviously. And I understand that as a mathematician, I am expected to understand such things. But I don't have enough information, I'm afraid. It's an equation without context, and a partial equation, at that. It could represent any of a thousand different things. I wouldn't know where to start."

Gabriel collapsed back into a chair. He felt as if he had been punched in the stomach. He wasn't ready for another dead end, not this soon. "Please, study it more, Everson. It's not just that you're a mathematician. You're the mathematician Helena picked, I'm sure of it. There is a reason she wanted me to come see you. This formula is the reason, I'm sure of it."

Wells looked at the other man with pity. "That may be true, Gabriel, but I don't know what her reason was. Mine is an extremely esoteric branch of mathematics. I'm not sure I have the insight that she expected."

"My wife was a very good judge of people, Everson. She knew you could help me. She pointed me here."

"Maybe not me specifically, Gabriel. Perhaps she meant that you should seek help in this department. Maybe we should enlist others?"

Gabriel shook his head. "That's not the way this works. That's not how Helena did things. She trusted individuals, not departments. It's you I need."

"Then I'm sorry, Gabriel. Even if I had one of my colleagues try some sort of computer match, I don't think it would work. They can try something like that if you know what field to search, or have the complete formula. But I can't tell from this how many elements are missing, and they're missing from the middle of the equation, not the end. It would be impossible, I think."

Gabriel tried not to give in to the increasing feeling of futility. "Let me ask you something else, then. What about the numbers forty-two and one hundred twenty six."

"What about them?"

"Are they special in any way?"

"Why do you ask?"

"Helena references those numbers in her recording."

"Can I hear?"

"No, not really. It's in code, sort of."

Wells looked confused, glancing back and forth between his guest and the image of the poor, deceased young woman. He sighed. "Well, as for one hundred twenty six, I can't say. But forty-two, of course, that's a different matter entirely."

"What do you mean?"

"Well, it's well known that the number is special, unique. Many would say it is the most significant of all real numbers, you know."

"What do you mean? More important than pi, than Euler's constant?"

"Those are not real numbers, Gabriel. They are of the class of imaginary numbers, important to the universe in their own right. Forty-two is a very significant real number. It is the constant that is most significant in our own world."

"In what way significant? I don't understand."

"Well, in hundreds of ways, really. It depends on your context. Mathematically, the number forty-two has dozens of special properties that make it unique. It is a meandric number and an open meandric number. It is a pronic number, an abundant number, a sphenic number; it shows up in Sylvester's sequence. It is a Catalan number, a Störmer number, a primary pseudoperfect number. And that's just off the top of my head."

"I don't know what any of that means."

"You're not a mathematician. Are you sure your wife wasn't a mathematician, Gabriel? She must have come up with this formula from somewhere."

"I don't think so, Everson. She had no formal education after seventh or eighth grade."

"Doesn't rule out the possibility completely. Less likely, but math is different from most other fields of study. Most mathematicians become successful through study, of course. But there is a long history of brilliant mathematicians who appeared out of the blue, or were mentally ill, even. Some have conjectured that there is a special relationship in the mind between mathematical insight and some forms of mental illness. There was a movie with that Crowe fellow, I forget the name. But it was a true story."

"Helena did do well in Professor Jacoby's graduate seminar, I know."

"Elliot Jacoby's seminar here? If she did well in that class, she's borderline genius. That man can't teach worth a damn. Students started calling him—well, I shouldn't say."

"Professor Jackshit. Yeah, I remember. I dropped the course after the first day."

"Oh, that was you? They still talk about a student—"

"No, that was someone else. I know the story, though. So if Helena was naturally gifted in mathematics, she may have discovered something, something to do with the number forty-two? Or something described by this formula?"

"Certainly, it's possible. But I don't see the importance of a purely mathematical discovery. Even if she discovered the proof of some long unproven theorem, such a thing would only be important to a small community of mathematicians. Might be worth a prize, but hardly earth shaking."

"No, Helena was no theoretician. Her research was very practical, I'm sure."

"What was she researching before her death?"

"I'm not entirely certain. It had something to do with mental illness, I know that. She was investigating a specific aspect of mental illness, using the brainwave analysis techniques we perfected. I'm not familiar with the specifics."

"Then it was some sort of physical phenomenon she was describing, most likely. Perhaps the property of some signal or a physical property, like conductance or something?"

Gabriel shook his head. "I wish I knew. That sounds reasonable. Closer than anything I've thought of. Does the number forty-two come up in any physical formulas?"

"All the time. It's like it's hard wired into our particular world. The critical angle between an observer and a rainbow? Forty-two degrees. What's more fundamental than that, I ask you?"

"Who doesn't like rainbows?" Gabriel asked, not fundamentally impressed.

"Oh, you'll appreciate this: Cooper did the calculations surrounding the thing in the book by Lewis Carroll, in the 1800's, where he wrote about boring a hole through the center of the earth to get to the other side. Turns out, if you did that, the initial acceleration of gravity and subsequent gravitational braking would land you on the other side at a dead stop. And the trip would take—wait for it, now—exactly forty-two minutes, not a second more or less. Impressive, huh?"

"Impressive."

"Not only that, but if the hole was bored through any part of the earth, not just the exact center, the transit time always works out to exactly forty-two minutes. Amazing."

"Somehow, Everson, I don't think Helena's formula relates to traveling through the center of the earth. Or off-center, for that matter."

Wells looked back at the formula on the screen, studying it anew. He fidgeted with his pipe, packing it with tobacco. "Do you mind?" he asked Gabriel, then went through a ritual of lighting it when Gabriel shook his head.

"Did I ever tell you about my grandfather?" Gabriel asked him.

Wells ignored the comment. His expression changed. "Gabriel, I might have a thought. Now that we know your wife's special affection for the number forty-two, and that this relates to a physical phenomenon, I think..." He trailed off.

Gabriel waited as the man rose from his chair and took a large reference book from the shelf beside his desk and paged through it. He got to whatever he was looking for and looked back and forth between the book and the computer screen.

"My god. I think I found it. Or something like it, at least. Look." Gabriel came around the desk to look at the screen again. "It's definitely in large part the Riemann zeta function, the sixth moment. I wouldn't have figured it out except for the number forty-two. Forty-two appears as a constant in the middle portion of the formula, see?" The professor showed Gabriel in the book where the complete formula could be seen to indeed include the number forty-two. "Obviously, constants are easier to identify in a formula than expressions. It's so simple when you look at it now."

Gabriel's heart leapt. This sounded important. "That's great, Everson. You're a genius for figuring it out."

"No, I'm certainly no genius. Actually, I'm a little embarrassed I didn't realize it before, now that I know what the formula is. This is really well within my field. Which really makes no sense, Gabriel."

"Why is that?"

"Well, the Riemann function relates to theoretical physics, involving higher dimensions and multidimensionality. Hardly something you'd use in analyzing electrical signals." They both stared at the woman on the screen and the formula behind. "And before we get too excited, I really think we're missing something else. The formula, including the area covered by her head, looks longer than just the Riemann zeta formula. There's something else missing."

"What do you think it is?"

"Truly, I haven't a clue, Gabriel. I'm sorry." They sat in disappointed silence for a few minutes. "I'm sure the answer lies in going back and reviewing her research. She must have left notes, documentation of some kind? The formula and its meaning must appear there."

"Destroyed."

"Destroyed?"

"Destroyed. All of her research, the notes, everything was on her hard drive. It's gone."

"Who would have done such a thing?"

"Helena. Just before she died."

"But that makes no sense, Gabriel. Why would your wife go to such trouble to leave clues about her work, but go to even more trouble to destroy it? That's insane."

"That is one explanation, Everson. I hope it's not the right one."

Gabriel packed up to head back home to San Francisco. He decided to skip the visit to his parents for now. He figured there would be plenty of time in the future to visit, when he wasn't so traumatized. Whenever that would be.

Arthur picked him up at the airport. Conversation was sparse between them on the way back to Half Moon Bay. Arthur told Gabriel that Chuck had resumed living at the lab, though he had no idea what he was up to. Arthur, it seemed, wasn't up to much of anything. He was taking Helena's death almost as poorly as Gabriel.

"So the math professor was helpful, then?" Arthur asked, turning into Gabriel's driveway. He turned off the car.

"Yeah, very. He figured out what the formula was, after a fashion. Most of it, anyway."

"That's great, Gabriel. What's next?"

Gabriel shook his head. "Not sure, Arthur. The whole thing is like a puzzle, you know? But the puzzle only has three or four pieces. If the puzzle had a hundred pieces, you can afford to leave out a few, if you can't figure out where they go. You can still make out the picture. When you only have three or four pieces, and one or two are missing? Makes it hard to see the big picture."

"Just gotta figure out the rest, Gabriel."

"Yeah. Working on it."

"Let me know if I can help, buddy. Dinner tomorrow? Sam would like to see you."

"Sure, Arthur. Pick me up whenever. Thanks for the ride. Night."

Gabriel carried his suitcase into the house. Nothing had changed, of course. His wife was still dead. And he still didn't know why.

He spent the night reading about the Riemann zeta function and remained completely lost. He was no theoretical mathematician. More important, he didn't believe his wife had been a theoretical mathematician, either. What was she playing at? If she wanted him to figure this out, why did she make it into some kind of scavenger hunt? Helena was a careful, studious researcher. Gabriel had read her reports for decades. She never, ever discarded primary data; she kept everything, forever. Until the day she died, of course. On that occasion, she melted it all down into slag. The professor was right: It was insane.

Gabriel thought he had figured out two big puzzle pieces. He had deciphered the importance of his wife's favorite number. It seemed forty-two was everybody's favorite number. His wife, though, was a true devotee. So much a fan that she had the tattoo to prove it. That tattoo, he realized, was at least thirty years old. She had it when they met. What kind of game was he playing that had started over thirty years ago?

That piece had helped him figure out the second part, the biggest piece so far—that equation behind Helena. By plugging in forty-two, Everson had figured out the equation. But what was the equation even for? On top of that, a part of the equation was still missing. Gabriel didn't have any idea how he was going to figure out the missing part. Hell, he thought, I don't even understand why it's missing. Why didn't she just turn around at some point in the recording and say, "Hey, babe. Here is a really, really important formula written on this board behind me. Let me duck out of the way a sec." Even better, why didn't she say what the fucking thing was used for? He was still stuck in the angry stage.

Gabriel played with his ring, twisting the huge gold thing on his finger. He had taken to doing that a lot over the last couple of days. He felt played. He had been ecstatic when he figured out the clues that sent him back to their tree. He thought he had the whole thing figured out for a while there. Wrong again. What was so important about the ring? He tried to remember exactly what she had said on their wedding night, when she had given it to him, but it was too long ago. How important could it be, anyway? She had stolen the thing. It wasn't a gift from her father at all. The whole thing had been a lie. Helena had stolen it years and years before they even met—hard to believe it had any special meaning for him personally.

Gabriel sat on the couch, head in his hands. It was dark, and he was jet lagged. Again. He wasn't thinking well, he knew. He'd get some sleep, start again in the morning. He needed a plan, though. He needed to know what he was going to do when he woke up, otherwise he'd never be able to fall asleep. He reviewed his situation. He had two angles to work: the ring, and the formula. Both dead ends. What next? Think, Gabriel.

Okay, he thought. All the records are shot, but the people who worked with Helena are still around. Unless she killed them, but Gabriel thought that Arthur probably would've mentioned something if that were the case. First item for tomorrow's agenda: Contact Helena's coworkers. Then there was the second item, the ring puzzle. He knew what he had to do; he had to find out who the ring belonged to when Helena stole it. He had no idea why; it was just that it was his only thread to pull on. Dad had said what Gabriel was thinking, however: Chuck could run it down, probably. If he called Chuck, though, he'd tip his hand. Helena had gone to a great deal of trouble to cover the trail to that ring. Asking Chuck felt like a bad idea. Who could he trust?

"Arthur?" Gabe said when Arthur answered his phone. "Sorry to bother you. Yes, it's really, really late. Three am. Yes, that's really, fucking late, Arthur. Listen; do you still play bridge with the FBI guy? You trust him? I know he's still pissed at me, Arthur. I need a favor. Get a pen and paper. I'll wait. Yes, this is important. No, it can't wait until morning. Yes, I know morning is in like three fucking hours, Arthur. You got the pen? I'll wait.

"Write this down: Robbery of visiting scientist exhibit at MIT, Boston. Scientist was Irish. Robbery occurred between twenty-five and, uh, say thirty-five years ago. You writing this down? It's important. A gold ring was stolen, never recovered. No, not mine. Yes, it was my ring, I think. Don't tell him that, though. Don't tell anyone, especially Chuck, okay, Arthur? No, I'm not being as fucking paranoid as Helena. And thanks for insulting my dead wife, asshole.

"Don't hang up. Ask your friend to see if he can find out the name of the scientist whose ring was stolen. That's it. Yeah, easy, right? The FBI is supposed to be good at this kind of thing. First thing in the morning, okay? It's really, really important. Yes, you can go to bed now. I'll see you tomorrow. Right, later today, then. Hi to Sam. No, don't bother to wake her up to tell her. Bye, Arthur. And thanks."

Gabriel had slept. He dressed and headed for the lab, the only place that felt worse at this point than his empty home. The place his wife had died.

Gabriel went straight to his office, studiously avoiding even looking in the direction of Helena's lab. It was early, at least an hour before the secretary would show up. Hell, he didn't know for sure that she even showed up at all, anymore. He sat at his desk and booted up his desktop computer. Chuck appeared in the doorway.

"Hey, buddy," Chuck said brightly, leaning against the doorframe. "Welcome home."

Gabriel studied the other man. "Hi, Chuck."

"Where you been?"

"Boston. Hung out with my in-laws for a while." Chuck just nodded, said nothing. "What've you been up to?"

"Not much," Chuck said. "Mostly trying to figure out your wife's message. Strange. Really, really strange."

Gabriel stood up and came around the desk, leaned on the edge. He had a feeling something wasn't right here. "Any luck?" Gabriel asked.

"Not a fucking bit," Chuck said. "I got the forty-two thing, we had that before you left. The rest is bullshit, I think."

"Why would it be bullshit?"

Chuck shrugged. "Who knows? Who knows what the girl was thinking? I mean, she was only a couple of minutes from offing herself at that point, you know?"

Gabriel cringed inwardly. "You said you had a deal. You don't think she kept it?"

"I don't know, Gabe. I really don't know. It was kind of an adversarial relationship, there towards the end. I don't think you and Helena were really being square with me at that point. Were you?"

"I don't know what you're talking about, Chuck." Chuck had taken a couple of steps into the office. Gabriel didn't like his body language.

"Of course not, Gabriel. It wasn't like you were calling the shots most of the time anyway, right? She had you dancing like a puppet there at the end, just like the rest of us, right? I mean, how many times are you going have to see that math professor, anyway? You must be getting a little pissed off, being pulled all over the country like that. And for what? It's all bullshit, anyway."

"You're following me? You know I was in Michigan?"

"I don't follow people, Gabriel. You know that. Just keeping tabs on my friends, that's all. Especially since my friends started lying to me, and destroying my work, and sabotaging my projects. That's all."

"Your work? That program was mine and Helena's. We worked our whole lives together on that."

"Yeah, that's right. And now it's at the bottom of the bay. How'd that work out for you? And in case you don't remember, I put in a few years of hard work on that program, too. You two wouldn't have made it except for me."

"You had your reasons, Chuck. Helena always knew what you were up to."

"Up to? I worked alongside you guys for years; I was the brain behind half the stuff this company came up with. Nobody complained about Chuck when I figured out all the signals stuff."

"You were figuring out how to interrogate people without pulling off their fingernails, that's all. Until you started working on how to turn the NSA into Big Brother. Helena was right about you. You're the Judas in our midst, the antichrist."

"Will you stop with that bullshit? I never had any other motive than to try to make this work to protect our country. I swore an oath. I spent years trying to make this work, and now it's fucked. All gone."

"She made a deal with you, Chuck. I don't know why; if it were up to me, I would've just burned the whole thing down. You say she didn't, and she left you what you need to get it back."

"That's a crock of shit and you know it. Maybe you can spend the rest of your life trying to run down a bunch of crazy-ass clues. I'm not that gullible. She lied to me. She lied all the time. Just like she lied to me about the drive and then tossed it off the bridge. I watched the police video, watched it sail into the ocean. That wasn't just my life's work, Gabriel. Our life's work. That was important, important to the security of this country. Helena was crazy—so crazy she had to destroy everything we worked on before she destroyed herself."

"She wasn't crazy."

"She wasn't crazy? How can you say that? You've been screwed just as much as me, chasing her crazy paranoid dreams just as much as me.

You know who I ran into at the wake, Gabriel?" Gabriel just shook his head. "Interesting guy, trucker who knew our Helena real well it seems. Spent a lot of time with her. Nice fellow. He's the guy who called Arthur, to tell us where she was when she landed in Boston.

"He told me all about her. How he had to spring her out of a mental hospital in the middle of Nowhere, Pennsylvania. About how she spent her formative years being raped in that orphanage on a weekly basis. Oh, and about how she was complicit in the murder of her kid sister. How she somehow managed to push her out a window or something."

Gabriel felt like he was being pummeled. He had no idea what Chuck was talking about. He latched onto the one thing that almost made sense. "It wasn't her kid sister—she had a twin, I think. I have a picture."

"It's all bullshit, Gabriel. Everything she said was a lie. How's this for a fun fact—your wife's name wasn't Fiona, either. Some surprise, huh? But you'll never guess this part. I did some checking of the trucker's story, pulled some old records."

"You said there weren't any records."

"There's not much, that's for sure, and half those orphanage records are complete fiction. They are a civilized country, though. They have to keep a record of who's born and who dies. So I found the certificate of the girl's death, I think. I mean, how many little girls are pushed out of a window to their death, right? Maybe they were twins, I don't know. Doesn't matter. Here's the good part. Ready?" Gabriel nodded, still stunned. "The girl who died, your wife's sister? Her name was Fiona. Your wife took her name, probably when she came overseas. How sick is that, Gabe? Impersonating her dead sister for all those years."

"You don't know what she went through. You don't know why she did that," Gabriel said in defense. He still felt like he was in a boxing match here, and he was feeling punch-drunk.

"I know what she went through, better than you, buddy. After that little incident, they had her hospitalized for almost five years. They fried her to a crisp back in Ireland. Face it. The recording isn't a map. It's the crazed ramblings of a fucking paranoid schizophrenic. That's why she killed herself, and now we're fucked. She fucked both of us."

Gabriel carefully considered everything Chuck had just said. If he were capable of thinking about it rationally, he may have believed some of it made sense. Maybe most of it. Gabriel, however, wasn't thinking rationally. He was still stuck in that anger phase. Maybe later he would get to the rationalizing part. Maybe someday make it all the way to acceptance. Today, he was still angry. So angry, that without realizing what he was doing, he smashed his fist into Chuck's face.

Chuck was down on the floor, holding his face as blood streamed from his nose. Gabriel looked at his hand in disbelief. He had never punched anyone before. "I think I broke my hand," he said.

"Who gives a fuck about your hand?" Chuck yelled nasally. "You broke my fucking nose."

"Get out, Chuck. Take your stuff, and your fucking broken nose, and get out. Go back to Washington, or wherever. Get out and never come back. And stop following me, too. If I find out that you're tracking me, I'll find you. I'll come after you with a baseball bat or something."

"You're almost as crazy as your dead wife."

"Yeah, almost. Now get the fuck out of my office."

CHAPTER 31

Gabriel waited until Chuck had packed his things and left. By the time he left, Chuck's nose had quit bleeding. Gabriel didn't shake his hand. Truth be known, he didn't think he could. His hand was painful and swollen. It was worth it, he thought. Faith had appeared at some point, asking Gabriel if he needed anything. When she saw Chuck preparing to leave, she didn't look in the least upset. Gabriel asked her to have Helena's coworkers; the musicians in particular, come by the office in the afternoon. He was going to the emergency room.

Gabriel came back from the hospital with his hand in a splint. He had indeed broken one of the bones of his hand, but the fracture was undisplaced and the orthopedic surgeon had assured him that it would heal fine without surgery. It was worth it, he thought again. He hoped Chuck wouldn't be as fortunate.

Gabriel sat in the lab with Helena's coworkers. Hannah and Zeke, the musicians who had worked most closely with her, still looked distraught. Gabriel listened as each described the work with which they had been involved, how they assisted Helena in her investigations relating to mental illness. They talked about how Helena had narrowed her investigations of late to that of schizophrenics with auditory hallucinations, how they had used the tonal analysis to identify when the hallucinations were actively occurring. Zeke had one sample on his laptop, which he played for Gabriel, the haunting loon sound echoing again through the lab.

Unfortunately, Zeke's single recording was all the documentation that remained. Gabriel was disappointed, but not surprised, to learn that Helena maintained all her own research records. These two were consulting for the most part, brainstorming with Helena. It wasn't their role to maintain any type of data or progress reports. That was all Helena. Now it was all gone with Helena. Gabriel thanked them for coming down and let them go, promising to follow up on Hannah's suggestion of a memorial fund of some sort.

Gabriel returned to his office and sat in front of his computer, his head in his hands. This was not nearly as comfortable as usual, however, due to his splint. His hand was throbbing. There was nothing for him, it seemed. He had come to another dead end. He was running out of things to pursue. He knew, though, that he had to keep at something. He had nothing else to do, and doing nothing was the worst thing he could do. He called his friend.

"Arthur? You coming here or am I coming to your office?" Gabriel asked, once he had the man on the phone. "I don't care. Really, Arthur. Fine, I'll be there in a bit." Gabriel hung up and shut down the computer. He had accomplished exactly nothing so far today. No, he thought, I've managed to break my hand.

Gabriel sat with Arthur in his office, looking out over the bay. It was clear this afternoon. They had watched the recording again, which made both of them feel pretty awful. The only bright spot had been when Gabriel explained to Arthur how he had broken his hand.

"I think you're missing something, Gabriel," Arthur said to his friend's back.

"No news there, Arthur." Gabriel didn't bother to turn from the window.

"You're focusing on what Helena said. I agree, there are a lot of coded messages in there. But we're ignoring her actions."

"You mean, like the fact she killed herself."

"That, too, of course. You and I know she wasn't the suicidal type—"

"Right up to the time she committed suicide, that is."

"It wasn't like that, you know it. She had a purpose. We're not looking at this from the right angle."

"I've tried, Arthur. Really, I've tried. I just interviewed her coworkers, tried to run down her thinking towards the end. No joy, nothing. I'm not sure she had a purpose."

"Of course she did, Gabriel."

"How can you be so sure, Arthur?"

"Look how she did this. It was some crazy experiment, like those old turn of the century scientists who inhaled strange gases or injected themselves to test new compounds."

"Like how they found out that chlorine gas will kill you, that sort of thing? Or what LSD does to you? You think that's what Helena was going for?"

"I do, Gabriel. Why else would she shave her head like that? You know how she was about her hair."

"Hardly cut it since I met her, I think."

"It must've killed her to cut it all off—sorry, that didn't come out right. But you know what I mean. She must've had a damn good reason to do that, to die with all that special recording equipment on. You've got to find out why."

"I know, Arthur. I've tried figuring it out, believe me. The way she was repeating that stupid poem over and over while she died; I'm sure that was supposed to have some special meaning for me. Only problem? I don't have a fucking clue what it is."

"Have you looked at the tracings?"

"About a hundred times, Arthur. I don't see anything meaningful; up until the point she dies, at least. I'm telling you, Arthur, I'm pretty much at a dead end here." He rubbed his throbbing hand.

"Then you have to keep running down the ring. If that's all you got, keep after it."

"Any word from your gun-toting bridge partner?"

"Not yet. He said he'd work on it, though. Turns out he's not as pissed off at you as I thought. He says hello, actually. He was saying that even though the guy never did time, at least we saved the little girl."

"Did he say how long it might take?"

"He said it could take a while. I don't know what that means."

"Then I'm back at that dead end, Arthur."

"Come on, Gabriel. Show some chutzpah, here. Go find out for yourself where the thing came from, what it means."

"How do you propose I do that, exactly?"

"I don't know, Gabe. Go to Ireland or something, ask around."

Gabriel turned from the window to look at his friend. "Arthur, I didn't even consider that. That's a great idea."

"It is? I was kind of winging it there."

"No, I'm serious. Want to come with me?"

"Honestly? No. If you need company, I'll go. But to tell you the truth, I'm not excited about it. And I don't think I'd be much help, anyway. And the food sucks, by the way."

"No problem, Arthur. Let me use your computer, I've got to book a flight."

Gabriel stepped off the plane in Dublin feeling great. A combination of the pain killers the doctor had given him and the Irish beer on the plane got him to sleep somewhere over Iceland, and he hadn't awakened until the wheels screeched their arrival. It wasn't even raining.

As soon as he had checked into his hotel, he went looking for jewelers. The receptionist at the hotel desk had given him directions to the jewelry district. The first three jewelers he went to were worthless. He might as well have just driven to his local mall. The most senior employee of each had no more knowledge than Gabriel regarding Claddagh rings. Less, actually, as Gabriel had at least been doing some research on his own. These guys could only spout a quasimystical sales spiel of utter fabrication regarding 'the long and storied history' of this ring. Gabriel wouldn't even take it off his finger for their inspection.

He did better at the fourth shop, a small upstairs establishment that required him to stare into a camera above the door before he was buzzed in. The owner was the only person in the shop. He was civil enough, but no one would describe him as enthusiastic in his welcome. The man was reasonably familiar with heirloom Claddagh jewelry, though he admitted it wasn't a passion of his, explaining that most of the rings were pure junk. He was impressed with Gabriel's ring, however. Gabriel took it off and allowed the elder gentleman to examine it, which he did with his jeweler's loupe. The jeweler pointed out an engraving on the inside, "WRH" in the tiniest of letters, which Gabriel had never noticed before, they being so small. It was the jeweler's opinion that the letters were possibly a maker's mark or the original owner's initials. Either was possible, he explained, especially in a ring so obviously dating to a period when individual rings were made as awards or special gifts for love or service. Either way, the jeweler was discouraging in regards to tracing down the owner. A ring of such antiquity and obvious worth would most likely have changed hands many times over the many decades, possibly centuries, since its manufacture, he explained. He was at a loss to even venture a guess as to how old the ring was. His greatest advice, however, was in pointing Gabriel to the Department of Irish Culture at Trinity College in downtown Dublin, just a short walk from where they were. He felt that if Gabriel was to have any luck in running down the ring's prior owners, the scholars there were his best avenue for investigation. He thanked the man and left him with fifty euros for his trouble.

Gabriel retreated to his hotel room. Here, he began to research the resources available at Trinity College. After a half dozen phone calls, he found a professor, in the Department of Irish and Celtic Languages, whose online biography admitted an interest in Celtic jewelry and ornamentation. He agreed to meet Gabriel the next day in his office at ten. Gabriel thanked the man and ordered room service for lunch, which felt like dinner. He fell asleep shortly thereafter, dreaming of his late wife.

Gabriel awoke with a sense of renewed purpose. He breakfasted in the hotel restaurant, pretending to read the local paper but mostly people watching. It was his first trip to Europe, and he was amazed by how both alike and utterly different everything seemed. Dublin seemed every bit as cosmopolitan and vibrant as San Francisco, but with a completely different vibe. Rather than his hometown's eclectic mixing of cultures and peoples, Ireland presented a uniquely consistent face. Everybody looked and sounded like they were related to his late wife. Somehow, he felt this comforting. A Midwestern Jew who had no blood relatives in this country, or even the slightest understanding of the native language, he somehow felt a kindred tug. It didn't look easy to be Irish, but it certainly looked like fun.

He walked around the downtown, paper tucked under his arm, trying not to look too much the tourist. It didn't seem to matter. He was greeted with either a smile or indifference on the sidewalks. Asking directions elicited a pleasant response, even though the young lady he stopped looked like she was in a hurry two seconds before. He stepped onto a bus at random, paid the fare and sat in an empty seat near the window. He watched the city roll by outside until he realized he was heading into a fairly seedy suburb. It seemed that in this town, the rich folk lived downtown, the poorer neighborhoods being further from the city center. Quite different from what he was used to back in the States. He bailed and spent an anxious few minutes at the bus stop until the next bus heading back downtown pulled up. He needn't have worried, no one gave him the least trouble; several others waiting at the stop with him actually smiled at him indulgently. He looked like an American from a half mile away, he realized.

He stepped off the bus at the same stop at which he had begun his journey, and began walking randomly once again. Before he realized it, he found himself in front of the main gates to Trinity College. He stepped through and stood at the front of the commons, students passing him in their hurry to classes from every direction. He stood and stared up at the ancient, imposing tower of the main building. For no conscious reason, his heart felt lightened for the first time since he had lost his wife. For no good reason that he could fathom, he felt optimistic. This elegant, ancient place, these people, were going to help him figure out what happened to his wife. At least, he felt they might.

Several minutes of staring at the campus map and two polite inquiries later, Gabriel found the office of the professor with whom he had scheduled his appointment. He was a half hour early. While he was debating whether to find a coffee shop and come back later, the man came up the hall behind him.

"Are you the American?" the man asked in a light accent.

Gabriel turned to greet him. "Yes, Professor, I am. I called you yesterday. I'm afraid I'm early," Gabriel said, shaking the man's hand.

"No, problem. Come on in. I'm embarrassed to say I've forgotten your name already. Never good with names, I'm afraid." The professor led Gabriel into his office and offered him a seat, taking one behind his cluttered desk.

"Gabriel Sheehan, professor. Thank you for seeing me."

"First time in Dublin, Gabriel? Enjoying your stay?"

"Yes, very much. Not vacationing, though."

"I'd offer you tea if there were any. Sadly, the assistant is out on pregnancy leave and none of us academics can figure out how to boil water. If she doesn't have the kid and get back soon, the college will have to close." He smiled at Gabriel indulgently. "So, if this isn't a holiday, what brings you to our city?"

Gabriel took off his ring and handed it across the desk to the older gentleman. The professor took it and examined it with open admiration. "My, my, Gabriel. This is a very impressive ring. Where did you get it?"

"It was a gift from my wife, professor. On our wedding night."

"Your wife is Irish, then?" he said, still admiring the ring.

"She was, professor. I lost her recently."

The other man looked up from the ring at that. "I'm very sorry to hear that, Gabriel. She must have been quite young."

Not for the first time, Gabriel realized he didn't know, exactly. "Thank you, Professor. I'm trying to track down the previous owner of the ring. It's important, I believe."

"Do you? Why?" He looked at Gabriel closely.

"I have reason to believe that the history of the ring somehow relates to my wife's death. It's complicated, I'm afraid."

"No doubt. It was rude of me to ask, sorry. Well, let's have a look, shall we?" He produced a jeweler's loupe from his top desk drawer and examined the ring closely. At one point, he placed the ring on his desk as he stood to take a book from a shelf behind his desk. He leafed through the book, comparing the ring to several pictures in the text. Gabriel waited silently, watching.

"Well, it's genuine, of course. Not any doubt about that. I'd date it to the mid- to late-nineteenth century, based upon similar work. That's the easy part."

"And the hard part?"

"Knowing it's approximate date of fabrication doesn't help us much in identifying the last owner. Even if I chanced upon this exact ring in a reference text, that wouldn't tell us the line of ownership."

"What about the engraving, the small initials inside?"

The professor picked up the ring and examined it again with his loupes. "Yes, the initials are quite clearly 'WRH', despite the wear."

"A maker's mark?"

"I don't think so, Gabriel. It's possible, of course. Many of the craftsmen who designed and fabricated these prime old rings did leave some type of mark. But three initials makes that unlikely. Most likely they are the initials of the first owner, particularly if the ring was a gift, or a token of honor."

"But not necessarily the most recent owner?"

"Almost definitely not. These older rings, the true collectibles such as this one, have changed hands dozens of times. I wouldn't expect a later owner to have his initials engraved like that, though it's possible, of course. More likely a token of the initial offering, though."

Gabriel felt his cellphone buzzing soundlessly in his pocket. He reached across the desk for the ring and placed it back on his finger. "Well, I appreciate your time and expertise, professor. I really do." He rose to shake the other man's hand.

"I'm just sorry that I couldn't be of more help, Gabriel. Please accept my condolences in regards to your wife. I am truly sorry for your loss. I hope that you are able to solve your mystery with time." Gabriel nodded a somber acknowledgment and turned to leave. In the hallway, he checked his phone, and saw that the missed call was from Arthur. He waited until he was outside the building and called him back. Arthur answered on the first ring.

"How's Ireland, buddy?"

"Impressive. Food's not nearly as bad as you said."

"What do I know? I've never been. Any progress with the ring?"

"Nothing spectacular. Everyone's impressed that it's the real thing. Most want to buy it. Nobody can tell me who owned it."

"Well, I hope this helps. Doesn't sound too promising, though."

"You heard from your agent friend?"

"Yeah, Ed called this morning. Don't get too excited, it's not much. There is no record of an exhibit relating to a scientist in which a crime was committed at MIT. There was, however, an incident at MIT over thirty years ago relating to a historic retrospective of nineteenth century mathematicians."

"What sort of incident?"

"All he knows is that a police report was generated, for insurance purposes. He can't get a copy of the report itself. There were no arrests, no follow-up. Just a line in a log, he said."

"How does he know it was mathematicians?" Gabriel asked, frustrated.

"He said the log entry had the title of the exhibit. It was: 'Riemann, Hamilton, and Lagrange—the Golden Era of European Mathematics'. Got that?"

"Yeah, Arthur. I got it. It's not much, though. I was hoping for a lot more from your friend." He typed furiously into his phone.

"Sorry, Gabriel. He tried. It was a long time ago. Good luck."

"Thanks, Arthur. Bye." Gabriel stood in the commons for several minutes, thinking. The previous crowd had dissipated, classes now being in session. He was disappointed and frustrated. He had expected more; more from the FBI report, and more from this Irish professor. He was trying to think of what to do next as he stared at the notation he had just finished typing into his phone, the name of the exhibition that Arthur had just related. Bells started to ring somewhere. Riemann, again. Somehow, 'golden' and 'Hamilton' stuck out at him. 'Golden' for the obvious symbolism relating to his ring. 'Hamilton' began with the letter 'h'. It was all he had. He headed back to the professor's office.

Gabriel knocked on the open door and poked his head in the office. "Sorry to bother you again, Professor."

"Not at all, Gabriel," the professor said from his seat behind the desk. "Think of something else?"

"I just got a call. Do you know anything about European mathematicians?"

"Not a thing, I'm afraid. We have a mathematics department, though. I believe it's a very good one, actually. Their building is just across the commons. Perhaps someone can help you there."

"Of course, Professor. Just a long shot. Thanks again." Gabriel retreated back down the stairs to the commons. Classes were letting out again and the torrent of students began to emerge from every direction. He stopped a pretty coed, noting how many students were redheads here, and got directions to the math building. He walked across the commons slowly, not wanting to burn too quickly through his very last lead. It was a very thin lead, at that. He walked leadenly to the building the girl had indicated and stood before it, gazing up at the sign. His heart seemed to skip a beat as he saw the name: The Hamilton Mathematics Institute, it read. He felt he must be in the right place.

Gabriel mounted the broad steps leading into the building. He stared agape at a bust just inside the entrance, reading the inscription. The bust was identified "William Rowan Hamilton". WRH. Gabriel thought he had just found the previous owner of his ring.

It took Gabriel over an hour to arrange an appointment with the dean of mathematics. The soonest the man could see him was tomorrow afternoon. It would have to do. Gabriel returned to his hotel, trying not to get his hopes up too much. It was hard, and he nearly failed. Large quantities of Irish beer helped.

Gabriel awoke the next morning and breakfasted alone in the hotel restaurant, again. He had several hours before his appointment with the dean. He returned to Trinity College and went to the magnificent old library, where he did some perfunctory research regarding Hamilton. Gabriel was still no theoretical mathematician, and he made little progress. He did succeed in using the subdued, ornate setting as inspiration to formulate a strategy. He doubted that the dean of mathematics would be overly impressed that he wore the ring of the college's namesake. He would have to take a different approach. Gabriel knew for a certainty, however, that the key to his wife's demise was somehow to be found here. Helena had led him here with a purpose.

The dean proved to be an enthusiastic man in his late sixties, happy to give Gabriel whatever help he could provide. He studied the formula that Gabriel had written out for him, particularly the central portion from which, Gabriel explained; he suspected some factor or factors to be missing. Gabriel explained that he had been charged with hunting down the missing portions of the equation, as the researcher had suffered a most untimely stroke, the man now being quite incapacitated. The dean was impressed and entirely in agreement with Gabriel's assertion that the formula related in some way to Riemann's zeta function. Otherwise, he was entirely confused as to why a nonmathematician such as Gabriel would have been charged with such a task.

"Surely, you can review his journals, his notes?" the dean asked, staring at the complex formula.

"Sadly, no," Gabriel explained. "Though several of his colleagues have tried to decipher the pertinent records, the researcher was a poor documentarian, it seems. It's almost as if the equation arose de novo, so to speak."

"It happens, it happens," the dean nodded, gravely. "It's a terrible shame. But why come all this way, to Trinity College? What is the significance of our institution?"

"Well, that's a mystery, sir. I must admit, I'm at a loss. I only know that my colleague felt that the work, or perhaps the character of Hamilton himself, to be in some way inspirational. He speaks of it constantly; though, of course, he's largely incapable of expressing himself with any sophistication."

The dean looked puzzled. "But you're quite certain that he is referring to our Hamilton?"

"Entirely certain, Professor."

"Curious. Are you at all familiar with our namesake, Dr. Sheehan?"

"I am embarrassed to admit I am not, Professor."

The older man stood up from behind his desk and took Gabriel by the arm. "Then this is a perfect excuse to get out of this office," he said. He gathered up Gabriel in one arm and his umbrella in the other, leading Gabriel out the door.

"It's a perfect day, Professor. I doubt you'll need that."

"What, this?" the dean asked, gesturing with the umbrella. "I can't walk more than ten steps without it. Come on now. If we don't get up a head of steam, we'll be waylaid by my secretary."

True to his prediction, they passed the dean's secretary as she called out to remind him of his next appointment. "Going to be late, I'm afraid," he announced as they swept past her desk without breaking stride. The dean led Gabriel at a brisk pace to the front gate of the college, where they caught up a sitting taxi. The dean gave the driver a destination that was lost to Gabriel.

"Where are we going, if you don't mind me asking?" Gabriel asked.

"To teach you about the greatest Irish mathematician of all time, Dr. Sheehan."

"Please, call me Gabriel, Professor. I didn't mean to take you so out of your way, sir."

"A perfect excuse, that's all, Gabriel. And since you're not on my faculty, you must call me Oisin." He offered his hand to Gabriel, who shook it firmly.

"A pleasure, Oisin. Thank you for taking the time."

"My pleasure, honestly. If I'm lucky, I'll have missed that meeting entirely by the time we return." The taxi stopped and the dean handed over the fare, and then led Gabriel out onto the sidewalk. "William Rowan Hamilton," the dean began, lecturing Gabriel as they walked together, now at a more leisurely pace, "was born in Dublin in 1805. He lived, studied, worked, and died in Dublin. His entire professional career was spent at Trinity College, you know."

"I did not know that," Gabriel encouraged as they were now walking along the Royal Canal. The sun glinted off the water as others passed on either side.

"Like your colleague, Hamilton was something of an enigma. Most mathematicians, then and now, are products of their upbringing, so to speak. They study under the guidance of a particular mentor or at a school, building their work and reputation from that which came before them. Rarely, though, true genius arises from seeming spontaneity. This was the case with Hamilton. He was already thought a genius by the age of twelve. He had mastered a number of languages by the age of nine, or so some claim. It is certain, however, that he had a talent for mathematics long before he was granted any formal training."

They had come to a bridge across the canal. Pedestrians streamed past them as Oisin brought them to a halt at the bridge's foot. "Hamilton is famous for an enormous number of insights and discoveries," the dean continued, "but you are here, most likely, because of Hamilton's seminal discovery; the discovery of quaternion mathematics."

"I'm sorry, Oisin—"

The old man waved at Gabriel dismissively. "I know, you have no idea what I'm talking about. You're no mathematician, I realize. Stay with me anyway, it's a great Irish story. Better than most, as it's true. Hamilton was already considered a brilliant mathematician, having made significant contributions despite belonging to no particular school or lineage. His discoveries, as I said, were uniquely his own. At this point, Hamilton was looking for a method of extending complex numbers to higher spatial dimensions. Others, of course, were pursuing the same problem, but none with much success. In October 1843, Hamilton is walking with his wife across this bridge, when the solution to the problem came to him in a blinding flash. The solution, you see, lay in a radical departure from the accepted thinking of the time, requiring the abandonment of the principle of commutativity. You know commutativity, of course, Gabriel?"

Gabriel nodded vaguely, murmuring, "Of course, Oisin."

"No matter. It was a brilliant stroke, a flash of genius. As Hamilton recounted it later, he was so shocked by his sudden insight that he took out his penknife and carved the solution into the side of the bridge, so as not to forget it."

"This is a true story? Really? Because it sounds—"

"I know, I know. Nonetheless, it is true. I'll show you." The dean led Gabriel to a stone plaque set in the bridge, and let Gabriel admire it, smiling.

Gabriel read the inscription:

Here as he walked by
on the 16th of October 1843
Sir William Rowan Hamilton
in a flash of genius discovered
the fundamental formula for
quaternion multiplication
$i^2 = j^2 = k^2 = ijk = -1$
& cut it on a stone of this bridge.

"That's incredible," Gabriel said when he finished. "I'd stopped believing such things happen."

"Then you're an unusual man, Gabriel," the professor said. "Most men never believe in such things."

"Actually, I experienced something like that myself once, when I was much younger. I called it my epiphany, at the time."

"As I say, then, an unusual man, Gabriel. Unusual and very fortunate."

"It was a long time ago, I'm afraid." Gabriel followed the other man onto the bridge. It was a brilliantly sunny afternoon, and the canal was a dazzling sight. They walked along, admiring the day.

"It must be difficult, wondering if such a thing ever happens twice to a person," Oisin continued.

"Not really. I never expected it the first time. I certainly don't expect such a thing to ever occur to me again."

"Then indulge an old man, Gabriel. I've given you my postcard version of the life of Hamilton. Tell me why you're here; because, no offense, but that story about the colleague with a stroke seems a bit strained." He smiled at Gabriel as they walked.

"Of course, you're right, Oisin. I'm sorry, but I didn't think you'd believe the truth from a strange American who just appeared in your office."

"All Americans are strange, Gabriel. But now that you're not so much a stranger, try me."

They walked along among the other pedestrians on the bridge as Gabriel related the story of his wife's death, the strange recording, and how he found himself at the dean's office. At Oisin's request, Gabriel handed over his ring for the dean's inspection. He tried to see the engraved initials in the sunlight.

"I'll have to take your word for it, I'm afraid," Oisin said. "My eyes aren't good enough."

"Don't feel bad," Gabriel said. "I didn't even know they were there until a couple of days ago, and I've been wearing that ring for over twenty years."

"Strange," Oisin said, handing the ring back to Gabriel, "that such a unique token should come to be on your hand. Almost an epiphany in it's own right, in a fashion."

"I suppose so, Professor. It got me here, at least."

"How did you come to possess it?"

"It was a gift from my wife. That's all I know."

"A generous gift. Well, we should be heading back, Gabriel. That's the third call I've ignored since we got here," the dean said, fishing his phone from his pocket and checking the number. "All from my secretary, of course." They turned about to head back across the bridge. "It seems your wife, or someone, went to a great deal of trouble to introduce you to Hamiltonian mathematics. Any idea why?"

"No idea. As you said earlier, I'm no mathematician, Oisin. This puzzle first led me to a formula with a piece missing. Now, I may have filled in the piece that was missing, but I still don't know what it's for."

"The fascinating thing is that both the Riemann function you showed me in my office, and Hamilton's discovery of quaternion mathematics, both relate to the math of higher dimensions. I doubt they've ever been combined in that manner before. Are you certain your wife wasn't a mathematician, Gabriel?"

"Everybody keeps asking me that. I don't think so. My wife was quite brilliant, in her own way. We worked together on discovering the principles of electrical analysis of brain function our entire lives. But I don't think anyone who ever knew my wife would describe her as a mathematician. That formula is the first time I've ever seen her do anything like that."

"Then what was she, if not a mathematician?"

"That's very hard to say, actually. Many things. Brilliant in her way, as I said, but I'm not able to say in what field, specifically. When we met, she was taking graduate astronomy and statistics courses at the University of Michigan. She had attended other universities before that, but she never had any formal training in anything, as far as I could tell. She never actually earned a degree of any type." Gabriel left out those aspects relating to his wife's expertise in thievery and motorcycle racing, feeling that they were probably less relevant.

They hailed a cab for the ride back to the college, continuing the conversation once inside. "How is it that she developed such a complex, unique formula, I wonder?" Oisin said.

Gabriel shook his head. "I have no idea. It seems to have just appeared out of the blue. Even worse, I have no idea what to do with it, now that I have it."

Gabriel walked the dean back into his office. They passed his secretary who said nothing, just shook her head disapprovingly as they passed. Gabriel shook the man's hand in farewell.

"Thank you for your time and your help, Professor," Gabriel said.

"It was my pleasure, Gabriel. It was a great excuse to get out and about for a while, before my jailer resumes the beatings." He smiled. "I just hope I've helped in some small way."

"I'm sure you have, Oisin. Will you have a look at my wife's formula, let me know if you think of anything more?"

"I will, Gabriel. Actually, I'm thinking of posting it to the members of the department; see if anyone has any thoughts. Many hands, you know."

"I appreciate that, Professor. Please let me know if anything comes of it."

Gabriel could think of no excuse to remain in Ireland any longer. He booked his flight home.

Upon returning home, Gabriel dedicated his time to the puzzle that was his wife's last words. He worked long hours each day in his laboratory. Chuck was gone, of course. Initially, the receptionist stayed on to deal with the practical aspects of running the office and answering the phones. After a time, however, the phones stopped ringing. One day, Faith came back to the lab to sit with Gabriel. She was sorry, she said. He had to let her go.

Arthur occasionally visited the lab, but these occasions grew more infrequent. Often, though, almost every week, he and Sam would have Gabriel over the house for dinner. Gabriel was reluctant at first, feeling his presence was an imposition. With time, however, it was clear to all that this friendship was meant to last and survive Helena's passing. Gabriel began to show up weekly, and after a while they all began to enjoy one another's company completely, without the sense of emptiness that was the missing Helena at the table.

Gabriel forced himself to religiously attend those dinners at Arthur's house, for other than that, he was alone. He lived alone, of course. In the lab, he pursued his research without the benefit of his lifelong partner. He received occasional missives from his new mathematician friends.

Both Oisin and Everson conveyed occasional insights into Helena's formula, or forwarded the thoughts of some colleague. Gabriel found none of it terribly enlightening, however. For the most part, it seemed that the two were being more polite than helpful.

Gabriel worked steadily. He was not a mathematician. Rather, he spent his time trying to apply the discovered formula to the field he knew, to the analysis of the electrical waveforms of the brain. It was all too easy to conceive of ways to apply the formula to the signals he had available. He still had a huge database on his own computer of subject recordings with which to work. His initial efforts to employ the formula in various ways all seemed to generate only a strange, but completely meaningless, distortion in the waveforms. Gabriel no longer was in possession of the program database, Helena's salmon of knowledge, and so couldn't directly analyze his results. He knew from many decades of work, however, nonsense when he saw it. He knew that his efforts so far were just that.

After a time, Gabriel considered contacting Chuck. The man was his equal, after all, in this exact area of inquiry. Electronic signal analysis was what he did, and certainly Chuck had access to resources unavailable to Gabriel. Several times Gabriel reached out to him. If Chuck was listening, however, he chose not to respond. Gabriel continued to work on alone.

In the face of increasing frustration, Gabriel was forced to return to his primary source, Helena's recording. He used every manner he had deduced to apply the formula to the recording of her brainwaves, but with a result no more meaningful than that he had observed with the other subjects.

Like many discoveries, his breakthrough was a matter more of circumstance than scientific method. He had worked hard that evening, trying a string of experiments without much success. It was late. Gabriel was tired, and frustrated, and depressed. He lacked the energy to leave, so he kept working on Helena's recording, though what he was doing could be better described as going through the motions of working. He fell asleep in his chair. When he awoke, it was to the disturbing but distinctive sound of loons calling loudly throughout Gabriel's laboratory. Gabriel woke up and looked about him in the semidarkness of the lab, disoriented. He half expected to find his Helena seated next to him. He was alone, though, and once he was fully awake he realized that the recording of Helena had run well past the point where Helena had died. He stared in amazement at the monitors. Where before he had seen only flat lines at this point, the formula had introduced a transformation that had a form to it that he recognized. For the first moment in a very, very long time, Gabriel felt a sense of hope.

Gabriel was fully alert now. He paused the recording and silence returned to the lab. He rewound the recording to a point before Helena stopped breathing, started it again. Unmitigated noise surrounded him, the tracings a meaningless jumble. He paused it again, sat and thought.

Gabriel checked the settings, wrote them down on one of Helena's yellow pads. He pulled up one of the standard recordings, applied his formula, and quickly killed the resulting noise. "Definition of insane," he said aloud to the darkness, "doing the same thing over and over again and expecting a different result." He thought for a moment, and then pulled up the recording of the schizophrenic subject that Zeke had left behind. He thought of Zeke, realized how long it had been since he had talked to anyone about this stuff: long time.

Gabriel began the playback on the section of the recording marked 'Hearing Voices' and the familiarly haunting loon sound boomed too loudly around the lab. Gabe reduced the volume, held his breath, and snapped switches across the panel to cut in his formula, the settings now adjusted to those on the pad before him. Immediately, the loons disappeared, replaced by a soft, almost inaudible, buzz. Gabriel slid the controllers to a higher gain and nearly fell out of his chair. He quickly snapped the switch to stop the playback. He had heard voices. He was sure of it. He hadn't understood what they were saying, but they were definitely voices.

Gabriel got up out of his chair and paced around the laboratory, switching on every light he could find. He started back to the console, instead went out to the office and turned on all the lights there, too. He went back to the lab and sat back down at the console. Gabriel took a deep breath, snapped the recording to play, and listened. Voices, two or three, all speaking at once. Gabriel could pick out individual words, definitely English, but the voices faded in and out, overlapped to a point where he couldn't follow. It was, in a word, disturbing. Deeply disturbing to the point that Gabriel had to stop it again. "Holy shit," he said aloud, then again, more loudly. He had found something. What it was, he didn't know. He did know that it scared him.

Gabriel looked at the big round clock on the wall across the lab. It was late, the middle of the night. He really should be getting home, grab something to eat and get some sleep. Really, he thought. I've been at this a very long time. One more night won't make any difference. A normal person would go home now. Gabriel didn't think he was a normal person anymore. He was more a widower. He drummed his fingers against the console.

Gabriel looked at the settings recorded on the pad, started the recording again. He adjusted the formulation in subtle ways that he didn't quite understand, mostly trial and error, listening and watching the waveforms as they became more distinct, separating as the individual voices became more articulate. They were talking to him, calling him Billy, commenting on some recent birthday, the weather, and—Gabriel snapped it off. "That's enough for one night," he said aloud. "I'm outta here." He nearly bolted from his own lab.

He had it now, he was sure. He thought carefully as he drove towards Half Moon Bay. He was close enough so that now he saw a way forward, a direction for his research. The long time spent groping in the dark was definitely over. Now, he wasn't frustrated or depressed. Now he was scared out of his freaking mind.

As he approached his home, he slowed. He was not excited at the prospect of sitting alone in his own house right now. He looked at his watch: twelve-thirty. That's not so late, he thought. He drove to Arthur's house. He was wrong about that, too.

Gabriel rang the doorbell three times without result. He didn't think Arthur had said anything about going out of town; he had just talked to him two nights ago. He pounded on the door. The house was dark, silent. Gabriel pulled out his cellphone, dialed Arthur's number. He heard the phone ringing inside.

"Hello?" It was Arthur's voice. The ringing had stopped.

"Arthur?"

"Yeah, Gabe? Are you home?"

"No, I'm—"

"Listen, I've got to call you back. Someone's trying to break in, I just called 911."

"Arthur, it's me. I'm right outside."

"That's you banging on my door like Charlie Manson?"

"Yeah, Arthur. Let me in already."

Arthur was in his pajamas, sitting at the kitchen table with Gabriel. Sam joined them with coffee and cookies. Gabriel ate most of the cookies without thinking. He told them what he had found at the lab. They looked at him, stared at him slack jawed.

"What the hell is it, Gabe?" Arthur asked.

"I don't know, Arthur. Really, I don't know. It's scary," Gabriel answered.

"Sounds pretty freaking weird, Gabe," Sam agreed. "What are you going to do now?"

"Now? When you guys kick me out, I'm going to go home and drink myself asleep, that's what. Unless I can stay here tonight."

"I meant in the morning," Sam said. "You're welcome to stay the night, though. If you want."

"Yeah, I think I should. You know, in case Helena's ghost drops by the house, trying to get me to stop all this shit. Better I'm here, if that happens."

"Get a grip, buddy," Arthur said. "Stay if you want, wimp. What are you going to do in the morning?"

"Sleep in, have brunch with you guys. You got eggs? I can make omelets."

"Gabe, really," Sam said.

Gabriel sighed. "Tomorrow I'm going to go back to Helena's recording. That's what I need to do. I know what to do now, it's just a matter of time and work."

"And then what?"

"That's the really scary part. I have no fucking idea, that's what."

Gabriel returned to the lab the next day, reluctantly. He kept all the lights on. Rather than go straight to Helena's last recording, he decided on another tack. If pressed, he would've realized he was avoiding the end game here. Instead, he found the recording Chuck had made of Helena during her last period of catatonia. He cued up the recording and adjusted the settings on the console as the sound of loons returned to the lab. He engaged the formula, listened with amazement and raised the gain as the loons were replaced with the voice of a young girl. She was speaking in Irish, and Gabriel understood none of it. He thought he knew, however, feared he knew, whose voice it might be. He switched it off. He dialed Arthur's cellphone.

"Arthur!"

"Gabriel!"

"Arthur, you got to get your ass up here. Now. Please."

"What's wrong?"

"I don't want to talk about it. Are you on your way?"

"No, I'm not on my way, Gabriel. I'm busy."

"What, busy? You don't have a job, Arthur."

"I've got a life, though, Gabriel. Later, buddy. Gotta go." He hung up.

Gabriel switched to the recording of his wife's death. He cued up the portion where she lay, eyes closed, quietly reciting. He knew this recording so intimately that he was able to advance to the fortieth repetition without counting. He knew what the waveforms looked liked on this side of her death with his eyes closed. He used to know what they looked like after, as well. Gabriel switched on his formula and slowed the recording to a tiny fraction of normal speed. He leaned into the monitor before him, staring at the waves now dripping across the screen like molasses. It had never before occurred to him that death was a process rather than an event, but he now had the proof before him. Where once he thought death had come too soon, he could now see, in the forty-second repetition, the transition his wife had made from the living.

It was only a matter of hours before Gabriel, focused on this narrow transition, was able to understand the transitive event. He understood now in a manner that allowed him to mimic the effect with the proper modifications and application of his formula. He sat, contemplating what he had just invented. He decided to go for a walk.

Gabriel walked around the streets of San Francisco, lost in thought. He had reached the last step in this experiment. He let his mind wander back to how this journey had begun, how he and Helena had started with the tiniest of steps, the initial six ideograms. How it led, somehow, to this moment. He had never imagined that it could come to this. Somehow events, beyond his control or intent, had seemingly conspired step by inevitable step to bring him to this point. He looked up and saw he was back at the door of his building.

Gabriel walked back to Helena's lab, so long untouched. He turned on all the lights, as well as the console. The monitors came alive around him. He retrieved his notes from his own lab and set up the console with the settings from the formula he had finally arrived at. He sat in the chair that his wife had sat upon, and donned the same electrode array she had worn. He didn't need to shave his head, however; nature had taken care of that problem years before. He snapped on the recorders and amplifiers, listening to the initial hum and then the sound of his own brainwaves broadcast noisily into the cavernous room. He turned the volume down and watched the waveforms, and waited. After a few minutes, he began to wonder what he was waiting for. What did he expect to happen, anyway? Did he think—

The room began to fill with an ethereal wailing that quickly built in intensity, a wailing that overwhelmed Gabriel with sadness and fear; a sound tragically, horribly, rending. He lunged at the console and swatted off the power to the equipment. The room snapped into ringing silence. Gabriel was ashen, sweating, his heart pounding. He had no explanation for what he had just experienced. He wasn't even certain he had actually heard the awful wailing, or perhaps experienced it in some other sensation.

It was gone now, however. He took a deep breath, consciously steeled himself. It was an experiment, after all. It was his device, his settings, and he was able to control it, cut it off at will. There was nothing to fear. He took another deep, shuddering breath, leaned forward, and turned the console back on.

"—abriel? Are you there? Where'd you go, babe? Don't be scared, I was just messing with you, hon."

Gabriel looked about the room wide-eyed. He looked for his wife. "Leena?" he said aloud, to no one.

"Hey, Gabe."

"Is it you, really? Leena?"

"Yeah, babe. You were expecting someone else?"

"Where are you, Leena? I can't see you."

"I'm dead, Gabriel. You figured that out, right?"

"How?"

"Haven't a clue on this end, honey. You'd know the answer better than me."

"Can you see me? I can't see you."

"I can kinda see you. It's weird. I don't think you can see me, though. How are you, Gabe?"

Gabriel thought about this for a while. He didn't really know the right answer to that. "Okay, Leena. I miss you."

"That's nice, Gabriel. I'm glad you miss me, honey."

"I mean I really, really miss you, Leena. Really."

"Yeah, I got that, Gabe. Buck up, big guy. It hasn't been that long."

"Yes, it has, Leena. Too long."

"Well, we always had a hard time being apart, Gabe. But a couple of months, I'm sure, with all the work you had to do—"

"Months? Leena, it's been years."

"What, years? What are you talking about Gabriel?"

"You died over three years ago, Leena."

"No way."

"Really." Gabriel looked at his watch, though he didn't know why. "Three and a half years tomorrow, Leena. Three and a half years."

"Gabriel, how could that be? What have you been doing? You haven't been schtupping Faith, have you? I can still haunt you, you know."

"No, Helena, I haven't been schtupping Faith or anyone else. I've been working. Working on this."

"Three and a half years? Come on, Gabriel. I left it all for you, in the recording. Those clues weren't that hard, babe."

"Clues? You call those clues? You left a whole part of the formula out, you know."

"Yeah, I know. Sorry, that couldn't be helped."

"Couldn't be helped? Why didn't you just move your head a little? Would that have been so hard? Huh?"

"Gabriel, you're yelling at your dead wife. That's not right, hon."

Gabriel realized she was right. "I'm sorry. It's just been very hard, Leena. I've missed you. Did you miss me, hon?"

"The truth? How about I just say, yeah, hon. Missed you, too."

"You didn't miss me?"

"Not really, sorry. It's just different here, hon. You'll see."

Gabriel had to think about this for a bit. "What is it like, Leena?"

"Pretty cool, Gabriel. It's great, really."

"You're not just saying that are you? To make me feel better?"

"No, no way, hon. It's fantastic. Weird, of course. Took some getting used to, at first. That was hard, the first part."

"Why did you do it, Leena?"

There was a long pause. "I'm sorry, Gabriel. I had to. I just had to, that's all."

"Why?"

"There was something that I had to do."

"Did you do it, Leena? Did it work?"

Gabriel heard his Helena sigh, sadly. "I tried, Gabriel. I tried very hard. As soon as I got here, it was the very first thing I tried to do. I didn't know, though. I didn't know, at first, that there are some things you just can't change, even if you're dead."

"What did you try to do?"

"I went back to try to save my sister, Gabriel. My kid sister."

"Your twin sister, you mean."

"She's my little sister, Gabe. She's nine minutes younger than I am. I had to try."

"But you couldn't?"

"No, Gabe. It's different, after your dead. This is a different place."

"Where are you?"

"It's weird. Like in all the stories, I'm kinda above you. Like in a higher dimension, you know. It's hard to explain. Like you're looking at a drawing in two dimensions; well, your world is like that to me. I can see it, but all three dimensions just look flat, kind of. But there's time. Time is the dimension above that. And I'm above time, now. That's where I am."

"So why couldn't you save your sister? If you're above all this?"

"It's different—like a picture, sort of. Like pieces on a checkerboard. I can move the pieces through time as much as I want, like you can move the checker pieces across the board. But you can't move the squares on the board. Well, I can't move anything physical in your world; I can't touch anything in space. Just in time."

"Weird."

"Yeah, and I didn't know. Not when I just got here. First thing, I went straight to that moment to save my sister, when she fell. I went straight there without even knowing how, and I saw her falling. It was horrible, to see her fall like that. I reached down to her, tried to catch her, but she went straight through my hands. I couldn't catch her. I kept trying, over and over. She kept going right through my hands."

"I'm sorry, Leena. I'm sorry you couldn't save her. You did all this for nothing?"

"Oh no, Gabriel. It wasn't like that at all. It was okay. I just didn't understand it, that's all. When I first got here, I didn't understand."

"Didn't understand what?"

"I didn't need to catch her at all. She was already here. Not already, exactly, because there is no already. But she was here. When I finally stopped—stopped trying to catch her, stopped going back over and over watching her fall, frustrated and cursing the whole time. I finally stopped, and there she was, smiling at me. 'You caught me,' she said. I really hadn't, but that's what she said."

"I'm happy for you, Leena."

"Yeah, Gabe. I'm happy, too. It's good to be with her again, finally."

Gabriel was crying a little, but tried not to let his voice show it. "I'm sorry you had to leave, Leena," he said.

"I'm sorry, too, dear. But it'll work out, you'll see. You fixed it. We fixed it, now."

"How did we do that, exactly?"

"Well, I'm not exactly sure myself, hon. I thought I knew part of it, when I was alive. From the voices, and the recordings. I couldn't be sure, though. My sister was trying to tell me things, but I never remembered what she said. All I had was your recording."

"But some people know they hear the voices. The recordings you had of the schizophrenic patients, some were labeled 'hearing voices'."

"Yeah, some people can hear us. Their mind is different, somehow. I don't know if the same glitch in their mind that lets them hear our voices makes them crazy, or maybe they get crazy because of the voices in their head all the time. I mean, who can blame them? Who wouldn't just decide to cash it in if you're being told all the time how much better the next life is, you know? Why wait, if everybody's treating you so crazy down there?"

"It's better, then?"

"Oh, yeah, Gabe. I think so. I mean, you're not here, so that's bad, of course. Miss you lots, babe."

"Yeah, right. Nice cover."

"I'm sorry, Gabe. It's just that, there's no time, you know? Just seems like we were just together. And like my sister, I just know I'm going to turn around and you'll be here, with me."

"I will?"

"Oh yeah, Gabriel. Can't wait."

"How?"

"We'll get to that. Are you alone, Gabe? Chuck's not there is he?"

"No, Chuck's gone, Helena. I punched him in the face."

Helena laughed, the sound like crystal droplets of rain falling around the lab. "Good for you, Gabriel."

"I'm alone here, Leena."

"Oh, Gabriel. Don't be sad, hon. You did great. Even if it did take you forever and a day. I can't believe you couldn't figure it out. I made it so clear, I thought. Except for Chuck. He's going to go nuts figuring out where I left that tracking number."

"You really did? You weren't just screwing with him?"

"Oh no, it's real. I went to a lot of trouble, just to keep my promise. He better get it, too. Not right away, though. Not without a lot of effort."

"What did you do, exactly? I still don't understand how you did this. Or why you had to make it so hard. Why didn't you just leave me the formula?"

"I couldn't, Gabriel. Don't be silly."

"Why not, Leena?"

"I didn't have it, of course."

"But you did. You figured out the formula."

"No, Gabriel, I couldn't. I'm no mathematician, you know that. I just tried to put things in motion, you know?"

"No, I don't know what you mean, Leena. What are you talking about?"

"Well, like I said, some things I guessed at before I died, so I put those things in place, for later. But I didn't really know a formula, didn't have a clue. I just had to believe it could be done. And I had to believe in you, Gabe, that you'd do it. And you did. Eventually. You did it."

"No, you did it. You gave me the formula."

"No, Gabriel. You found the formula. You have it on your hard drive, right now. I had to wait for you to discover it. I just shifted it back, just before I died. I couldn't give it to you, or move the drive, once I died. I just had to make sure that when you found it, it would be on the recording."

"But the missing part, Hamilton's quaternion function. That was the key. If not for Hamilton, and the ring, I'd have never come up with it."

"Yeah, that was a bear. My sister told me about the ring, I guess. I never knew. But that guy was clueless, I'll tell you. Maybe the smartest Irish math genius ever, but he was never going to figure that out. I was practically yelling the formula in his ear on that bridge, I'll tell you."

"He could hear your voice?"

"Yeah, he's one of them. Not all the time, but enough so I was able to finally get through. Had to just about scream at him, though. His wife was a trip—what a shrew. She kept yelling, 'Billy, Billy, who are you talking to?' I would've smacked her if I could. He finally got it, though. I made him write it down, right then and there. No way he was going to remember it, otherwise."

"You can't touch people then, or move things? No rattling of chains?"

"No, I don't think so. Some people here say they can move things down there, but I think they're just trying to be special."

"A lot of that going on there, is there?"

"No, not too much, really. Almost nobody here really pays any attention to what goes on down there. It's kind of like slumming, you know? No offense, it's just that most people want to move on. There's so much more, once you're here."

"Is God there with you?"

"I don't think so, not here. Or if he is, I haven't run into him yet. I did run into a bunch of guys dressed up in robes and all, pretending to be god. But I think they were just dead surgeons. Bunch of folks pretending to be angels, too, always mucking about in your world. Wackos, mostly, as far as I can tell."

"If you can move around in time, can you see the future? Do you know what's going to happen?"

"No, can't move in that direction. It's hard to explain. It's like when you travel to the South Pole, kind of. You know, in your world, you can travel East, North, South, or West until you get all the way to the South Pole, and then any way you move, you're moving North. In your world, time works like you're always stuck at the South Pole. The only direction you can move is forward. But here, I can move in every direction. I can't go to the future, though—that's like moving farther South, for me. It's dark there, like sunrise. When you leave here, I think you can see forward. From above here, I guess. That's what I believe, anyway."

"So you don't know what's going to happen. You don't really know?"

"No, not for sure. I'm pretty much winging it her, Gabe. Like the Chuck thing. I'm just hoping it works, what I left him."

"What did you leave for Chuck?"

"Well, that was a lot of work, too. Probably more than he's worth. But I promised, and it seemed important, at the time. I hope he figures it out. Did he figure out the part about the Book of Mormon?"

"I don't think so, Leena. What did you do?"

"Well, it just seemed so perfect, it all fell into place so perfectly. Like I was supposed to be right there, anyway, with that Hamilton fella—and then there was Joseph Smith. Another crazy, by the way."

"He could hear you, too?"

"Oh, yeah, no problem there. He was hearing our voices all the time. He's something special, I'll tell you. Wouldn't listen to me though, at first. Refused to believe me about the buried plates. More effort than I planned on, just to convince him to dig them up. I called him an effing moron so many times, he thought that was my name, you know?"

"Did it work?"

"I don't know, babe. Is there still a Mormon religion?"

"I haven't really been listening to the news much, Helena. Haven't heard anything dramatic, though."

"Probably worked, then. You would've heard, most likely. Chuck better figure it out. If he doesn't, I'm going to haunt him crazy."

Gabriel sighed. He wasn't sure if he was actually happy. He felt relieved, more than anything. "It's great to hear your voice, Leena. Really great."

"Yeah, Gabe. Great to be heard, you know?"

"Are we going to do this a lot, then?"

"Well, that's what we got to talk about, Gabriel."

"What? What's wrong, now?"

"We can't keep this up, babe. I'm sorry."

Gabriel was crestfallen. "What? Why not? We have to, Leena."

"It's too dangerous, Gabriel. Like what Chuck was trying to do with our work before, remember? I can't imagine how screwed up things would be if anyone found out about this. Can you?"

"Yeah, I can. I see what you're saying. But he's not here anymore, Leena. It's just you and me."

"For now, Gabriel. Not for long, babe. You know that. Everything gets out, eventually."

"What do you want me to do, Leena? I don't want to go back to being alone."

"You won't be, honey. You'll see. Trust me on this one. But you have to get rid of this. Get rid of your formula, get rid of everything. Right away, hon."

"Do I have to, right away? This is it, then?"

"You have to, Gabriel."

He sat, feeling more alone and abandoned than at any time since his wife had died.

"How will I find you? When I need to?" he asked his wife, quietly.

"It'll happen, Gabe."

"I don't even know your name, Leena. Not your real one."

"It doesn't matter, Gabriel."

"Yes, Leena. It does, it matters to me. I don't know if I'll ever find you again. I know your name isn't Helena, or Fiona, or any of those other names on the passports, or any of them. I don't know your real name. I need to know, to find you if you don't find me." He was crying again, but now he didn't care if his wife noticed.

"You're right, Gabriel. I'm sorry. I'm sorry I hurt you. I'm sorry I had to leave you. But if it helps, Gabriel: It was Grace. Before I died, my name was Grace."

"Your real name?"

"Yes, Gabriel. It was Grace; is Grace. You can find me now, if you want."

He stopped crying with an effort, wiped his eyes with the heels of his palms. "That's good, Grace. I'll find you, then. But there's some stuff I should do here, first."

"Get rid of it all. Every trace, okay?"

"I'll do that, Grace. I promise. But there's other things, with Arthur and Sam and all—"

"Yeah, well, Gabriel, about all that—you're going to want to hurry, okay, babe?"

"Why? Am I dying? I feel fine, Leena—er, Grace."

"That's great, Gabe. It's just that, I'm not sure how much time you have now. Sorry."

"What? Why? What's going to happen?"

"Well, I'm not sure, exactly. I can tell you, though, that I kind of started something, what with the recording, and the ring, and all. You've done something that wouldn't have happened, probably, if I didn't die and leave the recording. And the other stuff. So if I have this whole time thing right, I might have given you a little push, sort of."

"A push?"

"Sort of. I think. I'm pretty much spitballing a lot of this, to tell you the truth, Gabe."

"Maybe I should check on some things, Grace. Put some things in order, just in case."

"Might be a good idea, Gabriel. Get rid of the research, first thing."

"Got it, Grace." He looked up, for no good reason. "I love you, Grace."

"I love you, too, Gabriel."

"God bless the dead, Grace."

"God bless us all," Grace echoed.

Gabriel reached forward and, with great reluctance, killed the power to the console. He pulled off the headset and sat, remembering the sound of his wife's voice. He smiled.

"Grace," he said softly. There was no response. He didn't need one.

CHAPTER 32

Gabriel tore off the notes from the yellow pads and piled them on his desk. He pulled the hard drive from his computer and put it on top of the pile. He started to look around for a book of matches for a minute, before he realized that nobody in the lab ever smoked. No way there were any matches in this place. He tried to think of another way.

"Gabriel? You here, buddy?" It was Arthur's voice as he came down the hallway. Gabriel looked about, trying to think of some way to get rid of the pile in front of him. He realized he was feeling dizzy.

Arthur came into the office. "Hey, Gabriel. There you are. Who were you talking to? You okay, buddy?" Gabriel could only manage a slight nod. "What's so important, buddy? Been seeing ghosts? Talking to the great beyond?" Gabriel slumped back in his chair. "What's wrong, Gabe? You look like shit."

Arthur came around the desk to feel Gabriel's wrist. Gabriel felt like he was moving away from his friend, rising. He saw himself, at his desk, holding his chest, then slumping forward into his friend's arms. He felt lifting, and happiness, and relief. A soft, milky light suffused his vision. Gabriel tunelessly hummed to himself, the lyrics committed to memory through the countless viewings of his wife's recording:

T'was Grace that taught
my heart to fear.
And Grace, my fears relieved.
He would see his Grace, now; again and forever.

Epilogue: Charles "Chuck" Parnell, Apostle

"As man now is, God once was: As God now is, man may be."
—Lorenzo Snow, fifth President of the Church of Latter Day Saints

Chuck Parnell no longer worked for the NSA. He no longer worked for the government, or anyone else, for that matter. It wasn't his choice. He had been very close to leading a major government project, had presented himself and his ideas to a great many important people. When the project had collapsed, his career collapsed with it.

Chuck took on a new project; though it might better be called an obsession. His holy grail was taken from him, but he dedicated himself to getting it back. He lived with a new purpose now. He shaved his head.

It took Chuck several weeks of close study of Helena's recording to begin to sort things out. He wasn't destitute; at least, not materially. He holed up in his apartment in DC, and studied the recording. He needed a new purpose, and he found it in deciphering the recording of his former colleague and antagonist, Helena. He felt certain of only one thing: she wanted him to have the program. She wanted him to redeem himself. He was convinced of this. He was convinced he could.

Eventually, he figured out the reference to 'the golden book'. He finally realized Helena had been referring to the Book of Mormon. It took a while, of course. He was particularly pleased when he realized that her repeated references to him as 'a fucking moron' were actually code for the angel Moroni; not a comment on him at all. He was fairly certain of this.

Once he realized where to look, Chuck redoubled his efforts. Helena's clues always pointed to the number forty-two, of course. The problem was, this wasn't much of a clue. It occurred to Chuck, after considerable effort, that he would need to undertake a more intense study of the source material.

Chuck was chastened to find that the religion of the Church of Latter Day Saints was deeply secretive about many aspects of their faith. Chief among these was a reluctance to allow anyone outside the church access to the documents and relics upon which the religion was founded. This presented a challenge. Chuck, however, remained a man of great dedication and focus. He determined that his holy grail was only to be discovered if he made the necessary efforts and sacrifice. Chuck Parnell converted to the Church of Latter Day Saints.

Never one to stint in his efforts, Chuck moved his life to Salt Lake City. He not only joined the LDS church, he became an impassioned student of the faith. He rose in the ranks of the church as he pursued his research, gaining greater access as his intensity and enthusiasm for the religion were appreciated. Though initially a necessary means to an end, with greater involvement Chuck gained an increasing appreciation for the religion. While certainly no zealot, Chuck found in the LDS community a sense of belonging that he had only experienced before with his friends in San Francisco. He rubbed the bump on the bridge of his nose. The San Francisco friends, he thought ruefully, were no longer his friends.

Eventually, Chuck became a leading scholar of the source doctrine of the LDS church. His research centered upon his study of the initial Book of Mormon. Chuck's research intensified, developing a numerological interpretation of the scripture, taking as his model the similar studies that had been made for hundreds of years of the Talmud. He was stunned when he began to discover certain patterns and relevancies throughout the books. Years of impassioned research consumed him.

Almost four years later, he made his breakthrough. While he studied all aspects of the Book, of course he concentrated on those passages where the number forty-two was encountered. His goal, after all, was still to find the program that he had helped develop so many years earlier. He still felt the importance of that work, though the meaning had changed for him.

Chuck developed a program to scan through the multitude of numerological implications he had discovered within the text. The program could not be specific, however, as he really didn't know exactly what he was looking for. Every day, he poured over long reams of results, scanning for something extraordinary. Late one afternoon, Chuck found it staring at him from the middle of the page. A transliteration of the forty-second verse of the Book of Moroni. Where else? he thought. The transliteration had a numerology that caught his eye, generated by the program which assigned a number to each letter in the original text—the transliteration was nineteen digits, the same number of characters found in a UPS tracking code—and in addition, the transliteration began with "921", the same three digits which began the tracking codes in the exact month Helena had died. The odds against such a thing must be astronomical, he thought. He grabbed up his personal copy of the Book and thumbed through the well-worn tome. He found the corresponding passage: "Wherefore, if a man have faith he must needs have hope; for without faith there cannot be any hope." Nineteen words—the same number of letters and numbers which were in a UPS tracking code. Nine letters, two letters, one letter. He sat back in his chair, staring at the computer screen, trying to have faith, and hoping.

Parnell realized that Helena hadn't lied to him after all. She had, somehow, kept her promise. He looked at the combination of nineteen numbers and letters that represented a UPS tracking code from the year and the month she had died. Coincidentally, Chuck had received several more messages from Gabriel earlier in the month. He had ignored them all, feeling he had nothing to say to the man. Now that he did, he wouldn't. Instead, he called in a favor from his former colleagues at NSA. They were happy to help, the favor being an interesting challenge and by no means illegal. Perhaps inappropriate, but not illegal. With their help, and his appropriated key to the backup, Parnell gained access to the program that had eluded him for a significant part of his adult life. That next Sunday in church, he said a special prayer of thanks to the departed

Helena. Kneeling, he thought he heard the response, "You're welcome, you moron"—but he was sure he had just imagined that.

By this point, Chuck had risen to a position of considerable authority within the church organization. His work had proven revelatory on many fronts, and pertinent to important aspects of the religion. Parnell's religious studies and writings were the subject of lectures and commentary within the church. So when Charles Parnell, now an elder and respected scholar of the Church of Latter Day Saints, presented his adopted institution with this powerful new discovery, the ultimate authorities of the Church of Latter Day Saints received it with deference. These highest of church authorities retreated in contemplation. The question for their careful consideration, in conference with Charles Parnell, was to decide to what purpose this deeply insightful and powerful technique of reading and interpreting men's thoughts should be employed.

Once again, Chuck felt the influence of his departed friend, Helena, as he helped guide his church. Like her and her now recently deceased husband, Chuck had come with time to believe that a governmental program utilizing this tool for the purposes of state security might be something of a double-edged sword. As he had left government service, and gained the perspective inherent in belonging to his new institution, he developed a shared sense of deep approbation at the thought of his former department employing this power. He recommended that this powerful new tool, this 'Salmon of Knowledge' as he called it, be held by the church in strictest confidence, and be granted the church's highest degree of security.

Ultimately, the governance of the church sought Parnell's recommendation as to what purpose this powerful gift should be employed. Parnell took this responsibility as a sacred burden. He meditated and prayed upon the question for several weeks. Chuck felt that he had been given this gift and this responsibility for a reason, perhaps a divine reason. The purpose should be a high one, he reasoned.

In looking back, it became increasingly clear to Parnell why the program had come into his possession. He reflected upon the various uses to which the program had already been employed, and realized that it was Helena's work, towards the end, that impressed him as the tool's true purpose. During his short period of working with Helena back in her lab, he realized the true power inherent in their discovery; not in its employment to protect society from evil thoughts, but rather to discover the source and treatment of those disturbed thoughts. That had been Helena's mission, and Chuck took it for his own.

There was much about the Church of Latter Day Saints that Parnell had come to love. He was impressed by the sense of purpose and altruism expressed by the church, particularly as manifest in the practice of the church's missions. He was disappointed, however, that the church's highest purpose seemed in service to the church itself, in that the missions sought to convince others around the world of the correctness of the teachings of the LDS. Chuck felt there was an opportunity to achieve another, equally important work for the church. After all, the Catholic Church, in which he had been raised to a certain degree, had as the best part of its mission the care of the sick and infirm. The greatest good accomplished by the Catholic church, Chuck felt, lay in accomplishing that mission around the world. Why couldn't the LDS church accomplish something equally important?

So it was that Charles Parnell, elder and leader in his adopted faith, brought the LDS Church to its new mission of researching, treating, and ultimately caring for those individuals the world over suffering from mental illness of every type. It was important work, work worthy of one of the world's great religions. It was necessary work, for no worldly government or institution had yet come close to meeting this long neglected need. Now his church, with the tool entrusted to Parnell, could minister to those suffering children of god; these latter day saints, some of whom could truly hear the voices of the dead.

end of the first book

ABOUT THE AUTHOR

Evan Geller is a surgeon and critical care specialist living on Long Island, New York. He is happily married and the father of three extraordinarily pleasant children. He writes on the side.

~~~~
~~~~

END NOTES

God Bless The Dead is a work of fiction. Obviously, any resemblance of the characters in this book to real persons, living or dead, is mere coincidence and not the intent of the author. That said, much in this book is indeed true. The theories of time travel, the basic interpretation of brainwaves, distant sensing of brainwaves, and many aspects fundamental to the plot of this book are either already achieved in the laboratory or proven likely on a theoretical basis. In addition, much of what is not necessarily true is, nonetheless, based upon a unique interpretation of factual events. Allow me to elaborate, briefly.

Modern cosmologic and quantum theories now permit, and in some cases require, the existence of time travel. An interesting and approachable discussion of this possibility may be found in the March 1994 issue of Scientific American entitled "The Quantum Physics of Time Travel" by David Deutsch and Michael Lockwood. A deeper discussion is found in the New Scientist article by Mark Buchanan (2005) entitled "No Paradox for Time Travellers". These sources and other, more recent, articles are easily found in a cursory survey of the scientific literature.

I will leave a discussion of the mathematics of higher dimensions to those readers with a burning interest to pursue this topic. As a writer, however, I must emphasize the factual basis of the genius of William Hamilton, his strange epiphany on the bridge, and the repeated instances of mathematical genius coexisting with mental aberration. The unique importance of the number forty-two is a mathematical truth touched upon in this book and many other works of art, religion, and science. The astute reader will appreciate the many hidden (and some more obvious) references to this number incorporated throughout the novel. The fascinating mathematics underlying the works of Jorge Luis Borges has also been the subject of several recent texts.

I will also defer the discussion of the religious aspects of this work to a later time, as many of the issues and concepts raised in **GBTD** serve as a fundamental basis for the remaining two books in the trilogy. I would like to take this opportunity, however, to emphasize that I mean no disrespect to the teachings and beliefs of the Church of Latter Day Saints or any of the many branches of the Mormon religion. I am fully aware that some of the statements made in **GBTD** do not accurately reflect the exact nature of the religion and hope that I have not given offense. The liberties that I have taken are for artistic purposes only, which hopefully will become manifest in the rest of the trilogy.

Truly fanatic readers are referred to the Fenian Cycle (aka, the Third Cycle, the Ossianic Cycle) of Irish mythology in order to appreciate my obscure references and plotting regarding the life and times of my heroine, the significance of the Salmon of Knowledge, obscure punk music allusions, and the occurrence of digital amputation. Those readers interested in the ambiguous Irish historical references are encouraged to read about the life of Charles Stewart Parnell. I refer the interested reader to Katharine O'Shea (Mrs. Charles Stewart Parnell), *The Uncrowned King of Ireland: Charles Stewart Parnell—His Love Story and Political Life* (Nonesuch Books, Dublin, 2005). Those gentle readers who may be somewhat offended by the characterization of my heroine's experiences as an orphan are referred to the Ryan Commission Report (The Commission to Inquire into Child Abuse, 2009), and to the several excellent documentaries and reviews of what some have termed "The Irish Holocaust". Unfortunately, this aspect of the novel rings all too true.

~ ~ ~ ~

I would like to thank my wife Sheri, for her patient assistance and for tolerating a husband who occasionally spends vacations at the beach inside, typing. I would also like to express my heartfelt appreciation to Micheal McCormack, my friend and mentor, whose sage advice was always valuable and appreciated. Thank you to Mary Rabbitt, who was kind enough to spend a portion of her vacation in Ireland providing me with research materials.

Finally, I wish to express my heartfelt regards to all those individuals and families who have been touched by the ravages of mental illness. I share your pain. In a small effort to address this anguish, a portion of the proceeds resulting from the sale of this book is donated to the cause of researching the treatment of schizophrenia.

God bless you, dear reader.

Evan R. Geller, MD FACS
June 3, 2012

Made in the USA
Charleston, SC
23 March 2013